T0300776

Omerta

THE HUNGARIAN LIST

ANDREA TOMPA

Omerta

A Book of Silences

Translated by
BERNARD ADAMS

LONDON NEW YORK CALCUTTA

SERIES EDITOR
Ottilie Mulzet

Seagull Books, 2025

Originally published in Hungarian as *Omerta*

© Andrea Tompa, 2017

First published in English translation by Seagull Books, 2025

English translation © Bernard Adams, 2025

ISBN 978 1 8030 9 408 3

British Library Cataloguing-in-Publication Data
A catalogue record for this book is available from the British Library

Typeset at Seagull Books, Calcutta, India
Printed and bound by WordsWorth India, New Delhi, India

CONTENTS

PART I

Kali's Tale

I've done the right thing. Sure as eggs is eggs. Cos I've known for ages. I was thinkin' about it all that time, just didn't dare. You 'ave to give yourself some encouragement, cos if you don't you can turn back from the road when you should be turnin' onto it. Anyhow, this time I said to meself. Look 'ere, Kali, off you go, keep goin' as far as you can see. It's dark, but that's what you need, go now while it's pitch dark, leave ev'rythin' you've got, turn your back, wash your 'ands of it. Make for 'em 'ills, never mind if you can't see 'em, can't tell the sky from the ground. They blend so exactly in the distance.

Well then, I'm Green Kali Szabó, an' I'll tell you straight, whoever's listenin'. I'm goin' to tell you me story, an' it's startin' right now. But people don't listen to folk tales like they did in the olden days. They've got out of the way of listenin' to good folk tales an' stories. Women an' girls sometimes still do when they're sittin' an' workin' together, it's mostly 'em what still listens. And they only tell folk tales like that to children, but not once they've grown out of bein' children. And in our village ev'rybody used to know such lovely ones. I learnt 'em as well, from me mother, but ev'n I've lost the way of it cos there's been nobody to listen. There's only a folk tale if there's somebody to listen to it. Priests don't preach by themselves to the mice in church. Though they mostly do now. People don't care for priests these days.

But I can't keep quiet. I've always got to be talkin'. Cos if I shut up I get so miserable I feel like jumpin' down the well. Like that poor Sári Juhos. So either I must get away from 'ere or jump down the well, so that I can't 'ave no more story.

And I 'ave to tell folk tales so as not to be so lonely.

Cos the turn me life 'ad taken, there was nobody to listen. And I'd made that bad life for meself. Only perhaps I can still fix it. I'll just 'ave one last try, then it'll be the well for me, same as little Sári Juhos.

Me name's Kali, Kali Szabó, in full Green Kali Szabó. Cos there's two of us in the village of that name, an' when that 'appens both of you are given a nickname. And I'm called Green cos the fence by our 'ouse in Forrószék's green. Or rather, me parent's 'ouse, but that's in the past cos I don't live there any longer. And I went that way as I left the village cos it 'appened to be near where I lived, but I'll tell you about that when the time comes. The other girl was called Long Kali Szabó, she was as long as a summer day. Cos that's 'ow summer days are, so long they never mean to end, for people to leave the fields an' go 'ome.

But now I've turned me back on the whole stinkin' village. I've left. I certainly 'ave, an' straight away I'm into the thick of tellin' lies. Cos that's 'ow people are. When they start to tell about their own lives an' go off the way of truth they go farther an' farther into the dense forest with their lyin'. Only down our way in the Mezőség, there's not a bit of forest for you to enjoy lookin' at. So I don't mean a real forest with trees. Cos the first day of me life I went wrong tellin' lies. That's the way I am, I've been tellin' lies since I was a little girl. So that's why I'm also called Folk Tale Kali. Folk Tale Green Kali Szabó. Cos I don't always say straight away why I've come if anybody asks, I just tell a nice lie, an' I ev'n believe it.

I didn't ev'n need to go as far as Szamosfalva, I'd already worked out where to spend the night, if I got to where I set out for at dawn. So I made for the town of Kolozsvár. Kincses Kolozsvár, they call it, Kolozsvár the rich. Rich for anybody what's born a gentleman or a young lady in a tall 'ouse, but for anybody from the 'Óstát or some such industrial area, it's misery. By the time I got to the 'Óhér bridge, I knew whose 'ouse I'd go an' sleep in. Cos I wasn't goin' to the 'otel in town, was I! I'd got a bit of money, not a lot, an' I'd brought stuff to sell. Cos us from Szék, we're very good at sellin', that's one thing we're proud of, the way we can sell things. There's no bargainin' with us, you know. We state the price an' that's that. But you don't 'ave to pay for lodgin', I've never 'eard of givin' money for somewhere to sleep.

Cos I'd worked out that I'd go to me old boss's place an' spend a night in the straw if they'd let me. All the time I worked for 'em when I was a girl. Girl? I was a child. Cos in our village ev'ry child goes into service as soon as they're twelve. Cos that's one thing us Szék people are proud of, we make good servants. In the old days children went into service ev'n younger, at eight or nine. I was twelve. So I'd go to me old boss's place, I reckon it'd be quite late in the afternoon when I arrived, they'd 'ave just got back from the fields, or young Sára, their daughter, would be 'ome from the market if she's been to sell stuff, cos there's a market in the town ev'ry day. Ev'n on Sunday, the Lord's Day, they don't respect the commandment 'Thou shalt not work'. And there'll be the milkin' to see to, it'd be time they came 'ome. And I'd go out over the railway, what they call the Bulgaria district, cos that's where they live, well beyond the railway, an' they've got a big garden an' the whole area's called the 'Óstát. Me boss is from there as well. I can see 'em now, the farmers bringin' carts 'ome from the fields with all the cabbages, carrots an' onions. 'Ere they use 'orses more, not oxen like us. They're not used to oxen. 'Orses are cleverer, don't trample as much as oxen do. I 'ad a bit of trouble findin' the street I used to go down in the old days, I couldn't really remember it, an' all the 'ouses were so small, only the gardens were so enormous. I went up this street an' that, twist an' turn, but by then me legs were givin' out, really 'urtin', cos it was still dark when I set out from 'ome. And then in the end I found it, I knew the way from where the pub is on the corner, the Szatmári's still standin'. The gate was open at our place, the master 'ad just driven in, 'e'd come from the other direction cos they've got a garden over there as well, in the lower street. 'Is wife came along behind 'im, carryin' the wash tub an' clothes, an' she called out when she caught sight of me.

'Don't come in, love, we 'aven't done the milkin' yet, it'll be a good 'our before the milk'll be ready.'

All the same, I just followed 'er, a bit slower so as not to alarm 'er. Then I called out after 'er: 'Biri, love, don't you know me then? It's me.'

She turned round, looked at me an' said, 'Oh, love, see, my eyes are so bad, but now I know your voice, I recognize that. But just tell me your name.'

And she looked at me like a mole, squeezin' 'er eyes to see better. Then along came the master, an' I said to 'im, 'Good ev'nin'!'

At which Biri said to 'im, 'Look, my dear, see who's 'ere!'

The master looked at me an' said, 'Well, I never! Don't tell me you're Kali Szabó's daughter? Cos you're the same build, an' I can see you're nice an' strong as well, like your mother, just a bit fatter. Come 'ere, let old Furi take a look at you, cos I know your mother, that Kali, who was sent 'ere.'

And 'e came up to me an' put an 'and on me shoulder.

'Well, I never! You've grown up nicely, you're a woman now. And you're pretty, like your mother.'

Biri just stood there, starin' 'ard to see me. Then she came over as well an' took me 'and.

Oh, did I burst out laughin'! I was splittin' me sides. Me poor 'eart didn't know whether to rejoice or break for grief. Cos I certainly 'adn't laughed for quite a while.

'Biri, love, an' you, Mr Furi, no, I'm not Kali Szabó's daughter, cos she ain't got a daughter nor a son. It's me, if you please, recognize me, cos I was in service 'ere all me young days.'

'Look 'ere, Kali, you always were a crafty girl,' said the master, 'don't pull our legs like you always did with your stories, cos I remember the way you used to twist us round your little finger when you got started on 'em. We used to cry or laugh as you pleased. Don't pull our legs now, cos you don't look a day older. You've sent us your daughter, you're only pretendin' to be Kali Szabó. Just stop it, cos if I catch you, you'll cop it like you did when you was a servant.'

But I could tell that old Sándor was only jokin', cos 'e'd recognized me at once, just didn't want to show that I'd aged, 'e was just pretendin' the opposite. Now Biri gave me such a 'ug, kissed me cheek an' began to shed a tear.

'Oh, Kali, just fancy . . . but why 'aven't you ever been to see us? Aren't you ashamed, you 'aven't been so much as once!'

And we 'ugged one another again, an' they called me all sorts of things for never callin' round. But they'd 'eard a lot about me, cos they'd 'ad another girl from Szék after me, an' now they'd 'ad some from Magyarlóna, an' by the time they'd finished takin' trouble with 'em an' teachin' 'em ev'rythin' they'd be off gettin' married. And the way they answered back, an' their foul mouths! And by this time, there were another couple of women at the gate for milk, an' we was still there, complainin' an' weepin' for joy. And old Sándor said 'e'd better be unloadin' the cart, the cattle were waitin'. Then I asked 'em before they went off to do their work whether I might sleep in the straw there. Cos I'd 'ad to come in, I'd got things to do in town next day.

'Of course,' Biri nodded. If that was all I needed. Wouldn't I like to sleep in with the pigs? The servant would come out an' I could sleep on the bench in the kitchen. And she started goin' on again about 'er not bein' 'ome yet, that's what those Lóna girls were like, but you couldn't get one from Szék these days, they wanted so much that who could afford 'em. Now she'd sent 'er to the shop, but she 'adn't come back!

I asked Sándor whether I could 'elp with the milkin'. At which Biri said, goodness, I must be tired. That was true, but not so very, an' I'd just sit down an' do the milkin' for 'em. But then, she said, Tükrös an' Csárdás wouldn't know me an' let me milk 'em, an' it 'ad to be done quick cos women were already comin'. And those cows were so touchy, not like poor Fótos, she'd been so gentle. I said, I'll go an' introduce meself to this Tükrös an' Csárdás an' take 'em a bit of cabbage, cos I could see it all there in a basket, cleaned up an' ready for market next day. 'All right,' said Biri, 'you milk 'em, Kali, me dear, if you can 'andle 'em.'

I really enjoyed milkin' a cow, ev'n if it wasn't me own. 'Ere the farmer's wives put butter on the teats, yellow, but it's butter all the same. They don't in our village, they use bacon fat. They never water the milk to sell, that's not the kind of thing 'Óstát people do. If anybody found out that it was watered, the good name of the 'Óstát would be lost. And so in the end I sat down to do the milkin' an' ease me back, cos it was 'urtin' enough to kill me.

By the time ev'rythin' was seen to, an' the chickens ready for market next day, I went into the kitchen. Biri was puttin' out some lovely puliszka with túró, really rich, with sour cream, an' pickled onions. Old Furu 'ad always treated me like that. 'E'd made me work me, that was a fact, but 'e 'ad kept me an' fed me well, an' not just fed me, but absolutely feasted me! No regrets! But up there they worked like Black African slaves. Biri was only four years older than me, the master 'ad brought 'er there when 'is wife died an' 'e was left with the two motherless children. Sándor was much older than Biri. She'd been a poor girl, she'd been given a little patch of land outside the town, but she was a good girl cos she could work like the best of 'orses. Then Biri an' I 'ad become the best of friends, sisters. She wasn't me boss, more of a kindly sister. I'd seen 'er once again in 'Ungarian times, when we'd come into Kincses for the celebrations, when Miklós 'Orthy an' all 'em 'andsome 'Ungarian soldiers 'ad marched in, in procession. Ev'rybody 'ad come in from the village to see 'em, cos the main road didn't go our way. And that time we met at the station an' 'ardly recognized one another, she was wearin' such a beautiful dress for the occasion, the sort that 'Óstát people never wore except to the vintage ball, an' I 'ad a very nice dress on an' ev'n a tiara on me 'ead, though that's not part of our local costume, but I bought it for the celebrations. We was ev'r so pleased to see each other! But at that time people was pleased about ev'rythin', our 'earts were throbbin' cos we was back in 'Ungary again. Since then we've known nothin' about anythin' else. We didn't ev'n come into town, cos there was nothin' left to sell in the market cos of the war, an' me boss wouldn't ev'n let me try. I knew that Biri 'adn't 'ad a child, only the two orphans what she'd brought up. Perhaps they was married by this time, cos I didn't see either of 'em in the 'ouse.

Then Furu told me that the older child 'ad married locally. She'd found a decent, steady lad, 'e didn't 'ave all that much land but was very 'ard-workin'. The younger one 'adn't been so lucky, she 'adn't listened to 'im an' 'ad gone up to Borháncs in the other 'Óstát, an' there she was an incomer an' 'ad to work 'er mother-in-law's land as well as their own.

'And you, clever Green Kali, 'alf of what we've 'eard about you isn't true, is it?' asked Sándor.

'What do people say, then? Cos I can't know that, can I? It's not me they tell.'

'That your 'usband's not much good.'

'That's true enough, but there are others worse. The sort what beats their wives, an' can't do without drink an' the pub. Or don't work. Mine works, sees to 'is mother's land as well an' 'elps 'is family.'

We was eatin' the tasty, rich puliszka.

'He's been taken into 'ospital,' I told 'em. 'Pancreas trouble. I've got to go in tomorrow an' take 'im some medicine. 'E might be 'avin' an operation.'

'Oh, you poor thing,' said Sándor, 'you can go to 'ospital, but those thievin' doctors rob you blind. And now that operations are free for ev'ry-body you've still got to take so much in.'

Then Biri said, oh dear, what could she give me for me 'usband, what did 'e eat? She'd give me a bit of túró, some boiled greens to take. She'd never set eyes on 'im, but I should tell 'im what a good wife 'e'd got, 'e should look after 'er. 'E couldn't be such a bad man if 'e'd got a wife like me.

No, damn it.

I told Biri there was no need of anythin', 'e was given ev'rythin' in the 'ospital. Soft food, that was all 'e could eat. But she wouldn't 'ave it, she'd go to the market early, an' she told me off, there was no way I wouldn't take it. You couldn't get better on the stuff they serve up in 'ospital.

Then Biri an' I 'ad another long talk outside on the porch. Sándor went to bed early, 'ad to get up at four o'clock an' go out to the fields. Poor woman, she poured out 'er 'eart about 'avin' no children. She went on an' on, I thought she'd never stop. Cos that's what complainin's like, once it starts it's like a brook, it grows an' grows, becomes a river an' ev'n carries away big trees. She was pinin' like that for a child.

I told 'er to rest content, she'd brought up two orphans, that was more in the sight of God than rearin' 'er own. And she asked me quietly whether me 'usband wasn't really such a bad man, cos she'd 'eard that 'e'd always got a knife in 'is boot when 'e went to the pub. I told 'er that it was true, 'e was a strict man. And stingy, but whatever 'e did, 'e earned the money. But all the same, 'e wasn't such a good man, I said more quietly. And now it all came out of me. Not so good, 'e beat me when 'e lost 'is temper. To put it in a nutshell, 'e was a swine. A rotter. Cos in the end I needed somebody to tell. And then Biri tried to cheer me up.

'Leave 'im alone, Kali my dear, leave 'im alone, don't irritate 'im, look after 'im, especially now 'e's sick in bed. That's what men are like. Lose their temper an' 'it you. My father used to 'it me as well. I got it for all sorts of little things. If I was quick with work it was cos I 'adn't done it properly, if I wasn't it was cos I'd been lazy. 'E beat me, but 'e was fair. 'E never taught me any wrong. And the way 'e 'it my brother, beat 'im, thrashed 'im. 'E was still only little an' 'e damaged 'is new boots kicking things with 'em. 'E beat 'im so that 'e lay unconscious for three days. We thought 'e was going to die. And we couldn't call the doctor to 'im. 'E wouldn't allow it. It would cost a lot. Mummy wanted to take 'im to 'ospital, even put 'im in the cart. 'E wouldn't let 'er. But there was no 'itting 'im back. You don't 'it back. So it came as no surprise that my brother left us. 'E was a really nice lad, sixteen years of age. My father gave 'im another good 'iding before 'e left 'ome. With a stick. And 'e never came back. 'E went an' became an electrician, didn't work on the land again. I wasn't really so upset that 'e went. When people outgrow the 'ouse they leave. And my brother's working, doing well. Dad said it was shameful to work for somebody else, for your daily bread to depend on whether somebody gives you a job or not. We didn't ask for anything from anybody, did we? We work the land an' we've got all we want. But it did 'urt us that 'e left the church, 'e joined a sect, became a Jehovah's Witness. And 'e got married as well, an' she's a Jehovah's Witness. That really upset us. I'll say one thing, Kali: just don't leave 'ome like 'e did. If 'e's a good man, doesn't spend 'is time in the pub, 'as a regular job, mind you don't annoy 'im, just don't leave. I've been lucky with Sándor, cos 'e's got a very good reputation, 'e's such a good man.'

But that was why I'd come to see Biri, I wanted to tell 'er 'ow things stood. To tell Biri at least, to get it off me chest. Only when I saw the way they was sympathetic an' anxious I couldn't come out with it. And I ev'n thought at the time that perhaps I ought to go back to the 'ouse next day. So I didn't say anythin' about 'ow things were. I stuck to me story about goin' to the 'ospital. And Biri went on complainin'.

'But all the same, my Sándor's got one fault. Ev'rybody alive must 'ave one, mustn't they? Cos ev'n roses 'ave thorns, whatever the perfume's like. Cos 'e's very fond of money. Goes mad about it. Really watches it.'

Well, thought I, who doesn't like money? Ev'rybody does, whether they've got any or not. 'Avin' none's the worst thing what can 'appen to you.

'So tomorrow off you go,' said she, 'an' take in this bit of túró an' greens an' the carrots out of the soup, 'ave this tomato an' paprika I've just picked, look at the size of the tomato. Anybody this doesn't cure the Lord must be callin' for 'im.'

And so she put 'em in a bag. I did the washin' up for 'em, properly with two bowls, not like at 'ome under the tap, lettin' the clean water run from the tap onto the dishes, that was good enough for those scruffy people. Then I asked for a bowl of 'ot water, I said I'd better not take any infection from the cattle into the 'ospital. So I washed me feet an' dried 'em, cos they was still givin' way. And I couldn't walk, they were so sore. I asked for a drop of vinegar, soaked a cloth an' put it on me feet overnight. Well, they'll soon be putting vinegar-soaked cloth on me, cos that's the custom, it means the shroud. But mine was the shroud I got there in the big 'ouse while I was livin' there. I gave 'im twenty years, I wish 'e'd stayed in the ditch when 'e fell in it drunk. Why did I wait all that time, I'm an old woman now.

I wasn't goin' to the 'ospital, I 'adn't got anybody there at all, an' God save me from bein' a patient. I was goin' to the servant market more likely. Be there nice an' early an' 'ire meself. I'd got nothin' left only meself to sell, I'd go into service. It's no good Furu sayin' 'e's 'is own boss, ev'rybody' serves somebody. An 'Óstát man's a servant, an' so's the king if 'e's a good king, 'e just 'as to be. 'E serves 'is people, like King Mátyás did. It's only bad kings that don't. But since King 'ired for a nursemaid. Or to see to cows, or plant onions. You're a big girl, we 'aven't 'ad a proper 'Ungarian king to 'ave stories about 'im for children to learn. Oh, the stories I know about that King Mátyás. But what's the good if nobody will ev'r listen!

So I was goin' out up the town to the servant market. Like when I was a little girl, just turned twelve, I wasn't allowed any sooner. Me mother took me up to Kincses town to the market.

She said, 'Listen, Kali, I'm going' to take you an' get you 'ired tomorrow. I'll dress you up in kerchief an' overskirt, an' you'll easily be 'ow, useful on the land.'

Next day off we went. I was ev'r so 'appy at bein' a breadwinner! As early as four o'clock all the clever boys an' girls from Szék were standin' there, bein' 'ired by the 'Óstát people, an' they went like 'ot cakes. The boys wore sort of little pointy caps an' the girls 'ad nice white kerchiefs. Oh, it's been twenty-two years since I was in service.

Well, this time I'm takin' meself to get 'ired. Dear mother, if you did but know. She'll find out, won't 'ave long to wait. It won't take a day for 'er to know, cos that's what the village is like, ev'rythin' gets talked about.

Cos I've left 'ome an' come to town, forty kilometres on foot.

Of course, I'd made preparations for that big journey, I'd 'ad it organized for ages. But it's big not so much cos of the number of kilometres, that's just a good day's walk. But rather cos I 'ad to pull meself together an' desert the 'ouse for which I'd suffered so much. A great big 'ouse in the main street of Felszeg, though I'd never ev'n 'ave seen what it was like inside. Whatever would a Forrószék girl go to Felszeg for? In me mother's time a lad would've been stabbed if a Felszeg person wanted to 'ire 'im. But I'd got me eye on that great big 'ouse, it was painted blue on all sides, two windows on the street, three on the porch, a big cellar underneath, nice an' 'igh, such a big front room that I used to 'old dances in it. The yard was neglected when I was taken there as mistress of the 'ouse, not a single flower in it, just a stable, an' all the buildin's were sound, whether for animals or people, it looked as if there'd been a grand owner there at one time, only just then there was no mistress. There was a garden an' land an' ev'rythin'.

Me father 'ad told me not to regard the 'ouse when I thought of gettin' married, but the person. Well, yes, I thought, but what was wrong with this man? 'E was small, didn't 'ave a lot to say, didn't come courtin' with sweet nothin's, but always came, ev'ry Saturday, an' sat there. 'E never took me to a ball, we never went dancin', 'e'd just sit there puttin' away tészta an' pálinka, not sayin' much—an' that to me parents. Only when the ev'nin' was dark an' we was sittin' out on the porch, 'e'd start touchin' me up. But then the way 'e did it, me breasts 'urt, the way 'e grabbed 'em. I said to 'im, I wasn't afraid or anythin', just don't squeeze so 'ard, 'E never apologized, just couldn't control 'imself.

And I might 'ave thought that the time wasn't right to join two lives together. Cos as I was goin' to the wedding with me bouquet, out of our gate, all decorated with blue cornflowers, I tripped up. Nobody said anythin', as if it was usual. You're supposed to spit an' carry the bride through the gate to show that you'll always stand by 'er, whatever trouble she's in, if she's ill or anythin', you'll 'old 'er in your arms. That's the custom. But 'e didn't. If I'd turned back at that gate me life would 'ave been different. If I'd turned back people would 'ave been cross, argued with me, ev'n 'it me, then it would all 'ave been forgotten an' I've made a different life for meself.

One of me bridesmaids as well 'ad a bad cold at the weddin', she sneezed a good three times when we was in the church. It'd 'ave been much too late to run away then. And so that's what all that time 'ad in store for me. I've just been an' wasted it.

Well, you won't even be talkin' to me now, you swine, I think to meself, cos I shan't be there to 'ear you! Cos a year ago I made me mind up an' started gettin' some money together. I sewed a pocket on the inside of me skirt an' always put it in there so 'e shouldn't find it. Once 'e did find it, took it all off me an' 'it me so 'ard on me back with a stick that me mother put a cold compress on it. Right then, you swine! So I started savin' up again, scraped it together with me fingernails. Cos I was always weavin' linen an' takin' it to sell, walkin' over the bridge to Bonchída an' Szamosújvár, an' one time I sent some to town with me sister. Of course, linen don't bring in much. Then I secretly sold some to young girls, an' to young Filep, cos she was gettin' married an' was short of linen, it's a disgrace for a girl to be short of linen to take to 'er new 'ome. It means she's lazy. Cos never mind that you can get it in shops, you've got to make your own if you're a poor girl an' want to get married. Cos that shows what an 'ardworkin' girl you are. And I made 'emp sacks, cos we 'ad 'emp as well in Csukás pond an' the other one next to Palló, an' I stole it from me old man, I did. It made nice strong sacks, ev'n the 'ostát people bought 'em. And I put away a nice length of linen for meself, an' in the attic I tied up in a sack two blouses, a waistcoat, some foot-cloths, a kerchief, an apron an' me best skirt, an' then I'd made three pairs of knickers as well. Me bag was ready for the journey when that swine got that as well. 'E'd gone up for the pálinka still an' 'e noticed it, cos I'd put it by the big bread trough cos I didn't 'ave to use it, there was only the two of us so I didn't 'ave to make that much bread. 'E realized straight off what I was up to. 'E ran round to see me father an' told 'im Kali means to run away. But first 'e gave me a good 'idin'. The Ungváris' servant 'eard from the yard, 'e was goin' 'ome from the fields, an' I was shoutin'. Me father came an' said that if I went 'e'd shoot me. 'E'd take me to the Jew's, cos 'e 'ad a gun, an' 'e'd shoot me dead. But 'e could see that I'd been beaten up. Ev'n the sleeve of me blouse was torn. 'E took me 'ome an' let me stay for a week, cos me mother begged 'im, an' then 'e sent me back.

Then I began to think that I'd never get away. Where was I to go at me time of life if I wasn't allowed back to me parents' 'ouse? That thief was goin' to live as long as me or longer still. Cos God gives wicked people long lives so that they may suffer for their wickedness 'ere on earth. 'E gives good people not so much, cos the good enjoy ev'n the little they get. Cos that's the way it was with poor Sári Juhos. God gave 'er a short life, but she was 'appy with that. I couldn't wait for that man to turn 'is toes up.

Then one Saturday ev'nin' 'e came 'ome from the pub again. 'Is clothes were all covered in mud, 'e'd fallen in the water, or somebody'd pushed 'im in for misbehavin'. 'E'd lost 'is 'at an' 'is shirt was torn. 'E came 'ome, kicked the door open. 'E didn't say a word, not so much as 'allo, an' there was no visitor to say 'allo to 'im. I'd been in bed a long time but I 'adn't gone to sleep cos I was frightened. In 'e came, boots an' all, rolled into bed, gave me a shove, muttered somethin' that wasn't 'uman speech. 'E undid 'is *gatya* an' tried to get 'is boots off. I told 'im to go to 'is own place, what was 'e disturbin' me for. 'E said some filthy words, then pushed up against me. I pushed 'im away an' 'e rolled onto the floor, just like that, an' 'it 'is 'ead, Now you'll be for it, Kali, I thought, for pushin' 'im. But 'e could 'ardly get to 'is feet an' grabbed me duvet to pull 'imself up. 'E nearly tore it, an' it was a good strong duvet. I always 'id the pálinka, but this time I thought I'd give it 'im, at least I'd get some peace. I brought it, poured out a good glass, an' 'e climbed up. 'E drank it out of the glass, then out of the bottle. Well, Kali, I thought, you'll see no more of that. When 'e put the bottle down to stand up 'e fell over again. Then 'e shouted that I'd pushed 'im, insulted 'im, but by that time 'e was inco'erent. Right, Kali, thought I, your time 'as come. Only 'e'd got 'is boots on, an' there was a knife in one. I thought, I'll take 'is boots off, 'e can't stop me. I went to 'is feet, an' 'e kicked like a wild 'orse. I told 'im nicely to take 'is things off an' get to bed, it was the middle of the night. I wasn't givin' 'im orders, I'd bring 'im somethin' to eat an' some pálinka. And then 'e could fuck me, I'd just take 'is boots off an' take 'em out. 'E stood up, drank from the bottle again, an' then fell down on the spot. I went over, 'e grabbed me nightdress, then me, an' I fell on top of 'im. 'E was 'oldin' me an' pullin' me on top of 'im. 'E was goin' to brain me, evil witch. I caught 'old of a leg of the table an' got away from 'im, right, I thought, now you're for it, you old fogey. cos it's true, that much older than me. Ten or twelve years, but only as big as me. On the wall was the carved stick that the agricultural engineer 'ad left when 'e came to measure the land in 'Ungarian times an' stayed with us. Oh, 'e was a nice, kind man. I'd 'ave taken 'im to me bed. But 'e wouldn't come. I just 'ung 'is stick up so as to 'ave a pleasant memory of one man at least. I took it down an' said to 'im, 'Keep off me or I'll strike you! I've never in my life 'it anybody, but you'll be in for it this time.'

And again 'e roared an' went for me. Who was I keepin' me cunt for, 'e asked. Who needed me old worn-out cunt? That's the shameless way 'e was talkin'.

Then I let 'im 'ave one on 'is back. Quite a good one, it made 'im squeal. Then 'e turned round to grab me, but I belted 'm again, this time caught 'im in the ribs. And again on 'is arse. I really 'it 'im, might ev'n 'ave caught 'is balls. I didn't care. Then 'e fell face down on the floor. I gave 'im another on the back an' shouted 'Move an' you'll get some more. I'll beat the soul out of you, you swine.'

'E didn't 'ave a soul what might come out, just a stinkin' fart. 'E daren't move, cos I was standin' there over 'im watchin'. And I'd never 'it a child when I'd been a nursemaid, 'owever naughty they was.

Pista Mostis an' 'is family next-door must 'ave 'eard us if they weren't asleep. But they usually were, cos old Pista didn't go down the pub cos of 'is liver. By that time they was used to there bein' a shindig in our place on a Saturday night when the master of the 'ouse came 'ome.

I was standin' there over 'im like the 'albardier statue in the main square of Kolozsvár. Or like a dog catcher. I 'ardened me 'eart an' I didn't move. I waited a bit, then I 'eard 'im start to snore there on the floor. Three good whacks with a stick wasn't goin' to kill 'im. Or six, for that matter. So there I stayed for a while yet, till I was sure 'e was fast asleep. It was after midnight.

Then I went quietly, took the knife out of 'is boot an' the other two what I 'ad in the kitchen an' put 'em on an 'igh shelf so as 'e wouldn't find 'em. Then I began to get me things together. I went about quietly like a cat on the prowl, but I didn't let the stick out of me 'and. I quickly collected ev'rythin', I knew what I needed, an' I got out the bread, some bacon, a little pot of plum jam an' the linen what I'd got woven. I opened the cupboard, took out a nice kerchief an' an old one as well, to 'ave somethin' to wear for work, an' I stuffed a towel with roses on it in the bag, I might be able to sell it. 'E'd always got money in 'is waistcoat pocket, but I didn't go after it, if I'd woken 'im up I'd 'ave spoiled me luck. I 'adn't got much money cos 'e'd taken it all off me what 'e'd found, an' I 'adn't been able to get any together, I could only scratch a bit when I did some weavin'. 'E never ev'n gave me any that we took from the dances. I just 'ad to clean the floor under 'is muddy boots. Then I went back, put me coat on, ev'rythin' was ready. I sat back down on the bench with the stick in me 'ands an' waited. I'd 'ave to be off ev'n before dawn broke. If 'ed woken up 'e'd 'ave killed me.

I just sat there, listenin' to the death-watch beetles in the woodwork. I couldn't 'ear 'im breathin'. I wasn't listenin' for it either. Me thoughts were out of the 'ouse. I was anticipatin' me journey.

I 'ad a nice drink of water before settin' out, there was no tellin' when I'd get any more. It wasn't quite four o'clock when I left. The animals were still quiet, the whole village was asleep. I went out the back way, down the short street, then towards the Gypsy 'ouses so as not to be caught an' questioned. Down that way they don't chain the dogs, but they just came up an' sniffed at me. I'd brought some bread with me an' threw some to 'em so as they shouldn't bark. So ev'n more came, an' I'd got an 'ole army after me. They followed me, like the disciples followin' the Lord Christ. They went with me as far as the last shack.

Then I doubled back an' went along by the Palló. Perhaps I ought to 'ave gone in the Palló, right in the water, like that poor Sári Juhos when she was grievin'. It's a lovely story, I've been able to tell about Sári Juhos for ev'r so long. Cos she 'ad a real love, an' they wouldn't let 'er marry 'im. A Romanian lad, but 'e was all right. Cos there in the village we 'ad five Romanian families, decent people, respectful of all the 'Ungarians. The way they worked, 'em Bucsas, really tidy people. But they wouldn't let 'em marry. So they just carried on in secret. And so young Sári went for a walk by the Palló. She'd put on a big skirt an' filled it full of stones. And then the lad left the village, 'e was grievin' so, an' went to another, where there was only Romanians. It's a lovely true story.

That wasn't why I went by the Palló, I just 'ad to go that way, believe me, if I wanted to stay alive.

Instead I went out towards Pali 'Intás 'ill, an' a bit farther on there's a sheep-fold, an' I went round that an' along by the bushes. I couldn't see a thing, just followed me nose, it was dark, but I knew which way Bonchida was, only I didn't take the road but went through the fields. I didn't stop for a rest until I was well away from the village. I went past Bodon's Well, they only call it that now, there's no well there. I could 'ear the frogs croakin' a long way from Csukás pool, they don't sleep, they look out for one another. It was too dark to see anythin', there was just the saline soil crunchin' under me feet. The village area's so big, it's more like a town. Only the soil's so poor, its bein' big's no use.

By the time I came to old András Demeter's 'ill, it was beginnin' to be light. A bit farther on was Nucuj's Well. That's just a name as well, there's no well there. From the other side of the 'ill, you can see Bonchida church. Now, as I reached the top there was a bit of a landslip, I took one step an' lost me footin', the ground gave way under me. I slid down on me bum. Fortunately a bush stopped me goin' right to the bottom. I 'ung onto it. If I'd done that me clothes'd 'ave been torn shreds on the bushes. See, me skirt's not torn, just got a bit creased where I sat on it. So I stood up, but me legs started to shake somethin' awful. Goodness knows why. I caught 'old of 'em an' looked, why on earth were me legs shakin' so as I couldn't walk. I 'ad to sit down. They'd collapsed like a set of bagpipes. There I sat, nearly at the bottom of the slope. I couldn't get up, cos me legs wouldn't take me weight. Dawn was breakin', Bonchida church was comin' into view. I said to meself, Green Kali Szabó, either go back now, cos by the time it's light you'd be 'ome, or go as far as you can see, cos then you'll never be able to go back. Your father'd shoot you, that rotten 'usband of yours'd beat you to death. I could 'ave gone to me sister's an' to me dear brother Mihály, 'im what's become an Adventist, 'e'd 'ave been such a good man otherwise, but 'e'd gone an' joined that sect. They'd realize that I'd left 'ome an' I'd 'ave 'ad it. But there I was sittin' on the 'illside an' me legs wouldn't carry me, ev'n though I told 'em to. 'Ow much longer am I goin' to sit 'ere, I thought. Come on, Kali, this is where you'll end up. You'll neither 'ave got away nor stayed put. Like the stupid girl in the folk tale when the ugly king wanted 'er. She wanted 'is money but not 'is looks. Well that's just 'ow I was.

By that time I could make out old Gergi Filep's shack. It's got no roof, cos that man lives like an 'ermit. 'Is son went off to the war an' ev'r since 'e's been waitin' for 'im. 'Is wife died an' 'e was left alone. So 'e came out 'ere an' never went back. Somebody said to 'im, at least put some straw on the roof. What for? 'e asked, if it don't rain there's no need of a roof, an' if it does rain it'll trickle through. 'E's been livin' there, waitin' for death. Don't do nothin'.

I'd been sittin' on me bum like that as well since I fell down the 'ill. I couldn't get up. I wasn't 'urt, I felt over me legs. Me strength 'ad just given out. I sat an' waited for 'em to feel like goin' on. I'm not used to sittin' an' lookin' at the view. If anybody saw me in the distance, what would they 'ave thought: poor old woman, driven out of 'er 'ouse? Or she's been stealin' or somethin' else shameful, an' 'ad to run away? Nobody would think, to see me sittin' there, that I was a respectable married woman. Respectable married women don't sit on their bums in the middle of nowhere when the dawn's breakin', sheddin' tears.

I said to 'em, Now then, legs, come on, but not like in the folk tale for you to do as you please an' try to carry the poor girl to the devil. Why does the devil always 'ave to be temptin' women an' girls? 'E might tempt rotten men as well. Cos 'ow much better is that? Well, I started straight away to tell the story about the poor lad instead. Or the widower. The devil puts the man to the test, an' if 'e conducts 'imself well 'e's given the good woman, the good wife, or Goldilocks. If 'e withstands the temptation. In some stories 'e does, in some 'e's caught out. That's 'ow I tell it, about a man, not a woman.

There just needs to be somebody to listen. Cos I'm used to singin' to meself, but me tongue just won't tell stories. But while it was still 'Ungarian times a clever man came to see me mother an' asked for stories. And 'e wrote 'em down in 'is book. What's the good of tellin' stories to a book? They should be told to children, to men an' women, not to books. And 'e certainly couldn't 'ave written down the way me mother livened up all the stories, makin' the king speak one way, Goldilocks another, an' the lamb a third.

Well, don't just tell stories, Kali, but get goin'. Come on, legs, Left, right, left, right. The Lord 'as given me willpower, me mother was always sayin', 'Kali, you certainly know 'ow to wish for things. You're like Márton Ferenczi's eldest son when 'is two 'orses fell in the ditch. 'E pulled 'em out just like that. All by 'imself, an' 'e was only a little fellow. Only mind you wish for good things, not bad.' And who's goin' to say what's good an' what's bad, where I'm goin'? Whether I've done right or wrong in runnin' away? And what comes next? Into service or on the game.

So, now I'm well clear of Szék, I'm on the land of the big landowner in Bonchida. This is where the count lives. Or used to. As I look round, there's been no ploughin' done. The land's just bare, nothing's been planted. It's like the empty cradle in an 'ouse, brings tears to your eyes to look at it. I think the count an' 'is family 'ave been forced out of Bonchida, same as all the Ungváris in our village. They'd got enough acres to be taken away. They were loaded onto a lorry an' driven off, poor things. But the way 'e used to work! Aristocrat 'e might be, but 'e was a servant just the same. Never did 'e sit about like the idle rich, nor did 'is lady wife, they were on the land day an' night, 'ad just two servants, couldn't afford any more. We was never told where they were taken, prison or wherever. They'd become *déos*es, that's what they was called, *déo*es. What does *déo* mean? Must be Romanian. *Deo*. Not what's written on the wall in the church, surely?

The gentry were relocated from our village a year ago now. Maybe it was two years. In lorries, in the night. Their land's just been left, completely dry. Nobody dared touch it. Then this year men came an' the state ploughed it all up.

Well, Szék was well behind me by then. From where I was I could still see the 'ayfield 'ill, but there was no green on it. All the grass there 'ad been reaped an' grazed bare, ev'rythin' was all wilted, dry as a bone. There wasn't ev'n anywhere left to leave the 'erd, it 'ad to be taken farther up, towards Farkas wood. The sun was scorchin' the ground, wasn't it ashamed of itself not to cool down a bit. Cos it was September, you know, an' still blazin' 'ot. That's the time when big patches of salt appear down our way, an' all around the statice sprouts, though 'ereabouts it's grey. It's saline land. There used to be a salt mine 'ere in the old days. Then it was shut down. What became of the salt nobody knows. Cos salt's the kind of thing as tends to come to the surface. And if it's on the surface of the ground, stands to reason it's underneath as well.

Me damn legs was still as wobbly as an aspic when I crossed the village boundary. I'd taken me boots off now, I could 'ardly walk any better, but I carried 'em on me shoulder. I'd put me best ones on, what I'd got when I was still a girl, before I got married, an' me feet 'ad grown since then. They were good strong boots, solid, like tree trunks. I'd left me soft ones behind, couldn't make room for 'em. Me poor legs were shakin' cos they didn't know where they were goin', where their owner was takin' 'em. And then in the middle of nowhere I 'ad a good weep. That damn life with that swine of a man. But I was the one what 'ad ruined it, wantin' that great big 'ouse, I'd always 'ad me eye on it, I'd not ev'n been inside as a grown woman, just imagined plantin' the front with flowers, sortin' out the yard, paintin' the fence green cos I was Green Kali. All the poultry I was goin' to 'ave in the yard, ev'n get a turkey off the Gypsies, cos they 'ave those. I'd paint the porch green, cos that's me colour. I was a greedy girl, thinkin' of nothin' but money, cos I wanted to get away from the Green Szabós' little reed-thatched 'ouse. I couldn't see anythin' but that big 'ouse. What me man was goin' to be like was somethin' me short-sighted eyes didn't see. Me mother set me up very nicely, pillows, duvets an' crockery, a load of clothes, ev'rythin', an' I was given a bit of land as well. Just short of an acre, that wasn't much.

And now I'd left that 'ouse without sayin' so much as God be with me. Or crossin' meself. I went round pickin' things up, thinkin' of 'avin' ev'rythin' for the journey, an' I was just careful to shut the door quietly an' to walk without me boots creakin'. Not like somebody goin' on a great journey, but somebody escapin'.

I didn't go into Bonchida, somebody might 'ave recognized me. I'd already worked it out, if anybody asked where I was off to I'd say I was takin' linen to sell, I knew a woman in Bonchida, Szamosújvár, Zsuk, Apahida, whichever was nearest when I was asked. And I'd got a bundle, I wouldn't be lyin'.

I skirted Bonchida an' 'eaded for Felső-Zsuk. I plodded along, up 'ill an' down dale, an' there are some long 'ills in those parts, they stretch out in front of you like strips of spaghetti. There's no end to 'em, cos there's no forest or anythin' of note so that you know which way you're goin'. That's the sort of great big badland the Mezőség is. Then I caught sight of the church in Zsuk. I preferred to avoid ploughlands an' meadows in case a farmer saw me, an' I went towards the 'ills so as not to meet anybody. I crossed the Little Szamos below Zsuk an' sat on the bank for a bit. I could see the Zsuk mansion in the distance, all the windows at the back 'ad been smashed in. That's where Baron Kemény lived. Perhaps 'e'd been relocated as well for 'avin' too much land.

I gave me kerchief a good wash in the Szamos cos it was gettin' very 'ot, an' put it back on soakin' wet. And I wetted me undershirt as well. By that time me back was beginnin' to ache, an' me legs were feelin' 'eavy an' I'd still got quite a way to walk before I got to golden Kolozsvár. I stayed on the side of the Szamos so as not to lose me way. It does twist an' turn, though, it's not been straightened out by engineers.

I often sat down as well. But me back wasn't 'urtin' any longer, cos I was gettin' shootin' pains in me 'ips, as if I was about to give birth. As if they were splittin' apart. But the good thing was I'd got me back better. You can't 'ave pains in two places at once. And then I went an' trod on a big sharp thorn, I shouted out in pain, an' after that couldn't feel me 'ips. That's the way poor people get better. By then I was comin' to Alsó-Zsuk. But that river does wind about. I'd 'ave tried to straighten me route out a bit, but I'd 'ave got lost. A man can always judge direction better, 'e'll look at the sun an' be able to tell. But I can't do it. I just kept followin' me nose. By then Apahida was in sight, an' I started goin' quicker an' the pain went. I was walkin' pretty well. At Apahida the station was still in ruins, cos there'd been shellin' there, we'd 'eard it. We was afraid it was goin' to come our way as well, but it didn't. There's no railway or factory or prison down our way for the swine to shell.

Havin' nothin' to eat wasn't doin' me any good, but I could really 'ave done with a drink. I didn't drink from the Szamos, though, for fear of catchin' jaundice. So, I got to Sînnicoară, a Romanian village. I didn't know anybody there but the turkey-woman on the outskirts who used to go around in a cart bringin' 'em stupid birds to sell. Cos turkeys are really rotten creatures, 'Ungarians don't keep 'em at all. So there in Szinnikora I eventually 'ad a drink from a well. If there'd been a bridge, I'd 'ave preferred to cross, cos of the way the shadows were lyin' on the far side, an' I wouldn't 'ave 'ad to walk in the sun. I sat down for a rest under the trees an' started to cry again, I could 'ardly get back on me feet. So I sang a bit of a sad song an' went on.

Did you love me? Did you ever!
All I did was get to know you.
And the way I got to know you
I'll remember you for ever.

I certainly shall.

That song says it all. You can't ev'r forget anythin' bad. A bad 'usband. Like in the tale about poor Julis Bandi. She tried an' tried to forget 'er 'usband, couldn't ev'n when 'e was dead, but she didn't marry the man in the big fur coat, the devil, cos the devil's a man in a big fur coat with money comin' out of 'is pockets all the time. But she married a rotten man from Szék, a nice fat farmer, say no more. It made no difference that the rotter 'ad died, Julis couldn't forget 'im an' she went on grievin' the rest of 'er life.

So Kali, that's 'ow you'll end up as well.

After that I went past Szamosfalva without noticin'. I couldn't feel me legs under me any longer, I was so tired out, but I 'ad to press on if I wanted to arrive while it was still light.

From where I was I could see the 'ayfields in Kolozsvár, an' Kölesföld an' the 'Óstát lands, an' I began to control meself, me legs weren't tremblin' now. The 'Óstát people was all out on the land, the most marvellous land there is anywhere, it's like a chemist's shop. It's watered from tanks, an' lower down there are waterwheels as well what 'oist the water. It's as orderly as in a factory. The beds are laid out in straight lines, an' densely planted, an' the soil is black. It's manured all the time. Just then they were 'arvestin' the greens, dumpin' the manure an' spreadin' it round. I did a lot of that when I was a servant. We never went out to the land empty-handed. And the big mill wheels rumbled, bringin' water up from the Szamos an' irrigatin'. They weren't goin' to wait for the Lord to send rain, were they! Cos they could certainly 'ave been waitin' for it just then. The Lord 'ad business elsewhere, it seemed, not with the poor people. It 'ad been three weeks since there'd been any rain.

I pressed on, didn't stop to admire 'em. So, I'd got to go straight through the town, I thought, an' find me old master. Then I'd spend the night there. It's a good size, that town, damn it, as long as a vintage ball sash. The centre is small an' the outskirts are enormous. I was goin' to me old boss Furu's place an' to tell Biri 'ow things were. I'd pour me 'eart out to somebody. And next day I'd go to the market. I 'adn't worked it out, but it so 'appened there'd be a servant market next day. It's a Thursday.

I asked Biri in the ev'nin' whether it was still the way, that ev'ry first an' fifteenth of the month there was a servants' market, cos I 'ad to enquire for a friend.

'Oh, forget it, that sort of thing doesn't 'appen now. There'll be militiamen stationed on Karolina Square an' behind the post office.'

I was startled.

'So there's no servants market any longer?'

'Well, not exactly, but you can't 'ire a servant in the street.'

'How's it done, then?' I asked.

'Well, nohow.'

Then I told 'er that I 'ad to go to the market cos I'd arranged to meet a friend there. Well, I'd better be careful if I went, cos they were on the lookout for Szék people in particular. We could be known straight away, couldn't we, by our clothes, men by their little straw 'ats an' women by their red skirts. So that's that, Green Kali. You can go beggin' if you can't find work.

What's the world comin' to if I couldn't ev'n be a servant? What were those people after? Ev'n though I was worn out I 'ardly slept. I kept wonderin' what I was to do if I didn't find work as a servant? That was all I could do, be a servant.

Then in the mornin' I said goodbye to Biri with lots of kisses an' I promised 'er I'd come again when me 'usband was better. Well, Biri me dear, it'll be a long time before 'e does that. Maybe 'e's on 'is feet by now an' 'oldin' 'is back, cos the swine got a real whack on it.

I packed me things together an' set off for the servants' market, not all that early. The master an' Biri 'ad left for the fields, they 'ad a lot to do in September. I was left to pull the gate to. What time must it 'ave been? Six o'clock, I suppose. I played with a black an' white cat for a bit, to pass the time.

An' then the servants' market was like it used to be. I didn't see any militiamen. An' it's not good if it shows that you were standin' there at six o'clock, people think you'll go to the first that asks you. Then it was eight o'clock, I 'eard the clock strike. I could only see one girl from Szék with 'er mother, makin' a great fuss to an employer she was bargainin' with. She didn't spot me. Maybe the 'Óstát people 'ad already engaged servants, they always wanted to do so early so as to take 'em out on the land that same day. I wondered 'ow long I should wait. If I 'adn't been taken on by eleven there'd only be rubbish, the left-overs, who nobody wanted. I stood up straight, smoothed me apron, showed what a nice strong back I'd got an' knotted me kerchief neatly under me chin. So I wasn't goin' to look weak. It was important for me not to look old, cos then I wouldn't be engaged. A pale little woman was goin' around, screwin' up 'er eyes. And another 'Óstát man, but I turned away from 'im, I wasn't goin' to be an 'Óstát servant again. I'd done me time with 'em. Unless there was a child to see to. I'd 'ave liked it like that. It'd be really nice to 'ave a tiny little child to nurse, but for that young, cheap kids are taken on, twelve years old. One child to go with another. It doesn't take such a strong, expensive woman, an' I'd need a proper wage.

Women from the town came as well, all sorts of people, some better off than others. Only one woman asked me 'ow much I expected, an' she then moved on.

Then along came a man, didn't look like a workman nor a teacher either, couldn't tell what 'e was. A townsman. 'E looked at one an' another, like a well-fed chicken, bein' choosy, not likin' any of 'em. 'E walked round, then made to leave. Then 'e turned back an' came straight towards me. I turned away so that 'e shouldn't see that I'd been watchin' 'im an' was 'opin' 'e'd speak to me.

'Good morning! You're from Szék, I see.'

I said good mornin' back. 'E asked, 'ad I been 'ired. I said I certainly 'adn't, I wouldn't 'ave been there lookin' at the pigeons if I 'adn't been free.

'What are you lookin' for, sir?' I asked.

'I'm lookin' for an 'ousekeeper,' said 'e.

I didn't quite know what to say to that.

'Well, you'll certainly find a domestic at the market,' I told 'im, cos I'd got no idea what was expected of an 'ousekeeper.

'Say a domestic, then. So, 'ow much would an experienced domestic like you want?'

Well, experienced I certainly was, cos I'd been a servant all me life. Only not on the market, I thought. So I said to 'im, 'That's not 'ow servants are 'ired, askin' 'ow much they want, but first the servant enquires what the work involves.'

It looked as if I'd 'ave to teach 'im.

'What d'you mean, then, what the work involves?' 'e asked, lookin' me up an' down.

'Well, what about land, animals, 'ow many children are there, what ages, will she 'ave to cook or will your wife do that, is there another servant an' what does she do? When you know what the work involves you can state a price an' get 'ired.'

'There's land, but she's not allowed to touch it,' this gentleman told me, an' laughed aloud. 'No animals apart from mice. No children. She'd 'ave to cook an' see to the 'ouse.'

'Well, why don't you get married, sir?' I asked 'im. 'That's the sort of thing a wife does, an' you don't 'ave to pay 'er.'

'Don't tell me what to do,' 'e said crossly, an' was movin' on. Evidently, the nervous sort. 'I don't need a lippy servant to give me instructions.'

Well, I could see now, this one was quick-tempered as well, I knew the type. Now 'e was movin' away.

So I called after 'im, 'I was only jokin', sir, come back.' Then 'e asked, could I sell things. 'Well,' I replied, 'a Szék woman may know nothin' about cookin' an' ironin', but she'll surely be able to sell things. What would there be to sell?' 'That you'll see,' 'e answered. Then I asked where I'd 'ave to go. 'E said 'ed got a big garden in the Békás district. I asked whether the owner was an 'Óstát man, cos me previous position 'ad been in the 'Óstát. We discussed terms. What I asked for 'e gave me. And 'e said I'd 'ave to take two days a week off. 'A double day off?' I asked, I was surprised. I'd never 'eard of such a thing. 'Wednesday an' Friday,' 'e said, 'Those are your days off.' 'And not the Lord's Day?' So, it seemed that the world 'ad changed so much in that respect as well since I'd not been in service. Time off in the workin' week, I thought? What sort of a place is this? No Lord's Day, just work.

Then we set off. 'E went in front, takin' big strides, in an 'urry, so full of go. 'E strode out like the man with the magic boots in the folk tale, but 'e wasn't such a big man. Just rather active an' on the go like a puli. And 'e'd said 'e was in an 'urry. Me feet were still sore from the previous day, but there was nothin' for it, I 'ad to follow 'im. 'E'd steady up. It was cos of 'is age. When me dear mother was alive, 'ow often 'ad she walked into town to sell things, she'd never complained. She'd put chickens, eggs, sometimes vegetables in 'er basket, sling it on 'er back an' set off if she couldn't get a lift. She'd come in, sleep the night, an' go back next day. But by then I'd got pains 'ere an' pains there, sometimes me right arm went to sleep, sometimes me left ear buzzed, which 'appened, of course, when it was bringin' bad news, sometimes I wouldn't be able to see to thread a needle an' sew, sometimes I'd 'ave to sit on the loo for an 'our. And last Christmas I broke a back tooth on the roast piglet. Me youth 'ad gone, there was no denyin' it, it'd all been wasted. On that swine of a man. You did it yourself, you wicked Kali. Ev'ry day now you get a message from your body: don't forget, you're gettin' old.

The boss ran ahead an' 'e just called back for me to stretch me old legs or we wouldn't be there for midday an' 'e'd got a load of manure bein' delivered.

Then 'e took me bundle an' told me to 'urry up. Who ev'r saw such a thing, a boss carryin' a servant's bundle. 'E didn't ask, just took it off me. It was true, it was well an' truly full. Stuff that Biri was sendin' to me 'usband, cos I 'adn't dare leave it behind. And the four paper bags of walnuts what I'd brought from 'ome to sell in the market. I'd really 'ave liked some walnuts when I was little, but I wasn't given any. They were all taken into town to sell, ev'ry bani was needed for the piglet. So, I got used to 'avin' no nuts. And 'ere I was, takin' 'em to town like me mother did. You always think that your parents didn't do things right, they were mean an' unkind. And then you do things the same way yourself. It's in your blood. Cos I won't touch a walnut.

There was the boss runnin' along in front of me. But 'owever much I looked at that man I couldn't make 'im out. That 'e didn't spend 'is time indoors was obvious, cos 'e was as brown as a nut. 'E wasn't wearin' boots like a peasant, 'is shirt was a townsman's, an' 'e wasn't wearin' an 'at, an' 'is moustache was really yellow under 'is nose from smokin' cigarettes, like 'e was doin' then. Whether 'e was a decent man or a big-head, whether 'e was as coarse as they come, I couldn't figure 'im out. That'd become clear when we was under the same roof, that's where the mask comes off ev'ry man's face. In the street ev'ry man's like an archangel. As 'andsome as 'e's kind. But in the 'ouse! And the pub! And in the night! Like a pig. But I wasn't afraid of a man any longer. If 'e raised one 'and to me I'd be off. Only 'e'd better not get too bossy. And let's see what 'is wife's like. She couldn't be up to much if she sent 'er 'usband out 'irin' servants. That was a sign of a lazy wife. 'Irin' servants was a wife's job, unless she was a 'Óstát woman. With the 'Óstát people the man did it.

So I was goin' to be a servant again, wasn't I. Goin' to be, cos I'm thinkin' back to me story. It was like when I was a little girl, I was gettin' me youth back. Cos you're born twice. Three times, if you like. Only then I'd still 'ad 'opes of gettin' somebody, that I'd be nicely married, there's be little ones, one or two, no more, God preserve me. I'm married as I am an' I'm stayin'. Not like that Juci Mihók. What she was called before she got married I can't remember. Gyelek? Gyalak? Juci Gyalak. The way she was treated. 'Er 'air was cut off out of spite. The village was really revoltin'. Cos the poor woman ran away from 'er 'usband, she was caught an' brought back. And 'er 'usband chucked 'er out. 'Er 'air was cut off first. After that she 'ad to go about like that, with 'er 'ead uncovered. With 'er 'air short. She was a strong woman to do such a thing. There wasn't another in the village as wore 'er 'air short. Either it'd be long, down to level with the skirt an' woven with ribbons, or it was kept out of sight under a kerchief in a bun. She lived outside the village all by 'erself over Pandúr well way. And she didn't stay long, cos she was driven out. There was so much talk, she was run down, filth was daubed on 'er fence, an' she 'ad to go away. She went into town an' vanished without a trace. So it was said.

So, the boss an' me, we reached the Békás. From then on there were only the gardens, 'Óstát land an' an 'ouse or two 'ere an' there. All small, cos what matters to 'Óstát people is land, not big 'ouses. What would they want big 'ouses for? They don't intend to 'old balls. They want lots of land so as to live off it. Not like stupid me, always 'ad me eye on a big 'ouse. I saw we was goin' along a big fence, couldn't see inside, the boards were so close together. And in we went.

All along the fence was a solid 'olly 'edge, too 'igh to be jumped, an' if a thief climbed in 'e'd 'urt 'is bum. A big spotted dog came runnin' up, licked the boss's'an', jumped about. The boss just looked at it an' it quietened down. We went past the bushes. Once we was in the garden 'e locked the gate. That was the way there, 'e said. Well, I was really surprised at 'avin' to lock the gate.

Jesus, God, an' St Anthony! Was I dreamin', or was it enchantment, like when a comes to a poor man? I rubbed me eyes. Opened 'em again. I was still seein' things. What could I see? I 'adn't died an' gone to paradise, 'ad I? Or 'ad I gone off me old rocker at last, an' was out of this world? Cos I could see flowers what 'uman eye'd never seen. And what flowers! Roses by the million. An absolute rainbow. A rainbow come down to earth. First a row of dark red ones, then lighter red, more flame-coloured, then softer still, then pink, then purple, then lots of orange-yellow, then yellow ones an' right at the back white roses, but in so many shades, different reds, yellows, ev'n whites. There were more than I could count of the different reds. A row of each colour, each 'eight. And those along the edge, 'eld on a sort of enormous wire contraption. These must 'ave been the smaller sort, the bigger ones were behind 'em. They were in waves, like when the fairies took Goldilocks to their country, so as to support 'er as she went up, cos she'd died an' was goin' to be given a new life by the fairies. And what must the scent 'ave been!

Unfortunately I couldn't smell it. While I was still a child, I'd 'ad a fever what made me nose run non-stop for a long time, an' since then I'd 'ardly been able to smell anythin'. I could only taste things, if they're quite strong. I could cook all right, but I'd got no sense of smell. Well, me boss was no poor man if 'e'd got a garden like that. But 'e was 'urryin' through the garden, not lookin' at anythin'. And 'e called back to me to come along, get to work, the manure was comin'.

Then we went into the 'ouse. It was right at the back, away from the road, a big, stone-built, one-storey buildin', you couldn't tell which was the front or the back. An' there were doors ev'rywhere. On the inside you couldn't call it a 'ouse. But there was ev'rythin', kitchen an' rooms. One was a kind of science 'all. Rows of cupboards, masses of books in the shelves, an' ev'rywhere pots an' glasses an' boxes with labels.

I'd seen a man live alone, cos I'd known a widower what I used to visit, an' took 'im in food. I shouldn't 'ave been so surprised at that. There are women as well, who let themselves go. In short, the truth is that ev'ry man's untidy, an' I 'ate untidy people. I've never yet come across a man that's tidy. There's so much disorder in men. Ev'n those who've got wives. They're the worst. Cos it's 'er what 'as to tidy 'im up. They get to be as dirty as pigs. It's very seldom that they don't. Me father, 'e wasn't like that. Me mother made 'im ev'r so tidy. When she went an' married 'im she only put up with it until the first child was born, Then she told 'im straight, just like that, brandishin' the rollin' pin. She 'adn't come to be a servant. 'E wasn't to leave 'is clohes on the floor or she'd put 'im out in the pigsty. And 'e got the message. What 'is mother 'adn't taught 'im, me mother did. But I 'ad come as a servant, so shut your trap, Kali, an' do as you're told.

Then I asked the gentleman where the servant's place was to be. We went through two rooms, on through the kitchen, an' 'e showed me where I'd be given A big room with three windows, nice big ones. Well, they'd take some cleanin', Kali. A nice bed, a pink, carved wardrobe, table, washstand, jug. And a bedside lamp as well. I said to 'im, this isn't the servant's quarters.

'E said, This is where you'll sleep. I said, I'll sleep on the box in the kitchen. To which 'e spat out I'd better not be cheeky on me very first day, 'e wouldn't stand for it. 'E wouldn't 'ave anybody sleepin' in the kitchen. It wasn't that kind of 'ouse.

It seemed the world 'ad been turned upside down. People 'ad forgotten where the servant's place was, what 'er job was. Ev'rybody's 'eads 'ad been mixed up since the gentry 'ad been dispossessed an' reduced to nothin', an' it was all communism an' the rule of the people. 'Ow was the people supposed to know 'ow to rule?

Then 'e said I'd got to cook dinner. 'E 'adn't 'ad a nice 'ot meal for a long time. The pantry was the size of a dance 'all. There was a basket of vegetables, there was fat, bacon, sausage, plenty of ev'rythin'. While I was cookin' 'e was goin' muck-spreadin', 'e said. The manure 'ad to be shovelled off the cart, an' the farmer was makin' several deliveries. Then 'e'd 'ave 'is dinner. At the back of the 'ouse 'e'd got a sort of covered patio, 'e'd eat there. 'E said I was to sit down an' eat with 'im. Said I, dear sir, servants don't sit down to eat. 'E 'adn't engaged a servant so as to eat by 'imself all the time. 'E'd done enough of that in 'is lifetime. In this 'ouse this was 'ow it was. I was to sit down. So what was I to do? Down I sat, but all the same the food stuck in me throat an' I felt as if I was sittin' on pins an' needles.

'E said not a word about what the bean soup was like. But I'd done me best. There are men like that. Never say anythin' about the food. That swine of an 'usband of mine used to say that good food spoke for itself. No need to go on about it. I asked the boss what 'e'd like next day. There'd be a market, I'd go shoppin' for the Nativity of the BVM. That's a big festival for the Catholics, they're waitin' for 'er to appear. 'E's not religious, but it might be a good idea to mention it at such times as I'd be goin' to market. Oh my God, I really did like the big markets, at festival times. So I wasn't goin' to be a mere servant, but the equal of an 'ousewife!

Catholic wives an' women weren't supposed to work on such occasions, an' they didn't in our village. We was 'alf an' 'alf, Catholic an' Protestant, only these days they're not so strict about not goin' to work. Of course, people 'ave to work if they've got factory jobs, or land an' animals to see to.

'It's a festival for the Romanians as well,' said the boss.

'E asked me if I spoke Romanian, cos Szék people mostly didn't. 'I learnt in school,' I told 'im, 'I can count an' bargain, don't you worry.'

I certainly do like sellin' things.

'And then, what about cookin' for tomorrow. If there's any left you can 'ave me bean soup at midday, an' if not I'll make somethin' for the ev'nin' when I get in.'

Then 'e asked, 'Why are you called Kali?'

'How did you know that me name was Kali, sir?'

I wasn't to call 'im 'sir'. Nor 'boss'. I was to call 'im Vilmos.

'Kali, what's that stand for?' 'e asked.

'Well, didn't you know that I was Kali Green Szabó?'

'Oh, Green as well,' 'e went on. 'So why are you standin' in the middle of the kitchen with your 'ands on your 'ips, thinkin' now, Kali, what're you goin' to cook, cos the master of the 'ouse isn't goin' to 'elp you? That's why I thought you were Kali.'

So I asked whether I 'ad to work on the rooms. As I understood it, that was what 'e's asked for. Meanin' keepin' the place clean. There was one that I mustn't, an' two more that 'e'd show me. Then 'e was goin' to get ready for market next day. I was to go as well, 'e said, so as to know what there was to sell. Then we cut a great lot of lovely roses an' gladioli an' brought 'em into the cool store. I wasn't allowed to cut anythin', 'e wouldn't let me.

By that time it was dark, an' I went to bed. I 'ad a good wash, I'd got some soap, actually it was ev'n scented, cos it was white, not grey like washin' soap. I piled on the bedclothes, cos those were there as well. Satin quilt, big feather pillow, small pillow, ev'rythin', A nice 'igh bed. Was I goin' to be able to sleep in this, I wondered. I wasn't used to that kind of thing. Then I got in an' it was cold, like the dew on me feet.

But never as long as I live shall I forget the pleasure that I felt all over. I stretched out like a tomcat that's licked out the cream jug, an' I lay there with me eyes open, it was so comfortable. Oh, God 'ad surely taken care of me! I didn't ev'n want to go to sleep, just to 'ang onto that feelin'. Now none of me was 'urtin', not me feet nor me back, nor me 'ips. Well, Kali, you've fallen into God's pocket as a servant: satin quilt, embroidered pillowslip. Then I slept like a child. I'd never 'ad such a good sleep since I'd been a girl. When I woke up in the mornin' ev'ry bird was up an' singin'.

I was really ashamed of meself when I saw the boss 'ad been waterin' the garden at dawn. I got up a bit later. Then I actually asked 'im, 'What time do you get up, sir?'. 'E told me not to call 'im 'sir'. So I'd call 'im 'mister', like at 'ome. 'E said that while the roses were comin' into flower 'e watered 'em at four o'clock, cos the younger ones needed plenty. At 'alf past three, ev'n. It was a big garden, 'ad to be watered at dawn. The flowers sucked it up, then they worked in the daytime. I'd never 'eard anythin' of the sort. Least of all about 'em workin'. There's just the rose in the folk tale that grows all over the wicked man an' won't let 'im escape. But there was goin' to be a change in future, 'e was goin' to put in an irrigation system, then 'e'd just turn the tap an' wouldn't 'ave to carry water any more.

'E filled the barrow carefully for me, wouldn't let me do it, cos 'e'd only got one pair of gloves. I took it, covered with a damp cloth. Then to go with the bulgin' barrow 'e gave me a piece of paper that 'e'd written. 'E told me it was a certificate of origin. In case anybody asked where I'd got the flowers from. And 'is name was on it. I'd 'ave to show that they weren't stolen. I asked, was this really necessary? If somebody displayed three eggs for sale at the market, did there 'ave to be proof? 'E said crossly that firstly, this wasn't three eggs but six 'undred quality tea roses, secondly, 'is signature showed that I 'adn't stolen 'em, an' thirdly, that they came from the garden in Békás. And nowhere else. Cos 'ere people knew what the garden of the Békás wizard was. I asked what magician that was, but all 'e said was I'd better be off, not stand there chattin', get to work.

Early in the mornin', there I was at the market. I'd trundled the barrow carefully down the Békás 'ill, 'alf an 'our it took me. I bought a seller's ticket, that was expensive, an' there were a lot of people there! I saw an egg seller from Szék, she looked away, didn't want to see me. She was the daughter of old Nusi Pej from Felszeg, who was completely ash blonde an' nobody 'ad been willin' to marry 'er. 'Er 'usband 'ad been the same, no girl would marry 'im cos 'is one cheek 'ad been crimson from birth, cos 'is father 'ad struck 'is mother while the child was still in 'er belly, so they said, an' so 'alf 'is 'ead was red. The ash blonde an' the man with the red face then 'ad a lot of beautiful children, ev'ry one completely normal. So there was the girl, sellin' eggs. She was called a Szék egg woman, cos Szék people are so poor that they wouldn't put an egg in their mouths, they'd rather come into town an' sell it, not eat it. We'd always taken 'em to market as well.

I went to the flower sellers' area, I didn't rent a stall, that would 'ave cost money an' the boss 'adn't told me to. I set the flowers out nicely on the cloth by length an' colour. There was nobody with roses as good as mine. Some 'd brought roses that were droppin', some 'ad just got buds, the flower not showin' at all, might not ev'n open. The boss knew exactly when to cut 'em. People came to me, gathered round an' looked at 'em. Weren't they from the Békás garden? I said, an' what if they were? 'Ow was I to realize what they meant by that. 'Ow much, they asked. Oh, I did like talkin' about money. I'd start with an 'igh price, ten lei each, though the boss 'ad said five, six at the most. I tried to get ten. Then five for forty-five, there you are, pofteste doamna, or seven for just sixty an' so on. I certainly can count. Me father said, when 'e saw 'ow I 'andled money when I was still little an' we went to Bonchida sellin' eggs, 'Hey, Kali,' cos me mother was Kali as well, 'you sure you didn't 'ave this child with a Jew? She's got Jewish blood.'

When me mother brought me into the world an' the fortune-teller woman was called—that wasn't permitted, the old priest forbade it, but it was only done before the christenin'—she foretold that I'd 'ave an un'appy life, but that a lot of money would come me way. Maybe old Rébi was thinkin' of that day. Cos I put no small amount away in the front of me skirt.

I sold me few walnuts as well along with the flowers. It wasn't ev'n midday, an' I 'adn't got a single flower left. The lot 'ad been sold! I 'adn't asked the boss whether I was to buy anythin' that 'e needed in the market. I didn't dare do anythin' on me own account, not on me second day. I bought a bread roll an' some watery ludaskása with me own money at a sort of pub just outside the market an' went 'ome to the boss.

I reached the garden with the empty barrow, I'd 'ad to take it quite easy cos it was quite a long way out on the edge of town. In I went, but that great big damn spotted dog came runnin' up an' its master was nowhere to be seen. Who ev'r saw a spotted dog. I looked round the back, 'e wasn't there either. I went into the 'ouse, an' there 'e was asleep. 'E'd eaten the bean soup in the kitchen, 'adn't ev'n lit the fire. There was bread on the table an' a plate, ev'rythin'. Men. You've only got to look into a kitchen an' you'll see at once that a man lives there. I didn't say a word. Not 'alf an 'our went by an' I 'eard 'im stirrin'. 'E was a long way away, at the other end of the 'ouse. But I'd got sharp ears.

We sat down at the table outside, 'e brought 'is books an' we counted the money. I put aside what I got for the walnuts. Then I counted the money out to 'im. 'E complimented me an' was very surprised. Well, said I, I really bargained. I started at ten an' if anybody bought sev'ral I gave a discount. 'E said I'd ruined the market! I told 'im, I'd rather set one up. People respect expensive things. 'E wanted to give me an 'undred lei out of it. I said, when 'e gave me me weekly wages. 'Take it,' 'e said, insistin'. Looked as if 'e wasn't a miser. I asked whether there was anythin' I could 'ave bought. 'E said 'e'd been talkin' to a farmer down the slope that 'ad animals an' ev'rythin'. Butyka was 'is name. Milk, eggs, an' vegetables were delivered. Since I knew 'ow to deal with 'em, that was goin' to be me job. And once a week a chicken, but 'e'd always got that from somebody different. And 'e only bought one when there was somebody to cook it. Previously 'is mother 'ad come an' either brought 'im somethin' to eat or cooked for 'im. 'Óstát people didn't make bread, always got it from a shop once or twice a week. 'E didn't grow any vegetables, what there was, was experimental, not for eatin'. In general, nothin' in the garden was to be picked unless 'e said so. That was the rule of the 'ouse. If I broke it, I'd be out. I'd learn, cos it would be up to me to deal with buyin'.

I asked what 'e'd like to eat next day. I was not to ask such a thing, 'e knew nothin' about it, 'e said crossly. That was women's business. So in I went an' knocked up some nice pastry with túró an' fat bacon. And a drop of potato soup to go with it. I asked if 'e's got any ordinary bacon, a bit dried out, the fat 'ad shrivelled but I could use the lean. 'E said, if I asked 'im once more anythin' to do with the kitchen 'ed give me the sack. I wasn't to bother 'im with it. That was women's business, 'e'd told me. One thing 'e did say, let's always 'ave nice sweet pastry. 'E'd asked if I could cook an' bake. 'Well,' I said, 'as if a Szék woman couldn't, cos it's one of the things we're proud of, bein' able to cook an' bake.' Then 'e ticked me off, if I ev'r said any servant statements again about what a Szék woman couldn't do, then that'd be me lot! So I asked 'im, what kind of pastry. Didn't matter, just sweet. Nice an' sweet.

At dinner 'e made me sit at table again. I couldn't get used to that sort of thing. The food didn't ev'n taste right if I was eatin' with the boss. There was room in 'is innards, I could see. 'E was thin, but 'e ate for three. Nervy people like 'im are all thin. Then 'e said, when 'e'd lit 'is pipe 'e liked a nice cup of mint or lime tea, 'e'd got a paper bag full of such 'erbs. 'E started chattin', still made me sit with 'im. Well, you've now obviously become a lady, Kali. Sittin' an' chattin' with the gentry. I asked, should I talk about meself, didn't 'e want to know where I'd come from an' 'ow. 'E said, no need, 'e'd been able to work that out for 'imself, from the way I 'ad me 'air in a bun. I wasn't a widow, that was obvious, cos I wasn't all miserable an' didn't wear black. So I said, 'I'm certainly not a widow, I'm sorry to say,' an' we laughed. 'I've left me 'usband, 'e was no good.'

I told 'im 'ow things were. Why cover it up. Szék wasn't so far away that talk of me wouldn't reach the Békás. By that time ev'rybody in the village 'ad 'eard, I reckoned, that Green Kali 'ad gone on the streets. It'd 'ave been all the talk in church by Saturday what 'ad 'appened to that wicked woman.

And what was I goin' to do with the rest of me life, 'e asked.

Then we sat in silence for a bit while 'e sipped 'is tea. I told 'im I'd been in service all me life an' I knew nothin' else. Now, I'd better not start complainin', 'e wasn't goin' to listen to that. Said I, I 'adn't said a word of complaint, I'd only answered 'is question. Anyway, bein' in service wasn't cause for complaint, it was the way of the world.

And so I asked the boss what 'e did for a livin'. 'E was in service as well, 'e said. So who did 'e serve, I asked. 'Is roses, 'e said. And I serve me boss, I answered.

'E knew the song: Me sweet rose, a cheat was she, / But 'er 'usband didn't see, / Didn't care at all, so we . . . an' began to whistle the tune. I told 'im, we don't sing that to make fun of anybody. Did I know any songs, 'e asked. I do, I said, cos I've never seen any Szék women that don't. I know songs an' folk tales. That's one of the things we're proud of.

'D'you like folk tales, mister?' I asked, cos I 'adn't told a good one for a long time.

I addressed 'im like I did men at 'ome. Cos I couldn't call 'im Vilmos. 'E called me Kali. I called 'im mister. Then 'e said 'e didn't serve anybody, 'e'd only been jokin'. 'E was 'is own boss. 'E ruled nature. That's exactly what 'e said. Well, in me opinion ev'rybody's in service but I'd never 'eard it said that they rule.

All the same, it was obvious that the boss wasn't a man of peasant origin. Peasants, tillers of the soil, don't sit eatin' dinner an' chattin' while there's daylight. Nor do 'Óstát people. When it's too dark to see outside, only then do they come indoors an' eat. And straight afterwards they go to bed. When the stomach's full sleep comes quickly. When it is full, that is, cos it isn't always, is it.

While the light lasts 'e still worked, 'e said. But 'e wasn't workin', I could see, 'e was just lookin' an' lookin'. 'E was walkin' among the roses, takin' 'old of a flowerin' 'ead an' lookin' at it. Is that what you call work, I asked meself, cos I didn't dare ask 'im. If it was fine next day 'e was goin' to start the biggest job. What's that, I asked. I'd see, 'e'd need 'elp. I finished up in the kitchen, put ev'rythin' away. Put the curds to set. I went out to 'im an' asked, could I 'elp 'im. 'E was just brushin' some blue liquid on the roses. But not ev'ry one, only one 'ere an' there. Those that still 'ad buds. I 'eld the bucket with the blue stuff for 'im.

Well then, what story was I goin' to tell, 'e asked. Which one d'you like, I asked. Which did I know, 'e asked.

'All sorts. I know excitin' ones, true ones, then there's legends, sad ones, ones about devils, about lovers, unfaithfulness in marriage, then there's ones with King Mátyás, Goldilocks, King Burkus, an' true stories that 'appened in Szék. True stories. Which d'you want? If you like a song I can sing it.'

It was left up to me. So I told the tale about the devil temptin' the lads. Cos the devil could see the way the lads went for a pretty girl an' 'e tempted 'em so as to give the best lad to the good girl. Only in the end it turned out that none of 'em was any good at all. On Saturday ev'nin', when the devil turned out the light for 'em so that ev'n the moon didn't shine on the porch, an' it was pitch dark, each of 'em made a pass at the girl. 'Now, this tale's not about the lads but about the girl,' said the boss, 'that she could be tempted. Cos she was a bad girl.' But I 'aven't finished, don't be in such an 'urry to know 'ow it ends, mister! What sort of story is it, that doesn't end properly. Cos the lads would just wait for it to get dark. But the girl would smear the crotch of 'er knickers with earth an' ashes, well mixed up, got some black ink from the chemist's an' put that to it so that it should stick. And a lad would feel 'is way right to 'er knickers, an' then she'd say to 'im, 'Oh, there's a spider crawlin' on your cheek!' The lad would quickly brush the spider off with 'is 'and, but she'd say, 'No, your other cheek, no, it's on your forehead.' So you see, mister, the lad would touch is face all over with 'is 'and. And then the girl would suddenly say that she could 'ear movement in the 'ouse, cos she'd arranged with 'er sister to move about when she said 'Oh!' And the devil would turn the light on an' the lad would run away. Now, when 'e got 'ome 'e must 'ave scrubbed 'is face all over, it was so black, an' it would take 'im three days to get the ink off ev'n though 'e washed it with soap. And none of 'em managed to make it with the girl, cos she wouldn't give in to 'em. The devil fooled the lads, but not one of 'em 'ad their way with the girl.

'E 'ad a good laugh at me story.

'Kali,' said the boss to me then, 'you really do 'ate men, don't you?'

'Well, it's not that I 'ate 'em, frankly I despise 'em. Cos never in all me life 'ave I met a decent man.'

'And so that girl remained a virgin?' asked the boss.

'Not at all, she got the prince, I'll tell you tomorrow, mister.'

And so we joked an' brushed the blue liquid onto the roses. Then I told 'im that all the same down our way a great number of girls tempted boys before marriage an' the result was to be seen, cos their skirts were very short in front an' long behind. Then they couldn't 'old such a stylish marriage an' big do when the love-makin' was too obvious. They just 'ad to marry quietly.

So I went on tellin' the boss stories—at last there was somebody to listen to 'em. I'd tell one an' we'd say nothin' for a bit. We listened to the roses, as 'e put it. That was certainly 'is story. Silence. 'E was silent a lot of the time. Maybe that was why 'e was so jumpy. 'E didn't know 'ow to tell a story.

Next mornin' the boss was up before me again. Oh dear, what on earth could I do so as to be up before 'im? I asked 'im whether 'e'd got an alarm clock so that I could get meself up. What for, 'e asked. Well, it's wrong for the servant to be still asleep when the boss is already workin'. 'E'd give me a call, 'e said. But we couldn't agree on 'ow to do that. By then the sun was well up, it was time for breakfast. 'E asked what I would be doin'. Well, at 'is pleasure. 'E wasn't a gentleman, 'avin' people do 'is pleasure! I'd better stop thinkin' like that. Then I went out with 'im into the garden. 'E'd done somethin' terrible out there. The sight brought tears to me eyes. 'E asked what was the matter. I said, well, what 'ave you done?

'Why've you been angry with all 'em lovely things, an' ruined 'em? I asked.

Oh, did 'e laugh at me. 'E split 'is sides.

''Aven't you 'eard of breedin', Kali? This is the same sort of thing. Like when a bull jumps on a cow.'

I didn't understand what 'e was sayin'. What 'ad jumpin' got to do with it? 'E was doin' it there an' then. 'E was puttin' roses together, then tearin' all the petals off the one like a wild animal, like somebody with no feelin' for beautiful things. The flower was left standin' there stripped bare. Then 'e'd tear 'em off another. 'E'd take somethin' off the one an' use a brush to spread it on the other one, then slip a kind of paper 'ood over the one that 'e'd brushed. 'E spent all day doin' this. 'E gathered the petals in a barrow an' then a barrel. That was 'ow 'e produced new varieties. 'E took all different colours an' combined 'em. I said, we used to 'ave roses in the garden when I still lived with me parents, trained all round the door. But we never did this sort of thing. Again 'e laughed 'is 'ead off. People didn't indeed do it like 'im. 'E did what nature did, pairin' off father an' mother. Well, I didn't understand a word. I just carried the petals for 'im, 'anded 'im the tray of paper 'oods to put on the flowers. 'E stuck a label on each flower with somethin' written on it, letters an' numbers, I couldn't make 'ead or tail of what 'e put. Then 'e'd go down the row again with a book an' check. The first day 'e ruined at least ten rows in the lovely garden. I worked it out, I said, you could 'ave got a thousand lei for those. Maybe two thousand. 'E replied that I'd understand. If I stayed with 'im, I'd understand.

'E went on doin' this for another week. Did it to a good 'alf of the garden. It was like in books about Indians, when they scalp people. Flay the skin off their enemies' 'eads. No woman could 'ave done such a thing to 'er beautiful flowers.

I 'ad to go into market ev'ry third day with flowers that 'e'd left. But not the finest. Those 'e tore to bits. Those what 'e didn't like or 'ad somethin' wrong with 'em I 'ad to sell. And it was amazin', people went mad for 'em in the market. Some people asked when I'd be there again, an' what I'd be bringin' 'em. I did deals with one or two for ten white or ten red, an' with one man who wanted twenty-five dark red. I thought, that must be 'ow old 'is girlfriend is.

While there was flowers I did very nicely there. Then winter was drawin' on. Now, I thought, 'e'll give me the sack once we put the lights on the graves.

I'd been with the boss now for more than two months an' I was well settled. I cooked, washed, an' tidied up after 'im, an' I took flowers to market until the end of November. I bought 'im what 'e needed an' sometimes I worked under 'is direction. It took a month for me to put ev'rythin' away in cupboards, washed, ironed, an' repaired. Men always just drop their clothes, aren't at all careful. Pay no attention to their clothes bein' clean an' tidy. The boss didn't dismiss me for winter, I'd been afraid of that, cos there isn't the demand for servants in winter, there's no work on the lan', the animals are all brought in an' don't 'ave to be watched. 'Ere in the boss's place there'd been neither winter, spring, nor summer—as I saw it, they was all one, there was so much to do. 'E 'ad a lot of work indoors in wintertime, 'e just wouldn't let me work on me own. Cos I could only do 'ousework. Anythin' to do with work in the garden 'e wouldn't let me touch. 'E was readin', writin', always sortin' seeds to a system what only 'e could understand, an' there was lots of pots under 'eatin' lamps, sev'ral layers.

Only when the seeds were ripe on the roses did 'e let me cut 'em with 'im. Put 'em into thousands an' thousands of pots, more than you could count. An' again paper lids 'ad to be put on 'em. We took 'em all into the 'ouse an' the green'ouse at the back.

I could 'ave done with me loom in the ev'nin', so as to do a bit of weavin' as I'd used to, that wicked man 'adn't interfered with that cos the linen brought 'im in money, which 'e always took off me. I was never been allowed to read, an' if women came round an' I told folk tales 'e liked to mess up the tellin'. Cos what 'e really enjoyed was spoilin' the pleasure of others. So the women stopped callin' on me an' invited me to their 'ouses instead, they couldn't stand me 'usband. 'Ere the boss 'as got a nice lot of books, two bookcases full. In one are the sort of books what 'e reads, scientific ones, an' in the other are nice books, literature, 'istory, poetry. I'm allowed to take those, 'e don't mind. Only I couldn't see very well, the letters all ran together, like when I've got tears in me yes. One day I thought I'd try 'is glasses on, 'e'd left 'em there on the desk when 'e'd been writin'. An' bless me soul, I 'adn't seen so clear since I'd been a child at school. I picked up the book an' I could read ev'rythin' clear as the day.

So I asked 'im, 'Mister, where did you get these good specs, cos I can see ev'rythin' so clear with 'em.'

'E said 'e'd bought 'em ages ago in Debrecen, an' 'e couldn't give 'em to me. But 'e'd got another pair, I should try those. Well, those suited me very nicely as well, they weren't quite as sharp as the first ones but all the same I could make out the letters clear enough an' I could 'ave threaded a needle if I'd wanted to. After that, if I wasn't tellin' the boss folk tales, or if 'e'd gone out, I read a lot of books. 'E used to go out a lot, sometimes 'untin', sometimes playin' football. At 'is age! 'Is clothes would be so filthy as a result that I'd 'ave to soak 'em in expensive soap liquid for two 'ole days before it'd come out. An' 'e'd go out meetin' friends in an 'otel, as is the way 'ere in town. They don't go to each other's 'ouses, but they meet in the 'otel uptown. I used to use the electricity, but 'e didn't mind. I was a bit nervous all by meself, that was such a great big garden an' we didn't 'ave any really close neighbours, just a farmer a bit lower down, an' if I'd called for 'elp nobody could 'ave 'eard me. That spotted dog's no use. It just licks ev'rybody. It's a special breed, a posh dog, an' didn't do anythin'.

The boss is very kind, don't worry about a thing. 'E never says anythin' about bein' economical, I shouldn't waste electricity or use so much soap. An' 'e loves sweet pastry. I 'ave to bake a big trayful ev'ry other day, cos it keeps runnin' out. I just 'ave to be very careful about the garden. So as to do no damage. Mustn't pour away soapy water in the wrong place. That 'as its own soak-away to go in. The boss is as careful about the soil as old János Filep, 'er father, is of 'is daughter Borka. An' she let 'im down.

But nobody orders me about these days. But I'm a servant, on a weekly wage. Well, 'ave you seen, mister, you bad man, that bad Szék man in 'is big 'ouse? 'Ave you seen that Green Kali's enjoyin' life now? As she pleases she reads books or does the washin', or ev'n 'as a lie-down when the boss is 'avin' a nap an' she's got to keep quiet. What did you say, mister? A Calvinist don't lie in bed in the daytime ev'n if 'e's sick? So Christ can't love anybody that lies in bed? That Christ didn't die for the sort as lies in bed cos their body's weary an' their eyes are tired? Christ died for all men, ev'n the lazy ones. All the more so for 'em. All the more for bad men, cos they're in great need of Christ. But when they kick their wives with their boots it pleases Christ that rotten men should be kickin' the devil's arse.

Cos I've started straight away bein' mistress of the 'ouse! I do all the 'ousework. Oh, I do like to 'ave a nice 'ouse. Not for it to be mine, just nice an' clean an' tidy.

An' all the washin' I do! To me 'eart's content! All me life it's been me consolation. It isn't the washin' what I like so much, an' I don't mind it, it's good when I start on a Thursday mornin' an' put 'the clothes in the tub to soak for a day. Cos 'ere I didn't 'ave a tub available, so I told the boss to buy one. Previously 'e'd taken 'is washin' somewhere an' somebody 'ad done it for 'im for money, a girl or somebody. Only a man would do such a thing. Or 'e'd taken it to 'is mother, she lives by the station. So we bought two nice tubs, real tin tubs. I mean to say, we bought two, one for each of us. Friday's wash-day, that was always the custom, so that's 'ow I do it, it's put in on Thursday an' soaked for a day. But what really brings joy to me 'eart is 'angin' it out. Oh, I love it. I put the things on the line, cos we've got a clothesline between the walnuts at the back of the 'ouse. The boss bought clothes pegs as well, so I peg 'em out an' they swing in the breeze with that nice smell of soap what I like so much. The only trouble is, I can't smell it. An' of course I change the bedlinen ev'ry fortnight, that's really posh in these parts. I do the washin' an' me 'ands are red from it, but I like that nice crisp feelin'. That's livin'. I sleep in a nice fresh bed. An' if it rains I take it all into the stable—there are no animals there, we just call it that. That's where the boss worka on 'is flowers in the winter. An' I've got five nice clothes-lines to dry the clothes on. The boss gets a clean shirt ev'ry other day, though 'e prefers to work stripped to the waist if it isn't cold. Cos if 'e wears anythin' it always gets bloodied. 'E does 'ave gloves, but 'is 'ands get covered in blood, an' 'is arms an' lower legs as well. So ev'rythin' 'as to be properly washed. 'E tells me to take the clothes up into the loft to dry in winter, or into the cellar, cos 'e's got a nice dry cellar. No way! I don't like that sort of thing.

'Let our rubbish an' our dirt stay 'ere with us. It's good for clothes to be with us. Clean ones as well. It's our dirt, we must see to it an' clean it up. That's the way I like it.'

An' 'e lets me 'eat the 'ouse as much as I like. A stove 'as been installed in ev'ry room in the 'ouse. In some places that's not done, to avoid makin' a mess, but 'ere the boss 'ad done it cos 'e said there 'ad to be warmth. For the flowers as well what were indoors. Ev'rywhere there's a stove 'e takes the temperature, 'ow many degrees. I've 'ad to learn as well. Cos some rooms are lined with shelves one above the other with lots of flowers in pots on all of 'em. We've got lots of wood an' leaves that we 'ad to rake up. There was a sudden very cold spell in early November. 'E let me 'eat the 'ouse as much as I liked!

But ev'ry Wednesday an' Friday 'e's made me go out. I don't like that. An' sometimes on Tuesday as well. That's when 'is lady love comes. 'E's a man, 'as no wife, but nature makes demands. At first when I was sent out I just couldn't make out why a servant needed so much rest an' free time, an' to go out. An' where was I to go? I'd go to see Biri, I went to the church, on Wednesdays I'd go to the prayer meetin' though I 'ad no bible or 'ymn book, if you weren't given one in the church God could provide for 'imself. Then I watched from a distance the girls an' lads from Szék, when they met at the back of the post office. They sing an' dance to the words, just steppin' to an' fro. If I saw somebody that I recognized I'd go an' say 'ello, an' we'd ev'n exchange kisses. Then I'd see the boss emergin' from the garden as I arrived. 'E'd ride off, cos 'e was always on a bicycle. But if 'e stayed in an' didn't go out I noticed that a young woman came up to the garden. There was one what was quite tall, an' another came on foot. Each of 'em was carryin' flowers when they left. I don't suppose you gave money for those, did you, young lady? Well, that's 'ow it is with men. The one's rather an older woman, the other a bit younger.

Then after All Saints, we finished workin' on the flowers. The boss 'ad just a few chrysanthemums but didn't do much with 'em, just experimented, as 'e said. I don't like 'em as much as the roses or the gladioli. I took 'em to sell at the cemetery. Then we covered up, as the boss said, but not like on the land, 'e 'ad straw brought an' we covered up all the roses. That was quite a lot of work. There were some what 'e actually wrapped in cloth an' pinned it on. But I only dealt with straw. An' 'e collected a great amount of seed an' put it into thousands an' thousanda of boxes, which all 'ave to 'ave written on 'em what was in 'em. But 'e does all that. 'E sells seed as well, but not in the market. For that, people come to the 'ouse.

Then 'e said I was to smarten up the 'ouse an' ev'rythin for the comin' Saturday, cos guests were invited. I told 'im, the 'ouse was always smart, take a look, an' if 'e didn't like somethin' 'e should say I ought to do better.

'Cos there's one thing we Szék people do know,' I told 'im, 'an' that's 'ow to smarten up.'

'E didn't tell me to stop goin' on about it all the time. An' so the two big rooms 'ad to be arranged so that people could sit at table, an' benches brought in an' the cupboards moved to the two bedrooms. Me lovely room was absolutely full of pots, an' so was 'is. I said it 'adn't been me what covered the table all the time, I 'adn't dared touch it. 'E said I was talkin' like a bad wife. An' so the two of us organized ev'rythin', polished the tables, ev'n brought things out of the outhouse. We ev'n laid rugs what I 'adn't seen before. The boss brought out ev'rythin' what was 'idden away. Things from the attic. Lovely special decorated plates from a chest. Glasses an' all sorts. I would 'ave asked what I should cook, but I didn't dare, that always made 'im cross.

'What d'you usually cook in your village when there's a ball, Kali, me dear?' 'e asked.

Cos now 'e was so pleasant, it was dear this an' dear that. I said what. We usually made pasta, an' lardy cake if we really wanted to give people a treat. An' pogácsa, if there was goin' to be a lot of pálinka. An' sweet pastry, latticed with plum jam. There wouldn't be any pálinka, 'e said, only wine. 'E'd already bought it, nice Enyed wine. An' savanyúleves, an' if the ball was goin' to last a long time, then kaszásleves with sausage in it. I was to make lardy cake an' sweet pastry, an' whatever pogácsa I liked. The boss really enjoys entertainin', it seems, but 'e always slacks off puttin' things away when I say it 'as to be done, an' I've got it all to do. Men, you see, don't like doin' anythin' in the 'ouse.

Me lardy cake was ready on the Friday, it didn't matter if it stood for a day. The *pogácsa* was made as well. I bought some nice plum jam in the market cos I 'adn't cooked any plums that year, the boss 'ad sold 'em all. I'd only cooked apples an' pears, we'd got such a lot cos the boss 'ad been experimentin' with 'em. I bought the plum jam from a Szék girl, the daughter of Rózsi Bodon from Csipkeszeg. I asked if she recognized me. She said, 'Aunty Kali, so it is you!' She was very pleased, an' I was so pleased to see the black an' red skirt that tears came to me eyes.

So we 'ugged, but before that we just said 'ello. She said she was meanin' to get married an' was savin' up. If that's the case, all right, let me 'ave a nice kilo of your jam. There was no way she'd take money off me! Ev'rybody knew all about me, the way I'd run off, an' they were sorry for me. Cos me father an' me 'usband 'ad 'ad a row in the pub, an' if Marci Odorján 'adn't been there, 'e's the size of Gutin 'ill, they'd 'ave come to blows. But take me money for it, I said, cos I'm in service. I told 'er, 'Look, me girl, I'm not buyin' for meself, it's for me boss, 'e's got money, 'e's rollin' in it.'

'Gosh, that's good. I'll tell anybody what asks that God's been good to you, Aunty Kali.'

Then we gave each other another 'ug, an' I bought some eggs off 'er as well, though young Butyka from the 'Óstát 'ad brought me some an' all, well, it did no 'arm if we'd got plenty. The boss really liked to 'ave some fried for 'is breakfast.

I asked if she'd got a young man. She said she would 'ave 'ad, but 'e'd been taken away. An' she wiped away a tear. She'd been in love with the Ungvári boy, an' 'e'd been relocated. An' 'e'd loved 'er. But 'e'd been made *Déo*. I asked 'er, tell me what this *Déo* means. Is it a sect? No, it means somebody what's been turned out of their 'ouse. *Domiciliu obligatoriu*. She didn't know where 'e'd been taken, but wherever it was 'e couldn't move from there, all the bourgeois 'ad been taken away, 'adn't they. But now she'd got over young Ungvári an' she'd met somebody else. So I told 'er, listen to a poor woman what's 'ad some experience. You mustn't fall for the rich an' well off.

'Cos I was blind as well, I only 'ad regard for the big 'ouse, not the man. 'Ave regard to that young man's 'eart, an' whether 'e's 'ardworkin'. Don't consider anythin' else,' I told 'er.

'Ah, we're fine together, we can 'ardly be apart.'

I asked the boss 'ow many guests there'd be, 'ow much should I cook. 'E said, a good dozen, an' some would bring their wives. I asked what else I was to do. Cos I'd no idea 'ow 'e 'eld a ball, there 'adn't been one before. I was to take drinks round, but not give people too much, an' make sure the Gypsies got well fed. I was to cook a nice thick soup in case they were 'ungry, cos they really liked to eat. And make a cauldron of nice thick dried bean soup, an' put some bacon an' sausage in it. For next day I'd give the boss some savanyú soup for 'is stomach, that'd be good after a lot of wine, an' put millet in it as well. An' keep an eye open for anythin' runnin' out an' bring more. 'E'd brought two nice demijohns of wine. An' I was to keep an eye on the Gypsies, especially when they went into the kitchen to eat. They wouldn't steal, not for that reason, but so as to give 'em ev'rythin' they asked for. These were classy Gypsies. Classy Gypsies, well, I'd never 'eard of such a thing. An' there'd be Romanian guests, I should look after 'em as well, attend to 'em.

I'll look after ev'rybody, I answered. All right, don't answer back. Could I speak Romanian, 'e asked. Well not really, just a bit, the numbers, I needed those in the market, an' what I'd picked up at school, but that was a long time ago. I'd already told 'im I knew some, but 'e'd forgotten. All the same, I could manage in the market an' say *poftic*. That was all it took to serve people. An' an elderly man was comin', old Schultz, the gardenin' instructor, be very nice to 'im. If 'e asked for anythin' see that 'e got it. An' I was to open the windows when necessary, cos they'd all be smokin'. But I mustn't get in the way. I should stay in the kitchen. I should keep makin' mixin' cordials. An' serve 'em to the the wives. Wouldn't there be liqueurs for 'em, I asked. I'll get some drinks for the ladies, 'e replied. Now if only 'e'd said beforehand, I could've made somethin' with dried plums or an eggnog, that's what ladies are used to.

The guests are invited for seven o'clock, the Gypsies for nine. 'E's 'ired the Ruha brothers from Pacsirta utca, they're the best, ev'rybody likes 'em, an' they can play 'Ungarian, Romanian an' Gypsy music, all sorts.

The boss is puttin' out 'is lovely Korond plates, an' 'e's decoratin' 'em with 'is own apples, cos 'e's got apples an' pears in the back garden an' in another that 'e rents. 'E'll 'ave six kinds of apples on display. An' 'e's goin' to put some leaves to 'em, so that the leaves of 'is apples can be seen. Like a paintin', so to speak. 'E's goin' to put a nice sharp knife with each plate. 'E says I'm to polish all the apples with a linen cloth. An' 'e'll put the name of each with it. 'E knows 'em all—Batul, Pónyik, Sóvári, Cigány, all sorts. Me boss is a great expert.

An' for the middle of the table 'e's goin' to put out a nice embroidered runner out of a chest. So I asked 'im where that'd been until now, was it 'is bottom drawer? I was afraid 'e'd be cross at me talkin' like that, but 'e only laughed. 'E'd bought it 'imself when 'e was collectin' apples in the village, lookin' at apple trees. 'E'd bought 'imself some plates, bowls, tablecloths an' napkins, ev'rythin'. An' the Gypsies 'ad brought 'im some. If Gypsies ev'r came with items for sale I was to let 'im know. They knew 'e was a good customer. 'E loved that sort of thing. 'E'd bought embroidered boots as well. An' 'e'd been up that way. Nagybánya way, which was where 'e'd bought this Romanian runner, with roses. You could tell it was Romanian from all the strands of colour in the embroidery. It's Csiricsár style. Or rather it's weavin', not embroidery. So it's obviously Romanian. It's so many-coloured, it's flashy. That sort of embroidery's overdone. We only use red an' white, modestly. That's tidy 'Ungarian embroidery.

Among the apples we put the plates of lardy cake, well sprinkled with castor sugar. An' I asked, aren't there goin' to be any flowers on the tale? Cos there are still a couple of late roses. But the boss just said 'e'd be ashamed of 'em, they wasn't by any means the best roses in the garden. Let's not put 'em out. I said, they're fine. Who's ev'r seen a rose to be ashamed of? Very well, so 'e let me do that.

We brought the benches in from outside an' spread the woven rugs over 'em for people to sit.

I said, 'Well, I'm goin' to buy a good loom like this once I can afford it.'

'Don't you go buyin' anythin', Kali, I'll get the Gypsies to bring one.'

'That won't do. In the first place, I don't want any presents from a man. Secondly, looms all are different. I shan't be able to get on with ev'ry loom.' Cos you know, to a man they're all the same, but a woman needs to see 'em, there's a difference between one an' another. Same as with machines. There's so many different ones.

'Look 'ere, Kali, you're from Szék, aren't you? Are you sure you can tell a loom from the loo?'

It was Saturday, not a single guest 'ad come yet, an' I wished the boss an 'appy birthday. An' I gave 'im what I'd made 'im, wrapped up in paper. Cos 'e was celebratin' 'is birthday. We don't do that in our village, only celebrate name-days. I'd embroidered 'im a bookmark in the shape of a big red rose. 'E looked at it, turned it over, an' just said thank you. 'E's a man, damnit, didn't give any sign of pleasure.

The guests all came on time, 'alf an 'our an' they was all there what the boss 'ad invited. An' they all brought presents. Mostly books, but some brought some kind of tool, an' one a little pottery jug, an antique peasant piece, some people 'ang 'em on their fence. 'E said thank you for ev'rythin'. Some brought their wives. They weren't posh people, so to speak, but they all wore shirts an' elegant suits. I thought they must be 'is 'untin' friends, or some might be gardeners. The Romanians were some of the footballers 'e used to play with. Cos photographs of the team 'e'd gone abroad with were on the wall in several places. The Romanians spoke 'Ungarian, so the talk was mainly in 'Ungarian. The wives sat in a group, an' in these parts they drink more wine than down our way, or they drink cherry brandy, as one of 'em 'ad brought some morello liqueur. In our village you don't often see women drinkin'. 'Ere they certainly drink wine, but not pálinka. That can't make 'em drunk an' silly so quickly. And they drank an enormous lot of soda-water, an' there were two boxes of that. A lot of 'em cut their wine. That made it last longer, an' they couldn't get so drunk.

Then the Gypsies arrived an' the dog would 'ardly let 'em into the garden. Dogs are very aware of Gypsies, after all. It jumped an' barked at the cello player in particular, 'e was very swarthy. The first thing was that they 'ad to 'ave somethin' to eat once they arrived. They were so tired after the long journey. It must 'ave taken 'em a good 'alf 'our to come up from the Gypsy quarter down by the town gate, they live there close together not far from the small market. These were town Gypsies, an' they'd come up from 'Angász utca. Ev'n the Gypsies are different 'ere from 'em in the villages. Not so skinny, an' more polite. Better washed, as well. They can perform music ev'n as children, cos that gets 'em out of the Gypsy quarter. So, they was given such great big bowls of bean stew that their stomachs bulged. I kept lookin' in to see if they needed anythin'. Then each of 'em put a little cur wine at 'is side an' they started to tune up. Gypsies don't really drink much. They went inside, to the inner room. The tables where the guests were sittin' were out in the other room. At first they played nice an' quietly, softly, 'ere in town I don't know who's supposed to start the dancin' an' with who.

Back at 'ome we often 'ad dances until that rotter stopped 'em. Cos we 'ad a nice big room in that big 'ouse, an' for a long time people came on Saturday an' we 'eld balls. The men put up the money for the music an' dancin' an' the women an' girls brought refreshments. I used to clean the floor till me 'ands 'urt, before an' ev'n more afterwards, cos of the dirty boots. Then one day that dreadful man got drunk an' started arguin' an' bein' rude, an' people wouldn't come to our 'ouse any more cos 'e spoiled it all.

After the dances 'e always put away an 'eap of money. But I didn't dance much once I was married. Ev'rythin' was forbidden. It was silly of me not to ask 'im before we got married whether 'e liked dancin'. Cos 'e'd not ev'n taken me once. Well, you were daft, Kali, you deserved what you got.

Then the boss told me to take up the rug in the room. I pulled the chairs an' table back to the wall. And then 'e asked one of the young wives up an' they began to dance. The rest stayed sittin' down.

I could 'ear the music clearly from the kitchen. Good Lord, the way me 'eart melted then. It was as if I was flyin' in paradise. I really loved dancin' when I was young! The week never passed without me goin' dancin'. I was a good dancer, the boys used to take me a lot. Only with us there was order in a dance, 'ow it was at the start, in the middle an' at the end, an' 'ow the steps went. People didn't just make it up as they went along.

That's not the way a dance goes 'ere, people rather just talk while a couple or two take to the sand. I call it that like we do back 'ome, cos we always sprinkle fresh sand on the earth floor. Perhaps there'll be a few more dancin' a bit later on. 'Ere they 'ave board floors. All the same, I liked it when they struck up a tune I didn't know. Cos they played in such a Romanian style, strongly rhythmical, which you rather 'ave to be used to, me blood started to boil. I'd polished up me boots till they shone like the seat of a Gypsy's pants, as the sayin' goes. I was wearin' a snow-white blouse an' me kerchief was freshly ironed. Well, ev'n I 'ad 'alf a glass of cut wine, cos the boss didn't say I mightn't. The wine quickly went to me legs, made 'em tingle. Made me feel cheerful. I pulled the kitchen door to so as people couldn't see in, but there's also an 'alfway room, where people leave their coats. I shut the door an' did a bit of a twirl on me 'eels. Oh, that did feel good. I moved me feet cos just then they were playin' a *lépegetős*. I moved in time to the music, bowed an' swayed. By all that's 'oly, Kali, life isn't over yet if there's still dancin'! It didn't matter that I'd got no partner, I twisted an' turned as I pleased. I closed me eyes, I was enjoyin' meself so much. Me skirt was swingin' as it pleased. Now I could 'ear 'em playin' with a bit more fire. Perhaps there were more people dancin' by this time. There was one shoutin' out as well.

Just as I was spinnin' round, I opened me eyes an' saw the boss there in the door 'oldin' two empty soda bottles. The master of the 'ouse bringin' out the empties while the servant is dancin' in the kitchen. Really, Kali, you should be ashamed. You've been caught out.

'Kali, me dear, what are you doin' 'ere?'

I said, please forgive me, but they were playin' so beautifully. I couldn't control me limbs.

'You don't 'ave to do that, join the dancin',' said 'e.

'I'm not! Who ev'r 'eard of such a thing, the servant dancing with the gentry?' I asked.

'Stop that servant talk or you'll get a slap,' 'e exclaimed, but 'e wasn't goin' to slap me, I knew 'im, 'e wasn't that sort. Then 'e gave the order, quick march!

'You'll dance, Kali, or I'll spank your backside.'

The boss 'ad 'ad a little taste of that Enyed wine.

I took the soda bottles off 'im an' fetched full ones. I went inside. An the boss called out, 'Which dancer 'asn't got a partner? Cos I've brought 'im a young lady from Szék.'

Really, I thought, look 'ere, Vilmos, young lady! Do you mind! Up comes a gentleman, puts 'is 'and on me shoulder an' takes me into the room where they're dancin'. There were several couples there. They was playin' a *lépegetős* so that when the music starts the couples just walk, men an' girls the same.

They 'ave to be in step with one another. Then the man starts to pass the girl from one side to the other. Me partner wasn't the best an' didn't know what to do with the girl. 'E did it just a bit, but anyway it was dancin'. An' so we got through the number an' when it was over 'e let me go an' thanked me. It's never been the custom to say thank you for a dance, that was a new one. Then straight away the Gypsies started another tune, more lively. I was goin' to leave the room, cos I was still in there. But then another gentleman took me shoulder, an' this one was a better dancer. 'E wasn't remarkable, nor lively, but it was easier to fit in with 'im. Well, 'e wouldn't let me go. We danced three numbers together, gettin' better all the time. 'E didn't flatten is arms against 'is body, like we did at 'ome, cos there we 'ad so little space that people 'ad to 'old 'emselves in. And women always did. 'Ere there's plenty of room to raise your 'ands in an arc. Oh dear, I thought then, I ought to look in the other room an' bring some pastry an' tidy up, Then somebody in the other room did a *kurjantás: Ez a tánc a legényeké, nem a 'ázas embereké*—This dance is the bachelors', not the married men's—an' at that me partner let me go an' I left the room. An' I bumped right into the boss, an' 'e caught 'old of me.

'E took me shoulder, went up to the Gypsy an' told 'im to play a slow csárdás. The Gypsy did that, but so painfully slow it might 'ave been for a funeral procession. Gypsies can put such pain into a tune that I could 'ave burst into tears rather than enjoyed the dance. Well, I couldn't really show the boss what I could do about that. 'E was 'oldin' me so tight, I was almost trapped. 'E picked me up as if there was nothin' of me, like a silk 'andkerchief. I was light in 'is 'ands, there was nothin' I could do but relax. That's what a woman should do in a dance, an' it's marvellous the way she can. She needs to know 'ow to do it. The good dancer is the one that can really relax. She's picked up, turned round, spun. She doesn't do it 'erself, it's done to 'er. That's what makes the good dancer. The way the boss was 'oldin' me the perspiration was just runnin' off me. We didn't look one another in the eye, that's not the way it's done, the good girl dancer lowers 'er 'ead. She don't look at the floor, to see whether 'er feet are goin' to be trodden on, but at 'er partner's shoulder an' below. But not there! Not at 'is prick! The boss took tiny steps, slapped 'is feet—not too 'ard, an' not like somebody 'ose body's in pieces, 'ose 'ands an' feet are detached, but all nicely together, 'is 'ands an' feet inspired by 'is 'eart. Oh, the way 'e 'eld me felt splendid. Drove me mad. 'Is 'ole body was tense. You can tell from that the sort of man what 'as a great passionate nature, like 'e 'ad.

Then the lazy tempo began to change an' we moved more quickly. The boss began singin' the girl's words:

I'm a flower in the garden, I shall die for lack of moisture,
I'm a flower in the garden, I shall die for lack of moisture.

Then the man 'as to reply:

Be a flower in the garden, I'll be dew that falls at ev'nin',
I'll descend upon the flower an' shall lie there till the mornin'.

Finally the song ended with the refrain 'Oh, oh, oh', which the Gypsies drew out nice an' long, an' then went back to the start of the more lively part.

The boss put 'is 'and to 'is 'eart like so—cos the sayin' is that when the girl goes to right an' left 'e must first touch 'is 'eart—'eart to 'eart, that what the figure's called. So 'e did an' 'eld me, an' by God I nearly died. Then at the end of the number 'e spoke to the Gypsies, told 'em they could take a break.

'Run along, Kali, fetch a pastry an' some water for the gentlemen of the band.'

I did that an' then ran out to the kitchen, goodness, me face was burnin', it was red as a rose. Or as they say in the song, like a monkey's bum.

Then the Gypsies struck up again. Again the boss appeared in the kitchen, I was to go, 'e 'adn't got a wife to dance with. We danced a few more lively numbers together, an' 'e 'eld me nice an' tight so that I knew, whatever I did 'e wouldn't drop me 'owever I swayed.

The boss didn't get out of breath either, for all 'is turnin' round an' slappin' 'is feet. Cos actually 'e wasn't wearin' boots. Oh, I 'ate it when a man gets out of breath dancin'. If a man's breathin' 'eavily it shows 'e's not a good dancer. I don't mind if 'is forehead breaks out in perspiration or 'is shirt's soaked through, that's natural, 'is body's been workin'. But that 'e gets out of breath shows that 'e must be 'avin' to force 'imself, it don't come natural to 'im.

Never in all me days would I 'ave thought I'd 'ave such a good dance again. Cos it showed the kind of man what lived in me boss Vilmos. 'Is body was bakin' like a fiery furnace when 'e was dancin'. An' old as I am I was made to dance.

I no longer knew 'ow many turns we took like that. By that time 'em what wasn't dancin' began to stir themselves.

Then when the dancin' 'ad broken off, as they call it, when it was finished, the boss paid the Gypsies. They were given more pastry an' stuffed themselves. Then the guests moved off. It was quite late at night, if dawn wasn't actually breakin'. Not quite five o'clock. The boss said, I wasn't to clean the 'ouse but go to bed, cos 'e wanted to sleep 'imself. 'E'd 'ardly let me pick anythin' up.

I just couldn't get to sleep. The dancin' was still throbbin' in me feet. So I just cleared the pastries away, an' started to undress in me room, But I was so sweaty, I thought I'd 'ave a bit of a wash from me mouth. I took a mouthful of water, didn't need to warm it, that'd take the chill off it, an' wash away the worst of the sweat. Then the boss opened the door. I wasn't wearin' me kerchief, I'd taken it off. There I stood in me slip, I 'adn't put the light on, I knew where ev'rythin' was in the room. 'E came across an' started to run 'is 'ands over me. Not the way a coarse man would, enough to split me breasts, but gently, like somebody comin' to 'is lover in secret. An' 'e whispered, 'Oh, Kali, why've you been keepin' yourself a secret? I saw you dancin', you're not an old woman, you just make yourself out to be one,' an' 'e went on sayin' sweet words as 'e lifted me slip off me.

Then 'e carried me to the bed. 'E lay down beside me an' 'ad is way with me.

I didn't mind at all, things like that used to 'appen after dances. Then, of course, 'e turned to the wall an' went to sleep. Previously when there'd been dancin', we didn't go to sleep cos we 'ad to go out to the fields or to see to the animals. But now it was late in the mornin' an' the boss was fast asleep. I just lay there with me eyes open an' watched over 'im.

Then after that we went about the 'ouse all day with our eyes on the ground, I did the clearin' up, swept the floor, the boss was outside. Didn't come in at all, though it was cold. 'E asked me to give 'im 'is lunch at the back of the 'ouse. Now you're in a spot, Kali, you'll be given the sack by Monday. If you've let yourself go it'll be for that, an' if you don't, it'll be for that.

Monday came, an' we was still keepin' our distance like two dogs that don't know each other. 'E went out somewhere, was out all day, came 'ome in the ev'nin'. Didn't ev'n 'ave anythin' to eat, went to bed. Next day 'e was up at dawn, tidyin' up outside, cos 'e 'adn't finished ev'rythin'. I went out an' asked whether 'e wanted me to work outside as well? I could get an' clean the glass roofs before the frost came. I asked whether I should go to market on Wednesday, we'd still got apples an' pears. I should go, keep out of 'is sight, 'e said. I nearly said somethin' vulgar, but I 'held it back. That's what a woman can do, keep 'er trap shut. Damn an' blast 'im, the 'orrible man! 'E'd 'ad a good servant, well, now 'e's ruined it all. 'E's the one what caused the trouble.'E'll just dismiss me, God strike 'im.

Then I didn't go to market for 'im. Wednesday's the day I 'ave to be out from mornin' to ev'nin'. Wednesday an' Friday. That's when 'is lady loves come round, cos 'e's a man, isn't 'e, can't tie a knot in it. On Wednesday I asked 'im if I might go earlier, cos me dear brother Mihály was comin' to see me an' we'd arranged to meet. Cos 'e's such a nice man, is Mihály, it's just a shame 'e's joined that sect. Become an Adventist. Clear off, 'e spat out. Well, now I'm like I was with me 'usband. 'E's 'ad me, I was daft enough to let 'im, cos I was swept off me feet by 'im, an' now straight away 'e's turned sour like this. You've been really stupid, Kali. Won't you ev'r learn? Men are always like that. The devil made 'em an' 'e's kept 'em with 'im.

Oh, I was off at once, like Anna Mesés. Cos she'd 'ad to go out to the railway in Bonchida to be able to kill 'erself. So what wrong 'ave I done, for all men to despise me? The fault's in me, I thought, that men can only treat me like this once they've slept with me. This is the kind of thing that 'appens to servants. I know for a fact. And I 'adn't been impertinent, 'adn't said anythin' rude to 'im, not ev'n in me mind. And up till now 'e's been such a decent man. 'Eld me nicely when we was dancin', very nicely. An' then nicely in bed as well, 'e's a refined man. Only now 'e's all bitter an' twisted. Afterwards. It's ruined ev'rythin'. God strike men's tools. That's what always ruins things.

Now I don't ev'n feel like readin' a book. I was gettin' on so nicely 'ere an' the boss 'as soured it. Ev'rythin' was all right while 'e 'ad 'is lady loves an' left me alone. 'E didn't 'ave to foul 'is own nest straight off just cos the dancin' 'ad stirred up 'is blood.

I found a bit of relief in young Mihály. While I could see 'im me bad mood was gone. We met at the back of the post office, where people from Szék always get together. 'E'd brought 'is wife to be examined, that was why 'e'd come. Me sister-in-law's been bleedin' 'eavily down below. Poor woman, she's been admitted to 'ospital. Mihály told me all about ev'rythin'. 'Ow me mother's weepin' cos of me, me father keeps shoutin' at 'er, 'e'd told me not to marry that useless man, so she should stop mournin' me, she'll never see Kali again. An' our sister Sárika as well keeps sayin', that Kali was always 'eadstrong, an' she'd 'ad it comin'. Sári's not on me side. But Mihály forgives ev'rybody, 'is 'eart's as soft as butter, only thing wrong with 'im is 'e's an Adventist. So's 'is wife, an' the child. An' 'e says that in the eyes of God I'm livin' in sin, cos I'm married to that man. An' perhaps 'e'd still take me back if I went with 'im now.

'I'm not going back, not for all the tea in China. I won't ev'n visit 'is grave,' I said. An' I asked 'im, when a man beats 'is wife like 'is dog, isn't that sin? An' when 'e's always callin' 'er a swine, chicken-brained, a cow, fat-bum, worn-out cunt? When 'e takes all 'er money off 'er? 'Asn't got a kind word to say ev'n at Christmas? So isn't that sin? May God strike men altogether.

Mihály said I shouldn't irritate 'im. Let 'im take 'im somethin' tasty, cos that would be a token of atonement. An' 'e'd speak to 'im if I went back.

'Well, that'll be a long time comin', Mihály. 'E'll give you a thrashin' as well. You'd 'ear all the bad things about me what previously you've only 'eard about the devil. You'd do better to give the somethin' tasty to the pig.'

So then 'e'd just pray for us, that we'd come to our senses.

'E asked what me situation was like. I said it was very good, the boss was a good-hearted man, didn't tick me off, didn't 'it me, gave me money, just didn't give me the first two months' wages so that I shouldn't run away. We're gettin' on nicely, I said. Well, I couldn't let on that perhaps 'e was goin' to dismiss me. Cos Mihály was no better, I realised. 'E was tryin' to influence me. But anyway, I said no such thing to Mihály of all people, 'e's an Adventist, after all. It was so great a sin that perhaps 'e'd stop speakin' to me straight away.

An' 'e said nothin' about that wicked man, what 'ad become of 'im, an' I didn't enquire. What do I care. 'E can lie in a ditch, the swine, an' stay there. Don't talk like that, for God's sake, Mihály told me. I said, 'My God's seen ev'rythin', an' that wicked man raised 'is 'and to me. 'E surely knows without bein' told.'

So it was quite late when I got back to the Békás. Well, Kali, I thought, 'ow long are you goin' to be 'ere. Whatever am I to do. Perhaps I ought to leave of me own accord, not wait to be fired.

I went into the garden, an' the boss was at the back, I don't know whether 'e saw me. I called out to 'im did 'e want anythin' 'ot? 'E did. Well, you're 'ungry, I thought, 'are you, after your great passion. Cos it was Wednesday, wasn't it, 'is lady friend 'ad been round. Shall I bring it out, I asked. 'E didn't really want anythin'. 'E'd ave somethin' cold. 'E'd find it when 'e came inside. Damn 'im.

Then 'e did come in, didn't look at anythin', washed 'is 'ands, they was dirty, an' sat down. Isn't there any tea, 'e asked. Why did 'e keep a servant for good money if there wasn't ev'n a cup of tea when 'e'd been workin' outside an' was freezin. An' 'e ev'n grumbled—I'd better learn that there should always be a pot of 'ot tea for 'im in the ev'nin'. Now you tell me, I thought, an' I put on the water to make some. It was just lucky the fire 'adn't gone out. But I said nothin'. Then I asked, would 'e like some soup? I gave 'im the nice tarragon-flavoured soup, an' there was some *paprikás* as well. 'E started to relax a bit. 'E began to pick at the food. We was in the kitchen, in the light, but I didn't stay sittin' down, I was doin' the washin' up. 'E just swallowed a bit, bit off some bread. 'E stood up, stopped eatin'. I asked if there was somethin' wrong with it, as 'e wasn't eatin'. 'E just 'ung 'is 'ead. Well, I thought, ask no questions. Then I saw, 'e was in tears. 'E took out 'is 'andkerchief, I gave 'im a nice freshly ironed one ev'ry week. But nice 'andkerchief or not, 'e'd soon made a soggy mess of it blowin' 'is nose. 'E sobbed like a child. Then 'e took me 'and an' put it to 'is 'ead. To 'is for'ead. Then 'e lowered 'is 'ead into me lap an' sobbed. I stroked 'is 'ead, I'm not made of stone, an' it does sadden me to see a man cry. Cos I've got nothin' left to cry over, me tears are all dried up. Then I said to 'im, 'You mustn't take it to 'eart like this. Nothin' all that bad 'as 'appened.'

I knew what was upsettin' 'im. It was comin' into me room. Well, I said to 'im, such things 'appen between a man an' a woman. Especially if she's a servant. You mustn't keep thinkin' of sin, maybe that sort of thing 'as 'appened to 'er before. We aren't saints embroidered on the altar, that we aren't to do anythin'. And anyway, I don't know what church 'e goes to, cos by this time people don't think of religion in terms of what faith somebody else 'olds. In our village religion 'as been all mixed up. Certainly, parents don't forgive you if you change your religion. I kept talkin' to 'im, consolin' 'im. I'm the older, I thought, I've got to be the wiser. 'E just sobbed, wouldn't stop. Then 'e laid 'is 'ead on the table, pushed the dish away. By that time I wasn't 'oldin' 'is 'and or 'is 'ead, I was on the verge of cryin' meself. But I kept a grip of meself. So I brought meself to order. 'E didn't say a word. The soup an' the *paprikás* 'ad gone cold, but 'e ate 'em. An' that's 'ow we went to bed, cold.

Well, I thought, if 'e's wept like that to me 'e isn't goin' to sack me by winter. An' we just stayed like that, cool as an autumn mornin' to one another. We got on with our work. Didn't 'ave a lot to say to one another. Work cheers you up, makes grief pass off. So I just waited. I went down to the market ev'ry Wednesday an' took the apples an' pears. We'd nothin' else to sell. I didn't sell walnuts, I preferred to use 'em in pastry. The boss was runnin' short of money now, I reckoned. All the same, 'e 'anded over mine. I told 'im to 'old it back if 'e was short, give it me when 'e was better off. I'm not to argufy, take what's due to me. The boss was away from 'ome a lot but told me nothin'. When 'e was 'ere 'e worked indoors, makin' experiments, mainly writin' on sheets of paper an' in notebooks. Now an' then people 'ave come to see 'im, but then I've been out, didn't 'ear nothin'. An' sometimes they spoke Romanian, which I don't understand at all. I spent a lot of me time readin'. Cos now I was feelin' assured an' I could read again. At other times I listened to the radio a lot when I was by meself. I didn't care ev'n if they was speakin' Romanian on it an' I couldn't understand, at least it was a 'uman voice. I went to church, to the Kétágú, where 'Óstát people went. What an enormous church. On Sunday it was absolutely black with all the people. I couldn't do without 'earin' a 'uman voice. At one time I used to go to the Catholic church on the Főtér, cos we 'ad no service on a Friday. The boss 'ardly said a word, an' that was all right for 'im, but I'm a woman an' women need talkin'.

At one time I was so miserable at nobody sayin' a word that I took meself off an' went into the forest. Cos the Felek forest isn't far away. Not so as to 'ang meself, like poor old Pali Bodon, who wasn't found for three days. We never found out what the poor old chap 'anged 'imself for. I 'aven't the slightest intention of doin' that. Only I've been very worried. What the 'ell am I to do with me life now. Not that I couldn't go as a servant to somebody else, but it'll always turn out that the man'll just come an' 'elp 'imself an' I'll be no better off. I was clever when I was in service at Furu's, cos in 'em days I was still a virgin an' wouldn't allow it. Anyway, the forest cheers me up a bit. It's like a mother. But ev'n so, some mothers certainly 'ave 'earts of stone, they won't 'ear when their children are worried. If a child tells 'em 'e's got a problem, that sort just turn their 'eads away. Don't 'ear a thing. But the forest listens to ev'rythin'. I find a nice beech tree there an' it don't matter if it's cold an' muddy, I just put me arms round it as if it was me mother, I give it an 'ug an' I say, forgive me. What's it to forgive? What 'ave I done, then, in the eyes of God, that 'E should afflict me? I've left that wicked man, an' I don't ask forgiveness for that. Let 'im ask me what a terrible life 'e was givin' me. An' this new boss. What's 'e so sorry for? Why did 'e 'ave to wail like that cos 'e came into me room? Ev'n if I'd been a virgin. Or 'e'd been deceivin' 'is wife with me. But we're nobody, that we should 'ave to beg God's forgiveness. Well, it's true, there's no understandin' a man or what's worryin' 'im. Nor will 'e tell you. We can't understand one another. Anyway, at least it's beautiful 'ere in the forest. We'd got nothin' of the sort in the Mezőség. There was nothin' there except the poor soil, an' we was for ev'r quarrellin' over 'ow much there was an' who it belonged to.

So I told meself the end so that I should know, like in a folk tale, it 'as to be possible for anybody what listens to it know what the outcome is. Cos it's not enough to listen, they should learn. I said to meself, 'Well, Kali me girl, you've been a good servant. And what 'ave you become? The bad wife of a bad 'usband.'

I thought, what if me father dies, cos 'es got a bad 'eart, an' me brother Mihály was tellin' me that 'e was often laid up cos of it, then I'll go back. Or if 'e's laid up a lot, or goes into 'ospital, then I might go to 'im an' beg 'is forgiveness. If 'e was very ill 'e'd forgive me. But I don't want me father to die, not for that reason. Or perhaps I do, deep down. Who knows what's in a person's 'eart. I don't understand men, nor me own 'eart either. It'd be to me shame to slink 'ome to Szék.

So I left the forest an' went 'ome. I 'adn't cooked anythin'. There was yesterday's leftovers, if need be 'e could 'ave those 'imself.

'E wasn't in. 'E'd gone out. An' taken the spotted dog an' all.

I turned on the radio. I don't speak Romanian, an' when that's what they're talkin' on the radio I can't understand. Sometimes they speak 'Ungarian. An' sometimes the languages of the other nationalities in the country. 'Ungarian's spoken for an 'our at the most. When the boss told me, in the days when we wer talkin', that the reason 'e didn't buy a cow was that cows were finished. An 'e kept tellin' me I was silly, I knew nothin' about the world of today, an' so I bought a newspaper. *Világosság*—Illumination— that's the 'Ungarian paper round 'ere. I read it an' read it, as much as I could, but certainly no light came on in me 'ead. There was no way I could match up me own life with the newspaper. But the time was ripe, that was written an' printed. In the paper there was nothin' but politics, while we was stuck 'ere with our own trouble. I prefer readin' books, that's more me style. Now again I took a book off the shelf, one written by a wild man in Africa. So they're writin' books now! So I can start writin' at once. I ought to write somethin'. Cos there's nobody to tell folk tales to. 'E might at least keep a cow for me to tell 'em to. It needs to 'ave a mate as well.

In this wild man's book—Lobagola 'e's called—it says that there's some wild men what 'ave ten or twenty women. All 'em are 'is wives. Well, a world like that's gone wrong as well. If all the servants are to serve God an' man. Good 'eavens, men was crafty ev'n then, ev'n when they was in a wild state.

I went to see Biri as well, she's always feeds me up as if I was a starvin' beggar. She knows me situation now, I've told 'er. On Thursday ev'nins I went round the back of the post office, where the Szék people met up. I was still waitin' to see what the boss was goin' to do. Cos I'd got no work to do. But 'e didn't say anythin'. I was waitin' for 'im to fire me, I wasn't goin' of me own accord. I 'adn't stolen anythin' to be caught for, so as I'd go of me own accord. Let the boss say what I'd done wrong, I'd send word to me mother with Mihály, next time 'e came, that I'd like to see 'er.

Then by St Michael's day, we was back on good terms, an' 'e asked me to 'ave lunch with 'im again. That was all, we didn't discuss anythin', 'e'd just pulled 'imself together an' was lookin' pleasant again.

I'd been keepin' me eye on this Vilmos the boss so as to be able to make sense of 'is nature. 'Is face was so sullen when 'e talked to somebody else. So severe that they was frightened. 'Is mouth made 'im look as if nothin' on earth pleased 'im. 'E frowned, looked as if 'e was goin' to bite any minute. Only then when we was alone together, an' 'e could see that I didn't threaten 'im, 'is face become quite 'andsome, 'e lost the jumpiness. Then 'e was like a young man, started bein' kindly, friendly. But 'e certainly didn't pull that sort of face when there was a stranger present.

An' so we was on good terms again. Now 'e'was bein' nice, askin' me to cook an' bake this an' that. An' 'e told me when 'e'd got to go out an' what time 'e'd be 'ome. 'E'd never before said when 'e was comin' back. Well, I never know where I am with men. One moment 'e was cold, then 'e was sobbin', an' now 'e was tellin' me when 'e'd be comin' in.

So I asked about Christmas, 'ow did 'e want it. 'E said that on the first day 'e'd be goin' down to 'is mother's, an' the family would be there. So what was I to make for 'im? By way of cookin' an' so on. It's not a big festival to 'im, 'e only went down for the family's sake. Especially if 'is brothers an' sisters was comin', cos 'e 'adn't seen 'em for ages. 'E was very fond of stuffed cabbage. But 'e wouldn't 'ave a tree or anythin'. 'E didn't bother about Christmas. Just the stuffed cabbage, I was to make some of that. So I was goin' to be on me lonesome for Christmas as well.

What kind of a festival is that! 'E wanted some stuffed cabbage. Didn't want anythin' to with Christ our Lord.

We didn't get a tree, though we could 'ave, there was plenty up on the 'illside. Well, I thought, at least I'll make a kalács. What sort of Christmas was this goin' to be. No kids, no God. There'd just be the two of us in silence. I wasn't goin' to put meself out in that case. I just tidied the place up an' made the cabbage. 'E began to eat. It's not the way it's done 'ere. There's no sweetness in it, only savoury. Well, to 'ell with it. Do the cookin' yourself, then. But I'm sayin' nothin'. 'E just don't care for it.

I've 'ad a rotten life, but at least I 'ad an 'ome. We'd go to me mother's, the family would come over, we'd take golden nuts for the kids, the Romanians kept Christmas too, cos we 'ad a couple of Romanian families in the village an' they used to come round. So there was quite a few of us. Cos once a year we'd 'ave a lovely plentiful time. Once, at Christmas.

An' me thoughts went back to that wicked man. I spent twenty Christmases with 'im, I can't forget at a stroke, the way the golden ass carried the poor girl off so that she shouldn't remember anythin' any more, she'd be able to forgive that charmin' count, 'er 'usband. Cos it 'ad to take 'er memory clean away, otherwise she couldn't. Me 'eart don't want to be in that black rage again, like it was that time. To 'ell with 'im. Cos on the first day 'e still controlled 'imself, an' then 'e 'ad a bit too much in the pub. An' by the time New Year came 'e was simply knockin' it back.

That was a miserable 'oliday for the servant in the Békás. I thought, I'd do some embroidery for the boss, but when things were so cold between us I thought, the devil can see to you.

An' then 'e gave me an envelope with an 'undred lei. An' kissed me on the forehead. I felt quite ashamed of meself. I'd embroidered a few 'andkerchiefs to sell in the market an' I gave 'im some. But me 'eart wasn't in sewin' for 'im. But 'e couldn't tell.

Then 'e asked me to sing somethin'. I did, but me 'eart was breakin'. The little Jesus child 'ad been born, that's what I sang 'im. Somethin' else 'ad been born to us. Sorrow.

I considered a bit whether to go out of the 'ouse, cos Mihály 'adn't come an' I didn't know whether I could. I'd sent a message with a friend from Szék, a girl that I'd met at the market ev'n before the 'oliday, she brought eggs ev'ry week. She brought back word from me mother, it broke 'er 'eart, but me father wouldn't 'ave me back. 'E said let me stay where I'd gone an' go on the game. Well, if 'e won't, God damn 'im came out of me mouth. Then I was ashamed of meself, cos the Szék girl 'ad 'eard. She was the daughter of Mihály Salla an' 'is wife.

After Christmas the boss started goin' out a lot again. 'E went to a New Year's Eve party as well. I stayed in by meself an' listened to music. I read Jules Verne an' a lot of other interestin' adventure stories. A book's a good thing to prevent you bein' lonely in this world. I went to church a lot, an' to see Biri, but I got bored with goin' to church so often, an' Biri still 'ad 'er troubles. Well, Kali, you're goin' to grow old in silence. There's nobody for me to say a word to. Biri'd known for a long time 'ow I was gettin' on, she was very sorry for me. I got friendly with the farmers below 'ere, the Romitáns. An' with Butyka, an' there's the Bányai family as well. An' I went an' milked for 'em, then the milk was cheaper. Servants from Szék are appreciated.

In come the New Year. What could I expect, I wondered. I said me prayers, but without any feelin'. After all, God couldn't be able to repair me 'ole life after I'd messed it up. I didn't ask for anythin'. The boss said that per-haps 'e'd send somethin', cos now that I wasn't sellin' in the market 'e'd got no cash flow. I didn't know what 'e meant by flow. I asked 'im if there wasn't somethin' I could take? 'E could make some cuttin's, some rose roots, or some onions or gladioli, we'd got a lot of 'em. But just now they wouldn't sell. In another two months or so. Until then what was 'e goin' to do with me. I told 'im then not to worry about me, not to pay me, I didn't need anythin', only me keep, an' I'd work for 'im. 'E could pay me once we was goin' to market.

January was very quiet. The boss spent a lot of time sittin' at 'is desk, readin' an' writin'. 'E painted a bit as well in a notebook, with coloured paints. 'E painted roses. 'E organized the cupboards where the seeds are. 'E'd got a lot of cupboards made of little boxes, an' it was written on all of 'em what was inside. One ev'nin' after dinner 'e asked me to tell 'im a folk tale, an' did so on several more days. I told 'im the one about the devil quarrellin' with 'is wife. I always told 'im tales about bad men an' women, to make 'im laugh. So we shan't be so solemn all the time. One ev'nin' 'e took me by the 'and an' said, 'Come on, Kali,' an' pulled me into me room.

So there we was again. An' again 'e slept until mornin'. I was worried, cos I was afraid what 'ad 'appened last time would 'appen again. But it didn't.

This time the boss was very nice to me. In the mornin' 'e ev'n stroked me face. 'E said I should show meself round the 'ouse without a kerchief. I 'ad nothin' against it. So next day we was in a good mood. An' I did me best to please 'im. Only I couldn't find all that much to do. Cos in wintertime I'd always done weavin', or maize 'uskin', or what I liked most of all, basketwork. In a nice basketwork group with the other women. There'd be a lot of chattin', or somebody would tell a nice long folk tale. We met in me 'ouse for a long time. All the tales I told! The women used to curse me for playin' 'em like puppets, if I wanted they'd wail, if I wanted they'd laugh. But they couldn't stop listenin' to the storytellin'. An' we was like that a lot until me 'usband drove 'em away, so they wouldn't come any more. It 'urt 'im to see others enjoyin' 'emselves. It upsets me, makes me sad, to think about me old life.

This time I told the boss tales that were more fanciful, with fairies, magicians, miracles, kings an' Goldilocks. But these days people don't care for that kind of tale any longer, they just want reality, things what 'ave 'appened. The way the world is today, people 'ave no beliefs. Don't believe in anythin'. Cos things like that you've got to believe in. The boss just laughs, 'e don't believe. Don't go to church either. Gets cross as well when I mention church.

Then three days went by an' 'e took me by the 'and again an' pulled me. 'E was nicer all the time. So I wasn't so borin' after all. 'E slept in me room again. On Sunday mornin' 'e 'ad a strong urge to get up an' 'ave 'it off with me again. After that 'e was as 'appy as a man always is when e's 'ad what 'e wants. 'E' said, let's go for a walk in the forest. I said I've got to cook. But by then there wasn't much in the pantry, an' we wasn't buyin' meat. To 'ell with it, let's be goin'! 'E simply ordered me. Well, Miss Szék, 'ave you ev'r been on an excursion? Cos I never ev'r 'ad.

Out we went into the forest, an' we took a bag in case we found anythin' to eat. Vilmos the boss went in front at such a speed that I could only keep up by runnin'. You've 'ad it, Kali. It's not enough for you to be a woman first thing in the mornin', now you're out walkin' as well. Not that I didn't like it when the boss was so 'appy with me, but I wasn't as good on me legs as I was in me younger days. There wasn't that much snow an' it was meltin', so I was slippin' about. When we got 'ome the boss 'ad picked some snowdrops, bulbs an' all, an' wrapped 'em up in newspaper together with some other flowers. 'E called out, 'We'll improve 'em, what d'you say, Kali? Improved snowdrops. Never been seen before.'

Actually, the Gypsies used to sell things like that in the street. A serious florist didn't deal with it, but 'e said 'e'd show 'em. Cos if nature 'ad the idea of producin' a flower from under the snow, then man could take it an' develop it further so as to be bigger an' more beautiful. Cos in fact snowdrops are nothin' much. People don't usually pick 'em.

The boss was completely refreshed when we got in. 'E was writin' all ev'nin', an' towards midnight asked for a big mug of 'erb tea. After that 'e went to bed. At dawn 'e came into me room again.

An' so we went on for an 'ole week. 'E came in ev'ry second or third day. 'E got a good sleep, 'e couldn't complain. 'E was always bein' nice. On Wednesday afternoon, which was me day off, I was beginnin' to get ready to go out quietly. It was very cold, an' I thought I'd run down quick an' see Biri, take the bus rather than walk. The boss appeared suddenly in the kitchen as I was just off, cos we didn't say goodbye. 'E told me not to go anywhere, it was cold outside. I asked 'im, didn't I need to go? Cos I didn't go of me own accord, but that 'ad been the arrangement. No. Instead I should make 'im some tea an' finish the thick leg warmers that I'd promised, cos 'is legs were cold. Well, I wasn't goin' out if I didn't 'ave to. I fetched me knittin' pins an' wool an' knitted. I can't just sit there doin' nothin'. I stoked up the stove an' set to work. At the time 'e was workin' in the other room, cuttin' up some roots, but 'is 'ands was cold cos 'e wasn't wearin' gloves. It couldn't be too warm in there cos all the seeds an' pots were there an' they mustn't get too warm. I was to join 'im there. I took me knittin' with me. Well, tell me a tale.

'I'll tell you the one about the poor girl what ended up in the well, all right? This isn't about Anna Mesés, only like it. This is a tale, but what 'appened to Anna was real.' 'Don't make me sad, tell somethin' else.'

'Then I'll tell the one about the lad what died of grief cos the poor girl wasn't allowed to marry 'im. They walked together into lake Csukás with bags of stones on their backs. An' they always appear when there's a full moon, they dance on the bottom of the lake an' come to the surface. Cos in the lake they're 'appy in death.'

'Come on, tell me a nice 'appy story,' 'e said.

Spring was comin' in by then, it was still cold, but the boss was gettin' ready for spring. Oh, was 'e cross when I called 'im boss. Cos 'e was workin' outside in the garden, spreadin' manure on the flower nests, as 'e called 'em. 'E used to take a thermos with 'im, a sort of jug what keeps the drink 'ot, all shiny inside. An' 'e always took it with 'im to 'ave a drink of tea.

An' so we went on, 'e kept comin' into me room. By springtime we was quite cheerful. Quite like a sort of married couple. 'E used to stroke me face. An' kiss me forehead. Liked to look at me. 'E's an 'andsome man, is the boss, anybody what looks at 'im can see that.

The only thing what worries me is that 'e cries an awful lot. A lot for a man. 'E'll put 'is 'ead down on the table in the middle of dinner. Then I 'ave to cheer 'im up. 'E's just like a child when 'e cries. Just makes a face an' wails at me. But 'e can't say anythin' about what's troublin' 'im. That's what men are like. Can't say anythin'. 'Asn't learnt to let it out. 'E just cries an' says nothin'.

God damn 'im for not sayin' anythin'. It makes me so cross. Well, I can't see through a man so as to know what's the matter with 'im. What's gnawin' at 'is spirit all the time, why does 'e 'ave to cry so much, sometimes I just can't cheer 'im up. Cos there are times when 'e's grey in the face, an' 'is voice is ev'r so faint. 'E looks as if there's no strength left in 'im. Then when 'e's workin' 'e gets 'is strength again, cos work's what cheers a man's up. That's the way they were created. An' 'e's created ev'rythin' in 'is garden, like God.

People come an' admire it all the time. In fact, a woman finds cheerfulness in work, but it's not the same. If a woman's got trouble, she goes an' sweeps. Or does a good wash. But 'ousework, what good's that? Cos it don't produce anythin', Only that there's no dirt, there's clean clothes, an' there's somethin' to eat. Nobody regards that as anythin' much, that ought to be praised

When 'e cried, 'e was like a child. A little frog. Ev'ry man becomes like a little child when 'e's got worries an' cries.

I told 'im to go to church an' obtain consolation. At that 'e was so angry, but before that the way 'is tears were flowin' you'd 'ave thought 'e wouldn't 'ave the strength to raise the spoon to 'is mouth. When I said where 'e should go an' obtain consolation 'e fetched the table such a blow, I'd never seen the like from 'im. I should stuff the priests up me bum, 'e 'ated 'em, the fat slimy priests just drove people mad, took away their powers of reasonin', an' stole poor people's money. Pious people only considered the next world, but 'e believed you 'ad to consider this world an' raise it up, while all that interested the priests was keepin' the people poor, ignorant, an' servile, but 'e'd be able to fight 'is way out of it. Obviously 'e was tellin' me that I wouldn't free meself from servitude. Why do I always 'ave to be fightin', I thought. Stay where you are an' you'll be all right. I believed that anybody what's got such great trouble as 'e 'ad would do well to say a bit of a prayer. An' I told 'im so. That's what the church was for, to bring people consolation. But you didn't need a church to say a prayer. I'd come an' pray with 'im. Again 'e slammed the table an' made a speech like a minister. 'E was so angry, 'is face was all flushed blood-red. Since then 'e's been on edge like that all the time. It's a great pity if you 'ave no belief. A great pity. After that 'e didn't say a word all ev'nin'.

Well, I thought, you certainly can't bow the knee an' pray. The boss was so arrogant 'e couldn't kneel. It was a pity 'e couldn't. A great pity.

When 'e cried like that I wouldn't 'ave thought 'e was a big, serious person that could work all 'em acres of land by 'imself. Or that 'ed 'ave such strength when 'e came on top of me, cos the male power in 'im was somethin' amazin'. When 'e snivelled 'e was a little orphan child, the way 'e bowed 'is 'ead into me lap. It was better for 'im to weep 'imself out than to sit gazin' blankly at the stove, full of grief.

But when guests came or somebody to visit the garden an' they was exchangin' ideas, what a strong man 'e seemed to be. 'E gave the appearance of bein' very stern. Then there wasn't a vestige of any grief. 'Ow strong an' clever ev'ry man is in 'is work. But me boss's trouble must be that 'e dealt with such delicate material, flowers. Not that flowers aren't beautiful things, I love 'em, but they're not serious. The soil is serious, as are cattle, wheat, or greens, the sort of things that 'Óstát people produce. But flowers don't suit a man. Such a thing weakens 'im, makes 'im effeminate. In fact, all commercial gardeners, industrial gardeners, as they're called, all that do it on a large scale are all men to the last one. If anybody's ev'r industrial 'e's a man.

It's the same with flowers. If a couple of clumps grow in front of somebody's 'ouse, 'is wife sees to 'em. If there's two acres of 'em, that's man's work.

An' it didn't matter that the boss was 'ighly respected. Cos that 'e certainly was. Professors came to see 'im an' study the garden an' the species, an' the work that'e was carryin' out on the plants, flowers, trees, apples, an' pears. Mostly in spring, to look at the blossom. 'Ordes of students used to come. An' 'e proceeded more an' more scientifically, takin' samples of the flowers, uprootin' 'em, displayin' the roots, 'avin' 'em ready. 'E used to go all over the place, became an important man. 'E was invited to 'undreds of places by friends, colleagues, an' acquaintances. An' yet 'e was very depressed. But 'e 'ad nothin' the matter.

'E wasn't goin' to dismiss me now, I thought, I'd become 'is woman. 'Ow was I to know? Anybody me age, perhaps, gettin' on for forty, isn't goin' to be scared off a good thing. 'E kept askin' 'ow old I was.

'What do you mean, boss? Why do you need to know?'

'Out with it, Kali, 'Ow old are you?'

Well, old enough to know what people are like. Then 'e said 'e' get 'old of me ID card an' see from that. Look, me dear, if you don't believe your eyes. Cos what matters isn't the ID card, it's me actual face.

But when 'e come onto me, come into me room, twice or three times a week, I got no female feelin'. I'd run dry as far as pleasure was concerned. I won't deny, I was pleased for 'im when 'e found pleasure in me. But I didn't 'ave the pleasure in what 'e did. When 'e was on top of me, I rather thought what nice bedclothes we'd got, perfumed an' fresh. Or what tasty pastry I was goin' to make for 'im next day, with plum jam in it. An' 'ow nice spring'd be for us, to work in the garden at all 'ours, only not in April cos then we wouldn't 'ave anythin' ready. That's what I thought of all the time. I thought of the sort of good life what we was beginnin' to see a bit of. Cos that was just the gift of God. A bit of good, for me to enjoy as well. It was just that down below, I didn't get any kind of female thrill.

All the same I didn't mind this sort of thing, cos I rather liked me boss Vilmos. I just wished the man nature in 'im was a bit calmer. But 'is sort won't calm down ev'n when 'e's sixty. Once when 'e'd 'ad enough 'e said to me, 'Penny for your thoughts, Kali?'

At a time like that you mustn't tell a man anythin' unkind, it'll 'urt 'im. I told 'im I was thinkin' woman's thoughts. I wasn't goin' to say that me woman's thoughts was about makin' pastry, or that I was goin' to do a big wash next day.

I got no other pleasure, nothin' you might call female. Never mind, after all, such things fade away, like premature children. Anybody what's 'ad a bad start to life, like me, can't put it right by this time. I'd ruined me future as a woman with that other one, an' I'd loathed it when 'e was always comin' on top of me. An' it don't matter that I don't feel that way now, cos this one smells different an' 'is 'ands feel nice. I just can't forget what it was like when it was the other one. All the same, when 'e was on top of me I was just waitin' for it to be over an' done with. 'E needn't 'ave kept on goin' up an' down inside me, I didn't enjoy it. Only I didn't let on.

That wasn't quite 'ow me love life began, though. I used to 'ave a nice boyfriend, an' we used to 'ave it off together. 'E used to call round ev'ry Friday ev'nin, an' after dark 'e'd make love to me. Youngsters can't restrain 'emselves an' get married first. We was quite afraid, cos there was big trouble if it showed on a girl. That meant disgrace, but all the same that sort of thing often 'appened. So I 'ad this nice boyfriend, Pista Prózsa. 'E wasn't very well off but 'e was a nice-lookin' lad. 'Is land was a long way away. 'E used to take me dancin', an' we danced like mad things. But once we was stupid enough to fall out. Over such a silly thing. 'E said that if 'e 'ad a daughter she'd be called after 'is grandmother, cos 'e'd loved 'er dearly but she'd died young. So I asked what 'er name 'ad been. Jolán. Jolán Cubák. She'd been struck by lightnin' an' died on the spot. Well, I said, our daughter can't be called Jolán. There's no God in 'eaven to make us name our daughter after a woman who'd been struck by lightnin'. That was a bad omen for a child. It'd be an 'alf-wit. That was 'ow we quarrelled, an' 'e ran out an' slammed the door. Then I waited an' waited. I sent 'im a message, that 'e was forgiven. 'E never sent word back. Two weeks later, 'e was dancin' with another girl. Well, bugger you, I thought. I started measurin' me midriff with a piece of string, was I gettin' bigger. Luckily, no. Then I met that man who became me 'usband an' I went off with 'im, didn't wait any longer. I was only too 'appy to be rid of that arrogant Pista Prózsa. But 'e got on no better than I did. 'Is marriage to a rich girl went off the rails. She was so free with 'er favours, she'd go with anybody what asked 'er. Pista came to see me once, when me 'usband was out. I just saw 'im as 'e was passin', lookin' sorry for 'imself. So I asked 'im in for a bit. Sat 'im down. Then 'e gave me an 'ug an' kissed me. 'E said 'e'd come again as well. 'E did, but we was afraid, afraid me 'usband would catch us an' spill 'is guts. Then 'e took to the drink an' all, an' I didn't want 'im.

After that I really dried out down below. The feelin' was like churnin' with no butter. It was dry. It dodn't 'urt, that was all there was to it. It was nothin'.

I was sure me boss 'ad no idea at all that I didn't take the same pleasure in 'im. I mustn't show me thoughts an' feelin's. An' it wasn't 'is fault, 'e did ev'rythin', said sweet words, was ev'r so nice. 'E ev'n liked to 'old the soles of me feet, 'E said they as nice an' warm. An' me 'ands. When 'e was upset an' cried, I gave 'im a stroke, an' 'e said afterwards 'ow nice an' warm me 'ands were. Cos 'is mother's were always cold. Other women's as well.

'That's why I love you, Kali, cos your 'ands an' feet are lovely an' warm. An' not rough.'

'So now you love me,' I answered.

'Don't get conceited, now,' 'e said.

'I simply don't trust men. Don't you worry, mister. They're all like the weather, blow 'ot an' cold.'

Another time 'e told me, 'You're as beautiful as me grandmother.'

I replied, 'Even that's better than if you'd said I was as beautiful as the devil's mother.'

I can never make out whether a man's bein' kind or just pretendin'. It's possible for 'im to do both at once. I was better at tellin' when I was a girl. Or perhaps I was silly an' believed it all when people said, 'When she's old a woman can't be courted any more, can only pretend.'

Then 'e told me 'ow fond 'e'd been of 'is grandmother. She'd been really beautiful, 'ad a moon face. In all 'is life she'd been the nicest to 'im. 'Is grand-mother. She'd never 'it 'im, gave 'im an 'ug when 'e cried, was always givin' 'im sweets. An' when 'is mother gave 'im a slap, she'd pick 'im up an' take 'im to 'er place. An' keep 'im there for a fortnight. But then along would come 'is mother an' take 'im back, but not before there'd been a good slangin' match between the two women. So, that's 'ow nice 'is grandmother 'ad been. She was 'is mother's mother. There'd been the other one as well, but she didn't like children, was always tickin' 'im off an' 'ittin' 'im. She was a witch.

I wished I could 'ave been a bit kinder to 'im down below. I was always thinkin' about it. I ought to 'ave thought of somethin' nice so as to be a bit more welcomin' when 'e came inside me. So that 'e shouldn't churn with no butter I'd think of the roses in little pots that I'd take down the market in

March. Or I'd think of 'ow we'd unload the cart of manure an' take it to the beds in a little barrow an' baskets, an' 'ow marvellous it'd make the soil. An' I'd think of somethin' like us workin' together on the land, an' then I'd get nice an' slippery down below. Cos 'e came into me sev'ral times a week, an' 'e was so much a man, it was amazin'. You wouldn't 'ave thought it to look at 'im. 'E didn't look it.

But all the same, when 'e cried 'e was a proper *papalaptye*, as the Romanians say. A milksop, no sort of a man. Not a real man. I reckoned all 'em damn flowers 'ad made 'im soft. The way 'e was for ev'r lookin' ar 'em, 'andlin' 'em, drawin' 'em. 'E didn't do it for the money, to sell 'em, cos 'e only sold the bad ones. The nice, beautiful ones, the special ones, an' the varieties that nobody else 'ad made before 'e kept as experiments, an' the most beautiful 'e crossbred in autumn. 'E tore off the petals an' wiped 'em with another, that's 'ow you 'ave to experiment, by tearin' 'em to bits. An' 'e didn't do it to become famous, cos nobody becomes famous or a scientist through flowers, 'e used to say. 'E was just amusin' 'imself. Actually, by that time famous men, professors an' the like, were startin' to come to 'is garden an' look at the great things 'e was doin'. Perhaps 'e was becomin' famous.

Cos a man can't be 'appy workin' in silence. A man needs there to be somethin', money or knowledge, to be the strongest or to own a lot of land. To 'ave a reputation. Well, these days nobody can 'ave a lot of land any more, cos it'll be taken off 'im. Or be like the 'Óstát farmers. A man can feel strong when 'e keeps an 'ole families by the work of 'is 'ands. Me boss keeps nobody but 'imself. That don't make a man strong.

I told the boss 'e could be 'is own master if 'e bought an animal or two. The 'Óstát people don't always bring vegetables, milk an' meat. So I'd keep a few fowl for 'im, an' we' buy a little cow. I encouraged 'im, I said, 'Let's get one.'

All 'e said to that was: 'You're being' silly, Kali. Don't you know, then, there aren't any cows left? That cows an' bigger animals 'ave 'ad to be 'anded over, or the milk from 'em declared? So 'ow are we to buy one when they've all been taken away?'

Well, that surprised me. I knew that the big estates 'ad been confiscated, but I 'adn't 'eard that cows 'ad as well. Then 'e told me there was goin' to be a collective farm. I'd 'eard that, I said, only nobody in Szék 'ad wanted to join it. Ev'rybody was goin' to work together, 'e said, 'and in ev'rythin', an' be given a wage. Individuals wouldn't 'ave to work so 'ard.

'Maybe it'll put paid to the garden 'ere',' 'e said. 'I'll 'ave to 'and it over, cos it's too much for one man.'

Even if 'e wasn't a commercial. I could see I couldn't ask questions, cos 'e was so dejected.

I didn't 'ave to leave the 'ouse on Wednesdays any more. The boss went out now an' then, not as much as in winter, when there wasn't so much to do. Now 'e just didn't do it. But 'e wouldn't let me do anythin' on the soil without 'im. Sometimes 'e went dancin', cos 'ed come in in the small 'ours, an' I'd think 'ed been to a dance. But 'e'd just shake 'is 'ead, 'e wasn't much of a dancer.

'Not if I can't take you with me, Kali,' 'e said sorrowfully.

'Never 'eard of such a thing as a master takin' 'is servant to a ball an' 'avin' 'er dance,' I answered. I wasn't to call 'im master. Especially not now, people mustn't 'ear that, said 'e crossly. I must learn.

But when 'is mother came to see 'im, then these was trouble. Ev'r since was a bus from the station right up to the Békás she came once a week. Then the boss just sat without sayin' a word, but there was no sign of regret on 'im. When she came I always 'ad to bake some nice pastry. 'E didn't give 'er any indication of what I was to 'im. I wasn't ev'n to go into 'is workroom. I noticed that no women were comin' to see 'im by that time. Only 'is mother. She was a small woman, small but surprisingly strong. Thursday was 'er day. The boss said I 'ad to make a big effort to tidy the place. I always did tidy up for 'im, but 'ow was there to be tidiness in an 'ouse like that, where there was no furniture apart from tables an' shelves for experimentin', masses of pots an' ev'rythin', an' scientific books an' equipment. We'd move things from one place to another. I couldn't turn round without knockin' somethin' over with me backside. There was just one corner with a lamp, an armchair, an' a little carved table, an' that was where 'is mother used to sit. The boss was always grey when 'is mother was there. 'E didn't cry, but 'e wasn't a bit 'appy. An' they spoke to each other so 'arshly! I always took the tray in, like the maid in a posh 'ouse. Pastry an' ground elder tea, cos that's what 'e drank. An' I got a taste for it, was still makin' it for 'im in autumn. As I went out, I 'eard 'is mother say, 'Look 'ere, Vilmos, what d'you want a maid for? She just costs you money. Get a charwoman to come in once a week, she could do ev'rythin' for you. This one'll live in, eat you out of 'ouse an' 'ome, an' steal from you as well.'

'Stop interferin' with ev'rythin'! I'll keep who I like. I can afford it these days. All me life you've given me orders, so now keep your mouth shut. If I ev'r 'ear you say again about this woman that she'll steal from me I wo'nt 'ave you in the 'ouse, I swear.'

'An' then she'll go an' get 'erself in the family way so that you can't kick 'er out.'

'Will you just shut your damned mouth! You've never said a kind word in your life.'

Well, that was 'ow they went on, like gentry. Goodness, if I'd talked like that at 'ome I'd 'ave 'ad me ears boxed an' no mistake! I'd 'ave been thrown out, wouldn't 'ave touched the ground before the Király forests. That's not really a forest, just a poor thing like the whole of the Mezőség. I'd 'ave liked to tell 'is mother that we Szék people are proud of one thing, that we make such good servants. But what would I 'ave done if the boss came in?

There was a long silence after they'd finished their conversation, like dog an' cat. I peeped in. They were lookin' at each other like a pair of wolves. Then 'is mother said somethin' else about all the relatives, but only somethin' bad, or about what mistakes they'd made. One spoiled 'is children, 'e shouldn't do such a thing, an' 'e'd got so many, 'avin' em made in poor, they'd bred like rabbits, so many 'e didn't know their names. Another squandered 'is money, a third drank. I only knew about two of the boss's brothers. One 'ad got a lazy wife, couldn't cook at all. So, what it boiled down to was that 'is mother 'andt got a good word for 'er four children. It turned out that there was three boys an' one girl. And rather than create good feelin' among 'em by tellin' one nice things about another, all she did was make fun of 'em an' criticize.

The boss 'ad never said a word about 'is family when we was workin' together. Not a word. Not ev'n when 'e was bein' nice to me. Not ev'n where 'e was from, who 'is parents were, 'ow much land they owned an' where-abouts, what they produced on it, what 'e'd learnt in school. Nor about 'is siblin's. I'd never ev'n seen any of 'em. When 'is mother was leavin' 'e'd get out money from the box. 'Owever they'd been arguin', cos I could always 'ear the raised pitch when she was shoutin'. That was where 'e kept it, or rather, where we kept it, cos I knew, in an old painted box with a lid, an' I'd get some out when greens an' milk an' other things was delivered an' I'd pay. I did try to bargain but it couldn't be done. The boss 'ad told that Butyka the 'Óstát man to deliver forty lei worth of greens weekly an' milk twice a week. So 'e brought as much as 'e liked. Then when I asked for a chicken, I meant a nice fresh one, old Butyka said that'd be sixty lei. I said I only wanted one, an' 'e said that was 'ow much, sixty. So I asked what could that chicken do? Did it lay golden eggs? That was the price, it was a 'Óstát chicken. Well, I said, for sixty lei it can certainly read aloud from the Bible.

The boss just gave 'is mother money. 'E wasn't all that well off, I didn't really know 'ow much 'e'd got, cos 'e noted it all down in a book, but 'is mother took it an' never said so much as thank you.

When 'is mother 'ad gone the boss was so cross, 'is temper was on the boil, it'd flare up at simply anythin'. So I just kept out of the way. 'E'd be up till late, workin', but in such a jumpy mood, you could tell 'e was angry. If the least thing upset 'im 'e'd shout straight out. Or if I did somethin' wrong 'e'd find fault.

Then 'e'd come into me room an' cry. Cry 'is eyes up, an' then next day 'e'd be as cold as a churchyard. So I 'ad to cheer' im up. And so it went on, I got used to it. Dear oh dear, it's 'ard to stay well in with a man. 'Is mood's as changeable as the sky in summer. The colour of blood, or rose pink, then pitch black, an' then the sun'll shine again. It's important for a servant always to keep an eye on a man's mood. Somethin' for a woman to do. God damn it. A woman can't get on by 'erself. She's always thinkin', well, the next one will be better.

I kept me eyes open, an' 'ow. If 'e was in a good mood I 'ad to talk to 'im kindly, if 'e was grievin' an' cryin', then quietly, an' if 'e was angry I 'ad to leave the room an' make meself scarce, keep out of the way. The boss was so jumpy all the time. This was no good, that was no good, 'e 'ardly took pleasure in 'is flowers. As 'e didn't 'ave a wife to 'it, 'e'd go out. To 'ell with all men. The boss was quite right, by that time I loathed 'em all. Cos they was all decorated bone china eggs, only just rotten, the devil's work the lot of 'em. I preferred sittin' in me room in the ev'nin', I'd shut the door so that 'e couldn't come in when 'e felt disposed. I read or sewed or knitted. Especially when 'is mother 'ad been round I'd avoid 'im for two 'ole days. I'd knit socks to sell at the market, an' gloves. I used to watch the money, cos I was savin' it all up so as to 'ave some. There was no knowin' where I'd 'ave to go.

Marriage is certainly a lot of worry. Ev'n if you're equally well off, acre for acre, as the sayin' goes, a reasonable age, neither older than the other, an' in good 'ealth all considered. Ev'n if you're well suited, if the parents aren't difficult an' against one other, or are nasty to the other's child, an' will ev'n 'elp if that's the case, ev'n then there's nothin' but trouble. The one will simply interfere with the way the other does things. Perhaps the wife interferes cos she's argumentative, so that the 'ole district 'ears what she's got to say. An' there are men that stick their noses into women's affairs, ev'n cookin' an' bakin', or the way to keep poultry, or 'ow wide open a window should be. There are ev'n 'em what knows better. Me father for one knew all about cookin'!

'Hey, Kali, isn't that stew burnin'? You should put less fat in, you know. Don't waste it. Goodness, all that bread's gone, are you feedin' a regiment?'

But 'e never ev'r lowered 'imself to cook a meal. Me mother once threw the wooden spoon at 'im an' said, 'You do it, Marci Szabó, if you're that clever.'

Well, that time we got dry bread for two days. After that father said no more, 'eld 'is peace, as they say. 'E kept quiet for a month, then 'e started again.

So it wasn't that Vilmos me boss was so quarrelsome that 'e'd tick me off for ev'rythin', it was only when 'e got cross or 'is mother 'ad called. It didn't matter that she was such a little woman, she was such a controllin' sort. Well, if she'd known about our relationship! That would 'ave been all it needed. Vilmos was indifferent towards cookin', wasn't as devoted to 'is belly as other men are, wasn't interested in ev'ry plate of meat. 'E ate well, but still was so finicky. 'E never saw anythin' in the 'ouse, that there was dust or we'd carried mud in, I didn't, cos I'd got woven slippers made of straw, but 'is 'ighness walked in 'is shoes ev'n on the rugs. The only sort of thing that 'e saw was if there was a tiny bug on a rose—it was amazin' 'ow 'e'd see that. Then 'e'd go to work somethin' awful, washin' an' cleanin' 'is roses.

In early summer 'e 'ad more an' more callers, a lecturer or somethin' from the university, a Romanian, what's more. Officials would come, look, examine, 'e'd spend all day explainin' to 'em an' they'd go out into the grounds an' the fields. Then big groups of university students would come an' 'e'd give 'em lectures. There was somebody ev'ry week, sometimes two lots. And then officials came who didn't look at the flowers but discussed somethin'. The boss didn't 'ave much to say to 'em, then when they'd gone 'e was very thoughtful. But 'e didn't tell what was the matter.

When I asked 'im whether I was to go to market, take some bulbs or roots, 'e just went round the garden impatiently an' I 'ad to follow 'im. 'E indicated the stocks from which I could take stems, an' ev'ry stem 'ad a green tip which I'd painted on it in winter, there was a bag of all 'em little green sticky. Green an' red sticks. Them I could dig up an' take. I put a label on each sayin' what sort of rose it would be, cos of course there's no tellin' from the root. I just 'ad to put the colour, an' whether it was a bush, tea or rambler variety. 'E'd noted down a long time ago 'ow many leaves there were an' the scent an' all the many other things there are to be known about that sort of rose, but such things don't interest the people who buy the flower in the market. I'd be perfectly able to sell 'em.

Then that Romanian lecturer who was always comin' brought 'im a flower of some sort. I don't know what it was, but 'e presented it as Christ's cerecloth. Right at the end of the summer 'e brought it. Well, the boss was so interested in it, the way 'e fussed over it, covered it up, 'ugged 'imself for pleasure. That was goin' to be such a marvellous rose. I asked no questions, was careful not to touch it, cos then I'd 'ave 'ad a tickin'-off. Then when 'e was a bit more friendly towards me 'e told me the rose's name, some foreign name. It turned out that roses 'ave names as well. An' 'e'd always yearned for one of these, an' all of a sudden this lecturer brought 'im one from abroad. Cos this rose 'ad brought about the end of the war. 'E was goin' to tell me a folk tale if I behaved nicely. Well, I thought, perhaps you've always behaved so nicely? I've told you tales all the same. 'Ow would it be if only good people was to 'ear folk tales? Cos it's the bad people what ought to 'ear 'em, so as to improve a bit. Well, it's not saints what need to go to church. Look 'ere, I'd go into the prisons an' I'd arrange for all the wicked people there to listen to folk tales. The sort what 'ad killed, lied, swindled, mothers what 'ad killed children. An' men what 'ad beaten their wives an' left 'em crippled. They're the ones what need to. An' good people could listen as well, cos actually it wouldn't do any 'arm. I'd ev'n 'ave women what were good at tellin' folk tales paid by the state.

Since 'e'd 'ad 'is rose, this new foreign variety, an' it was planted in the best position, where all 'is treasures was, 'e was a changed man. It was like when old little Sándor Minya's wife died, an' 'e got together with the widow of old János Sári, Aunty Kali, cos she was a Kali as well. They lived to a good age like a pair of love-birds, you know. Maybe Vilmos'll get old, an' then won't be so jumpy any more.

But 'e didn't tell the story about the rose. I asked 'im 'ow it 'ad 'appened that a rose 'ad caused the war to end. Cos wasn't it all the American machines what 'ad come along, an' they stopped it? An' the Russians. In that case it's an American variety, I thought.

'Come off it, Kali, what do you know about the war?'

'Well, if I don't know, you tell me! But I can tell you a great war story! A great one!'

'About strife between men an' women. That you do know, Kali. What do you know about the war?'

Get a life, I said to meself. You think the war didn't affect me, only you? So didn't we 'ave nothin' to eat? If only it 'ad carried off that rotten 'usband of mine. But it only took 'im for a bit, an' 'e was sent straight 'ome cos 'e was shittin' all the time. 'Is innards was so delicate, 'e 'ad dysentery an' typhus. If only 'e'd been kept in the army an' never come back. I'd 'ave done all right, in'eritin' 'is 'ouse, drawin' 'is war pension as a widow, I'd 'ave been comfortably off. If only! But I wasn't goin' to tell 'im about me war.

Anyway, this rose certainly brought about a change. I no longer 'ad to be out on Wednesday an' Friday, when the gentry attended to men's affairs. 'E'd dropped that girlfriend what I'd seen, who always used to come. Or she'd dropped 'im, 'ow did I know, 'e never said a word about 'er an' I never enquired. I'd only seen that when she'd been in the mud she took 'er shoes off while she was still down on the paved path an' put slippers on. But mostly she was brought in a car, cos she was posh, wore an 'at, 'ad a snooty look, an' was as thin as a rake. I never saw 'er in the same clothes twice. 'Er skirt an' top was always a perfect fit, an' the same colour an' material. A woman like that must 'ave a big wardrobe, I thought. Once she came in trousers, very wide flared. An' she 'ad a feather in 'er 'at. Like a man. What did a posh woman like 'er want with a gardener? Why did she keep comin'? Well, the demands of nature drives men an' women just the same.

Early one mornin' I went out into the garden cos I couldn't find the boss anywhere. I looked round the back, in the trees, 'e wasn't there, among the plants, in the stable, no sign of 'im, so I went on into the garden. I could see the dog standin' by a row of roses, where it wasn't allowed to be, waggin' its tail. I went over an' what did I see, Jesus an' Mary!, I 'ad a shock an' cried out. There was the boss, lyin' on the bed. I didn't know whether 'e was alive or dead, cos 'e 'ad is eyes shut. I ran over, I'd gone out in me slippers, an' I shook 'im. At that 'e gave me a fright an' shouted out to leave 'im alone, 'e was workin', Gosh, ev'n now me 'eart misses a beat.

'What are you doin', lyin' there on the ground, workin' at dawn? You'll get a chill, the ground's cold,' I said

'Go away, you silly woman,' 'e shouted at me.

And I'd 'ave gone. Straight out through the gate, if that was what 'e wanted.

'Don't talk like that, boss, I'm only afraid of you catchin' your death. You'll catch cold in your guts, then you'll be runnin' to the loo all day. Please get up off the soil.'

I 'ad to speak to 'im like a child. I 'ad no feelin' for flowers, 'e exclaimed. Go away. So I went. To 'ell with 'im. What sort of science is that, sprawlin' in the bed, who ev'r 'eard of such a thing. Men can only be lyin' on the ground if they're drunk. It can only lead to trouble. It means that the soil's ruined.

'E didn't say another word all day. Then in the ev'nin' all 'e said—bein' mysterious, like ev'ry rotten man—was: 'There's goin' to be some big changes.'

I asked no questions an' 'e said no more. Oh, I do 'ate men what can't say anythin'. Neither about grief nor 'appiness. The devil take ev'ry last one of 'em. 'E could stuff with 'is secrets till 'e bust.

'E never 'ad to ask me to talk if 'e wanted me to tell a folk tale. Then I'd go on for an 'ole 'our tellin' the one short story. An' if I wanted, I'd spin out for two 'ours tales about 'ow Goldilocks was still' married an' was bein' tested, an' then the wealthy count who'd married 'er was wallowin' in wealth with 'is friends, so I told it at such length, it was like a winter day, never goin' to end. Well, if I too was to take a long pause at the end of ev'ry sentence, was I to tell the story or not, just so as to be asked to go on? What kind of storyteller needs to be asked? Really, I ask you!

All I said was when should I give 'im the nice cow pea soup, I'd bought some from a kind 'Ostát neighbour, the first crop. There was nice thick szalonna still crisp on the surface, an' I'd put a big spoonful of sour cream on top, cos 'e was like a child, 'ad to 'ave sour cream on ev'rythin' before 'e'd eat it!

An' I said to 'im, 'I don't care much for changes. No good comes of 'em.'

At that 'e looked at 'is bowl an' said, 'Kali, isn't this the eighth time this week you've kindly made me a nice bean soup?'

An' 'e laughed at 'is joke. Kindly, by the 'orse's arse! But I said nothin', just didn't eat with 'im. As 'e wanted me to. Are you cross, or somethin'? Then eat by yourself. If I ask what to make you're cross, an' then you're cross if I give you bean soup. I can't do right for doin' wrong in this 'ouse.'

'Well, it's Friday, after all,' I told 'im. 'We usually 'ave bean soup on Friday.'

'An' what did we 'ave yesterday?'

'Yesterday I 'ad to work, an' there was some left over from the day before.'

'An' what was before that?'

'Well, that was completely different bean soup, couldn't you tell? That was Juliska beans.'

'E laughed at me.

So there were to be changes. The boss was goin' to be a state employee.

I said to 'im, 'Listen to a peasant woman, cos I told you before, it's not good for anybody who's always been 'is own master if somebody else starts layin' down the law to 'im. Cos anybody employed by the state is goin' to 'ave others tellin' 'im what to do.'

An' 'e came 'ome from the interview like somebody whose mind 'ad been taken off 'im. 'E'd 'ad to go for the interview in order to get the state employment. 'E was goin' to be a lecturer. But 'e was frantic when 'e came 'ome. 'E'd 'ave to tear up all the roses! Roots an' all. What 'e'd thought about an' cared for so much that I wasn't ev'n to speak aloud when I was workin' with 'im. Mustn't upset 'em! The inanimate world. Well then. Now 'e was going to take an axe to 'em, 'e was so angry. But I'd thought 'e'd be celebratin' after the exam. 'E was such a great scientific man, I didn't think e'd fail. But 'e 'adn't failed, 'e was just very angry. I daren't ask what was wrong, or 'e'd ev'n 'ave used the axe on me. So, 'e'd been accepted as a state employee in the university, an' now 'e was as angry as if 'e'd been fired. There's no pleasin' some people, is there!

And we 'aven't been on very good terms since 'e's been goin' out to work. An' 'e brings all the university students round an' teaches 'em 'ere in the garden. An' a lot of officials came to examine the garden. An' they said it wasn't a productive garden but an experimental one. It was surveyed. When they came to survey it, I thought, well, Kali, you can be off, like old Gergi Moldován when 'e drank away the cello an' couldn't make music any more. 'Is wife threw 'im out. Cos if 'e was goin' to 'ave to give up the garden it'd be goodbye to the servant. But I 'aven't been thrown out yet. Signs 'ave been put up ev'rywhere namin' flowers, trees, ev'rythin', ev'n the wild roses, cos there's some of 'em as well. An' 'e's 'ad to 'and in copies of ev'rythin' that 'e's written about it, lists, all the drawin's that 'e's made, an amazin' amount of paper. 'E's doin' a 'uge amount of work now. But it's mainly with the university people an' deskwork. 'Is experiments with flowers an' pots aren't so respected, but ev'rythin's deskwork. Now I'm 'avin' to do the sort of thing 'e wouldn't let me do before.

A great change came over 'im at this time, an' not entirely for the better.

But all the same, 'e still came into me room. Sometimes once, sometimes twice a week. Then on one occasion as we was lyin' there I whispered in 'is ear an' told 'im—'e 'adn't asked, but I told 'im. It pained me, but I 'ad to tell 'im. I whispered in 'is ear as 'e lay beside me that there was good reason why I'd not 'ad children. It was cos me 'usband an' I 'adn't got on well together. We certainly 'adn't! Only abnormal children are ev'r born under those conditions. An 'ealthy child is only born if people love each other an' get on well together. In the first year I did ev'rythin', tried 'erbs an' potions, an' at the time I really wanted us to 'ave a child. But that rotten man couldn't 've cared less, an' when I went to Bonchida to see a doctor all 'e did was complain that I was wastin' money. All the doctor did was poke around down below, which I didn't want, but there's no other way of carryin' out an examination. Ev'rybody can poke around, but they can't cure anythin'. It's no good, it's not doctors what gives people children, it's God. God could see 'ow badly we was gettin' on, me an' me rotten 'usband, an' didn't give us anythin'. I drank up ev'rythin' I was given but no child came. I went round all the women, the 'erbalists, the fortune tellers, an' it all cost money, chickens, an' szalonna. No sign of a child. I ev'n went to a Romanian woman, an' she exorcised me of an evil spirit. Then I thought I'd try fastin'. I fasted for an 'ole year, ev'ry Wednesday. Never ate a thing. Cos there are those who God 'as 'elped. Aunty Győri's 'usband was cured of drinkin', for example, cos 'e fasted 'imself off it. It pleases God when somebody refrains from food. It pleases 'im an' 'E grants their prayers. Anyway, 'E didn't grant mine. That wasn't the plan. An' now I was really grateful, cos in the third year I realized what a rotter me 'usband was, an' so I stopped wantin' a child. Why should I put up with that as well? It'd 'ave been stupid in such a marriage. An' in the second year I 'ad a lover as well. The 'andsome Pista Prózsa. So I whispered that as well into Vilmos's ear. I was thinkin' it would 'ave been all right if I'd 'ad a child by 'im, Pista, that is. It's not written on 'em whose they are. But nothin' came of it. Actually, with 'im it was just a passin' affair. You get no thanks for 'avin' a lover. You've always got to be afraid, on the lookout, an' ev'n then the word'll go round that you're an 'ore. An' I didn't like livin' like that, 'avin' to be frightened all the time. I much prefer a quiet life.

I talked like that into the boss's ear for an 'our or so. I ev'n shed a tear as well when I told 'im about the little child that I wanted an' struggled for in me first year of marriage. An' when I got to that 'e gave a loud snore. Didn't reply at all. 'E was asleep! Well, 'e might 'ave said somethin' back when a woman 'ad told 'im 'er life story, what 'ad been painful for 'er. But 'e didn't say anythin'. 'E'd got an 'eart of stone, or a rose bush.

Then first thing in the mornin' I saw 'e was gazin' sorrowfully at the ceilin'. I asked 'im what 'e was lookin' at. There was no cobwebs, I'd seen to that. Did 'e want me to tell 'im a nice folk tale an' cheer 'im up, 'e was in such a grey mood. I told 'im an amusin' story from Bocaccio. I'd just been readin' it in a book off the shelf. About the priest, the insatiable woman, an' 'er fat 'usband. Cos it came to me mind 'ow the three of 'em managed. I said that three priests came to see the insatiable woman, all of different religions. To that 'e said that 'e'd better turn onto 'is other side, cos 'e couldn't 'ear. 'Is left ear was no good. 'E'd 'ad inflammation in it when 'e was a child, the eardrum 'ad been perforated an' 'e couldn't 'ear anythin' with it. Just as well, cos 'e 'adn't been called up, bein' 'alf deaf. So I told 'im the story in 'is right ear, an' I worked it up, turned it round so that that woman needed so many men that there wasn't enough in the 'ole village. 'E laughed an' laughed, but by that time I was feelin' gloomy.

Well, I thought. It was 'is left ear what I confessed into last night, cos that's 'ow 'e was lyin'. I didn't think 'e'd 'eard a word. So I asked 'im, 'Did you 'ear me story in the night, mister?'

'What story was that, Kali? Are you tellin' stories in your sleep as well now?'

'Well, what I told you about me own life, mister,' I said.

'E 'adn't, then, cos 'e'd been fast asleep. 'Ow in creation was it that when a man'd 'ad sex with a woman 'e immediately turned over an' went to sleep, while that was just when she wanted to tell 'im about 'er own life. Cos then we was feelin' good an' satisfied. An' 'e 'adn't said 'e'd like to 'ear about me life. I'd 'ad to tell the story to meself so as not to forget. That it 'ad been so nice. As nice as the devil's aresehole.

Then once again the entire day was turned upside down. 'E was on edge, couldn't settle, couldn't be spoken to. 'E was in an 'urry, shoutin' for things, an' there always was somethin'. The students came, after 'em officials. Then somebody from the newspaper, took photos of ev'rythin'.

But 'e didn't tell me anythin'. An' I didn't understand whether this 'ad now all been discovered, the great work that 'e'd been doin', all the diff'rent things, or whether it was to be destroyed, an' so an assessment was takin' place, cos presumably all the gardens an' the land was to be confiscated. Mainly the outlyin' parts, goin' into the collective. That was a big piece of land, if not so very big, a good two 'ectares, almost three. I was gettin' a bit worried as to what was goin' on. Cos previously it 'ad been nice an' peaceful, but now there was this pandemonium all the time.

One thing I did like that we did then. We went to the culture centre. As the boss 'ad been discovered as a famous gardener an' plant breeder 'e was asked to present a culture programme. Cos now that the people was bein' educated an' elevated, programmes was bein' presented for any what didn't 'ave one. The only thing wrong with it was that it was scheduled for ten o'clock Sunday mornin', when I went to church. But in 'em days the church wasn't in favour, an' the boss didn't like it either, always told me off if I went. 'E was to go into the culture centre to present the programme, 'e'd been put in charge. 'E'd invited musicians, not the usual swarthy Gypsies but 'Ungarians. An' 'e'd invited experts who could teach dances. 'E'd invited a man from Méra an' 'is wife as well. 'E told me I should go to the culture centre if I wanted to dance. No way. Goin' dancin' at me age. So one day 'e grabbed me an' took me. 'E said 'e 'adn't got a good partner, an' we was goin'. Well, I was really embarrassed. But then, I thought, nobody'll see me. So I said, wait a minute, I'll wear me best skirt or two, if there's dancin', an' me best kerchief, not this tatty thing what I wear in the garden. Well, there they was all organized an' all sorts of people came in. Not of their own accord, but an activist 'ed brought 'em, somebody called Tompa. First we 'ad to listen to what the activist said about culture. 'E 'ad a lot to say, goodness, the way 'e droned on an' on. Then an expert 'ad to come on, somebody called Jagamos, an' 'e talked an' talked as well. All about the values of the people, what was then bein' discovered. But the audience kept fidgetin', they wanted to get an' dance. 'E talked so much, I thought 'e'd never stop. Well, at last 'e finished an' we clapped. Then the two youngsters began to demonstrate dancin'. The girl 'ad a pretty skirt on but there was too much decoration on 'er blouse, it wasn't nice an' plain like down our way. Very colourful. Over in Kalotaszeg ev'rythin's flashy like that. All the girls are like Christmas trees. An' they're all Calvinists over that way as well. The lads wear loose-fittin' *gatya*. Not trousers like ours do. I think they look much more manly. Some are so tight they show off their pricks. In the old days the girls would look at 'em as they danced an' giggle.

Two musicians 'ad been 'ired, fiddlers. But we couldn't really dance, the man 'ad to teach the people 'ow the steps went. Cos it was diff'rent from down our way. So I wouldn't 'ave known 'ow to dance if it wasn't a waltz. But what need was there to teach people all that? Dancin' just follows the music.

I said quietly to the boss, ''Ow long do we 'ave to sit 'ere?'

'E didn't answer, but 'e got the message. 'E went up to the lad what was demonstratin' an' whispered in 'is ear, to demonstrate 'ow to 'old a partner an' strike up the music, cos people was goin' to be bored to death if it was just learnin' an' learnin'. What they should do was strike up, an' then people would pick it up. Wasn't that 'ow small children learnt from big ones? Nobody taught 'em. They'd form couples an' try to follow. That was 'ow little ones danced.

So the lad demonstrated 'ow to 'old a partner, took the girl, slapped 'is boot, an' told the fiddlers to start.

So, at last we was gettin' some action. That I liked.

Even if it wasn't the quite same as a nice dance in Szék, cos I didn't recognize a single face there, not a single Szék woman or pointed 'at was to be seen. What we called a Szék 'at. What would a Szék woman be doin' in the culture centre. The 'ole buildin' was strange to me, with the great big rooms. It was more like a school or a factory. But I wasn't concerned with anythin' but me partner's 'ands. 'E spun me round, picked me up, we moved so fast, so lively, an' me boss started slappin' 'is shins—'e wasn't wearin' boots, only shoes. 'E slapped 'is legs an' picked up 'is feet. 'E swung me round on me 'eels, an' wow, the room spun around me. Then they began to play a *ritkább*, an' the lights came on, it was gettin' a bit dark, I wondered if there was a storm comin'. Well, it seemed the young people were gropin' one another as they danced. The boss was just 'oldin' me nicely, swingin' me round as sadly as if 'e was buryin' 'is mother.

The old folks used to say: those who dance well together, do well together in bed. An' they said it more as a catchword, but many a true word is spoken in jest. A good partner fits in all the time. Then the activist, who wasn't dancin', just organizin' ev'rythin', told me boss to bring it to an end, cos by then the dancin' was gettin' out of 'and,. 'E said there'd be one more number, so that the young people wouldn't be so sorry to leave. We was the old ones, weren't we? Then they struck up a lively tune, an' the way they played, repeated, tore the 'airs off the bows, the end wouldn't come. Ev'ry time I thought that the dancin' would stop we 'ad to dance that figure again. The boss, as well, was clappin' 'is 'ands an' spinnin' me round like a top. Oh, it was really good to be spun around. May it never end, was 'ow I felt. Cos it's definitely better than bein' in bed. When the end came there was great applause. That's a new custom as well. I was gaspin' for breath as if I'd been runnin' away from wolves in the forest. The boss an' I walked 'ome, there was sweat runnin' down 'is back, an' me knickers was soakin'! We went past the cemetery an' turned uphill to the Békás. The boss said, let's go into a pub an' 'ave a soda. I went in with 'im an' 'e got one for me as well. Only it wasn't soda, it was watered wine, a spritzer, as 'e called it. Wow, it did me good. It went straight to me boots, or rather to me feet, an' they got tipsy on it.

When we got 'ome, the boss said, 'I've 'ad the straw delivered, Kali, start coverin' 'em up. You can do it this time.'

Cos the roses 'ad to be covered up for the winter. I said, all right, if necessary I'll see to it. Cos 'e said 'e couldn't spare the time.

'There's goin' to be big changes now, Kali.'

I answered, 'Not again? There was big changes not long ago, when you went into the university to work for the state. So what else is goin' to 'appen? You're gettin' to be like Mostis the farmer, always tryin' somethin' new.'

'Why, what did 'e do?' asked the boss.

'Well, the way it was, if you please, there was a very poor man an' 'is son.'

'Look 'ere, Kali, I'm busy at present, I can't listen to your folk tale. It'll take an 'our.'

So once again I'd got nobody to listen to me tale. What's life comin' to when people 'aven't got time for a folk tale, they'v got to be runnin' about like that? To 'ell with it. The boss is like Kati the Runner, who always did nothin' but look for work. She paid no attention to anythin', children, grandchildren, rather the sucklin' piglets, was they gettin' fatter? She kept 'er 'usband busy, made 'im work all the time, an' 'er son. An' it ended up badly for 'er, cos 'er 'usband put 'imself on the railway lines in Bonchida, 'e was so fed up with the life 'e led.

I was quite upset, cos I'd been thinkin' 'ow nice the dancin' 'ad been, now there'd be a lovely quiet ev'nin', with the boss sittin' at 'is desk workin', writin' essays an' me knittin', cos I was beginnin' to knit things for winter again, what I'd be able to sell. An' then I'd tell the boss a nice folk tale while 'e smoked 'is pipe after dinner, an' 'ere 'e was talkin' about changes.

Oh, I really don't care for changes.

Men can't sit down an' keep still. That's the truth. They just can't cos their blood drives 'em forward, there's always got to be change, development, organization. It's always the case that one thing 'as to be better than another, that they're jealous of what somebody else 'as got, an' they want that as well. Or they want to see which is the stronger. There are some who are quite ill with jealousy of what somebody else 'as got. An' at that time in particular, when 'e'd been drawn into state affairs, the boss 'ad no peace. There'd been a piece in the paper about 'im. 'E put it away but I found it an' read it. So what did it say? Not a word of truth. I knew better, livin' 'ere under one roof with 'im. Such was the stuff that paper, the *Világosság*, wrote, that 'e was the wonder-gardener of the Békás, cos it didn't mean that 'e was a magician, that's not nice, I wouldn't 'ave recognized 'im from it if it 'adn't put 'is name. I didn't know anythin' about 'is life or 'is family, but 'e couldn't 'ave been recognized from that article. Ev'n 'is own mother wouldn't 'ave recognized 'im.

An' I'm to get 'im ready for the journey, cos 'e's got to go to Bucharest next week. 'E'll be there a week. So I asked, 'What about your garden, then?'

'Well, what about it? You'll be 'ere, won't you?'

'I'll be 'ere, but the garden needs its master.'

'Well, there's nothing to do in the garden just now,' 'e replied.

All right then. I'd never seen there be nothin' to do.

Then 'e started bein' nicer. We'd sat down to dinner cos we was starvin', but first 'e'd caught me by the waist, carried me into me room an' stretched out on me. I 'ad to take off me kerchief cos 'e couldn't stand it. 'E ate like 'e 'adn't eaten for a week. 'E nearly ate me an' all in bed. We 'ad a nice *paprikás* with a side-salad, an' 'e asked for some bread. Then 'e was a bit more relaxed an' asked for the story while 'e smoked 'is pipe.

'I'd like the story an' all,' I said. So 'e told me what changes there was to be.

'E was goin' to be officially designated a research institute. A *Station*. It would be state-run, an' 'e'd be given men an' more land. A lot more, twenty 'ectares at least.

I asked, 'Why aren't you satisfied with the way it is now?'

I simply didn't understand, 'e said. 'E couldn't achieve anythin' big by 'imself. Somethin' like the collective farm, I asked. Is the garden to be confiscated? 'E really shouted at me then. I left the room, I wouldn't be shouted at. I told 'im straight. If I was 'is servant, then all right. But when 'e'd 'ad sex with me as much as twice I wasn't 'is servant any more, I was 'is woman.

'Look 'ere, don't you shout at me!'

I told 'im straight. An' I called 'im *te* for the first time. When 'e'd finished 'avin' sex, 'e immediately felt no need of sayin' sweet nothin's. Until then it would be this an' that, Kali me dear, Green Kali, beautiful woman from Szék. But 'e's just shouted, 'e knew 'is business, I didn't understand a thing, peasants knew nothin', they'd just got two or three 'old an' wouldn't let go of it. Well, 'e was goin' to 'ave an 'ole station an' carry out research. Did I remember 'ow it 'ad been in the summer, when we'd 'ad no water cos the Békás 'ad dried up? Well, would I 'ave been able to dictate to water an' make it come? Anybody could make a garden in a desert as long as they'd got the water for it!

So I said, 'Well, water 'as been taken up into the mountains an' all, it's written in one place in the Bible that it was taken up for the sake of Nebuchadnezzar,' I told 'im. 'Just recently there was a sermon about exactly that from a Cath'lic priest in the main square, not the bishop, cos their bishop's been arrested an' put in prison. Cos I went down there to listen to 'im. There was so many there, they was outside in the street listenin'. 'E said that people could make a garden anywhere, they just 'ad to work at it an' want it, an' not worry about anythin' that tried to stop 'em. That's what 'e preached. It was the sort of sermon that you could understand was about the fate of the 'Ungarian people, only 'e took it from the Bible. It was a very fine sermon. Ev'n if 'e was a Cath'lic.'

Oh dear, was the boss annoyed. When I mentioned the Bible to 'im, 'is face went as red as the fieriest of roses. I was afraid 'e'd 'ave a stroke. Them clerical bloodsuckers, 'e said, they're still foolin' the people. 'E got so worked up at once, an' 'e stayed like that all ev'nin'.

Well, what good this change was goin' to do us I didn't know. I don't care for changes.

Anyway, it 'appened. The change was in 'im. Cos after that 'e was 'ardly in 'us garden any more. 'E'd either be up in the university or directin' the Station. An' it was enormous. I said to 'im, ev'n Count Bánffi didn't 'ave all that much land at Bonchida. An' 'e'd got more. I told 'im straight, I'd be off. Cos 'e 'ated God an' 'e 'ated the count. It was February when they came with big machines an' did it all. They built a big greenhouse an' ev'rythin' there, laid on water, an' all 'em big machines goin' around, they was like dragons. An' the way they 'urried, you'd 'ave thought the Mongols was comin. If it rained they ruined all the paths, we was up to our eyes in mud from all the tractors, trucks, an' machines. An' the noise all the time. Never a minute's silence, ev'n at night. The boss brought in all 'is saplin's an' stored 'em behind the 'ouse, where there was room. I just 'ad me own work to do, an' I saw to that. The boss showed me 'ow to prune the roses, an' I did that in the third week of March. Cos we'd certainly 'ad a long winter an' now they was sproutin'. That year the spring was late. The way I 'ad to prune 'em was to leave the outside shoots an' three leaves from the bottom. So that the rose would grow outward, not inward. If it grew outward, it'd form a bush an' be nice an' round. If it was cut from the outside, the 'ole thing'd just be a mass of sticks, not beautiful, wouldn't be able to develop, an' the sun wouldn't warm it. Now the boss wasn't doin' anythi' in the garden, just a bit of work on 'em few roots what 'e'd discovered in autumn. Them few was an 'undred or two, that's 'ow big the garden was.

I asked if I should plant the gladioli corms what we'd taken up in autumn. Yes. Where? Didn't matter, wherever there was room. All of 'em? As many as I liked. I asked whether to take some small roses to market. Yes. 'Ow many? As many as I liked of 'em over there, 'e pointed, what 'e'd done in autumn.

'E was off to Bucharest for a week again. While 'e was away I went to the theatre an' all, oh, there was such a lot of singin' there, there was a good play on about peasant life. I went with me sister Sári, I loved 'er as if she was me daughter, she'd come to town with 'er 'usband, an' we 'ad a good laugh. After that we went down to Unió utca, where the Szék people all used to go, an' 'ad a beer. Ooh, it was bitter. Why did so many people drink it, if it was that bad? One glass an' I was tiddly. Then I said they could come to our place an' see the garden. They came an' were amazed. Such a big garden, nothin' but flowers in it, all roses. I was ev'r so pleased to see young Sári. It was really nice not to fall out with relatives all the time but to make it up. But of course she'd got 'er 'usband, didn't need 'er sister, she'd got 'er own problems.

I went to church a lot when there was services. I didn't go to the Cath'lics any more cos the one what 'ad invited me was a woman at the market who'd been a nun before, an' now she was sellin' 'oney for somebody, an' she told me that that good priest what I'd 'eard in the winter 'ad been a communist priest all the time. She told me in confidence, cos it was a secret.

Then the boss came back from Bucharest. 'E was loaded with presents, a Turkish delicacy what stuck me teeth together, some rose water, a towel an' a box of all kinds of stocks for 'imself. So 'e was bein' nice again an' came to me room ev'n in the daytime an' gave me a surprise.

'Now then, Kali,' 'e said, 'the change is comin'. The Station is goin' to open in the summer.'

So I asked 'im, 'Dear boss . . .'

'Don't keep callin' me your boss,' 'e answered, 'e'd get locked up if 'e'd got a servant.

'Well, that's just the point,' I said, 'cos now *I've* got to tell *you* about a change.'

'Are you leavin'?' 'e asked. An' 'e just looked at me, screwed up 'is eyes. But 'is face gave nothin' away to show that 'e was alarmed at the thought.

'Maybe that's just what I ought to do,' I told 'im. Cos I'd 'ad to think a great deal about what I might do.

'So, where would you go, Kali?'

'Well, I've got to figure that out.'

'Into service?'

'Everybody's in service. Bosses an' all'

'Will you stop that stupid talk?' The boss was gettin' cross.

So should I tell 'im or not.

'So, who wants you, Kali?' 'e asked. 'If you want to work in the Station, come on in. There'll be land, pots, ev'rythin' for you to work. You'll 'ave a state job an' you'll receive a salary.'

'E just looked at me an' didn't speak.

'Are you goin' to join the Station or not?'

This wasn't a good time for me to say it. But I 'ad to say, it couldn't be put off. It concerned us both.

'Somethin' else 'as changed,' I said quietly. 'I'm in an interestin' condition.'

'E understood at once. 'E said nothin', didn't answer. So I watched 'is face to read 'is thoughts. I 'eard 'im whisper, 'Are you sure?'

'Yes,' I nodded. 'I've taken a piece of string an' measured me waist ev'ry day. It definitely won't reach round any more.'

A woman 'as to put an off'rin' on the Lord's table when she begins to 'ave a little pleasure. That's the price. I'd known there was goin' to be a bit of trouble. Cos I was beginnin' to find a bit of 'appiness 'ere. An' the boss 'ad been comin' into me room an' onto me a little bit too much.

The boss an' I were quiet for a day, two days. 'E said nothin' Then 'e asked, ''ave you been to see a doctor, Kali?'

'Well, there's no need yet. 'E wouldn't know any more than me, just go proddin' all the time.'

Then 'e asked what 'e was to do about me. I replied that 'e didn't 'ave to do anythin'. An' I shut the door behind me an' went out to the kitchen. I was cookin' the food an' workin' in the garden. just a bit. There's always somethin' to do in a rose garden. To 'ell with 'im. I didn't want to 'ear what 'e would do about me.

I 'ad been to see a doctor, though. I'd lied to 'im about that. I'd sat an' thought for a long time an' kept inquirin' what 'Ungarian doctor there was in those parts cos I wouldn't be able to discuss in Romanian. An' then a nun told me to go to a certain Dr Szabó. So I went. I told 'im what the situation was at me age. 'E laughed so much 'e thumped the table. 'E asked for me ID card. What was I on about, me age? 'E looked at it. You're not ev'n forty yet. You're capable of 'avin' a child for another ten years, me dear. Then 'e asked where I lived. I told 'im, up in the Békás. So I wasn't from Szék? cos 'e'd been lookin' at me clothes. I told 'im I'd left there a while since, but I was from Felszeg. Cos 'e was a Szék man as well! The second son of Márton Szabó. 'E'd come away a long time ago as well. Oh, we was so pleased to meet. Two Szék people, two lives, an' we'd gone separate ways. Neither of us lived there now. Actually, I'd 'eard that 'e'd become a doctor, but it 'adn't occurred to me that 'e'd 'ave a place in town. 'E wouldn't ev'n take any money. I asked if I could bring 'im somethin' from the garden, there was a lot of lovely flowers. I wasn't to bring anythin', 'e wouldn't accept it. We was pullin' ev'rythin' up. In that case, 'e said, bring me some bulbs if you've got any, flower bulbs. 'Is mother-in-law 'ad got a garden on the Kerekdomb. An orchard. All 'e'd got was a little official flat as a doctor. Two little rooms in a block. But 'e was always goin' to the Kerekdomb. 'E couldn't do without a garden an' a bit of soil. I'd bring as many bulbs as 'e liked. What about a rose? Please, 'e'd accept it with pleasure. A rambler, 'e'd train it up the outside of the 'ouse.

Then I told 'im, an' it didn't trouble me to tell 'im, 'e was a doctor, an' like a priest I could tell 'im in confidence. Especially as 'e was a Szék man. That me passport said that I'd got an 'usband, but I'd left 'im an' it 'adn't been changed in the document. This child was by somebody else. What should I do, please tell me. Don't worry! About what, I asked. Well, your belly will show. No, I wasn't worried! Not a bit. I'd told me new 'usband—

that's what I said, new 'usband, but I only called 'im that to the doctor—I'd told me new 'usband.

'I need this little child. I want to 'ave it. I need it so as not to be alone in the world all the time. I want to 'ave this little child.'

'That's fine,' said the doctor. 'So you should. A child is always a pleasure.'

So then I asked 'ow to deal with the passport. Cos the child would 'ave to 'ave a name an' ev'rythin'.

To that, Dr Márton Szabó said—that was 'is name, Szabó, same as mine—that first I should divorce legally. So I told 'im, that certainly wouldn't be good for me, cos I'd 'ave to be goin' over to Szék, an' for legal proceedin's to Bonchida. That was not good for me at that time. Then secondly, I should lose me ID card, an' when I applied for a new one say that I was unmarried. An' won't that cause trouble, I asked. Well, no. 'E asked if me new gentleman friend would let me take 'is name. Of course, I said. But I didn't really know whether 'e would or not.

So I reported that I'd lost me papers. An' they gave me new ones, an' put me name as Zöld. Cos me original could now be recorded. An' it said *necasatori*—spinster. There, you see, you pig, I've shaken you off like dust, you've been blown away. You're nowhere now! So it was. Fortunately me belly wasn't showin', cos I'd been able to get the documents in good time. An' I wore me skirt in such a way that it didn't show what I was gettin'. If me belly 'ad shown perhaps I'd 'ave 'ad to explain that at the police station.

Well, after that the boss 'ardly mentioned the matter. 'E just came to me more an' more, cos now the way was clear, there wasn't ev'n any bleedin'. Not ev'n the week a month when I wouldn't let 'im. I just 'ad to be careful not to let 'im crush me. But 'e was more involved with buildin' an' layin' out the land. Cos by that time things were startin' to get organized in the institute. It was all nearly finished, buildin' was complete.

It'd be ev'r so nice to 'ave a little girl, I thought. Well, if it's a boy, it won't matter. But a girl would be better, I thought. Only I didn't say a word to the boss.

I wasn't seein' much of 'im in the daytime. 'E'd vanish, 'e was very busy with the Station. 'E was startin' to go about like a minister. The *shlep* was always followin' 'im. That was the word 'e used—'ere comes me *shlep*. Technicians an' all sorts of lecturers, experts, Party men. 'Is office was down at the university, the Station was up 'ere. Actually, it was neighbourin' land, but 'e was there all day. I 'ad to see to ev'rythin' in the garden.

An' 'ow roughly all the 'Óstát owners were forced off their land where the Station was to be! If they went into partnership, then they could 'ave been given pensions or somethin' instead. As it was they was all forced off. Some didn't ev'n manage to 'arvest their carrots, the tractors went over the lot. Cos in 'em days, it wasn't the way to plan an' discuss, but bang! ev'rythin' was done at a stroke.

Then 'e recruited the people what was goin' to work there. 'E asked me why I didn't go for a job. Plantin' things.

So I asked 'im, 'Do you want to kick me out, boss? What about the child I'm 'avin'? You want me to work for you there an' put the child in the crèche?' Cos there was this kind of child-mindin' place, little children was left there. It wasn't an orphanage, cos they was taken 'ome after work. 'Do you think I'm 'avin' a baby so as to 'and it over?'

I'd rather work for 'im in the garden. Cos 'e was no longer payin' me. Not since I'd been in me condition, well, it was as if 'e was me 'usband, 'e stopped payin' me. Why should 'e, when there was a child on the way any time? I was prayin' 'ard that I'd 'ave an easy birth. An' then what was we goin' to do with the garden? Who was goin' to do all the work there? To which 'e kept sayin' that that garden was finished, there was goin' to be a 'uge garden, ev'rythin' would be an experimental garden.

I used to go an' take 'im is lunch, cos 'e didn't 'ave time to come to the 'ouse for it. 'E'd be sittin' over documents, tables, nothin' but figures.

'Stop for 'alf an 'our, mister, while you 'ave your lunch. Get away from the papers.'

Well, when we was workin' in the fields we always used to sit down properly in the shade, that was 'ow we 'ad lunch. Oh, the way 'e shouted, I should shut up, I'm a stupid woman, why was I interferin'. Stupid I was too, I knew I'd only annoy 'im. Ev'n when it would 'ave been for the best, I annoyed 'im. Men are always like eggs. They break in your 'ands ev'n though you're ev'r so careful.

Then I saw all the women what was goin' to be workin' for 'im. All young an' pretty. Blondes, brunettes, black-'aired, Romanians an' 'Ungarians. It was only fair that ev'rybody should 'ave a chance. But they was all too pretty. 'E'll try to get off with 'em all, I thought. They'd want more pay, better positions for themselves.

It was only when me belly began to show that I stopped goin' down. Why should I, I'd only be makin' trouble for 'im. We wasn't married. 'E comment on that was, that was in the old world. In that of today it didn't count. Nor did ancestry, where you went to school, 'ow old you was, nothin' at all. But ev'n so, I wasn't to go.

But now me poor mother was comin' to see me once a week. Poor woman, she wept an' wept like when the count 'ad rejected the poor girl an' put 'er patience to a great test. It was a great disgrace for a mother when 'er daughter turned out that way. Well, it was for me too.

''Alf the village knows, I suppose,' I said to 'er when I saw 'er cryin' all the time.

'It's common knowledge, me girl,' she said, as upset as if King Mátyás's crown 'ad fallen off.

'Well, what if it is. Too bad. That means all the more will wish me well,' I told 'er to cheer 'er up.

But it wasn't only cos me pregnancy was showin' that me mother was wailin', an' gossip 'ad gone all round the village. But I'd stopped wearin' Szék costume.

Cos of course I'd stopped wearin' it, a bit at a time, when I became pregnant. When she was there, I'd only worn little boots, an' I didn't wear a kerchief at 'ome cos the boss liked me not to, an' I only put one on when we was workin' so as to keep dust off me 'air. I left off the close-fittin' waistcoat an' wore looser blouses that I got an 'Ostát woman to make me. Of course I couldn't wear that nicely pleated skirt for work all the time, I'd 'ave been for ev'r ironin' it cos 'ad to be rolled up damp so as to keep the pleats in. So I'd bought a bit of tergal material an' made meself a simple skirt or two, an' wore 'em. So our costume was a lot of trouble. An' once me mother came up earlier than she'd promised, just turned up, an' I wasn't dressed up in Szék costume. That time she caught me. I looked exactly like a town woman. She ev'n gave a squeal when she realized that it was me, 'er daughter, Kali, she just 'adn't recognized me. The way she cried! I used to put it on to go to church an' such places. And to the market, cos women from Szék, the 'ostát an' Györgyfalva was well thought of. But why go about in Szék costume when I'd soon be 'avin' a child by a father other than me 'usband, an' I wasn't ev'n divorced?

'You've let the costume down,' said me mother, an' she 'ung 'er 'ead as she sat on the bench in the kitchen, an' wouldn't ev'n 'ave a bit of pastry.

'An' 'asn't it let me down?' I replied. 'An' 'asn't life let me down? Just tell me, mother dear, which of the commandments I've broken, 'onestly. All right, I didn't marry for love. There I went wrong. But the Lord Jesus never gave us any such commandment. All 'e said was 'onour. An' that people shouldn't make statues to themselves. That's exactly what the sermon was about. So 'ave I made a statue to meself? 'Ave I stared at me face in the mirror?'

'What statue?' asked me mother, all puzzled. She'd never 'eard of any statue in the commandments. Where 'ad I been goin'? She 'oped I 'adn't gone mad an' joined a sect, like poor Mihály.

'Only place I've been is the church in the main square, cos that's where such things are! A famous bishop used to preach there in the old days, an' 'e was a Catholic, but 'e gave such great sermons while 'e was at liberty that all the 'Ungarians wept at what 'appened to 'im. An' now, when other priests preach in the church, they talk in such a way that anybody what listens to 'em thinks of that bishop, what's now in prison. Cos 'e was arrested an' jailed an' 'e isn't preachin' any more cos the communists was angry with 'im, 'e 'ad so much influence. 'E's just like Strong János, when the witch put 'im in captivity, an' 'e escaped in that 'e was inside an' outside, cos she could see 'im in the cell all the time, but only 'is body was there while 'is spirit was goin' about in the world, doin' such great deeds that ev'n the White King bowed down before 'im cos 'e'd set 'im free from the Black King So this bishop's just like that, carin' for souls from inside the cell there. Ev'n though 'e's a Catholic.'

'Oh dear, what ever are you up to, Kali? Now you've shamed your religion an' the church,' an' me mother's tears flowed again, more an' more.'

'I'm goin' where the Lord Jesus is properly preached. I go to the Kétágú an' to the main square, so there. I go where it does me a bit of good.'

Then she became so upset that it was ev'n better, cos she stopped cryin'.

'Well, I never 'eard of such a thing, a person 'avin' two religions.'

What was I to say to that?

'If you 'eard 'ow they speak in the Catholic church, Mother, you'd get on the bus ev'ry week an' come. I tell you, the sermons are so good. 'E used to come out into the street for ev'rybody to listen. 'E was always talkin' about the case of us 'Ungarians. Probably that was why 'e was arrested.'

The child in me belly was growin', I was takin' care of meself, I wasn't workin' nearly as 'ard as before. The boss was now spendin' all 'is time on paperwork. Plannin' all the time. 'E wasn't bendin' 'is back to the soil any more, 'oein'. So what was all this plannin'? These days it's all plans in this world. I'd got a child on the way as well, an' who planned that? I 'adn't, that was for sure.

I asked the doctor, dear Dr Szabó, tell me when will it be me time. Well, that's for you to know, Kali Szabó. We're not related, it's just that the name's the same. Well, 'ow am I supposed to know that, if you please? I 'aven't only just started 'avin' sex. So when you plant red onions in the soil only you know 'ow long they'll take to ripen. It's the same with women, you know. Well, I said, it's not like that. In one year the sun 'eats the soil, it's nice an' warm, an' 'eaven waters it. Next year it's freezin' cold in April, or there isn't a drop of rain all spring. The soil isn't somethin' like a cuckoo clock, what always sings out when it's wound up.

'Well, then you'll know, when your waters break come in quickly.'

Then 'e examined me once more.

'An' Kali Szabó, don't let me 'ear that you've called in some midwife an' given birth like that. That's where people go wrong these days. Stupid Szék women say that if they go into 'ospital to give birth they're lettin' the village down. Don't let me 'ear that you 'aven't come in. The number of children that midwives kill!'

The boss told me that now 'e was Uncle Vilmos, but to me 'e was still just the boss, ev'n though 'e wasn't payin' me—'e told me: these days women do as they please with their children. They give birth to 'em, go to work, put 'em in the crèche, etc. Women are liberated. So, if that's the case, very well. And, said the boss, they can arrange to 'ave a child when they want to.

That I knew. Cos women 'ave always wanted it to be good for 'em to 'ave a child at one time an' not another. It's just that God 'as 'is ideas about it, an' 'e doesn't agree with 'em. Take me, for example: when I'd wanted to, nothin' would make it 'appen. When it never ev'n crossed me mind, an' I wasn't all that young any more, there it was, just like that.

Vilmos 'ad told me I was 'is companion on the way. So I asked 'im, where we was goin'. 'E couldn't dismiss me any more. There was that big crock cabbage pot, an old one, an' all the money was in it, an' I took what was necessary. 'E never counted, nor asked.

We was gettin' on very well by this time, like the best of married couples, cos actually we didn't see much of each other. 'E'd come in late in the ev'nin' from the buildin' site, construction was in progress, 'e'd give me quick directions as to what I 'ad to do in the garden, an' 'e only complained if 'e saw that somethin' wasn't th way 'e liked it. Then 'e'd be off at seven in the mornin', I'd 'ave 'is food ready for 'im an' 'e'd either take it with 'im or forget it in 'is great 'urry. Where the man got 'is strength from goodness knows. 'E was never still, kept goin' like a machine. An' so on edge all the time. Much more so than before the Station.

Only one thing upset me. Oh, the row 'e 'ad with 'is mother when she came an' caught sight of me. This stupid peasant woman's made a fool of you, I told you, Vilmos, she's got 'erself in the family way, I told you to be careful, not to let a woman under your roof.

'So now she's goin' to 'old you back, son, when you're makin' somethin' of yourself. She's just after your money, she's a scroungin', scruffy peasant. She's ev'n run away from 'er 'usband, ev'rybody knows. You could 'ave your pick of women, Vilmos, a good-lookin', well-off, strong man like you, you could 'ave chosen a smart town girl, any one you wanted.'

She called me ev'rythin' under the sun, an' the boss as well. They'd got the door shut but I could 'ear. Well, when I couldn't 'ear, I put me ear to the wall an' the words come through, especially the way they was shoutin'.

'Get out of 'ere with your foul mouth!' the boss shouted at 'er, an' 'e drove 'er out of the garden. Vilmos wouldn't stand for such bad language. 'E grabbed 'is little mother's arm, 'eld it really tight, an' led 'er out of the garden, pulled 'er after 'im, an' the dog barked at 'er as well. She wasn't to set foot there again, 'e'd 'ad enough of it. She turned quite white an' didn't speak, just stumbled towards the gate. Then she shouted that 'er arm was 'urtin', don't 'old so tight, an' Vilmos shouted that 'er filthy language 'ad 'urt 'im, an' she was gettin' a bit of 'er own medicine. Ev'n if she crawled back on 'er knees, 'e wouldn't let 'er in.

Well, thought I. Firstly, she'd really deserved it. Ev'ry word that 'ad come out of 'er mouth was full of poison. And secondly, that I was now becomin' a mother, an' 'er son 'ad taken that mother to the gate an' put 'er outside, never to return. So that was what the children 'ad done to 'is parent. But 'ow 'ad the parent behaved as well! Only badly, always, an' been settin' the children against one another.

Nor did 'e ev'r let 'er back in. From then on they'd fallen out. The boss 'as never said a word. Oh, but was 'e wound up when 'is mother 'ad gone. I 'id in the kitchen so as 'e shouldn't see me, cos 'e'd just go for me when 'e was like that. Why 'as ev'ry man that's been under me roof been so 'ighly strung? It's God's punishment to me.

That ev'nin' 'e came in, didn't do anythin', just lay down, then cried like a child again. I really loved it when the boss cried for me. When 'e did, I knew 'e was mine. In the old days I used to be frightened, didn't know 'ow to deal with 'im. When 'e wasn't drunk, no relation 'ad died, an' 'is land was there for 'im, what was 'e cryin' for? I took 'im in me arms, stroked 'is face, an' dried 'is eyes with a corner of me apron. Then 'ed give a good snore an' go off calmly to sleep like a child. But 'e was a big man, such a big man, givin' orders on the buildin' site, workin' in the university, been a Party member for a long time, ev'n went to Bucharest, never sat down all day for a bit of a rest, one day, I told 'im, 'e'd be eatin' standin' up like an 'orse. An' then 'e was in such great pain that 'e was cryin'. But what a nice man 'e was. Cos 'e was nice to me. Especially since the child 'ad been inside me, very nice, in me view, nicer an' nicer. Our little girl was certainly goin' to be nice. Or little boy, didn't matter at all. 'Ow good it'd be to 'ave a little daughter.

An' above all, 'e didn't drink. Oh, 'ow grateful I was to the good Lord that I'd got a man what didn't drink. I 'ad another once what didn't drink. But on the other 'and 'e was always grievin', an' goin' around as if grief was bowin' 'is 'ead to the ground. All the time 'e could 'ardly ev'n work. When I told me mother 'ow lucky I was, 'e didn't drink, she wouldn't believe me that there was such a man in the world.

She said to me, 'Even your grandfather used to drink. Your father does as well, when 'e's thirsty.'

But Father doesn't get drunk, just 'as a drink. 'E'll 'ave one when 'e comes in from the fields an' when 'e's goin' out in the mornin'.

'An' the way your 'usband drank, God rot 'im.'

An' I said, 'An' a lot of women drink as well, they just don't go into the pub. They drink so as to 'ave a bit of pleasure.'

'There's no such man as doesn't drink,' said mother. 'Maybe they just give it up, cos they 'ave to restrain themselves. Don't you believe it if a man doesn't drink, Kali. Beware of 'im. The ones what don't drink are the ones what are ev'n more addicted.'

I said to me mother, 'Why should I beware now? Just take a look at me.'

Cos by that time me belly was an amazin' size. Dr Szabó 'ad been listenin' to see if there were goin' to be twins. Oh dear, I said, God forbid. Not that I'm all that old, but ev'n so two at once.

An' I insisted to me mother, 'This boss of mine drinks two glasses of wine. Never a drop more.'

'Well, it's not really anythin' to do with us,' she said, 'that sort of thing's men's business.'

So what was I to say to tha? I said, 'Don't be like the old woman what it 'urt when the sun shone. Let's be glad that 'e doesn't drink. You remember that old witch Aunty Bodon, 'ow ev'rybody in Csipkeszeg 'ated 'er. It always 'urt 'er if anybody 'ad a bit of 'appiness.'

I asked me mother, 'Will you come in when I'm expectin'? An' when I'm 'avin' it? An' will father come?'

'Mihály an' I'll come, an' 'is wife. Your father might as well.'

Then she told me that Mihály an' 'is wife an' she 'ad clubbed together to get me a sewin' machine, an' me sister Sári 'ad contributed as well. I was gettin' a little sewin' machine from 'em, but they'd 'ad to scrape it together an' keep it from me father. Me grandparents 'ad chipped in as well, an' it would be brought over next week. With that I'd be able to make things for the child. Well, I'd be glad of that. If I couldn't do any more weavin' I'd take up sewin,' cos I liked that very much. I'd just 'ave to wait for the child to be born, cos I wouldn't be able to sit at it for the time bein', so as to reach the cloth an' keep it straight, an' so as to use the treadle. I'd just 'em a couple of nappies for it. Well, once the child 'ad arrived me belly would get smaller. Me grandmother 'ad sent a lovely shawl, a bit yellowed by then, she'd brought it down from the loft, it 'ad been put away cos it 'ad been used for 'er poor little Feri. 'E'd been born an imbecile, an' the poor child 'ad died just turned eight. She was givin' me 'is shawl, with 'is name on it. I'd bleach it nicely with soda, it'd be as good as new. Oh, look 'ere, baby, you'll be all right tucked up in that.

Ever since the boss 'ad been a great man we'd 'ad the telephone installed. Dr Szabó gave me permission to ring 'im at the 'ospital an' go in if I was in labour. Well, by then I was beginnin' to feel it was near, cos I could 'ardly walk. I told the boss 'e'd 'ave to get somebody in for the garden, cos I could 'ardly do anythin' for 'im now. I gave 'im a note sayin' where I was to go when the time came. Dr Szabó told me to do that, ev'rythin' 'ad been arranged for me. Oh, what would I 'ave done if I 'adn't 'ad somebody from Szék! The boss told me to take some money with me, cos I'd 'ave to make a donation. It was all free of charge, but that was the custom. I told 'im, Dr Szabó was from Szék like me, an' wouldn't accept a thing.

Late one ev'nin' the boss came 'ome. I told 'im I'd be goin' that night, I could feel it. Couldn't I last out till mornin'? Now, there's no 'oldin' out with this, it's not that sort of thing. Then I asked 'im, cos now I 'ad to know stuff like that, 'Would 'e give the child 'is name, or was I to give it mine?'

Did I need to ask? 'E'd give it 'is name. 'E was absolutely delighted about this child.

Well, thought I, won't the weddin' ring fall off your finger if you say a thing like that? Cos until then, like the mute child in the story about Little Dunno, 'e 'adn't said a single word.

'An' what if it's a girl? Or a boy? 'E 'adn't given it any thought yet. I said, well, you'd certainly better do so now, cos it's goin' to be 'ere in the mornin', I feel sure. Then I said, 'If it's a girl, let it be Klára, like me. An' if it's a boy . . . Vili. Vilmos. That'll be nice.'

'E didn't like that an' said that 'e'd already given that name to a rose. Vilmos Décsi. You couldn't call a child after a flower. That was goin' to become a famous rose, 'e'd 'ave to enter it for competitions. A rose is one thing, a child's another, thought I, there'll be no clash. So I asked 'im what it was to be.

'Do as you please.'

'E'd never before addressed me in that formal way. I said, come with me as far as Furu's, cos I 'ave difficulty walkin' an' I can take your arm. There I'd be given a cart, it was all arranged, an' be driven in. Why 'adn't I spoken, 'e'd 'ave a taxi brought. In a cart I'd be shaken to bits gettin' to the 'ospital. 'E phoned, an' the taxi would be sent. In less than 'alf an 'our there it was outside, an' we was off. Shall I come? 'e asked. As you please, I told 'im, like 'e'd said to me. In that case 'e'd rather go to bed, cos 'e was worn out. An' for sure, the birth wouldn't be a matter of a couple of minutes. 'E'd phone the 'ospital, tell 'im which one. Emergency, or which department? I told 'im, the corner of Pap utca. Obstetrics, I couldn't remember the Romanian for it. Ev'rythin' 'ad been arranged with Dr Szabó. Márton Szabó.

As I was leavin', I called Dr Szabó an' told 'im I was comin' in cos I was splittin' in two. I spent a day there in the 'ospital an' nothin' came. Dr Szabó looked at me ev'ry couple of 'ours an' said, was I certain I was 'avin' that sort of pain? The problem was, of course, 'ow was I to know, I'd never 'ad a baby before, but I just felt I was dyin', I was in such pain. Well, after I'd lain there for a day 'e gave me an injection an' then me waters really did break. 'E said 'e'd given me somethin' to speed things up. Then they put me on a trolley. Well, I thought, this is what ev'ry woman wants, but it don't 'alf 'urt. I dyin', it was so painful. By then I was 'avin' to scream, ev'n though I was ashamed, but I couldn't stand the pain. But there ev'rybody was screamin', women, babies, ev'n men an' all. I prayed, but not for meself. Never mind about me, ev'n though I could die. I was prayin' for that little child.

I remembered askin' me mother, when we was 'avin' a chat, didn't she regret 'avin' children?

'Does it 'urt a woman, 'avin' a baby?'

She said, 'Certainly it does. It 'urt your mother. The first one in particular 'urts. I thought I was dyin'. I ev'n asked the nurse to kill me, I couldn't stand any more. The way I was screamin', your father fled straight to the pub, 'e couldn't stand listenin' to it outside the window. An' after that it was all right. Mihály didn't 'urt as much. An' 'e was small. An' you just popped out. The nurse said that a child what 'as an easy birth will 'ave an easy life.'

'Well, they were wrong about that. What's been easy for me, mother?'

'You've been lucky, me dear, cos you never let it get you down. 'Owever bad an 'usband you got, you didn't really get depressed. Anybody else might 'ave given way, jumped under a train, gone on the pálinka or become generally 'ated. But you didn't at all. You wasn't blessed with a child, but you didn't moan about that very much. There are some what die of grief, abandon themselves to it. You've never been seriously ill. Nobody's fallen out with you, 'eld a grudge against you, an' ev'rybody's loved listenin' to your folk tales when you've told 'em. You see, you've come through, you've got a new 'usband an' you'll soon 'ave a child. Not quite the way you wanted, but there it is.'

Well, it wasn't quite true that I'd 'ad it cushy. But what was I to say to me mother now? An' me father, who'd adored little Kali when she was little? 'E'd never once 'it me. The others 'e did, especially poor Mihály, 'e gave 'im many a slap. 'E sent word, when the child was born 'e'd come into town, an' I could go an' visit 'em. But me man ev'n now didn't come into the 'ospital to cool me fevered brow. 'E phoned yesterday, said 'e'd got a lot on at the moment, 'e was in a conference, was goin' to a committee meetin', wouldn't be able to come in. Well then, off you go to your conference, to 'ell with you.

Then along came little Vilmos. Just like that, out 'e popped, like Tom Thumb to 'is old parents in the folk tale. 'E just said, 'ere I am, look at me. It was only while 'e was gettin' ready to emerge that 'e gave me trouble. The doctor gave me a tranquillizin' injection so that I shouldn't feel so much, cos I was screamin' me 'ead off. 'E was a bit reddish an' ev'n 'is 'ands were all wrinkled, but Dr Szabó assured me that they'd smooth out, I'd see, 'e'd become whiter, not a single baby stayed red once it 'ad come into the daylight. So, I 'ad to stay there another four days for me milk to come. But they wouldn't give 'im to me. I didn't like that at all. They'd bring 'im in for a bit, then take 'im away again. To give the woman some rest. Well, that's 'ospitals for you. I wasn't in charge. Me mother told me that in our family not a single woman 'ad given birth in 'ospital. It looked as if I was the one what wanted to do ev'rythin' diff'rently. Wanted be blowed! 'Ow would I 'ave given birth up in the boss's 'ouse? I didn't know the midwives round 'ere. Townspeople go to 'ospital, it's free, they don't 'ave to pay a *bani* like in the old days. Only they knew what to give to good old Márton Szabó, cos you couldn't leave the doctor empty 'anded. So that was 'ow I 'ad me baby.

Little Vilmos Szabó. Cos on the card it said Szabó. They asked me at the time what 'is name was. I said Vilike, an' they wrote down Vilike Szabó. Or rather, Vilmos. I didn't say that, they did it themselves. I gave 'im me name, but I 'adn't meant to. But I could see that the boss wasn't keen on bein' a father. Well, 'e was keen on makin' children all the same, but 'e preferred attendin' conferences. So 'e'd kept the name of 'is rose, cos that was exactly the way 'e'd wanted. An' 'e wasn't ev'n there when we gave 'im the name. So I could see that to other people 'avin' a child was like 'avin' a tooth out. I actually asked 'im, are you pleased, boss? 'E asked what 'e was to be pleased about, 'e 'adn't ev'n seen 'im yet. That's what 'e said. An' on me papers it said I was married, an' me name was Szabó. Me maiden name 'as been Szabó an' all. Such things do 'appen. 'E'd give 'im 'is name, 'e said, we'd go to the registry office in City 'all an' get it changed so that 'e'd 'ave 'is father's name.

So little Vilmos Szabó would really be mine. But the child wouldn't ev'n be mine, cos 'e wasn't a kerchief or a shirt, so as to be mine. That little Vilmos was so pretty, an' the minute 'e came into the world, the world pleased 'im. 'E looked at it with those clever eyes of 'is. 'E was as clever as the boss. 'E couldn't deny that 'e was 'is. So, when the boss wanted us to change 'is name I didn't mind.

The boss came on the third day. 'E took note of the card sayin' Vilmos Szabó, but 'e said nothin'. 'E looked at it, turned it over an' put it down. Goodness knows whether 'e was pleased or not. 'E asked me whether I'd been in pain. I certainly 'ad, what was a woman to say, givin' birth is quite painful. Me chest 'urt as if it was bein' split in two, it 'urt down below, an' neither mother nor child could 'ave anythin' to eat yet. So I didn't say to 'im what did 'e know about it. I said, well, it's all over now, it won't 'urt for ev'r. 'E looked at the child when 'e was brought in.

'Well what 'ave you to say to Uncle Vilmos?' 'e asked. 'You splutterin'? So that's all right. I'll give you back to the nurse,' an' 'e put 'im in the nurse's pram. She 'ad a little pram with bars that was used for bringin' babies for mothers to suckle.

Uncle Vilmos? So you're goin' to be 'is Uncle Vilmos.

'E asked what time the taxi should come to pick us up. Then 'e attended to the money for the doctors an' nurses, ev'n gave the cleaner somethin', 'e was so much the gentleman. So I asked 'im 'ow much 'e'd given to Dr Szabó. That was none of me business, 'e got what was due to 'im.

When mother an' Mihály came in the boss quickly shot off. But they weren't on bad terms, an' in fact 'e already knew Mihály. An' so 'e couldn't stay long, like the tom cat that wandered into a strange 'ouse. We needed to know where 'e was from, who 'e was related to, what 'is background was. An' they brought enough food for an entire 'ospital. After all, somebody in the world was pleased with little Vilmos.

Uncle Vilmos asked why I was lookin' so miserable. Well, said I, I thought as father you'd be pleased. Was I blind? 'e asked. Can't you see, Kali, I'm over the moon. What was I to say? I said nothin'. Cos there wasn't a spark of 'appiness to be seen on 'im. 'E was just in an 'urry, 'ad to go to the site, on edge.

'E's the sort they call a flower child. That's the Romanian word. A young woman there 'ad 'ad a child, ev'r so young she was, didn't ev'n want to take 'er baby 'ome. It 'ad no father, not nobody, nobody at all 'ad been to see 'er.

I gave 'er food all the time, cos the poor thing was so 'ungry. I couldn't talk to 'er, only by signs an' facial expressions, an' I kept tellin 'er, *bine, bine, poftic*, take some, an' I asked the nurse 'ow that young woman was. Well, she's just a little girl, said the nurse, she's not grown up yet. She's 'ad a flower child. I asked what that meant, I'd never 'eard the term. *Copil de flori* or somethin' like that in Romanian. The nurse wasn't Romanian or 'Ungarian, sort of mixed race, an' I couldn't understand what she said all that well, she talked a bit of ev'rythin'. What it meant was, born among the flowers. The girl an' boy 'ad gone into a wheatfield, made love together, the result was the child, then the boy 'ad shot off, taken fright, an' as I thought, experienced woman what I am, she was left with the child by the flowers. An' why 'adn't she slipped away or got rid of the child? She'd preferred to 'ave it, it would be very 'andsome cos they'd made love among the flowers. That was what the Romanians call it if a child is only out of lovemakin'.

Well, in that case I'd got little Vilmos out of lovemakin', cos 'eaven only knows 'ow 'is father was goin' to regard 'im. But 'e'd said 'e was over the moon. An' that young woman kept on cryin' cos she'd be leavin' 'er baby in the 'ospital. Didn't the law prohibit that, I asked. Well, no, they said there. There'd be no punishment, the state would take it into an orphanage an' give it to somebody else. There are women what are glad to get somebody else's child.

So, milk was comin' out of me tits nicely. An' I 'ad to go back to the garden. To Vilmos's place. Dr Szabó gave orders not to let 'im come into me for three months. A woman needs that time. So, thought I, the devil can 'ave 'im now.

This little Vilmos was a very quiet child. You can see 'e's a love child, said me mother, cos 'e's so pretty. A love child? I asked. Well, I didn't contradict me mother, but love, of all things? What the 'ell. Was that love? I'd aged enough an' loathed men for love to come all of a sudden. 'E'd become nice an' white all right, as old Marci Szabó 'ad said—that was what me mother called 'im. Father 'ad called once as well, looked at 'im an' gave 'im 'is blessin'.

That's sayin' a lot. All the same 'e told me mother not to, but she came up ev'ry week, an' when the boss was away on business, as 'e called it, or in Bucharest she's stay with me for three or four days. Father was really annoyed at 'er makin' a fuss of me. There was nobody to be with the animals. Mother said, an' Kali 'asn't got anybody to be with the child. It was amazin' the way she was fond of the little thing! She's got all the milk she needs, said father, meanin' me. Mother said, 'is 'eart would draw father to me more an' more, but 'is mind wouldn't allow 'im to go so much, cos 'e was a man, an' 'is mind came first, not 'is 'eart. I could see little Vilmos not able to walk yet, an' father sittin' 'in on 'is knee an' tellin' 'im stories. 'E told a very good story. The way Vilmos used to open 'is eyes wide when I told 'im the tale about the dog stealin' the bacon. That was the kind of story I told 'im, ones with animals, the cheeky cat, the mischievous magpie an' the faithful dog. Lots about donkeys, bears, an' sparrows. But I didn't tell 'im about devils or anythin' suitable for grown-ups, for fear of frightenin' 'im. I told 'im folk tales all the time when 'e wasn't sleepin'. The boss used to listen an' all. I'd take 'im into the kitchen, put 'im in a bread trough, an' tell 'im a story while I did the cookin'. The boss would come in, smoke 'is pipe an' listen. 'E looked at the child all the time, an' took photos of 'im with 'is camera.

Now I didn't 'ave to work in the garden in spring. The boss sent men from the Station to attend to ev'rythin'. By then the Station an' the boss's garden formed a unit an' ev'rythin' was taken from 'ere, flowers, trees, food plants. The boss didn't 'old anythin' back.

On one occasion, when me another was there, 'e asked me to go outside with 'im, just for an 'our while she looked after the child.

'Now then, Uncle Vilmos is takin' your mother away. Mind you behave yourself,' said 'e to little Vilmos, an' pinched 'is cheek.

'E'd got a car an' a driver an' we went out into the country. I asked where we was goin'. 'E'd got somethin' to show me. We was goin' by car. Where to, I asked. You'll soon see, don't be impatient. We left the edge of the town behind, though we was already there. We wound our way farther an' farther uphill to where there was nothin' but the 'Óstát lands. I didn't know whether they'd been confiscated or not. Then we turned off an' took a side road to Györgyfalva. That's a village, nothin' special about it. A nice muddy street, as long as a stallion's tail, an' straight. Lined with nice 'Ungarian-style 'ouses an' Romanian ones at the end, cos it's mixed. You could tell by the entrances; a carved gate meant 'Ungarian, an' the Romaian ones 'ad curved porches an' was better painted. It was rainin', though it was July, an' a bit on the chilly side. I'd 'ave brought a kerchief with me, I said, but I'd been so surprised at Vilmos the boss takin' me in the car. It wasn't a good sign if 'e was doin' that. I went in the car when I was 'avin' me baby.

So, then we stopped somewhere on the edge of the village. By that time I was thinkin', there'll be an edge an' an end to this 'uge village somewhere. We stopped outside a little 'ouse, an' 'e said to the Romanian driver, '*Asteptaci, nea Nelu*'. Nelu was the driver, a very nice man. In the car 'e 'ad a crucifix 'angin' in front of the mirror, but Vilmos said to 'im take that down, it's not the good Lord drivin' the car, it's Nelu *bácsi*, an' you drive so well, you don't need Christ an' 'is Virgin Mother up there. Cos 'e'd also got a Romanian miniature of Mary stuck up.

Vilmos got out, Nelu *bácsi* jumped out, produced an umbrella, an' 'eld it over 'is 'ead. Uncle Vilmos set about openin' the gate, which was chained up. There's nobody livin' 'ere, I thought, if there's a chain an' a lock. I'd never seen such a thing as somebody in a village lockin' up their garden gate. A dog'll stop thievin' Gypsies, a lock won't. 'E was fiddlin' with the key, couldn't get it to open. Me kerchief in me 'and was soaked by that time, cos I was just standin' there, like Balaam's ass eatin'. Then it worked an' in we went. Vilmos told Nelu *bácsi* to stay outside.

'Look 'ow big the garden is,' an' pointed.

I didn't look at anythin'. Not a garden. I looked after 'is other garden. Then 'e opened up the 'ouse. It was a nice, solid 'ouse, not 'igh, but solid, the bottom part was stone an' the top was brick. 'E unlocked ev'rythin'. Two nice rooms an' a little porch. 'E showed me ev'rythin'.

By then I was beginnin' to wonder.

'Why are you showin' me this 'ouse? Are you thinkin' of gettin' married?'

'E burst out laughin'. Exactly that, that's right, 'e said. Then 'is expression became very serious again. I didn't like the look of that. 'E pulled a face like that when 'e'd got an important job on. 'E said, 'You're goin' to live 'ere, Kali. You an' the child. I've bought you this 'ouse.'

I was completely taken aback. I was at a loss for words.

'Well, say somethin',' said Vilmos.

Well, what was I to say, I was thinkin'.

'An' where are you goin' to live in future?'

'E didn't say a word. Looked at me as if 'e didn't understand 'Ungarian.

'You're goin' to live 'ere, I've bought you the 'ouse,' 'e repeated.

We stood there like two angry dogs. Just stood there an' rolled our eyes. We was waitin' for the first to attack. To see which would bite 'ardest.

'So I'm bein' dismissed?' I asked.

That's it, then, Kali. 'Ere you are standin' in the middle of an 'ouse with your master, an empty 'ouse, an' there's a nice big garden. Might well be bride an' groom. But that's not the way it is. You know, Kali, nothin's ev'r worked out for you. You've messed up ev'rythin'. Don't go into this 'ouse, ev'n if it's bein' thrown at you free of charge.

'E went out an' snapped, 'Well, come out of there. This is where you're goin' to live. Full stop. It's been bought on your behalf.'

'E shut the 'ouse up an' replaced the padlock. 'E tossed me the key.

'It's been bought on behalf of you an' the child. You're gettin' an 'ouse as a gratuity. Shame on you.'

'E reached into 'is pocket, took out a little notebook an' gave it to me.

'See, money's been deposited in the CEC bank in your name. Buy some furniture, an' whatever else. An' go 'ome an' tell your mother that you've been given a whole 'ouse an' about four thousand square metres of garden. Only you 'aven't actually said thank you'.

We went 'ome in deathly silence. I said nothin' to me mother, what could I 'ave said. Then not a week 'ad gone by before some lawyer come along with a briefcase an' a mass of papers for me to sign. 'E kept explainin' to me what I was signin'. I also 'ad to bring the child for 'im to see that there really was a child, an' 'e 'ad documents an' I 'adn't found 'im in the street an' 'e 'ad a birth certificate. Registration, primary contract, ev'ry document in Romanian an' pages long. So to 'elp me understand, I said, 'Listen, Vilmos, come 'ere an' tell me what all this is I'm to sign.'

'Just sign, Kali,' 'e said. 'You won't come to any 'arm. You're gettin' the 'ouse an' the land, you an' the child between you.'

'Land as well?' I asked, cos 'e 'adn't mentioned that.

'I mean the garden. That's land, isn't it? Land you can't buy these days.'

The lawyer's name was Ozsvát, 'e was all 'Me dear Vilmos this, me dear Vilmos that', an' 'e said, 'Me colleagues over in Vásárhely are 'avin' a difficult time. Now they 'ave to draw up ev'rythin' in 'Ungarian since there's been the Autonomous Territory in Székelyföld. Well, I admire the 'Ungarian lawyer that can draw up a bill of sale in 'Ungarian! 'Ere ev'rybody knows the law in 'Ungarian but 'as to write documents in Romanian as there's no 'Ungarian legal system, is there? Oh, that Professor Neumann's a real laugh! I'll tell you about it one day. The old lawyers could draw up 'Ungarian documents, but they've all left the country. I'm from the Nyárád valley meself, came up to Kolozsvár to study an' managed to stay on. But I'm not goin' back now, autonomy or no autonomy, I'm not goin' to start studyin' again as I'd 'ave to learn to conduct affairs in 'Ungarian. Isn't that so, Comrade Décsi? I've never seen a single statutum from the Autonomous Territory, we've adopted the Soviet pattern. But as a lawyer I'd make sense of it. So, me dear Mrs Szabó, sign 'ere, then, an' initial ev'ry page there. If you please. Clara Szabó, your full name 'ere. And your initials.'

Oh dear, writin's really 'ard.

This autonomy, I'd 'eard it mentioned in the market. It was said that independence 'ad been granted to the Székelyföld. So that they was completely independent now. An' that the Székelyföld didn't belong 'ere any more, not to Romania like us, but to the Autonomy. A Little 'Ungary 'ad been made of it. Maybe the old chap 'ad got the wrong idea. But 'e was pointin' to the newspaper, it was all there. Maybe we should be pleased about a thing like that.

That's that, then, Kali. I was goin' with me child into a village where ev'ry dog would bark at me cos none of 'em knew me. I've 'ad me ups an' downs. Keep straight on, Kali, you're a Györgyfalva woman.

I'm an incomer 'ere, an' that's that. Like an unwanted child. A woman in the market what came from there said that in the old days there used to be a lot of such unwanted children in Györgyfalva. They called 'em 'royal children', cos if women didn't want 'em, they was taken there straight from the 'ospital, an' the 'ospital was the 'Royal'. An' families would be paid by the state for lookin' after 'em. Nobody was goin' to take me in there an' make a fuss of me. God strike ev'ry man what thinks about 'is prick all the time. An 'ere I can go around in black from 'ead to foot so people will think I'm a widow. Goodbye, red Szék skirt.

There's a little lake near the village, like we've got in Szék, an' this one 'as no bottom either. Ev'ry lake is said to be bottomless. This one's called Emberölő—Mankiller—cos if anybody goes in it won't let 'em out. Same as Nemtudomka—Little Dunno. 'Ow did it 'appen that the poor man said over an' over I don't know, I don't know? Gosh, it's been ages since I told anybody that lovely folk tale. So I'd better tell it in case I forget it completely. There was this lake, or at least this man must 'ave known where it was. When 'e came to the lake 'e walked into it. Cos God 'ad made it the sort of lake that people are afraid of. 'E made it for men an' for big fish. An' that miracle-workin' woman as well, what appeared now, an' kept foretellin' the end of the world, an' was in a state of ecstasy, that woman would stand in the middle of the lake an' talk like that. An' she saw visions of Mary, the god of the 'Ungarians. Cos the woman loved the Virgin Mary very much. The people would just stand on the side of the lake an' listen to 'er. An' there was one that went into the lake cos 'e didn't believe 'is eyes. The water swallowed 'im, it was a greedy creature. 'E was an activist, an' it ate 'im. That's 'ow I was told it by old widow Vajas, who 'elped me out when I 'ad nothin' in the 'ouse, no salt or pepper, things like that, she 'ad an 'ouse farther along Méhes utca. A woman like that, a prophet of doom, appeared in a village in the Aranyos valley. She 'ad the second sight an' foretold the end of the world, an' she was taken into 'ospital an' got better. But people really believed 'er.

Since I'd been dumped out 'ere in Györgyfalva I thought a lot about this 'ere Emberölő lake. I just thought that 'ere I'd got little Vilmos, my dear child, an' I'd got to wait for 'im to be able to look after 'imself an' then I'd be able to go into the lake. At that time 'e was still suckin' 'is rag an' the breast. Me mother kept askin' why I didn't prefer to go to Szék, cos 'ere I was dumped in a strange village. Well, why should I go there, the child would be farther from 'is father. 'E was always comin' round, takin' photographs, couldn't do anythin' else with 'im. 'E said 'e'd 'ave to wait until 'e could talk intelligently, then 'e'd come an talk to 'im, teach 'im stuff.

Me cousin kept sayin', on behalf of mother an' 'er brother, that I should go an' live at their place, as they'd got no children. Ev'n though they was big farmers, cos poor Boris married well an' Pista was such a kind-'earted soul an' more decent than words can express, God 'adn't blessed 'em with children, just a lot of land. If I'd give 'em the child, Boris said, 'e'd give 'im 'is name, an' it would be as if 'e was in King Mátyás's court. Well, I said, I couldn't give 'em little Vilmos cos God 'ad ordained 'im for me, an' it was up to me to take care of 'im. They both come up to Györgyfalva, Boris an' Pista, an' brought the child a bottle with a rubber teat. They brought me mother as well, so that I'd be afraid with 'er there an' ashamed of meself, an' that'd do the trick. They gave me a lovely goose an' a cushion. I 'adn't got anythin' to offer 'em, only a bit of doughnut, I'd ev'n cooked it on the Friday, I always did in case that wicked man came up. But 'e 'adn't come, an' the doughnut was stale by then. I was embarrassed. I 'adn't got any pálinka to offer 'em.

Then they said to me, 'Kali, why don't you let us 'ave the child? 'E's just a millstone round your neck.'

'A millstone 'e certainly is,' said I, 'only it was God what 'ung 'im there. That's the way it 'as to be.' I thought I couldn't give the child away if God 'ad meant to give 'im to me. An' what was I to do then, poor woman, if I 'adn't ev'n got a child to tell folk tales to.

'God won't be angry if you give 'im away so as 'e shall 'ave better prospects. 'E'll see that you've given 'im to a good 'ome. Look, we aren't goin' to torment 'im with lots of work, like we was tormented. I promise you that, Kali, I'll swear to it before the crucifix if you want.'

An' they said they'd give me a bit of a job ev'ry month, 'elp me out with this an' that. I knew they would too, they'd keep their word.

'Look, Boris, there's all these unwanted children 'ere in Györgyfalva, why don't you do that, get one from the 'ospital, they'll gladly give you one. It wouldn't know 'ow it'd come into the world.'

'It wouldn't be our blood' said Pista. 'I'm not takin' strange blood into the 'ouse.'

'Isn't little Vilmos an outsider?' said I. They'd never seen Vilmos senior. They'd read in the papers about what a great man 'e was. That was all they knew.

''E's 'alf our blood, that we'd raise, not somethin' else. They might give us a Romanian or a Gypsy. That child wouldn't be able to speak yet an' say whose it was. We're not takin' pot luck, that's for sure.'

But I wouldn't give 'em little Vilmos, though the way they looked at 'im they was eatin' 'im with their eyes. They ev'n put me under a spell.

Then Boris asked again, 'Why won't you give us this child? 'E'd 'ave such prospects with us. We'd pay for 'im to go to school.'

'You aren't goin' to 'ave to pay for anythin',' I replied. 'The state provides all the schoolin', it's not like in the old days. Ev'n goin' to university an' academy is free. An' 'e's got a father an' a mother, an' I'm not givin' 'im away. 'Is father would likely kill me if I did such a thing.'

'Just look,' said Boris, ''ow the Gangó boy's got on. Feri an' Julis Gangó's child, back in Felszeg. They gave 'im to their brother-in-law cos they couldn't afford to keep 'im. 'E's been raised somethin' wonderful.'

''Is mother went off an' took service in Debrecen, an' nobody's 'eard from 'er since.'

'An' the boy went through school an' went to become a priest. 'E studied up in Enyed an' then 'e came 'ere to the town.'

'Don't take somebody else's child off 'em, I'm tellin' you, Boris. I'm not givin' 'im to you, an' that's that. I need this child as well, an' God didn't give 'im to me when I was a married woman livin' with me 'usband, but 'E 'as now. You go on waitin' as well. Maybe 'E *will* give you one. 'E did to Abraham an' Sarah, an' they wasn't all that young, 'ow old was they? Seventy or ev'n eighty.'

'Well, I'm not goin' to 'ave any children by this time, you stingy Kali. I'm not if I 'aven't by now,' said Boris an' burst into tears. 'The Bible's fairy stories, kids' stuff. A pack of lies.'

What exactly did it say in the Bible? I was thinkin' while poor Boris cried 'er eyes up. I was wrong about Sarah, it'd been Ester. Or was it Rachel? I couldn't remember for sure, it'd been ages since I 'eard it. Perhaps it'd been Abraham, 'e'd 'ad two women, or ev'n more. That 'orrible man couldn't ev'r tie a knot in 'is willy for a bit of peace. Didn't the boss 'ave two? At least two. Or maybe only just the one now, cos that was what 'e kept comin' out to see us in the village for, 'e couldn't manage by 'imself. What was the wicked man to do, 'e couldn't change 'is ways. 'E was forever askin' me to go in to 'is place so as 'e could get somethin' decent to eat if I cooked for 'im.

When she'd calmed down, Boris's reply was: 'You're the fairy story, Kali, for a woman to 'ave a child when she's as old as it says in the Bible. That's a fairy story. You aren't goin' to fob me off with stupid talk like that, cos any doctor'll tell you that a woman can't 'ave a child any longer once she's stopped 'avin' 'er monthly trouble.'

That was what Boris said. She paid too much attention to doctors an' science. It's no good, if anybody studies too much, they find no consolation in 'Oly Scripture.

Pista was winkin' at me mother all this time, but she didn't look at 'im at all. She just looked at the floor.

All the same, it grieved me to see Boris in tears. Me 'eart began to go out to 'er. Let me give 'er the child if she needed 'im. I couldn't bear the sight of distress. I thought, it'd be easier for me as well. Perhaps I wouldn't 'ave to stay in that 'ouse. I'd go somewhere else. By then we was sittin' in silence, an' Boris was wipin' 'er eyes with 'is 'anky. Pista was gently strokin' 'is leg an' lookin' at the floor. And so, just at that moment the child began to gurgle in 'is cot. I got up an' went to look at 'im. I put 'is dummy in 'is mouth so that 'e'd stay quiet. Well, I couldn't give that child away. The very idea! Who would I 'ave left in the world? What would God 'ave to say about it if I gave away 'is child that I'd borne? An' 'is father? Ev'n if it wasn't quite the way it should 'ave been, properly by me 'usband.

But I couldn't 'elp it, she wasn't gettin' the child.

I said to 'er, 'Look 'ere, Boris, dear girl, I'm ev'r so fond of you an' you've been like a good relative to me. But I can't give you little Vilmos 'ere. Who'd I 'ave left if I gave away this little thing? You've got good old Pista 'ere, you see, an' 'e loves you ev'n though you've not 'ad a child, just as much as the day 'e proposed to you. You two are all right as you are, cos that's what God 'as planned for you. You two are never lonely for a moment, cos you're always goin' out to the land an' Pista's right there at your side, strokin' your kerchief when you're milkin'. You're so suited, there isn't another couple like you in the whole of Szék.'

After that Pista was no longer lookin' at the floor. An' I told a folk tale. It said in the story about 'ow György Lél 'ad been an unwanted child, an' what great strength 'e 'ad. Well, it didn't ɯean that ev'ry unwanted child was amazin'ly strong. They listened to it right through in silence, never said a word.

But then I just didn't give 'em little Vilmos. 'Ow could I? 'E wasn't a bread trough what I might give to a neighbour.

They went off in a big sulk without the child. Pista said later to me mother what a woman that Kali was. A bad woman, cos she 'adn't given 'em the child, an' 'e'd only come cos it 'ad been decided between 'em. A mean woman. Well, thought I, I'll tell 'im who's the stingy one. An' that poor Boris 'ad already embroidered the shawl. She'd run about ev'rywhere to get a child to come, from one doctor to the next, ev'n been up to Vásárhely, cos there some specialist doctor 'ad been recommended to 'em. What if the two people just aren't right for each other.

I'd been such a bad person, not to 'elp me dear relations. But I might 'ave been worse still if I'd given that lovely child away. Who could say which was the greater evil in practice? I didn't give little Vilmos up. I couldn't do it. Maybe it would 'ave pleased God if I'd obliged me relations an' not thought of me own interests. Who says you 'ave to make the right choice? When 'e grows up, I'll ask little Vilmos: if Aunty Boris an' Uncle Pista bring you up, perhaps you'll be able to become a doctor. Like old Marci Szabó. 'E's from Szék as well, isn't 'e? Would you like to be a doctor, Vilmos? Cos 'ere on the midden, where you're goin' to grow up (I always call the place 'the midden' cos I was dumped 'ere like a piece of rubbish), you aren't goin' to get much schoolin', are you, ev'n if it's free? Maybe if your father looks after you, you'll go away to school. Cos you're goin' to 'ave to 'elp your mother, aren't you, you'll 'ave to learn to use a scythe an' sow seed. An' by then maybe it'll be machines doin' the sowin' an' reapin', men won't 'ave to follow the plough an' lead the 'orse. We 'aven't ev'n got an 'orse, anyway, That's the kind of poor place this is. You'll be all right 'ere in the bread trough, that was where 'e slept, an' I'd sewn 'im a nice cushion an' put it in, an' 'e was comfy. Just now 'e wasn't asleep, cos 'e could always 'ear the wind, it kept 'im awake ev'n though I put 'is dummy in 'is mouth. Only 'is father might want 'im to study, mightn't 'e, an' make somethin' of 'imself. Who knows what Uncle Vilmos 'as in mind? 'E never says a word about what 'e wants for the child, 'e just comes along, takes ev'rythin' that 'e can from the shop, puts down the money an' takes the photographs. 'E's so obsessed with machines.

But me mother 'ad just sat there like somebody crushed. She 'adn't said a single word. Just looked at the floor an' the 'em of 'er skirt. Didn't tell me to give 'im up, nor not to. Perhaps she thought this little child would be better off with Boris. But in 'er 'eart she knew that if you've borne a child, you can't just give 'it away. Not ev'n if you've brought it into the world in such a rubbish situation as I've got meself into.

I didn't give 'im away, an' 'ere I stayed in this rubbish village. It's pretty, cos there's a nice view from the 'ill over the 'ole of the Mezőség, but to me it's rubbish. It was no good the boss tellin' me it'd be quiet up 'ere, not like at 'is place next to the Station with the noise of machinery all the time. Out I 'ad to come.

If the boss got an idea into 'is 'ead 'e 'ad to carry it out no matter what. 'E didn't manage to cross paprika with tomatoes, though 'e tried for years an' years. Tried an' tried until it 'appened. It 'appened, an' then nothin' came of it, cos it was inedible. But 'e stuck me out 'ere in Györgyfalva. 'E was ev'n goin' to get me in a little cow, but there was nowhere 'e could buy one an' 'e 'ad to give up. Then one day, as the pig 'erd was comin' 'ome, I was brought a little cow, an' the lad said it was such a little thing but all the same it was 'ealthy an' it would do for me. It was mine. It isn't, I said, I've never 'ad a cow, that's for sure. But the boy said it was mine, an' 'e looked at 'is papers, a young calf an' the papers to go with it. The licence. It was certified that Klára Szabó might keep it, cos she'd got a child an' so it was permitted. An' so it 'ad been driven through Ajtony, or whatever that village is called what this dirt road leads to. So in come the calf, or rather it wouldn't, 'owever 'ard the lad pulled at it, cos it was a clever calf an' knew that it didn't belong 'ere. Its 'ome was somewhere else. An' the dog kept barkin' at it, cos Vilmos the boss 'ad given me a dog as well, it was called Bundás, The poor creature didn't know that it 'ad been exchanged an' from then on it lived 'ere. Then the lad told me to keep it inside for about three weeks not to let it out in the field, cos it would go 'ome to the next village where it 'a come from. When the time came, 'e'd take it to graze for me, an' ask for twenty litres of milk in exchange. So I told 'im, 'ow could I give 'im a cupful, cos I'd only got this one calf now, that was all. Then 'e asked for two tubs of plums. That you can 'ave, I said, cos I've got some. But I neither made nor drank pálinka. That bad 'usband of mine 'ad been enough. But I was pleased with the calf. It 'ad a lovely red back. But it was obstinate, as obstinate as 'im what 'ad sent it, that conceited Vilmos Décsi. I went quick an' cut a bit for it's dinner, an' goodness, it liked me grass. Then the lad 'elped me tie it in the stable cos it was obstinate an' strong, an' 'e told me to go out on the road while 'e did that an' keep the cows from strayin', cos that little lad took the cows that 'ad been brought in from the village to the collective farm land. They was all state owned now. Did I know 'ow to look after a cow, 'e asked. I certainly did! I preferred 'em to men. Cows I did at least like. I was definitely more pleased with this nice calf than I would be with an 'andsome man. I didn't need any more men in me life, I'd 'ad enough.

Then 'e said, 'Weren't you expectin' this calf at all, then?'

No, I said, if I'd been expectin' it, if I'd known that it was comin' to see me this ev'nin', I'd 'ave out on me best kerchief for it. But I knew nothin' about it, did I.

'So you've been given it as a present, aunty?' 'e asked.

Well, I thought, I don't much care to be called that, but in this black dress I suppose I'm 'aunty' all right. An old woman.

'Somethin' like that, it must 'ave been,' I replied.

'Or the 'Oly Spirit's sent it,' 'e went on.

'Must 'ave been an 'oly spirit to 'ave sent me the calf. Only one with claws.'

Cos in fact nobody but Vilmos the boss could 'ave arranged for me to 'ave a calf, in times like that, when ev'ry animal was bein' impounded an' confiscated. Then Vilmos said that you could 'ave one cow. One, an' no more. If you 'ad more you 'ad to give 'em up. An' ev'n from the one a quota of the milk 'ad to be surrendered.

So now I too 'ave begun to make a few lei. Cos next door I 'ave got this woman an' 'er 'usband, an' they take in children from the city an' look after 'em, an' I give 'er little Vilmos to look after, as I've got nobody. I don't shut 'im in the cellar, like mother did when they went out to the fields. I don't do that to my little Vilmos! She used to lock me an' me brother Mihály up, an' 'e was older than me. Sárika 'ad gone into service in town, by then she was a proper servant. Mihály an' I used to cry an' cry all day, but there was nobody to see to us, they was all out in the fields. Mother used to leave us some porridge but we'd 'ardly touch it. So I prefer to 'and mine over for 'er to see to an' so 'e can play with the other children an' look at ev'rythin'. 'E's a quiet little thing, is Vilmos. I go into town. At first I just took eggs to sell, an' a few plums or apples if there was any. But then I 'ad a better idea. There's a lot of 'ungry students, what 'as got nothin' to eat. An' each of 'em 'as towel vouchers. I buy these towel vouchers off 'em. At first I used to give two eggs for a voucher later I've only been givin' one. The students are so 'ungry that some take the egg an' crack, suck it up as the 'en laid it, not cooked at all, nothin'. By this time they know that when they see me they can exchange their vouchers. So, from the soft little towels which I buy for the vouchers in the shop I make skirts with my machine. There's some soft tergal in the shop, sold by the metre. I'd 'ave me backside through 'em skirts in a couple of months, for sure. They aren't the sort of thing I made when I was young. They don't take much material, cos they aren't full-length like what I wear, just cover your legs an' bottom. I dye 'em nicely, an' that I buy in the shop. I put buttons on 'em an' they're finished. We don't crush stone for dyes any more an' I don't ev'n know what it's made from. Down our way in Szék there was that red stone an' we used that a lot. But this time I buy it in the shop.

I make skirts from the towels in a range of sizes, for the larger woman an' slimmer-fittin' for the more slender, an' I take 'em into town an' sell 'em. I'd go to the side of the market, cos I don't buy a ticket an' be a seller, no way, or I'd 'ave to pay for that. Then I go along Farkas utca to the university an' on to Majális utca as well. Me skirts sell like 'ot cakes. I don't allow bargainin', just state the price, an' that's that. One 'undred lei an' one 'undred an' twenty for the larger sizes. Some people take 'em into the bushes to try on. I don't worry about 'em undressin' there, it's not me bum showin'. I make about ten skirts a fortnight. In the main they're blue an' black, that's what's wanted. Young girls don't go for brown. That's more for old women. There's no fine decoration on 'em, they're quite plain. But then there's a demand for that. I wouldn't wear 'em, not ev'n as an underskirt, not these days. A thing like that would make me bottom stick out somethin' awful. When I was a slim bit of a girl I'd wear four or five skirts to make me backside nice an' broad. I've got enough of a backside by this time, no need of so many skirts. A nice skirt's like a bell. And almost as modern as trousers. But all the trouble we 'ave to take with things like our Szék fashion! Put it away like this, 'ang it up like that, put lace on the 'em, do it up at the bodice. None of that. These you just take, put 'em on an' drop 'em off, don't take a moment.

The boss come when 'e wanted, sometimes ev'n took the child to town an' for a ride in the car. If 'e didn't come we didn't shed a tear.

I never shed tears these days, I've got none left to shed. I've run out. They've dried up since I was a youngster. Why that is I don't know. Maybe it's cos of me wicked 'usband. I used to cry, an' I cried at first when 'e beat me. But then I controlled meself an' gritted me teeth, I thought, I'm not lettin' you make me cry, you rotten devil's spawn, I'm not goin' to shed a single tear for you, I'd rather you killed me. Well, then 'ee'd get 'old of me, 'it me, beat me up like beatin' puliszka, then all 'e'd say was aren't you goin' to cry, eh? You was so wicked you couldn't admit what a swine you was! I can't remember what I'd done, burned the dinner or the pastry, 'ow do I know. Or I'd left the chickens out of the pen an' some 'awk 'ad taken one, or I'd broken some eggs bringin' 'em in, cos the yard was always slippery, an' if it 'adn't been swept an' sanded you could slip. Then 'e'd give me an ev'n better thrashin'. One day mother came along an' called out: 'Leave that girl alone, can't you see she's 'alf dead, she's not ev'n cryin'.'

'The reason she's not cryin' is cos she's bad an' wilful! I'm not stoppin' till she starts to cry,' was 'is answer.

I seemed to 'ave been turned to wood, I 'ad no sensation. 'E only stopped when 'e got bored. Then mother wrapped me up nicely in cool clothes an' I lay down in such a way that it didn't 'urt me back. I lay like that for an 'ole day, didn't get up, didn't do anythin' but lie on the bench, an' 'e daren't look, 'e was so frightened. Would the doctor 'ave to be called. 'E was very worried about that, cos it cost money, an' 'e wouldn't pay for anythin'. An' the doctor would tell the police if a woman or a child was beaten like that, an' 'e'd 'ave to be summonsed. When I didn't cry or utter a word when 'e beat me 'e was afraid that 'e'd beaten me to death, like old Bodor did 'is son, 'e gave 'im such a thrashin'. The policeman come round, but 'is wififled that the wood pile 'ad fallen on 'im. But their neighbour 'ad seen, Aunty Szabó, cos 'e beat 'im in the yard. So the policeman said 'e should take more care over that wood-pile so it don't fall over onto any more children, an' 'e was satisfied with that. Seven kids 'e 'ad. Then just six.

Maybe that was when I started to dry up so that life wouldn't be able to 'urt me so much. I dried up so much that all me tears left me. Me 'usband couldn't do any more to me. 'E just kicked me with 'is boots. 'E'd brought 'im back from the army an' 'e wore 'em to work, not shoes.

So, I didn't cry then either when the boss put me out 'ere in Gyurfalu, cos that's what the Romanians call it, Gyurfalu. They can't pronounce György. I didn't cry, though God does love tears, that was said in the Bible class when I was still able to go. There's no Bible class 'ere in this stinkin' village, only what's in the church, nothin' else, they don't meet in an 'ouse, it's not the custom. God loves people's tears, cos then 'E's able to bring 'em consolation. 'E don't bring me any, I'm a wicked woman, cos I wouldn't bow down. Me father always said, that Kali won't bow down till Satan comes to

Szék. Well, thought I, 'e's already 'ere an' 'e's married me. I didn't go to the boss's place very often an' do a bit of work for 'im. I just go now an' then. We're clearly the sort what come an' go.

Then I took that little child an' 'ad 'im baptized, I asked the priest to take 'im as a child of Jesus, an' I said that me 'usband couldn't come, 'e was a Party member an' wasn't allowed to. They aren't allowed to enter a church. Oh dear, when I told the boss! 'E was like lightnin' in the fields, absolutely blazin' with fury. An' 'e 'adn't yet been christened. 'E 'as been now, an' Uncle Vilmos didn't say a word.

Well, why should 'e? 'Ow does it go in the folk tale? The poor lad wants to marry Goldilocks an' she loves 'im, but also cos she goes mad if she can't see 'im night an' day, the poor lad what saved 'er from the dragon, but then they can't just run to the priest an' Bob's your uncle. An' in our lives as well it's not the case that we plan ev'rythin' very cleverly on' on paper, like the cadres in the factories. Cos things turn out different from what's been expected. The poor lad doesn't 'ave to undergo one trial, two trials, an' a third, cos the first trial becomes three, don't it, an' so on, an' the poor lad's given more an' more trials. György Lél 'ad to pass ev'r so many an' all. The way I tell it, nine. But when I was little I once 'eard Father say twelve, cos 'e also tested 'im with the dragon, but I really 'ate the dragon an' I don't tell it like that. An' the Gypsies tell it ev'n better an' longer, cos they like to make it last! They'll make it last all day while they're shovellin' manure, an' the sun's 'igh. There was one such Gypsy, used to live over in Kormos utca on the edge of Csipkeszeg, if you please, 'e used to tell it with twenty-four trials. Lajos Ciffra used to come as a day labourer, but nobody wanted to go in front of 'im, they all wanted to work beside 'im so as to listen to 'im. That Lajos 'ad to tell 'is tales nice an' loud while the rest brought 'im water now an' then cos 'e got dry, an' for lunch they all fed 'im well on their cheese. An' next day 'e'd got a sore throat.

Only I don't know what me trial 'ad been, an' 'ow many more I'd 'ave to endure. What other dirty tricks life was goin' to play me. At first the situation was that Vilmos the boss didn't come all that often, but once the child started to toddle—'e was certainly an 'andsome child, little Vilmos, cos 'e was by a flower, as the sayin' is. Then 'is father come more an' more often, made more an' more of a fuss of 'im, brought 'im presents, more than any child in the village 'as. Clothes, a little toy car, a cart, ev'rythin', a train, a car with wheels. 'E pampered 'im so much that I began to be afraid 'e'd make a fool of 'im. By that time 'e was completely attached to 'ere, 'e was comin' an' goin' so much. 'E ev'n listened to an 'ole folk tale when I told it to the child. Vilmos the boss said 'ere 'e didn't 'ave to run about all the time.

'Where do you run to?' I asked. 'Ev'rybody runs, don't keep runnin' after 'em,. You shouldn't be in such an 'urry. Learn to sit still, like János Culi's wife.'

'An' who may she be?' 'e laughed out loud, clutched 'is belly, an' stuffed in some lardy cake. 'Tell the story, me dear.'

'For a start, if you don't believe that she's still alive, go an' look for 'er in Forrószeg. An' this isn't a folk tale, not a tale at all, but a perfectly true story.'

János Culi's wife was left a widow at a very early age. She'd got two nice children but, of course, she was very poor. But she was such an obstinate, stiff-necked woman, an' she said that the Grim Reaper 'ad come an' carried off 'er 'usband, who she'd so loved, an' she'd 'ad mass said for 'im ev'rywhere, an' she'd fasted, but the Grim Reaper 'ad laughed at 'er. Well, after that she surely didn't stir a step from the 'ouse to get a new 'usband, she wasn't goin' to look an' get 'erself a man. She brought up 'er two children nicely, fitted 'em out an' married 'em off. Cos there are widow women who start runnin' around to get one for themselves. Then in the end the most slimy villain came payin' court to 'er when the children 'ad left 'ome. A big farmer started to make up to 'er an' she was beginnin' to feel interested, cos 'er 'usband 'ad been dead twenty years an' 'e'd been well an' truly mourned, when 'er son Miska Culi came 'ome with 'is new wife, a foul-mouthed young woman. An' Miska asked who the strange man was sittin' in 'er kitchen. An' 'e drove the suitor out of the 'ouse, sayin' that no stranger was goin' to shack up with 'is mother. An' 'e got a stick an' threatened 'im, so that 'e just 'ad to run away.'

'Well, Green Kali, what does that prove? Tell me that, now,' asked Uncle Vilmos.

'Well,' said I, 'don't you get it? If somebody's well behaved anybody they want can come in.'

'But 'ow could she get what she wanted once 'e'd been driven out?' asked Uncle Vilmos very shrewdly.

'After that Miska moved into town an' got a job at the glassworks, an' didn't keep comin' an' bein' tied to 'is other's apron strings. An' she went an' started seein' an' talkin' to that villain, oh, I've just forgotten 'is name, I'll 'ave to ask me mother. So then ev'rybody could see 'ow they were, like man an' wife. Only when the children came to Szék she 'ad to be quick an' go away, cos that Miska was a foul-mouth an' always in a bad temper.'

But the boss didn't really care for true stories. 'E preferred the sort that the child listened to all the time. When 'e came an' spent the night 'ere 'e didn't give me any peace. An' 'e preferred makin' it 'ere in Györgyfalva, rather than me goin' there. 'Ere 'e 'ad peace an' quiet. An' then I 'ad to tell 'im tales about János the Strong, György Lél, Laci Vas an' the rest. 'E liked stories about powerful men.

An' I was certainly well supplied with stories.

Once people came from the university in town to Szék, one was a young woman as well, lookin' for people to tell 'em folk tales. They were sent to old Zöld Szabó, cos ev'rybody in Szék knew that the Zöld Szabó family was the best storytellers in Csipkeszeg. But me father didn't tell any stories. Cos 'e said 'e'd dried up, couldn't do it any more. Then me mother told that young woman to speak to 'er younger daughter, she knew stories. That was me. An' to wait while a message was sent, for me to come. An' then me mother an' ev'rybody begged me, we was goin' to be studied, to go an' tell stories cos I knew better than 'em cos they'd grown old an' couldn't remember ev'rythin'.

So since then I've 'ad to go to Szék again with me stories. By then the boss would 'ardly let me go. I was employed, a workin' woman! I've always taken little Vilmos to Szék with me cos the way 'e looked at me when I was tellin' a story was wonderful. An' me old folks were 'appy as well, cos they 'adn't 'ad any young children there for ages. I didn't want to keep goin' there so much, cos dogs an' people all recognized me, an' there'd be gossip about me. But me mother said it 'ad all been a long time ago an' me leavin' 'ad all been forgotten. 'Ad it though! Aren't we the ones what tell true stories about other people, things what 'ave 'appened 'ere, who's done what that was wrong? It's amazin' 'ow informative such tales are! That's 'ow we know about 'alf of Felszeg, 'ow ev'rybody's goin' on, that their mother-in-law's 'ad a fall, that their father's died! Forgettin's not like you've left, a year goes by, or five, well, as many as me, an' that's that, you can slip back cos by then it's been forgotten that you're a runaway woman. An' by then I'd been given a bit of a ring by Vilmos the boss, to wear on me finger so that nobody can say there, you see, life's been 'ard on Aunty Kali. Ev'rybody knew that I was a married woman an' 'ad a tidy life in town. An' I didn't go to see me former 'usband. I didn't go, but I knew that 'e'd recovered. 'E'd been taken ill, an' the doctor 'ad said that either 'e'd die or 'e'd 'ave to take good car of 'imself, an' 'e'd pulled 'imself together. An' 'e'd recovered. Wasn't settin' foot in the pub. Quite a turn around.

Vilmos the boss too kept tellin' me to go an' tell me folk tales, cos the people was bein' studied an' they was all the people's treasure. Furniture, all the kinds of embroidery, textiles, carvin's, costumes, ev'rythin' under the sun, songs an' dances, there was only the spoken word that wasn't bein' sufficiently studied. Well, I said to me mother, what fool don't know about Mad Istók or the three devils an' the priest, they all know that, other people will tell 'em, why should I come all this way to tell 'em. That's not the point, said me mother, cos the young woman what was collectin' 'em 'ad told 'er that it didn't matter if a folk tale was well known, they wanted the person what was cleverest. So I said that was right, it did matter! Cos Rózsi Bodon told tales in a monotonous voice, I'd 'eard 'er very often in the past, an' then nobody 'ad asked 'er to tell any more. Then old Pista Alig couldn't tell 'em with much detail, just that Jóska Lüke went 'ere an' there with 'is donkey an' this an' that 'appened, but 'e simply didn't know 'ow to give it a bit of a twist or work up the devil's trial an' liven things up when the borin' corn-huskin' was goin' on. An' old Mitruly knew such a short version. 'E was such a dull an' borin' person, didn't know the story an' didn't tell it well. That was when I was asked for tales all the time. Cos they 'ad to laugh when I told 'em, gosh, I do like it when there's a lot of laughin'. Once poor Lajos 'Omoki's wife gave three such farts as she laughed that the women all thought that the devil 'ad obviously come to Szék, cos it was a tale about the devil an' she'd made such a terrible smell.

I've told Vilmos the boss I'm not goin' to Szék so much. Last month I went with little Vilmos, stayed there a week an' told about thirty tales. But then the young woman asked whether I knew any more. Well, I do, but they're not fit for children to 'ear. But I do know some for children. So write down the titles of 'em. But they don't 'ave titles, they're just like tales about St Peter, then there's true stories, some about animals, Goldilocks, the devil, foundlin's, then there's King Mátyás, or the crafty old man, an' tales about marriage, cos those I really like. An' then there's tales from the Bible, but the way I tell 'em it's not like what you 'ear in church. An' then there's some about 'usbands an' wives, playin' nice tricks on each other. That woman just wouldn't leave me in peace, I 'ad to tell 'em to 'er an' she noted 'em all down, filled about eight books. Then I said I knew one from Bocaccio as well, cos I'd read 'it. Oh, the way she laughed! That wasn't a pure source, but she wanted to 'ear it, so would I tell 'er what I knew.

Then when I'd finished the folk tales the young woman asked me to tell the true stories. Well, 'ow could I finish, no one alive 'ad ev'r tried to see 'ow many stories there were in 'em! I knew a good 'undred about animals. Lots about donkeys an' all the animals.

'Well, let's see 'ow many tales there are in Aunty Kali.'

'Do you want true stories as well, young lady?' I asked.

'Ev'ry last one,' she replied.

'About the village an' all?' said I, an' I winked at 'er.

Then at last me father gave a laugh cos 'e'd 'eard that, an' 'e knew a thing or two about the village. An' 'e asked, 'ad I 'eard 'ow the son of Peter the Jew from Felszeg, that Peter the Jew junior, got a wife. 'E went into town, an' became the leadin' worker at Teknofridge. 'Is picture appeared in the news-paper in the works, it 'ad its own paper printed. This Peter the Jew junior 'ad a girlfriend who wouldn't marry 'im cos 'e wasn't all that good lookin' an' very short. But when 'is father showed this picture in the council, cos 'e was very proud of 'is son, an' the daughter of Miklós Puji caught sight of it, she went to 'is father an' said that when 'is son came to Szék she'd go an' see 'im to congratulate 'im. Well, congratulate 'im she certainly did, cos the child's just been born.

An' so the young woman sat there all day takin' notes, an' when I'd fin-ished, cos I was worn out by that time, I'd 'ad to 'elp me parents a bit, the talk went on. Me father wasn't sayin' anythin', me mother an' I went on dis-cussin' an' the young woman took notes. Then it turned out that I 'ad to tell 'er all about meself, who I was an' what I did, where I went to school, where I lived an' what sort of a life I'd 'ad. Just like that, she said, the story of me life! Goodness, me girl, I'm not tellin' you that, cos it's been such a bad life, so sad, why should I trouble others with it? An' that bad life 'ad been all me own makin', all of it. I was to tell 'er, she'd listen. Well, she was such a young thing, but she'd got four children at 'ome.

An' when she got it printed, she said, me name would be in it.

I told Vilmos the boss, listen 'ere, mister, cos I've got somethin' to say the like of which you've never 'eard. I'm goin' to be in a book! 'E looked at me, just like I'd always seen: I could never tell anythin' from 'is face. 'E just asked what kind of book.

'A book of folk tales. I've been tellin' folk tales to a young woman, an' she's taken 'em down an' she'll get 'em printed. Then people what don't know 'em can read 'em all. Like that.'

He replied that they surely would, cos from then on the people was goin' to be discovered, all ethnic groups an' individuals, in the Soviet Union as well there was amazin' peoples bein' discovered. An' the workin' class as well was bein' discovered.

'Books are bein' written about 'em, ev'rybody what's got treasures is goin' to be studied in future, ev'rybody. It's not like it used to be, when only rich people or the educated sort, or 'em what's done somethin' big, could be put in books. But any ordinary person.'

Well, I said, I never would 'ave thought that you would consider that I'd got any treasures, cos you've never said a single word. 'E 'adn't meant me, but the people. I'd understood 'im to mean, well, to 'ell with 'em, 'e kept goin' on about the people an' the people all the time.

An' I should be warned, the village won't look kindly on me if it's published. Well, said I, quite the contrary, an' I told 'im about Peter the Jew an' 'ow 'e'd got a wife after 'e'd been in the paper. But I said I thought they would look kindly on me cos I'd told true stories that ev'rybody knew. Not cos of that, said Vilmos the boss, but cos I'd got a name for meself, an' after that nobody there was goin' to like me. Cos I'd 'ave a name, an' it'd be talked about when I was dead an' gone. Well, I said, I don't really think so.

Well, I said, Vilmos, as you're leavin' Györgyfalva, mister, you won't forget us 'ere, an' only think of the girls? You won't bother about us any more, just roses, roses an' more roses. Oh, was 'e angry when I said that.

An' now I'd be able to live 'appily 'ere in the back of beyond, nobody'd see me, with me child, the rickety fence, a bit of land, an' this red calf, an' I'd got a nice black-an'-white cat an' the good dog Bundás. Said the boss, that's not so, I was distortin' all the good things an' considerin' only the bad. When I told 'im the rotten way 'e'd put me out of 'is 'ouse, 'e said it 'adn't been like that. Then I said to 'im, 'Well, you say 'ow it was if you know better.'

'E said, when 'e came out just once a week by then, an' I went over once a week, an' 'e 'eld the child an' put 'im to sleep, 'e said, an' 'e 'ung 'is 'ead, 'I miss your folk tales, you know, Kali. D'you 'ear me? I'd never 'ave thought I'd miss 'em.'

What was I to say to that? 'E shouldn't 'ave put me out. 'E 'adn'! 'E'd rather been thinkin' of me an' the child. 'E'd 'anded over ev'rythin of 'is, the garden, an' now 'ed got nothin' of 'is own. Well, said I, from 'ere in Györgyfalva it certainly looks like you put me out. So 'e was missin' me stories. Comin' from 'im that was a love letter, as I took it. Well, I thought so.

Uncle Vilmos said, 'Take that as a confession of love.'

'Well, then,' I asked 'are you tired of your other girlfriend? Or 'as she gone off the boss? Cos girls are like that. A sugar daddy is nice, very nice, an' then they get tired of the old man. They need a young man as well.'

Oh, did 'e lose 'is rag. Men 'ave always lost their rag when I've told 'em the truth to their faces.

Cos I told 'im on me own be'alf, the way I saw it. 'E couldn't stand me bein' in 'is 'ouse, an' when 'e became an important gentleman, 'e dumped me. 'E was an important comrade now, not a gentleman. All the gentry 'ad been sorted out. I was speakin' on me own be'alf, not 'is. Ev'rybody can tell the truth on their own be'alf. Only the priest speaks in the name of the Lord. But it 'as 'appened that a priest 'as spoken the truth so wickedly as ev'n 'ere in Györgyfalva. I once walked out of the church, I 'ad to, I was in tears. What our priest said was that a man of filthy life was comin' an' goin' 'ere so as to cover up 'is past. People should reveal their past, not cover it up. They're only shown mercy if they reveal it. An' 'e read out the parable from Scripture. So what was I to say in reply? Church isn't a place where you can't know what to say. People aren't questioned there, they 'ave to listen. It's only the Lord what examines 'earts, the priest's job is to preach. One person can't answer another. I've only told the Lord me situation, 'aven't 'idden anythin' about me past. That's the truth. 'E can clearly see me soul an' me life. But other people can't 'ear.

I told the truth on me own account, the way it is. There was only one thing what I couldn't really tell. 'Ow I 'ated that wicked man with all me 'eart. Cos anger's a sin, a great sin, most of all when you give it room in your 'eart. So there, I've got one sin, an' God's punished me for it.

'You go on an' tell me your story, mister, cos it's sure to be different,' I replied.

'E left the 'ouse, all sullen. As 'e was goin' 'e shouted at little Vilmos not to get under 'is feet. An' this time 'e couldn't take 'im with 'im cos 'e'd got to go on a journey. 'E was so worked up, there was no talkin' to 'im. Why ev'r did God create men an' not give 'em a bit of patience? Just so as to be big men an' 'ave their own way all the time! All of 'em want to big men all the time. Dear little Vilmos was wailin', wailin' at me.

'Cry, you dear child, you poor orphan, you cry! 'Ere you are, four years, eight months an' three weeks old, an' you're weepin' tears as big as the Nádas stream. Do you know, you poor orphan, the way Ámánka cried when the witch put 'er eyes out? She did, you know, So that she couldn't see the prince, cos she'd 'ave fallen in love with 'im. An' if she did that, she wouldn't. So what could that Ámánka cry with? Well, she couldn't after that, poor girl. Nohow, poor thing, cos she 'adn't got no eyes to cry with. So she 'ad to cry with 'er 'ands. She just made with 'er 'ands as if she was cryin', poor thing. So along come the witch an' took 'er 'ands away. So Ámánka went on cryin' with 'er mouth. So then the witch took 'er mouth off 'er an' she couldn't cry any more.

That's 'ow the story goes, but it's diff'rent in real life. Cos we don't only 'ave to be grateful for what God gives us, but for what 'E takes away as well. I was grateful that 'E 'adn't given me a different child when I wanted one. An' you see, 'E's given me one now by this other man. 'E's not that bad, but 'e is a bit. So 'ere I've got you, I told Vilmos, an' I don't 'ave to sit in the kitchen ev'ry day with your father an' watch 'im eat 'is dinner an' say all the time that nothin's any good. That was 'ow me mother used to cook, so why shouldn't I cook like that? Don't you think so? Aren't the two of us all right? So we aren't, but never mind. 'Ow would God be able to test us if 'E made ev'rythin' perfect for us? So ev'n poor Ámánka gave thanks to God for takin' 'er eyes away, first the one, then the other. And then 'er 'ands, both of 'em, an' then 'er little voice as well. An' the witch took 'er place in the coach an' became the prince's wife, an' she got what she wanted. But as soon as 'e'd put the ring on, the prince saw that 'e'd been deceived, an' the witch sat beside 'im in a great rage. But by that time the prince 'ad said 'e'd be faithful unto death, an' couldn't do anythin' about it. An' it isn't the story that 'e didn't keep 'is word. Cos 'e 'ad to, didn't 'e? Kept 'is word. If it was no good, then so it was, but the prince was faithful. Only I wasn't. Cos your mother was clever an' got away from that other one. But so did poor Ámánka, didn't she?

Now then, little Vilmos. Little Vilmos Green Szabó. You've 'ad your name changed now an' it's the same as your father's. You've been good an' stopped cryin'. I'll tell you this folk tale now, as it should be. We've got a long ev'nin' ahead of us, an' you'll go to sleep durin' the story, an' it doesn't matter. It'll go into your little 'ead if you go to sleep. I'll tell you that there was great love between Ámánka an' the prince. Cos it turned out that Ámánka was Goldilocks. Oh, they lived ev'r so 'appily together to the end of the world an' seven days, only previously she'd been the witch, ugly an' old an' as thin as a dry stick, an' she'd 'ad to take Ámánka's eyes, 'er eyes an' 'er 'ands an' 'er little voice. But they lived together, an' Ámánka was magicked back, an' the Count didn't dismiss 'er when she'd got no voice, but she got 'er 'ands an' 'er eyes. 'E was nice to 'er, didn't turn 'er out. Like the boss did me. Cos that's 'ow it was in the story, an' in real life it's diff'rent.

Vilmos the boss said 'e 'adn't turned me out, but that I'd done all right out of 'im. For ev'r. With 'im, the Lucky Gardener. So there.

An' 'e'll tell you better 'ow it all turned out.

PART II

Vilmos's Tale

A rose grower has blood on his hands. Don't I know it. It's just that now an attempt is being made to frame me. Because I'm having to sit here in the Securitate and explain and write a statement.

And then it's a bit of luck, isn't it, that round here I'm known as the lucky gardener. May his hands drop off that stuck that nickname to me. Because everybody just thinks that it's my magic wand that does the work, I just command it, and like in the folk tales it does a dance and works instead of me. That I've only got to look at a tree and it produces half-kilo pears.

'What great luck you have, Vili, you trod in mud when you were a child!' all the gardeners tell me, especially Werner, when they see all my results.

Well, in mud is just where I did tread, as there was nothing else in our street, only horse manure and all that mud, there the other side of the railway, because I'm a Kerekdomb man. Or I was, because I'm not now. Why do they always talk about luck? Don't I have to work for it like other people? They should come up here in early summer at four in the morning, because that's when I'm up and out in the garden. What gives people the idea that everything works for me? I don't talk about what's not been successful, or rather it doesn't have to be obvious. It has to be my misfortune, I don't blame anybody else for it. And I don't make a show of it like others do, even though they know that their flowers or fruit or hybrid is no credit to them, there's something wrong with it, they ought to forget it or work on it, but they think that maybe they'll be lucky and it won't be noticed. If something isn't a success I take hold of it, cut it down and chuck it out. Or I go halves in it with the Hóstát farmer down the hill here, and his wife takes it to market. People buy the stuff because they don't understand crossbreeding, and my name isn't on it. I don't show anything that isn't successful. So now I can explain my statement.

People generally forget that for luck, you have to work, fourteen hours a day. Because then luck will come to you and in spades. They're trying to ruin me for being a green-fingered gardener and the 'Békás Magician'. I'm near the Békás, that's where I get the name from. But they don't consider the work involved. They want to ruin me because neither am I a commercial gardener, like the big ones with hectares of land, who've all been nationalized now or have had to join collective farms, nor am I a scientist in the university. Anybody like me, just getting on with my work by myself on the edge of town, not part of the urban set-up, is despised.

It begins with a stroke of luck for me, because my gladioli are open on 26 July—St Anne's Day. That's what's made my fortune, because they've never had so much as a bud by that time. People don't consider that the sun that shines on the Békás is the same that shines on the other slopes where they are. And I haven't got any wonder-fertilizer to force gladioli into flowering specially. But there have been seven years when I've produced early gladioli here. They don't consider that I've tried all this time, not just for the colour, like everybody else, and that they should be dark red, have sixteen flowers, but that they should open early, for St Anne's Day. I've selected the early openers corm by corm as the chance arose. Really, they should have got up earlier. Definitely. Not only in the literal sense, that they should be up and about at four o'clock and watering, but they should pay attention to how to make them come together. In other words, think a bit. But flowers won't wait while you think. Flowers look for feeling. Anybody who has no feelings should go ploughing. Everybody's got land. Especially nowadays.

Not so as to annoy them, but I'll have my say. I'll tell you what I've put in my statement, I'm not ashamed, which is what the Securitate want now, isn't it? And I'll tell the other farmers so that they'll learn. That is to say, what the situation is here with me and my damn great luck. Because it's true, my star rose so quickly that in all my life I'd never have thought it. I started with gladioli, then antirrhinums, then roses and so on, up and up. The sky's the limit, I thought. There've been three articles about me in the paper, people have come from the university to visit me. It's a new world.

In this world it's no longer just a matter of how much somebody's studied, but of what they know. I never went to school, that was how the world was in those days. My father wouldn't let me, and when I was ten I had to be apprenticed. But to them, the trained gardeners, all that matters are things like trade schools, industry colleges, universities, high schools, special schools, they couldn't give a toss, they look down on the uneducated. They were green with envy, of course, when they saw my reputation here and elsewhere, everybody bought from me, King Carol of Romania, Miklós Horthy, even the Dutch used to buy from me before the war. And it was a big deal to sell a single seed, a single bulb, to the Dutch. And the things they bought! Whole plants, specifications and all, patents, they called them. Patents. Because then the antirrhinums that I'd developed became patented worldwide. My big red Lya Roşescu antirrhinum and the sulphur-yellow Marika, because those were the names I gave them. The Dutch dreamt up something different, but that was their business. Before I took an interest, the antirrhinum had just been the peasant snapdragon, a simple everyday flower.

Looking at my statement, the security man asked, 'Who's this Lya Roşescu, then? Some bourgeois aristocrat?'

'Just a girl,' I stammered.

'You and a Romanian *boyar* girl had an affair?'

'She was the daughter of the fire-brigade commander,' I said, which in fact she had been. I'd worked there a long time ago, when I hadn't yet got even a small garden. The commander had a lovely young daughter, but I hadn't meant that. She was pretty, but too young for me. Then he didn't ask about Marika, as she didn't strike him as *boyar* enough.

But he was interested in what I'd done with antirrhinums. And King Carol, and Horthy, and the Dutch, and that's where the trouble is now, because here I'm having to sit with this security man and explain. When things begin to go better for you, they drag up the past. I'm having to establish my innocence because I've done nothing wrong. Only they think so, don't they? But those who wish me well would be happy if they knew that I was sitting here writing a statement in the Securitate on Majális út! That Vilmos Otto Décsi is sitting there in the cellar over a piece of paper, explaining it away. Because I've had to state that Horthy and Carol bought my roses. The way the world is these days, everything has to be clarified and explained.

But so that they shan't be all that happy I'll tell them. I'll give an account of the main stages of my life. Because if you don't do that, somebody else will do it for you. And I shan't be grateful for that.

It was just coming to the Nativity of the Virgin Mary, and I decided that the time had come for me to take on an assistant. I'd give them half the cut flowers to sell in the market, only what I didn't need myself for experimental material, of course. I'd do that until I was losing too much. On the other hand, what I could sell on that day would be enough to pay a servant for three months, and that would bring me another benefit as well. Because I could do with a woman in the house. I don't mean because she'd be a woman, but a helping hand. Then after All Saints Day, when the flowers were over, we'd tidy up and I'd pay her off. And then get somebody else in spring.

I took my mother's advice: I didn't get a young girl. It would be more than a man could stand. A sixteen-year-old, fresh from the country, would always be a distraction for me. Under the same roof. Even if she wasn't good looking I'd fall for her. Not what I needed. And knowing what I was like, I'd have sex with her once, then twice, and once she was crazy over me I'd chuck her out. I wouldn't want her round my neck and fussing over me. She might even fall pregnant, God forbid!

The only trouble with an older woman, of course, was that she couldn't work as fast as a young one. But I didn't get an old woman but a good one. Nice and strong, sound in wind and limb, and her tongue wagged as well, so I wouldn't find life dull. She could tell a good folk tale. I made a point of not asking where she was from. That's not the sort of thing a gentleman asks. She was a real Szék servant, such as Hóstát people have.

So I engaged this nice strong Szék woman and took her home. But how was I to explain to her what the job was? She'd see what had to be done around the house, she was a woman, after all, no need to teach her. I asked her not to start with the housework but with dinner. I was really looking forward to something nice to eat, I'd been having to eat dry stuff all the time. I used to go down to Mother's once a week, and I'd bring home a pot of something, but that had given out by then. I didn't like to keep on getting cooked food from my mother all the time. And I told her one thing, to get to bed because she'd have to be up at four o'clock to be in the market by six. I'd cut all the flowers for her, that day if it was cool in the evening. If it was too warm, I'd get up at three. Or perhaps I'd cut them in any case and put them in the cold room. I'd got a nice big cool store room, and I sprinkled the floor as well to prevent it being too dry; flowers like to rest in moist air. And first thing in the morning, she would take them to market in a wheel-barrow. Then she wanted me to give her a knife so that she could cut flowers as well. I said to her, dear lady, in the first place we don't cut flowers with knives, like Gypsies do when they're stealing them, we use secateurs. And secondly, you won't know which to cut. Only I know that. Because I'll only send the inferior ones to market, not the ones that are fit for further devel-opment, know what I mean? She gave me a funny look. I could see that she'd never heard of anything so strange. But she didn't ask any questions. Otherwise the lady from Szék caught on well, I didn't have to tell her any-thing, she knew it all. Her bean soup with a little bacon was, as she put it, her introduction. I had a double helping. Apart from that, she could see what the work involved, and I didn't have to show her. She got a bit under foot, like a new dog, but soon settled down.

Then she said apologetically that she hadn't got a workbook so couldn't give me one, because she hadn't been a servant for a long time. Because . . . and she dried up. I got the message. She'd only said that once she was installed and had been engaged, rather than in the market when we were still discussing, because she was a crafty woman, wasn't she? Didn't want me to turn her down for having no workbook. To which I told her that the world wasn't like that these days, she didn't need a workbook. There weren't any servants either. That wasn't what they were called. What then, she asked. Staff. Assistance, or something of the sort. And if anybody came round and asked who she was, she was to say she was a relative from the country. If anybody was daft enough to believe it, she answered. I told her to leave it to me.

Late that evening we cut the roses, and I showed her how to take the leaves and thorns off, gave her the trimming knife. She worked quickly, wasn't bothered by the thorns, though a lot of women are a bit put off by them. Women like roses but don't care for thorns.

Then I told her the price. She wasn't to sell anything for under a lei. One lei, like a cat at the dog-pound, she said and laughed. Because that was what the dogcatcher gave for a cat, it was written up at the Hóhérek bridge, she'd seen it. What did they do there with a one-lei cat? We counted the flowers, tied them in bundles of thirty, wrote it down on paper. I gave her money to buy a ticket for the market and to get herself something to eat, because there was hot food there if she wanted something, not expensive. She asked me to give her three of the apples that were inside on the table. I said I couldn't give her those, they were for experiments, but she could pick what she liked off the tree. She wasn't used to picking them, she said, only to windfalls. I gave her some gladioli as well, I prefer to cut those in the morning, and I told her, no cheaper than the roses. I gave her lilac ones, pink, and soft white ones. She placed them carefully in the barrow, covered them with a damp cloth, and looked at them like a woman in love does at her groom before the altar. I saw straight away that she had a feeling for flowers. Not from a scientific aspect, not a bit of it, she just loved them. That can't be taught. It's something you're born with, Mendelian genetics, modern science calls it. Though it's not yet certain which is the stronger, nature or nurture, Mendel or Michurin. These two great forces are in conflict in science nowadays. But you can see as quickly as the colour of their eyes whether a person has a feeling for flowers or not.

Any ass can study at university, because these days every illiterate is admitted, the younger generation en masse. That's a good thing, and I don't say that because in my time it wasn't possible, but even so if I were a teacher there I'd first make applicants take an exam in feelings. Anyone that has feelings would be able to study. How it would be possible to examine whether or not somebody has a feeling for flowers I don't know. They'd also have to have a feeling for the soil. To that, experts will say that in that case every tiller of the soil makes a very good gardener. Poppycock! You've only got to look: take two peasants, both with land in the same area. One gets one sort of yield, the other something else. Some people have gone and lived in the country, such as old Károly, the famous writer who lived in the small village Sztána. He'd never owned any land, nor his ancestors before him, they'd been artists, intelligentsia. To the best of my knowledge. Károly Kós, the famous architect and man of letters—my friend Lali, Lajos Jordáky, knew him well—great artist though he was, had a feeling for the soil. What he did with it was to break it up where nobody had ever sown anything before. He removed stones by the cartload, there were so many. Then he cultivated it. And wrote about it, about the soil, the horses, everything that he'd learnt by himself. The other one, a dyed-in-the-wool peasant like all his ancestors, just plundered the soil, had no feeling for it. So it seems that he hadn't inherited anything in the genetic sense. I didn't know that man, but I've got an article about Mendel and his genetics. But I don't go in for breeding people, only the German fascists did that, so as to produce the best people. I know of one exception, where there's a sort of innate understanding of the soil—the Hóstát man. In them it's genetic, it really passes from father and mother to son and daughter. The Hóstát people are like the folk tale horse that had wings and never stumbled, as the lady from Szék told me. I didn't give it a thought, because it was from the Hóstát. In fact, never in all my life have I seen a bad Hóstát farmer, man or woman. So new university students should be tested as well, but now the world is in such a chaotic state.

Everything is having to be rebuilt from the bottom up, at university there's no time for that sort of thing.

But without feeling, knowledge is rubbish. That's my humble opinion.

So, I took this working woman on to assist me, and in the morning she took the flowers to market and sold them. I'd have liked a new greenhouse for spring and had to make money somehow. I had visitors in the morning. I was getting used to the numbers that came to the garden, as my reputation was spreading more and more, there'd been articles in the papers, and other gardeners had gone out of business, hadn't they, especially the big commercial ones with lots of employees and extensive acreage. I even had a lot of visitors from the university and I had to do a lot of explaining, so half the day was spent on it and I couldn't get any work done.

So, these visitors came. These were definitely 'coats', I saw that straight away. The vizsla rushed at them and barked. There were two of them, and they stood motionless at the gate, not daring to come in. The dog didn't let anybody in. It used to catch Gypsies as well, because it scented them at once. They greeted me in Romanian and I replied likewise. At first sight, I thought they'd come about the couple of boxes of plums that I'd sold to the factory workers, and which hadn't been declared. They inquired how much land I had, and if I had any help. I said, only a relative, an elderly woman. She was down in the market. They admired the garden, the rows of plants. Then one asked: 'And which one might be the king's rose?'

Coming suddenly like that, I didn't understand. *Trandafirul regului*, he'd said, but there's no such variety as 'king's rose'. Well, they said, I'd named a rose after the king. Damn it all, they were coming back to that! I'd already spent half a day sitting in the Securitate writing my statement. I told them plainly, I'd said everything already, written it down for the comrades. I'd got a copy of my statement, because I'd written it out for myself at home so as to know, if asked, and in case I might put something differently, I wrote it out straight away. If I'd omitted something as I wrote, I'd put it in. You can't say something in exactly the same way twice. It was just a kind of listening. Because I'd had to write in there, hadn't I, and it was no use my asking to be allowed home to fetch my books, I couldn't recall everything from memory, I didn't just scribble general remarks about roses, but I had to know exactly the day when I did something to a rose and what, where I'd taken it from, which generation etc. They wouldn't let me go. They'd come out and look at those books, they said.

I put everything down in my statement exactly as it had been. As far as I could from memory, without my books. All the years I'd been searching. When I'd started bringing on that hybrid tea which the king had bought seven years later during the royal dictatorship, because he'd been Carol II, a great dictator. I'd been at a very early stage of my career, if you please, and was beginning to make headway. The king had actually been to the world exhibition and made his gardener buy it. I hadn't sold it personally, I hadn't gone to that exhibition, old Schultz went on my behalf. I'd written that I could only go to the Kolozsvár exhibition, I'd booked a place, that was in 1941. What the king bought was from my father plant Charles P. Killham, and the mother plant had been a cross between a hybrid tea from Harrison and the famous Ville de Paris. I even traced the ancestry for them. The father had been bred in 1928 by a Dutch gardener, the mother by an American in the nineteenth century. My flower was of medium height and leaf-size, less strongly scented, but all the same a delicately perfumed rose with thirty petals. It was a bright medium yellow. At first I'd tried to produce the golden yellow that I wanted, with a tinge of dark red. But it lacked brilliance. I hadn't given a thought to the scent, because in my climate that is very difficult, and I've never yet managed to achieve a strong perfume. I only brought out the brilliant colour in the fifth year, when I pollinated it from a classic Ville de Paris. The flower belonged to the Pernetiana class, created by Pernet Ducher. And then in the seventh year I got what I'd been after. That rose had precisely the qualities that I'd been looking for. And I thought that it was going to be the first rose that I would register officially.

While I was writing my statement, they actually came in twice saying *gata*, was it finished? In the Securitate, you're actually addressed in the second person. I said no, because there were a great number of important details that had to be noted. So, it took me seven years to grow the rootstock of that rose and then another three or so to keep an eye on it. Then there was no time left to select carefully the best ones to take further, it was a rushed job. That hadn't been my first rose, I'd made at least eight of my own. I hadn't been at all keen on going to Bucharest to exhibit, I couldn't afford it, what with the transporting, vases, exhibition stands and all that. Some people even employ a designer to make their table look good. But old Schultz, my master, really assured me that I'd definitely got something to go with. That I'd got a flower of that quality. I said to him, who'd take seriously a gardener with neither reputation nor garden and not a single registered flower. He insisted that I could make my fortune if I'd make it known. He was going anyway, not taking much, so let's go together. Old Schultz just wanted to show people what a pupil he'd got. By that time he wasn't being taken all that seriously, there were much bigger gardeners, but he could still go because this was Romania: Jews could take part and weren't banned as they were in Hungary. Well, I didn't have to write all that down in my statement, they knew. I told old Schultz to take mine as well, and if he sold any of them, I'd give him a share. So we agreed. Before the train left in the small hours, I took him myself what I'd cut in the night. I'd disbudded every stem by lamplight, so that nobody should steal the buds off them—I knew that low trick. I had to make special big boxes to protect them, line them with strong, damp canvas and cut holes in them for ventilation, otherwise the flowers would suffocate. So I went along with big boxes, and a farmer took me in his cart. I told my master that he could sell all my varieties, because I'd sent seven new kinds of roses that I'd grown, only what I'd put my name to, those he was not to sell. He slapped me on the shoulder, gave me a hug, even shed a tear. Never mind, he was a sentimental old man. I was his best pupil, he said, and I'd see what it would bring me when I got my flowers acknowledged.

Then five days later came a telegram from old Schultz. The king's gardener, one Negulici, was going to call on me, he wanted to buy 'your one'. Less than a fortnight went by and Negulici appeared, wearing a suit and riding in a car. We discussed for more than an hour, and he urged me to sell him everything. He'd had a contract written under which, once I had handed over the stocks and the certificate of origin, I might never cultivate it again. And as the rose was not yet officially named, he urged me to give it the king's name. I was given a lot of money, 800 lei. The more I said that I was reluctant to sell, the more he sharpened his tone: instead of my being glad at my roses adorning the king's garden, he would act in the king's name, confiscate them and take them for nothing, as the intellectual property of the treasury of the Kingdom of Romania. I could see that that refined gentleman was the sort that would do what he threatened, and in the end I took the money. I also won a minor prize at the exhibition. With those eight hundred lei, if you please, I bought four thousand bricks and at least thirty rafters. I live in that house now, because I bought the land with the antirrhinums that were sold to the Dutch, while the bricks and wood came from the king of Romania. And with the money from Miklós Horthy—well, the Securitate wasn't interested in what I spent that on. I never saw my work blooming in the king's garden because I never went to Bucharest. But the whole rosarium was destroyed when the city was bombed, so that the king's rose, as I like to call it, no longer exists.

Then the Securitate men came in again: had I finished my statement? I asked whether I should write about Miklós Horthy's rose, or was that about King Carol's dictatorship enough? I'd better give an account of the Horthyist rose as well, said one of them.

The big Flower Exhibition in Kolozsvár took place in 1941. Regent Horthy's idea was to take a plant from every gardener in Kolozsvár and have a special Transylvanian section in his garden. It was said that the victorious army took a plant from every village that they passed through. They collected all kinds of other Transylvanian bric-à-brac, clothing, buckets, carvings, gates, even tore the wood off houses. They even took peasants for the Budapest zoo as examples of Kalotaszeg peasants or Székelys in local costume. People could see what Transylvanians looked like. It was in the papers, with photographs.

Then they bought all kinds of items, including roses. But here in the Securitate, I only had to write about roses and needn't mention the rest.

Then the comrades said: when did a poorly educated gardener like me go wrong, who had worked hard all his life, got up at four every morning, sometimes at three, and been born into a family where there wasn't a pair of shoes or enough to eat, and if he hadn't stood up for himself would have been a house painter to this day? And today too, when the people was in power, and the country was a people's democracy, even so the poor were plundered. So then I had to tell them the story of my life from the very beginning, and in particular how I did business first with the Dutch and then with the king of Romania and finally with Miklós Horthy. Because these three were now our enemies.

The rose that Horthy bought, to continue, was also a hybrid tea that I had produced and developed further. The father . . . At this point the security man interrupted me, leave out the fathers and mothers, I was obviously trying to confuse them. Excuse me, I said, I only wanted you to know that this was not some ordinary species, but the creation of my own hands. So I described how I crossed it. Its parents were Max Krause and C. Vandal, and it took its habitus rather from the mother. Never mind habitus, said the interrogating officer, nobody wants to know about that. Then I'll explain what it means, I said. He wasn't interested! I'd really have liked to put something about yellow and orange roses, what the fashion had been at the time, before and after the war, and what it meant. The gardener has to know and understand plants, but even more so the world beyond. To know what's wanted, what's in fashion. I'd have needed a whole book to write the history of colours. I might have been able to put it into words that even non-experts would understand. Say why orange flowers in particular were so much in vogue in those days. But I wasn't allowed to put any more, nobody at all was interested.

They told me to leave the statement. They kept me sitting there for about two hours, shooting questions about this and that at me, trying to confuse me. Then they let me go.

And now here were the two coats in the garden. And again I had to explain about the king and Horthy. So just show us that yellow rose, said the two security men, standing in the middle of the garden. And the Miklós Horthy kind as well. Look here, I put it all down. I agreed not to produce any more like the one the king bought, so I can't show you that. And what are these yellow roses, then? I could see that they'd read the statement, but I thought that they didn't believe it, so here they were to verify it. I said that yellow hybrid teas were my speciality. I was continuing to experiment with them. I hadn't put that in my statement, they said. No, because just look how many yellow roses I'd got, and I pointed to at least six long rows that were coming into flower. There are thirty-five yellow hybrids here. To their eyes they were all the same, they couldn't see any difference. And there were a lot more under experimentation, and the polyanthus at the back. I told them to take a good look, everything had a name—not that they were all written down; I wasn't a shopkeeper, I knew them all by heart. The way a mother knows her children's names. One of the two looked at them, scratched his head, and couldn't make out that there were so many varieties. Look more closely, I advised. Look at the thorns on this one. And the way the leaves are on this other. And the number of petals on this third. The shade, the brilliance, the whole shape, the habitus, the external presentation of the rose as a whole. There's external presentation and internal. And the scent. I could see that hybrids didn't interest them.

They'd go inside, they said, they had to look round the house. They looked to see what sort of books I had. Turned out the whole bookcase. At first they put them back in place, then just piled them up one on top of another. And they seized the article on the desk, one that I'd just started. On the cover sheet, it said *The Rose*. That was put into a briefcase. Then they examined the other manuscript books. They asked, which is the one with the king's rose in? Because I'd got two similar shelves of hybridizing records. I told them and pulled out the ones from 1936 on. They took those away. I asked whether I would get them back. They said nothing. Only they ask the questions, we merely give the answers. They're allowed to say nothing. We have to talk and keep talking.

The king took my rose way back and in fact he paid for it, but I couldn't have said that I wouldn't let him have it, because he was the king. So he took it and christened it in his name. The comrades took away my rose books in which I'd recorded observations year on year until I'd exhibited the twelve stocks that I believed were suitable. Suitable, not perfect, as old Schultz used to insist. There's no such thing as a perfect rose! Eight years' work, from the first crossing to the final flowering. Didn't mean a thing to them, they knew nothing about roses. So *colac peste pupăză*, as they say in Romanian, on top of it all they even took away my article from my desk—in it I meant to sum up my knowledge of roses to date. It didn't even have my name on it. Why should it have, when I was actually working on it? And there I was with nothing left of that flower. I could have put aside a couple of stocks, and who would have known that I still had them? But I hadn't. Firstly, it was honest dealing: once I'd said that I would sell my invention, it was sold. Secondly, I'd thought I'd be able to produce it again when the time came, because under the terms of the contract I'd sold it for twenty years. What are twenty years to a rose grower?

But these days you've got to be very careful. If you see a coat like that you're duly nervous. A lot of great men are in prison these days.

When the comrades had left with my books and my article in their brief-cases I was absolutely shattered, and even a folk tale from Kali failed to cheer me up. The rose that I'd meant to give my name to, its entire biography and the course of its development had gone, leaving not a trace behind. At dinner I was so overcome with bitterness that I burst into tears and cried like a child. I laid my head in Kali's lap. God damn this life!

At least Kali's here. She's a very sensible woman, what's more. She's like a remontant rose: strong, nice and prickly, and disease-resistant. And just then she showed her true qualities. I said to her: 'Kali, you've turned out to be flowering for a second time.'

Kali's Rose—that would be a nice name for a rose. Astute people like her are a feature of the peasantry, and of the working class too. If they're born into another class, they become scientists, university lecturers, famous inventors and painters. The way she can tell a folk tale, you lose all sense of time, and suddenly it's evening. But these peasant elements philosophize away, and it's nothing but rubbish. Kali has no ambition. That's why she's still only a servant.

And unfortunately there's no way of liberating a woman like her. For all the intellectual revolutions in the world, women like her just want to be in servitude. When I told her that she ought to be liberated, she replied that she already was, liberated from the clutches of her husband, and if ever his foul mouth reached her here, his hands wouldn't, because he wasn't going to take her back to his house. She was her own boss now, she said. And if I gave you the sack, I asked, who would be your boss then? Then she would go and be a servant somewhere else.

'Everybody's a servant,' she said, and began to talk about God.

I shouted at her so loudly that she shut up. That's what the Church does. How can the common people be freed from it? It deprives you of the power of reason. At least the sects have been prohibited now, and all the Church schools and the pious monks and nuns. But everybody knows that the problem isn't just to do with the sects. Jehovah's Witnesses, Seventh Day Adventists, Baptists, Sabbatarians, there are so many you can't count them. And the Greek Catholics have ceased to exist, they say, so that the Romanian people may be united. United in faith, and everybody who is religious may be Orthodox. If that's the case, then the Hungarians can be united as well, and one or other of the churches be abolished, the Papist or the Protestant. Only the Hungarians aren't interested in being united at present. It's just not right that they should be united. Let them rather be split up into all the religions they please. They think that the more they're divided among themselves the better.

I've described how I was made to spend half a day in the Securitate cellar and write down everything as it was. Not only my life. In simple terms, in the words of an uneducated man who knows a thing or two, all the same, about the world of plants and biology. That I'd never been interested in anything, absolutely anything on earth, apart from roses. I swear to it, comrades. For a little while, antirrhinums and gladioli. Although I had a bit of an interest in the last two, I bought a piece of land solely so as to be able to attend to my roses and develop them better. I sold the antirrhinums to the Dutch gardener. But the gladioli brought me the good luck that I'd got red ones on St Anne's Day, and they were so much admired. As early as 1938, I was producing red gladioli with sixteen open buds. Nobody else had any, except the thief who stole them from my garden, as in fact happened.

And twice a week, the fair sex had interested me. Or even three times. So what! You don't put down such things as a woman twice a week. That was just a passing thought.

Then the question was: why had I sold my flowers to the king and Miklós Horthy? By way of business, so as to buy land, dig a well, be able to water. And to build a house and not live in a shack, like primitive man. Not so as to make a name. A rose grower doesn't consider his own name, passing it on and extending it. World renown isn't to be achieved with roses. Least of all by anyone that's not born to it. Or into a great gardening nation, like the French or the Dutch, or even the Germans. The truth is that the Germans are quite good all round. Just now I'm not sure I did the right thing in putting that down about the imperialists and the fascists, or whether I made things worse for myself.

But roses: how was I to tell these leather-coats? Roses, comrades, roses, I explained to them, roses aren't just flowers when you look around in the garden. How might I tell anyone who doesn't know, what The Rose means? There's no explaining roses to anyone that doesn't love them, any more than the soil to anyone that doesn't have it in their heart. But I didn't add that, I had no idea of the background of these two comrades, they might even have misinterpreted it. Thought that I was alluding to them in mentioning the soil.

Was I going to get more trouble from my hybrid tea?

Anyway, off they went, *gata*. We carried on with the autumn jobs. Peasants don't appreciate the beauty of the work of autumn. The autumn sowing can be explained, but there's something else, a beauty in work on the land that can't really. The peasant considers only what's there for him at once, the very same year. The Hóstáter understands and knows. I live among them and I know the type. The Hóstáter is actually a separate breed—he's not a peasant, nor a townsman either in the sense that he's alienated from the soil. Working on the soil in autumn is like caressing a girl. In time you'll want back what you're giving now. In autumn the soil has to be improved, and this is the time to plan the following year. And country people can't plan. They're like horses in blinkers. But they can see that it's no use taking onions to market in autumn, so they don't do it, whereas I do send flower bulbs. And how much better things grow that are planted in autumn. Onions don't sprout so well in spring but can be sold straight away. The point is that if a thing is nice people always want it quickly. They have no patience.

Now I'd got to preserve what I'd achieved so far, cover up the plants and protect them for winter. At this time I had to select the seed that I'd obtained from the new varieties. From roses, of course, but also from fruit, as I've been trying to learn about fruit. In autumn one has to use one's brain, one's imagination, as one has to discover and work out what people may want. The physical work will come in spring. That's when one can actually see the plants. So it's the same as with a girl.

At the end of September, I grafted an amazing number of new roses. Onto at least 800 briar stocks. I cut the last of the flowers. Kali took them to the little market, because she also goes there, not only to the big one. At other times I'd sold them not as cut flowers but as petals. Before the war the Catholics used to take them to church for the feast of the Virgin Mary, Our Lady of the Hungarians, which is in early October, I can't remember exactly when. They had to put them in different baskets by colours. The church paid handsomely. I knew that they used to spread them outside the church for decoration. They no longer buy them, they're not allowed to process round the church or to give any indication of religiosity in public. In my opinion that's correct. The purpose of the church is to keep the praying inside. I asked Kali to cook the petals for attar of roses. She was outraged, it was as if I'd said skin and cook the dog! I told her to add plenty of sugar and I would cook them myself. And I did. There was no way she would taste it. I told her to take it to the market and sell it. Nobody at all would buy it! And she would be ashamed. A Szék woman selling attar of roses. I told her to label it *dulceață de trandafir*. The Romanians like *dulceață*, it's a thickish liquid. She took some labels from me and put them on the bottles She wrote in capitals, she couldn't write any other way, only in capitals. She said she'd never learnt to write. Who would she have written to? We just kept back a couple of bottles in case visitors came, it was something special.

Previously I'd written up my books in winter, and every comment on the experience of the year. I didn't know whether to start on a new article. The current one wasn't returned although I asked for it. And I'd even asked a mediator, as I knew a policeman in the militia who I'd played football with as a boy. It wasn't returned. Once something's been taken it doesn't come back.

As autumn went on, I'd had no more trouble, the comrades hadn't come back. All that had come was a letter confirming that I'd made a statement and that the investigation had been terminated. Then another article about me and the garden appeared in *Falvak népe*. Well, thought I, this is like being rehabilitated after being in prison. If my name can appear in the paper there's nothing wrong. Werner must have laughed out loud when he saw the article, because I sent it to him. It was full of praise for my results. And it emphasized that I wasn't a trained biologist.

In October, Meilland sent their latest catalogue. I was actually amazed that it came through. I hadn't received any foreign papers since the war. It seemed that the international post was running again. It had been taken out of the big envelope and there was a Romanian stamp on it. It had been posted in Bucharest, and checked, I thought. It was a fat book with coloured pictures.

As I turned the pages, my heart was pained and my arm too felt numb. I was so envious that even my voice was choked. I had to control myself, and I closed it and put a big book on top of it so as not even to be able to see it. I thought to myself, that Frenchman can have all the enjoyment he likes! There was a buzzing in my ears, an internal throbbing. I'd have liked to go on turning the pages, reading, studying, because everybody knows that Meilland is the greatest rose grower in the world, but it was a month before I could bring myself to take it out. I only looked at it later when I was able to do so in a calmer frame of mind and when my envy had abated.

On the first pages, it showed the land on the French Riviera that Meilland had acquired, and how big the greenhouses were in which observation, experimentation and production took place. A family tree was traced, and beside each name, that of the most famous rose that that person had produced. Rose-growing was now in its third generation! The third! Beside the portraits was depicted the rose with which that person had won the most prizes in exhibitions and made the most money. There were separate pages on the history of the rose Peace; these I had difficulty in reading as my French isn't strong, and the dictionary wasn't much help. As it was about Meilland, however, I made a start but didn't get very far. I have no talent for languages. Nor much patience either! Then came his best roses that were offered to dealers. I could see the system: the more one bought, the cheaper they came. That's how to make oneself known in the world. The patent numbers of his new roses were also given! Because nowadays it's not only the names of flowers that are officially protected but new roses are registered in the same way as inventions. I looked to see which was the rose of the year for 1949. His hybrid Eden Rose, which was pink. And Gran'mère Jenny, yellow with red-tipped petals. There were both densely compact cutting roses. A franc and a half apiece. Anything that was patented was a dollar or more, no less could be asked. Werner too had said that, when he'd mentioned the way that patenting was practised in other countries. I hadn't believed him, he often exaggerated, and always talked as if he knew what would happen tomorrow. What were the dollar and the franc worth now? In Romania we had no conception of money. In any case, Meilland dictated the fashion in roses. After all, that was where fashion in clothes came from, the French. He always tried to find out what 'the market' wanted, as they say. Or they controlled the market. They, the biggest growers, Meilland, Tantau, Kordes, Poulsen. I couldn't make out which controlled which. He dealt wholesale, in millions. It was interesting that there were no new red roses. As I looked through the catalogue, the principal colour was no longer red. It looked as if this was the century of the hybrid yellow tea rose. So much for revolution.

After looking through the Meilland catalogue, in November I picked up neither my pen nor my knife, and not even a spade. I had no energy. I simply drifted about like a fly does in autumn before finally expiring. All my innards were in pain. I went out and watched a bit of football, as our new national team was playing; that always cheered me up and brought to my mind the good old days when I too had played quite seriously. Now, however, I knew nobody in the new team, nor the trainer nor the referee. They were all new. There were only two Hungarians in the team, not five or six as formerly, especially in Kolozsvár. I hung about, slept, spent time with friends, even went hunting with them—one day I bagged three pheasants. Didn't do a stroke of work. I didn't even go to that show-off Werner's name-day party. And wasn't he cross!

When I looked at the Meilland book at first I just felt envious; I had a tickling sensation in my throat that made me choke, and I coughed as if I needed to be put in a respirator. My whole body was wracked by envy. After that came bitterness—I was going out of my mind. I had no family that might found a rose-growing dynasty, nor the money to undertake great projects, because I was always having to look for something to sell. And furthermore, in Romania roses weren't as highly esteemed in those days as in the bourgeois half of the world, where there were people who gave their lovers 500 roses a day if they felt like it. Gentlemen, aristocrats, men of property. Meilland was one such, I thought. Working men didn't buy flowers. The churches did, I supposed. They were the best at taking people's money off them. A speck of dust might not be able to argue with a mountain, because I was a speck of dust compared to Meilland, and yet it was human nature to be simply green with envy at what someone else had. To want to compete, to be better, more famous. I didn't have that regard for money. Perhaps I would if I'd lived there. I hadn't the means of competing with the likes of Meilland, born into a French rose-growing family, imbibing with his mother's milk the notion of a fully compact rose, because in fact Madame Meilland too had been a gardener. I had the gardeners here to compare with, Werner and old Schultz, and above all whoever there was in Bucharest. In any case, Schultz was retired by then and no longer did any big jobs, because since the hail before the war ruined his garden, he'd produced no more flowers. I'd been lucky on that occasion, really and truly. The hail didn't touch the south of Kolozsvár, only the north.

But if you pay much attention to what others produce, your blood runs cold. Because if they do better, then you, you're green with envy, and if worse, then you're happy and flushed with Schadenfreude. You shouldn't worry about others. Nobody at all. You'll go mad if you're for ever considering others and comparing yourself to them.

But this cockchafer, this Kali, now, she was good luck, she didn't disturb my mind. So she was a good woman. The rest just drive me mad.

That Kali was a green rose-chafer, not a cockchafer. I wouldn't have swapped her for anything. For a start, she really was Kali Green, and secondly, there was such a lovely peasant aura about her. I don't know how to explain it. I saw her the other day coming up from the market as I was going a roundabout way home. I caught sight of her in the distance. I just watched her go past the cathedral, the Roman Catholic church, it's nearly as big as the Catholic church in the main square. She was going along primly, swinging her Szék skirt on her finely rounded rump. I liked the way it swung. She wasn't hurrying anywhere but stepping out nice and firmly. That's how I like to see a woman move. Not fussing, just knowing what she's doing. I actually got off my bicycle and went on watching her, as if she weren't my employee. Nobody paid any attention to her. That didn't matter, it's only 'pretty women' that get stared at in the street, the sort that wear such tight skirts or trousers that people lust after them, like a stray dog after a stick of salami. I once tried to talk to her about Meilland, but she didn't understand a word. She shrugged: 'Why worry about 'im, mister? 'E's a long way away, won't be comin' 'ere.'

Then in winter, when envy wasn't tickling my throat any more, I looked to see whether Meilland had produced anything like my rose. Fortunately, he hadn't. Perhaps it wasn't worthwhile by then. What had been a success ten years previously was now quite ordinary, didn't have the force of novelty. Perhaps so. There was no knowing.

Meilland had had an agent at the Bucharest exhibition even before the war. Old Schultz had met him and had given him my name. Goodness knows how he found out where I lived. It could be that by then I was known as a rose grower. If my name was known abroad, that was good. If I was in the public eye here in Romania, possibly not so good. On account of the garden. That was actually the time when the outer suburbs were being assessed, because big factories were being built all over the country. And there I was on the edge of town. Surely nobody was going to site a factory on top of a hill?

And then, bored as I was, I celebrated my birthday—something I never did. I brought it forward a bit so that it didn't clash with the public holiday. There was a woman in the house to take care of all the arrangements. If only Werner didn't have so much to say! I was fed up with him. The way that man was always gossiping! He knew everybody, was in with everybody, went around in Bucharest, was even allowed out to Hungary, had been to Szőreg and Tétény. He'd always got to be spreading scandal. Or name-dropping. How many he'd sold, what he'd exhibited, what he'd had sent. Who could prove it? Or that there was a gardener in Bucharest who'd been awarded a big state pension and wouldn't have to work again. Soon the state was going to hand out scholarships to Party members in support of the great powers that were to come from the common people. All the same, nobody'd yet heard of anything of the sort. And Werner said that Meilland's people were close to producing a blue rose. I asked him how he knew what Meilland was close to producing. He'd heard in Szőreg, when he was in Hungary. The Szőreg rosarium was still there in Szeged, and it had been nationalized. It was unfortunate that since the war there'd been no official connection between our rose growers and those there. We were like two foreign countries. At the birthday party, old Schultz kept looking at my apples and sniffing them; he very much liked the Batul and Pónyik varieties. He also tasted my Gypsy apples. He asked whether it might be possible to produce something better and bigger from them, something that would crop heavily. That would be a marvel! The flavour was divine, but the fruit were so small. I asked Kali to cut some apples up and offer them round. They would go very well with the fine Enyed wine.

But that Werner so annoyed me that I got up and joined the dancing instead. I couldn't bear to listen any longer, he talked nonstop, and half of it was rubbish. And he told such lies that it made my blood boil. One can become terribly bored with a man who's forever spreading rumours. He ran me down too, I think, when my back was turned. I watched him while he was eating, his mouth was full of apple and pastry yet he'd still be talking to whoever was sitting beside him. Obviously, there's something wrong with him, the way he talks so much. Doesn't his face get tired? Anyway, I went and had a nice dance to calm down, I was so cross. I got hold of Kali and danced with her. That woman knows how to dance. She felt just like pruning-shears in my arms. Then I went and sat with Popescu and the others—there were four of them from the old team, him, Filotti, Avram and Kovács. At least they weren't running people down. They were their usual selves. But they've put on some weight! They were tucking into the lardy cake.

But I could stand it no longer. It was night-time. Or perhaps, dawn was coming, but it was still dark. I went into Kali's room. She was getting undressed. I looked at her. She was quite another woman. I wouldn't have believed it. That Szék costume that she wears is lovely, lovely, but it makes a mockery of a woman. Every Szék woman looks the same wearing that. The individual doesn't show through.

I went into Kali's room and I've stayed there. That is, I've been going frequently.

In spring Emil Pop came to see me. We're talking about May now. We'd never met. He'd come at old Schultz's suggestion, and he'd given him a letter of introduction. Who am I, that he'd need a thing like that? And he let me know in advance that he was coming, towards the end of May, when flowering was beginning. This Emil Pop was assistant dean of the Faculty of Agriculture. Or of Biology, I'm not sure which. He was a university lecturer. I'd read something by him. *The Ageing and Death of Plants* was the title. At the time he was director of the Botanical Garden. Old Schultz said—he's got a former pupil on the university staff and he'd let it out—that Pop had been severely criticized from a scientific point of view for not using Soviet but Western literature and methods. So Pop had criticized himself and apologized at a meeting, and it had all been smoothed over. What, I wondered, could a clever university person like him want with me? He arrived in the morning and thanked me politely for giving him my time. He'd heard a lot about me from Rudolff Schultz—as he called old Rezső. He'd wanted to meet me for a long time. Well, really. I'm not a giraffe, that people ought to come and gawp at me. All the same I was touched. I took him inside to entertain him. Got Kali to make coffee, and bring some pastry and syrup and soda. He preferred tea, which I drank. He seemed a straightforward man. I'm afraid of those clever men. I'm dim, got no small talk.

He asked politely how I had come to be a rose grower. *Selekcionar* was the word he used. I didn't recognize it. I did my best to tell him. I speak good Romanian, but only the ordinary sort of language that I'd just picked up playing football. Nice earthy swear-words, that's what I'm best at. When had I started improving and crossbreeding, *ameliorarea și incrucișarea*? He was of peasant origin as well, he told me. Came from Alba county. Fehér county, to a Hungarian. We could speak Hungarian if I preferred, he said, because he'd been to a Hungarian primary school, a Roman Catholic school during the monarchy. He just didn't know Hungarian scientific terms. I didn't know them in Romanian. So I explained carefully this and that in Romanian, and what I didn't know I said in Hungarian because I didn't know the Latin either. I told him about my revered master, old Schultz, who'd taught me everything when I was starting out. And I told him about my flower breeding and the results I'd achieved. Then I brought out the albums, the books in which I'd drawn them all, because I hadn't had a camera, but that wouldn't have given the colours or the texture of the plants. Well, no more need be said, we got on like a house on fire. He gained my confidence by first asking about my background, and then he said he too was a son of the people.

He asked me which of my numerous inventions—*invencii* was his word—I had on the premises. All that I had were my antirrhinums—they also used the Hungarian name for them, *tátika*—my gladioli, and about ten of the rose varieties that I'd developed. I hadn't sold them, was still keeping an eye on them all. Had I got the famous one? he asked. Well, I hadn't got what I'd sold. How did he know about that, I wondered, was it from Schultz or from the Securitate? Perhaps he was from them, checking up on me. Or perhaps the Securitate had sent him to ask, as they didn't understand flowers. Let's go into the garden, I said. There aren't all that many open yet, but there are a few. It's been a warm May, the roses are developing beautifully. I've been trying to improve lily-of-the-valley and tulips, to get stronger stems, experimenting with colour in hyacinths, trying to get a yellow one as there isn't such a thing. Yellow and orange. Then we were out in the garden. I apologized for having no snowdrops to show him, but I'd been planting them for the last five years, trying to make them stronger and bigger.

Where was I to begin? I showed him everything I had. He asked all sorts of questions. What varieties was I currently working on, what had I crossed, which were in what year, how much longer would I persevere until I achieved the desired colour, perfume, disease-resistance, showiness and leaf colour?

What mattered most to me was *light*, I explained. But I couldn't just tell him *lumina* because that didn't give my full meaning, I couldn't find the right Romanian word. Would it be *lux*? Because that was the Latin word, I remembered, and there was a variety of rose about which old Schultz had used it. Because the *light* that I meant was contained in the plant, it was its power and mirrored that of the sun. What description, what explanation could one give of *light*?

'*Caut lux*, I try to achieve light,' I said.

'*Lux?*' he queried. He didn't understand the word.

'No,' I laughed, 'not *luxus*, nothing like that!'

He also looked at the edge of the garden, where I had a row of dog roses along the holly hedge and kept a bed of young dog rose stocks. What were those, he asked. That was my hotbed, I replied, I started from there actually. That was where I started grafts off. They were strong and pure. I always keep dog roses, but I was anxious about their being pollinated by something else in the garden. I had to transfer them to the greenhouse.

Could a graft take even when it's in full bloom, in the height of summer? It could, I said, but I'd had the best results in early June. at the first flowering. By then we were deep in conversation, but I heard Kali asking whether I'd like my lunch. The guest as well, there was a place for him. She'd laid up at the back of the house. That Kali knew her stuff, she'd laid a nice table. There was a cloth, which we didn't usually have. Emil Pop was very reluctant, but in the end he accepted. It was a proper lunch, quite filling, but all the same suitable for a guest: *lucskoskáposzta* with plenty of sour cream. I asked Pop what he would have called it, and it turned out that the Romanian name was the same; it was followed by Kali's túró doughnuts. And rose jam to go with them! Enjoy! The lecturer joked that we were eating our children. He was referring to an ancient myth in which some god had eaten up his children.

Then he asked me what trees I had there behind the house. I said that I'd been experimenting with local varieties of apple, studying their resistance to disease. I'd infected them with pests. I'd found cold hillsides in the Bükk and elsewhere, and planted seedlings with no protection, in the open air. Because, of course, the land wasn't mine. It belonged to nobody, was common land. Pop remarked that it no longer belonged to nobody, everything belonged to the state. I told him how I'd studied the effect of cold on trees and their acclimatization. I'd planted about fifty, apples and pears. I'd tried to discover what the trees could tolerate, and to breed from the stronger ones. But I didn't yet know much about fruit trees—which he didn't believe.

He invited me warmly to call on him at the Botanical Garden. I'd never been there. I was to phone when I wanted to go, and he'd give me a ticket, otherwise I'd have to pay. How was I to phone, I wondered. He'd show me round the garden. Although it was state property it was effectively his. And he like to have my advice.

Pop came to see me several times more that summer. He used the familiar *te* to me, a great honour. He was a university lecturer, for one thing, and twenty years my senior. He often came for lunch or dinner. Then he didn't come for a month, as he'd gone abroad. One day he told me that he'd brought me something, nothing special, that he hoped I'd accept. A little coloured, cylindrical bag, sticky-taped. On the end was printed the word *Peace*.

It was so sudden that it took my breath away as if it had been cut off. Oh goodness, I almost died of surprise. I had Peace in my hand. It took several seconds for me to relax. I hoped I wasn't going to have a heart attack. A stock of Peace. Pull yourself together, Vilmos.

'It's the most famous rose in the world.' Who wouldn't know that? But I'd never seen one before. Would I ever?

But that's what I'm like. Envy overcame my pleasure. Envy fit to choke me. 'There are eight million of them.' It said that in French on it, because they were just sold in garden shops, it said. I can't speak French, but eight million I could understand. When I read a thing like that I felt unwell. My head started to buzz. When was I, here in the Békás, going to produce a single patented rose, buy a fifteen-year licence for it, like Meilland, and sell even a couple of thousand?

I thanked Emil Pop. He said that he didn't know how it would shoot. He'd ordered it from abroad for the Botanical Garden, but it had been kept on the train for almost two months while it went through Customs, and everything was scrutinized root and branch. Especially root. I was amazed how well Pop spoke Hungarian. And he had to account for everything on paper. He'd been able to bring one, the rest belonged to the Botanical Garden, there'd been a dozen altogether. He'd report it lost, the thieving French had sent one short of what was on the invoice. He'd had to pay in foreign currency. An astronomical amount. If he hadn't had high-level connections he wouldn't even have been able to buy them for the Garden. But it might be that it wouldn't even shoot, it had been held so long in Customs.

Emil Pop was always saying that I was too modest, although what I had done was tremendous, my research and crossbreeding, all by myself on the edge of town. Schultz too said, because he was my real father, that my modesty would hold me back from being the greatest in Romania today. I hadn't even a name card, nor a garden, I didn't enter competitions, held no state honour, didn't teach, wasn't a trade union member, in fact I didn't really know whether there was a trade union. I didn't socialize so as to be known, because, you know, anybody that wants to be somebody has to keep in with the big names. I was hiding my professional ability, said old Schultz. Well, my father used to preach at me as well—a really great gardener would have been living in a villa by this time and hunting with greyhounds. But there was I, still sitting on the edge of town in my little dump. This is no little dump, I said, there are eight thousand bricks in it! And there've been articles in the papers about the wizard of the Békás, saying what a modest element of the people I am, and that I live incognito.

What my anonymity had cost me, nobody knew.

If anyone could have seen my innards, how soot-black they were when I thought about that Peace. Envy was really gnawing at me.

Emil Pop said that he hoped that I would graft it and make more. Best of luck!

'Is that allowed?' I asked. 'Grafting, I mean.'

'Well, why not?' he replied. 'There'll be no Frenchmen coming this way to see what we're doing.'

'If it's patented, it's not permitted. That would be theft,' I told him.

'Quite so.'

We laughed.

Ever since I'd heard of Peace—*Pace* in Romanian—I'd wanted to see a two-year-old bush, I told him. Werner had told me two years ago that he'd give me one, but he hadn't any. He was always lying and exaggerating, that was his style.

That evening I took the Peace indoors and put it on my green-baized table, where I kept everything that was dear to me. We ate dinner in silence. We worked in the evening, as there was a lot to be done at that time. We were dealing with the first flowering and had to watch how it turned out. Next came selection. I said 'we', because Kali did everything that I told her. Fortunately she did nothing of her own volition, just the woman's work, cooking, washing, things like that. I gave her paper to cut up, and from that we made little caps for the flowers after they'd been cross-pollinated. Some people had that done by a printer, but I'm not such a gentleman, I have to glue them by hand. I used to do it in the old days, now she did the gluing.

Kali said she'd tell a folk tale. Go on, my dear, said I, let's hear it, because I enjoyed her tales. But I couldn't pay attention, that Peace was all I could think of. She told me about the envious woman who had to give all she possessed to the devil because she envied everybody the food they ate, Makes me look good, Kali. Could she read me now, if she was telling a tale about envy? Or perhaps it was just by chance that she'd said that. The envious woman was rich, but she envied the poor woman's chicken that laid three eggs a day. The devil deceived her and took everything off her. So then she was poor as well, like the other one. But Kali told the tale cleverly, gave it a twist, varied her voice, made the one character sound one way, the other another, gave the devil a deep voice, played on my enjoyment. She was like a great actress. But damn that envy, because he'd got everything. but even so more was needed. It was a real people's bourgeois tale. After all, the common people had always been socialist, and the story raised up the poor and despised the rich.

Since then I've been visiting Kali all the time.

All the same, I was curious about what this Peace could do. What had made it the most famous rose in the world? That evening I was going to moisten it; I cut off the bag, and was about to wrap the root in a wet cloth before planting it. I was going to try, although I didn't think it would be possible to plant a stock in July. I looked at it, and the root hadn't even been put in soil, it hadn't dried out, but it had been held in the Customs for two months. It was in sawdust or something. Something yellow. I'd have to analyse it. Glory be! Is soil no good to you now? Has something been discovered to take its place? We'll soon have to plant roses in chemicals, not soil. The root was covered in wax, the ends of the branches were cut back and waxed. There were a couple of little buds on it, but they were puny. I'd heard about this waxing. It was as if the plant were asleep, had been put to sleep. But now it had got to be brought round. I'd never heard of this being done in Romania. Of course, we didn't have to send stocks thousands of miles by train. Or by ship, come to that! Because that happened as well in those days. They were sent all over the world. And since air transport had become commoner, roses could be sent from hot climates as well. So I was finished. Where the sun shone all the time, roses could be produced in January.

I considered how long I could hold Peace back. Should I wait for autumn or plant it at once? Who'd ever heard of planting a stock in summer? The risk was great. But if it was strong it would work. And after all, the poor thing had been made to travel, go through Customs, and was too late for the spring planting. In fact, autumn would be better. I thought I'd ask the water diviner, because not only could he see water in the ground but he could also dig a well and knew about the weather. I asked him when it would be a bit cooler for us, so as not to do it during the drought of the 'dog days'. Or should I plant it in the shade and bring it into the sun in spring? Would it stand it? I just cogitated for five days, enquiring, waiting for the right idea to come of its own accord. For the time being I put the stock back into the mixture of sawdust and sand, because I felt that that was where it had been. I thought that there must be some artificial nutrient in it, in which case it could survive. Then along came a heavy thunderstorm and it became a bit cooler. So I watered it and planted it.

And so, I know of nothing at all that is finer than waiting for something. Time just went by as I waited. Three strong little branches. Then nothing for a month. Every day nothing but hope. And then—oh goodness! That delicate, pale bud sprang into life. Right at the root, by the part that had been watered. A real dark red. And then another. That was dark red as well. I looked at it every day. I thought I'd keep a record of it day by day, go back to the hotbed again and again as I'd done when I was starting to grow roses. It had been a long time since I'd had a bare root and I'd got something new. Since I hadn't been getting anything new—I was producing every rose myself—exchange with abroad had ceased completely.

While they were closed up tight those tiny leaves were red. I had to look up in the specification what colour they would be. Then one day, all of a sudden, they began to turn green. And what a green! I'd never had such a lovely summer. I watched the rose, wrote down everything that I could say about it. By autumn it had become a little bush, no flowers were to be seen that year. It was certainly holding out on me. Then I covered it up well for the winter and in spring began observing it again. It was like a girl. The one that blooms early grows old quickly. The one that retains her secret can drive you mad.

When the first vigorous leaves appeared on Peace and it was becoming a little bush I was beside myself, all tense, and that night I called on Kali three times. When I asked the third time she turned her back on me. All the same, she wasn't like that. She was worried about her breasts. Nature hasn't given the same desire to women as to men, because women are quickly satisfied. That flower was driving me quite mad.

When Emil Pop came to see me a lot we got on so well that I had no secrets from him, and took him to see the seedling house. You couldn't see it from outside because I'd hidden it away. From the house it looked as if there was a stable. But behind that was a low, glass-roofed seedling house, in which were my most interesting plants. I used to start filling it from the end of February. If I could have heated it I'd have kept it open all year round. I'd tried to keep it for winter, covered the glass with matting like the Hóstát people do their greenhouses, I even double-glazed it, but it didn't work, everything froze. I could achieve flowering in there as early as the start of May. I could produce seasons as if we were in the south.

Pop was simply amazed. He said I was a whole research station all by myself.

Then one day, university lecturer and director as he was, he asked why I didn't go into state employment. With the tremendous amount that I knew, said he, I ought to put my knowledge to the service of the socialist state. I felt my face blaze, he had to be joking. One should be at the service of advancement, not keep everything to oneself like in the old days. But, I said, how could I work for the state? Where was there a place for me? And what was I to do there? Was I to leave all this fine work here, my life's work? No, he said, I might be able to take my research straight over. Then I said, whatever he knew about me, I was ashamed. Because I had no qualifications, I'd only done six years in school. I'd taught myself, and all that I knew was from experience. These days what counted was knowledge, he replied, not certificates. So that was what I ought to take along! To the university, for example, or a research institute. I said, you can't just walk into the university and announce that you know ever so much and want to be a lecturer.

'The professor will know how to arrange it, if somebody's needed, they're invited. And you need somebody to know you. So you'll see, my dear Vilmos,' was his answer.

I told him that it was out of the question. I'd done six years of school, hadn't been allowed to stay on, had to go as an apprentice. That didn't matter these days, I should be quite clear. There was one lecturer, said Emil, a working-class writer, in the Hungarian university, who had only done two years of school! He hadn't studied, but he'd been a great activist. I know, said Emil, what working people were allowed to study at universities. I told him modestly that I didn't know the sort of things that were needed at university, scientific things, theoretical stuff. I didn't know anything about the structure of cells, couldn't describe hybridization in chemical terms at all, I just produced hybrids. I had no theoretical knowledge.

Then he said that I wouldn't be allowed to stay for ever here in my garden all by myself. Firstly, I must share the enormous knowledge that I possessed. It was my duty. Secondly, there was no great future in such selfishness. That was *proprietate individuala*. Private property was at an end. Not just as concerned belongings, but nowadays people didn't act for themselves but for the common good. I should read the papers. It was true, there was nothing about individual affairs, just what people could create together, a village or a team. Nowadays what mattered was not the person but the whole *personalitate*, what I'd been able to discover for myself here in my garden. That sort of thing was egoism. In the old days, the gentry had kept everything for themselves. I should just look at the state now. Hospitals were free of charge, and anybody that went into communal ownership, a collective, got a pension, school was free, child care was free in factories, university was free. Had it been like that in the old days? Of course not. If it had been, you would have studied as well. Look here, Vilmos. An equitable world is coming, we've just got to do something for the purpose.

How much land did I own, he asked quietly. Because there were laws. Two hectares and a bit, I replied, all my garden.

'So, intensive cultivation will work wonders,' said Emil.

'That's the case now, it's intensive. Dawn to dusk.'

That wasn't what he meant, he said.

I knew what he meant, I'd read about it in books. Extensive and intensive. The Hóstát people were intensive, just didn't know that was what it was called. Not much land but it was much fertilized, and there was rotation, when one thing was harvested something else was planted, several times a season. A lot of produce, a lot of work, and a lot of irrigation too. And the peasants were extensive—a lot of poor soil, as far as the eye could see. Left water to nature, didn't irrigate, and all just plundered the soil.

What mattered was not how much land you had, but the way you worked it, how much you did to improve it. Manure, that was the thing.

'And chemical fertilizer,' Emil added. 'That's the revolution these days. Artificial nitrogen. There's granulated chemical fertilizer too nowadays.'

Then I replied:

'*Domnu professor*, I believe in horse manure. Horse and cow. Organic manure. That's what I trust. *Faecal* in Romanian, or something like that, I think.'

Oh, we had a good laugh.

'It makes a difference, doesn't it, Vilmos, whether you bring nitrogen in a bag in your pocket, like ours, or whether you have it carted in heavy loads from farms. Because what's in a bag is nitrogen, and what's on a cart is *balega*.'

Balega is Romanian for shit. I knew that.

'So, call it two and three quarter hectares, it makes no difference. Toiling by yourself. Individual work. You need to do big things, think big these days like never before. The whole of Romania's one huge garden, you mustn't think in terms of three hectares. You belong in the university, Comrade Décsi. You'll be famous.'

My summer was full of this. I was so on edge I could hardly do my work. Being famous. I was with Kali. At least I wasn't on my own.

By now this Kali'd been with me for almost a year. At first she was like a servant, and now she kept telling me not to pay her. I understood. If she wouldn't take money from me she was thinking of herself as a wife. You can always tell if you've got somebody there close to you. Even if she'd gone to the market the warm feeling was still there. She was more than a dog. And fortunately, less than a wife! Above all, you've got more than one parent. She was a kind of human exhalation, or rather photosynthesis. She gave off warmth, and it was better for me than keeping a lover all the time. Only she cawed a lot. Then I sent her away, I couldn't stand listening to her.

Now I've only got Kali, because I began to drop Mrs M. in spring. I'd been with her for three years. One of those had been the flare-up, the second the fire. By the third it was just like a smouldering bonfire, taking a long time to die down. The third year smelt like that too. In the first year, however, we'd spoken about divorce, about her leaving her doctor husband. She was such a passionate woman, she could never get enough. Never tired of it. The first time she came was to visit the garden. When her husband gave a dinner at their place and had invited his hunting friends, as he'd bagged that fat deer. He gave a dinner like that every year. He roasted the deer whole, a demijohn of his wine went with it, and there were about thirty of us guests. She asked me in the kitchen when I went out for salad whether I was the famous gardener. Famous? thought I, What am I famous for? Those big roses. She adored flowers. Yearned for them. That's what she said. Yearned. Well, later I found out what she yearned for. She was trying to get something done about her garden at the time. When could she come, she asked. I told her, just them I'd got nothing to show her, only seedlings and the stocks covered up for winter. What sort of seedlings, she asked. The kind that would later become stocks. Because it was February, wasn't it, the master of the house was actually wearing a mask, dressed as a Turk, and she was wearing big feathers, because it was Carnival time. She wanted to plant all sorts of things and pointed to the garden, because we were in a villa on Erzsébet út. Would I help? I asked which way her garden faced. She didn't know, would ask, but it was nice and shady. That's not good for flowers, I said. So she'd have the trees cut down. Could she come and see my garden, where was it, because she wanted to learn. I said she could come any time. Wouldn't she be bothering my family? Not at all, I said. Wednesday? She asked for my address, she'd come by taxi. She certainly did, and in the morning, though she'd promised the afternoon. I took her straight to the seedling house, I hadn't even got anything together for her, I thought I'd give her twenty or thirty stocks and of course wouldn't ask for money. I explained which was which, how big they'd be, what colour. She knew no more than anybody else. She'd like some yellow ones and some red, knew no more about them. She leaned so close over my shoulder that I couldn't help swallowing. The way I felt her breath on my neck. Then we were swallowing one another's tongues. I caught the smell of a door opening in her.

What a woman! Her underwear was all silk. Such was her skin that I felt I should put on gloves for fear of my rough hands doing harm. Then I was to go to her house and look at her garden and say what should be planted where. I was afraid that I'd run into her husband and feel like a thief with him there.

After that we settled into a routine. Wednesdays and Fridays were her days. At home she said that she was taking piano lessons. She'd found that in a book as a means of deceiving her husband. But the way she played, she could have been giving the lessons. We could never have enough of each other. She always had to leave me half-satisfied. Sometimes during the two hours that she was there, I wanted to have her as many as three times. She was always ready, no mistake about that. Her flower was always open. Her husband couldn't have paid her much attention. She would say things to me like 'You're my peasant husband, my dear little peasant, my strong peasant lad.' So there, Ottó Vilmos Décsi, you're a peasant. A peasant, with a name like that. I told her, not even one of my grandfathers had been peasants, I'd known them and I didn't remember that. I'd only known one of my grandfathers, in fact, the other had gone to the war, he'd been a craftsman. A proud craftsman, a painter and decorator, and the other was a cobbler, because his father had been one as well. Neither had worked on the land. It would have been a disgrace in an artisan family to till the soil. I don't do that, I told her. What do you do then? and she laughed so loud that my ears hurt. To a bourgeois element like Mrs M., a *mic burghez* as they call them these days, there was no difference. What was down there beneath her was all one class.

In spring she wanted me to go round and plant her garden. I told her that in the first place, spring wasn't the time to plant flowers, autumn was best. But she had to have it done now! Couldn't wait until autumn. Had to have a garden made now! And secondly, I had so much work that I couldn't do hers. She should call on a gardener, it wasn't such a big job. Pay him double the going rate. But I had to go, her husband was often out operating in the morning. She carried on asking until I went down and planted about forty rose stocks for her. When I asked in July how my roses were getting on, she said she'd go and look and let me know. She pouted like a child that was offended at being caught out. She'd just had to have those roses.

Then when my roses began to open she was always asking to take some. Some I gave her, some I didn't. I used to say they were experimental, I couldn't give her them. They were the most beautiful, of course, she wasn't blind, she could see that. Then she would start pleading, like a child. But on that one point I dug my heels in. After that she didn't come for a week, and then she came in tears, I didn't love her at all if I wouldn't give her my most beautiful roses. Who was I keeping them for? We cried, we made love. Then she talked about leaving her husband, he didn't love her, didn't care about her, she had to keep asking him for money. Because I think he was tighter with money than I was with flowers. But she'd got those two little girls. Twins. What was she to do about them? I'd seen them a couple of times. The first time when I'd been at their place for the hunting party, they'd been introduced; they were like two little angels, in identical frilly white dresses. Then when I went round to do the garden I'd seen them again. On that occasion her husband happened to come home from the hospital and was surprised to find me working there. He asked whether his wife hadn't seduced me into making her a garden. I didn't know what to say. Then he slapped me on the back and asked me to stay for tea. I had no idea what he thought. She just shrugged it all off.

Then when Kali came along Mrs M. began to twitter—why didn't I get a charwoman, who'd come in once a week? It was as if she was my mother, began to tell me how to do everything. These women always knew all about doing housework, but they wanted to give me orders. I always sent Kali out of the room when she started. She'd go on about my always being untidy, I should clear up the garden, put it in order, throw out all the rubbish, get everything together. It was terrible, the way she began to tell me what to do.

But at that time I didn't have that relationship with her, I didn't need her like that. And she was middle class, lived in another world. Class was always coming between us. All the same, even love can't put it into Esperanto, so to speak, that all class distinction must be overcome.

Well, I'd got bored. Every woman bored me. Everyone else as well. And most of all myself.

When Emil Pop the lecturer brought me that Peace stock I asked Mrs M. to be so kind and read me what it said on the wrapper, because she spoke French like a native. She'd even read books. Other languages as well. Just then she was learning Russian. She kept putting it off, didn't feel like it, she was tired, would rather have some tea. Well, then I was annoyed, I had to know there and then, I said, it was very important. I could say my life depended on it, and if I didn't find out I would die. I wasn't asking her to translate a book for me, just what it said on the wrapper. I got so worked up that I started lecturing her about Peace. It was the most famous rose in the world, I'd never had the chance to see one, that rose was going to change the world, it would bring peace, because I already knew what the name meant. From then on mankind would be taking a new road.

Then in the end, she sat up a bit and began to read. Slow down, I said, I want to write it down, I'll get my notebook. She read in such a bored tone, but she'd always boasted that she didn't have to look up anything in the dictionary. If there was something she didn't fully understand, she added, 'That doesn't make sense, but that's what it says.' But what sense it did make! What did it mean, father and mother? She asked with such a bossy look, had I finished, could she go on. When she'd finished translating she dropped the empty wrapper on the floor. Now are you happy? she asked, and it sounded as if she was mocking me. Then she lay back exhausted, looked at the ceiling, and said that my servant didn't clean very well, she could see a cobweb in the corner. As I looked on in surprise at her dropping the wrapper and staring at the ceiling, her one breast was free of the bedclothes, all her clothes lay tossed onto the armchair, and she was just picking at her nails, and I was so, so tired of her. Her nails were always dirty, that was why she painted them. Only someone that washes, washes clothes, uses water, only they have nice clean nails. She painted over the dirt. She exuded boredom. I got up from the table and left the room. I'd never felt like that about a woman. My head was aching, my ears were ringing, there was a numbness in my arms. I pulled on my trousers and went out into the garden, shirtless and barefoot.

To hell with her. That woman could clear off. Then I put on an old coat, went out of the gate with a spade and my goat-skin gloves, carrying on my back the basket that I used for collecting plants. I took the dog as well. I don't know what she did then. I just kept going straight ahead. I dug up about eight biggish wild rose stocks on the far side of the hill, on the edge of the forest below the Felek. Of course, I'd already got some, but they always came in useful. One gave my neck a good scratch when I lifted the basket onto my shoulder. Never mind, you had it coming, Vilmos. By the time I got home it was dark.

After that she wrote me a letter. I'd humiliated her, plundered her, discarded her. Never mind. We'd gone on for long enough. Fortunately, she didn't come again. We'd have been bored to death in each other's company. I mean, sometimes I worked like a maniac, even kept the light on at night, writing, making notes of everything, sometimes my mind was a blank. She'd driven me out of my mind. Then, by the second year, it had begun to calm down. We were friends and lovers, so to speak. Then the third year, it had become so embarrassing. She no longer talked about leaving her husband because she knew that she wouldn't. But she was always asking me to get her things here, a rocking chair in the house, a garden chair for her to sit on when she came, and once she gave me a kind of silk apron, all tassels. It made me look like a Persian shah at Carnival.

All the same, perhaps I ran out to collect plants on the hill when we finally finished with each other, rather because I'd finally realized how that 'Peace' had come about. It was the most beautiful, most mighty rose in the world. Because a story like that, one so inexplicable, was a pure fairy tale. You couldn't expect to believe it, perhaps it had been made up as an advertisement and written up so as to improve sales.

But when Mrs M. was reading it out in her grey, boring voice it seemed I could scarcely hear her, I just wrote in my book so as to remember. Perhaps that was why I had to run out to the edge of the forest for a few wild rose stocks. I was in despair.

She'd driven me mad. And not with love.

Previously she'd merely pottered around, then came into the garden, was fascinated by the flowers, and then asked for this and ordered that. And in the end nothing was any good. Flowers, those are good, only those. But she'd announced by then that she deeply loathed gladioli. They were middle class. To her, gladioli were bourgeois. That's exactly what she said! Mrs M. considered herself an element of the people, because her father had worked on the railway, but she was no more 'people' than 'Bonjour, papa'. She knew 'the people' by hearsay. Then what a shambles I had, tools and chemicals and all that around the house. A shambles! I should destroy those huts and sheds and make a proper granary. A granary! At least she didn't want a stable. Or a barn. Well, let's say a nice barn like the one I saw in Méra, I'd like that. A nice big one. Big enough to hold a dance in. Only roses didn't need a barn, did they? But Mrs M. knew it all, she was a great biologist, a Mrs Michurin. She liked a nice orderly garden where there wasn't so much coming and going all the time. I said, this isn't a French garden. Here we're conducting experiments. She didn't understand. All she could see was something different. That it was male and untidy. But she wouldn't do any tidying up! She wouldn't pick up a tool, wash the chemicals out of a hose. No, she criticized.

And she wanted me to wash. It was all she thought of. Wanted me to wash all the time. Didn't expect me to take a foam bath every day, did she?

What could be the point of all that washing? I didn't get it. Was I filthy, that I needed to bathe so much? And underwear all the time, it had to be like this and that, and stockings. I didn't go about in stockings all the time. She didn't understand. I was a working man, my clothes got soiled, and my hands were always dirty and scratched. Sometimes bloodied. If I went anywhere, I didn't have to scrub with a nailbrush, because the others there wouldn't be gentlemen with shiny nails either! According to her, I was a biologist, there were articles about me in the papers, books would preserve my achievements. A famous man. But, I told her, I'd achieved things wearing soiled clothes. I hadn't developed a single rose sitting at a desk

Kali did the washing in the tub once a week as well. And I couldn't bear to watch the way she'd wash herself on a Saturday evening. She always chased me out of the kitchen, but I always went in if I was home. The way she scrubbed her soles and heels, it hurt just to see it. She really polished herself up. But on weekdays she didn't bother, went about barefoot even in October. And then face-cloths and foot-cloths were separate. Once I wiped my hands on a foot-cloth of her's, and she shouted out, 'Boss, put that down at once, it's a foot-cloth!'

Why, I asked, is it infections? To her it was a commandment that she should be clean for Sunday. Whether she went to church or not, I didn't stop her, but I'd told her my views on the subject. Even so she had a good wash on Saturday. When she was smartened up like that she wouldn't let me near her. She'd explain this way and that and push me off her. She'd had a good wash, now she wanted to feel clean. Why, I asked? Was I going to make you dirty?

'Everything's dirty if it's to do with men.'

I'd better not dirty her with myself, then. And she laughed, didn't she just!

I won't bring you any dirt, I said, If you like I can wash as well. No, she said, no need for you to wash, I just mustn't go to her. Not on the Lord's Day, she said. You mean Sunday, I asked, just for fun. The Lord created men all dirty, let me give her at least one day when she could lie in bed clean. But the more she rejected me, the more I wanted to go to her. In particular, I hadn't been dropping in at the Darvas on a Saturday, because the old crowd were starting to meet again, but that restaurant was really going downhill by that time. Nor did I drink a lot, but I liked a drop of Enyed wine and a chat when I got home. A chat yes, anything else no, said Kali very sternly. Never mind what suits you, what do I keep you for, I said to her. Not so as to come on top of me when the urge takes you! I might be something in the larder! That's what she said, and she shut the door to the kitchen and didn't let me in!

'Calm down, sir, take a drop of bromide like the soldiers do! You've got all them chemicals, it'll only take a spoonful of bromide for you to relax. If you 'aven't got any, I'll ask my brother-in-law for some, 'e's a warden at Szamosújvár prison, 'e's always getting bromide there an' bringing it to Szék an' sellin' it.'

'Who does he sell it to then, Kali?' I asked, because I didn't believe that about the prison warder.

'Well, to them poor women whose 'usbands won't leave 'em alone. The amount 'e sells! You wouldn't believe it, mister, 'e's made so much out of it that 'e means to buy new furniture for their livin' room, from the furniture factory in Vásárhely. Modern furniture, veneered.'

By then I was really stirred up, so I asked her whether she really thought that every woman avoided it like she did.

'No,' she said, ''cos some are 'ores an' they like it. I know one like that in Szék.'

But she also knew a woman in Szék that was happy with her husband! Every three months, her brother-in-law brought her bromide, she was a regular customer of his, and she gave her husband a good dose, after which the rotter didn't want to do it. Just occasionally that woman would miss a week or two, and then she'd give in to him. But that was only so that he wouldn't suspect anything. And he was ashamed to go to the doctor and ask what was wrong with him. They got on ever so nicely, nothing disturbed their tender affection.

By this time we were in a heated argument, Kali in the door to her kitchen in her slip, and me in a good mood because I was looking at her nice big bristols, and she wouldn't let me hold her, just hold her, it wasn't right. Well, all the same she was pleased that I was so interested. I told her to send for that bromide, I didn't care, I just didn't want to wake up all by myself.

'What are you, then, mister? A child? Frightened of the dark, need the light on?' she asked.

'And what have you got that nobody else has, Kali? Look here. I promise you, here in this holy place, that I'll take you dancing within a fortnight. Do you hear? Because I know that dancing will put you in the mood. The way I'll whirl you round, your heart will really pound. Only give me a little advance just for now.'

On and on, until I simply gave up. And Saturdays got harder and harder. I said to her, look here, Kali, you've become a right Saturday Jew, they're forbidden to do anything on Saturdays. I didn't ask whether she enjoyed it or not.

One evening I explained to her about Peace, and I wanted to tell her about how a flower had put an end to warfare. The most beautiful rose will come from this stock, I said. To which she said that every rose is beautiful. Even the one that's wilted, I asked. Even the one with black spot? Because there's one that's spoiled by black spot. Even the one that wilts when it's put in a vase? That as well, she answered. Or the one that I strip of petals so as to work with it? Because she'd been so upset about that. She said, certainly, that as well, because they've all been of service to the boss. Drop the boss once and for all, I told her. She served me because I was her boss. I should realize that every rose only declared the praise of the boss, and she laughed, and she was only answering back to tease me. She was a real provocateur. Then I told her, don't be silly, Kali. Always that feudal way of thinking! If you give me any more, God, your career in the Békás is over.

All the same, I can't understand the French doing it.

I noted down the day when Peace began to open. I'd never seen anything like it. Great rejoicing in the Békás. Kali was circling like an eagle there all the time, watching it open. The bush was no more than forty centimetres high, if that. Don't ask what its habitus was like, I couldn't even bring myself to draw it.

I thought I'd wait another couple of days and enjoy seeing it. Should I invite old Schultz? He'd be ever so pleased. Or show it to Werner? He'd be so jealous he'd pass out, and he'd say he'd already got ten of the sort open. I'd have to show it to Emil if he came, after all it had come from him. From him and the Romanian state, because that had brought it to me.

But instead, I preferred there to be nobody at the great celebration. Not even Kali. I said to her: 'Look here, Kali, if I see you going anywhere near this bush I'll give you a good hiding. Understand? You're not even to look at it.'

Well, she was startled, quite offended as well. That Kali's always taking offence. That was her biggest problem. I once asked her:

'So what is it that Szék women are best at?'

'What, then?'

'Taking offence, of course.'

What did Kali say when she finished that folk tale? She ended with 'So great was the love between the prince and Goldilocks, words can't describe it.' And because words couldn't describe it, she said no more. That was the end of her tale about Goldilocks. Peace was like that as well. Words couldn't describe it. The most famous rose in the world. What was it derived from?

And so I sat beside it for seven days. Seven glorious days. And that was still the first flowering. I sat there with my notebook, observed and noted. After that I was able to write ten full pages, because when I looked at the flowers I did find the words.

I heard nothing from Emil Pop. It was September. Would the university be opening?

One day I heard Kali's voice in the market; I didn't mean to spy on her like I usually did, not at all, so as not to feel guilty afterwards. I went over to see what was on sale. My early gladioli that had been stolen, for example, because down our way, what happened was that somebody would jump in, uproot them, they'd be gone, and in future somebody else would be selling them. And to see what was in fashion at the time, colours, bunches, how they were put together. Rucska the florist knew how. The Túróses did good business, even the little girl was selling. Sometimes in a bunch, sometimes as single stems, the way they sold them changed all the time. I couldn't see the Buci garden sellers or the Réz brothers, but I'd heard they'd closed as florists. Banga wasn't there either. Out of interest I looked at the Hóstát people's new plants, because they certainly replanted everything even in June, lettuce, late tomatoes, kohlrabi. I like plant varieties, so I looked around them. I could hear Kali shouting her head off.

'Here you are, perfumed roses! Look, red perfumed roses, only twelve lei a stem. Here they are, perfumed roses, the most beautiful flowers from the Békás garden, come along! Vilmos Décsi's flowers. Take a sniff, no other roses have such perfume!'

I slipped out at the back to Hosszú utca so that nobody should see me.

When Her Grace came home and very proudly displayed her empty hands, because she'd sold everything like lightning, I nearly struck her. But I don't hit women.

'Look here, don't you feel the slightest shame?'

She was taken aback, didn't understand at all.

'The way you shout in the market, you're like the worst red-necked cockerel, do you want to give me a bad name? Look, everybody in town knows who I am, what do you think you're doing?'

'Well, if you weren't so well known in town, mister, I wouldn't shout,' she snorted angrily. She slapped the cash down on the table crossly and wouldn't take her share.

Then I forbade her from going ever again and lowering my reputation in that fashion. She went into the kitchen and slammed the door. That evening I ate her bean stew without a word, didn't even say it was good. But it was. I was fed up with it, that was all.

Because she was so keen on it that we had to adore bean stew three or four times a week—green beans, kidney beans, dried beans, broad beans, haricot beans, runner beans, the lot—and she explained that they were all different, so she never made the same thing twice. But it was all nothing but beans. Yes, she might put a bit of smoked loin in, some sausage, a pig's trotter, something or other, celery, even tomato. It was all right, I mean, but I was finding it rather boring. I said to her, look here, Kali, has your God created nothing but beans? We're farting so much that we could keep all the lamps burning. She burst out when she heard what I said, what a foul mouth I'd got. Why? I asked, how do you all fart in Szék? I suppose people do break wind? Or do they let out cooing doves? I was so worked up, she could be as offended as she liked.

It was terrible, she was thoroughly upset. And there was no placating her. The next evening I sat her down so that we could make peace. I said to her: 'Look here, Kali, my dear. Maybe, at one time, those roses were perfumed. Quite so. A long time ago, before I worked on them, they certainly must have been. But since we rose growers have tinkered with so many varieties, cross-bred them, the scent of tea roses has been lost. That's how it is with tea roses. The scent is very faint. There's nothing to be done about it. Either there's scent, or there are the new varieties of hybrids that flower repeatedly, open two or three times a year. So smell them, my dear. Is there any scent?'

I wasn't to call her *maga*!

Then she burst into tears. Put her head in her hands. I'd never before seen Kali cry. She said she had no sense of smell, there was no way she could tell. Well, now she knew. Only she mustn't tell people that they were scented. Otherwise ladies would bring them back and want their money returned. And she ought not to be asking so much for a single stem. People could bargain with her, she said, she was even prepared to and liked doing it. Szék people didn't like bargaining, but she certainly could! And why shouldn't she ask a lot if they'd fetch it? Look how much the boss had worked on them, they were worth it.

Until then I had been working on the roses, but perhaps everything was just about to change. Things were suddenly coming to a head.

University, Party membership, it was all happening now. Time was flying! I didn't tell Kali. She wouldn't have understood. Wouldn't have understood and wouldn't have liked so much change. Too bad, anyone that's been accustomed to the soil for centuries, seen no change for generation after generation, life has just meant constant servility, they don't understand which way the world is turning, that there's a whole new life now.

And I was admitted to the Party. I was invited as an independent developer. Emil Pop had proposed me for membership in spring, and he hadn't said a word to me about my being offered a post at the university because I would first have to undergo screening, and that was a lengthy process. At the time only very few were being accepted, fewer still Hungarians, because of all the screening, and many were rejected as unacceptable. It was a great distinction for me to join the Party. Only really excellent people, people who'd done something, were given membership cards. You couldn't apply to join, as in the old days after the war, when two sponsors signed for you and you were in. You had to like the Party, act in accordance with it, believe in its principles and so on. Now, on the contrary, you were invited; the world had changed. When I was admitted, I had two sponsors, Emil Pop and an old Hungarian colleague from my footballing days who had been screened at the time. Doncsev, a Bulgarian by origin. Pista Doncsev.

What happened was that first of all one's entire life history and character were revealed. Who and what my father and his father had been. The family was atheist, my father was a Communist. I was actually surprised at where they'd got so much from. They knew who my father had been, his brothers, his children, my mother, everybody. Where I'd been to school, even so briefly. Then my successes, my research along Michurin lines, my single-handed gardening. The great things that I'd done were, of course, exaggerated. The old regime had offered no assistance to such a marvellous self-taught head. Indeed, it had obstructed my training. It hadn't been in the interests of the exploitative regime that the splendid achievement of such a mind—the hardy varieties of vitamin-rich fruit and vegetables that I had always tried to produce—should be brought to the common people. It had been to the advantage of capitalism to bring in from abroad all manner of foreign varieties, and with them alien pests. Such as the Californian shield mite. 'This Kolozsvár gardener, an uneducated son of the people, spent years in his struggle against the Californian shield mite, and not without success. Meanwhile the regime continued to import expensive protective agents, because on such is founded every regime of greedy, feudal landowners.'

Every word was exaggeration. There had indeed been a shield mite that I'd tried to deal with, but I hadn't been successful because I'd only been able to work on the adult form! Well, they made a fuss about it. But when you've got half an hour to give an account of someone's life, everything in it is an exaggeration. Because all that gets into it are the important big things in which you've been successful, but your disasters and failed experiments don't—we keep quiet about them. And I hadn't quite managed to get the better of the Californian shield mite.

The speaker gave an account of my property. Two and three-quarters hectares of experimental garden. He said that I had bought every square metre through the sale of varieties developed with the work of my own hands. I had several thousand varieties of plants in this garden. Well, that was about right. He said of me that my practical knowledge was outstanding in every respect, but that I lacked theoretical experience. When he spoke of the sale of varieties something of a lump came into my throat. Was he going to mention the rose that had got me into trouble? He didn't. And yet he then started to!

In the 1930s, Western gardeners had bought the young gardener's varieties at rock-bottom prices. Discoveries worth millions, which could have brought praise to the country at an international exhibition. Under the exploitative bourgeois regime, however, he had only received altogether 500 heavily taxed marks for what had then enriched Western usurers.

At this a sour taste came into my mouth. I had grateful thoughts towards that Dutchman who had bought my snapdragons. He'd given me a fair price. But perhaps they might have been worth more.

Then came an account of my character. I was a modest working man, worked alone, had no help, was occasionally irritable. An atheist, no chauvinist or nationalist feelings, no connections with bourgeois or clerical circles. Had an adequate knowledge of Romanian. A bachelor, lived alone. Employed a housekeeper of whom nothing was reported. My simplicity was made much of. I was a simple man, of a nervy disposition, passionate.

When my life history was being discussed, a certain comrade spoke up. Made a long speech. If we wanted a new world for the nationalities to build together, every remnant of the Iron Guards and Horthyists had to be liquidated. Legionaries and Horthyists, those were the main enemies now. All nationalism, because that was the main obstacle to building the future. And selfish, individual interests. Individual interests had to be nipped in the bud, replaced by communal interests. We wanted the sort of members who, as he put it, had even before now come to the service of the new humanity with all kinds of scientific inventions. Not helped themselves. *Nu pe propria perzona*. He spoke in Hungarian and repeated it in Romanian.

Everybody called everybody *te*, that's how it is in the Party.

And I didn't have to be a probationary member, I was admitted straight away. They said that with anybody else, screening could take a long time, months even. Not in my case. I was surprised. In the meeting, Hungarian and Romanian were spoken half and half. At first, mainly Hungarian, and then it changed to Romanian. There are a lot of Hungarians in the Party. In the old days, before the war, there were a lot of Jews, but they spoke Hungarian as well. Then there became fewer Jews, as my friend Lali said, because they failed screening.

Poor Lali! Lali Jordáky. Bubi to others, to me Lali. He doesn't say so, but it's his greatest grief that the Party doesn't need him. And now he's in prison. It's dreadful! Him, of all people! I can't make out why he's been put in prison. Mari said he was just being questioned. She's his wife, and Oh my God, how he loves her! He and three other old comrades like him from before the war have been imprisoned. And how long will they be interrogated? Anybody they take in isn't released very quickly, they can always find some pretext. He was a very big man after the war, number one in independent Transylvania, in the Social Democratic Party. And if ever there was a real left-wing man, it was Lali. Jordáky Lali. Mari, his wife, just keeps on writing petitions, she writes them and then has to get a translator to put them into decent Romanian. One was a request for mercy, because she showed it to me when I took the poor thing some flowers for Lady Day; she'd addressed it straight to Gheorghiu-Dej and said that she was going to go mad and commit suicide! I told her to take that out. Women are forever threatening to commit suicide. But she said no, she'd written it. I'd gone to town to see her and taken a bunch of roses. Lali always took her red ones, in particular Princess Esterházy, one of Rudolf Geschwind's lovely roses to which I'd added a touch of dark red, because originally it had been plain pink, but it wasn't a success and I'd rather spoiled that lovely full rose. Lali always says that that is the one he likes, but it hasn't been given a name. But on this occasion I preferred to take something smaller, a pink Poulsen variety, so as not to remind the poor woman of her husband, she'd got enough problems, stuck there with the child. I thought, if Lali's not there now, because he was always taking them, at least she can have a bunch of roses. The way she howled, I couldn't get away. She really might be going mad.

These days there's no admission like that to the Party. Rather more are thrown out than are admitted. They're very choosy about who they take, and they just go for excellence. *Eminență*, that's the word they use. Filotti called me *Eminenciás uram*, Your Eminence, like addressing a cardinal, because he's a member as well. Nowadays they pay no attention to nationality in the Party, that's a fact. My father would never believe that I was here.

He was what they called a hatted Communist. They used to wear black hats with wide brims, because in the twenties that was how they went about. It was a sort of uniform. Then when it became prohibited and they were all being rounded up they stopped wearing them because everybody knew what it meant and they had to be afraid of being arrested. Over there on the other side of the tracks, there were a great number of Communists among the workers and tradesmen. Then after the war, they were all kicked out that had informed and got their comrades into prison. But of course they would, when they were being arrested and tortured. Especially the women. But I've heard it said that some women were harder to break than men! That's true now as well. I look at that Kali, if she were taken in on a false charge and accused, she'd stand up for herself. She's like a rod of iron. The good Communists were just the same. They were beaten half to death, tortured terribly, but they couldn't be broken.

And there's something called candidate membership. Somebody whose acceptance is postponed. With me, one meeting and that was it. A long meeting, that's true. And there'd been other candidates, professors, writers, working men.

When Hungarians are being admitted, one of the chief activists gives an account of how they behave towards minorities. Under the monarchy, before 1918, here in Transylvania, there was a feudalist and bourgeois oppressive attitude towards the minorities, especially the Romanians. Then after 1919 there came a new oppressive policy, when the Romanian population oppressed the Hungarians, when it was the kingdom. Well, when I hear the word king, it makes me feel sick. But after the abdication and after 1945, the rights of the nationalities came into force for everybody. Now at last after the war, there's equality. Count the Hungarian successes, the university, and how many Hungarians there are in regional government and offices.

I was accepted. And I've got my membership card. I look at it and look at it. Oh, Lali would be pleased.

I've written to thank Emil Pop for the membership. But I haven't heard a word from the university.

I've got to go in for a meeting, but look here, it's summer and I've got so much to do. I've got to look out for the second flowering of the new varieties, every moment counts, because I'm making very important observations of the first generations. It's nice and hot, and at least I'd be able to see how the roses behave at such times, how they stand the heat. But I've got to go, no question about it. And in fact, I'm even a little bit curious. Actually, a colleague whispered, though I didn't really believe him, that Hungarian autonomy is being granted, it's been in the papers and it's going to be in the constitution. *Scânteia* published the draft and then *Romániai Magyar Szó* too, word for word. I've always thought, how can there be Hungarian autonomy when the rights of the nationalities are already so fully granted, what can Hungarian autonomy mean? But I've never talked about it to anybody, I don't make a habit of passing on stupid rumours and then having to look silly. But if it's in *Scânteia*, then I've got to go, because if that's the main paper, it knows. But I don't look at it very often. I've heard that Sándor Mogyorós's wife is Russian—he's in the Party Centre, responsible for agriculture. Eszter, she's called. Eshtera. Mogyorós gets his wife to read *Pravda*, and from there they find out everything. Somehow I've never been able to understand newspapers, they just don't interest me.

Summa summarum, it turns out that the draft constitution has appeared in the paper, we've got to discuss it and our opinion will be submitted. In fact there's a kind of proposal to create a Hungarian autonomous region where the Hungarian population is solid. Then one of the big men says that it will only contain a third of the Hungarians. So I wonder whether Kolozsvár's going to be included? Because Kolozsvár isn't pure Hungarian, is it? How many Romanians are there, 35 per cent? Or even more by this time? Perhaps only Székelyföld will be granted autonomy? We follow the USSR in this respect as well, because they've got regions where the nationalities are all mixed up. Even the Jews have got their special autonomous region quite a long way out in the east. On the other hand, it's emphasized that autonomy doesn't mean independence. I still don't really get it. But I think, all right. Once there's autonomy, it's good. It's got to be, otherwise why would it have been done? We'll see when it's in operation, I think. At the end of the meeting, an actor member read out a fine, inspiring poem:

S hol a völgyeket a	*There where Maros courses*
Maros szeli át,	*by autonomy*
dolgozó magyar nyer	*shall in full rewarded*
autónómiát,	*Magyar worker be,*
közös birtokunkban	*wider still and wider*
tágabb térre lép.	*shall his bounds increase.*
Így forr jobban össze	*Better thus together*
az ország és a nép.	*folk and land find peace*

On the back of the brochure, it showed what we were going to share in our district. It talks about the Maros. The Maros, not our river, the Szamos. Then perhaps we aren't included. I don't know, because I'm not an agitator, just an ordinary member, but I was given one as well.

If, let's say, autonomy is designated only for Székelyföld, it won't really interest me as a gardener and research biologist. There's no developed fruit and cultivar industry there. Perhaps there'll be a start on development, because experiments on adaptation have begun in colder areas. Székelyföld happens to be very backward and, in particular, cold. 'From the rose point of view, uninteresting,' as little Werner, son of the great and clever, commented, because roses don't do well there. In the autonomous region, the only good soil is in Maros country, along the Nyárád, over by Vásárhely, I think that'll be in the autonomy. Soil as good as ours here in the Hóstát. But in Székelyföld? That's hilly and cold. I don't know it all that well, I confess. Politically, however, it's very important now, because it serves unity, that of the Romanian People's Republic.

From now until September all I'll be able to do on Sunday mornings is attend meetings about the autonomy question.

I keep wondering how this Hungarian regional and administrative self-determination will work in Székelyföld, but we can't yet see that. Because the Centre is still very much in charge of everything. Bucharest. Institutions are beginning to be taken down there from Kolozsvár, everything here is being closed. That's not good, though, but it's my good fortune not to be tied to Hungarian interests.

I've heard that in autumn, a number of Hungarian Departments of the university are closing, and from now on instruction will be in Romanian. Law, mechanical engineering. No university for me in that case, I think. The theatre university as well is being moved to the MAT in Marosvásárhely. The MAT is enticing everything away from us these days. A lot of wailing, but it's only being moved, not shut down. Also, at the Bolyai, the arts faculty is being suspended, because that was closed this year. My dear friend Lali Jordáky is still inside, though he was only taken in for questioning. Seems to me, in his case overenthusiasm for Hungarian interests must have been the trouble, but after all he was a member of the illegal party, a left-winger. There are terrible charges against him and the 'professors', because there are four of them in there. Lali still has his mind on Hungarian interests, Hungarian national and socialist interests, because in his opinion there's room for both. Mari, his wife, is completely distraught.

But good heavens, I don't understand territorial autonomy either. Because who's going to be in charge then? Bucharest or Vásárhely? What's the point of taking institutions away from Kolozsvár? Because Vásárhely is the centre of the autonomous territory. I've been reading what it says in *Előre*. Because of course that's the Hungarian *Scânteia*, that's where the autonomy question has been transferred from. It says that 'The creation of the MAT will focus on and intensify the struggle against nationalism.' All right, that I understand. Sort of. Because if we're going to talk about an autonomous Hungarian territory, that's where Hungarian interests above all are valid. But the true purpose is that we shan't split off but be united. 'The opposition fosters isolationist ambitions and tendencies towards cultural distinctiveness in the ranks of the nationalities that live together.' That's the same everywhere, no need for the MAT for that. And we aren't in it. We've got to see to our own affairs.

When Emil Pop asked why I don't enter state employment, I told him that the job that would suit me hadn't been invented. I preferred to pay the land tax, I hadn't got to surrender anything. He talked to me for a whole evening about the Hungarian-language Agricultural Institute being reorganized, and the need for experts with practical experience. I ought to offer to go and see them and give a demonstration lecture, so that they'd get to know me. These days there's no call for the sort of theory that's no use to the farmer, and science needs to be put on a new footing. Science purely for its own sake wasn't worth a thing. That was Engels's principle, and that's what Romanian higher educational establishments were now applying. Profitable sciences. In the old days, quite a lot was useless, just cleverness for its own sake. He knew, because he'd been through a lot of schooling.

Emil asked, straight out, would I be prepared to do that? I hardly knew what to say. I began making excuses, I'd never been a lecturer, I wasn't the sort to go on the dais. Yes, I read things, because they interested me. But my excuses were feeble like that. What should I talk about, I asked in the end. I must decide, there was so much I knew about.

He meant to discover me! He wasn't going to let anyone else. He was amazed that the Hungarians hadn't done so before. Neither have they, I thought. Because either they were envious or they looked down on me for having only done six years of school. Hungarians are like that. Such is inter-Hungarian friendship. That's the way we stick together. So that a Romanian had to help me. But I didn't say a word, just held my tongue. He and I didn't talk nationality topics. You can't discuss such things with Romanians. Nor will it ever be possible.

I spent the whole evening alone in my room, even locked the door. I sat at the table, picked up a book, turned the pages, found another. None would stay in my hand. My head was aching fit to split in two. This is blood-pressure trouble, I thought. What d'you want then, Vilmos? University! You've lost your marbles.

Oh, but how I'd love my uncomprehending father and my uncle, the proud craftsmen, to be here and hear what Emil Pop was proposing to me. For my painter and decorator relations to see what I am. And especially what I can be! Because my mother anyway would simply say:

'Forget it, Vilmos, you're not university material. Go there and the learned gentry will laugh you out of the place. Perhaps they're inviting you to make fun of you, so as to see what a man can do that hasn't studied. You'd do better to rent a bit of land down by the Butyka, plant a few flowers, and sell them. You haven't learnt a trade, as is the way in our family, and you've preferred tilling the soil.'

Because in their eyes I'm a tiller of the soil. According to Emil Pop I'm university material. Well, a man can't be a prophet in his own family. But my poor little sister would fling her arms round my neck if she were still alive, and say 'Oh, I'm so proud of you, my dear Vilmos! Oh, it would be so good to listen to the lectures you'll be giving at the university!'

Why did she have to have a child? Poor little Erzsi. Curse it, that was what she died of. She and the baby, septicaemia.

What my mother said hurt me deeply, dragged me into the depths like a millstone on my neck, and I felt like jumping into the Szamos with it. Because that's how people commit suicide around here. But I was going to the university whether they laughed at me or not! Because a university professor had invited me, the director of the Botanical Institute, who was always coming to study here. And I'd produced roses for his garden. Nowadays it doesn't matter whether you've been to university.

And what did Kali say? Not that she influenced me, but in general. Typical of a peasant.

'You go to the university. And if the gentry there don't like you, they won't listen to you. Even a bad priest gets turned out.'

Priests again! Oh, I was tired of them. But she isn't very impressed with such a thing. She's got no peasant drive of her own, though. No ambition.

'You'll see when you've had a go.'

So I began to calm down, perhaps there was really was no need to get so worked up and nervy at the university calling on me. But when I went up there and introduced myself I came home with my hands all trembling, couldn't think straight all day.

Then Kali said, 'You know 'ow it is in the folk tale, mister: Marci Vas tried and tried and couldn't succeed. Then along came the devil an' 'elped 'im. And then 'ow well things went for 'im. He was even able to get Goldilocks, because the devil showed 'im 'ow to get a woman like 'er. But then 'e asked the price of 'is assistance.'

'Now look here, Kali. Can't you see how on edge I've been?' I spoke sharply, and before that I'd broken a pot but it was a cracked one, and it would have lasted another winter. 'Don't talk to me in riddles like that. Either tell me Marci Vas properly, or belt up that silly talk.'

Belt up. That's what I said to her, that's the way she talks, peasant style. She told me the tale of Marci Vas, but I couldn't concentrate. And there was the devil again! It does irritate me. These constant religious elements in folk tales. Though the devil isn't exactly religious, more of a persistent trouble-maker. Only at the end could I laugh aloud, when the devil ruins Marci's pumpkins. Oh, how can Kali say such things! When the devil takes revenge, or the cudgel dances on the man's back. That Kali's quite happy when men are getting a thrashing! You can really see she hates men. We had a good laugh at the tale, but we couldn't laugh at our own situation.

After that I couldn't get off to sleep. I could see myself on the rostrum. Drawing grafting on the blackboard. I thought I'd choose to talk about hybridization. Hybrid tea roses. I'd done quite a bit with those. You have to put your best horse in for the race. What had Emil said? Fifty minutes at the most. That will mean a lot for people to listen to, not to get much said. And I'll have to say something about flower development, the history of selective growing, so that people will understand why the new varieties and hybrids are required. And about the observations and the minimum seven years that it takes to produce a new variety. I might entitle my talk 'Patience grows roses'. Because seven years is the minimum. If you're in a hurry, go and be a butcher. If you can't sit and wait, observe and improve, don't try to be a rose grower. So I'll talk about grafting, hybridization. And what if I say something out of order and they laugh me out of the place? All night long I tossed and turned, sweated like a pig, the sheets were wringing wet. I opened the window and shut it again, first I was freezing, then I couldn't stand the heat. I dozed off in the dawn, then I was up with the birds, but I was usually before them.

I took a blanket and a nice old sack, and went into the garden. Everything was still damp. I lay down in the middle of the tea roses and the yellow multi-floras, sprawled and looked up at the empty sky. Should I go to the university? Or should I stay there in the garden and please myself what I do? Who could stop me from being silent for ever? I just lay there and my heart was pounding, I could hear it, my watch was a drumbeat, hammering in my head: go, go, go, it said. Go, then you'll be well and truly turned down.

Of course, Kali would stick her nose into this as well. You never get a minute's peace if you take somebody into the house.

Perhaps I ought to tell them about my best results. And my crossbreeding techniques. And something that was quite novel, my experiments with the environment, at adaptation. I'd been told that the rector would be present as well, he was a working-class writer. István Nagy by name. I ought to read his books. What a marvellous thing it was that nowadays even somebody who hadn't studied at university could get to the top. Because he must know his subject. He'd done five years of elementary school. That was why I'd been invited, I was a practical man. If that working-class writer was there, I certainly shouldn't need to use so much Latin or technical language, as nobody would understand. They wanted to see if I could lecture, was I self-confident, did I know my stuff. But I'd say straight away that I was a practical man. Because these days, practice comes before all else, even I knew that.

Then Emil told me that 'Patience grows roses' wasn't a good title for my talk. Historical time is making huge strides, and in his opinion I should think again, as 'Patience' didn't sound good. 'My most successful crossbreeds', I suggested. No, that was rather too subjective. In that case, 'Hybridization'. That would be all right.

I received my invitation to the university. I was to take documents and so on. My only documents were my ID card, and my birth certificate if required. I hadn't got an *iparkönyv*, because I never finished my apprenticeship as a painter and decorator and I had no other qualifications. I did eight years in the fire brigade. I hadn't even got a baptism certificate, but that wasn't required in those days. On the other hand, I'd got a few certificates from exhibitions, awarded before the change of regime. Should I show those, I asked Emil. A distinction, a bronze medal, a *cum laude*, I'd got them for various things, gladioli, snapdragons, but mainly for roses. Yes, take those. And my military service book. That is, my exemption from war service. Perhaps they wouldn't employ me if they saw what was in that. That my hearing wasn't too good. Perhaps they'd ask how I was going to hear students when they mumbled from the back row. Fortunately they wouldn't ask for that either.

At the university I was greeted by the dean and two lecturers, one of whom introduced himself as the local Party organization activist. They were all Hungarians. They welcomed me warmly, though you wouldn't really think that they would welcome new competition, but we got on together and the conversation was friendly. They'd heard that I too was working on Michurin biology. I didn't know how to answer that. I'd read something about Michurin and Tyimur and their revolutionary ideas in a pamphlet, I'd forgotten what it was called, and I'd seen the exhibition as well. And actually I have experiments of my own on adaptation. That's very important, they replied, I should bring that out prominently in my lecture. They asked what botanical items I'd experimented with by the Michurin method.

Mainly with roses, as those are my main interest. And a few apples and pears. They asked me chiefly to give an account of my experiments with fruit. Could I bring any demonstration material? Of course, I'd be delighted, because it would be autumn and my lecture was scheduled for 1 October. Unfortunately, however, experiments with fruit couldn't be carried out in a place as small as mine, and continued over so short a period. By my reckoning two or three decades were needed to get good results. A new rose variety could be produced in one decade, or seven years if things went well.

It wasn't desirable, they said, for me to emphasize excessive length of time. The point was that at present, in the period of revolutionary change, things were moving quickly, there wasn't time to experiment for two or three generations because the aim was for the population of the country to have access to good, vitamin-rich fruit. The university course couldn't be prolonged to infinity and had to be kept short so that experts might go out as soon as possible into the real world, into production.

I asked how long the course was at present. Four years, they said. I said nothing, because what was there to say. You couldn't even observe a new rose variety in four years.

They also asked what fruits I was continuing to experiment on. I said that in my collection garden I had eight types of apple and six of pear, all pure Transylvanian varieties: batul, pónyik, gógyi, sóvári and Gypsy apples were my favourites, and for pears I listed veresbélű, torzsa, autumn mocskos, hosszúkó havasalji, pergamott and small széki, but the names didn't interest them. I used nothing but native varieties, Transylvanians. They were very pleased with the answer. They drew attention, however, to the fact that nowadays Romania was unified, and it would be taken amiss if we Hungarians now wanted to be different in terms of apple varieties as well. You see what we mean, Comrade Décsi? Because nowadays separatism is a big danger. I said that I hadn't taken them as Hungarian or Romanian varieties, just from the aspect of region. Transylvanian, local. For example, I'd been experimenting on Gypsy apples, which were neither Hungarian nor Romanian. But I hadn't yet achieved any results, hadn't been able to improve them, to increase their cubic capacity. Then let's forget about Gypsy apples. I should say instead, local varieties. Or Romanian. Or if I really needed to, Transylvanian basin varieties. We had to adapt ourselves, not only apples, said the dean with a laugh. Everybody called him Stefi. There was informality everywhere there, equality.

'We'll stick with fruit, shall we, Comrade Décsi? Well, the name suits you,' and he winked. I stared like a fool. What was he thinking of? Was he saying that the Magyardécse wasn't the best fruit-producing area in the RPP? He didn't think that at all.

Let's agree, then, I said. The activist comrade said that roses weren't as important in present-day agriculture as they'd been in bourgeois days. Now the national aim was the use of vitamin-rich fruit on an industrial scale, not flowers for flowers' sake. I should talk about the achievements of the Michurin method in Romania, especially with regard to fruit. 'Adaptation and the inheritance of registered properties'—how does that sound, they asked.

The activist comrade also said that he would visit me in my garden next week for us to finally shape my talk. As a leaving present, I was given a couple of new brochures, things the university had printed, dealing especially with Michurin and Lysenko methodology and the achievements of Soviet agriculture.

They asked me whether I was happy with the systematizing of the subject in this way. Let me have a little while to think about it, I replied. To that they said reassuringly that society, the university, and Romanian science had great need of practical people, people like me that had considerable knowledge and who were going over of their own accord to the methods of Soviet biology.

But what was I supposed to say? I'd been a coward. A cringing cur. I just said cautiously that I would prefer to talk about my improvement of flowers, because I'd spent almost twenty years at it. But what was I supposed to say? That I'd been right at the forefront of experimentation with fruit, and I was hardly able to hold forth about the process of adaptation. And secondly, that I'd never used and definitely not studied the Michurin method, the most I'd done was to hear of it. Then again, I was to say how important it was to extend such useful knowledge as is of immediate use in agriculture. Towards the end we just sat facing each other and they waited for my answer. But my neck was beginning to sweat, the smile was frozen on my face, and I just looked to left and right. I tried once again to say that perhaps what I ought to show the learned lecturers and the distinguished university was what I knew best and had learnt in the course of practical work. They said that I ought not to be so bashful, they'd heard about me and my achievements.

Then two weeks later, I was to submit the text of my lecture and after that I'd able to deliver it.

I had no enthusiasm as I left the premises. Because I'd agreed without a word of objection to talk about something of which I knew next to nothing. And which pleased them. Now was I to run to Emil and ask him what we could do? I couldn't be such a baby. That he should help me in my difficulty. What would he say? At the university things should be taught that were useful and true. Everybody toed the line to some extent. What was being required wasn't such a big deal, was it?

Now I could see it all. What I knew best of all I had to throw out. Nevertheless I wrote it all as best I could. It was passed. If I was supposed to refer to Michurin, I would.

So, the 1st of October came. 'Adaptation and the Inheritance of Acquired Properties'.

I was talked up something awful. In his introduction, the dean said that science repeated itself. As had the great scientists, Russian and Hungarian alike. Lobachevski and Bolyai had progressed in their work in ignorance of one another, far apart, without any connection, and yet they had reached the same revolutionary results. Ivan Vladimirovich Michurin had found a counterpart in Romania who had been driven to the edge of town by the repressive regime to carry out his large-scale experiments, likewise involving the hybridization of plants. Now, however, before every member of Romanian society that possessed valuable practical knowledge the way lay open to attain their potential, to work for the community, by way of university education and large-scale experimentation and development, and through the national university too!

I gave an account of my previous experiments in adaptation. All the same, I brought roses into it, because I'd started by seeing the Charles Kingham rose as such a pale yellow when I began to grow it under local conditions. And then how I'd obtained that brilliant colour by a process of adaptation and gradual transmission, and, of course, mainly by crossbreeding. Then I turned to apple varieties. I brought in two baskets of fruit, individually wrapped in paper. We set them out on trays. In groups by stages of development, where each was from, which way the slope faced, and its elevation. They were tasted and liked. Well, of course.

You know very well what you understand and what less so, what you only guess and assume, and then what is dead certain. Because if you're dead certain about something there's no need to say so, because that's the way it is. It's a fact. The only thing you say more about is what you assume. Because there's no certainty about it. The devil's for ever deceiving you into saying things that you're not too sure about. Because you want to show off? Then I plucked up courage and said that there had to be several kinds of university experimental stations in a variety of situations and elevations so as to show results in fruit production, if serious Michurin experiments were required. They are! That's how I finished up.

I'd been allowed to invite guests to my lecture. At the end old Schultz was in tears as he embraced me. Said he was proud of me. I was his greatest pupil. I was on the way to the top, he said. But I felt deflated after the lecture, and all their congratulations—from Emil Pop to the dean and all the lecturers—didn't mean a thing. The rector's a very down-to-earth man, you can tell where he comes from. I'd have liked to go and hide in my garden, be as young again as I'd been when I first saw my rose opening that I'd have given my name to if it hadn't been taken from me. There was a reception laid on in the dean's room, the clinking of tiny glasses of pálinka. I only stayed half an hour, because a reporter came to interview me. I had to go into another room and talk to him. When we'd finished there was nobody left at the celebration.

My brother didn't turn up, though I'd sent him an invitation. I wasn't surprised. Just a bit hurt. He didn't even send a card to reply, that would have cost him a lei. I hadn't invited my mother, she's not the university sort. It doesn't matter that your origins are regarded differently these days. And then she'd want to be talking all the time. It even crossed my mind to invite Mrs M., but I didn't want to impress her. People always cling . . . Whom else was I to invite? I asked Werner, who replied that he'd got to be away. Didn't even congratulate me. So, thought I, he must be going out of envy. Old hunting friends came, people I'd played football with. Filotti, Kovács and all sat there respectfully. Kali asked if she might come, and I said that only people with qualifications could be admitted. But that wasn't true at all. What would a Szék woman have looked like on a university bench?

I've been summoned to take my documents to the personnel department tomorrow. There was some explaining to do there as well.

I was so deflated after my lecture as I went through the town that I completely avoided the Főtér for fear of meeting somebody that I knew. I went round the edge of the town, because I went out first of all down Monostori út, then below the beech forest and then towards the south-east. I like going that way, round the outskirts of the town, because it's quieter. But this time I felt no relief. How had I got into the university? Actually, only so as to be laughed at. By the time I got home it was late afternoon. Some scruffy dog was going along with me, and I threw a stone at it, but I don't usually hurt animals. Only I was so worked up. I was seething. Kali grinned at me, she'd got a celebratory meal laid on. I told her to hell with it. I had to keep myself in check so as not to shout at her when she tried to ask again when I wanted to eat. She pestered. In the end I had to come out with that she should take me at my word, or I'd chuck a budding spoon at her. She came back with 'All men are the same, the devil created them all so that nothing's ever good enough for them.'

I went straight to my new experimental row. I took an axe. Now then, let me see you, you famous remontants. Because up till then I'd tried to get that yellow rambler to flower more than once. I gave the outer bush a good kick with the toe of my shoe. But it didn't even move. It had a good strong root. I'd grafted it, I knew, onto a nice thick stock, so that it could stand anything. Then I took the axe. Right, I thought, won't you flower twice, you swine? You Ville de Paris, or what the hell. You're famous. Ever since Pernat created this rose in 1925 and won the prize for the best new rose in Paris he's made so much money that he gave it all up and just dangled his legs for the rest of its life. It didn't have to be examined by the committee! I'd grafted the precious Ville de Paris to a rambler. You aren't going to be a remontant, eh? You aren't disposed to open more than once in our climate? I'll give you what for. I took it and cut it off right by the graft. You can go and rot. I took the next and cut that clean in two as well. Die! I was feeling so furious, I was going to cut the lot to bits. The whole garden, every unwanted rose. By that time I was bellowing at the top of my voice. Everything that I'd grown and discovered, all of it, I'd now betrayed. The whole thing was nothing. Just a load of shit. Twenty years' work. A load of shit.

By this time I was cutting the fifth stock of Ville de Paris. It was painful and felt so good. Demolition always makes you feel so good. Because it's so easy! And it's black as poison, and washes the body clean from inside. Then I felt something tugging at my shirt. Kali was clutching at me from behind. Stop it, you idiot, stop it! Has the devil got into you? Why are you destroying yourself? She was shouting like that, louder than me, squealing like a stuck pig. I said to her, 'Go away, Kali, I'll hit you with the axe.' She hung onto me, so tight that we might have been tied together. She wrenched the axe from my grasp and threw it into the road. Who would have thought a woman could be so strong? Well, she said, it's not the end of the world if you haven't managed to get a job at the university. You've been doing well here in the garden, the university's not right for you. You have to be born to it. Everybody fails now and then in the exam of life, she said. When she could see that I'd calmed down and wasn't going to do any more damage to the flowers, she let me go.

'It's better like this,' she went on. 'You don't need anything of the sort. What's going to become of the flowers and the garden if you want to work somewhere else? Haven't I told you what happened to Marci Vas? You don't want the devil helping with something you can't do yourself.'

I had to wait a moment before telling Kali to listen to me, and then I said, 'I've been taken on.'

She didn't understand. I told her again.

'Just like that, I've been taken on.'

'Well then, I came in good time,' said she drily. 'Then why were you behaving as if you'd taken leave of your senses? Go indoors and wash your hands and face.'

That Kali Green had one cure for everything. Go and wash your hands and face.

We ate the celebratory dinner in silence. At least it wasn't bean stew this time. There was meat soup of nice fatty brisket, meat fried in breadcrumbs, and for afters pancakes with caster sugar. Kali was trying to impress me and produced a bottle of rose *dulcsáca*. The table was laid with a pink cloth. She had to ask whether I'd noticed, because I hadn't personally. Roses. You're done for. I've finished with you. God damn all roses.

There was a cut-out from an article about me on the university wall-newspaper. I didn't stand there and read it, how would it seem if I looked at my own picture? Instead I got a copy from personnel. I took it into the loo, because I could find no peace in the building. My stomach heaved as I read. I was afraid I was going to have a bilious attack, like after my first lecture. The article was all about my person, my family, my past. I was the third child of peasants. But we hadn't said anything about that. How I'd begun research. There wasn't a word about the king's rose, although the reporter had asked a lot about it and made notes all the time. Then came how I'd been discovered and brought into the university. There was a lot about my experiments with fruit, how I used a Michurin method, and what I'd discovered myself. And that there was now the possibility of fruit farms in the

Romanian Republic, based on the system of the great Soviet Michurin, to adapt domestic varieties to climatic conditions and further safeguard their properties. Not bringing in foreign varieties, but just as Michurin had confined his work to local ones, taking them further and further north and obtaining plentiful, tasty, vitamin-rich fruit. In conclusion, the article wished me much success for my plans.

It was like reading about someone else. Not that the writer of the article was telling lies, but this was about a different person. A great man. A man of science, with lots of fine goals achieved.

The article had been printed in *Igazság*, and my workbook was made up at the university. Or rather high school. Another reporter, from *Romániai Magyar Szó*, the national paper, came to see me; he wanted to write about the results of Michurin biology in Romania and the progress that the RNK had achieved through me.

I had to reread the report that had appeared in a quiet moment. I looked at it again and again in peace at home. Only where could I get any peace? In the loo, that's where. But I was full of loathing. Loathing. I read it in the evening at my desk under the lamp. I just had that bitter feeling all the time that the piece in the paper was about some other person, not me. Because here was this man making sweeping statements about what must be done and how to do it, knowing everything, like a kind of prophet. But what I'd said at the university was what might be attempted! That experiments must be made! Not that things are that way already! That a lot more fruit could be produced if we took up in a big way experiments in adaptation on the lines of the Michurin system. Old Schultz had always said, 'The whole of Transylvania could become an orchard.' And that in the olden days, there'd been a famous photographer and inventor, Ferenc Veress, who had three hundred or so kinds of apples. Three hundred apple trees alone, and with those he experimented. But in my lecture I can't have said that Transylvania had to become an orchard, because firstly, we're in the RNK, and secondly, it all had to be experimental. The whole thing must have been badly explained. I'd only talked about the possibility of improving the industrializing of fruit.

But after that it emerged, when I began to discuss more fully with a colleague, that the reason why new people had to be brought into the agricultural school was that there was a shortage of teachers. Members of the former EMGE, members of the Farmers' Union, had been imprisoned. Why hadn't anybody told me before? Perhaps if I'd known I'd have been more careful.

But as a member of the university staff, I was completely at liberty. I put together the university curriculum, wrote up the plan for it, submitted it, and not a word was said. There were separate classes for reproduction, plant protection and industrial fruit production. Everything had to be submitted for permission. I gave practical classes, some of which I conducted in my garden. This was officially inspected in advance, and the class always had a minder with them. I could hold those mostly in spring, and until November. Where I put roses in my plan, it was always crossed out and 'botanical unit' substituted. I had to place the emphasis on fruit. I didn't know which way to turn so as to be able to prepare. I took a heap of books out of the library and then only read one, because there were some that I didn't understand, they were solid chemistry, and of others it was said that they were out of date, ignore them, things had progressed. The main thrust in Soviet science was not Mendelian heredity but only adaptation and the inheritance of acquired properties, and we too had to take that line. I'd always studied inheritance in roses, and so had to marginalize it and keep quiet.

I had, however, to educate myself in terms of theory. Now I was a member of university staff, it was essential. Lamarck, Darwin, Mendel and, most of all, Michurin, Timiryazev and Lysenko, the greatest disseminator and developer of Michurin's teachings. Only when I read them, I dozed off. When they weren't obligatory reading for me, I would leaf through them, found them interesting and could get the hang of them. Now that I had to, I just opened them at random, and I was always afraid that I'd trip up in class. But Lysenko had had some astonishing results! I didn't know why vernalization hadn't been tried in Romania. Or was it vernalization? I wasn't sure which was right. It was very revolutionary.

Not every class that I took was a waste of time. When we were in my garden and I was teaching bud grafting, taking cuttings and cross-pollinating, I felt certain that I wasn't misleading the students. I took the knife and demonstrated. Then I'd take off ten or so buds and show them which were viable and which were empty or decayed and couldn't be used. Then I'd give them all knives and let them ruin a couple of stocks each. There were those that were clever, but most were not. That's what I must have been like at first! I did well not to cut a finger off, or not to slice clean through the branch. Then came the selection of grafts, their storage, binding, shaping. They could do those too. Nice jobs, those. Then I gave classes in crossbreeding. If there was anything that I knew about, it was crossbreeding. All the same, I had to do a lot of preparation. I wasn't able to sleep at night. Since I've been teaching, I've got used to not sleeping, I've been so on edge. I sleep on Saturdays, get a good sleep then, because there's no work the next day.

As for as crossbreeding was concerned, I had only to teach technique. Technology, as they call it. Crossing varieties or methods of creating new, beautiful hybrids, never before seen, was not a permitted subject. Or rather, not approved, not profitable from the industrial point of view. That I realized in the first place, but it was pointed out several times. I'd stuck firmly to the rules. In my opinion, however, varieties new to cultivation might be introduced and cultivated on a large scale. But I didn't argue. Let them say what it's profitable to teach. All that was only possible in September and early October, when the time for bud-grafting was approaching. Crossbreeding is delicate work, and I could demonstrate to no more than five students at a time. What was I to do with the rest? I set them work that would be useful. Each group watched crossbreeding for half the lesson. I didn't say what the varieties were, what I was doing with which and what I expected. It's like when a doctor teaches how to make an incision, how to hold the scalpel, but pays no attention to whether the patient is ill, what's the matter with him, is it really necessary to operate. Perhaps they couldn't even understand what it was all good for. A crossbreeding procedure takes seven years. What could be learnt from this? Who had the time for that in education?

And now I thought, oh shut up! While the students watched I crossed a nice Charles Kingham with Harisonii and Ville de Paris mothers. There was one of each left. In a lesson I made about three crossings. Then I said, we'll do it again next week. If there's time, of course. I hadn't thought that I was going to do precisely that, hadn't put it down in the curriculum. But I didn't have to detail such things as what I was going to demonstrate. Only the methodology, the technology, and this was good for that purpose. Quite, but they didn't know that. It was as if I'd given away some secret in front of an audience. After all, it was my rose! The greatest that I'd ever created. The king took it off me, but I'd made it again! Because I knew what I was doing, what my aim was, but it was all the same to them, because they were studying the method. Then at midday, off went the class. I just had a bite of lunch and carried on. Did perhaps thirty stocks. Didn't hurry. You can't hurry with a thing like that. The flower will sense that you're rushing and it'll take its revenge. That's how you get freaks.

Now for the first time since I've had to teach, I began to work for myself. And this is how it all turned out: as they came to class, the autumn term was beginning, and I told them that we would be meeting rather more now, because in December and January, I wouldn't be able to demonstrate any experiments for them. I'd be able to teach more often, but not so much. They were there by nine in the morning. I brought out a table to the side of the Kingham row, and the tools. I'd already prepared the mothers the previous day. Because they had to stand for a while, to get wet and be nice and tacky. You can't go into a woman like putting on a shoe, I gave them that simile. Only one boy and one girl laughed. They'd understood, the others hadn't. The rest were still a bit green, they knew nothing. But from that one can best understand what kind of work this is. You have to open up and wait. Some people open the mothers towards evening, and only pollinate in the morning. The Ville de Paris was already bare. I demonstrated with a couple of flowers how to strip off the petals so that the mother exposed itself. Then we took those that were already nice and ready for the pollen and pollinated the Kingham and brushed it over. Then I showed them how to close it up. With little paper caps that Kali and I had made in winter.

In the evening, Kali and I had dinner. It was the first time for ages that I hadn't grumbled at the poor woman. She'd cooked stuffed summer cabbage with rib of pork and marrow, covered it with buffalo sour cream. Nothing had ever tasted as good. When I'd finished, I went out again to the row I'd been dealing with. I put the tools in a basket and brought them in, sat down and asked her to bring me some tea and tell a story. I was just in the mood! At last I'd done a good job of crossbreeding. I was surprised she hadn't told any stories for quite a while. Well, she asked gloomily, what was she to tell? 'Cos I didn't like her stories, didn't listen. Don't take offence, I said, because she was always touchy. Just go on.

'King Mátyás and the crab apples. Will that do?'

'That'll do nicely.'

'Well, it so happened that King Mátyás used to go about to get to know the country. The sorrows and suffering of the people. 'E disguised 'imself so that people wouldn't know that it was 'im. An' 'e came to Szék, which at the time was a big, thrivin' town.'

'Steady on,' I said to her, 'Wait a minute, madam. How could Szék have been a thriving town? When it's a village.'

'Quite,' she was touchy straight away, 'nowadays it's not a village, it's a community. But in King Mátyás's time, there were great big salt mines. It was certainly a town.'

'Well, I never heard of such a thing as a thriving town getting run down and becoming a community.'

'Anyway, that's what 'appened. An' if you aren't goin' to believe it, mister, I'm not goin' to tell you the story, because you won't listen to it.'

Why should she tell stories if I wasn't going to believe them? We were silent for a little while. I told her to go on.

'But believe me, then.

'Well, so King Mátyás came to the town of Szék, where all sorts of rich people lived in great big 'ouses, because everybody used to work and trade in salt. In them days there wasn't a Gypsy shack in the town, because even the Gypsies worked and was rich. Only on the edge of the town was there a miserable 'ovel, where there lived an old woman. But nowhere would the rich people give Mátyás bed and board, 'cos 'e was so poorly dressed. 'E went out to the edge of the town where the old woman lived, and 'e asked 'er too for bed and board. She couldn't see all that well, and she told Mátyás that she didn't mind if 'e slept in the kitchen, she'd got nothin' else, only the one room. That'll do for me, said Mátyás, because by then night has fallen an' it was pitch dark. Then the old woman asked 'im whether 'e was 'ungry after 'is journey. 'E must surely be. The old woman said:

' "I've got some nice cold water from the well, drink your fill. And I've got some fresh crab apples, take them and eat your fill."

'King Mátyás drank a pail of water and ate a basket of crab apples, because he was as big as Kakas 'ill. And them apples was so tasty! But they was so small, more like like oak apples. Then said King Mátyás that 'e would pay in gold. The old lady said:

' "Don't give me gold, young man, what would I do with it, and all the greedy people would kill me if they saw it. 'Cos 'ere in Szék all the people are so greedy, they scratch each other's eyes out. Rather let me 'ave a sack of wheat, young man."

'King Mátyás said: "Go into the village in the morning, granny, because the king is coming. He'll give some out."

' "No, I'm not going to push and shove, 'cos the greedy people will just trample me if the king comes, 'cos the greedy always crowd around the rich."

'Next morning the poor young man, that is, the king, went his way. Along came the town drummer and proclaimed that whoever gave King Mátyás bed and board, theirs would be the golden apple and three sacks of wheat too. Everybody ran home and smartened up their houses. Then into town came King Mátyás with great pomp and ceremony, in a gilded carriage drawn by twelve white horses. 'E went up to the first big fat 'ouseholder and asked: Will you give the king bed and board, my good man? Gladly! was the reply. An' will you give to a poor man? 'E would. Gladly. An' did you give bed and board to anyone yesterday? Well, of course 'e 'adn't. An' 'ad anyone asked him? No. Are you sure? asked Mátyás, you aren't misrememberin'? Well, then the householder remembered. Well, a young man did ask. Then why did you not give it 'im? The guest room 'adn't been swept, said the rich man, 'e'd 'ave been ashamed. Then the king asked other 'ouseholders likewise, and it became clear that nobody had given bed and board the previous day. Let 'im come forth that cleaned the guest room yesterday and gave somebody bed and board that asked for it. Well, nobody came forward. Then King Mátyás saw the old woman at the back of the crowd and made 'is way through to 'er. 'E stopped in front of 'er and asked whether she 'ad given anybody bed and board the previous day. Yes, young man, I did, 'cos my guest room's never dirty, it's as clean as God created it. 'Cos my guest room's outside the house, under the crab apple trees.

'The king laughed aloud and said to her: "Take a closer look at me, please!"

' "Well, what am I to see about you, my lord king? Your clothes are gilded, your crown is agleam with many precious stones."

' "And can you see my nose?"

' "It's nice and large, as a king's should be. It must be good for smelling out falsehoods."

' "And did you see this nose yesterday?" asked the king.

' "Yes, but it was pointing downwards rather a lot as it pleased you to chew crab apples. But it was certainly good to see." So then the king brought the old woman to the front. 'E set 'er on a gilded horse, 'cos she was such a little bit of a thing, light boned. 'E showed 'er the bags of wheat. And 'e brought out the golden apple from 'is pocket. What a big apple it was! And the people of Szék could only look at the old woman, as she was now made rich.

'Well, from then on, the district where the old woman lived was loathed. 'Cos even when she was dead it was loathed, she who had been so kind and done such good. 'Cos that's the kind of village it was. Such a bad village that that old woman actually had to move to another, such was the anger directed against her.

' And so, I hope you enjoyed it,' said Kali at the end, because that was what she always said, as if we were finishing dinner.

So said Kali, black with venom, as she reproached her village.

'And what became of the crab apples?'

'Well, along come a clever gardener, 'e grafted them and got from them great big half kilo apples and left them to the old woman, and they spread and spread,' said she and laughed. ''Er garden became full of such wonders 'cos she went on 'ybridizin' the crab apples. But the rich people kept criticisin' 'er, wanted to dig 'em up an' 'ave 'em planted in their gardens, but the trees couldn't stand being transported an' they all died,' and crafty Kali laughed so much that her ribs hurt.

'Heavens, what a Communist that Mátyás was,' I said to her. 'Because Mátyás was always on the side of the poor.'

''E was no Communist,' said Kali, 'but 'e was a good man. ''E was the best-hearted of the 'Ungarian kings. 'E was born, you see, at the back of the post office. Since then we 'aven't 'ad a good 'Ungarian king that we can tell folk tales about, because the rest didn't eat crab apples, just spat at 'em when they was put in front of 'em. The others 'ad to 'ave nothin' but rich people's food, and were forever dishonest. An' not one of them knew the common people, they didn't go among 'em, just sat in their palaces all the time. An' they preferred to have all the trees cut down.

'Very well,' I said, 'let's get to bed,' because I was very sleepy after the folk tale. Even after that I went in to see Kali for a bit, because I hadn't for a long time. It wasn't as if she'd complained. She'd developed an interest in herself, I suppose.

The following week we 'Békás farmers' went in for a meeting. They're almost all Hóstát people up that way, and I'm the exception. There had to be a discussion about the collective. It was compulsory. Anybody that didn't go was given a warning. I had to set an example. I could no longer be ashamed at being discovered. Activists came, two of them, and spoke about associations. They would be given machinery with which the land could be cultivated communally. There would be wages, some of everything would have to be given in exchange for payment. Here none of the Hóstát farmer had so much land, for the most part the area was small, but it was farmed intensively. Then one farmer was called on—he was a great drunkard, I'd picked him out of a ditch on one occasion—and he said that he'd already joined the association, given in his cow, his cart and everything, and his land. All he'd retained was the garden by his house. And since then he'd got new living-room furniture and a radio with his wages. He was in the Infracirca association. It was a 'Brotherhood'. He only worked as much as was laid down, never on Sunday. They did everything communally, were always singing, and the work went better. Then somebody said in an undertone, 'You can sing all right, farmer Hancz, mostly when you're on the pálinka.' He used to go down Méhes utca, where the only pub in the Hóstát was. Then a woman was called on to speak as well. She was a widow and lived alone with her two children. She was pleased that she didn't have to work on the land. She spoke quite quietly and was hard to hear. Then the activist asked everybody what they thought. Application forms were distributed. One farmer said that he'd take it home to read, he hadn't brought his glasses, and he'd have to have a word with his wife because she owned land as well. This isn't women's business, the drunken farmer told him. So if it's not women's business, why did old Böske Furu speak? When my turn came, I said that I didn't cultivate productive land, I was an experimenter, that must be understood. Comrade Tompa, the activist, actually said that he would come next week and pay me a visit. He told everybody when he would come to their houses for a discussion. Activists like calling on people at home. You have to visit people in their own homes, he told the meeting. It's effective.

The collective wasn't obligatory, explained Comrade Tompa, but voluntary, yet the farmers still couldn't understand why it was good for them. They ought to know about it. And be a bit more trusting. So who was there here, that could be trusted? Who was the leader of the Békás people? asked the activist. At that the drunkard Butyka said—he was called that because there was another Butyka in Bunaziua district, who wasn't a drunkard— that the best farmer was always the leader, and pointed to me. I said I wasn't a farmer, I hadn't got a single cabbage, what was he talking about?

Then the activist came to visit me as he'd said he would. He'd done his homework, I could see, about the university and everything, he'd read the paper, he knew that I was an experimental gardener. He said, what wonderful things I'd done there myself and that I should help their work, because I was a member. I told him I hadn't got a moment to spare, he could see. Garden, university, activism. Well, then we agreed, and off he went, he would put in a report about me, who and what I was.

Since I've been a member of university staff, an *adjunktus*, I haven't have a minute's peace. I was scarcely to do any work for myself. I could only gather my rose seed on the side, so to speak, one evening; I had to light a lamp for Kali to hold, and took it indoors to put into boxes. I'd been afraid there would be a frost the next day, it was already getting cooler, after all it was early November. I didn't take any pleasure in collecting the seed—that was what you waited for, wasn't it, the first seed from the crossbred plant. I simply had to ask Kali to hold the lamp, though I liked to do that sort of thing by myself. The WC was absolutely the only place where I could be alone in those days. The next day there was hardly time to sort out the seed, clean off the flesh, pack it up, leave it to rest. What I'd previously done so nice and patiently now had to be done at breakneck speed. A year before Kali and I had sat in the evenings and sorted the seed by lamplight. White, soft, rough, we stored them all away. I'd had plenty of time to pick over the seed with my shining tweezers! I only potted the undamaged ones. Kali didn't care for such delicate work as sorting out the seed, because she said she couldn't see very well. But I'd given her some glasses. Meanwhile she told lots of tales. There was time for everything. But now? At the stroke of twelve, I dashed out for a bite of lunch, then had to run back to the university. There were times when I couldn't get out to eat and had to find something in town. Then I stole an hour from my afternoon nap and did the potting-up. I was always having to go to the university, sometimes there was ideological training, sometimes a professional meeting, then I'd have to take some no-good class for which I couldn't prepare fully because I had to give out so much material that I couldn't see the end of it all, I was constantly on edge, couldn't think straight. Then I'd have to give back students' work and enter marks for it. What could I give marks for? I asked a colleague that I knew well, how he classified things. It was easy for him, he only taught a theoretical subject. There was a written exam, then he gave a mark. Then if any was a bit uncertain, he would call them in for a discussion. Then I asked at the *katedra* for my exam to be rather later, so that as many roses as possible were open. Let the candidate demonstrate cross-fertilization. I would see what they knew as soon as they took hold of the stem. Some would mess about for half an hour opening the flower. Afraid of it. You just had to use a nice firm grip, and that was all there was to it. Then you had to trim off the stamens, bring the pollen from another flower and brush it on. I laid out all the tools. One set about tearing the petals off with tweezers. I asked what the young gentleman was doing. Trimming his moustache? There were thirty of them. When I asked what they were going to cross-fertilize they looked at me like Kali did at the electric iron. Because I'd bought her an electric iron as a present, and she almost threw it at me, she certainly wasn't going to iron with that contraption. Because I'd brought out about fifteen varieties for them to choose from, and a few dog roses as well; actually, wild roses open nicely. And did a single one notice? Yes, one did. A sharp-eyed girl. She was clever. She said when she'd picked it up that we shouldn't cross-fertilize it because it was a wild one, wasn't it? She selected a bush rose. She said that we'd put together a multiflora with a *grand fleur*. A clever idea. And what will be the result, I asked. She'd get the bush rose from the mother and the *grand fleur* from the father. How nice it would be, I told her, if it always worked like that, only bred true. And what if it turned out the other way round and there were tiny single roses? Then we'd have created a little, scrawny, insignificant thing. That little girl had something about her . . . but women don't make rose growers.

By the time that we got to the end of the examining, I could see a caricature of myself. A lunatic tearing leaves off roses—because that was what I'd been, that was my report on the examination. Such was teaching.

I'd been thinking of writing about the new rose which I was then going to graft. More correctly, I was still only waiting for the seedling, but in any case I could visualize the grafting of it. I'd planned it, I would describe how I would achieve the colour that I wanted, what stages there would be in the search, how we would divide up the seven rose years. A real, proper, nice thick book on rose-grafting about a single flower, and I'd also bring in, of course, times when I wandered off my main course, when I went exploring, because I wouldn't hit the target first shot. And in this way I'd give an account of the Ideal Rose from the plan, the idea, right up to the ultimate reality, as it happened. Like a scientific journal, as part of the work of a rose grower. The seven years, every step, mistakes too, blind alleys. But I didn't even manage to jot down a couple of words. Month by month, I thought, like a log. To hell with the whole idea. Was I to observe it and note it down properly for myself? I didn't have a minute to spare even for myself.

On the other hand, I was now getting regular money. No time, but regular payment. I signed for payment every month, I had a travel allowance, and at the request of András Sütő I wrote little articles for *Falvak népe* on pruning fruit trees in accordance with Michurin principle, and those brought in good money. In addition, the university paid me extra for the use of my garden in practical classes. and I could charge for materials. Suppose the students broke pots, did a certain amount of damage, time was required for repairs. Now there would certainly be money for development, as at the start of every month I went down to the CEC, the bank, and paid in two or three hundred lei, only there wasn't time for development. I had to get used to money coming in every month, it had never been so steady for me. And perhaps I soon got used to being paid for everything. Then if I wasn't paid for something I didn't feel like doing it, wasn't willing to work for nothing. And I was always being told to write a popularizing book for a series on farming. The State Publisher was offering good money for that too.

But the trouble with the university was that I was always hearing too much evil.

Professors were being removed from the arts faculty. Straight to prison! The rector had been replaced at the Bolyai, he was being investigated. Did I have to go into the university? Everybody was inclined to be a bit right-wing and separatist. The previous rector too had been ousted, there were accusations against him. We reviewed the case at a meeting. Now László Luka too had been dismissed. He'd been supporting the kulaks, holding back the development of heavy industry. And there'd been dissatisfaction with his financial reform. He'd been 'insulated from the masses by his aristocratic lifestyle'. I didn't know, I'd hadn't known him personally. He spoke nicely in self-criticism, but then the fool withdrew it. Why did he do that? Didn't he know that could only lead to trouble? People were sentenced to death for that sort of thing in those days. Anyway, he was in prison.

I couldn't get on with anything. There was so much going on that I was afraid now to go in for a meeting. What was happening in the Magyar Autonomous Territory, in the university, in prison, what were we to make of reorganizations, constantly increasing tasks? So much instability. If I kept paying attention to what was going on I wouldn't be able to do my own work. We in education weren't to consider what went on. We didn't understand, we weren't in charge, it was none of our business.

In January, Dej announced that the nationality question had been resolved. A final solution to the nationality problem, said the paper. And not ten years had elapsed since the liberation! Obviously this too was the result of self-determination and the creation of Magyar autonomy, the MAT. That too we contemplated in a meeting. Then later we heard that the

Hungarian People's Union, MNSZ, had dissolved itself, because that was the Magyar party. Elderly people who'd been in the association were very worried. The paper didn't have all that much to say about the dissolution as a whole. I would have spoken to Lali, but he was in prison. Mari, his wife, kept on at me to do something. What was I supposed to do? Who did she think I was, that I could get somebody out of prison? If the nationality problem was solved once and for all that meant that there was no need for a separate party, I thought. What mattered now was unity. Not that I'd been a member of the MNSZ, but I could have joined when it was formed in '44. I'd never given it a thought, as I don't care for parties. But now there wasn't a separate Hungarian party, from now on everybody that wanted to belong to the Communists, and Hungarian affairs could be dealt with by the Hungarian members of people's councils. If there were any Hungarian affairs. But I just didn't know what separate Hungarian affairs there could be. Every Hungarian was now absorbed into the MAT. The only problem was, of course, that we weren't in the MAT. There wasn't a word said about Kolozsvár, just MAT and more MAT.

Then the university sent me to Bucharest, where a Michurin Institute was being set up. Every delegate had to make a presentation to the foundation session about how they would develop and disseminate Michurin principles in their areas. I had to work on that day and night.

I described one by one the stages by which the gigantic Michurin garden here in Transylvania would be developed. I didn't put like that, of course. First of all, a collection circuit staffed by experts had to be organized, and all local varieties brought together in the Western Havasok mountains. Then young, strong seedlings of local varieties would have to be taken back—I too had a couple of hundred apple and pear seedlings—and allowed to acclimatize to conditions in hilly and higher areas, so see what they could withstand and tolerate. In this way the Havasok would be planted nice and slowly, experiments in adaptation carried out, and acquired qualities rendered permanent. The whole of the Mezőség would have to be planted, poverty in the Mezőség and the Havasok eliminated and vitamin-rich fruit grown almost free of charge for families. In the Mezőség, irrigation would be a problem requiring urgent attention, and in the Havasok, there would be that of frost. A research institute must be established in Kolozsvár and small observation stations in the Havasok. The Kolozsvár institute would have premises outside the city, on the best soil in the surrounding hilly region, in places such as Békás, Bunaziua, Borháncs and Szopor. Before making my presentation in Bucharest, I had also to introduce my plan at the university. A slight correction was made in that I should call the Mezőség, which I had referred to as Campia Transylvaniei, a *regione deluroasa*—a hilly region. I'd never ever heard the word, *deluroasa*, I had to get it right, must be careful not to say *dureroasa*—painful. I was told also to exclude Magyardécse and the surrounding area from the Mezőség as the best fruit-growing areas. Only there ought there to be industrialization, and work carried out only on local varieties everywhere. No foreign ones. We would drive out the many alien and dangerous diseases. What we cultivated in Romania would be made resistant.

The institute was established as was the committee, on which I represented Kolozsvár. It was my part of the country, there was no backing out. I gave my presentation and many questions were asked. Reading aloud in Romanian was hard going, practising hadn't helped, but fortunately everyone was given a typed copy. I was anxious all through my talk that when the questions began I wouldn't be able to give them due regard, would fail to understand. The questioner would reach the point of a very long question but I wouldn't even know what he was talking about. The more I concentrated, the more I'd lose the thread, because I'd be completely confused. I wouldn't know what answer to give, I'd be so on edge. What was I to tell him? I'd seize on the final words and blurt out something. I'd repeat my principal idea, that we would adapt young seedlings to cold places. Perhaps that wouldn't be what he was asking and I'd look stupid. Academic surroundings like that terrified me. What was more, I was a Hungarian, couldn't really follow Romanian when people discussed technical matters among themselves at full speed, especially these southerners with their unfamiliar accent. But fortunately for us, we were now most politely treated, and one couldn't be laughed off for not speaking the state language very well. Petru Groza actually spoke Hungarian all the time when dealing with a Hungarian. I've heard him do that. He opened the meeting. And then over coffee he spoke Hungarian again with some bigwig.

I really wished I could have told my mother: I was on top of the world. Appointed lecturer, university post, Party membership, elected to the committee, and perhaps I'd have to set up the Michurin branch in Kolozsvár. But I didn't dare say anything. I was always so on edge when mother came round.

On the last afternoon I went into Bucharest to do some shopping. I bought something for Kali, I could see that everybody was buying things, it was the thing to do. A little porcelain object from a new factory, I didn't know what it was for but it was nicely painted. By that time I wanted to get back to my own bed. But I wouldn't the first day, I thought, but I'd go with her in the other room. I told her so.

So I went up to Bucharest for a week to a congress, and it achieved all sorts of things that couldn't be read in the paper. Political matters. And in particular, that until then I'd been sitting in my garden and not bothering about anything. Just roses, roses, roses. But now things were moving so fast that I was out of breath. We spent all blessed day in session.

I was only sorry that when I was so far from my garden I could see how trifling it all was. Everything that I'd done until now. When I was away from my work and looked at it from a distance, it all seemed so small, so ill-starred. It saddened me that for twenty years I'd searched, deprived myself, cross-fertilized this way, adapted that way, bowed to the soil a million times, and the whole thing had been a great zero. Seen from afar, every life was a great zero unless it was that of some great man. One was no better than another.

'What are you lookin' at, Vilmos, my dear?' asked Kali. By that time I'd become Vilmos. 'Are you looking at nothing, like Pali the coachman, when 'e climbed the wild pear tree?'

'I'm looking at precisely nothing. The rose leaves. The bursting of the buds.'

'What are you lookin' at there, mister? Ev'rythin's still completely green.'

'I can make sense of the green as well,' I replied.

Because I'd been looking at the tiny, glistening leaves of the new shoots; they were still round, mint- or rather Eocene-green at the time, and by summer they would fade slightly to emerald green, lose strength. But when the leaves opened they were even reddish inside. Healthy, thick leaves. I looked at that nothing which I myself had made. Oh, that double manuring last year had done the trick. One lot in spring, and another in November or December, on the early snow. How good it was to look at nothing.

At last there was nothing to occupy my eyes or my ears after a week of talk, because even in the hotel I'd had to share a room with the delegate from Arad. I liked those early leaves even more than the flower buds, because at such times I'm even so full of hope that tremble as I look at them. Then the flower appears, bursts, then opens fully, it's lovely, lovely, but it's over, hope is ended because reality is there. And reality is never like in our dreams.

We didn't speak. Kali's very good at silence. I'd never before seen a woman who could keep quiet when need was. Previously I'd only come across chatterboxes. It was a warmish evening, and I even brought out a folding chair. Then I said to Kali: 'Go on, then, tell that tale about Pali the coachman, who looked at nothing from the wild pear tree.

I listened to her tale while I worked. What a dinner she'd made! A nice cabbage laska, with apple doughnut for afters. At last I was eating something good, and not in a restaurant. Then I called on her a second time. She didn't like me to go twice. A woman doesn't like that sort of thing. Only when she's very young, only just starting to get used to it. Then when she's really mature and starts to enjoy it, then a second time. But not everybody feels that way. Goodness only knows what they're afraid of. That's biology for you.

We were the same in spring, except that I was dashing from one place to another. Kali had to do the pruning, because I was at the university all the time. She did it well. Not hard enough, though—I like to see the stocks even shorter. But women don't know how to prune, that's the truth of it. They regret cutting flowers down.

Kali asked, were we having a dance? Not because she was bored, it's just that she would enjoy it. I said that we could go to the cultural centre, there's dancing there on Sunday mornings. That was when she went to church. Especially at this time, having fun wasn't permitted before Easter. What about in the afternoon?

'I'll dance with you here at home, Kali.'

'Oh, it'd be fine to have a good dance together. Only it'd be a bit expensive, wouldn't it, 'irin' a band just for the two of us?'

'I'll see to the band, it'll be here day and night! We can get it on the radio.'

But we couldn't find any. There wasn't a note of folk music anywhere, least of all Hungarian. Those days it was all nationalist songs and choirs, what they called 'movement' music. No folk music at all. So we were left with the culture Centre, there was nowhere else to go for dancing.

Then in May we took the little seedlings outside, those that I'd done to show the students. There were about a hundred and fifty of them in pots. Each one was marked *DV* so that we shouldn't mistake them; the first selection would be from them. I knocked together a separate table for them, with a surround so that they wouldn't fall off. I gave Kali orders that if a big storm came she was to take the lot inside. I was now reducing the seven years of observation to five, because I wasn't making Vilmos Décsi for the first time. I knew, of course, what I'd added to what in order to get the rose that I'd had previously, and all that I had to bother about now was the selection. The world was going so much faster now, and I with it; there was something new happening every week. This week I was given a memorial tablet for my research. So roses too were speeding up. One year and everything would be done. My rose would be there once more, and I'd give it my name.

Seven years with me, fourteen with Meilland. The story of the Meilland family was written on the Peace packaging. Time had been on their side! It had been easy for them! Meilland's grandfather had been a rose grower as well, the families had united and both had become rose growers. They were in no hurry. Even his son became a rose grower. We've had this one life. Did have. I say 'did have' as if we no longer had, as if we'd all died. Because we haven't any more. My father used to be a factory worker, my son . . . who knows. What 'my son', I mean. For us in Romania the clock runs faster.

And here's an example. I was moved up another rung, higher and higher!

Now I was asked to establish the branch of the Bucharest institute. I was called into the university specially for this, and a committee came from Bucharest. They asked where the best land might be. The best is all in Hóstát hands, Békás, Szopor, Bunaziua, Borháncs, Eperjes; I listed the places outside the city, of which I'm one too. The next day the committee reported to my place to look at the garden, and an elderly man from the surveyor's department came as well. It wasn't an official visit, they said. How could it not be official once there was a committee involved? Never mind. It was evening by the time I got home, and I was so on edge. Everything ought to have been tidied up quickly, but of course that was impossible. That was how we lived here, and when students came I didn't particularly care. But now officials were coming. I couldn't take everything out into the garden now and tidy up. Kali said no need to worry, everybody would realize.

'You know the saying, mister, when the oxen aren't in, the manger is clean. That means that where there's tidiness nobody's workin', no animals bein' kept. Where there's life—as they say in the village, life is when there's animals about—that's how it is. Not all nice and tidy.' We were in disorder. And the yard was muddy.

'Oh, what a clever woman you are,' I said to Kali.

'If you think so, read the Bible,' she replied very sharply, 'for that's where I got it from.'

I told her to stop irritating me with the Bible, and instead pick up the tools and clear up around the house.

I told her to bake a dish of pastries, make some coffee, fetch some pálinka from the Furus's down the road, and have a box of soda water ready.

The committee arrived, three in number. One was a university lecturer from the capital, another was an activist, and I don't know about the third, though he was something on the ideological side. And the surveyor as well, so they were four. The lecturer was most able to discuss what I showed them. He was interested in the roses, but he said that this wasn't the time for such things. Now fruit and vegetable production was being revolutionized. He caught sight of the seedlings and asked what the experiment was about. He wanted me to tell him about it. I told him what I'd crossed with what, and asked whether he'd done anything with roses. He'd tried, but without success. Then he went over to the morellos. He knew about those, was experimenting on increasing productivity.

They took soil samples. We went out further into the Békás and looked at the land. They took samples from there too. All the Hóstáti plots were planted at the time, with lettuce, red onions, radishes and other vegetables. The tomatoes were still ripening. All the people were out there, working. The horses were tethered between the paths. When the trowel was brought out to take a sample a little Hóstáti girl stopped and looked on. Nobody there had joined the farmers' association yet. Everyone was working their own. It was no use agitating, the Hóstátis didn't want to know. They didn't believe in 'common'.

The following week they came to measure up. The decision was that here in the Békás would be the best place. It was a very great piece of luck for me that the Michurin Research Station was to be next door. I was deputy chairman of the planning committee; Avram, the chairman, came from Bucharest. The dean invited me to hand my classes over to an assistant lecturer while planning was in progress. I was somewhat startled, and said that it was all right, I'd be able to manage. But I wasn't to worry, my salary wouldn't be affected. So I spent all day calculating and drawing in a big, smoke-filled room—could hardly see a thing. There were a lot in there. I was so on edge from head to foot. I didn't have to write ideological material. My job was to plan the research sites for fruit and vegetables, and I was given an economics assistant.

It had to be done by the end of May, as the intention was to plant in autumn! What a hurry all the time.

By that time the land had been expropriated. The Hóstát farmers all came asking me to save them. How could I save them? I wasn't the one taking their land off them, was I? Appealing to me was futile. We said it would be possible to wait until autumn for owners to get the crops in. Anybody not in a hurry could still leave their onions in the soil, but there was nothing to be done with seedlings, nowhere to put them. Everything was being ploughed up. There was farmer Butyka, who had no other land but this here and a bit by the house. I told him to join the association, he'd get a wage, have no worries. A little girl came running to Kali, for Aunty Kali to help, speak to me. What could Kali say? She couldn't stand in the way of the machinery when it came. It was a state decree, there was nothing to be said. Sorry.

Kali announced that she was in the family way.

Outside the tractors arrived at six in the morning, then the students appeared, because there was nowhere to do practical work, and I spent all day either running somewhere or sitting in the planning Centre. I hadn't had a hoe in my hand for a month. When I sat down late in the evening it wasn't with Kali, but there were three of us, weren't there! I wished to God I could have been alone for a bit. And then there was the child here as well. It was like a weed. It hadn't actually arrived yet, but I could sense its presence everywhere. It was lurking in every corner. Everything was interrupted, my work, my sleep, my meals. It was the end of my life, and I had to give it up to somebody else. Kali said she needed the child, she should keep it. So what did that mean, needed the child? Was it a handkerchief? Or a side of bacon? It was coming. So come it would. There was no stopping it.

I shut myself in the WC, because there I could at last be myself for a bit. Maybe I would actually go mad. To think how I'd used to live here just a couple of years before! What had become of that fine, quiet life? I couldn't even get any decent sleep any more.

Emil Pop was quite right. Peace and quiet were at an end. The only place I would find peace and quiet was in the WC. Peace and quiet to take a hurried look at my seedlings meant stealing time. I could now spare a quarter of an hour for what had previously been my whole life.

The Michurin Research Station, as it was called, was taking shape after only four and a half months. The pace was frantic. There was even a USSR delegation at the opening, headed by the biologist academician Ushakova. I was surprised at the leader being a woman. But she wasn't so much a woman as a scientist. They brought a beautiful samovar. Perhaps they knew I liked tea, only we didn't know how to use it. One said it was like a tea kettle, you had to make tea in it, put it on the stove, or on charcoal. Somebody else said you only put hot water in it. Perhaps it's not for making tea, only for decoration. It was very pretty, and I put it away in my director's office. We drank toasts in pálinka. I didn't like the Soviet comrades. Over-spiced. Smelly. They say that vodka has no smell.

Comrade academician Ushakova and the delegates looked at everything and even came through into my garden. She asked which of my experiments were written up. I said that I hadn't really written any up, had just been making observations.

'We too would like to learn from you, Comrade Décsi. We don't just want you to learn from us.'

Because we've based the station on Michurin's revolutionary experiments, haven't we, and on his followed Lisenko and Lisenkoism.

Comrade Ushakova said that the national economy of Romania would complete the next five-year plan in four years, and for that numerous schedule schemes were available. The task of plant research was to make agriculture effective, to find new and productive vitamin-rich varieties, to spread them all over Romania and to share in industrial production. The Soviet government would give its Romanian friends every assistance in attaining their goals, and was prepared to send even more experts to help in the development of the national economy and the rapid growth of industry and agriculture. Sovrom, the Soviet–Romanian general share company, was already in operation.

Comrade Ushakova could see the basic function of the station as mainly in research into fruit and vegetables. No question of roses now.

The opening was a great success. A little wooden platform had been constructed which had to be taken down afterwards. The dance ensembles that had won in culture competitions gave a performance, and there were Soviet dancers too, Russians and other nationalities. Their dancing was very interesting, quite different from ours. Of course, the Romanians too dance differently, they don't slap their feet, their style isn't so masculine. They have that stick dance. The Soviet instruments too are different. The balalaika makes a painful sound. I was only sorry that, as I so enjoyed watching the dancing, I couldn't take a turn myself. The dancing was very well rehearsed, they didn't spin around whenever they felt disposed, but only when it was time. Then we drank vodka. I didn't like that very much, but then I don't go in for pálinka very much either. We had some Küküllő wine.

I had to recruit the workforce. I brought graduates from the university, who, of course, knew as much as students. It was dreadful that they had no practical knowledge. Werner pleaded on behalf of his son. What could I do but take him on? He was such a quiet little Jewish boy. I was actually taking in the enemy. Werner was as jealous as a dog and only said bad things about me. Perhaps he'd shut his mouth if I did that. I had to be very careful from the nationality point of view, not to take on only Hungarians; half had to be Romanians, and a couple of Saxons or Serbs and an elderly Jewish accountant. Old Schultz was in charge of that while he was still running a big business. International was the watchword. In the new era there were no such things as Hungarian, Romanian and Jewish, those distinctions had slipped below the horizon, and everybody was now the same. I was given a secretary from the Centre, and a member of university staff as my deputy. They were party people, reliable. As manual workers I took on eight planter-women—there were plans for six greenhouses.

Kali said sourly that each of my planter-women was prettier than the next. Why should I take on freaks?

While planning was in progress, I had to send to Bucharest for permission for everything. Our title was *The Michurin Experimental and Plant Research Station*—in both languages. We were given permission to supply the central flower distributor. There was no quota laid down, just what was spare from experimentation. The main building wasn't yet in use, but it had to be set up, heating installed, laboratories and water supply. Until then we were given premises in the university for planning, one big room. But at the time we were mostly on the land.

I planned just two big rose-houses and fifty ares of outdoor beds for commercial use. And, of course, there were separate houses for the carnations, geraniums and other annuals. When the request was returned the rose-house was crossed out. Not approved. Nor was I surprised. Then I leafed through and read the recommendations, and saw that five rose-houses and five hundred ares of open ground had been inserted. I asked myself, hasn't there been a mistake? At first I just looked at it and thought, what should I do? Better not say anything, we'll do it and keep shtum. I had a word with my deputy, Stefan Velican. Stefi, by that time. He could see the same on the page as I could. But we didn't want to get into trouble over it. They've made a mistake and we pay the penalty. When we were down at the university, I asked my secretary to ring up the Centre. I asked for Comrade Avram, told him that everything was clear, only we hadn't yet worked out the plan for the rose-houses, had we? How were we to take this? Well, he said, Comrade Décsi, you'd underplanned. Under? I asked.

'Comrade Décsi, you're the biggest rose grower in Romania,' he replied, calling me *te* like everybody else did by that time. 'That's why you've been given the establishment. So carry on, now you can grow roses for the state.'

'In five greenhouses and five hundred ares?'

'Quite, and we're giving you Central Park as well, Parcul Central.'

'You mean the Sétatér?' I stammered, because I knew of no other big park.

'Yes, that's right.'

What else was I to ask? I was losing my voice completely, beginning to choke. I thanked him, could scarcely get the words out, and rang off.

Grow roses for the state? The state wanted me to go on experimenting with my roses? A vein started to throb in my forehead. The way it was pulsing, I was in danger of a stroke. I felt dizzy, had to sit down. Couldn't think. Then I sent for the economist. We'd have to do the calculations again. So look here—one greenhouse, so many stocks. One *are*, so many hybrids or floribundas. That made altogether—I couldn't believe my eyes. You just wait, Frenchman Meilland. I've got five rose-houses and five hundred ares of land. We worked on calculating for a while, then I simply ran home, didn't wait for the bus, ran out of the university. I ran and ran, felt nothing, didn't get tired. Gave that fat Kali a hug. Couldn't remember ever having done that. If she hadn't been so fat by then, I'd have grabbed her and started dancing. She was getting a bit tubby with the pregnancy, of course. I ran out into the garden and looked at it, so, what was I to do with you all, you wonders of loveliness?

Kali said she hadn't got a celebratory dinner ready.

'Anyway, there's some nice bean soup, I'm sure you'll enjoy that, mister.'

'Oh, look here, Kali, have I ever in my life tasted bean soup like yours? Let's have it, quick!'

'Just stop makin' fun of me, sir!' she replied, but this time she wasn't taking offence, she could see how delighted I was. 'What's come over you then, mister, that you've given up bein' sarcastic, like Mad Kati, when she . . .'

'Dry up, Kali, I'm so delighted that I can't listen to your Mad Kati because I've gone completely mad myself!'

'Well, tell me about it. I hope you can keep hold of it like Pista the Strong did the iron bar!'

'There's Pista the Strong in it as well now? That I must hear this very day!'

And then I told her. Five rose-houses, five hundred ares open land for roses. It was down in black and white. It's been approved. Think what that means! They've given the go-ahead.

Well, her face registered nothing. You'd have thought it would be a great pleasure, in future others were going to be working in those greenhouses if I'm to be in charge. Storing the stocks would be somebody else's job, not hers.

'Oh, come on, you're always spoiling my enjoyment! Listen, Kali, there's going to be five rose-houses, understand, I'll be able to heat them as much as I like even in winter. And five hundred ares just for growing roses, do you see? I'll do so much to be proud of!'

'Well, that's nice, then. Eat your soup 'cos it'll go cold.'

But I couldn't understand why they said I was the biggest rose grower. When until now I've only been told that rose growing is a sort of bourgeois relic, a thing of the past, just plain surplus to requirements. I'd got to go completely over to fruit. And I'd gone over, in my heart too, given up roses. Now, the students' practical work was all in the Western Havasok, they were having to collect varieties, carry out the experiments on adaptation. They wouldn't be interfered with all the time in the hills by armed terrorists, partisans, whoever there might be, fascists or whatever, all talk in my view, there was no opposition these days, it had all been eliminated. It was from the hills that seeds would be collected in autumn, and it wasn't such a good idea to entrust it all to students. But students come free of charge. Then why had I to produce eighty thousand new rose stocks at this time? He was a clever man that could obey such a production directive, because I certainly couldn't. But never mind! I didn't care a bit. We could produce almost ninety thousand stocks. If every square metre held four or five bushes—let's make it five, as we're into intensive cultivation—then five hundred ares would hold a hundred thousand or more! Good Lord, not tens of thousands but a hundred thousand! Five rose-houses additionally, in which we could put them even closer together, as they would be in pots. That is, we would have to bring in experimental composite medium, and not earth, because long ago I'd seen factory-produced seedlings on coconut matting. I'd have to consult the soil scientists about finding something to use for the purpose. Perhaps we could make some nice ground bark ourselves.

I simply couldn't grasp that number. A hundred thousand rose stocks! I couldn't even imagine it on a human scale. Eight and a half thousand, yes, that had been the most I'd dealt with. But a hundred thousand was off the scale.

Sleep deserted me completely. Long ago—not all that long, two years ago—when I was only pleasing myself and searching for the blue rose, as the saying goes, because we've discovered everything else by now, just can't produce a blue rose—I'd always slept well. Even if I'd had too much on my mind, I would just lie down and go to sleep. Kali always said it was typical of a man. Sleeping like that is what men do. Women are always waking at the slightest sound, and then quickly asleep again, that's their nature. But a man sleeps like a log. I would sleep until four o'clock or half past, because then I went watering. Just occasionally it happened that I couldn't get off to sleep because I was waiting to get up and go out and do the watering at first light, and after that start work. But now I couldn't sleep. Something wrong with my bed, I thought, so I bought a new mattress, horsehair-filled, a hard one, flexible, never mind what it cost. Made by the best upholsterer. Even then I couldn't sleep. Got to get used to it, I thought. Three weeks went by—it takes that long to get used to new secateurs. But I didn't. I would wake up in a sweat, and unrested, as if I'd been bending down all night. I was weak, wilting, like aspic in the sun.

I dreamt—the whole thing was a nightmare—that the Station was open, but one day hail smashed all the glass in the greenhouses. Hailstones the size of children's heads reducing everything to splinters. Then I grabbed Kali and we danced on the broken glass, I could hear it crunching under our feet just like that. We went quite mad, the way we whirled around. We were being punished for something and had to dance until we'd danced all the fragments of glass into the ground. And Kali told a folk tale, I can remember it: along came my dog in my dream and my own dog barked at me, and it cut its paw. It ran off whining and I couldn't catch it, but there was blood everywhere it went. I woke up in such a sweat and went quickly and told Kali about that weird dream. She looked at me sadly and said that they'd had a woman in the village who could interpret dreams, say what they meant. It would be very nice to know whether or not broken glass meant good luck. The Romanians always say 'Good luck!' when they break something. *Sa fie cu noroc.* Once I was at a name-day party in a restaurant and a waiter said that when he dropped a tankard. I needed that damn great Station on my shoulders, all those people, the money, the responsibility, I had to carry the can if anybody did anything wrong—there'd be fifty or a hundred thousand rose stocks, not to mention the fruit section—and to answer for everything. For the fruit industry of Romania.

I had to plan for the roses as well. A stratagem was called for. Everything had to be done at the double. We had to show results in two years at the most, that was all the latitude allowed. Two years for a rose? Why not make it this morning, then? I had a lot of arguments about this with the Centre. There wasn't even any start-up material. I passed over a couple of hundred stocks of my own. I put in a list of what ought to be obtained, but of course I didn't really know the new varieties, only the pre-war ones and what I'd seen in Meilland's catalogue. And Peace. Couldn't have that, it would have meant foreign currency. I explained that even if we bought them there'd be some that didn't colour up too well for a year or two. They would be too pale, we'd wait a long time for the second flowering, the flower would be thinking, maturing itself. it would take time, perhaps it too would adapt, but I hadn't done enough experiments on it yet. Then what would we do? We'd do some bud grafting, not spend foreign exchange on it. Steal it, not to mince words. Bud grafting is child's play.

There were a thousand things to do, but I had an urge to graft a rose again. Now I was dreaming of a completely new variety. When I went to bed my head was full of it.

That strong, slender, flesh-pink mouth. I'd seen a girl in the market and kept looking at her mouth, it bewitched me entirely. I didn't even notice the rest of her face, just her mouth. That's what I would make. Not one with a big, open flower with a cup as big as the spread palm of a hand. What did I care that the fashion was for compact, full roses. That tiny, closed, strong mouth before it began to open out. As tight and small as the bud. That was the kind of flower that I'd produce. I knew the fashion: what won everywhere in those days were big quadruple flowers with at least fifty petals, or better still seventy or ninety! Those were what people went for. Packed full, the bigger and wider the flower, the more people were attracted. But there was no obligation to follow fashion. I liked small, strong, compact flower heads. Which only opened when sprayed. Which held a secret. Only a few petals, like wild roses, but not showing their stamens. Twenty petals is enough. But I didn't want it to open fully, I didn't want to see its sexual organs. I've never liked that sort of thing, only in wild roses. Exposing the stamens is exhibitionism. The same sort of thing as a prostitute. And I wanted to find that shade of pink. I'd start with Charles Kingham again, because I liked its bud. It was small and compact, and even when it was open it was modest, unpretentious. That Kingham variety, however, was too thorny. It was small all right, but had a lot of thorns. So it took a good thorn-stripping knife for me to approach and open that delicate little rose. Where was I to find that colour?

And most of all, when?

Shall I reach for another brush and do some cross-pollinating? Or shall I stay seated at my desk, giving orders to the people working under me, signing everything, asking for approval from the Centre, getting machinery, sending for trees and tiles, fertilizer from the nitrogen works, begging for peat? Because I beg the Centre for everything. Machinery can be ordered from Soviet industry. Tools for the workers are mostly made in Romania, although we have no good hand tools such as secateurs or knives for bud grafting or thorn stripping, because we'd never known such delicate items and had always imported them. What our factories know about is more on the lines of big iron jobs, massive castings. Small implements for research work tended to be French or English. Now, however, we couldn't buy them as that required foreign exchange. I'd thought of having a dozen made by the knife grinder who used to work for me, but we weren't allowed to purchase from a private person, only from a factory. I really had to beg to get that approved. If there was no factory in Romania that made budding knives, they could only be obtained to order from a knife grinder who had a shop at the market, like his father before him. You told him what you wanted, gave him an old one to copy, and he could make them.

I've never ever missed the flowering. In the old days I'd be there as the buds began to loosen and the colour became visible between the green sepals. The final colour, however, would be a long way off. Every day I checked twice, early in the morning and in the evening. That was my work. Every day, when I had to leave the light—there's no more grievous moment in the day—first each colour seemed to draw a little of the darkness into itself and become stronger, more intense. Then colours blended slowly into one another and darkness covered them up. At night I couldn't imagine all the indescribable colours of the flowers that lived in my garden. I'd looked at them in the evening too, as we said good-night to one another. If I looked for too long my heart began to feel crushed, and then I'd be unable to sleep, I was so waiting for light, for the dawn. Sometimes I'd run out with a torch and look to see that they were there.

I could look at them until October, when all the petals fell. But August I heartily loathed. There was nowhere to put the flowers out of the heat. I suffered and so did they. Then there were another two months of hope from

September on, and if we had a warm autumn perhaps even more. I would look at the healthy, dark-green foliage of those that didn't flower a second time, because hybrid teas don't really care to do that. Each variety has its own leaf colour.

It's been twenty years now since I first experimented with my own rose. The bud is what I like most, as it still holds promise. It's not reality, and scarcely anything can be seen of the colour. I could just about tell red from white. But white and yellow were the same at that stage. I could see the healthy, swelling bud, and my bosom swelled with hope. But at such a time the rose was in my head, not my garden. The most wonderful rose just as you'd imagined it. The nuance of colour at the tip of the petals, the green of the leaves. It was splendid, beautiful. But more than that, it wasn't what I'd been looking for. There was too much yellow in it. The leaves were pale. The petals were stiff. It didn't bush out but grew forcefully upwards, straining for the sky, as if there were no softness about the whole plant. There were people that aimed for this. I'd contemplate it for a year or two, and then by that time I knew, damn it: it wasn't right. That wasn't what I'd been dreaming of. I'd close my eyes and begin to search again. To search for what was in front of my eyes.

But Emil Pop was right—no more pleasing myself. I was no longer at all able to observe the opening of the buds.

The Station was open, and so great were the expectations that I could no longer get any sleep, I had so much to do. But I did miss the flowering. I just ran quickly round the garden and saw that the plants were there. I told Kali exactly what she could cut and sell, but she couldn't manage the barrow any longer. She wore her skirt in such a way that it didn't show that she was pregnant. I could tell all the same. She talked with a farmer about taking her down in a cart, but she was afraid that the jolting might be bad for her. She preferred to take her time going down. Didn't utter a single word of complaint.

But when did we ever have such a spring? What a spring it was! And I saw nothing of it. We got some rain, and plenty of warm sunshine. But I was just run off my feet and raced from one place to another. On the go all day long. Station, university, meetings, delegations, Bucharest, all sorts of things. Didn't have a single day to sit in my garden and see my flowers.

But then I didn't know what would happen in autumn, and how. There was the university. There was the Station. Some people can take it. Every month to Bucharest, supplementary training. And on top of it all there was the child, of course.

Then when I had to take the train to go to the Centre I felt that I was somebody. I was questioned about everything and I always took care to have an opinion. Took great care. We Hungarians in particular really had to be careful. There were several there in the ministry, on committees, and there were Hungarians in the Centre as well. Sándor Mogyorós, for one, was an important man. It made no difference, there had to be equal opportunities at that time. All the same, I had to be very careful about what I thought and said, as there were a lot of people actually in prison at the time, including poor Lali. He hadn't even been sentenced, had simply been arrested. I heard about one important man who'd been a member of the Hungarian party, a writer at the opera as well. József Méliusz, he'd been in prison for four years by that time, and still hadn't been sentenced. Not even charged. He'd had simply no way of finding out what the accusation was. Poor Lali. And poor Mari and her child!

Soviet comrades came, and there were always delegations from collective farms bringing machinery and instructing workers on collectives. There were some very odd-looking people among them, minority nationalities, because some came from remote regions of the USSR. In Romania, progress had been made on the minorities question. So they said. I didn't know how it might be possible for us too to make progress, what we had to change for that purpose, or how we ought to adapt ourselves.

Then I would travel home, worn to a frazzle. I really looked forward to a good night's sleep. But then I had to hold meetings in the Station at once, to give an account of directives. Then came Sunday. Oh, I'd so looked forward to being at home, seeing to all my jobs, the things that I'd planned before going away. But no such luck. I just couldn't go on. I had to have a good sleep and get my strength back. But I couldn't get any sleep at home now. Not since the child had been there. Since little Vilmos had come into the world.

I took a good look at myself. Because at home I was a great nobody. On the train I was somebody, in the garden I became a great nobody. So, which was I to be, I asked. I'd rather be nobody, but I couldn't. As I'd acquired a taste for important affairs, lecturing, writing in the paper, leading a culture circle, advising a farmers' circle, along came committees, the Station was set up, and I was asked for my views on everything. How could I have remained a nobody once it was so good to be somebody! But that wasn't the end of it. Because I would go down to the Centre, and up would come academicians, advisors from the Ministry, leaders of institutes in various parts of the country, one had more people, the next had more territory, a third had published two books. So I became jealous. Why didn't I do as much? Why wasn't I being asked how things should be? And then it was even decided who were to go abroad on study journeys, some to the USSR, some to Germany! My mouth was dry with jealousy. Why isn't my name being spoken? Why are you jealous, Vilmos? Haven't you got enough money, position and everything? What more do you need? You wouldn't like to be the Lord God? Be damned to my thoughts. The main thing wrong with me was jealousy. I'd become worse than the great Werner.

I was thought well of there at the Centre, since I was neither stubborn nor wilful like some Hungarians, who couldn't be talked to about anything because 'No' and 'Not allowed' were all they ever said. I wasn't conceited, like certain others, who couldn't shrug off their ancestry. Straightforwardness was written all over me, I was down-to-earth, I'd improved a lot in all respects, and they said so when they read my character and biography. And I wasn't lazy, I could bend my back. And I shouldn't be given work involving nothing but planning at a desk, because that would drive me mad.

I'd found some clever young people who could work and discover ever-newer things. One had constructed the 'hospital'. He was collecting diseased plants in special large glass tanks and experimenting on them. If anyone had a good idea, I didn't stand in their way, and if something was required, I obtained it. Little Werner was clever too. True, so was his father, but he was so conceited as to be useless. The boy was not.

Young Werner loved roses deeply. There was nothing else that I could use him for. So, let him have roses. He said he'd like to experiment on white varieties. If I would let him have a whole greenhouse-full, he would collect every variety. Not a whole house, I said, start with half of one. The varieties that he wanted were Virgo, Agnus Dei, Little Sheep, Little Mermaid, City of York, Blanche Mallerin and Five Nunns. The last-named was a bushy variety with tiny insignificant white flowers, I said, not worth bothering with, but he had an idea that something might be made of it. We had come by two Star Roses catalogues, those for 1948 and '49, and there was hardly a white rose in them. They weren't in fashion these days, I told young Werner, but here we didn't worry about American fashions. Young Werner—otherwise known as Benjamin—said that he would graft a tall trunk shrub from one, and from the other he would try for a resistant floribunda. He would like a flower with a bigger head from the polyantha, not the tiny Five Nunns variety. He would like to achieve a much purer colour for the Agnus Dei, not that off-white but a genuine snow-white that would gleam like sunshine.

'Why white varieties exactly?' I asked him. Because every gardener has his own colour, his shade. And white is the most delicate. The hardest thing is working with white, the plant has no resistance. Because humanity has made red, the rose of the heart, so resistant that even the clumsiest of gardeners can't ruin it.

He couldn't reply. He just gave me a wan look, like an examiner on receiving a bad answer.

'How am I to give you a whole greenhouse if you can't tell me, why white exactly? You know what is meant by money and responsibility? And that I shall have to tell the Centre why we're doing it? What we shall be producing for the Romanian People's Republic? What results there will be? Because we'll have to show results. So, why should we produce white roses?'

Then he said quietly: 'Because the whites are the most beautiful.'

'Now you're talking.'

Because if he'd embarked on some complicated account, some reasoning that white roses had not previously been dealt with, that nobody was struggling with them just now or some such casuistry I would have cut him short. Who was I! But if those were the most beautiful in his eyes, that meant that he'd fallen for them, and so would achieve results. He'd go on looking until he found. Only love can tempt the gardener. The rest is empty words.

But I didn't tell him that I didn't believe in the project. Because I doubted whether he would succeed. To make white roses as resistant as red or yellow? Nature wouldn't allow it. They're the most fragile, actually. You can't send virgins into battle and win. But let him experiment, I didn't mind. I was going to have to commend it to the Centre.

Because, that is, roses had to be justified in terms of ideology. Fruit, vegetables and other plants did not have to be explained in this way; just results were sufficient, and the quicker the better. Positive results, even during experimentation. I've been experimenting with apricots and bitter almonds, for example, for the past twenty years. If I described anything of the sort to the Centre, it wouldn't so much be crossed out as I'd be out of a job the next day. Fired, as the term is these days. Here in Transylvania, in twenty years' time, there's got to be an orchard such as the world has never seen!

Roses had to be thoroughly justified. But since I'd been given five greenhouses for them, which could be heated and irrigated at all times as required, it wouldn't be so difficult. We didn't have to cultivate for the market. But Romania had to be given a helping hand as far as roses were concerned. The 'Romania in Flower' movement had already been founded.

Because of all the planning I'd missed the third phase flowering of the new generation. I went home to find all my lovely flowers in the fourth or fifth phase; at such times we merely hurried between the rows with secateurs. I should have gone at the most beautiful moment, when the colour was appearing on the buds, under the sepals! Curses! I'd seen nothing of the second flowering, when they opened fully and began to reveal their real selves, That was when I ought to have been in the greenhouse, to observe and consider what would be good for them.

I ought always to stay in the same place, not do so much rushing about being active. It was only while I was a nobody, an unknown, only searching, that I worked to good effect and was able to keep a close eye on the flowers. Once I was a great man, had been discovered, I had no time for work, not a minute to attend to things, because of constant demands on me. Then there was only a hollow greatness. A past glory. By now I could see that I was not going to be able to do any further big jobs. When, then? Damn all the travelling to Bucharest. Wouldn't it have been my duty to create a flower capable of competing at an international level, which was what the Station expected of me, as did the whole government, all of Romania?

Kali always said: it'll work next time. If some flower hadn't been very successful, or had become diseased, she said: next time. If the plum jam that she'd made didn't set properly, she said 'It'll be better next time, you'll see, mister.' And next time so I did.

'You shouldn't be running about like that all the time,' said Kali. 'You're always in such a 'urry. Stand still. And take a good look at what you're doin'. Keep lookin' until you're bored to hell. Like the pretty girl that became bored with lookin' at 'erself in the mirror, you know, in the folk tale. And what became of 'er? She did all right, ended up jumpin' down the well.'

Kali hadn't told me that tale. But now I'd heard another—about myself!

Every two years there was a Party report in the *aktiva* on members, myself included, and I had to be present. An assessment. And not behind my back! In the course of it, my activity was verified, and they considered whether I had offended against the spirit of the Party or directives. Development too was considered. There was certainly no fault to be found with my work and the Michurin Gardening Station. In that we were in the forefront at a national level, that was clear, and no one was going to say otherwise. We were the first after Bucharest.

Mogyorós too supported me strongly, and that meant a lot. Alexandru Moghioroş was a Hungarian. His name is Hungarian, but all the same so important a man answered better to the Romanian form. They said he was also a Jew, but those days that didn't matter. One's origins didn't count.

Comrade Décsi has been very active in every sphere of activity relating to the development of the Station, said the assessment. He has produced outstanding results in the dissemination of Soviet scientific methods, especially in the search for new, vitamin-rich fruit and the improvement of the mass cultivation of native varieties. His theoretical grounding has developed considerably. He is in close connection to popular elements, collects simple peasant tools in villages, and when he goes on visits to Bucharest, his is not a petty-bourgeois lifestyle. He enjoys hunting and football. He regularly takes part in cultural competitions. In terms of personal characteristics too, he is modest, very disciplined, not talkative, but sometimes on edge, and at times has been authoritative in the collective. A hesitant nature, he does not handle responsibility at a corresponding level. He does not maintain contacts with nationalist or chauvinist circles, nor with any inclined to mysticism. He directs the collective well. His private life is disorderly.

It said no more on the subject. I thought, what is that supposed to mean? The child, obviously. I don't imagine they don't know. The child and Kali. When there's something in a report to the effect that my life is disorderly it has to be taken as a hint. That I should tidy it up. Because this local report will, of course, find its way to the Centre and onto my record. Then if anything ever happens, it will be brought up. It would be seen that there had previously been this black mark. So I had to sort it out.

What was I to do about that Kali? She's was a good woman, and I don't just mean nice to me. But anyway, how shall I put it? Her moustache was prickly.

That other girl, just when I called at her house, was drinking milk. I'd run over to see her, if I thought that her father wasn't at home and maybe I would catch her in. There was milk around her mouth. On her top lip as well. It wasn't a moustache, just down. She worked on the land, and so did I, I told her, and we laughed. We hadn't all that much in common. Because I was a biologist, a lecturer, director of the Station, and she was a little Hóstát girl. How old was she? No more than fourteen. Thirteen at the most. Or even less.

My mother had told me that I wasn't husband material. When I did my first big deal with the Dutchman, how old was I, not even thirty yet, I boasted to my mother, because I couldn't keep quiet about it. She told me not to ruin my life with such stuff. Look how much she'd suffered from her children. Your father never got you anywhere, she said.

'You couldn't go to school, your father wouldn't let you, took you with him whitewashing. Then when you grew up, reached twenty-five, you didn't sit still. You've done all sorts of things. You've made money,' said my mother. Because all she could see was a pile of marks. The Dutchman had paid me in marks.

So, I asked, didn't she want a grandchild? She'd got enough even without me, she replied.

'Look at young Sándor, he can't tie a knot in his prick.' Sándor is my elder brother. 'And that woman as well, why doesn't she do something? They've just had their fifth child. Five girls. Well, God has afflicted them, they were both conceived under unfavourable stars. And that Sándor is so pleased with her all the time, you'd think he'd found a full purse in the street. Marriage isn't for you, my boy. You need something big to do, not to sit around as a married man, letting your wife tell you what to do. Because you're the sort of dope that a wife will push around.'

If for some reason I were to take a woman out, it was only to score on my mother a bit. But I wasn't that way inclined. To meet a woman, go with her to the council and get married—Mother was right for once, that wasn't for me. Nor do I feel so disposed. Now I'm going to have an international exhibition, maybe I'll be sent to Trieste now or in the future. They hold a rose competition there every year, but nothing has come about it yet.

Kali and the child are now living in Györgyfalva, and now I'm able to work in peace. I've bought a little house for them. It's not big, but she's got a garden and she can keep some poultry and plant onions if she likes. She was very upset. So too bad. I took her into the CEC and she took out a little loan as a single parent with a child, but I shall repay that for her. I had to arrange an income for her, because, of course, they asked in the CEC what income she had. I'll put her into one of the collectives, I told her. Rather, take me on at the Station, she said. How can I do that, I asked. How does she imagine that I can put her in there? I'm very highly regarded now. I simply daren't put it on paper. I'm not in a position to keep you with me at the Station.

'What position are you in, mister? Tell me.'

And she just looked at me. Looked with her smooth face, because there's not so much as a single wrinkle on it. Just her clear blue eyes, which can look at me in such a way that I see right through her. She's a woman, so she wants a quarrel. They all adore it. I've never seen a single woman who wouldn't have given anything to have a row with her husband. But I'm not her husband, that's a fact, but she thinks I am. I said to her: 'Look here, Kali, you're getting a house and garden in your own name. Do you understand that?'

She said that she certainly did understand.

'That we're being put out. Because you need the room, mister.'

What room? She's off her rocker.

'For your girlfriends, of course.'

Then she said nothing.

'You had a break for a bit, and now it's come over you again, and you're off.'

'What's come over me?' I asked.

'Being male, of course. You can't do without it, mister, your prick's always up and away.'

She so annoyed me, I didn't speak to her for at least a week. But now I've ensured her future. House and all. Even a loom! Because the loom was brought for her. She likes weaving, she's said as much, so she's been given a loom, she can do some weaving if she's a married woman. Well, said Kali, when it was brought.

'Put it together now, Kali Green. because you've never seen anything like it in your life.'

She turned it this way and that, the pieces wouldn't fit together.

I asked her: 'Kali, my dear, have you any idea how to weave? You can't even assemble the loom.'

Then Kali picked it up and read out what was carved on the base:

'*Razboi de Nae Gheorghe*, Balani, 1899. I can't understand a word.'

I looked at it myself.

'*Razboi* is Romanian for war.'

'So, what was this Uncle Gheorghe doing at war? Where did you get this contraption from?' asked Kali.

'When we were getting the students to collect things,' I replied. 'We were collecting apple varieties in Szilágy county.'

'Well then, round me up a Wallachian who can tell me 'ow it works. Because we're going to get on with this like when King Mátyás presented the rich man with a plough. You know, mister, 'cos I've told you the story. A plough that ploughed by itself, but that man didn't give 'im as much as a sour apple from 'is garden. 'E certainly made a bad bargain with 'im.'

Then the Romitáns, a Hóstát farming family on Pata utca, said that they had a Romanian woman who stayed with the little child when they went to the fields, and she used to weave. They'd have to bring her round. She came and looked at it this way and that, then said that she didn't know at all how to weave with it. Then Kali went down to see her friend Mária, and it turned out that she had a Lónya loom, there was carving on it, and that was different. The devil would be puzzled by all these looms. By now I was sorry I'd bought it rather than put it on the fire, because that was what a Gypsy had intended, so as to cook in the yard where we'd collected the apple varieties. I bought it when I saw that there was something carved on it. Gosh, the amount that Gypsy wanted for it. We bargained as if I were buying on behalf of a museum. He asked enough for five cartloads of firewood. Kali's been given it so that she can do some weaving out in Györgyfalva and sell it, if she likes, because she's always talked a lot about weaving. And now she's sewing, because she's been given a machine by her family.

Whether she understands or not, I've got the Station here to attend to, and it'll be better for her to live quietly with the child out in the village, in the country, away from the bad air of the town. She's got chickens and onions. I'll go and call every week. Sometimes twice. I've told her I'll marry her if she so wishes.

The verdict has been pronounced. You couldn't make it up. They're saying now, and I've heard it in the university, that the lecturers have been sentenced. And Lali. There's been no detail in any paper, just a bald statement. The hearing wasn't public. Lali's been given the most. Twelve years with hard labour and confiscation of property. The rest all got less. It's beyond belief. They've already been inside for two years, and now comes this sentence. Trial of Transylvanists, it's been made out as. Trial of university lecturers, more like. Transylvanists—what's that supposed to mean? Hungarians, born in Transylvania, therefore Transylvanists. I could even understand all the clergy, the dissidents, the chauvinists, that agitated against collectivization, I understood that the world had to be purged of them so that a new way could be constructed, But Lali? And Edgár Balogh? Well, they were merely left-wing. That Lali's never coming out. No chance, he's going to die in prison. Twelve years. And Mari as well. She's bound to kill herself now, she's always been threatening. Lali and the rest are in Jilava. Everybody's talking about it. I don't feel disposed to be in any company, people will know that I was a friend of Lali's.

Over dinner I started to sob. Then little Vilmos joined in. Kali was offended that I didn't tell her why I was sobbing. How could I tell her that my dear, handsome friend, of whom she of all people had always said what a really refined gentleman, had committed such a great crime as to be given twelve years? I didn't want to upset her as well. God damn this life.

Well, I haven't gone to Trieste this year. Nobody had said that I wasn't going, they never do. The year just went by. But at least one thing pleased me greatly. I wanted to say a great kick in the backside, because these days the sort of pleasure that I get from above equates with a light smack on the bum. I've been given tickets—not one, but two—for the Romania–Hungary B team match. It says on them, to take place on 19 September 1954. They've come from the Centre, so I can't not go. Why shouldn't I go? I like watching people running after a ball. These days I mostly watch others, don't play myself. I asked young Werner if he would like to come. He said he didn't understand football, didn't even know the rules. It was simple, I said. One side wears red, the other blue, and at half-time they're all so muddy you can't tell the difference. What did he mean, didn't understand football? I asked, hadn't he played as a boy?

'Where I was as a boy, there were no footballs,' he replied, and kept his voice down.

That's what these Jews remember about everything. Where they were in those days. In that camp, lucky to have got home. He needs to be able to break free, I thought.

'Well, these days the way the world is, every Jew can get as high as they care to. Take Ana Pauker, for instance.'

He said that he knew about Ana Pauker.

'The Jews have been dropping out for a long time now.'

I said, that wasn't the case because they were Jews. Why then had a Jew and a Hungarian dropped out together and been condemned to death? For wasn't it true that László Luka too had been marginalized? Serious errors had been made in agrarian policies, in the organization of collectivization, because Pauker hadn't been sufficiently active? Hadn't shown enough results, had acted too weakly? Well, what did people expect from a woman? Young Werner said that he didn't understand politics, but . . . That was obvious. I didn't tell him what a stupid business it was, didn't want to keep arguing, after all he was my colleague, but anyway, if somebody Jewish was arrested, it was immediately said that Jewishness was the reason. Or that he was a Hungarian. And just as well it wasn't because she was a woman! Because there wasn't another woman in the government, was there? I'd heard there wasn't another woman minister in the whole of Europe. Ana Pauker was the first. A Romanian Jewish woman. So there.

'These days there's no need to consider anybody's origins, it's what they do,' I explained to him. 'These days nationality politics is completely different, but people don't understand, it doesn't penetrate. Because all they've got in their minds, even good minds, is the same old thing, Romanian chauvinism. So it's lucky that many young people are beginning to think differently today. They can see how high a Hungarian can rise in the Party and the leadership of the country. What, there aren't any Hungarian ministers? I beg your pardon—Mogyoros. And there isn't a Hungarian Autonomous Territory? Can't they see it?'

If he didn't come to the match with me never mind, at least he'd been getting on with budding. The summer weather was still good enough for that. Only I hadn't prepared enough wild rose stocks. You could even buy wild rose stocks in Western catalogues. Curious.

Then I asked young Tibor, my junior secretary, whether he would come. A very clever lad, young Tibor. Tibor Dáné. He's done some marvellous work, domesticating wild flowers. It's fantastic what can be achieved when you can master nature. It looked as if I'd be going by myself. I didn't know which of my old footballing friends I might take. I didn't want to take a Romanian to cheer on his team against the Hungarians, and I didn't want to take a Hungarian for fear of repercussions. Just this once it wouldn't matter, though, I felt, to cheer for Hungary. Just this once, because it was a match, wasn't it. But to hell with it. I was always being cautious. It hadn't always been like that. We were a team and we'd shout and kick, that was all, never mind in which language, and mainly *bozmeg*, which every Romanian knew. The ball was what mattered, not who was what. Then I went up to town early, there was always something for me to do at the Centre; this time I had to ask for a whole list of things for the laboratory, which was as empty as a barn.

There was a procession to the match with big Romanian banners, and some turned up already drunk. They were let in drunk as well, as only tickets were checked. I went into the stand by myself. The whole office and the chiefs of the Centre had all turned out. People had come from the MAT as well, Comrade Csupor. Lajos Csupor, First Secretary of the MAT. He'd been in prison with Dejzs. Or was that Mogyoros? Sándor Mogyoros was there, as was János Fazekas, who was on the Centre committee. He had a good knowledge of Hungarian affairs and handled them well. All the leading Hungarians. There were also two actors from the MAT, from Vásárhely. Unfortunately, everybody likes football. There was little Ceaușescu, he too had come out.

This match had to take place at just this time, because a couple of months previously, the Germans had beaten Hungary in the World Cup. Even if it was only a B team match. The Romanians were ever so pleased that the Hungarians had been beaten. The golden team, as it called itself, had lost for the first time. That wasn't the team that had come here, this was the B team. I didn't know where to sit so as to feel comfortable. The Hungarians were all seated in a bunch, all shouting things like '*Na, acum va arátám vouá!*' Now we were going to show them!

Before I left Kolozvár, my old footballing friend Filotti told me how lucky I was to be going to the match in Bucharest. So this was luck! The way I was being watched, stared at! I didn't feel comfortable being looked at like that. But I couldn't support the opposition! This is my homeland, the Romanian People's Republic, this I must serve, this tells me that I'm to be an important man or whatever. But even so I couldn't see it like that when the Hungarians were running around the pitch as if they were Hottentots, with whom I'd nothing in common.

How was I to behave in that situation? Let it not be said that I'm lily-livered. Are thinking people all lily-livered? The Hungarian fans were in the stand opposite. Not all that many, but they'd come down from Budapest by train. I could see that they weren't being allowed to wave Hungarian flags. I'm not ashamed to say that at first I hardly saw the ball, I couldn't watch, or rather couldn't enjoy watching, I was so on edge. I didn't know how to behave, and I didn't enjoy it one way or the other. Mogyorós and Csupor weren't bothered, they weren't cowards, they appreciated this and that, every move. '*Ce faza, ce faza!*' howled the commentator. He only said that to Romanians, when the Romanians had possession. Then I thought, when there had been good Hungarian possession—towards the end of the first half, we were on the attack, we kept the ball as long as we wanted, and then it was rolling in the tatty Romanian net—well, I thought, to hell with this nationalism. Isn't it better to watch the football, see how skilfully the ball is carried and passed from one to another, how quickly it's passed back and controlled, then dribbled—that's what should be watched. And not what's Romanian or Hungarian. From the way we looked at each other, it was just as if the match were being played in the stands. Oh, when there was Hungarian possession and we had the ball, the whole stadium immediately resounded with 'Shoot!' There was cheering and even throwing of bottles. People ran out to get them off the pitch, while the players too picked them up and threw them aside. And then the Romanian national anthem was sung—you couldn't hear the loudspeakers for it, and they were really big ones. It would have taken a miracle for the Hungarians to win.

When, however, the Hungarians scored, the pitch was invaded. They were hooligans. Frightful bellowing, fighting, I couldn't really see what was going on. There was no more need to take an interest in anything, what went on was absolutely disgraceful. Oh, that little pumpkin seed did indeed grin from the VIP seats! He even raised his eyebrows and laughed aloud. Damn him, I thought. And the other one, Comrade Mogyorós, was clever, and only after a long time, when the uproar was in full swing and drunken hooligans were all over the pitch and shouting, did he stand and call for order to be restored so that the game could continue. Mogyorós didn't care, he wanted the match and that was all. One of the Hungarians was substituted because the hooligans that had swarmed onto the pitch had beaten him up. I was absolutely trembling, as if I'd been him. The police restored order in a lazy sort of way. I'd have been after them to get a grip and sort things out. I'd have expected better, especially at an international match. Finally the match was abandoned ten minutes before the end. The hooligans were driven off the pitch and the Hungarian supporters had to be escorted from the stand to protect them from the people who were invading it again. We Hungarians had lost, and we, citizens of the Romanian People's Republic, had won. Such is football.

I shall never again go to a match. To hell with it.

It would be better if I never went anywhere, not to Trieste that year, nor in the future. It was preferable for nothing to happen in the new year, such was my wish to myself. Let me have some peace, do my work, keep quiet, not have to go off anywhere. All I was interested in was flowers.

But the expectations of the Station in the new year! Spring brought results. No frosts, no new diseases, and we were able to begin budding in August. Now I was running about every morning as if I were twenty and looking for my first rose. Those rose-houses were now two years old. I was also conducting experiments on all the apple varieties that the gormless students had collected. But I wasn't looking forward all that much to beginning my classes at the university, I'd already lost so much time.

I went in at the end of August to see whether I still had any examinees from summer. Some, of course, had just failed in some state exam as well. The second year cohort had just left. An important matter.

Word got round that I was there and the head of personnel called me in. He asked if I'd decided.

'Decided what?' I asked.

'Whether the comrade will go and lecture in the Romanian Department or resign?' said he. He'd been waiting since then for me to look in and tell him. I didn't understand what he was talking about. Everybody else called me *te*. The head of personnel alone did not. Had I received the notification? he asked.

'What notification?' I asked, 'I haven't had anything.' But word had been sent to my address for me to come in, posts in the Romanian Department were being offered only to me and the Hungarian dean. I still didn't understand. He said that as of autumn agronomy was to be taught in Romanian only in the Agricultural High School. How was that possible, I asked. He didn't know. It was a *decizió*.

'And don't expect me to explain, comrade. You should have come in when you received the letter.'

'I've told you I haven't received it!' I replied irritably. Until then the head of personnel had been looking at me quite dismissively, but now he became more insistent.

'Admission to Agronomy hasn't been announced. *Gata*'

Then he asked again for my decision. No way, I replied, because I'd only just heard about it. He had to know, they'd sent it out a month previously.

And so it came to me like a blow on the head. In 1949, when the Hungarian Agriculture Department was formed, it had been such a bonus for the Hungarians, and now, if you please, six years later it was being closed. That was what this meant, wasn't it. The letter had been sent to the lecturers during the vacation so that they wouldn't be able to get together at the university and protest.

In came Sándor Nagy, the door of the lecturers' room was opened for him and he began to pack up his books. He had to show everything when he left in case he'd stolen something. He was told that they had to check that nothing was from the library. He was leaving as if he'd been a thief. Because the rooms had to be cleared by the end of August. When the head of personnel had left the room, Sándor said, 'You're the lucky one, Vili. Only two have been invited to transfer. We from the High School Department have been invited to join the Biology Department at the Babeş.'

Yet again this confounded good luck! It wasn't enough for me to hear only now that there was no more Hungarian agronomy. Well, it was good luck, I can say, from my point of view. Now be sensible, Vilmos. If I join the Romanian Department to lecture, I'll get it in the neck from the Hungarians for betraying them. But if I don't, it will be said of me that I'm being pro-Hungarian and snooty, that I favour isolationism, or I'll simply be accused of nationalism. Perhaps the Station would be taken off me.

I asked where he was going. Where would he be?

He was a sound man on theory, and had written a book on animal feedstuffs. I asked which colleague was keeping his post. He hadn't spoken to anybody yet, everybody had been away in summer, all over the place, he'd only heard about Balla. He was leaving, he said softly. He'd met Gazda and his wife. Gazda was said to have had a nervous breakdown and had been in hospital. He was now at home. I asked, hadn't he been able to speak to anyone else? He could either have gone to see the rector or up to Bucharest to discuss the matter. He just winked. It was all settled, he said, and you had to be careful. The students had played a sort of joke, had set up a candle outside the university at night. Written on it had been *Agronomy Department 1948– 1952.* Meaning that the one course had been able to graduate three years ago. One student had been arrested and taken into custody. He didn't know what had happened to the rest.

No meeting had been called for it to be debated. The decision that agronomy was not something to be studied in a minority language had come from the Centre. That the soil was, of course, neither Hungarian nor Romanian, neither baked by the sun in Hungarian nor rained on in Romanian. It was enough if agronomists studied in Romanian because that was in their interest. Perhaps the whole business was some wider policy. But for that matter I hadn't have been so interested in the university, not a bit, that wasn't what pained me. I was a terrible lecturer, because I didn't like it, only cared for practical subjects. Students just upset me when I saw that they had no feeling for either the soil or plants. What in heaven's name did they want? Not that it did my salary any harm. But it did harm in other ways.

I told Sándor to write his address down so that I could keep in touch. We hadn't become such friends that I knew where he lived. It was only been three years since I'd been appointed.

I left the head of personnel and told him that I'd be in the following week. What was I to tell him about what I was now going to do in the university? Whether I would lecture in the Romanian Department. A great honour, it was said. They could keep it. It was important, but I just had to be able to reply properly to such a thing.

When I'd been taken on the rector was István Nagy, the working-class writer—I'd bought his book for Kali to read as he was my superior—and he'd said, at the very last department meeting in June, that we ought not to consider whether or not we'd been well off for buildings, because he wasn't explicit but alluded to the fact that the Romanians had been given the the-atre, hadn't they, and the Hungarians could go back to the chamber theatre as before the war, and use the girls school, the Marianum, which used to belong to the nuns, as a university building. The new regime, however, was going to do away with nationality boundaries, would no longer take into account whether one was Hungarian, Romanian, Jewish, Saxon, Armenian, or whatever. We must take the USSR as an example of how clearly and simply the nationality question was resolved. We were working on this together. Then, perhaps, it would be resolved in such a way that instruction in Hungarian would not be required. The specialist schools would all be closed one by one. We must wait patiently for the time when everything would be sorted out.

I'd intended to call at City Hall on the way home, but now I couldn't. I just fled, I was so on edge. A heavy storm broke and I was soaked through. I didn't attempt to run, I let the rain beat down on me, nice warm, summer rain, and at least I came to myself. I didn't see anybody, and my tears too were pouring. By the time I reached home, even my underclothes were sodden. Kali was there again with the child, because she made a point of coming over once a week, and she got me out some dry clothes, made some tea and gave me a drop of pálinka. I didn't tell her anything, I didn't know where to begin.

Once I was dry I said, 'Let's go into town, go and see a film. Have a bit of a laugh.' Though I really didn't feel like laughing.

She was amazed, I'd hardly ever taken her to the cinema. Her favourite films were musicals. She looked out of the window. The rain had passed over by that time and the sun was shining.

'Is this the best time to go, when it's easiest to pull weeds?' she asked. ''Cos that machine, the cultivator you bought, is out of order, isn't working.'

Let's stop in, she said, and do some work. Then she cooked me ever such a nice *pánko* filled with sour cream.

She must have taken the child down the road to the neighbour, because little Vilmos had had a *tejtestvér* there. Kali had provided milk as the other woman had had none. So she was able to take the boy down there to be looked after, the two children played happily together, and it was a shame to waste the good weather. I thought to myself, she's just a peasant woman. So out we went into the garden.

What a heavy vegetable smell! You could cut it with a knife after the rain, in the warmth, when the oils were moving. We went to the Annabella row. The heads were as big as my palm. Kali brought the stool and a bucket. She pulled up the chickweed separately to give to the farmer in exchange for eggs. Weeding was easy work. Kali asked whether she should tell a tale, as she could see that I was upset. Not now, I said, I'll tell you one at dinner. I won't thank you for that, she said. Then we worked in silence. I got stuck into the weeding like I did in my young days, when I'd first had the garden. Then I fetched the secateurs and did a bit to the flowers as well. You could tell that there'd been no gardener there, I'll say.

Then Kali made a very wise comment.

'You should come out weeding every time you're upset. You'd see, it would make you feel better. It clears your mind nicely and you can see what you need and what you don't. What you don't falls away. You lose one thing and get another.'

'Really, Kali, who didn't you become a priest? You're so fond of philosophizing.'

'I'm your priest, mister. That's quite enough for me. See, the good Lord gives with one 'and and pulls weeds with the other.'

So it was, because I'd received. On Monday approval had come. I could take on five experts to work only on the roses. I'd asked for three and been given five! And two women for the five greenhouses. Who would have dreamed of such a great opportunity! But would I in fact have five that I could rely on? Young Werner would be seeing to his resistant whites. I was looking for one to experiment on cutting roses, so that I could bring them into cultivation. I had to find one that flowered repeatedly better, yielded most in a year. One man, the very best—but who was it to be?—whom I could take to my side, with whom I would work on the selection of varieties, and who would go to international competitions. Because my brief now included bringing honour to Romania in competitions. It no longer meant improvement, because that didn't ring at all true, but a selection of varieties. Then I had two places left to fill. Five greenhouses, with a man carrying out experiments in each. I had to engage experts whose cadre sheets were in order, and it was required that one should be suitably trained. But paper was meaningless if they knew nothing. I'd heard of a young man, a Romanian named Mocean or Moceanu, who was very clever with roses and had his own garden in Erdőfelek. But if he lacked the documents, what could I employ him as? A planter.

I ought to have gone and looked at new varieties abroad. I didn't know whether I would be allowed to. I could go to the USSR, delegations were always going there and plenty came from there to Romania. But I didn't know what the situation was there with regard to roses. Perhaps things like roses too were being moved along quickly. One could mainly visit the Michurin gardens, and even in remote, cold, Asiatic regions, Lysenko too had achieved fantastic adaptations, and it had turned out that the whole of Siberia could be amazingly transformed by vernalization: varieties could be transformed through the transmission of acquired properties and the cooperation of varieties. I ought to go to France or Germany, but at the time I didn't dare apply for a passport to go there. Not even to Hungary, nobody was going there just then. I didn't want to attract attention by needing to go travelling all the time.

But then all of a sudden there was a great thaw! It was as if the world had been renewed. The order came. Mogyoros phoned that I should get ready, I'd be going to Trieste next time; I'd only been waiting four years for that. Lali too was released from prison. He, Edgár Balogh and János Demeter, of whom Lali had nothing good to say, had been inside for three years and were released in May. Lali came up to the Station in June to see the flowers open. He didn't admire the flowers as much as the Station itself, and how much it had expanded. He'd lost thirty kilos, and gone grey all over. Kali didn't recognize him. Previously he'd been such a proper young gentleman, a bit of a dandy, and so he'd been called Bubi. Now he looked like a retired factory worker. Completely shrunken. He burst into tears when he went into C greenhouse, where fifteen hundred Cluj Superstar were opening; that's the name I'm proposing for it as it comes into production. I created it, it's my variety. Lali had become very sensitive. He's lost his faith in people. Or rather, not people, just the Party.

In September he took me to the theatre. He was mad about the theatre. He'd been secretary, literary secretary, and had directed plays. He said that in prison he'd yearned for the theatre. He took me to see a new Hungarian play. Well, I mean, I'd have regarded it as a new Hungarian play as well, it was about our present lives. It was by Anna Novák. A woman writing a play—I'd never heard of such a thing. Well, if that's what was on in the theatre there was no need to go there again. It was a sort of kitchen-sink drama, it tried to be like real life, because it was performed in a room and showed a family, and there was an anarchist and an Arrow Cross man, who later committed suicide, but it wasn't like real life. They spoke from written scripts, a STAS-script, as nowadays anything is called that has no soul. STAS, I don't even know what it means, what the letters stand for, because these days it sounds like a bit of officialese, so that's what it must be, STAS. I'll have to ask Lali.

Lali criticized it severely all through, muttering to me during the whole performance as we sat in the royal box. In his opinion that ancient nest of Hungarian culture was being foully soiled. The author might be a Jewish woman who had survived the camp and come home. Being Jewish didn't mean she could write plays. Lali believed she was in line for a State Award for the play. When he went backstage to congratulate them, Lali addressed her as Zimra, her original name. Lali worshipped actors, and they gushed over him. He said that there were a lot of good people in the theatre, but not future people. They were such petty-bourgeois elements, lived in the past. So when he later invited me to some Russian ballet or an opera, I told him I'd had enough of the theatre.

He'd do better to come and see me in the Station, there was always something for him to look at there. I said I was a bit alarmed, we kept being given more and more land that had been taken from the Hóstát farmers and annexed to ours. I was still having to expand and plan all sorts of further things on the site, I was at my wits' end. At least I could talk things over with Lali, there wasn't really anyone else. He said sadly:

'*Forma fără fond.*'

I asked him what that meant. I understood the words—form without foundation. What did it mean? He replied: it's a philosophy. The Romanians' philosophy. The basis of the whole modernization of Romania. Its basis was that it had no basis! It aped a sort of form from the West, a sort of external form, but there was no content to it. It would set up a university or a factory or some cultural body and it had no academics, no skilled people to staff it.

It would buy machinery from abroad but didn't know how it worked, there was no one to maintain it, it just wanted to mechanise.

'*Forma fără fond*. Form without foundation, get it? These days it isn't modernism, it's socialism.'

But all the same, he said, sooner or later these forms just fill with something. Once a university's there. Or a Station.

That was right, *forma fără fond*. That was what mattered in those days. I was rushed off my feet. I was expected to come up quickly with rose production on an industrial scale. Everything was ready, a huge amount of land had been appropriated, I'd got 360 hectares, I was to fill them up.

How was I to know about commercial rose growing? I'd never been a commercial grower, only in a small way, a private concern. Now I was having to do everything as if I understood industrial affairs. Perhaps I ought to work with miniatures. People didn't have such big gardens in those days, only smallish ones, and a lot of people grew things on their terraces. Because, of course, they were starting to build big blocks. But I deeply detested miniature roses. They looked as if they were manmade, and not his best work. Nature wasn't short of space, didn't have to create suppressed, dwarf things. I didn't like it if the hand of man was to be detected in a thing. In real creation, it isn't. That's pure nature.

The question was which varieties I meant to grow. Commercially useful, quick to flower a second time, long-lasting when cut, resistant to diseases, and with flowers as showy as the leaves. Only beauty must not be emphasized in plans for development. Indeed, nor could it be. Beauty was not to be prescribed in commercial terms.

After twenty years' experience of growing roses I knew that one must not make a rose too beautiful. Or perfect. It's not allowed. No rose grower will acknowledge the fact, but it is so. While the war was still going on Werner produced Regina Elisabeta, named for the queen of Romania. He called it that then, whereas we knew that it had originally been Queen Erzsébet, for the queen of Hungary. When he had to say what it was being named for, all he could put on the registration certificate was that he had given it the name of the most delicate queen. I knew, of course, which queen that was, because she'd been the queen of Hungary, but Werner had been clever and had been able to bring a new name into circulation. People went mad over it! But that rose was too beautiful, and I said so. It had big, heart-shaped, blood-red petals that darkened towards the edges and were paler on the reverse. Its leaves were a very deep colour, almost black, solid, shiny, almost lacquered. It was too beautiful. Among thirty other varieties in a garden, it was too conspicuous. It flaunted itself and its power, trying to outdo the rest. Werner had gone too far, piled in everything at once: strong colours, posture, shape. Like when a woman has everything she wears too cleverly made, has even her skirt tailored to fit closely, and promenades like that in the main square. You shouldn't show everything at once. You could tell that that rose was manmade. That's exactly what should not be obvious. Nature is cleverer in such respects.

We had to look for complicated simplicity. That was my philosophy. Mere simplicity means that of the wild roses, *Rosa indica* or *gallica* or *canina*. We had to see what nature could do by itself. That kind of simplicity could only be attained in such a complicated way. I didn't know whether I'd been able to explain to young Werner what 'complicated simplicity' meant. He seemed to have understood. The other colleagues in the rose-houses were either envious or slave drivers. With such thoughts I was on my own, couldn't share them and had to keep quiet. Or put them in a good book, but for that there was never going to be time.

Werner senior was still claiming that he was going to develop that rose further still, to be completely full; he wanted as many as seventy or eighty petals. What he had done so far was very strange, actually, fantastic. The final form that he produced was fourteen centimetres across. It was never able to open fully! That is, it would have been capable of reaching that size, but its strength, the plant's inner strength, had failed. He'd asked too much of it.

In my opinion simple was more beautiful: the kind of thing that pres-ented itself as commonplace at first sight, not so showy, though it had a certain novelty that there had never been before. For example, if someone should produce a white multiflora with tiny buds, snow-white and very small. It would look something like a bush sprinkled with snowflakes, so that one should see it, at a glance, as merely a trifling thing, insignificant. The Five Nunns was rather like that, and so not significant enough. There's no need for terribly great beauty and perfection. Anything too beautiful soon becomes boring.

When a gardener thinks of something simple and natural, not too showy, which seems to everybody to have always existed but never did—as nobody had ever noticed it before or thought of producing it—well, I'm jealous. Very jealous of Peace, for example. But that too is from two colours. Now I've found out what it came from: we have Charles P. Kilham in common.

I'd told Kali as well, explained 'beautiful' to her. Because I couldn't contain myself, I was always chattering. I'd told her my line of thought, complicated simplicity. My theory of beauty.

'The way nature makes things isn't that the back is like this and the edge like that, and in the middle there's another shade. Simple is beautiful, there's no need for display. It's possible to produce something which is red inside and white outside, but a thing like that is excessively attention-seeking.'

'Goodness me, that's a nice Calvinist idea you've got, mister, you might even preach that in church,' said she to that. We were working one Sunday afternoon, with the child asleep in the basket. My reply was to pick up a lump of dried manure and throw it at her. How I hate that endless talk of religion!

'You've thrown bread at me, not a stone. 'Cos this nice manure is bread to the soil,' she said, 'And I'm not cross about it.'

Then I went on: 'Therefore anything beautiful must be simple and natural, because we've got many varieties, haven't we, and we put a lot side by side and it's called a rose garden. They have to blend in with one another. But on the other hand, if we produce a variety that's nothing but a jumble, where there are so many colours on a single stem, it just won't do in company, it looks out of place. Because one rose has to blend in with another and a third, and so on. If they're individually this way and that, they'll never make a garden.'

'Exactly like in the Calvinist church!' Kali clapped her hands theatrically. "Cos look 'ere, if we're all alone we're nothin', the wind blows us away, we're weak. So we 'ave to be a congregation, there was a sermon about that just now. And certainly the universal priesthood's just the same, 'cos there in the Lord's 'ouse we all preach equally, 'cos you 'ave to stand up by yourself, and in front of the congregation. That's what the reverend said in the Kétágú.'

'Look here, Kali, dry up, I've told you to leave out this stupid church talk that the cabbage under your headscarf is rinsed with every week. The priests really do brainwash you.'

Because, of course, it was possible to produce something that would win in competitions. That was what I was having to do in my research. You just had to know what was fashionable, what was novel, the world situation, and there had to be something personal in it.

There were those three flowers that I was producing. One was the excessively beautiful, because I wanted to outdo nature. Number two was the one that would win in competitions, would be better than the rest, surpass everybody. And the third sort would be neither the one nor the other, only, to tell the truth, just for my pleasure, and it would have to be the complicatedly beautiful one.

Finally I told the university whether or not I would join the Romanian section. I'd taken a week to think it through and I had to be clever to cut the Gordian knot with which I was faced every day. I told them what in fact they knew: I had the Station, which was no small undertaking, and the forty employees in addition, the planning wasn't yet completed, some things had yet to be approved, and we were in a fluid situation. And so I'd have to leave the university even if the Hungarian agronomy were not closed, because when was I to give lectures? By that I didn't only mean that I had at present a huge amount to do. I suggested now to the university that it was possible to come to the Station for practical work, I would undertake a quite serious half-year course in the Romanian section up there, because we would have plenty of material, *material de demonstrare*. Only practical. No one questioned my ability to lecture decently in Romanian and give instruction. I therefore took that for granted. And so I would extricate myself, like the clever girl did with King Mátyás, as Kali told the tale. I would then be taken off the university staff and transferred fully to the Station. I would cease to be a lecturer in Hungarian at the university. I happened to bump into ex-rector István Nagy in the street; he had then been ejected from the Party, even though he had made a declaration of self-criticism, because there had been fascist writers with whom he had collaborated. He told me not to resign in haste but to think. Not to worry. One had to be very careful. He was no longer rector, but had been rehabilitated and awarded a State Prize. He said that I should remain on the staff but my norm would be reduced. Oh dear, I didn't understand that university jargon. What *norm*? Whatever was I to do?

Then I ran into Werner; he'd come to look at the site and the new land. Because, of course, we hadn't yet finished building and never shall. He'd heard what had happened at the university.

'Vili, how lucky you are even now,' said he.

I thought I'd burst with rage. Really, how was I lucky now? Not to know what to do with myself so as to suit everybody? Then again, there was the unfortunate Sándor Nagy as well; I called him unfortunate now because it had turned out when I enquired that he'd got some medical problem, his hands were trembling, so I couldn't offer him experimental work though I'd thought he'd be good at it. After all, he was a member of the university staff. I'd thought of him as a scientific assistant as long as the Centre gave permission. I'd have made good use of him when I had to write reports as well, because as a researcher he'd also know how to write, there had to be so much verbiage in those reports and it needed a man of learning, not a practical one like me. So I asked him, but he could scarcely hold a pen, his hands were shaking so badly.

As for the white roses, young Benjamin Werner said that his father had advised him to forget Virgo, Agnus Dei and Five Nunns. They were all very fragile flowers, and he couldn't see world famous flowers coming from them. Don't work on those, his father had said. I said that he should, because in the Station I'm his father. They're tiny, soft plants, one's a floribunda, another's a polyantha, and they wouldn't lead to strong park roses with big thorns, that was true, but there had to be a place for ones with small heads and tiny, delicate, dark green leaves as well.

Werner was sick with jealousy, it seemed to me, and was jealous of the Station; there we were going to achieve great results. Because now, of course, I had been awarded a State Prize (Fourth Class), something that no Hungarian gardener had ever received. And my first book on the Michurin results had been published—not exactly a slim monograph. The institute was developing nicely, and at the university I'd been kept on the staff; they hadn't let me go and I was on a half-timetable.

But we would give new roses new names. That was the prime business of the moment.

I set up the Naming Committee in the Station. I obtained authority for it, though my request was rejected three times by Bucharest. Finally it was accepted up there that once we were bringing in serious rose results and showing our new varieties at international level we would have to keep to the highest standards in all respects, and in that too would have to follow acknowledged procedures. We couldn't take plants to competitions with nothing but numbers. We didn't have to do it yet, of course, but we had to consider that in three or four years' time there would be something to take. International success was expected of us.

I had to explain to the Centre why a Naming Committee was necessary. *Comitetul Nominazarii.* I hardly knew what to call it in Romanian, because, of course, no such thing existed. They must not have known what roses meant in the Michurin Institute in Bucharest, nor in the office, as they didn't look for new varieties like we did. We were the only Station in the whole country to grow roses. The Naming Committee had to be formed to give names to flowers, because it alone knew what growers had intended to conceptualize in them. They would use them to remember the beauty of some woman, to commemorate some historical event, on account of some great work of art or in honour of somebody. That was the easier way, wasn't it. I would take a name and attach it, *Dante* or whatever. But if the intention was to convey to the world some feeling, some notion, the right name had to be found. It had to be something that would stick in the mind, not too everyday or commonplace, nor yet too strange, because then nobody would think much of it. And what was more, if we were to compete internationally, it should also be something international.

I too had a name-giving father and mother, because we weren't baptised and didn't have godparents; father had been a Communist when we were born and loathed priests. So my name-giving mother had been my father's half-sister. My father's mother had died young, so she was from my grandfather's second marriage. They'd decided that I was to be Vilmos. Vilmos Ottó. What conceit! They were thinking of the heir to the throne's brother. My father didn't give it a thought, just wrote it down. All the same, he liked it. Maybe he wasn't a committed Communist at the time. My mother wasn't herself, she was having a nasty dose of lacteal fever, and wasn't consulted. Later she was very pleased that I had such a noble-sounding name. My brother, however, they had called Rudolf, So Vilmos, Rudolf, Erzsébet and Ferenc. They certainly hadn't convened a naming committee. But I didn't refer to any of that when I asked for permission.

I put the best people into the Naming Committee: young Werner, as he was becoming a serious 'christener'. Let it be said that he was not readily accepted. Firstly because of his name, secondly because of his father. Jews were never liked, of course, but one thought that after the war the situation would improve; it wasn't so. Especially since older Jews had dropped out of the Party leadership, such things were taken very much amiss. But him I crossed out and young Werner I appointed. Then I called on academician

Emil Pop, director of the Botanical Garden, to chair the committee. His name ensured his acceptance. Then I needed a linguist, as I knew no foreign languages. I had my dictionary and we'd chosen a good few, but that wasn't the way to proceed. Even I could sense the way a name sounded. But it wasn't for me to say that the effect would be this or that, or that a word was Latin. So I asked at the university for suggestions. I consulted the Hungarian Department. A member of staff told me quietly that their best man, T. Attila Szabó, had been dismissed, investigated and reinstated the previous year; he'd previously been in some academic language institute and had lectured at a seminary If he'd been dismissed, he was no good to me, I replied. But who hadn't been investigated? I had to get people approved by higher authority. There was László Szabédi; the name was spoken so softly that I hardly understood. So if I wanted a good man I should speak to him, but not take him onto the committee, he'd suffered a house search and everything, and now had become a State Laureate. But he was the Head of Department. What did all this whispering mean, I wondered. Did he have a bad name? Head of Department, and they had to speak his name in an undertone? Was there nobody who knew their subject and who could get authorization, in other words, who would be in order with authority? What did I want from these linguists? Was language such a risky thing? It seemed that knowledge of languages was a kind of foreign currency, you could be caught with it and put in prison. I didn't understand it at all.

So I said, 'Tell me of someone who is firstly a good linguist and knows his subject, and secondly, whose name can be submitted. The minute they see the list, they'll cut out anybody they don't like. Perhaps the entire committee will be crossed out.'

Well, he knew of nobody. T. Attila Szabó, perhaps? He didn't really know.

'Why do you want a Hungarian?' asked this young linguist, a certain János. Because, of course, I'd said that flowers didn't have to have Hungarian names, they can be Hungarian or international, so it's quite a problem.

'Isn't there some elderly professor?' I asked. 'Somebody who could do research for us, somebody with the time to come up with good ideas, who understands the world of today?'

'Well, no,' he replied.

They'd all gone, or had left while they still could, and foreign citizens had been dismissed.

How many would there be on the committee? Benjamin Werner, Emil Pop, the as yet unknown linguist, myself for sure, and someone else. So I needed a good Romanian. Three Hungarians, two Romanians. One always had to balance things carefully. Werner counted as a Hungarian. Fortunately he was a Party member. I'd introduced him.

By the end of January, permission had been granted. Last of all Rodica Sas had also been added; she was from the central Michurin Institute and didn't know the first word of Hungarian, so that the language of the committee had to be Romanian, and we only spoke Hungarian now and then among ourselves. Never mind. Everything went along as it should in a big plant-research establishment. People were always appearing with varieties. We could deal with one at a time, but not at once. Photographs were taken too, as we documented everything. Young Werner's job was identifying varieties. There were six of us in the end, but permission had still not been granted for the linguist, and we were still looking for one. I would have liked to have László Szabédi; he also knew Turkish, and had done research in Old Hungarian. He would have suited me. So in that company, young Werner and I understood roses, Emil Pop was an expert on the plant world, but the remainder knew zero, nothing, only politics and words, and as we saw the two were then very closely connected. We had to come up with the proposals. That, of course, was when we could have done with the linguist. Werner brought along such fanciful names. I've no idea where he got them from. He said that Peace was the most famous rose in the world. Let's consider its name and develop a style from that. It was no good my saying that that had been a different era. Not all that long previously, but different.

The first meetings were all mainly procedural, *De metodologie*, as we stated in the minute book. Rodica came up with the idea that we should have a rose named for the Liberation. I told her that our brief was to compete with roses at international level, displaying the scientific achievements of the RNK. That was what we had been created for. It would be a great honour to name a rose '23 August'. Let's say that that wasn't exactly what we were working on just then, it was too soft and somehow rather feminine for victory, but would suit another in the future. If, however, we took it to a competition abroad we would not be able to make it widely known.

'A French gardener isn't going to understand what 23 August means,' I explained.

'We don't understand what Peace means,' she replied.

Professor Pop asked:

'What do you mean, comrade, we don't understand? It means *béke* in Hungarian, *pace* in Romanian.' He was being astute, helping his colleague.

'Then what does that mean? Why call a rose that?'

'Because it symbolized the end of the war. That the war had ended and World Peace had come. Do you get the idea, Comrade Rodica?'

Then Rodica asked how roses were named in the USSR. Well, said I, there is no Soviet rose business and no institute that looks into new varieties, such as we have in Romania. In that we're unique. I mean, there's another rose grower in Hungary, but he doesn't rank as an institute. That's Gergely Márk.

'So a rose can only be given a foreign name?' asked Comrade Rodica.

The reason why we'd set up this committee was to find names. Slowly we succeeded in finding common ground.

Werner's proposal for his new little white rose was Calm. It seemed very suitable. But to come out with Calm ten years after Peace? How would that be in French? Or should we give it a Latin name? I asked Mrs M., because we still hadn't got a linguist. Tranquille (don't pronounce the -*lle*), and there was a similar Latin word, rather longer. Ah, that was no good.

Then Werner said that he had another suggestion too: *Expectation*. (In Hungarian *Várakozás*, in Romanian *Aşteptarea*). That was only a guide, said he, we'd have to find a final form, but as an idea he was thinking of something on those lines.

'You couldn't call a flower *Expectation* at an international exhibition in a Communist country,' said Emil. 'It'd be misunderstood.'

It was for such sensible thoughts that I'd invited Emil. He knew what we expected of him. He didn't have a lot to say, but when he did speak it was to the point.

'*Deşteptarea*?' he suggested. 'I'm thinking particularly of the meaning *Rising* or *Awakening*, in Hungarian *Felkelés* or *Ébredés*. It's in the Romanian national anthem, or can be, as it's just been changed.'

'It would be *Ébredés* in Hungarian,' said Werner. '*Ébredés*.'

'That's fine,' I said. Because it really was good. '*Ébredés* can be descriptive of the opening of a flower. But *Deşteptarea* is not so good. That tends to mean an armed uprising.'

I'll have to discuss with my friend Lali what *Ébredés* means in his opinion. I ought to bring in a man who is sound on ideology. Somebody sensible, clever, judicious, cultured. Old-fashioned and up-to-date.

I asked Emil quietly whether there hadn't been some such fascist Romanian organization. What had Codreanu's organization been called? Because now the Iron Guard was very dangerous even to mention. The legionnaires, they were all in prison. I didn't know, I wasn't so well up in history. T. Attila Szabó said, when I asked him—because while we still had no linguist approved, I'd been put in touch with him so as to consult, he was a real bourgeois element—that in his opinion it wasn't certain that it was good. Because perhaps it was misunderstood that it was sectarian. I mean, that anyone was awoken in religious terms. Because there was such a thing as a revivalist movement. So we could discard that name because it was either sectarian or Iron Guardist. Out went *Deșteptarea* and *Ébredés*. But it was a shame.

That Rodica hadn't actually been talking such rubbish. Perhaps we ought in fact to produce a 23 August rose. I was already thinking what it might be like. Because, of course, that was the time when Romania had dropped out of the war and allied itself to the USSR, and then had been victorious. It would have been good if it had also occurred to the Hungarians to drop out and turn on the fascists and Horthyists. I could now visualize what 23 August would have to be like. The name would certainly not be much good for international competition, but we couldn't produce everything just for the sake of winning in competitions and carrying off prizes. I would produce a big, tight-packed red rose, more of a spray or polyantha type, to pour forth flowers, as the people had gone over more and more. Something that flowered continually, because since then our victory had not diminished. Nor had the spilt blood that had flowed for the fatherland. In my view that was hardly the sort of thing to win in Paris just then, because the shedding of blood must not be made much of.

A compact spray rose with big, dark-red flowers. But then let it blaze for me! There was to be no black in it, not even at its densest. This rose didn't intend to mourn but to celebrate, yet modestly, like Peace.

In my opinion, true greatness doesn't call for display. Greatness is immediate and straightforward. It's as if it has always been. It has very little perfume, like hybrids in general, such is the price of grafting tea-hybrids. It doesn't clamour for attention because it's quiet and calm, as its name indicates. It doesn't make itself conspicuous, but it's there all the same. There it stands like someone that can't be destroyed even though the world is in ruins. That was Werner's word, 'someone'. Young Werner was a bit of a poet. Poetry was in his blood, and when all's said and done, blood will out. But he was too quiet, was that Benjamin. It was to be understood, the Jews had been so repressed, they couldn't speak out and the world begged their forgiveness in vain; they didn't say a word.

In those days I was in complete turmoil. I'd have liked to see that young girl again. There was so much going on, I couldn't organize myself to get on with my own work. All the same, if I had a horse I'd have mounted and gone to see Kali and the child. Perhaps I ought to have cycled out. It's only six kilometres.

Lali had been bothering me as well lately, we'd had a bit of an argument and now he wanted to make up. He invited me to the theatre. I told him I'd had enough, I didn't want to see those political plays. So why didn't I go and see *The Silent Knight*, there wasn't a trace of politics in that. Not a kitchen-sink drama for once. We laughed. Oh did we laugh! Béla Horváth was divine. Lali told me that it was rubbish, that was why it was a success. I said that the audience needed plays like that so as to laugh a bit. Lali grumbled that Kolozsvár was being made into a collective-farm theatre. The sacred home of Transylvanian acting had been corrupted. He criticized it severely. He even wrote in the paper that it was rubbish. I don't understand why the theatre is so important. If he doesn't like things, he shouldn't go.

He was always wanting to give me tickets and admission cards. In exchange he took flowers from me. Or came up to visit the Station. It was no good my saying that I should be grateful to him, not *vice versa*. It meant a great deal to me that he was always visiting. I'd really missed him when he was away. In prison, that is. 'You're a big man now, Vilmos,' he was always saying. Oh, I got so on edge when I heard that. I hoped I wasn't going to have a stroke. A big man.

I'd been given another copy of *Falvak népe*, which carried a picture of me sitting in front of the roses. 'The wonder-gardener of the Békás.' The caption said that I was admiring the fruits of my labours, my new variety *Superstar*. Well, every reporter that writes such stuff should be flogged. Has anyone said that when I've been standing it was to admire my flowers? Never ever. Yes, I have stood and looked a lot, but I'd been working! I wasn't at all accustomed to being in raptures. Ages ago I was, over the fair sex, even now very occasionally, over that young girl. But when I'm standing I'm at work! Not admiring the flowers, but watching them. How they're filling out, what diseases they've got, how long they last, generally speaking, what's been happening to them. Do they look good, are they healthy, can they be made better still? It's not like when an artist paints a picture and never looks at it again. He'll look at what he's done, even if he can't do anything to improve it. But he won't glory in it. It's bad taste to glory in what you've done. What did this paper pick on me for? Everybody else, workers and peasants, were hard at work in the paper. And I was just sitting there being proud? What did anybody who didn't work with them know about roses? The devil had got into this reporting. Most of all, saying that I was in the Békás. Now of all times, when the farmers on whose land I was with the Station were so angry with us. Was it my fault that they'd been turned out? I think there were some laughing up their sleeves. Now it's one Hungarian against another. The Hóstát people against me.

Now, in any case, we were having to get ready for the international competitions. It had been given out that we had to go, had to introduce novel rose varieties. We couldn't be ordered, of course, to come away with the Grand Prix, but now I'd been given everything that I'd asked for, I'd better get on with it. I asked for another two laboratory assistants, and was given them straight away. Previously I'd been sent to Trieste with a delegation, to see how to behave in an international event, and the next year I had to go to the world competition. I represented Romania, no one else was sent from here. Old Schultz told me that there'd never been such a thing. 'What do you mean?' I asked. 'Well, that a Hungarian should be entrusted with representing Romania in an international contest.'

'Do you see, Rezső, it's not just so much hot air now when they say that there's equality and Hungarians are being accepted everywhere. We mustn't feel sorry for ourselves, we've never had it so good. Especially not when there was a king. Here's a gardener, who never studied except in his garden, having his work recognized.'

We produced Cluj Superstar. That was the name given to it. It was spot on. I named it. A hybrid with big, milky or rather snowy single flowers and long, handsome buds. Suitable for cutting or for the garden. As strong as a chased sword. The buds were very slow to open, and so the flowers were long lasting. I now regarded the slow opening of this rose as a point in its favour. How could this be demonstrated at a five-day competition? No way. Slowness isn't a virtue anywhere in the world. On the other hand, perhaps this will be our greatest success here in Romania. The point is that to the public it matters quite a bit whether a rose lasts for four days or for ten. *Cluj Superstar* was good for ten. It was healthy, big, and didn't overcrowd the bush.

Cluj Superstar came from a simple cross. Actually, two ladies met in it: Louise Criner and Mrs Charles Lamplugh. Two women, one French, the other Irish, it says in my book. I don't care much for Irish roses, but the man who produced it was the richest rose grower after the First World War, Samuel McGredy II. I haven't got any plants of his father's, but I have of his son's. And so the Roman double is in his name, as his father before him had also crossed roses. So it's easy, dear boy. To sum up, it's from two women. Who these were is not recorded.

We introduced Cluj Superstar officially at a little in-house celebration after it was named. It was a great success. But old Schultz shook his hand and asked, 'Wasn't this . . . ?'

'No,' I replied very firmly. 'This is Cluj Superstar.'

Whether he remembered or not, I didn't know. Or did he just suspect? It was better not to say anything. Because this certainly was Carmen Sylva. I had produced it as long ago as 1937. How I'd got away with not being questioned about it by the Securitate I didn't know. After all, she had been the queen of Romania. But nobody remembered by this time. Perhaps the lovely Carmen Sylva too was beginning to be forgotten, like those French women. Was it wrong to give this rose that name? What were we to do? Throw away the past completely? Because we were at the most giving it a new name. Carmen Sylva, who had tended the sick and the war-wounded. In that name she had written poetry and tragedies. As our Queen Erzsébet, she obviously couldn't have put her name to them, and in the Kolozsvár of the 1930s nobody would have had anything to do with the queen of Hungary. Because in those days Hungarian society was a world apart. The people, by which I mean the Romanian people, were very fond of Carmen Sylva. She had a real, sturdy Romanian beauty, but she wasn't a Romanian by birth but a blue-blooded German, I believe. She had a fleshy nose and a stately figure. She was a good woman and cared about the people. She loved forests passionately. And rivers. Her poetry was about nothing else. I was glad to have got away with it, I'd forgotten the Carmen Sylva rose, and no more will be said about it, and I hardly think that anybody who comes across it in my books will split on me. So then, here was Cluj Superstar.

But old Schultz shook his head. He was certain that he had not developed anything from Louise Criner. Rather, he wanted nothing to do with it, said he. Why, I asked him, because in my view this was a good rose, quite unique with its big flowers, and resistant to disease. He replied that that Frenchman had produced this flower even before the war. It had been standing on the table in the château of Trianon when the decision on our fate was being signed. I should look at the photographs.

He said in an undertone, 'No Hungarian should touch this flower.'

I didn't want an argument with him. So I didn't take the opportunity to tell him what I'd always thought.

The other one over which we were likewise prepared to fall out was a dark-red cutting rose. I'd been looking for one that wouldn't turn purple as it faded. It had to grow old gracefully, so to speak. I wanted the colour to age nicely but not to change. We'd combined Mrs Henry Winnett with Étoile de Hollande and then with Lady Helena Maglona, because the first generation was unsuccessful. There was a lot wrong with it, but the colour was very long-lasting. The main problem with Henry Winett was that in summer it produced light purple flowers, and only the first flowering was really bright, after which it began to deteriorate. Through a great deal of selection, we'd found what we've been after in the sixth generation. So what were we to do if there were no historical Hungarian woman to name it after? *Egri nők*—the Women of Eger, who defeated the Turks in the siege of 1588—should rather be a sword lily. No other ladies came to mind.

When the Naming Committee sat to name the new rose, I'd had to go to make the monthly report and couldn't be present.

I went to Bucharest, where I had an appointment with Sándor Mogyoros, or rather Alexandru Moghioros, as that was the name that he mostly used in the papers. He was in the Centre office and took all the decisions. I had to get his permission to prepare for the exhibition with all the transport—carriages for watering, storage, cooling, everything necessary, because going to such an event meant no small expense. I was advised that I'd do better not to speak Hungarian to 'Sándor'. Gheorghiu-Dej always called him 'Sanyi', but only so as to pull his leg about his Hungarian origin. I'd better not speak Hungarian, I didn't want to get his approval just because I'd asked in Hungarian. By then my card named me as Vilhelm Deci, and was also in Romanian.

In any case, the meeting with this dreaded man was very brief. He spoke curtly and questioned me. He was a top man in the agriculture ministry but mainly dealt with questions about horses. Any taken into collectives were his concern. There were supposed to be too many horses in those days as the country was becoming mechanized. There were tractors, weren't there, which did the same work? International rose exhibitions weren't his field, he didn't even understand what we were doing.

'Ennobling? Don't tell me we've got the nobility back?' he asked ironically. I'd said in Hungarian that we were taking new varieties, because I was so tongue-tied in his presence that I'd forgotten the Romanian word and begun to stammer. So I'd tripped up in Hungarian. Damn and blast. And I'd practised so hard to get it right.

He asked me straight out what benefit my roses brought to the Romanian economy. I was ready for that and I said, 'They'll win honour for the country.'

'We can indeed do with that,' said Moghioros, and said that he'd attend to it. He'd come and visit 'la Cluj'. *Iti dau o vizità la Cluj si vedem.* He'd come down and pay a visit. He called me *te*.

The ten minutes or less that I spent with him really brought me out in a sweat. Damn and blast it. I'm no good at role playing. I went back that evening to Kolozsvár absolutely shattered, on edge. It was officially stated that this was a plant research station and that I was to go to international competitions, but even so I had to beg for the means. But there was nobody I could complain to.

The naming session had taken place. I was excited to hear what name had been given to my deep-red flower.

Duiliu Zamfirescu was the name it had been given. When I heard that, my stomach gave a nervy twitch.

'What?' I couldn't hold it back.

I just asked the chairman whether they thought that was a good name for us to enter competitions with. Something that would sound good. A Romanian name, representing the country. I didn't want to seem stupid, but I simply didn't know who on earth that Duiliu Zamfirescu was. I'd never heard of such a name as Duiliu. I misspelled it when I had to write it down. I didn't know whether he was a professor or a partisan. Then I got a book from Anisoara, the new girl in the calculation department, because it turned out that he'd been a writer who had written about the decadent lives of the boyars. *Viaţa la ţară*. Life in the Country. I liked the title, and that somebody should have written about life in the countryside. I thought I'd better read it if my rose was to be christened by that name. So one evening I conscientiously started. To tell the truth, I'd never really read anything like a novel in Romanian. I put a second cup of tea at my side, and two nice apple pastries, and I read. That is, I would have read. I was brought up short in the first line. There were words in it that meant nothing to me. I looked to right and to left. I found the language terribly hard and struggled through a page or two, but I couldn't get on with it. But it hadn't been written all that long ago. There was a bad taste in my mouth and I had to shut the book. I couldn't understand it at all. Was I now going to have to study Romanian, to read books like that? I was quite happy writing reports by that time, my deputy director was a Romanian and knew everything, as did the secretary. But books were another matter. After that, when I looked at Duiliu Zamfirescu, the silky, dark-red rose with its long, slender buds, which it didn't hurry to open in summer as if it were daintily holding back its colour, I thought, 'Were you really like that, my friend?' Because this was no kind of countryside rose, was it?

Roses are at their most lovely in September. The big exhibitions are always held in September. And so who could tell what the Party had in mind when I was suddenly to travel to Trieste, because of course that had been promised three years previously. And in fact I was sent. Three weeks before I hadn't even got a passport, but now there I was, but I couldn't make it out. To us, Trieste is the West. Indeed, in the geographical sense Budapest is the West as well.

Since the year before, everything had suddenly become strange. Perhaps this great liberty had sent me a little mad. In Hungary, de-Stalinization was in full swing. That was all the talk there, and now people had begun to use the term and personality cults were being unmasked. Lali came up to the Station and talked of nothing else, didn't even notice the new row of Five Nunns; well, it wasn't really all that striking, it took patience for one to see it. All he could talk about now was what great things were about to happen. Everything was going to change.

Since the Soviets had held the Twentieth Party Congress, great revelations were being made, huge crimes were discovered, and our lives too were going to take an upward turn. Well, thought I, mine did that yesterday when Annus sat on my knee, but I didn't mention such a thing to my friend. He's a married man.

'I don't think,' I said to Lali, 'that our lives should be directed by a Soviet congress.'

It had only been the year before that Lali had been released after three years in prison, and he was already politically active again. Lysenko had come a cropper, he said. Could an academic biologist come a cropper at a Party congress? I was amazed. It turned out, said Lali, that everything that he'd done had been deception, but Stalin had made much of him and so he'd become a great man. We shan't have any of this de-Stalinzation, I said, because there's nothing to be unmasked. Lali snapped at me, and we nearly came to blows. What had he been in prison for, then? Because feeling had been turned against him, and his good name besmirched! I should remember that they, the professors, had been the first for whom the death sentence was demanded. They'd been full of immorality and corruption, said he. In Romania everybody just expected others to think for them. Society was completely passive, and the Transylvanian Hungarians and the Romanians did as they pleased. Take Bányai for an example, he said, the rector. I should consider him. A dictator. I was lucky he wasn't my rector, because I was in the Babeş. Under Daicoviciu. There was need of a democracy of achievement, he said. The country should go by a liberal socialist path, free from fear. In Romania everybody was cautious, scared stiff.

'Me, scared stiff?' I asked, because he was being offensive. I was so on edge.

I said to him, 'My dear chap, I'm not going to fall out with you over politics.' He said that it was only over politics that people did fall out. He hadn't got a reliable friend left.

'But anyway, you're out,' I said, 'why are you lecturing me?'

So I wasn't a reliable friend to him. I'd have liked to ask what I meant to him then, if not a friend. But one doesn't ask questions like that. I'd meant to discuss with him what we should take to compete with in Paris, because it was Trieste now, wasn't it, Paris next, and I'd have liked to show him what I was doing. Perhaps this was the end of my friendship with Lali. So I didn't even ask. I'd make my own mind up.

Then it was Trieste. Trieste, but I couldn't get that girl off my mind.

It's when your troubles are most numerous that the really big one comes along. As the Romanians say, *când ţi-e lumea mai dragă*. When you're loving the world. At last the time came for us to go abroad, and then—out of the blue came that girl. Anyone with so much sex drive is always wanting, and there are those who can't control it, don't even want to, their blood carries them along. I'd been completely content with Kali there, well, not completely perhaps, but the main thing was that I'd got a woman. But this girl came down the hill on horseback like a little Amazon. She brought me vegetables, milk—she's the daughter of the Butyka family, Annush, the poor thing whom her father used to beat something terrible. It wasn't the first time I'd seen her, and once I'd made an effort to get a good look at her. In fact I never saw her when she was delivering vegetables, milk and *túró*, because those she would give to Kali—she always dealt with such things, and she was spending longer here than in Györgyfalva. Then the girl came down the hill one evening and ran straight into the kitchen, asking for help because her load of carrots had tipped up. She'd been on their land up on the hill, had piled the cart high, it had been too heavy for the horse, she'd been unable to brake, and it had crashed on a cart track in the Békás. The horse wasn't hurt, but the harness had broken and she was in tears. Would Aunty Kali come quick and help her pick everything up—Kali and the child had come for another couple of days—and she would fetch more people from lower down? As she ran, her headscarf flew behind her. I went out as well and helped, as did the porter from the Station, and the three of us soon had it reloaded and gave her the reins. Kali told her, as she was already there to stop at our garden and she would take three basketfuls; she'd put them in the cellar so that there'd be no need to keep coming in winter. The deal was done, and Kali began putting them in the cellar. The girl said that at home they laid them out in a semicircle, that made room for more. That way looked better as well. Looked better in the cellar, I asked. Who was going to see them? It just looked better, she replied. She asked for some water, and I told her to come into the house because I'd developed a thirst as well, and she could have some soda water, I always had some by me, it was delivered on Tuesday, and she could have some raspberry syrup in it. I took her inside and gave her a big glass, Kali would bring out the raspberry syrup, I told her. So that was that, and she just took the glass. She was flushed and even panting like a small dog.

What a mouth she had, good Lord! Her lips were firm when I kissed her, but she didn't push me away but yielded, or perhaps even felt pleasure. Her whole mouth was as small as a kitten's and sweet, and her tongue was strong. I was driven mad by something so novel. I'd thought that I'd never have my tongue in so youthful a mouth. Not that I'd have said so, but I'd been thinking that it was all in the past, after all, I'd become a significant, big man, I'd even got a child, I wasn't going to mess about with girls like her.

She tasted so finely of strawberries, because I'd brought some strawberry syrup out of the larder. The Gypsies had brought two buckets of wild strawberries, and there's nothing to compare with them. I couldn't have enough of those strong little lips, released her mouth and at once wanted it again. She all but bit me, so strong were her lips, because now it was she that was doing it. Then I gently stroked her breast, small and firm as a Gypsy apple, and as I held it her nipple stood erect. That held a message. Either she was frightened or she too felt that way.

'Mr Vilmos, Mr Vilmos, for heaven's sake!'

What did she mean? That I should stop, or that she wanted it and was overcome with pleasure? I just stroked her with my mouth, tasted those gorgeous lips, her little breast. I could hardly make myself let her go. She closed her eyes as if embarrassed and turned away. Gave a great swallow. So she was still a virgin, I thought, still a little girl. I called out as she left the kitchen:

'Come again, I'll expect you, Annush!'

Now Kali was calling as well, she'd done the carrots, she could be on her way. Annush turned and left the kitchen like a startled fawn. I could still feel on my palm the shape of that warm little breast. And her kiss in my mouth. In my whole body. So, Vilmos, you're looking well.

'When will you come?' I said to her back.

She didn't answer, just hurried off. I went in her wake. Then she said that she'd be coming that way less often, because their lands had been put into the collective, which was higher up in the Borháncs. She wouldn't have to come so much now, she'd lifted the carrots so they were finished, there were only the cabbages left. When would she be selling in the market, I asked. Well, this town wasn't so big that I mightn't run into her somewhere.

It was a good thing I had my work, or I'd have gone mad.

I'd only been given a transit visa for Hungary to go to Trieste. I didn't even ask where I could stay, my head had been so full of being able to go to a rose competition. If I were going so far I wouldn't have minded a stop-over in Budapest or Szeged. I didn't know whether the Hungarian or Romanian governments would give me permission, but at all events it was possible, there was such great freedom in those days. An agreement had been reached and we could travel from one to the other. Previously neither would have let me, but would have dug their heels in. The regime was the same, but it hadn't been very easy to travel to Hungary. Now you could go as much as you liked. There was such to-ing and fro-ing as if the frontier didn't exist. This had happened three months before. In Budapest, as I heard, even the papers too were completely at liberty, the Central Committee no longer checked the press. I didn't know what the sudden result of this was to be.

We'd been standing in the Budapest station for some three hours by the time we set off for Italy. I would at least have bought some papers, but I hadn't changed any money. I'd thought I wouldn't beg and try to use lei, I'd have been embarrassed to ask and be laughed at for wanting to spend Romanian currency in Budapest. But oh! the tasty sausage that a man was selling there, he had a pot slung round his neck. He would have given me bread with it as well. His sales patter was very persuasive, but I couldn't be tempted. All I had was an envelope of Italian money which I'd picked up at the CEC. I didn't know what it was worth, I didn't dare produce it, but a shady looking dealer offered to get it changed for me. I was always afraid of being swindled, so I didn't buy anything.

That's what I saw of Budapest.

I read quite a lot on the way. In my tense state, of course. Anything that has *rose* written on it I always buy as a present. Or anything decorated with roses. You never saw so much tatty china! Kali likes it, she's got two shelfs full. So there was this slim little book, *The Six-Acre Rose Garden*. As far as roses were concerned, it was rubbish. It looks as if the writer wasn't interested in roses, only symbols. The fellow had no idea what roses there were in the big rose garden. But Lali told me what a great poet this Mihály Babits was. What he'd got to say about marriage, however, and women was sensational! Only I couldn't be sure whether liked women or not. He was sure as hell afraid of marriage.

The rose exhibition in Trieste, now I ask you! How can I put it? It was pure theatre. The flowers weren't the principal actors now. It was held in that enormous pavilion on the bay. Every country that was exhibiting was given an area. Every area was furnished like . . . I don't know, a room or a hall. Quite big pieces of scenery were set up. Signs in French and English. 'Rose show.' Parade, in French. Paradé. Rose parade? That was publicly displayed and printed on all the tickets. The interpreter that I was given by the embassy said that it was all a sort of performance. A show. So, I didn't know how we were going to get a kick at the ball there. I'd been sent to see what would be required if we came in future. Our debut was planned for September 1957— Mogyoros had shown me the official decision.

'This time you're going so as to prepare yourself, next time you'll be going to Paris.'

Because, of course, it wasn't just that a special railway carriage had to be built—I didn't think we'd be taking flowers by air—that could be chilled and carry water, because flowers had to be kept moist. But then, who was going to design the way in which we were to present our flowers? As part of the scenery. Not me, that was for sure.

I didn't know why, but everybody was so pleased when they heard the name Romania. That I was from there. But we had nothing at all on display, we were merely visiting. Nobody had come from Romania for ages. That I could believe. I handed out visiting cards so fast that the next day I was out of them. I was quickly resupplied from the embassy a day later with type-written cards, and I was given so many that I couldn't get them all into my pocket. And catalogues. The interpreter carried them in his briefcase as well.

There were some wonderful things. French, Dutch and American. Nobody's seen anything finer, that's the truth. How did the Americans get there? By ship? Certainly not, no sort of cut rose could have stood such a long journey. Rather they'd been brought by air. Incredible. Roses by aircraft. But, of course, the new People's Republics didn't come. Nor was the USSR represented.

I looked at the many marvellous new varieties, chiefly Star, but Meilland could still do great things, and so could Kordes too. And what about Tantau! That was the leading German. So what was I to say? I lost my voice, I choked, I coughed, I could hardly get a word out. It was envy. It made me really on edge. That's the way I am. But when I looked at them I was so happy that tears came to my eyes. Then I left the pavilion because I needed a bit of a walk, I couldn't breathe in there. And yet it was lofty, like a hangar. Perhaps my blood pressure had gone up. There I was, and yet I was not, because I hadn't brought a single rose. I wasn't an exhibitor, was I? I'd only come to study form.

The interpreter came everywhere with me. I told him to stay where he was for a bit, I was going for a little walk. He came with me. I told him to stay where he was. How was I going to hold conversations, he asked. I'm not going to, I said, I don't know a soul in the place, couldn't he find something to do, I'd like to take a half-hour stroll by myself. He'd been told that he couldn't let me because I'd get lost and wouldn't be able to speak to anyone. So I said that even in a forest I didn't get lost, surely he didn't think I couldn't find my way to somewhere in a town? Bloody hell! Well, in the end he left me to my own devices. There was a bakery across the road. I had to get something to eat, as I'd had no breakfast and my stomach was rumbling. In I went, and it was amazing. There were at least thirty sorts of bread. So I thought, do people really need thirty sorts of bread? Aren't three enough? And there was milk in glass bottles, several sorts of that as well. I'd have bought a croissant or a bread roll, but there was nothing of the kind. I pointed at one that looked like a croissant, but it was terribly sweet. That's capitalism for you, I thought. For people to have thirty sorts of bread. All around I could see many poor quarters and tenements. A big economy must always need a lot of poor people. That area was mainly heavy industry, ship building, because that's what seaside towns are like.

I must say, I'd never before seen the sea. That was odd. We'd got the sea in Romania, but I'd never been to look at it. Why? Why not? Goodness knows. That was our custom. The sea was too chilly for Hungarians, especially there. They should get used to it. I hadn't got a single friend that had been to see the sea. I'd been given a *Bilet de trimitere* by the Centre, a sort of voucher, to go to Sovatara. A week, and valid at *menü házak*. They wanted to build hotels in Constanța as well, meant to develop seaside tourism. But I didn't go to Sovatara. I'd got nobody to go with, and at rose-opening time? Why go by myself?

Trieste was beautiful, but so . . . alien. And there were too many churches. As big as mountains. Where did churches always get so much money from? They should have built more low-price housing. And schools. But the palaces there were! Who'd want to live in places like that? I didn't know. I didn't think we'd ever be comfortable there.

By that time I wasn't sorry to have to be going back. But I'd hardly seen anything. It would have been nice to take a boat trip. So, if we mean to exhibit we'll certainly have to make an effort. And the organizers will invite us to the celebration dinner. Next time, a Romanian exhibitor will be assured of a warm welcome. Given discounts. I didn't understand the figures. Everything seemed to me astronomically expensive. Had I any requirements or requests that they could fulfil? I said that it wasn't only up to me, it would be a corporate decision, and the Centre would pronounce. What Centre, they asked. The Party Centre, of course.

I thought that perhaps I might be able to study the delivery carriages. That wasn't really possible because they were privately owned. There was a standard type of carriage and they could make recommendations. Yes, please. Everything would be sent to the embassy. It would certainly be cheaper if we built one ourselves.

So then Paris was to be next. What would be better, I wondered: to go and fail, or never to exhibit a single rose and not compete? Now show some sense, Vilmos.

But it was just as Móric had imagined in jest. Or Mózsi the Wise had in Kali's folk tale. Were we supposed to do our utmost to prepare for an international rose competition when all that was happening in Hungary! A revolution. Or a Freedom War. It had been just as well that Trieste happened in September, because by October I couldn't have gone anywhere any longer, that was for sure.

But what hopes we too then had in the autumn! To me they were hopes realized, because I'd been to Trieste, hadn't I? To Lali, however, the trampling underfoot of our national traditions continued. He'd returned from Vajdahunyad in tears. There had been a great Hunyadi celebration, a great academic conference, people had come from the fraternal countries and Hungary. But Hunyadi had been made out to be a kind of Dacian hero, the epitome of Romanian national aspiration! Not a word of Hungarian was heard! They'd done better to keep quiet, said Lali, because if ever anybody had said anything! That would have been the end. They'd just had a basinful and it had turned their stomachs. A wreath had been laid in Gyulafehérvár Cathedral, and bishop Áron Márton, who had been in prison until recently, delivered a powerful sermon. As he described it, Lali wept. Wept like a child. Since he's been in prison, he's always crying.

In Hungary blood flowed in the streets of Budapest.

Once again I can only say how fortunate it was for me. In my case, in the Station not a hair of anyone's head was curled when the balloon went up in Hungary. None of my people were arrested, no one had any trouble or was mixed up in anything as far as I was aware. To a man they neither wanted to demonstrate nor to show off. Nor did anything happen, because I kept an eye on all of them. I didn't go to Hungary, however, though I might have gone in autumn. After Trieste I'd held discussions with the Szőreg people. Because that was the first year that we'd been able to go, didn't even need a passport. Just your ID card was enough. Great liberty had come in, and in mid-August it was announced that one could go freely to Hungary once more. How long did it last? Five minutes. All right then, two months. And then look. The frontier was closed. We'd had no official contact with anybody in Hungary since the war, and now it was officially permitted, at state level, and we began negotiations with Szőreg. They visited us, but first we went over to Szeged. We swapped experiences and plants.

A week before, I'd been back in the university as I had to deal with admissions. There was a Hungarian Department after all; the first and second years had been started, but had been closed in '55. For bureaucratic reasons, it was stated. In any case, the Hungarian agriculture course had been stopped and now it was on again, decision reversed. It was nice when the Party realized that the ministry concerned had made a mistake. Nice but rare, like blue roses. Perhaps we'd operate as a department again, and then I'd go back from the Babeş to the high school. Then I saw from the list of admissions, however, that all sorts of students had been sent from other departments—Chemistry, Biology, Technical Training—just so that we should have students. So there wasn't even one that was specializing in our field. There were some that hadn't seen even a patch of soil. Never mind, at least there were students. It had really pained me that I couldn't have taught my subject in Hungarian. Not that it would have mattered to the soil, the trees, and the flowers, because there we all spoke the same language. But all the same, we needed the Hungarian university, and it was in keeping with the Party's nationalities policy. That had been a great bonus for the Hungarians.

What hopes there still were that year! A Debrecen University delegation had actually been here in spring. Hungarians had come for the first time since the war. I'd had to show them the Botanical Garden, we went to the Romanian opera and the Hungarian opera, and there'd been great mutual affection. Romanian dancing, Hungarian dancing. Not for us to take part, we'd just been spectators. It was all very well organized. After all, people were here from Hungary! Then conversation over dinner. Very careful conversations. Choirs came as well and sang the Romanian and Hungarian anthems.

Daicoviciu made a fine speech on behalf of the Babeş; he began in Romanian and went on in Hungarian as fluently as I would have done myself. He hit it off with them straight away. And then in May, a Hungarian delegation went to Debrecen. I too could have gone, but I asked to be excused and that was approved. How could I have gone anywhere for so many days in May? Five days! There was a lot repeated in speeches about Danube and Olt having a single voice, and the building of bridges between peoples. Indeed, a fine thing. Everybody said that this was the year, 1956 was the year of the great change. Hungary had been de-Stalinized, but that wasn't necessary in Romania because conditions were different. All the same, people who had been in prison were set free in Romania as well. Lali had been home since the year before. Not only set free but also rehabilitated. Great! There'd been abuses in the past. Excess. Their crimes were washed away. Poor Lali had done three years.

I didn't regret not having gone to Debrecen in that great liberation because of what happened. Professor Emil Pop told me about how he, as an academician, had delivered a lecture there. When our university people, from the Bolyai, that is, went onto the platform the audience wouldn't let them go, such was the applause! There was nothing that they could do. It turned into something more like a demonstration. At the end the Bolyai choir sang the folk song 'Elmegyek, elmegyek'—I am going, I am going. But that hadn't been authorized. The Party had scrutinized the programme before passing it, and that hadn't been in it, The audience wept and sang along. But it ought not to have been included. There's always trouble. Apparently lecturer András Bodor, the leader of the delegation, was hauled over the coals, but he wasn't the outspoken sort, very conforming ideologically. He was spoken to severely for agitating among the Debrecen student body for Transylvanian interests. He should have taken greater care, he didn't understand the situation in Hungary, one mightn't put on a programme like that. Red boots and Hungarian dances. He told the students off. Then here at home too he was castigated, for not being sufficiently alert. So even dancing was trouble in those days. It was no use his explaining that he hadn't been to Hungary since the war, didn't understand the situation, didn't know what was and was not in order. No one had briefed him. He'd been the leader of the delegation, he should have known. Then the clever philosopher Miklós Kallós argued it away. He turned the problem round by pointing out that as for dancing, if we went to Iaşi, Romanian got more applause, and in Debrecen, Hungarian did, for the one was done in *bocskor* and *opinca*, and the other in red boots, so it wasn't a big deal. So when all was said and done, the philosopher was the clever one, always finding the pertinent form of words.

However, I'd begun corresponding with Szőreg. There'd been a big rose garden there in the past, and I'd lost track of what had happened to it. It too had been nationalized, and had become a sort of collective farm. I'd begun exchanging things, and what really pleased me was that at last I had a fellow specialist to write to. Gergely Márk lived in Hungary, near Budapest. He too was a Transylvanian, and had studied in Budapest. He was a trained rose grower, but didn't look down on anyone that hadn't been to university, though I admit that I wrote to him on university letterhead. He wrote that Hungary too wanted to hold a big international exhibition, so let's get together. That would be good! We discussed exchanges with Szőreg, with both of us sending material. I didn't send any new varieties, of course, for fear that they'd be stolen. That sort of thing did happen. I'd been given some stocks of new Meilland varieties, not officially, nor were they officially produced. I'd written and told Szőreg that I could send some cut roses, but the problem lay in transporting them. So I'd bring them in person when the chance came. Don't hold your breath, Vilmos!

That summer, friendship with Budapest was so great that a Hungarian journalist spent a month in Transylvania. He went everywhere. I didn't meet him, I wasn't important enough, but receptions were attended rather by writers and intelligentsia, and the well-known travelling circus of bourgeois elements. He spent about a couple of weeks in the MAT, after which he wrote an article for *Szabad Nép*—and the trouble started. I only knew about it from what was said in *Scânteia* about an article in hostile tone that had appeared in a paper in a people's democratic country. That article then had to be studied at the Party congress. How kindly and warmly that journalist had been made welcome. Such a visit ought to have encouraged the reconciliation and friendship of our peoples, not to have stirred things up. To that the Hungarians said, in self-justification, that they had no censorship and so articles like that might be published and it was broadcast. That too was completely permitted, there was nothing to prevent it. I realized that nothing but trouble could result. Didn't articles have to be authorized? It was odd, because in Romania everything had to be vetted. From over there, from Hungary, everything was seen as misfortune, there was no regard for achievements or attainments, only the lack of them. That chap Pándi had said that autonomy didn't mean the universal use of Hungarian, it wasn't sufficiently widely accepted, and the leadership was simply dependent on the Centre, which wasn't really autonomy. And he gave an account of a lot of slights endured by the Hungarian minority as well. Was that called for? Rather than saying that we were glad for one another in this great liberty. That's what was needed, in my opinion. Because what a great thing it was for a journalist from Hungary to be here for a whole month. Such a thing hadn't happened since the war.

Now, however! Now what was going to happen?

Since Kali hadn't been in the house, I'd stopped having the radio on all the time like she always did. Perhaps I should have given her the radio, she was always complaining how lonely she was. She wasn't, though, she'd got the child. She talked as much as the radio did, but I didn't listen to her, because I had to be among people so much that my ears wouldn't stand all that chatter. Yesterday, quite at random, I switched it on. Good Lord, what was happening in Budapest! In the morning I ran into the Station quite early so as to be there before anybody else. In fact, I only had to go through the garden gate and I was there. The dogs were still dozing and didn't even get up. Only the gateman greeted me and asked whether it was so late. I said I'd got a lot of work, so I'd come in. What should I do, I wondered. Phone the Centre? Or the Ministry? To ask whether there were any instructions. Perhaps our people didn't even know yet that civil disorder had broken out in Budapest. Perhaps I'd only be doing the wrong thing if I rang. Or perhaps I ought to go into town and see if anything was happening. I'd be going into the university that afternoon in any case, and I'd get all the news there. Until then I kept things normal. For a start, I didn't hold a meeting because I didn't want it seen that there was something going on. And then it wouldn't be good if too many people got together. Everybody stayed in their places and worked. I decided to allot jobs: we had to hurry with the earthing-up because there'd soon be frost, check the heating of the greenhouses, clean the water system, and the inside workers were to write up the plans for the next two months, which was quite urgent.

The experimenters were to lift the potatoes and cabbages, wash and dry the potatoes for storing, as the experimental potatoes had to be protected from frost. The cabbages had to be sprinkled with salt to deter snails. What was to be done with the experimental green tomatoes, which were both out-doors and indoors? In the greenhouses a lot of them were ripe, but outside they were still green. We'd ripen them indoors. Once they'd done that, could they do some digging, they asked. No way, I said, cultivators would be coming. Jorgu, the boss of number three brigade, said that he preferred to use a spade, because like that bigger clods could be left, and cultivators broke the soil up too much—his way it dried out better. If he cut quite big clods the water in them froze and it was all more lumpy. That Jorgu was right, he was a very good worker. But I told him that here cultivators did the work.

'I do as much in a day as a cultivator!' he replied.

'You can't, it's planned for cultivators, it has to be left to them. You've got other work to do.'

'Suppose so, if I can't even dig any more,' he replied gloomily.

'Make out your own work plan,' I told him.

I gave them all more to do than they would manage. They wouldn't have time to chatter. I reorganized number nine brigade so that everybody had a new man to work with. With a new man they couldn't come out with some-thing straight away, they'd have to sound him out first. Groups that had become used to one another had to be split up. I told them all to stay where they were at lunchtime, as we had to close the canteen for cleaning. All morning I waited for something on the telephone, but nothing came. At noon I went into town, telling Nicu the driver that I was going down to the council; there I stopped to take in an envelope. Then I went towards the police station, then along Majális út to the Botanical Gardens, where the Securitate was. There were more civilians in the street than officials, and not all in uniform. I hurried back. At six in the evening I told Nicu again that I was going into town, to the university, he was to leave me there and not wait for me. I didn't like to keep the car waiting all the time, it would be constantly on my mind that it was waiting and I wouldn't have a minute's peace for conversation. I told him I'd get myself home. His answer was that he couldn't leave me at such a time.

'What time, Nicule?'

'You know, Comrade Décsi, *Cu evenimentele*. With the events.'

But so far there hadn't been anything from Bucharest on the radio. My neighbour and I sat there all night listening to the Hungarian radio. He knew enough Hungarian to follow it. Well, I said, Nicule, you just go home, look after your family. He, unfortunately, hadn't got one.

It was a Wednesday, I didn't have to go into the university, I had no classes, I just stayed up in the Station. I took down a book as an excuse to make the secretary type out a passage from it. I'd go along on the off chance, I thought, that there'd be somebody that I could speak to. Classes were being held as usual. I could detect nothing out of the ordinary. I went into the lecturers' room. Two Hungarian colleagues were still there, fortunately they'd been reinstated. Gazda and Nagy, and they suggested going for a coffee. We sat down on Karolina square. We couldn't even have a proper chat, we were so agitated. And, of course, cautious. Nagy said that the students had intended to do something that day, they'd asked the Romanian students to be with them so that it shouldn't become a Hungarian demonstration as that would lead to serious trouble. But the Romanians were told that what the Hungarians intended would be an anti-Romanian revisionist demonstration, and they were not to go but stay where they were. Neither of them knew whether there would be anything else that day. Nagy thought not.

'Just as well,' said I. 'Better if we wait a bit. Let's see what happens.'

Nagy thought that we ought not to wait. If we intended anything, today was the day to hold a demonstration in sympathy with Budapest.

If we intended, I thought. But I just didn't know what I should intend. I was responsible for the whole Station, he could go and demonstrate, he was just a lecturer. Certainly, he'd been reinstated once things had eased up a bit, but perhaps for that very reason he ought to sit still.

I let Nicu go and set off across the town. I could sense in the air that something was up. Everybody was so on edge. There were a lot of police about. The two big bars were closed with signs up saying *Pauza sanitara*. Just what I too had invented, cleaning. And they'd be open next day. I ought to ring my gateman in case anybody had wanted me. What was I to do? Go home? Sit by the radio? I didn't care to be alone at a time like that. I'd go out and call on Kali. Only I'd just sent the car away. Never mind, there was the bike, I hadn't used it for a long time. I didn't think she would have any information, she'd got no radio or anything. But some know-all in the village had spread the news that revolution had broken out in Hungary, and the Americans were coming. Kali was so pleased she was beside herself—I didn't know whether it was at seeing me or at what was going on in Budapest. I preferred not to comment on the stupid remark about the Americans.

In the ten o'clock news, Bucharest also announced the counterrevolution in Budapest.

I went in early again next morning to find the gateman still asleep.

I began to write *Ordin de deplasares*—travel passes. I didn't usually do it, the assistant director did, but now I wrote down all the Hungarian names. They were all only to go on official business. I checked my lists so as to make no mistakes. The only people who weren't sent away were those working outside on the land. The rest all had to go, especially the younger, unruly men, well, they all had to go. I began phoning and arranging who was to go collecting and where. They had to take samples, or at least something from there, be given a sapling or the like. Every last thing had to be thought of, they were to go away, I didn't want a single one here getting in my way. I included a couple of Romanians, so that it shouldn't be too conspicuous. At other times travel had to be pre-authorized, but this time I did it on my own authority.

At this point I began to take up professional links with the Magyar Autonomous Territory and set up an office there, to begin adaptation experiments with them and to see how our trees withstood the climate there. The coldest place in the country, Csíkszereda, was in the MAT, but I wasn't going to send a single person there, least of all a Romanian, there would have been no point. No one had better go to the MAT at present, as I hear that the Bánát too was beginning to stir, as there had been leafletting in Temesvár according to Radio Free Europe. No one was to go there, but that was where we had connections. First I had to send young Tibor Dáné away, as he couldn't sit still. That morning he'd turned up dressed in his best. I asked him what he had come to? A wedding? He was taken aback and didn't reply. He looked at me and thought I'd understand. I don't understand, I said, why you're dressed like that. Put your overcoat in the cupboard, then once we've written the assignments just go home, pack your case and be off to the Mócvidék and look around the hills for possibilities for adaptation. Collecting has to be organized as well. Hold discussions with the collectives about going to collect data on fruit varieties.

'I'll do it by phone, there's no need to go out for that,' he said.

'You're going, that's an order, no more to be said.' I replied.

'Comrade Director, I'll give the collectives a ring and that'll be that. You'll see, there'll be no mistakes.'

'Look here, Tibor. Don't answer me back. You'll be on the afternoon train, and you'll ring me this evening and tell me you're there. If you don't I'll stop your salary. Understand?'

He huffed and puffed, but off he went. I had to argue with everybody before they would go. Nobody understood why I was sending them away at the end of October. Because I said so, that was why.

I didn't send anybody to the Centre but rather all over the country, down to the plains to find me warmer climates in the Bárágan and Moldova. They were to take measurements and bring back samples. To see whether it was possible for us to establish biggish rose plantations. Warmth was there, we would bring water and improve the soil. Everybody spent five days on their missions. This cost me a lot, I paid for train tickets, had to make daily allowances, money for meals, everything. It was repaid from the Centre when I was eventually authorized. In fact that daily allowance for such as young Tibor was such that he was able to afford cabbage soup—he had as yet no years, had been taken on straight from university. I was hoping not to have to pay for a hotel, he would just find a bed with the local religious. However, not one was to come back before Monday, I told them. They had to be away for the weekend. Hot-blooded youngsters like Tibor couldn't have kept quiet, Now they were all cross with me for sending them away. None of them could understand. Too bad. I called it good fortune. I was thinking about them like my sons, anxious about them, looking after them at such a time, and so bullying them.

By afternoon and evening they were all safely away on their trains. I actually escorted that dear Tibor to the station so that he wouldn't wander off, and put him on the train to our Romanian brothers in the Mócvidék. All the frontiers were closed, of course, and not a single train was entering Hungary now. Everybody had gone to the Romanian countryside, and the farther from me the better. It was a big country. So there.

Next morning the instruction came from the Centre. Everybody was recalled from holiday. I'd only got two on holiday, one a manual worker, the other a married woman—she'd gone into hospital with her legs. My staff were allowed to take leave in winter, and fortunately all were now at work. Working hours were extended slightly. The remainder were on official missions.

All sorts of rumblings could be heard from the Bánát. Leafletting and everything. I went into the university again, to the Hungarian Department, as it wasn't prepared to come to me. I learnt that a number of hot-headed students had been arrested, as had one of us lecturers. More too from another department. I asked where Ferenc Gazda was, the linguist whom I'd wanted to put on the naming committee, because after all he'd been recommended for not being all that conspicuous and very sensible. Then it turned out that I couldn't, as he wasn't ideologically suitable. I'd been without a linguist on the committee for two years by then! I couldn't make out what was expected of those linguists. After all, they dealt with such harmless subjects. I understood about Lali, he was actually a philosopher, he'd been in another party, and of course he'd wanted Magyar autonomy even after the war. That made sense. But a linguist didn't.

My people up at the Station all excused themselves, didn't want to come to work, one because of illness, another because of his mother-in-law. Of course, they all wanted to stay at home, and listen to the radio. It was as crowded as usual on Saturday evening in the Ursus, but we asked for a table and said we'd come by six. Everybody would rather be out of the house. A couple of policemen went up to a group of youngsters, about six of them standing chatting, ordinary working chaps, to break them up. I could sense electricity in the air. University students, another five or so, were moved on from the Politechnika. I asked Filotti whether Sunday's match would take place.

'All the Utémistas, the young Communist organization, have been told to be there. Several thousand, to create a good atmosphere,' he said. He was into football, and they'd got a good team. 'The Utémistas have been given tickets.'

There'll be no trouble at the match then, I thought. It'll all be under control. Kornyél Muntyán said that the statues of Lenin and Stalin had been knocked over at the hospital.

I heard a lot of such idle talk. There was no making sense of it. Transylvania was to be reunited with Hungary. The Serbs would be given the Bánát, because Gheorghiu-Dej was just back from Yugoslavia and had been given instructions by Tito. He'd not been a friend of Tito before, but now he was beginning to warm to him.

And it was said that revolution had broken out in Marosvásárhely. Really, there of all places! A good thing it wasn't in Piski. Quite, because Marosvásárhely was being very much promoted, it had been made capital of the Autonomous Territory. That had been done to demoralize Kolozsvár. I didn't know whether it would. Was anything going to happen here? Kolozsvár was under tight control, I didn't think there'd be anything. People were always very nervous here.

The Soviets marched across Romania into Hungary. It said in the paper, insofar as you could believe the paper in those days, but in *Scânteia* it said that a Soviet train was going to the aid of the Hungarian state. It said that there had been opposition, and that a fifteen-year old boy had caused the train to be held up. A fifteen-year-old! He'd tried to divert it. Tried to set the points or something, I didn't really understand exactly, so that it would be derailed. His father was a railwayman, he'd got the idea from him. So his poor father must have gone to prison.

It said in the paper that a number of trouble-causing hooligan elements had held a meeting in the Fine Arts Institute, where painters and sculptors were trained, and had taken advantage of their fellow students' good nature. Rabble-rousing speeches had been made, rowdy behaviour had been in evidence, and such conduct could only benefit nationalist and chauvinist elements.

On Sunday morning an extraordinary meeting was convened for the first time in Kolozsvár. Two days previously, Miron Constaninescu was here, because a top man had been sent from the Centre to each of the Hungarian areas to bolster the work of state and Party. Miron was sent because he had good Hungarian. Directives were given on the attitude of the Party to affairs in Hungary. I'd never attended such a long meeting, and was so hungry I nearly fell off my chair. I wished I'd taken a couple of apples with me, as we weren't given any refreshments. There was so much debate, this way and that: weren't those rebels right in a way, yet the Hungarian Communists had not been wrong, or why had it all happened, and must help be requested from outside, or could Hungary sort things out. Debate raged on, and there wasn't time to say everything in both languages. We only spoke Hungarian. Nor was it easily moderated. It was obvious that the Romanians were afraid of Hungarian interests—and that once again these were in the foreground—for fear that there might be greater cross-frontier Hungarian collaboration. It was clearly stated in the meeting why the Soviets had had to enter Hungary. Everybody was asked if they had understood, and were there any questions. When there were no more questions we broke up.

When I called to see him in Kőkert utca, Lali said that I should see what all was going on, because he was perfectly able to tell me, and he said that in Romania Stalinism was not in any way going to diminish. Rather, it would gain strength. Because however offended the Hungarians were, there was nowhere for them to take their complaint, no organization or party or anything, because the Hungarian People's Union had been silenced. There was only the Communist Party, but that was entirely governed by sectarian Communists. The Twentieth Soviet Party Congress had brought no change for us, Lali explained, because he had always believed that the Twentieth Congress was a turning point. But in Romania it had produced nothing! Nothing for the benefit of the Hungarians. He spoke so courageously, it was amazing. He said that he was actually keeping a journal. He was doing it for posterity, so that there should be evidence. I didn't understand why anyone should think about the future when we had our own lives to lead. I would have asked him, but I suppose I didn't want to cross swords with my best friend, did I, about whether he would be able to record everything in his journal with full sincerity and clarity. Because if not, what the hell was it for?

Lali said that even in early October, it had been possible to raise points with the Party. Points had been raised concerning Hungarian interests. He wasn't a Party member, he hadn't been accepted, but he helped with Party work. They'd been presented to Miron when he, Fazekas and all the rest had

been there. Such as, for example, that there was no indication on the outskirts of towns that they were Hungarian. Well, that was certainly so. There
was nothing to indicate. And the question of schools. Thirty per cent of the
pupils enrolled in Kolozsvár primary schools were Hungarians. Thirty per
cent! That was the figure for this year, 1956. Shocking! What could I say?

We chatted in the kitchen until late in the evening. Lali asked whether
I'd read the list of new academicians? It had come out in summer. He'd made
a note of it, if I wanted it, got it from the paper. Look here, Lali, I said, in
July I was reading flowers, not about the Academy. He meant the new
members of the Romanian Academy of Sciences, those who'd been honoured. Not a single Hungarian. Not one.

He said, and immediately burst into tears:

'It's true! It's a Romanian Academy of Sciences all right. That's what it's
called. What would a Hungarian be doing in it? Their place is in Hungarian
science.'

I told him to ease up a bit, not to be so negative all the time. There were
good things as well. Wages were going up. There was going to be more in
the shops, it had just been announced in parliament. According to him this
was just pulling the wool, they were doing it to distract attention from the
revolution in Hungary. He began to shout, he was so upset.

'Do you really believe it, Vili?' he asked.

'That's what was said,' I replied. What answer was I supposed to give?

Then I had to listen to some Bartók piano concerto on the radio with
him. I know nothing about that sort of music and it actually irritates me.
I'd rather have silence.

From my point of view, the most important element of the Party directive was that there would soon be a revision of salaries. There were to be
increases, and we'd get them within days. And more in the shops, which we
would feel as of next week. Salaries were very important to me. I could pay
people so little that I felt ashamed. We didn't reckon overtime, they had to
do a standard working day, so the standard was paid in such a way that it

could only be earned by overtime. I paid a better worker six hundred lei, while a pair of shoes cost four hundred in the shops. Well, I thought, this socialism might really be a bit better by this time. It was no use my telling a man that I didn't set wages, that wasn't how it was done. The Centre told me what to pay. The details were all set out in a table and that was that. But I could see the state his clothes were in. It had been said when the Station was opened that every worker would be given annually a suit of overalls to wear for work. Blue ones, like every worker wore. But nothing had come of it. Women put on aprons and all the men wore tatty shirts. So I was delighted at this wages business. And at the improvement of supplies. As early as Tuesday I could feel that the shops were better stocked. Everybody, but most of all the women, asked for time off to go shopping. Especially for bread, oil and rice. There was more meat about as well. Previously there'd hardly been any cornflour, they said. I didn't know, I didn't have to go shopping. Things were brought to me from the Party canteen. Nicu, the driver, always brought them. If I asked for something he could bring it from there. At the weekend either my mother sent me something or I'd go and see Kali, so I had cooked food. But it also happened that there weren't even potatoes in the shops. In fact, that year had been hit by the weather, there'd been such a drought! We hadn't been affected, and in the Station we used all the water we needed for research. I never even thought about water. I irrigated regardless. If we wanted results we had to irrigate, not save water. Now I was really looking forward to seeing the new salary tables. To my staff being pleased. And the women. Those women watched the money! Some of them understood money better than their husbands.

But I was very worried about the students. They were closely watched, and for every five students, there's a supervisor. They were given so little money, of course, their whole allowance was thirty lei, and what could they get for that? Toothpaste and shoe polish. A lot of them used to sell their meal tickets and others went into the students' canteen with them. They were then able to buy a pair of socks or a book. I realized when they come to the Station for classes that they were weak with hunger. I always had bread and bacon brought, set out on big tin plates for them to take between sessions. There were some who only took the course so as to get something to eat. Never mind, at least they came. There were some who came wearing *bocskor*. Hungarians too, though *bocskor* is a Romanian thing. But they'd got nothing else. So it was a fact, I always had to worry about the students. That taught me a thing or two. They couldn't sit still. I was like that too, though I'd never ever been a student. I did my best bits of work when I was serving with the fire brigade, and I'd cross-fertilized things which turned out very well. Courageous things. Even now I was living on them. In the canteen at the university, the Budapest radio would be blaring forth. A lot of the students were Romanian and couldn't understand a word, but they didn't go away, just sat there. Then in would come some officious person and switch it off. Lunchtime over, he'd say, and that was that.

It was the 29th, a Monday. A directive had been received that all institutions were to hold meetings about the counterrevolution in Hungary. The Party line had to be stated so that the workers might know what it was. I wasn't making it up, I had to chair the meeting. My deputy director was a Romanian, but directives were expected to come from me, though I was a Hungarian. Such was my good fortune. I said straight away at the start that the meeting was to be a brief one because we had a tremendous amount to do. I summed up what we'd received in the written synopsis, speaking first in Hungarian and then in Romanian. It's usual to do it the other way round, of course. But this time it had to be different. To let it be seen that I was a Hungarian and that first and foremost I spoke Hungarian. I didn't repeat what it said in the papers about monstrous, inhuman atrocities being perpetrated in the streets. Anyone who wants to can read about that in the paper. There was nothing on the subject in the synopsis. Then I asked, were there any questions? Was everything clear? There was no time for analysing everything, let's get on with our work. But I paused in case anybody did put a hand up.

There were no questions. And I wasn't sorry. After that I changed the subject to the work ahead of us in the weeks to come. My estimates had been sent in but hadn't yet been returned. New fertilizers would be tested and we'd work on them. I went into it all in detail. Then we stood up, and off we went.

I'd now arranged everyday affairs in the Station so that I had nothing to do but supervise. That was the way it had to be now. I had to keep an eye on everything. I dropped in everywhere, checked, gave people jobs so that they should be busy and have no time to spare. On Wednesday my people would be back from their missions. They'd been away five days, and Sunday. Perhaps I'd send them again to somewhere different. We'd see what the mood was like.

The entire staff were called into the university on Tuesday. The students had to be watched, and might only go anywhere, to practicals and outside classes, under supervision. We were told what to do if they quarrelled or began demonstrating and becoming disorderly. If a free fight developed, it had to be broken up at once. Hooligans must be identified. Well, all that it took to make me happy was having to shepherd university students. I hadn't got enough people to keep an eye on the Station. I escorted students there myself, gave my lecture and took them back. That wasn't in orders, just common sense. There were thirty of them, all were present. A group came up to me every day. That was all I needed. They also wanted to put me on duty to watch the student hostel, and I had difficulty in getting out of that, so as not to have to spend all night with them as well. I wanted to hear the news at home as well. By now I was popping out several times a day, some days going over to the house five or six times for one thing and another, and listening to the news.

The students went completely mad. We'd become reconciled to Tito, we'd abandoned the Soviets, and they sympathized with the situation in Hungary. They all wrote on their fingers, their four fingers, indicating Tito. Some painted them all. That became the fashion. Because if there was Tito, there were no Russians. So what did you mean, my boy, if you painted something on your fingers? Was that your idea of revolution? But I didn't say a word. I pretended not to notice, and kept out of it.

On the weekend, dancing was not allowed in the nightclubs, because it had led to trouble in Bucharest; people had got worked up, shouted rubbish and then made to go into the streets. Now all the youth had become bullish at once. A young poet, Nicolae Labiş, was arrested. He'd begun to organize something on the lines of the Petőfi Circle. I could see in class that no one was paying attention, they all had their minds on something else. Another group had been discovered, also in Bucharest, because letters had been written to the papers, demanding that they tell the truth about Hungary. Which truth, I thought. Because number one was what Hungarian radio said, number two what *Scânteia* said, and three what Radio Free Europe said. The radio championed the cause of the clergy, all the bishops would be let out of prison and begin to be in charge once more. Perhaps the clergy wanted to be the masters again. I wouldn't obey a priest, that was for sure. According to Lali, the clergy would only destroy the entire achievement. They wanted a return to square one. That was how Lali viewed all politics. Politics were his life, and he'd only just been released.

But it wasn't that easy to decide for oneself what was the truth. But priests ought not to be carried shoulder-high. Priests ought not to be running the country and saying how things should be.

Perhaps Romanian and Hungarian Radio Free Europe were saying different things, perhaps the two accounts could not be reconciled abroad. I didn't know, I didn't listen to the Romanian. But which way did the Transylvanian tend? What was it that Kali always said? Not between two stools but under the bench? In Lali's view, however, there was no Transylvanian business involved. Now there was only internationalism, international left-wing business.

It was announced that there were to be more parties in Hungary, and elections. And agreement with the Russians had been reached on this. Everybody was so crazy about having many parties. I'd never understood such a thing. I'd been invited to join the Party because I'd been found acceptable and I had a good record. But I hadn't looked for parties of my own accord, not even one. I didn't even know about them. I knew there was the Tsaranist, the Peasant Party, and the Liberals and the Communists. About six in the old days. But I hadn't understood which the Social Democrats were or the Socialists while there were several. Nor had I gone and voted, though I could have. The writer István Nagy had said in parliament that many parties always resulted in a tug-of-war. Everything was torn apart, whereas people should strive for unity. What a kerfuffle there had been a couple of years ago when the Hungarian People's Union was dissolved. A silent kerfuffle, of course, because it only took place between individuals, cautiously. But I didn't know what we wanted all those parties for, when what mattered was unity, and Nagy said that as well. He had a good understanding of politics, he'd been a party member for a long time and an exiled Communist. Parties weren't necessary, just good people that worked, didn't steal, didn't take risks, but set an example to others. In particular, that didn't lapse into the wickedness of the personality cult. Was that so difficult? Yes, it seemed.

Lali ran up to ask for a couple of flowers if there were any left. There were a few, because it had been quite warm even in late October. He asked for red ones, as his heart was full of happiness and pride. Hungarians were proud again! I could hardly get him indoors to talk more quietly. In his opinion there had been stirrings everywhere and everybody was proud of the Hungarians again, and it was only in Romania that Stalinism was so deeply ingrained. There'd been no change here, certainly not in the attitude to Hungarian interests, and everybody was just cautious and afraid. Here Stalinism was of such a degree that the press simply denigrated the Hungarian revolution, and so debased itself. Lali was quite rejuvenated. He'd even put on weight.

Romanian students were agitating in Temesvár too, according to rumour. I thought that the Hungarians were overly nervous. Several hundred had been arrested in Temesvár. They'd handed in protests, held meetings. They didn't want to study Russian, their grants weren't enough, they didn't want a collective. Yesterday Radio Free Europe announced that there'd been a student gathering in Temesvár and the Minister of Education had been present. Anti-Communist slogans were shouted and the organizers taken into custody. I think they'll be jailed. Lali said that Temesvár was the most advanced town, it was always ahead of the game. Hungarians, Romanians, Serbs and Germans lived together very well there. They had common interests. That was how it should be here too. But in Kolozsvár there was always friction. We couldn't live in peace. That's the kind of town it was. That's why there was such anxiety about Kolozsvár, and it was more tightly controlled. That's why it had had to be left out of the MAT, clearly.

Now the light was dawning, it couldn't be stopped—this was the word in the university as people went out to visit the dead. I told my staff in the Station that they wouldn't be given the day off, I wouldn't let them take it, and they couldn't ask for it in advance as I'd dock them a day's money. It was a working day like any other. Anyone that wanted to go to the cemetery could go in the evening. I would hardly be going, it wasn't my custom. I didn't like cemeteries and all the piety in them.

The day before, I hurried home in the evening. I was just running from one place to another in those days. I was surprised not to be more on edge. I switched on the radio, and it didn't light up. I looked, flicked the switch, twiddled one knob and another—nothing. Something had burnt out. Confound it. Just when I wanted to listen to it. Tomorrow I'd ask Nicu to get somebody to attend to it. Damn it. Now I couldn't find out what was happening. I burst into tears like a child. I've never been able to hold back tears. There was nobody there, I looked around in the pitch darkness, not a soul. There was just a cold pillow for me to cry on.

In the morning I was up late. Never mind. The workers went in whether I was there or not, signed on at seven o'clock. My first thought was the Station. Yesterday those I'd sent out had kept arriving back. Young Tibor appeared in the afternoon, he was as excited as a puppy. He hadn't heard the radio for a week, only rumours. Now that he was allowed back, all was quiet.

The moment he was back. So we too could relax. As long as they were successful over there, in Budapest, presumably nothing would be required here. That frontier was paper thin, every sound could be heard through it.

I went in late. I couldn't get started. I was so tired, it was like wearing lead boots. But I looked through the back window. I'd left two quince trees at the back of the house, the old Constantinople variety. I hadn't been able to find a Transylvanian one. The fruit were shaped like the Tartós Gusztáv apples here in the orchard. I'd meant to graft something onto them, but they'd just been left. I might have tried grafting a bitter almond. I'd never done enough work on quinces. They're not a commercial fruit and I'd abandoned them. They're the sort of thing you find in a peasant yard. They can't come up to commercial standards, so they're no use except in the home. Kali always wanted to have them cut down, wasn't familiar with quinces. I told her to cook the fruit until they were sweet and roast meat with it. She'd never heard of such a thing, mixing meat and fruit, she didn't cook anything like that. She only picked them for pálinka, made nothing else with them. I looked at the trees, couldn't take my eyes off them. They were the last to shed their leaves. The fruit too was the last to ripen. The trees were full of tits, which came to pick off the grubs. We'd had so much rain, and when I'd sliced up half a dozen quinces, they'd all been full of them. I hadn't treated the tree with anything, I hadn't thought about it. The tits kept coming and pecking busily, and there must have been a dozen on each tree.

There was silence, I had no radio. I didn't know what had happened. But now I was thinking that things must have settled down, there and here. Now there would be no more fighting. A week had gone by since I'd sat alone and looked around. I needed to do that. I needed to look at Nature, then I could put two and two together. How I could develop plants. But I had to look in silence. I'd spent a week just running about, organizing everybody, escorting them, calming them down, telling them to be quiet. Now I looked at the nice round leaves and the black trunk, because everything was wet and looked black. I had to summon up the strength to get up and go to meet the day. But it did me good to look at that tree and the busy birds. All of them knew what to do. It was just a shame that the fruit had all fallen for lack of somebody to pick it. I don't like to see fruit on the ground. It looks as if the land has no owner. That's not nice. Even a wild apple tree in a field is untidy. It's better for some animal to eat it up.

Then I went out.

Today I had to hear the reports on what those who'd been away had accomplished. The whole thing was boring, and I hadn't send them out on real jobs. They might have found something of interest even so. Some were the busy sort and even brought something back from the edge of a forest. All those journeys hadn't even been authorized, and they might have been accepted in the Centre but there had been no time to give me approval. And when would we have got the money?! I'd had to take it out of my own. That would never do. But what could I have done? Luckily, nobody knew. I'd even omitted to keep account. Anybody that went away was given a hundred lei in an envelope and had to manage.

When I went back to the Station I couldn't calm people down. It was Friday, they were tired, I'd driven them hard all week, that was true, and they all now wanted to go to the cemetery. The Romanians didn't so much, as they had no family graves in Kolozsvár. Or was it Thursday, not Friday? I was quite confused by that time. Anyway, I let them go at five o'clock. They were supposed to work until six. Go quietly, then, it's still daylight, I said, don't disturb the dead. In the end I didn't go out. I'd thought, though, I ought to go to my grandmother's grave; she's in the Calvinist cemetery. And to go to my father and say to him, 'Well, Sándor, are you pleased with your son? He's a director. And a university lecturer. And he's had three books published. What do you say to that? Or should I have been a painter and decorator, like you and the rest of my relations?'

Anyway, I didn't go. Why should I disturb the dead? He's dead, we've evened the score.

It turned out to be just as well that I didn't go. Yet again our students couldn't keep still. They went to all sorts of graves with wreaths and speeches. I learnt about this not from the university but from the radio, because it was on Free Europe the next day. In our faculty, agriculture, not a word was said about it, it wasn't certain that they were ours, but perhaps they'd been in the arts faculty. There was always trouble with them. The radio also knew that those responsible had been arrested. So either I believed it or I didn't. There was so much exaggeration. The radio technician had come in the night and said that he'd got more work than he'd ever had. He said that if I hadn't sent a car he wouldn't have come, he was run off his feet. He didn't ask for payment, he'd rather have some fruit from the garden. I said I'd give him some of my own but not the Station's. He was happy to pick up the quinces, his wife would make cheese with them. Take them, my dear chap. At last somebody can use them. I told him not to overcook them, that would destroy the vitamins. I also gave him three bags of walnuts, there were so many that I hadn't got the time to break them. But I did like them. I used to sit for two or three hours of an evening just breaking walnuts, listening to the cracking, and Kali would tell a story. What had become of that life? How could I even find time to break walnuts?

But I wish the radio had remained silent! I'd had just about enough, I went into the Station; I was beginning to twitch in case somebody had done something. Then to the university—I'd had no good news from there that autumn. There'd been a disturbance in the cemetery.

One know-all colleague said of the Bolyai that what had happened at the cemetery wasn't as the radio said—that they'd gone there for the express purpose of showing sympathy with the Hungarian revolution. It had been quite different, because it had been discussed long before, Lali said that the situation was that of only a little flame and everything suddenly flaring up. Speeches had been made, the workers had arrived from the Herbák shoe factory. The crowd had swollen as darkness fell.

Never mind, said I, as long as they came to no harm, got away with it. Lali said that originally it had been agreed as long ago as spring by the Sociology and History Departments that each assistant or assistant lecturer would take care of a grave, do the right thing in the Házsongárd. There were some youthful talents, among them Dávid Gyula, he said, but I didn't know him. And so wreaths had been laid on great Hungarian poets and scientists, and candles set up, it had all been quite orderly. Nothing wrong at all. Only this was not the time to place a Hungarian flag on a wreath, considering what was happening in Hungary. Apparently, the day before it had been forbidden for students to go to the cemetery. You couldn't prohibit a thing, just like that.

It was Saturday, 3 November, my God. There was a big gathering, university people from the Bolyai and the Babeş, all departments and high schools. It was fortunate that it was only in the evening. because I'd just begun to do some valuable work, sorting out and selecting the year's best seedlings. I was trying to make myself work so as to take my mind off things. The seedlings had been sorted and I was just looking them over—they were from the new hybrids, and I was seeing what they had produced for the first time. The little plants had no names as yet, nor did they need them. Perhaps they never even would have. There's no telling what you've created, whether it will come to anything. Such is experimentation. All the same, I was trying to produce 'Kali's rose'. But now she had the child. I'd thought of putting together a grandiflora and a little polyantha. Almost impossible! But in the end I began to enjoy the work so much that I completely forgot to go home and listen to the news. Where was I to escape events, except in work and experimentation? Things were starting to calm down in Budapest. At last. There were to be several parties, apparently, reforms and everything. At last there was peace. Peace.

Miron Constantinescu was still here, and he presided over the meeting. We weren't personally acquainted. He now assured the territory that he had full authority. We could learn the opinion of the Centre at first hand. The counterrevolutionary problem had been resolved, and, according to Constantinescu, order had been restored in Hungary. I didn't know what he was talking about. I'd been hearing something quite different on the radio. At the time, however, nobody dared ask a question. The meeting was conducted entirely in Romanian, not in two languages like the previous one. Constantinescu announced that those responsible for the actions in the university had been sought and had been found in the Bolyai. The cause of the disturbances had been the liberalism and lack of awareness of the pro-rector. Ernő Gáll delivered a judicious self-criticism. So, he hoped for the best, that there would be peace and that we would be able to get nicely on with our work undisturbed. He and the comrade shook hands and that was that. But it seemed that more was still expected of him. He was not being dismissed.

It turned out later that there had been a university meeting that morn-ing, but I'd missed it. I didn't understand how I hadn't received the sum-mons. Nothing came by telephone and nobody said a word. I just wasn't summoned. Fancy missing a meeting at a time like that. But I heard that there was a big debate in the Bolyai. This was a moment of truth for the Hungarians: would we remain faithful to the Romanian Workers Party? Professor Edgár Balogh spoke very well and convinced everybody. Now we had to be at unity. That evening the sub-dean called on me and got me to sign the document that had been drawn up that morning by the staff. It was just as well that it was brought for me to sign. The Bolyai and the Babeş signed it jointly. If I'd accidentally not signed, I thought, I'd have been fired. I asked if I might read what had been drawn up, but he said that there wasn't time, he'd got to hurry to the *Igazság* editorial office and hand it in, as it was to be published the next day. It would appear with the statement of the Kolozsvár writers: they too condemned the counterrevolution. We were defending the fruits of the joint endeavours of the two peoples, said the sub-dean. It would all be in the paper, I could read it there. I should buy the paper in the morning, 4 November. There was to be a special edition.

It was Sunday. I was late up, almost seven o'clock. The previous evening had been so painful that I'd stopped listening to the radio, I could stand no more. When I turned on to pick up Budapest I didn't know who was speak-ing, but I just heard somebody shouting 'Help! Help!' like a drowning man.

Then in a foreign language. Then in German. Then in Russian. Calling for the world's help for Hungary. Jesus Christ!

What was going on? I knew nothing, transmission broke off early in the morning. Something had gone very wrong. It had been three days since I'd been able to get Free Europe. Where was I to turn? I picked up Bucharest, but it was saying nothing. It was always so late in announcing everything. Should I go to the university? Whom was I to disturb on a Sunday morning? I had no car, I hadn't called for one. I had no ideas. Should I do some work? I'd rather go out to see Kali on foot. An hour and a half's walk. I might cycle. But I'd rather go more slowly. I was having to rush about so much. This time I'd take it easy. Perhaps Kali would be in church, it was Sunday. Never mind, I'd take my time.

The postman brought the paper. Two!

The paper was in my hand at ten o'clock. The lecturers weren't individually named, because the entire Bolyai staff had signed, as had the Hungarian lecturers at Babeş. It said: 'We express our commitment to the democratic and socialist attainments of the Romanian People's Republic. These are the fruits of the joint endeavours of our peoples. For that very reason, the principal evidence of our defence and further development is the unity and brotherhood of the workers of the Romanian, Hungarian and other nationalities . . . under the leadership of the Party!'

Everybody signed. Anyone that had a name. Anyone that had a reputation worth five bani signed. All the writers, all such as were in the university or in science, were party to it. So anyone who had no reputation didn't have to sign. That's the way it was. Even the awkward people all signed. The only exceptions were those who were in prison.

Lali hadn't signed. He came up yesterday to look at the last of the roses, the November roses. He was so downhearted that I couldn't cheer him up even with a Peace. He'd been down in the dumps ever since coming out of prison. He said that the intelligentsia of the Transylvanian Hungarians, all the writers put together, had no backbone. No backbone, no will. And the students despised their teachers, all of whom had signed. I didn't argue. What argument could I have offered?

'It was forced on us,' I told him. 'Anyone that didn't sign the "greetings telegram" will be able to look themselves in the face.'

'It wasn't a greetings telegram either, but militant solidarity. Never mind. It doesn't matter, whatever we call it, it comes to the same thing,' answered Lali dolefully.

He hadn't signed. It didn't matter to him, he'd been in prison, and now he was to be rehabilitated. He'd appeared in court in Bucharest, even been given compensation for his time inside, he and the other three professors too. Perhaps they even agreed on some important point and said as much, but Lali very much doubted it. I didn't think they'd give him much of a position after that.

Lali said how much he owed himself to remain silent if he could no longer speak. Or to grieve if he couldn't fight. Because even the students had all dressed in mourning on the Day of the Dead.

The students didn't have to sign because they had no reputations. Only the leaders did. Apparently the linguist who'd made such a damning speech on the radio, a man called László Szabédi, whom I'd wanted to take on, had had misgivings. He was talking of killing himself, said Lali, who was a friend of his.

In the MAT, the Marosvásárhely writers had by then made a declaration and condemned the events in Hungary. It had appeared that day in a special edition of *Vörös Zászló*. It was interesting that I wasn't a subscriber but the postman brought it that morning together with *Igazság*. The MAT was nowadays cleverer in every respect, more advanced, more mobile, better informed. Miron had complained to us of just that, Kolozsvár was backward, only doddering along. Lali said that a separate condemnatory statement from the Kolozsvár writers was going to appear in *Igazság* the next day, the Monday issue.

I looked at the paper. It was filthy. Kali was quite right. If you picked it up your hands were black. Even the theatre column was better than what was on the front page. János Tompa, the activist, always wrote the theatre reviews. He was writing about some anti-Soviet play, a French piece, that was on in the Romanian National Theatre. By somebody called Sartre. I had to read it twice, and even then I didn't understand it! 'The club of those to be shot in the head' was the title of the review. A title like that these days? What was that supposed to mean? Some satirical play, I supposed, and therefore anti-Soviet in such a way that in the course of it we would have to laugh at people that were anti-Soviet, or rather at the stupid French. Oh dear, everything in the theatre was so overcomplicated, I could hardly make out what was intended. Why couldn't there be plain, straightforward plots?

I still couldn't get Free Europe. How many days had that been now? I'd rather go and see Kali.

By the time I got to the Györgyfalu forest, entirely new thoughts were beginning to stir in my head. Things that I would work at. I ought to try something completely new, a variety that had never been, that I would be the first to exhibit. Not that I meant myself, but the Station. Something that we'd experimented with, the combination of paprika and tomato, or some high-grade apple. I felt so enthusiastic! That's what a good walk does for you. By the time I arrived, I was feeling really keen on Kali as well. I had to wait for her, because she was actually in church, but the bell was ringing by then. She and the child came home, and was he glad to see me! Made a real fuss. I sat on the porch, didn't go inside. I said to him, 'Hallo, son, I haven't brought you anything, just my good humour.'

'What are you so pleased about, mister, on this sad day?' said Kali. 'Can't you see . . .'

And she began to sob. Something awful. I'd never seen Kali cry like that, but I wasn't going to admit it. Damn it all. I came in high spirits, and she was crying. So I asked what the matter was. There was nothing wrong with the boy.

In church they'd been praying for Hungary. Didn't I know? What didn't I know? Hungary was done for. War had broken out. The Russians had come, there was shooting in every street. Now the boy began to cry when he saw his mother, so I said to her, 'Stop it, Kali. Anyway, can't you see, there's no shooting here? We're not in Hungary. Why don't you make me an omelette? I'm starving.'

I stayed with her all day. We were like we used to be in my garden. I didn't even feel like going home. Then when the boy went for his afternoon sleep, she didn't mind and we had sex. And the last time hadn't been the day before. She said, 'Well, you don't mean to be an old man, mister. 'Cos you make music like a youngster.'

And we laughed. She'd have cried all day, but we laughed instead. We had a nice bean soup, because that Kali certainly could make. I played with the boy, then I fixed a rope to a tree for him so that he could climb and swing. Kali watched and was so pleased that tears came to her eyes. When I was leaving, she said, 'Where are you off to in such an 'urry? Perhaps your girlfriend's waitin' for you at 'ome? You're goin' to walk like the devil with the Gypsy.'

'Well, how did he walk?'

'I can't tell you that at the gate, mister, 'cos you're always in such an 'urry.' I was in fact standing by the dilapidated gate. 'Where are you always off to in such an 'urry?'

'I've got to listen to the news as well,' I said.

'Never mind the radio, 'cos what's on now is the devil sayin' Mass. So as people don't 'ave a minute's peace. You can even 'ear it in the privy.'

That was true, too, because she'd got a neighbour, a teacher, and she could overhear his radio in her privy. Kali always had maize husks in there to wipe her arse with. She'd never got used to newspaper. She said that newspaper was filthy. When she handled the paper to read it, her fingers always went black. So she didn't blacken herself in that region. Nor could she get used to having a lavatory indoors.

I told her how I felt, I too preferred the nice wooden privy down the garden to the flushing toilet indoors. I was used to the outside one. I didn't mind about winter. Everybody was surprised that I didn't knock it down. Why should I? The fresh air was pleasant, and it was good for the soil. At home, when I went outside, I always turned the radio up so as to be able to hear it. Then I didn't listen to it because it wasn't like the human voice, all I got was background noise. But at home I couldn't do without the radio any longer. 'I've got to go and get on with my work,' I said, 'I'll come and see you again', carelessly calling her *maga*.

I wasn't to call her *maga*, she wasn't my wife.

Oh blast you, Kali!

I asked, 'What do you want? Shall I take you to the council offices? Shall we get married?'

She wasn't goin' to have any more to do with filthy men. They could all go and rot.

Once more we parted on a sour note. The boy came running after me, caught hold of my trouser leg, wouldn't let me go. What was I to say to that child, what indeed? But I really enjoyed myself with him. At least I wasn't alone, wasn't always thinking of revolution and the Soviets. The boy did me good, stopped me thinking about the outside world all the time. I could play with him and not have a care in the world.

On the way home, a cart picked me up, a farmer taking a big load of dried maize stems. The horses were very listless. So was I, although I'd had a nice day. But I was as tired as if I'd been carrying stones. Family life wasn't for me. And the boy. He always wanted to play if he saw me.

I asked what was in the cart.

'Maize stems,' said the driver. He was taking it to his sister because she used them for heating. 'I wish I hadn't collected them.'

Then he said no more. I asked why.

'Well, then I wouldn't have seen what I saw.'

'What did you see?' I asked, because I could see that he wanted to talk but only if I asked questions.

'Well, those big vehicles. Army vehicles. Some were tanks.'

'What tanks?'

He'd looked down into the valley, onto the road to Szamosfalvi, and seen tanks going along the valley. Two days ago, he said.

'How come we knew nothing?' I asked.

'They certainly hadn't been in the city,' he answered. 'People wouldn't have liked that. They'd have been alarmed to see Russian tanks and soldiers at a time like this. So they must have been going from here to Hungary.'

Then he just shook his head like a horse, and said, 'That little Hungary has no luck. We have no luck, God's always striking at us. Mary's country! Load of shit! Excuse the language.'

The peasants are very coarse, I'm afraid. Awareness is at a very low level. That's exactly what István Nagy, the worker-writer, was saying in parliament.

In the morning I set the alarm for nice and early. I was in the Station at six o'clock. I couldn't face working now, I just went in and shuffled papers. Moved them from one place to another. I'd hardly got there before I had a row with the doorman. I asked him why he didn't tie the dog up in good time? Well, Comrade Director, say what time, and he'd tie it up. I said, first thing. When we start work. In came Miora, asked if I'd like a coffee. I said that she'd been working there a year, wasn't that long enough for her to learn that I never ever drink coffee? Damn these Romanian women they've landed me with. I asked if she took such good note of everything. She went off in a huff. I was so on edge, there was a throbbing in my temple all the time.

On the stroke of seven, young Tibor appeared. Dressed in mourning.

I called him into the office, shut the door, and asked, 'Have you lost your marbles, Tibor?'

'Why do you ask, Comrade Director?'

'What are you wearing?'

'Mourning clothes.'

'Take them off at once. Or go home.'

'My mother and cousin have died.'

'Do you usually mourn your mother and cousin? And the neighbour's cat?'

'She brought me up, if you don't mind. I've been with her ever since I was a child.'

'And can you show me a document proving that she's died?' It was hard to make out young Tibor.

'What document, if you please? Does one have to have a document to mourn one's family?'

'Look here, Tibor, let's not pull each other's legs. You are not to go into town today dressed in mourning, understand? You're a clever chap, you've got a bright future, why must you ruin it? Now, leave that jacket here. Put this pullover on, here, you can wear it home, but you're taking these black things off this minute. Understand? You're going to get us into trouble. Don't just think of yourself all the time. Here you have to consider us and the whole Station. Do you understand, my boy?'

Fortunately it was that day that I was able to announce the increase in pay. And there would be money after having a child and on going into retirement. I held a meeting at nine o'clock. I spun it out a bit. In my view that was what was needed. Hungary was finished, and I was giving out money. I spoke of the growth of the economy, of equal distribution, and of how we recognized the difficult position of working people and meant to do our utmost to improve it. The papers contained a full account of the rise in the general standard of living. So, there you are, we've also improved salaries. The payment of railway workers too has gone up significantly, as has that of those that joined collectives.

'Why did the railwaymen mean to go on strike in Bucharest when the events began?' asked some know-all.

'If the comrade wishes to say something, I'll give him the chance. Just let me finish.' So he said no more.

There was no way other than that of socialism. That I knew. And I said so. We couldn't relapse into the unfair bourgeois system, into poverty, inequality, so that a child was unable to go to school because there was not a single pair of shoes in the family, or couldn't enrol for the university because of working-class origin.

'Yet again people can't study because of their background,' said another know-all. 'The child of a doctor can't, because his father was of independent means, and for no other reason. Here he's taken on as a manual worker.' Good Lord, how brave everybody's getting. People used not to speak like that.

'You can't defeat socialism by any arguments, because it has such a foundation laid in the human spirit,' I said. 'Improvement, that's what's needed. Needed every day. There are mistakes everywhere, but we shall correct them.' I went on by asking, 'Does everyone know what they have to do? If so, let's adjourn and get to work. We aren't paid for talking.'

This was the time when I always worked up all my research, from November to February. Until then I would carefully put all the bits of paper on which I'd written into a box. This was when I brought them out to write them up. But I couldn't face doing it. I just couldn't get going. I checked on things here and there, but they raced about in my head and I couldn't make decisions. And the new book was expected for spring, the National Library of Agriculture and Forestry in Bucharest had given me an advance. And a big one! Because Hungarian publishing was interested in it now. *The Practical Results of the Application of Michurinism*. That was what I had to do. I ought now to be working on just those types of green plants which were difficult to shape, less plastic, could not easily be influenced. Those in which inherent characteristics were established. Conservative plants, hard to prevail on. I'd been thinking of writing a short chapter on what a futile experiment meant. Such there were. The young plant developer or researcher for whom the book was intended needed to know that I had carried out many experiments that could not have succeeded, produced any result, like Plovdiv's 'elephant's trunk', the marriage of paprika and tomato. But you have to keep trying, working, seeking. Results will come in time. It takes a minimum of ten years, or rather fifty, to show whether something's really proved, has really propagated. It's as well that we can't see it completely, because by that time we too will be well and truly laid out. That I call really good fortune. I can never know the fruit of something that I've spent ten years working on. Mendelian genetics aren't the only thing that can't be worked out by formulae, neither can the behaviour of plants in general. Anyway, I shan't write about Mendel, he's ideologically unsound.

Why is a conservative variety hard to affect? Firstly, the more distantly related things are, the harder it is to try to crossbreed them. Secondly, the more ancient a species, the less it can be influenced. Thirdly, even so, many things happen that cannot be anticipated. Fourthly, if we succeed in something, it may be that it was purely accidental, and we are unable to repeat it.

Now that I had this clever secretary, Mioara, I would have to type the manuscript. Previously I could at least have dictated it. But now, of course, Mioara was from the south, a handsome, black-haired, fine figure of a woman—only she didn't know the first word of Hungarian. I took on one Hungarian typist, Mari Nagy. She could write to everybody. She was Lali's wife. They were so strapped for cash, they just couldn't get by. Lali hasn't published a single book, nor will he, in my opinion. Because of the prison, of course. There are some, however, that have managed to get books out, it's not such a cut-and-dried matter. He and I have been back on speaking terms again since the events started. His being in prison kept us apart as there were no visiting political prisoners. That was three years, though. He's aged badly.

I was doing nothing else now, I held meetings when I had to, I went to the university when I was called, like an automaton, and I wasn't nervy any longer. I'll write up our new varieties. What shall I write! Like Kali in the folk tale, when she got to the bit where 'and so great was the love between

Goldilocks and the prince that there are no words to express it'. Then she fell silent, that was the end of the tale. It's just the same with a successful rose. What words are there for it?

Alexendru Borza had been wonderfully successful. I didn't like the name, and when I heard it I said straight out that it would irritate me so much that I'd burst. But that was what the Naming Committee had given it. On the other hand, the habitus of that flower! Such was its bearing that I was ashamed of myself in comparison. And it was lasting, slow to shed its petals. It was a brilliant colour, like freshly spilt blood. It had rather a lot of thorns, but we'd improve on that. Though I was afraid I'd ruin it. It didn't fade to purple in the vase, which is the shortcoming of red roses. It was named for the Alexandru Borza who established the Botanical Garden. He took over the Hungarian University's animals in 1919. The rose was derived from three women. Every rose grower names roses after women and girls, that's the source of most names. Does it take three women to make one man? If so, too bad. I thought we'd have three beautiful women. Or maybe one was a mother-in-law! I didn't just write, I could see it in front of me. Because there it was. I could hardly wait for next May, to see the real thing again. Previously I didn't think so, even if we kept it under glass. It wouldn't like being in the greenhouse, it'd open late. I'd put it into circulation if we managed to produce a commercial quantity, and the town would go mad over it. Only we mustn't make too much of the name. Names don't count. It's going to outshine Cluj Superstar.

I was ever so tired. There was another mass meeting today in the Aula Magna, but there wasn't room for everybody. We declared that we, Bolyai and Babeş alike, supported the new Hungarian government. I was still in Babeş with my book, as Bolyai had no Agriculture Department for me. But when the Bolyai people had to sign, I was duly summoned!

I'd asked for four new appointments in the Station, and I was curious to see what I'd be given. Someone was needed for the research, scientific work, two more for the land and one who knew about machinery. I was given a translator and an artist. I'd asked for an artist a long time ago, when we opened, and I'd forgotten since then. And the translator. I'd also thought that one was needed when I believed that the institution was going to concentrate on research rather than production. Now I'd been given one. And the name was stated—it was Mrs M. She knew three languages, French, English and Russian. And she could draw. Because, of course, it wouldn't be possible to take photographs, especially of the new hybrids. The camera wouldn't know what was important, what had to be given prominence. That the artist would know. Or I'd tell her, Mrs M or not. I couldn't object. I really hadn't asked for her. Let's say I didn't mind.

Every day there came a new declaration in the paper. Militant solidarity with Hungary. University lecturers, writers, the entire progressive intelligentsia. In all factories the workers held spontaneous meetings and made declarations. Foremost of these was the János Herbák footwear factory, because there were a lot of Hungarians there; the paper carried that on the front page. In Kolozsvár Pista Tompa chaired the meeting. I knew him well, he was secretary of the regional Party committee. A kind man, and very convincing, able to answer any question. Not as forceful as . . . Never mind. Mogyorós. Moghioros. He was fearsome. Tompa was the kind of man that the situation called for. A man of refinement, not the sort that attacked people violently and handed out great dressings down. A man of sincere belief, unwavering. Who knew how to persuade. Furthermore, a few old Communists were now being readmitted to the Party. A clever move, because then as Party members, they'd keep quiet. The attitude of the intelligentsia and the working peasants to the events had to be consolidated. That was now the main requirement. Consolidation. Now we were only holding meetings once a week, making a resumé, saying what declarations the intelligentsia and the working peasants had made, and then getting on with our work. *Igazság* kept carrying dreadful pictures of lynching in the streets.

Now we could only learn about events by listening to Free Europe. Lali said that he could get it again. I could only get it in the morning, never in the evening. And, of course, the story from Budapest was different. I didn't know. It wasn't good to listen in my situation, but I couldn't break the habit. Even when things were on the boil. There was nothing to be done now about affairs in Hungary. Here one had to be careful to avoid trouble.

In December two students were sentenced. They were given seven years each. Seven years lost from their lives because of some stupid behaviour. They'd been arrested back in October. One was a Hungarian, Balázs by name, the other was called Vid, but I didn't know his nationality; they were from the Fine Art University. Fortunately, not two of ours. I didn't know what the Temesvár students were given. For next to nothing. They'd been stirring things up, reading out complaints, and the sentences had been revenge.

In view of current circumstances, I really didn't think that I'd be going to the big exhibition. Nor was anything said to me about holding a national exhibition. I didn't even dare mention Paris to Mogyoros. All the same, I'd have needed to know if I was going, so as to have something to display in September. So for the time being I'd been getting ready with my competitive material. But then the Trieste people sent a complimentary invitation for me to go on the jury. Me, to be a judge! Well, I ought to have taken part in at least one international competition before going as a judge. Or I'd misunderstood the letter, because, of course, it had had to be translated as I didn't know Italian.

Then in spring came the trial of the students who had caused a public disturbance in the cemetery. Lali brought the news, and was very upset. There was no hiding the fact that since his release from prison Lali had been a frustrated man. He said that our entire intellectual life was Stalinist in a bad sense. Three youngsters were now sentenced for the events in spring in the cemetery. They were all very talented, said Lali. So there, what good's your talent in prison?! All the same, it was as well that the agriculture students hadn't done anything foolish, or they might have been up before the court.

But we were having to think of nothing but Paris. This was to be the year of the great assessment, and perhaps after the events in Hungary that wouldn't happen either. I was doing my job and getting ready.

Yes, yes, they said, I was going to Paris. Hell's bells! There'd been a revolution in Hungary, we'd been well and truly scared, and *o altă ordine de zi* had started—a different order of the day. I didn't even know what to call it. A new agenda? But now even the Soviet forces were leaving us. In Lali's opinion a great easing up is now on the way, the end of Stalinism in Romania. Mogyorós rang me about what was happening.

'What's happening?' I asked, and I became so uptight that I had a spasm of coughing and couldn't speak. I kept on coughing and choking, Mioara brought me a glass of water, and I said 'Comrade Minister, I'll have to call you back.'

So I called him again.

'What's happening, Vili? I haven't had your plans yet.'

'What plans do you mean, Comrade Mogyorós?' I asked, because I always sent everything off on the dot.

'Well, you're off exhibiting, you've got to say where to.'

Jesus, Paris. It was decided, done and dusted, I was being sent. I picked up the phone to make preparations. No precedent, because since then there hadn't been anything said, and now bang! Put in the plan at once, do all the planning, the travel orders, everything.

At the most I'd only got Sunday to get ready and think about Paris. Then there was no Station, no university, nothing to bother me, and at last a bit of peace and quiet. Then I'd sit and think how it would be and what to take. But even then I wouldn't be left alone! I didn't get a nice quiet Sunday. Either a meeting would be laid on, or I'd have to watch some cultural programme, confound it.

Or I'd be invited to a christening. So had that brother of mine Sándor had a child? It was the fifth or sixth. And they were always so hard up, my mother funded them and I gave money to my mother. So I was funding them. 'It's a christening, you can't not go,' said mother. Nor, of course, not take a nice fat envelope.

I asked, 'Why had he never been over? When I gave a public lecture at the university? Hadn't I invited him when the Station was opened? I'd held an exhibition and invited him, sent an invitation. No sign. A book of mine had been launched. Had he read it so much as once? Or a an account of me in the paper? Had he ever come to one of my public events?

'They have no time for anything, with all those children,' said mother. So they haven't got the time to write a word of congratulation and put it in the post? Even no congratulation hardly mattered, I didn't get that much. But I'd been present for every child, christening, funeral, everything. I was always giving money. That was all very well. Money was all right. I'd sent him books, dedicated. It didn't worry me if a university man didn't read it, or if somebody wrote a review on it. That didn't interest me. But coming from my brother, it hurt.

Having a brother like that hurt me, but there was nothing I could do. I didn't open the Station for his benefit, lay on an exhibition for him, write books, take university classes. I shouldn't expect anything. We were like strangers.

And what did they say to that? That it was easy for me, the family hadn't interfered with my work, my successes. I was very fortunate, that was true. They hadn't disturbed me. But it had failed to acknowledge me in everyday life. Even my mother said, 'Marriage isn't your cup of tea, Vilmos. You've become a man of learning. You've got no place for lots of kids and a wife.'

When I had to have the house painted because rain had come through I called my brother and told him to come and paint. How much would a house like this cost? And you have to pack things up. And don't touch my study, that must be left alone. So I spent a week packing things up. Then sometimes he came, sometimes he didn't, because the collective sent him somewhere else and he had no time for me. I waited and waited for him, and everything was like that. Then he came, worked for one day but didn't for two.

'Look here,' I said, 'are you working somewhere else as well?'

Well, things weren't as they used to be, when he could go off and work in somebody's house, he was in a collective now, that was where his money came from and they told him where to go.

He spent a month painting my three rooms. I paid him generously. He took the money without a word, didn't even say thank you. But neither did I, that's for sure. Mother said 'You're good brothers, you help one another.'

The Minister would thank me sooner than my brother.

I had to prepare for the exhibition and write this book about Michurinian biology. I preferred dealing with that rather than with my brother.

I believe in acclimatization. Actually, I'm only saying that I believe in it. You have to believe in a thing that isn't there. In church, that's where belief is called for. But I can see, experience and demonstrate the power of nature, and acclimatization and the inheritance of acquired properties. Until just now I'd dedicated my entire work to that—apart from searching for beauty and new varieties of roses. I'm capable of doing that, it's a natural thing. Acclimatization. Because we, the human species, can live in a hot zone, in eternal snows, live well and frugally, in palaces and thatched cottages. I too can become accustomed to everything. Such is nature. That is likewise the basis of Michurinian biology. We too can become accustomed to our new homeland and love it.

After the Plant Research Station opened, in 1953, we started conducting experiments and still did. We'd taken our seedlings out into cold surroundings and trained them to be resistant. And so all the colder regions of Romania would blossom, places where the poorer classes had been unable to afford vitamin-rich fruit. In this we would change the quality of life. One means of doing this, therefore, was acclimatization, by which I gradually accustomed small but very adaptable and resistant fruit trees to colder surroundings.

The other means was to find local varieties and improve them. It was the collecting tours that gave the Station its *raison d'être*. We went round the regions looking for varieties. But what did one find? One could see at a distance desiccated crowns, signs of disease or premature ageing. We went into every yard, every garden, and examined trees. Sometimes the owner, or more often his wife, regarded us with suspicion. We showed them the official order. People were so afraid of being used, of collectives. If we liked their tree, we said that we would, at the most, only take cuttings for grafting purposes. All of them praised their fruit trees as if they were their daughters. They produced this and that, were so flavoursome, so perfumed. But I'd never seen as many bad fruit trees as I did in the villages. Because how did the peasant think? He planted the tree and it grew for him. When the fruit was ripe he picked it, and when the tree produced nothing more he burnt it. But how did he care for it? Older students gave courses of instruction in all the villages on pruning, spraying and grafting.

Until the state had an all-embracing plan, it had been possible to bring in all sorts of foreign fruit trees. Here they all failed and caught diseases to which they had no resistance. Scale insects, to which they were least resistant of all, raised three generations on them every year. We brought home cuttings, nicely noted, and grafted them onto strong resistant stocks. We couldn't, of course, display quick results from what was collected, though that was expected of us. Quick results. Ana Pauker was actually dismissed because her progress in collectivization had been too slow. And not because she was Jewish. Reshaping nature isn't a quick business, but I daren't say so.

And I had to bring results back from Paris.

That had been written in an article in an article that appeared not long before in *Falvak népe*. It was by András Sütő, sometime editor-in-chief; he'd only just been promoted and was no longer running the paper, and he wrote about me: 'A forward-looking man'. I was always going forward, looking to the future, studying how things could be improved, how we could help and serve the people. He had a good understanding of our Michurin work and acclimatization altogether. Nobody had ever written so kindly about me. I confess to buying four copies when I found out. One we kept in the album at the Station, one I sent to Mother, one to my brother, and one was for me, as I had my own album, there's no shame in that. And I've often read it.

In Romania there's always discord. And Romanians are kept in a state of alarm. I don't understand why this must always be so. I knew Raluca, the rector of the Babeş, very well, through the Academy too. I didn't find her a beautiful woman, but she wasn't elected to the Academy for being beautiful but for being a chemist. Raluca Ripan was a Moldavian, and spoke such a Moldavian patois that I couldn't always understand her. She held a confidential leaders' meeting in the Babeş not long after the events, at the end of November. She said that if the revolution spread to Romania the Hungarians would demand the return of Transylvania. 'The Hungarians want to steal Transylvania, and our Hungarians will stand firm with Budapest,' said she. That sort of talk was bad. How could Transylvania be stolen, I ask you? From whom? It's not the branch of a tree, to be picked up and carried off. I didn't speak up, because a Hungarian was the last that should speak during such a speech, and there were rather few of us left in Babeş, just a couple from the abolished departments. Whatever a Hungarian said, it couldn't have been said without causing trouble. So I kept quiet. You have to look forward, not back.

That sort of talk was not good, so there. Firstly, I didn't know any Hungarians in the leadership here who supported it. In the way in which it was expressed. I don't mean that I knew what everybody thought, I'm not an X-ray doctor. I know nothing about organization or the like. But all the same, I've worked among people, that was a fact, Romanians and Hungarians mixed up, and I would hear things. Secondly, such a thing was just scaremongering. That which was in Hungary was in Hungary. Or had been, rather. In my view we all had to keep quiet now, we didn't want trouble. Let's get on with our job, say no more.

And that was our job.

May was nice, even lovely, if only September and Paris weren't approaching. I went around the countryside a lot, villages, farms, hillsides, strips of forest. If an area was pointed out to me I soon had a plan, but I'd just got to look at it. We would secure exposed areas and cleaned edges of forests with fruit trees, and once we'd improved the saline soil with manure we would plant the undulating hills with apples and pears. And rows of walnuts along river banks. Every household was to be given a couple of dozen fruit trees suitable for the region. Only quality plums, not cherry plums that were only good for making pálinka. Nice crunchy morello species. No foreign apples but improved native varieties, such as *pónyik, batul, cigányalma, bóralma* and the rest. Their shade would provide cool in summer. And they would provide kindling when they were pruned. So really, wouldn't this be Fairyland? A fairy garden? What writer said that? Somebody had. I asked Lali and he really laughed. But he was always so sour in those days.

'You mean you don't know, Vili?'

Well, I'd had to go and ask. Why hadn't I kept quiet, and now I'd disgraced myself. It was the great Hungarian writer Zsigmond Móricz. Hadn't I read it? When did I have time for reading, for goodness sake? He wasn't even a local writer, he was a Hungarian. There you are, he too could see that it was a Fairy Garden. We're the only ones that couldn't.

But since so much had been written about me I didn't feel like going anywhere. I'd recently been to a silver wedding celebration. When they'd had a few drinks a university colleague said to me 'Well, Party-Vili, have you been allowed to come? You've descended to the level of ordinary people, to talking to people?'

Party-Vili. That summed me up. That's what I was called when my back was turned. I'd heard it before. Nobody dared say it to my face, only when they were drunk. They were jealous. Then they began to call me names. The drink was talking, I paid no attention. Why had I left the fire brigade? Had the bread and dripping been better? How could I teach in the university? Could I get them jobs that paid better? I was a big man, well in with Dej. Hand in glove with him. And with Mogyorós. Not one of them knew what I was doing, what my research and development were about.

Party-Vili. That was what was going around then. And Party-Marci, because Márton Káli Nagy, my colleague at the university, was also called that. And Mózes Kun was Party-Mozsi.

And apparently, he said, I wasn't the same sort of dirty dog. By that he meant that I didn't drink pálinka from so big a glass. Anybody that didn't drink like them was a dirty dog.

I didn't want to be drawn into conversation, just as I hadn't wanted to before.

Then, when I had to be preparing for Paris and I was stressed enough to die, I was sent to the country to be a judge in a cultural competition! I wasn't judging roses, but dancing. And then to organize the dance-ensemble competition in the Kolozs region. When I told Lali that I was going to the country he said that the country was dreadful, worse than the town. I asked why.

'Corruption, robbery, and intolerable nationalism,' he replied. 'These three things are rife in the country. It doesn't matter whether you're a Hungarian, a Romanian, or a bit of both. And there's hatred.'

Lali was always making grand statements like that. Definitive statements.

'Even so,' I said, 'I've got to go, and to all sorts of villages, call the dance ensembles into the village houses of culture, and see which is the best. Wouldn't it be better,' I asked, 'for them to say which were the best and for those to be sent in for the competition?' Couldn't be done, because then they'd quarrel. An outsider must go. I hadn't got enough to do. I had to prepare for Paris, and now I'd got to go out to even more villages—always on Sundays, of course, because that was when dancing took place in the cultural centres. I went out to Frata, where I'd never been. Magyarfrata, they call it, only there wasn't a single Hungarian there. I asked whether people in that village were keen on dancing. Of course! And which was their best dance ensemble? Well, the Moldovans, so I had to go there. They knew the street dance, the invitation dance. I was thinking that they would be in the cultural centre if they were the best. They didn't go there because they were too old.

So how old was the Bágye Moldován? About forty-five. Maybe fifty. So, I thought, you call that old? To hell with it.

So in I went to the cultural centre and looked at them, they were clever, nice-looking Romanians, all wearing tricolours round the waist, all young. I asked which were the Bágye Moldovans. Well, they weren't inside. Bring them in, because here was the committee from the region, four of us, three men and a woman comrade from the council to pick the dancers.

In came two couples. The one was a man, so to speak, like myself, how can I put it, neither old nor very young. They came in two couples. Not specially dressed, just a sort of smart folk costume, with colourful embroidery. They had two fat women, so fat that the men couldn't put their arms round them. One of the men had a good paunch, the waistband of his *gatya* was folded outwards. Well, not all that attractive in my view. They'd brought their own musician, just a clarinettist. Well, it was unusual these days to have a clarinet, and I liked that. All the same, the clarinet sounded a bit shrill to my ear, but the *joc*—as the Romanians call the dance—was lively. They danced in Romanian style, a slow number, but with such great spirit. I said I definitely liked it. Only, of course, they weren't particularly young people. I asked what the dance was called. *Preumblat.* A street *preumblat.* What did that mean? It turned out that the dance began with this, outside in the yard, even in the afternoon, and they only came indoors after it. I asked where their costumes were. The women had kerchiefs, but they wore aprons as if they were cleaning carrots. One of the men had no hat. Where was the folk costume? They no longer had any, it had been abandoned long ago. Then we still had to go to Urka, a Hungarian village, so there was no time for debate. Nobody danced the *joc* any more, it had been given up in 1950 or '51, when people had begun to go into the factories and dancing in the cultural centres had begun. There was no longer a clarinettist to accompany the *joc* but one only played at weddings for payment.

By the end of May there had to be twenty ensembles. That was what was required, twenty. So I said, if twenty were wanted, twenty there should be. If we could but find that many in the region. I asked how they were to be divided. Half and half, Romanian and Hungarian. I had to take account of the census which had taken place not long before. It had turned out that Kolozsvár was half Romanian, half Hungarian. Half and half? Incredible. It was a Hungarian town. And still the Romanians were more numerous by five hundred. Lali had heard that when Gheorghiu-Dej learnt that the proportions were so good he called for champagne.

'In the entire region?' I asked. In that case the Romanians had to be the more numerous, because there were more Romanian villages in the region—that was how the regions had been created and delineated, so as to regulate the proportions. Therefore Kolozs region had a Romanian majority. So we were not to rely on memory of what we thought the proportions were, but had to apply statistics. There was no way out, that was how it had been laid down. And since the regions had come into being the proportions too were different. This gave the Romanians an advantage, but anyway, what could we say.

Annush pestered me for a Hóstát ensemble to be picked to compete. So I said that they might only be picked from villages and local areas. Well, the Hóstát sequence was a special dance, she said, I should go and watch it. So where was I to do that, my dear?

'Come when the Anna-ball is happening or the vintage ball in September.'

She told me how the ball programme went. I should watch it, because they always danced out the whole sequence at the ball. They began with the slow *csárdás*, followed by the quick *csárdás* and the *keringő*.

'I don't think the *keringő* can be displayed. This has to be folk dancing, my girl, not ballroom.'

'It's not a ballroom dance, Vili, not at all. It's what we dance.'

Annush didn't get the point at all. Never mind, it wasn't for her great brain that I loved that girl. If only she hadn't been so young. Or damn it, that was what was so nice about her, that she was such a little girl. So I said, local area, that's the basis for selection. Well, wasn't the Hóstát one? That was a local area. So it was, she told me. See—Magyar utca, right down Téglás utca, the whole Cukorgyár district, the Pillangó estate, the Tököze, the Hídelve, though that was almost demolished then, all the Bulgária estate, the Kőmál, Bornyúmál, Kölesföld, Eperjestere, Szopor. Wasn't that a local area, she asked. Only I shouldn't include the Lupsa, because there were all sorts of wicked Hóstát people there.

'This is a town, my dear. This is all Kolozsvár,' I replied. It was all part of the town, they were the only people to recognize those suburbs. Referred to them all by their own names. They lived in another world. In the town, but another world.

Ballroom dancing wasn't admissible, I said. The waltz was a ballroom dance, it had no place in a culture competition, get that straight.

'Why won't you help, Vili?'

She really would have liked to dance.

'My dear, I would help. The only thing is that the Hóstát people live in a town and want to do the walz. Neither is acceptable, do you see. My dear, Hóstát people aren't recognized like people from Mezőség, Szék, Kalotaszeg, Urka, Frata and Magyarlónya. And you can't dance the waltz in a culture competition.'

'You mean, Hóstát people don't count?' asked the little angel.

'Not at all, my dear, Hóstát produce sells in the market, it's highly regarded, you can get half as much again for tomatoes and onions compared with people from Szilágy county and other places. You think well of yourselves. And people pay you for them, because those who've lived here a long time know what Hóstát produce is and they'll pay for it. But that's not what's wanted in a culture competition, take my word for it. You're not a country girl,' I said. 'We're not accepting dance ensembles from towns. The villages have to display their treasures, do you understand? We've got to bring the peasants out these days.'

'Why do you only want that old woman from Szék all the time, Vili?'

Ouch! A young girl knows how to hit where it hurts. She went for me over Kali. Then she snivelled and snuggled up to me, and that was really nice.

'And then why take an ensemble from Torda? That's a town, isn't it? And aren't I a peasant myself?' and she wailed as bitterly as if her mother was being buried. And that's right, she was an orphan.

'There's a great folk-dancing tradition in Torda, you see, such a big ensemble, about fifty people. We just had to pick them.'

The other nuisance, gnawing at me on the other side, was Kali. Whom was I going to take from the Szék ensemble? Surely not that András Demeter's wife, she'd got a wooden leg. Nor Rózsi Sípos, she was a loose woman. Nor Zsuzsi Szováti, she was light-fingered. She'd go stealing everything when she came into town for the competition. Even the newspaper from the bog. János Csorba I should take. He'd once twirled her around so much that her innards nearly fell out. The way he could do the *sűrű*, it made every girl wet her knickers. What makes you wet, tell me? Because I don't know things like that. Perhaps it was when she found a mushroom, 'cos then everybody was just so pleased. That János Csorba used to organize the dancing so that it went on until morning.

'Take some little ones, mister, look at the little ones dancing.'

'We can't put children in the culture competition. It's not allowed.'

'But it's unusual for children to be dancing. And the way that János Csorba dances the *magyar*. I once took a turn with 'im. Or was it twice? A *magyar* lasts an hour, even an hour and a 'alf. That's the sort of thing that you should take to the competition, mister, 'cos such a thing 'as never been seen!'

Well, how was I to take a dance lasting an hour and a half? Who was going to sit and watch that? How many ensembles could I put on in that time? And if a Hungarian ensemble was on for an hour, then a Romanian team would have to have that long as well.

I asked Kali, 'Why is it called a *magyar*? Isn't it just a Szék dance?'

'It's called the long *csárdás* down our way.'

'But it's not just a Hungarian dance?'

'I've no idea, go and ask the teachers what are always comin' and watchin' the dancin' an' writin' about it. We don't know. We just use such words as *csárdás, szökős, lassú, hétlépés*. And the *verbunk*, but that's only for men. Go and watch that Márton Juhos, 'e's gettin' on, 'e's got a paunch like a Turkish pasha, but he picks 'is feet up like a young girl. You know, mister, like the stick in the folk tale what's a magic stick, that's what 'is feet are like. Like Moses's staff before Pharaoh, that's what. 'E can do wonders. 'Cos 'is feet does what 'e tells 'em to. Yes, ev'ry woman gets turned on with that Márton Juhos. 'Cos 'e won't let any of 'em alone. The way 'e can dance, 'e drives 'em all mad. 'Es not much to look at, 'e's fat, but 'e drives the women mad.'

But in those days we didn't dance together much.

Nor had I been to Paris.

In January I was sent off to Bucharest again. I was hoping to have to discuss Paris, and finally to be going that year. Because a month previously such a silence had fallen, it was as if the world had died. Everything was just as before. The same hotel, the same comrades. Quite, but even so, the atmosphere was somehow different. Goodness knows what it meant. There was a sort of chill in the air. In the old days, before the events in Hungary, there had been such a relaxed feeling, almost like being in a completely foreign country. The way Hungarians had been spoken then, I felt that the brotherhood that the USSR and its peoples dreamt of had been achieved. A great dinner had been held in August two years previously, when the pact with Hungary had been signed. The Hungarian guests and all the diplomatic corps had been at separate big tables. Everybody who was alive and kicking had been present at that dinner. I didn't hear it, but I heard that Dej had made a speech in Hungarian! The Hungarians had made speeches in Hungarian, and there were tables where Hungarians and Romanians were mixed. It had been an event of world significance. Even those who had been in prison together were aware of it. Especially when the mood began to lift. As the vodka had flowed, so did the pálinka. There hadn't been enough pálinka glasses. Either there'd been a miscount or it hadn't been thought about, but suddenly there was only a demijohn on each table. There were about fifteen at each table. There were a lot of people from the MAT. I was sitting there with Pista Tompa, the economist, and there were writers present; there were so many in those days. So, there were no pálinka glasses, but there were wine glasses. Spirits rose greatly, and all we needed was a good Gypsy band, but there wasn't one, it hadn't been considered. Such a thing is the making of a good dinner! There are summer gardens in Bucharest where the way the Gypsies play is enough to drive one mad. But not only were there no Gypsies, there were no women either, so that dancing wasn't possible. There were a few Party women, but I didn't get up to dance with Pauker. She wasn't even there, of course. She'd been sacked long before. That was the first time that fine Murfatlar wine had been produced. It had a delicate *aszú* taste, was harvested late, being left to ripen on the sandy soil. I talked to the writers a lot of the time. They were all called István. They had been invited as decoration—artists and writers were liked in the Party. Actors too were invited. Another Tompa, the financial expert, was there as well in the Autonomous Territory. The writers were known as 'Istváns's literature'. There were Asztalos, Horváth, Nagy, and a second Tompa, not the economist. Tompa's 'portfolios' were appearing in the papers by that time.

I knew Asztalos, he'd been up to the Station when a film was being made from one of his books. He'd needed an orchard in it. He was portraying a kulak. It was no good my telling him that the fruit in the Station was no good, a blind man could have seen that a kulak couldn't have had fruit like that because we'd improved it, it was the big and special Décsi favourite, my hybrid. I told him not to film that, it wasn't correct from the historical point of view. If he wanted his film to be historically accurate, he ought not to take the Décsi favourite, as everybody knew that hybrid varieties hadn't existed in the 1930s, when the film was set. But he insisted that I shouldn't make a fuss, that was what he wanted to film. They filmed everything there, about the kulak making love to a pretty girl He had such a big paunch, I didn't know whether it was the actor's own or whether it was padding. But they kept on rolling about. I watched from a distance, because I'd never seen a film being made. Two lovers don't really roll about like that, but it's not for a gardener to point things out to an actor that doesn't deign to know. They trampled flat everything around, cut down a couple of trees, had to bring in an electricity supply, and churned up all the C-4s. Then the comrade writer invited me to go to the premiere—*Szél fuvatlan nem indul* was the title of the film. What did I care? I went. When I saw the kulak rolling about in my orchard, I burst out laughing. So such faking of history was eternalized! The *Décsi favourite* hadn't yet been registered as a new variety, because we were only in the tenth year with it at the time; I'd started work on it before the Station even existed, and in the film you could even see the little sign marked X, indicating that it was ten years old. These writers treat history as if it were a face flannel, twisting it this way and that, using it however they please.

There were writers, actors and painters, and of course all the bigwigs, but this had been before the events in Hungary in October. The Autonomous Territory had brought an actress for people to lick their lips on seeing her. Her shoulders were bare, round and soft as a cushion. Her complexion was flawless and her curls looked as if they were painted. I couldn't talk to a woman like that. To me she was like a painting. I looked and looked at her, really enjoyed looking, but to talk to her would have been beyond me. I'm at a loss for words when I see a woman like that. I thought that she'd been brought just to give people something to look at. But the very idea of dancing with her! Her dress wasn't suitable for dancing. It was completely tailored to her body, it was tight-fitting. And long. She couldn't have danced a *csárdás* in it.

We'd had such hopes that evening! Long before the events in Hungary there had been high hopes. I too had achieved great success, taking along several boxes of apples and pears; there was a selection on every table. I'd had some special fruit knives made, on which was engraved *Statiunea de cercetare Horticola Cluj* and on the other side in Hungarian *Növénykutató*

Állomás Kolozsvár—Plant Research Station Cluj-Napoca. It required nerve, I thought, to put Hungarian and Romanian. I'd asked whether it was in order, and no one had said no. I took that as a yes. Little penknives, with neatly engraved blades. And nice boards to go with them so that people could cut and taste. The *pónyik* apples went over well with the writers, and the common *sóváris* were a success, as were my favourites, the *batuls*. Neither the colour nor the shape of the *sóváris* were attractive, only the bitter-sweet taste and the white flesh. The *Décsi favourite* was warmly praised. There was one writer, a János somebody, who asked a lot of questions about apples and made notes. There was a great atmosphere. People felt as if this was their homeland, as in the olden days. We were at ease, local Hungarians and Romanians alike. We could trust each other.

Now, however, everything was so frosty, it was just as if we were to blame. For the events in Hungary. Or as if we were demanding revision of the frontier. Leave the bloody frontier alone!

In January came the document. I was going to Paris in September 1958. That was all it said. Then I got a phone call. From Mogyorós himself in the Ministry. I was to start getting ready, as a Hungarian delegation was coming. When he didn't say, but it was a high-ranking delegation. We had to prepare in advance plans for the collaboration of the two countries. Please, said Sándor (or rather Comrade Minister Mogyorós), I was to tell him what I wanted. Present a plan. He spoke briefly, hurriedly. I said to him, 'Excuse me, I would need official guidance, a detailed directive in order to be able to plan properly.'

I didn't tell him that he ought to open a drawer in the Ministry, because ever since the Station had existed, for five or six years, that is, even in the year of its establishment, I had made such a plan and sent in a written report to the effect that professional contacts at international level should be developed with the people's democratic countries. I'd also written a report or two on ways by which foreign currency could be acquired. This was all there in writing. So I would produce it, then they need not go to the trouble of opening a drawer. Because now we only required the heading Hungarian People's Republic. So I asked for the planning directive.

'You can do that, Vili, even without a directive.'

'If you wouldn't mind, just say by when,' I said, and would he write something for me to integrate with.

He didn't write, and I didn't like such a verbal arrangement. Not at all. Then he would back out, saying that Décsi was always agitating, self-motivated, sending in on his own initiative schemes for Hungarian-Romanian professional connections between experimental stations. Whereas nothing had been asked for in writing. Then Décsi would be in hot water.

'In a week', he replied.

'A week?' I asked. 'And when's this delegation coming?'

That he couldn't know. That's how planning goes here.

What could I do? Hurry everything up. I got out what I'd already written and dictated it carefully for Ancuta to type, then it could go off. Thirteen pages. Not a good number, said Ancuta. So let's add a title page—*Raport cu privire la*, etc.

By that time I was tired of what I'd said. There was so much of it. Ages ago there'd still been enthusiasm in it but now there was none. There hadn't been a single response. Things like exchange of varieties, letting the Hungarians use a testing garden in colder regions, in the hills, sharing of advice, exchange of workers when roses were opening in September in Szeged and Kolozsvár, perhaps in Budapest as well, because the institute had been set up in Budatétény and development was being carried out there too, swapping of specialist literature—all were common goals.

I wrote without any enthusiasm, but all the same we ought liaise with the Hungarians.

At that time further land had been allotted, another couple of hectares or so that had been annexed for us. I thought I'd ring Mogyorós up, as in fact I'd have to ask him for more workers because the extra land had not been provided for.

He became very agitated when I spoke to him. And I hadn't even asked what was happening about the Hungarians. Were they coming, or weren't they? Well, the way he was shouting I couldn't ask. To hell with you, Sándor.

He said I was to wait for the delegation. The very highest. I was so on edge!

My great rose-friend Lali took me to see a great actress, because he'd worked as secretary of the Hungarian Theatre before going to prison. Now informers were always after him, and they were trying to pin on him that when the events in Hungary were taking place he'd stirred the students up. The greater trouble was, however, that he hadn't signed the condemnation of the counterrevolution. He was becoming politically active again, saying how many terribly dogmatic and Stalinist people there were everywhere in leading positions, the old guard were still in power even in the periodical *Korunk*, and he definitely couldn't put his name on the front page.

But roses, not politics, were our shared interest, and he'd chosen what we should take to the actress, because we would take the last of the roses from the greenhouse, after which there'd only be carnations left. I'd seen this actress on stage a few times, but, as I've told Lali, I'm not all that interested in the theatre. The play was *Bernarda Alba*, which he'd taken me to see before, and it had been interesting, there were a lot of lovely women in it, but too serious. It was all so tragic. Lili Poór was shocking. She wasn't even a woman, let alone a man. She was made of stone! She was sixty at least, but still clearly a woman. She had such dignity, the way she sat down, the way she held her cigarette holder. And her voice! We took her a bouquet. Lali kept insisting, though he knows how much I dislike taking flowers. He said that I should take a tidy bunch. 'Why?' I asked, 'Do I usually take untidy ones?' 'No, but make it a big one! Fifty stems.'

'Lali, my dear chap, you know that here in the greenhouse we struggle with winter roses, because we have to maintain a minimum twenty-five degrees for them to open. If I can let you have three in winter it'll be a miracle.'

We managed to get together fifteen of the 23 August. I didn't tell him, nor have I told the bosses in the Centre, but really, we haven't had much success with winter roses. People don't want roses in winter, damn it. We can't imitate sunshine.

Well, we weren't taking these to just any woman, but to one of the greatest theatrical talents in Transylvania.

She was such a great woman, a mighty actress, and it appeared that until just then she'd been marginalized. Not only she, but the whole theatre! The tendency in those days was to put down theatre in Kolozsvár. All that would be left was the Székely Theatre in Marosvásárhely. All there was left in the MAT. Because, of course, that was highly delighted. It was ten years old, said Lili. But the Hungarian Theatre in Kolozsvár was a hundred and sixty. She asked me whether I knew, as a man who was somebody in those days, how the hundred-and-sixty-fifth anniversary of the Kolozsvár theatre had been celebrated? I said not a word, I didn't know.

Lali interrupted: 'Look here, Lili darling, let's not start criticizing again.'

'Bubi darling, don't butt in.' (Everybody called Lali Bubi.) 'I wasn't asking you, I was asking Vilmos, a born-and-bred Kolozsvár man. My dear young man, tell me straight: what did a hundred and sixty-five years of Hungarian theatre in Transylvania mean to you?'

Well, what was I to say! I sat there like a like a schoolboy that hadn't done his prep. I had no idea. So, a hundred and sixty-five years was quite something. I didn't know what to say, so I made the mistake of asking 'How old is the theatre in Budapest?'

She replied, 'We predate Budapest in this regard, darling.' As she said that she laid her hand with all its many rings on my knee. There was a little bottle of liqueur on the table; we drank coffee from tiny porcelain cups, and there were little plates of *dulceață* and biscuits. Rose *dulceață*, as she'd wanted to give us a treat, she'd been sent them from Bucharest. And her cigar had such a fragrant scent.

'Bubi darling, you know very well, I don't really want to make a fuss about that and my husband.' Lali had in fact told me that her husband had been a director in the first Romanian period and even before that, then had been marginalized and had only returned after the liberation, because he was Jewish, had been hidden in Budapest; his name had been Jenő Janovics, and he was no longer alive. 'But that there shouldn't be a collection of verse, a clinking of glasses, is pure ignominy,' said she. 'I felt I deserved never to set foot on the stage again. It's been the cradle of the national culture in Transylvania, and now, if you please, we're rehearsing another piece of French buffoonery. I'm supposed to play comedy and make people laugh. I, Lili Poór, the spirit of Janovics, who was brought up in a culture both universal and national.'

She was a marvellous woman. A real somebody. What women there are. There's such a great spirit in an actress. One wouldn't think so, to look at them, some believe that every actress is just a sort of ornament. A Persian cat. But Lili Poór was a great human being, she had dignity.

Lali said that Kolozsvár now had to be destroyed. It didn't exist, only the MAT and Tompa. It was said that Tompa had taken over the direction of all the theatres in Bucharest.

'Which Tompa?' I asked. I knew of two Tompas, one of whom wrote theatre criticism in *Igazság*, and the other was a bigwig in the Ministry of Finance, and I knew that they were related. I believed that he was on the Néptanács. I was surprised at either of them directing theatre. But it turned out that there was a third Tompa, a producer, and that was who was meant.

Lali then asked, 'So, now there's only the MAT, and we're not in it. Do you speak Russian, Vili?'

'I don't,' I replied.

'What about you, Lili?' She didn't and didn't even wish to. Hadn't wished to, rather, but now that she's seen Moscow companies playing as visitors she'd been most impressed. She'd realized the meaning of psychological realism.

Lali said, 'How could the Soviets have allowed us to call our autonomous region that? Because it's based on a purely Soviet pattern. What the papers call MAT, isn't it?'

'Like in chess?' I asked, 'Mate?'

'Well, it's certainly true that they've got us mated, but that's not what I meant,' said Lali. 'But in Russian *mat* means "bad language". Cursing. Swearing.'

Then talk turned to discussion of a new show that Lali had been to see. The way he criticized it! Stupid Party-line Soviet tripe, a pack of lies from start to finish! It was disgraceful what went on there, in that hundred-and-sixty-five-year-old theatre that Jenő Janovics had directed.

I went home, and that little liqueur had gone to my head.

That winter was nice and quiet. There's never been one so quiet. At Christmas I spent a lot of time with the child. The holiday is better with a child around. But I wrote not a thing for my new book. I'm writing the history of rose growing. If I live that long. I slept my winter sleep. Kali and the child came over a lot. I couldn't work, so I became irritated and sent them home. And Annush couldn't come while Kali was there. I'm being split in two, and it's nonsense. I'm so on edge that I have to take something for it. These women, they're all dreadful. Mrs M. torments me nonstop, because, of course, she's working as a translator in the Station. Kali torments me as well. At least Annush doesn't torment me. For not showing my feelings. According to Mrs M. I haven't got any! I can only show my feelings to a rose or a peach. According to Kali I'm heartless. According to Mrs M. I'm a Party-line man . . . what on earth, a Party-liner! That's what she said! That Mrs M. She can travel as much as she likes. I'm the course-man! Last year I wasn't allowed out to the world exhibition, but I was promised, and still I'm the Party-liner! But what will this year bring for me, 1958? Shall I go to Paris, or shan't I?

It was almost the end of January when my night porter ran over. This is what we usually do. The telegram had come! There's still no phone in the house. I was to go to Bucharest in three days' time because the Hungarian delegation was arriving on 20 February. How many days I'd be there it didn't say. If I asked I'd be snapped at. My time was not my own, someone else organized me. I put young Tibor in charge, and said that I didn't know how long I'd have to be away. Who was coming, who we were having talks with, what about, what had been sent ahead, what we ought to have discussed, read, held a debate so that we could thrash things out, nothing. Not a thing. Only that something ought to be approved or something of the sort. We just weren't going to say on the spot this way or that. Without permission.

I went, took my hat and got on the train. It turned out that we were leaving the MAT on a special train! I was seated with a comrade from the MAT, an educationist called Péter Csoboth. Therefore hopes were high. Such a high-level delegation was coming from Hungary. Such a thing had never happened since the second Hungarian period. There was the writer Győző Hajdú, and an activist, and a factory hand from Vajdahunyad, an actress from the MAT, and a painter, people who had just been rehabilitated, then from academic life, a lecturer from the Bolyai and a woman chemist. Anybody that wasn't in prison was there, said Lali when I told him that damn it again, I'd had to go. There were about forty of us. Lali told me and laughed fit to bust. He'd heard from the university that some Hungarian language professor had to be on the list, and they looked for him everywhere but couldn't find him. Then it occurred to some know-all—steady on, he's in prison! So, we were nicely gathered up from the country, and we had to leave the MAT by train because the MAT is now the centre of the world. So we had to go by air to Vásárhely. I'd never flown there before, and it only took twenty minutes. I didn't mind looking at the world from above, but, of course, I didn't see anything because there was so much cloud. In the MAT we were given instructions on how to talk to people, how to introduce ourselves, and then the programme. I was to be introduced as a biologist, but I'd gladly have said rose grower. I couldn't have said *hybridisator* because nobody who wasn't in the business would understand. 'Rose grower' wasn't permitted at the time, as it could be misinterpreted as little short of kulak. Biologist, in that case. When we were introducing ourselves we were lined up, and it was even laid down whom I came after. Győző the writer, and then Pál Péter the collectivist from Kispetri, and after him the woman chemist, then the factory-hand. János Kádár asked Győző, 'What do you do, comrade?' meaning what was his profession. He replied, 'I'm a writer,' and Kádár said, 'That's something we certainly need.'

Then the poor collectivist from Kispetri (because, of course, that had been the first model farm) was so nervous when his turn came that all he could say was 'Pál Péter, collective'. The fathead even got his name wrong. Then in the evening, as the wine went round, so did the joke—the whole collective was there. All I said was 'Research biologist from Kolozsvár'.

'Good show, my boy,' Kádár replied.

János Kádár gave a big speech; I'm not sure what his title was, whether he was First Secretary or Minister of State. He spoke in a factory in Bucharest. I'd never heard him speak before. We were given flags too, Hungarian ones. I'd never seen so many Hungarian flags in Romania. So we waved them. I'll confess, I was delighted. It was great to have a Hungarian flag in my hand. Kádár expressed thanks to the Romanian People's Republic and the Party for their overt moral and material assistance in putting down the counter-revolution, and to the writers of Hungarian ethnicity who had set an example to those in Hungary when they spoke against it. Our Hungarian writers had declared sooner than those in Hungary. Loud applause! Of course, the declaration of the writers of Marosvásárhely had been published on 3 November, hadn't it? He expressed his regret that two years previously, when the turbulent events of November were taking place in Budapest, their Hungarian counterpart had been unable to welcome the delegation of the Romanian People's Republic and Party with appropriate ceremony.

Every word that the Hungarians said would now receive attention. That .was possible, was the gist of what he said. He was speaking straight to us,

Hungarians of Romania. Imparting a message of sorts. I heard the words, even noted them down, but I couldn't catch the sense. I'd read them in the paper and then understand better. But I always turned my head so as to hear with my right ear.

Kádár praised the work of the Romanian Party and how equality had been realized; it was obvious that Hungarians and Romanians were living together here in hard-working peace. That evening there was a dinner, more speeches, Romanian dancing, Hungarian dancing, fraternal dancing, in which Romanian boys and Hungarian girls danced together. There was singing, a fine cultural programme, the usual, but then I couldn't feel much enthusiasm. I sat there in silence, looking forward to a worthwhile conversation, not a cultural programme and the drinking of toasts. Everybody thanked Romania for its help once more. It was only to be expected, they said in Hungarian, then in Romanian, then vice versa and at length. Then dancing. The *hora* was danced by only the Hungarian delegation and the Romanian notables. We just sat at the tables. I don't much care for the *hora* because it isn't a partner dance that a man dances with a woman. There was hardly room for them as round in a circle went Kádár, Kállai, Dej, Sándor Mogyorós, Sălăjan, Joja, Ceauşescu, and the students' representative, Ion Iliescu. Peasant origins are now in evidence! Even that Ceauşescu is such a clever dancer. Mogyoros is clumsy. They say that Ceauşescu is heir apparent to Dej.

The following day we went on with the delegation into Moldova, for a tour, and that was their next stage. We travelled by the special train. Then we went south to Craiova. Speeches were made at the station as soon as we arrived, and Romanian women brought a huge loaf and salt, and we were given a tot of *cujka*, soft, not so strong. Pálinka makes me hiccup. Then up came a brisk young girl wearing *bocskor* and beautiful national dress. She had a scarf in her hand and she began to twirl it. There was going to be trouble! This, of course, was the *perinica*, the Romanian dance in which there is even a kiss. A band struck up a *pattogós*. Now the girl caught János Kádár, put her scarf round his neck and took him to the dance, took his hand and danced with him. A second girl and a third came out of the crowd, as did more. What lovely black-haired girls had been brought! All the members of the delegation were pulled in. Even that writer from Marosvásárhely with the wooden leg was pulled in, though he couldn't dance, only hop. By then only two girls remained without partners, and suddenly one of them grabbed me, slung her scarf round my neck and pulled me into the dance. Oh, did she spin me round, her legs were like machines. And it was cold, so they were wearing *pendely* and *katrinca*. The men kept up a whistling from the side. So what, that was all right by me. This was dancing and this was a girl. Then, when I was released, I was given a big kiss on my cheek. But Kádár was given two, and did he blush! We stayed in Craiova a while longer and had a bit to eat, then left as there was a factory visit in Bucharest on the programme for the afternoon. We were taken aside for a lecture, while the delegation went on the visit.

At dinner that evening we ate suckling lamb. All of us at the table said that we hadn't eaten anything so good for ages. Suckling lamb in February? We only have it in April, at Easter-time. Evidently Romanian custom is different. It was so tasty and tender, I'd never eaten anything like it in my life, and it was on a barbecue. Everybody was given a plate on which to be served. Only the greater big-wigs were served at table with second helpings. Well, I was sorry not to be sitting at that table. I could have eaten more. As special-train people, we were seated at two big tables, and I looked to see whether somebody would tell the waiters to give us seconds. I didn't dare. Then Toma, a Bucharest actor, who was always joking and telling such sharp political stories that I was afraid to laugh—I didn't know whether perhaps he was employed to do it, but he was very brave—so he caught hold of a waiter's coat and said '*Ia mai aduce tu . . .*'

And something more. Well, a Bucharest man could. They have no shame, least of all actors. A famous Romanian actor like him. He's been in films, in the theatre, everything. 'Bring some kore over here . . .'

The waiter recognized the actor and began '*Domnule* this, *domnule* that,' might he not have a photograph in his pocket, asked the waiter, that he would sign for him, because his sweetheart had fallen for him. '*Monser*,' said the actor, because in Bucharest the Romanians speak a soenwhat different language, rather stilted, there happened to be such a thing on him, and then we were given such a dish of roast lamb—and some mujdej—that I took two pieces.

Indeed, I shall never forget that milky lamb as long as I live.

This Toma, a bit of a character, asked where we had to go the next day. One of us replied, to the MAT, which in Romanian is *Regiunea Autonoma Maghiara* or something like that. He replied, 'That'll be nice for you. That MAT. Because that means *cîntece şi dansuri*.'

Singing and dancing? So I quietly asked Lajos Csupor what he was saying. Csupor just pulled a face, and I asked him again, and it turned out that in Bucharest, it was considered that the MAT was a kind of House of Culture where people danced and sang in Hungarian, a theatre of sorts—completely untrue.

So I roared with laughter, but Csupor was quite offended. *Cîntece şi dansuri*, that was good.

Well, the next day we went to Marosvásárhely, capital of the MAT. Another Station. The delegation went by train from Bucharest to Transylvania. What rejoicing there was in Marosvásárhely! From the station all the way to the furniture factory, the streets were lined with people. Peace and Hungarian-Romanian friendship incarnate. There, however, flags were not handed out. I had my own, but didn't bring it out. If we weren't told to, I wouldn't. I couldn't bring myself to throw away a Hungarian flag.

We went to the Simo furniture factory, and there a big speech was delivered. Géza Simó had been a big Communist. Now the Hungarian Minister of State Gyula Kállai was to speak. He began in the same way, with thanks to the writers of Marosvásárhely for supporting the achievements of the Communist Party, setting an example to their fellow writers in Hungary and condemning the counterrevolution. And the counterrevolution had meant to bring about a change of frontier, because it had been nationalist,

Horthyist, and was directed by revisionist forces. Well, everybody could relax now, there was no change in the frontier.

Then Kállai spoke decisively: the Hungarian People's Republic made no territorial demands of the Romanian People's Republic in any respect. Hungary had, he said, enough land to cultivate and the working people to cultivate it. Hungary made no demands, neither territorial nor otherwise. When he said 'nor otherwise' and the interpreter put it into Romanian loud applause broke out. I thought that this 'nor otherwise' meant that they had now visited us, and it could be seen that international politics were in order and differences nicely resolved. I looked around and could see no surprise. If they weren't surprised, neither would I be. Of course, it was natural that there were no demands.

Comrade Kállai went on to say what a great achievement the Hungarian Autonomous Territory was. Equal status of the languages everywhere was a dream come true. That was to say, the Hungarian Autonomous Territory had come into being in what had been the Székelyföld. Loud applause and cheering. The government and Party delegation was bringing a Hungarian-made radio to the factory.

Furthermore, the speech was being broadcast by radio to the entire city and could be heard everywhere. Csoboth said, because once more I was sharing a room with him, that when Kállai began to speak, Romanians in the city had left the square and gone to make a disturbance. Romanian hooligans, trouble makers.

At this point it was certain that talks with the Hungarian delegation would take place in the MAT, if they hadn't done so in Bucharest, because so far we hadn't been talking with anyone, merely clinking glasses. There was a big dinner in the evening, dancing, all sorts, but their pálinka had very little aroma. Those plums weren't from Beszterce, I thought. At the dinner János Kádár spoke again and personally thanked the writers of Marosvásárhely for their assistance. They were still there, celebrating at a separate table. Kádár spoke appreciatively of the MAT, and added that people of Hungarian ethnicity lived there too. The interpreter hesitated slightly, because at first he didn't understand that this was a pointed remark, but then he extracted himself by interpreting literally that people of Hungarian ethnicity too lived there. Of course. In the lovely Székelyfóld? Even in Marosvásárhely? In the MAT? Of course.

Just as well he didn't ask, 'Do you still?'

The Székely Folk Ensemble, because that too existed in the MAT, gave an excellent performance. Only Hungarian songs and dances. The delegation had come, been entertained, and would be gone the next day! In the morning we went to Dicsőszentmárton to visit a collective farm. There were so many people that it was almost impossible to see anything. I wasn't prepared to push and shove to get a glimpse. The delegation were invited into a peasant's house, given refreshments, and on leaving were presented with some fine peasant embroideries. Well, I wouldn't have minded having one to take home. I asked Csobor, the educationist that I was always with, to get one for me as well, as I hadn't any Székely embroidery like that. Certainly, said he, because about a hundred had been sent to that collective member's house for him to give to everybody, there'd surely be some left over and he'd bring it. He promised and then went and forgot. I don't like asking for things.

A short lunch, then they went on to Kolozsvár by the special train, we went in ours. So perhaps that was where we were holding talks? But it would be good if there were a train like that between Kolozsvár and Marosvásárhely and I didn't have to go by car all the time, because always having to wait to change trains was a miserable business.

A smaller crowd greeted the Hungarian Party delegation at Kolozsvár. There were no flags handed out. Kádár only spoke at the station, but in such a way as if he were in the main square. That's what he said, 'in the historic main square of Kolozsvár'. Well, perhaps he didn't know which was the main square in Kolozsvár. Or perhaps he thought that he *was* speaking in the main square? Or was he simply in a great hurry to get back on the train?

There wasn't all that much applause after the remarks in Hungarian, that was kept for the interpreter. Or perhaps there were no Hungarians in the audience? That I couldn't imagine. Or perhaps they were afraid to let it be seen that his words were understood. There was no festivity in Kolozsvár, just that speech and that was that. Nothing was visited, no dinner laid on. After all, there was now only the MAT. Kolozsvár was finished. We weren't connected to the Autonomous Territory, delegations like this no longer mattered here. They would pass through as if they were being pursued. Wouldn't even go to Budapest, but back to the Regát.

I'd seen enough of them. Home you go! It was nothing more to do with me. I'd applauded, I'd raised my glass, eaten the roast meat and the lamb at the dinners, watched the cultural programmes, and that was that. If I'd known that I'd have to do all that, I'd have admitted myself to hospital. Somebody else would have done it! It all had to be in February of all times, when I'd got so much work. I'd got to write my new book; in fact that was done, but all sorts of revisions had been recommended by the Direcția de Cultură și Societate, which housed the censor department. Directives, instructions, rationalizations. I was to write a complete new introduction, differently angled. What the role of the Station was in the industry of the Romanian People's Republic, the position of research and development in capitalist society, etc. etc. I must think in much broader terms, I was told by the Direcția, which gives the *imprimatur* for printed material and other such things as theatre, dance and orchestral music.

March came, and there was nothing, not a word about how our shared affairs were to be after the visit of the Hungarian government and Party mission. Whether there was to be any result or follow-up, some realization, or in fact discussions. But one thing pleased me. Péter Csoboth remembered that Székely scarf and sent it. That was just the thing, and I hung it on the wall in the office. Young Tibor, however, said that a Hungarian scarf on the wall was not a good idea. I said, 'The whole of the Hungarian government and Party mission were given them.'

'That's different,' he said. 'Take it down, Vilmos. Or put up a Romanian pin-up as well.'

'All right, but I haven't got a Romanian one.'

So he'd provide a pin-up. We've got a lot of people that have come from the country to work here, and one of them would give him one.

Until then the Hungarian scarf was taken down, the point had been made. It didn't do to be provocative. especially just then, of course. He was right.

I read all the speeches again in the papers. They printed Dej's words, Kállai's, Kádár's, everybody's. Even Antal Apró's, though by then I couldn't remember which he was. But I couldn't, in reading them, find any message in them. They were clear enough, but only one conclusion could be drawn, that there was no territorial demand and that was all. Since the solidarity shown in the counterrevolution, Romanian-Hungarian friendship was unbreakable.

Therefore it was odd that there was no mention of the delegation coming to Kolozsvár. If anything, just that they got off the train. But not a word more. So did Kolozsvár no longer exist? Did we no longer count? Kádár did well to ask, in his speech in Marosvásárhely, are you still there?

There had been a Hungarian reporter who spoke to us that were on the special train. His name was Szántó. I kept asking him what Kádár had said, what did he mean, how should it be taken? Maybe he knew better what the Hungarians meant, he would be able to express the message more clearly. Only there simply was no message.

Not a single beautiful woman had been included in the whole of the special train delegation. That is to say, Dej's daughter was there. She's a lovely woman, I'm not saying otherwise, she's been in lots of films, though according to Lali, she's not much of a talent. But who'd want to chat with Dej's daughter? There was no way I could have had a serious conversation. I didn't say a meaningful word to anybody.

I even did better to keep quiet. For a meaningful conversation, I have to take a position, reveal my thoughts. If I just talk for the sake of talking it leaves nothing behind. I've divulged my plans, and then been unable to achieve them, and then been like a blown egg.

Sometimes in winter we carried out analyses. I meant to get down to it, but once more I became so edgy because that dreadful Mrs Szőke came to mind. Last autumn she completely ruined a year's work. Actually, she stole it. My doorman was a very kindly man, one couldn't fault him in that respect. If somebody was carrying a net bag full of apples he didn't say anything, but he could see that they weren't carrying stones out of the Station, but nice apples. Or pears. I'd not said anything about net bags, especially to anybody who had children. But this time I'd caught one. Well, I didn't, but my new doorman Horváth did, when he carried out an inspection. It made me look into what was being stolen here.

He came into the office and told me that my property was being stolen. I asked what exactly was being taken. A spade? Or the selector? So he'd stopped Mrs whatshername and said that she'd been taking experimental material home. At that I was furious. Experimental material? Good God! Well, I didn't say that, just thought it. Now the siren had sounded for the end of work, and we went out to the greenhouse.

The woman was waiting there outside greenhouse number 10, with two men watching her. She'd got a nice big net shopping bag, and Horváth asked me to look at it. I said, wait, first I'll go into the greenhouse and look to see the situation. Damn and blast the woman. She'd picked the lot, hardly left a couple of fruit. All my experimental material had been picked.

I took her bag, emptied it and set out the contents on the examination table. The paprika-tomato cross, the greatest fruits of my most promising Michurin results, on which I'd been working for six years. Then the 87/1954 hybrid, which still wasn't fruiting anywhere, it was only four years old. And there was the (f) *Solanum lycopersicum* 'Alice' x (m) *Physalis alkekengi* hybrid, going home in her shopping bag! She'd picked their splendid, hybrid fruits. The vandal! The tomato-groundcherry hybrid, pure artifice! Pure artifice, because it hadn't yet had any result. Who could say what would become of it. I was trying to produce a perennial tomato with high vitamin C content. My finest Michurin experiments, study material. She didn't even know what she was taking! They weren't even named yet!

'Now then, look here, comrade!' She was quite a hulking brute, that Mrs Szőke. 'You've been working here for me for quite some time.' In fact her husband had also been a greenhouseman who'd been dismissed for being absent a lot, and when he did come to work, he'd been drunk. 'I've never said a single word before this about you taking an apple or two for the good of your health. But are you trying to stop an epidemic with these, eh? Don't you know that these aren't for eating? Perhaps you meant to steal them for some competitor, so that they'll have the advantage over us? What the hell were you going to do with them?' And I pointed to the fruit.

Well, nobody ever ate those. So she'd wanted to taste them.

'What do you mean, wanted to taste them? Was that why you picked all my fruit?'

Well, she'd read in the paper that I'd said what a high vitamin content it had. And her husband was ill, he was obviously getting weaker and perhaps it would make him better.

'Have you heard of anybody eating these?'

'Then what are we doing all this for, if they're not for eating?' She started to answer back. 'Because we've been watching over them like Christ's coffin.'

So, I thought, you're another that wants to tell me what to do.

'If we're watching over them, what do you mean by taking them home in your shopping bag, comrade? Do you realize that if I report you to the Securitate, you'll be charged with the theft of the people's property? Do you realize what will happen?'

'This must be reported,' Horváth interrupted.

I said to him, 'You go off home, Comrade Horváth. Thank you for drawing the matter to my attention. Tomorrow all the greenhouses will be checked.'

To hell with the lot of them. How good it had been when I was on my own and didn't have to look out for anyone. Now I must keep my eyes open in that case. Somebody like Mrs Szőke or that Horváth was going to make me go to the Securitate. An offence against public property. How many I read of in the paper, how many there were, and how heavily they were sentenced. It was said that there were those that weren't even to do with the economy, were just put in the paper in those terms. A lot of accountants were imprisoned, mostly from the old guard. I too had had a Jewish accountant, but he'd gone into retirement, or rather I'd had to dismiss him because I'd been given another. It was said that the prisons were full, there was no room for people. You could go to prison for every little thing, even a couple of bags of potatoes. You had to be terribly careful in those days. And how many anonymous denunciations there were. Or not anonymous, it made no difference. A whole body of denouncers. Then investigation committees had to be set up. And once you were investigated, you were caught. How often had I seen it? How often had I too been put at risk of investigation? I had to be very careful not to be the subject of an investigation. If that sort of thing happened and somebody was caught and the findings of the enquiry were made public, then we'd get a committee and be investigated.

What was certain was that the work of the whole year was ruined.

I told Mrs Szőke to go wherever she like, get out, it would be investigated the next day. So she began to cry, don't put her in prison, Her husband was enough of a prison for her, he was such a hooligan. He had no work, wherever he went he was fired, and then the police were informed. I said that the damage would be assessed and her pay would be docked. God bless you, dear Mr Director, and she started kissing my hand. Then I became even more irritated. I told her she shouldn't have stolen so much. A bag of fruit was being stolen, the doorman spotted it because there was a new man on duty, wasn't there, but who was going to get it in the neck? I was.

With people like her how I was going to achieve significant results? Here we were in the middle of the five-year plan, and now look, at the end of September everything's been picked that I was going to analyse. What was I going to write a report on?

I intended to dismiss Mrs Szőke, and then she wailed at me so much. She'd got an idiot child, she hadn't put it in an institution but she might. Her husband, of course, was work-shy, so one day he'd be suddenly taken away. She wept to me—where was she to go with such a record. I said that she wouldn't have a record, she'd merely be transferred to another section where she wouldn't be able to do such damage. I was so cross, the blood was throbbing in my head. The common people had no idea about science, all the weekly lectures on ideology, the broadening of outlook, our holding meetings, our explaining theory, achievements, goals—it was all a waste of time. Mrs Szőke went and picked all the results of Michurinism. That was what I'd begin my new book with. The stupid common people could only understand what they could eat at once. They didn't understand the first word about experiment, crossbreeding and our search for new varieties.

But then I had to go down to the cinema where the new Soviet film about Michurin was being shown. Which cinema? The Maxim Gorky? Which was that? Fortunately it said in the name Universității, so that meant Egyetem utca, the old University cinema. I was to give the introduction, which was ready written. The cinema was packed, young people, school children, entire classes. I liked talking to the young. But there was a lot of misbehaviour in the cinema, the teachers in charge of the classes were all drunk. Then the film was shown. Well, it was as if I were seeing myself. I hadn't even known that the great scientist had spent seventeen years as an accountant. That was how it was in the old world. In modern times things were different, because everybody went to school, then to university, and became whatever they liked. It certainly hadn't been like that in my time, dear Ivan Michurin. I'd borne the yoke in the old world, and when I finished work I hurried home and did experiments. All the work I'd had to do as a firefighter. There'd been nobody to explain the system to me, nobody had given me a single book on science for me to teach myself.

Otherwise, this film was marvellous educational material. and if anybody couldn't understand from it hybridization and northern adaptation I couldn't have given them a better explanation. With coloured illustrations. And mentor plants. But I was sorry that I hadn't invited Kali, it just hadn't occurred to me. So that she could understand what we were doing. Of course, she wouldn't have been able to make much of the Romanian subtitles, and the soundtrack was in Russian. It would have been greatly to my advantage if I'd studied Russian, and could read books and wouldn't always have to wait for Hungarian or Romanian translations. But, of course, I'm not much good at languages. I never even learnt Romanian properly.

According to Lali, this Michurin film was propaganda rubbish. It seemed to me he'd failed to appreciate the scientific parts.

Paris. Was there to be Paris? Mogyorós had said that I'd got a document about it. I was supposed to have read it in January, in the plan for the year that the Ministry sent out. The French invitation had also been sent from Paris. I'd been very surprised, because it had come straight to the Station, addressed to me by name. I didn't know whether it had been torn up, or what. Probably, I thought, if it had come from abroad they must have known what was in it. I didn't take it too seriously anyway, because I'd been given plenty of such invitations, but I'd never taken any of them up except the one to Trieste, and there'd been no follow-up to that. I didn't even have it translated, because I could see from the invitation what the date was and that the organizer was the big international rose society. Signed by Francis Meilland. Francis Meilland! Creator of Peace. Was I ever going to meet him? I went up to Bucharest a week later, in early April—the usual regional summons to the Ministry, and I reported, gave an account of results, failures that had been rejected, and then what I was planning. When I'd nearly finished along came Mogyorós and spoke to me in Hungarian. He asked whether I'd brought the invitation. It was so sudden, I was completely surprised, I couldn't even think what invitation he meant. Didn't I want to go, then?

'Go where?' I asked. I was so disturbed and on edge because the way Mogyorós spoke to me I felt less than well.

'Well, aren't you going to represent the country at the big international rose competition?' he asked, giving me a piercing look.

What was I to say? I was at a loss for words.

'I haven't yet contemplated international competition.'

'Then why did we send you to Trieste?'

But that had been a good two years previously. In September 1956, since when it had all gone silent.

'Mind you go. I'll give you two weeks to submit your proposal. I'll have to get it accepted, things aren't the way they used to be. You must write a serious proposal, a plan of action. Something may have to be added in order to get it approved if it won't do as it is.'

'Two weeks?' I asked in horror. 'And what's to be in this plan?'

'How should I know? Don't you want to go, then?'

Oh, the way he spoke. What did he mean, didn't I want to go? How did I know where I was going? I was going where I was sent. I began to perspire. Was I to tell Mogyorós now how things stood? I'd been invited as a judge of new varieties of roses, but I wouldn't been allowed to go, I'd been invited as a member, they'd have said that the country couldn't afford the dollars, personal membership meant nothing to them, they didn't like individual things, I didn't work for export, for the market or anything, and there was no way I would bring in the money for such a thing. And now here was Mogyorós asking whether I didn't want to go. Perhaps I was going to have a stroke on the spot.

He had said I could go, and I didn't want to let him change his tune.

'I'll go, but let me know what I must submit by two weeks from now.'

'The whole plan. Preparations, means of transport, members of your team. You'll be the leader, of course. I might come as well. Don't put anything about money, that'll be dollars anyway. When does it take place?'

I hadn't even looked at that, I hadn't taken it seriously.

'Late September. It's always held in September.'

I put it like that so that he should see that I hadn't been born yesterday. I knew what went on.

When I was released from the Ministry, I had to go and sit on the boulevard because I was so on edge. Then I calmed down and bought two thick notebooks, a sharp pencil and a rubber. The latter was soon worn down but not the pencil. I would think and think, then want something better and better and rub it all out, leaving the paper nice and grey. I hadn't been able to get such quality notebooks as I'd hoped for in order to plan myself a world exhibition. Never mind. I didn't sleep a wink on the train, just kept writing notes all the time but in such agitation that I broke the pencil. I was thinking, 'How was I to do it? What should I take to exhibit? In what should I take it? How much should I ask for? If I asked for a lot, it wouldn't be granted because it would cost too much, if for too little it wouldn't be taken seriously. If the team was a big one it would be too expensive, if it was small we'd look too modest.' I had always, always to be a politician, play it canny, as Mogyorós would say of somebody that he didn't quite approve of. Actually, I'd never heard him approve of anybody. Other than Dej. He'd been in prison with him as an illegal Communist.

But only two things interested me. Firstly, what to take with me, which flowers to compete with? Second, how to take them so that they would arrive fresh and fit to display, not dried up and lifeless?

Which flowers to take was also a political consideration. By which I mean that the colours of the flowers to be taken to Paris had to be decided. Crimson should not be taken, as it was not such a good colour over there. I mustn't take white, because my whites weren't good enough. Perhaps it ought to be a fine soft pink. That was so bourgeois, as my Naming Committee always said. Suitable for young ladies. What should it be, then? Orange-yellow? Oh, you couldn't base a world competition entry on that. And above all, I didn't like orange roses at all. Forgive my saying so, but there's never yet been a rose grower that's made his name with an orange colour. That left yellow hybrids. What about Cluj Superstar?

For me to be going was in itself a political statement. There was no way I could go abroad without making a political statement. Really, I was not only going but representing a whole country, achievements, development, beauty. If I didn't win anything I wouldn't exactly be put in jail, but who could say what reprisals would result?

Three days had not gone by when Mogyorós phoned me at the Station.

'How are you getting on?' he asked.

'Fine,' I answered, because by then I knew how to reply, but I was so on edge at hearing his voice. 'I'm working on the plan, it'll be ready in a fortnight.'

The response was that he couldn't wait a fortnight, he'd got to present it at the meeting next Monday for it to be discussed.

Nothing on earth could be planned in an orderly fashion. There was a fortnight to make the plans, no, there wasn't, there was a week. Then I waited two months for approval, it didn't come, and there I was, not knowing whether to make a start or not. A special carriage had to be constructed, I couldn't cobble that together myself, could I? Other rose growers knew two years beforehand that they'd be going, what they'd be taking, how they'd get the flowers there without spoiling them. Why did they think that I'd got everything ready, I'd only got to cut them when we were just off?

What could I say? I danced to the music that was played.

Whom should I put on the preparation committee? Young Werner first of all. I'd take Anisoara from the Naming Committee, Horváth was included and at least one competent person from the technicians. Six people. That was unbalanced—five were Hungarians. If I increased the number it wouldn't work because it would be too many, and if I took one off I'd be losing good people. I put down two people and left it at that. I'd hold weekly continuity training sessions for them, ask them for reports and plans in writing and that would be that.

On the Monday the plan went in, and on the Tuesday Mogyorós phoned. I could see that this exhibition was very important now. Why? Goodness only knows. Since the Station had been there I'd always been asking to do something. Then, of course, in 1956 I'd stopped. What could I have asked for? I could see the situation. And now *Realizare de prima importanţa*. Mogyorós called; the draft wouldn't do, he wouldn't take it to the meeting.

'Why are you being so modest, Décsi?'

'What do you mean, modest?' I asked. Because I'd said that I'd be able to manage, but wasn't asking for too much or too little.

'For example, what do you mean to exhibit? With what will you represent the country and the successes of the Party in the Station?'

'How do you mean?' Because I'd written five varieties of rose, and named three.

'Whom are you reserving the *Vilmos Décsi* for? Why aren't you taking that?'

'Well ... er ...' I stammered. That Mogyorós was always going for me.

'Well, what have you to say?'

'I'd thought that the ...' but what was I to say. That I'd been hauled in by the Securitate over it? And didn't want that experience again? He knew why I hadn't named it.

'I'll take it if I must,' I replied.

'You do that.'

Well, I must say, I was ecstatic. After all, I was bound for the centre of the universe. For I was alone.

I had to find an old colleague in the university who also knew about the matter, so that I could look out the former plans for the carriage to transport the flowers. Because that had to be constructed, of course. So as to contain refrigeration, ventilation, shelves and everything. We could do with somebody from the old guard, somebody even from the EMGE days, who, of course, were all in prison. Fortunately, some were now out. Dániel Antal or Bikfalvi or Andris Szopós. Antal had written a book about storage, only with reference to fruit and plants, it was true, but he probably knew a bit about transportation and refrigeration. His book had actually been published, and if that was so it must be available.

I'd only got a book from 1938 on the technical side. Since then, I thought, science has advanced greatly. But everything cost foreign currency. Where could I get some from? There were people had some, of course. I'd even read in the papers about priests always being given foreign money. Those days a lot of priests were being locked up. Where did they get it from? Most of all, how were they not afraid to possess it? And then, what would anybody want foreign currency for if they weren't going abroad?

I didn't know about foreign currency. I was given what I was given, and that was that. Because, of course, I'd now had to pay for registering names. And for taking part. And also for the size of the pavilion that I wanted. I didn't make the arrangements. I'd said that a couple of big tables would do for me.

Mogyorós called saying that I hadn't provided for a stage designer, transport, decorator, interpreter or vase maker; he hadn't even taken my proposal to the meeting.

'This simply won't do,' Mogyorós shouted. 'We aren't going there to pile things up on a couple of tables like they do in the market. We're not shelling out for that. There'll be a whole Romanian pavilion built. By a stage designer, the full works.'

'A stage designer?' said I. 'I've got a good stage designer that I'd like to work with.'

'Let's have a look,' he replied. I was to send in the name and the designs.

Well, I ran to the theatre. I had to watch a performance that Gyuri Szakács had designed. It was pretty boring, very political, I left at the interval, I'd seen what I needed to see, I hadn't got the time just then to sit in the dark and watch. Gyuri said that there was nothing beautiful on the stage, I shouldn't base my ideas on that, because in the Kolozsvár theatre there was no money for it, all the money was now going to the MAT and the Székely Theatre. Those days they were rather having to go for simple things, weren't making big sets, having to economise. Nowadays expensive, beautiful things weren't even in fashion, there was another style, realism. I should see one like that, *An Inspector Calls*, that was a really daring show. I asked Lali what he meant by daring? He said that in fact there'd been a scandal over it. It was the sort of play that showed that we were at last awakening from suppression. László Szabédi had criticized it severely, said Lali.

Gyuri said that he would be delighted to design the pavilion for us and had no commissions. The sort of thing that he imagined would be nice and folksy, stylized, as he put it. I didn't know how to take that. He meant so that it wouldn't be immediately obvious which part of the country it came from. Then he shouldn't do something with a Hungarian slant, or I'd be kicked out! Not at all, he replied, only folksy, that would be right for the people's democracy. I said that in my opinion there was no way that it wouldn't be Hungarian or Romanian or, what should I say, Saxon, but a bit of everything. Such a thing I couldn't imagine. Leave it to me, he replied.

Well, if I'd got to lead such a regiment to hell with it. There certainly wouldn't be the funds for me to go with ten or a dozen people. In that case people from the Party would have had to come as well, and I hadn't counted on that.

Then in May it all went quiet.

It was June.

Not quite. Somebody else was appointed as designer. A very important man, a great designer, who already held a state award. Furthermore, he was teaching here at the Kolozsvár Academy of Fine Arts, though at the time he was in Bucharest, working on a statue. He asked for pictures of the roses to be sent so that he could begin planning. Unfortunately, I said, I can't be sure of the colours. Was there nobody that could paint them? Well, yes. But would he not rather pay a visit to see the garden in flower? It was by that time in full bloom, of course, and the design was still nowhere.

So he graciously came down.

Virgil Fulicea came from the capital by chauffeur-driven car. All the same, he was astounded at the sight of rose houses G and F, from which we were going to take the competition material. He asked to be allowed to walk around by himself. As much as you please, I said, as far as I was concerned, he could stay all night, I'd even put a bed in for him. Especially if the night was warm and we shut off the external ventilation, then he could also catch the perfume. If he wished he could take some flowers, but let me cut them for him to keep at home and be able to draw what he wanted. He sat in there for an hour or more, but it wasn't cold inside. I didn't know what he would design, but he was a man of feeling. An artist, well, obviously, though I'd never heard of him. I could tell from the way he looked at the flowers.

He sent two designs, rolled up in tubes as surveys used to be, for me to get approved. That is, he was going to do the work, I would just look on; in the end it would enhance my flowers, but I had no say in the matter. He said of the one design that it was symbolic, and I couldn't understand it at all. There were all sorts of silks fastened to the design, waves and lights drawn. Oh, it was all so puzzling. The other one was clearly a Romanian peasant room. National costume and plates, tiles, embroidery, carved furniture. But too ornate for roses. One wouldn't be able to see where the roses were, because they were not the main actors. Where was I to place the flowers in this room? There were even dolls in Romanian costume. Were there to be full-size dolls standing in the pavilion? Or who were they? They would make a mockery of it all.

My main concern was the construction of the railway carriage. I'd made no progress with that, only squabbled, telephoned repeatedly without result, couldn't find out anything. No licence came, nor did the money. I didn't know how to obtain railway licences, I wasn't in the CFR. But on this occasion the whole route had to be reserved, so that one carriage could go all the way without being detained at frontiers. If it were held up for a day at

Customs, that would be the end, I could throw the flowers away; every hour counted. I wrote to Mogyorós. I could have phoned, but when we spoke he was always in the saddle. I wrote and said that I had worked out the countdown, and if the carriage were not ready by the middle of August for me to test all would be over. I wouldn't need a pavilion or any vases, I was well supplied with those.

What was his answer? What I was to say in the brochure about the Station that I was producing. Gheorghiu-Dej, no less, was writing the introduction, I was to deal with the technical part. I must write about mechanization, what plans there were for development, Michurin-based achievements, that I was mechanizing rose production. So I had to ring him back and say that I couldn't do it even if he crucified me. Roses couldn't be mechanized, it had to be manual work.

'Then say nothing about roses!' he exclaimed at once.

'What do you mean? It's a rose exhibition I'm going to. I'll do a separate brochure in French.'

'There won't be a separate brochure. Just write it and that's that. But something progressive.'

'The new varieties I've produced are all progressive. The ones I've put into industrial production. Cluj Superstar, Duiliu Zamfirescu, Alexandru Borza and 23 August!'

He wasn't interested, don't bother him with lists. In that case I was to write as much as I liked about roses, but it could only be two pages of the brochure. Full stop. I couldn't include one more photograph.

'But wait a minute, I didn't mention the Vilmos Décsi.'

'That's not in industrial production.'

'What do you mean?'

'Well, like that, with a name like that. It's unacceptable industrially.'

'And why's that, may I ask?'

'Personality cult. Especially after the Twentieth Party Congress.' So I said, 'See here, I'm well informed ideologically, I'm not stupid.'

'Then change its name and put it into industrial production.'

'What? Rename it? Again? It's been changed once already. Do you want to take my name off it?'

'Don't you want to put the best flower into industrial production? Why weren't we informed of that before now? Whom are you reserving this flower for, anyway?'

'There are seven varieties in industrial production, I've reported that every year. I bring in new varieties according to demand. I'm working on more than a hundred varieties in the Station, developing them, carrying out experiments.'

'The Vilmos Décsi must be put into industrial production. *Asta nu se mai discută.*' Nothing to be discussed.

Not a word about the carriage. There'd been no production, I should understand, it was an annual holiday, there was nobody to sign my document. So I wasn't going.

When I put the phone down, I swore to myself that even if I were dismissed from the Station, I wasn't going to put 11-16-45 into industrial production. That's what I was then calling the Vilmos Décsi: 11-16-45. What did that number indicate? Firstly, that overall I'd been developing it for eleven years. Then the 16 meant that I'd found it by sixteen related selections. And lastly, I worked myself in, saying how old I'd been when I last produced it. I didn't want to say my name all the time, as that was a dull and conceited thing to do. I might be able to put it into production, but I wasn't going to if they killed me. And I hadn't shared that thought with anybody at all, because I trusted nobody. I'd promised solemnly and that was that. Not that I was sitting on it and not letting anybody have it. If someone asked for it, I gave it to them. But I didn't want myself to be spread abroad on an industrial scale. I wasn't churning out my name on a production line and releasing copies by the million. Just nicely, anybody that asked for one was given one, and that was fine. There were a hundred or a hundred and fifty stocks out-side, sufficient for my requirements. One can put oneself about a bit, make a show, give people pleasure, even a little admiration does no harm. And then it fades away. One has to vanish. I didn't want to commit myself to being scattered everywhere in ten thousand, a hundred thousand or a million of a single variety, so as to be here for ever even when I am no more. To hell with it. It didn't give Meilland a headache. Perhaps I was simply afraid, and that was why I didn't do it. I couldn't contemplate going down Ferenc Deák utca and finding my name bandied about in Flora Park.

Also not satisfactory was the fact that August was almost there, and I still hadn't got my refrigerated carriage. Everything would be ready at the last minute with the exception of young Werner being dropped from the team.

I didn't know how I was to tell him. I didn't want to go anywhere with-out him. I was going to ask him to become responsible for all the cutting, because the roses would have to be cut into A1, A2, A3 and A4 lengths before being put in the carriage. Whom was I to rely on if not him? Nobody knew how to do it, and so I would have to. I hadn't got enough problems, I'd do that as well. And the placing of them all in boxes. Because, of course, I was having separate boxes made of light cardboard, but lined and ventilated too. I kept asking and asking for things, but then went and had them made at Station expense.

When on Tuesday the approved team list came, saying who should send in their passports for visas, a day, two days went by, and I said nothing to Werner. How was I to go about it? Look here, my boy, now you've been dropped?

At lunchtime on Friday he came in, tapped the door and asked Anisoara if he might have an audience. Well, we weren't on audience terms. Come in, my boy, said I.

I closed the door so that we could talk.

He was clutching his cap so tightly that his fingers were white. I kept my hands down under my desk where he couldn't see them. But they too were white. Perhaps he guessed something, or somebody had dropped a hint. I'd got so many well-wishers.

He tried to start and cleared his throat, not knowing how to. How to say that he couldn't come to Paris, and he looked at the floor.

'I know,' I replied.

'How?' he asked, looking up.

'The approved team list has come.'

Yes, he was no longer on it. So did he know? He was getting ready to go. Where on earth to, when he was supposed to be going to Paris with me? But I said nothing, just looked at him speechless.

'Where are you going, Comrade Werner?' I asked, because I couldn't endure saying nothing. My temple was now throbbing painfully, even my teeth were hurting.

To that he said some word which I didn't catch. *Alja* or something. I was beginning to be on edge.

'Stop mumbling, speak clearly.'

He was going to Israel, he'd sent in an application, he'd been wanting to tell me for a long time but hadn't known how to say it.

They'd been able to emigrate again as of that year, and all the Jews in Kolozsvár wanted to go. Not all of them, as young Werner said, but very many, because he'd had a terrible long wait before he could go to the office where it was dealt with. There were huge queues for passports at the police station. Previously nobody had been allowed to go. Now at Yom Kippur permission had been granted. Israel was awaiting her sons. Now he'd handed in his application, and so I had to terminate his employment at the Station.

So it hadn't come from the Centre yet, but he'd been excluded from the team.

He'd thought that would happen. Because if someone wanted to go, their house would be taken, they'd be dismissed from their place of work, and they could take only thirty or forty kilos of property. Gold and objects of value all had to be sold. But they were keenly awaited in Israel.

'Who's waiting for you, my boy?' I asked. I hadn't known that he had relatives.

'The new state,' he replied quietly. 'We have to build it together.'

The state . . . that was no good. But why hadn't he told me what plans he had? Perhaps he knew that I'd have tried to talk him out of it, and if that didn't work, I'd have told him off as they do in Party meetings. But he'd wanted to go and had persuaded his father. Now I'd got to sack him, he'd lose his home, and he was hardly allowed to take anything with him. I said to him, where would he find another job like the one he'd got? Out there in the desert? He said that he was going to work on a farm. I said that here he could create roses and dream of anything he liked, could do anything. He was a modest young man, worked like a slave, had a feel for flowers and, most of all, knowledge. He'd learnt all he knew from his father and myself, and from books. Now he wouldn't be able to repay it. He was off. There wouldn't be any roses growing for him over there, I said. Don't worry, he replied, everything grows on that soil. Everything there is. Not for nothing is its name The Promised Land. He said that so modestly. Not like some Jewish know-all. I would never have another man as good. I told him that I didn't even go to Hungary, I stayed where I was and worked, and that was that.

'I'm certainly not going to Hungary,' he replied. He wouldn't go there for anything.

I could see now that all the Jews were being moved out of positions of authority, but young Werner hadn't even been promoted to anything of the kind. He was a very small man, never bothered by irritation or bad temper, but that was what I was for, because dealings were always with the director, never the technician. He was employed as a technician, but knew as much as a researcher. I'd told him previously that I would help him, he should matriculate and go on to higher and higher things. The poor chap had been to the Jewish school, and then that had been closed. It was nicknamed Zsidlic, short for Zsidlic Liceum.

I wasn't allowed to give young Werner a leaving celebration, it wasn't like a retiral. He left with nothing more than a handshake, and I gave him a present when the two of us were alone. In my room where nobody would see. A nice album had been produced about the Station with photographs and newspaper cuttings. He was so pleased, it moved him to tears. When he looked at it he said 'Don't suppose I'll be able to take this with me either.'

I didn't have a man like Werner, the young Jew; hadn't had one before him and never shall again. He would walk along the rows with the eyes of a cat, reaching out and picking off insects, crushing them in his fingers and wiping them on his apron. His hands were never still. He would sweep his hands upward over a bush and lift off the white netting. My sight is good but I couldn't see them, while he would pick off twenty in a row. Roses in industrial production could be sprayed with insecticide, but not experimental varieties. In those cases I had to see how the plants were developing and how naturally resistant they were. I mourned that Werner as if he were my own son. I didn't like his father, though, he was a real Jewish big-mouth and I couldn't stand him. I'd never even seen him laugh, ever, Nor seen him come for a glass of wine or a beer at the Ursus. It was amazing that they'd both come home from the camp. Mrs Werner and their daughter did not. The latter actually died on the journey. Now all was ready and the two of them were off to Israel.

Damn and blast it. Why on earth was he given permission? Didn't we need the Jews here? Once that handful had returned, we should at least hang onto them. What kind of a country is it where there are no Jews? Werner was the best. Young Werner, that is. The cleverest, the most capable. Nobody recognized him, because he just stayed in the shadows. The shadow of the great Décsi. But I'd kept telling him, pestered him, to do his own thing, produce his own varieties. It's always the most capable that have the least self-confidence. Anybody that is solidly average can climb very high up the tree and be so successful that the daily paper and the Party resound with the praise of them all. What was this young Werner going to do in Palestine? Or Israel? Was he going to feel at home there?

As he took his leave, I asked whether he couldn't wait for a year. See, I was getting ready for the big international competition, I had to make preparations, and there was no one better able to help than him. I'd write again and say that the team couldn't go without him.

But he'd been given permission, he had to wait for just two documents and he'd be off.

Well, that was that.

I look at that team list. A fine set of names, twelve people. Which of them had any experience of working with flowers? One. Myself.

I'd managed narrowly to avoid sitting on a new committee. Was I to do that as well, just before departure? I'd go completely mad. Committee! 'A committee dealing with the problem of the cohabiting nationality.' I'd almost been put on it. I had a word with János Fazekas, as he was the only person who could do anything about it. I went straight up to Bucharest to see him after the telegram arrived saying that there was a session, and I was a member, because, of course, that's how things are done here. Or rather not cohabiting *nationality* but *minority*, as the term had been for a long time. I don't know how long. Words keep changing their meaning. Lali preached a little sermon about what the former meant and what the latter did, and that both meant that we were being suppressed. Words? How could words show that we were being suppressed? I didn't understand. Ever since he'd been released, Lali was always going in for exaggerations, and negative thinking had such a hold on him.

I spent all afternoon typing my report.

I wrote: Firstly, I appreciate the vital importance of the question of the nationalities. We have to adjudicate on a textbook for use in school or university, I don't know which. When Edgár Balogh—whom I hardly knew except by name as a great man with whom Lali had been in prison after the lecturers' case—telephoned me and asked me at all events to take this on, he explained that the textbook contained verse and other items from nineteenth-century Hungarian literature such as criticized nationalism and, deliberately or otherwise, excluded works on the class struggle.

He suggested meeting in person so that he could persuade me. Very well, so we met yesterday in the Karpáci. He said, 'Look here, Vili, you're a level-headed man, you won't have to do anything, just follow our lead and back us up. We're not seeking confrontation, but we must achieve collaboration. We've already been trashing this book,' said Edgár, 'Now the voice of calm reflection must be heard.' What, me? Level-headed? But I didn't argue. Then too, however, I was on edge.

One could talk to Edgár Balogh, and Lali also said that he was a melting pot of a man. He could talk to anybody, was always optimistic and a solver of problems. A little soft-hearted, it was said, because anybody that could always soften others must be that way himself. So I asked him.

'Comrade Balogh, don't be cross, is it your opinion that I'm an authority on Hungarian literary textbooks?'

'You aren't, Vilmos, we didn't even suppose that you were, just say what we say.'

'Is it your opinion that I'm an authority on the solution of the problem of cohabiting nationalities? I'm going to solve it, correct? You don't also want me to sort out industrialization straight away?'

It was all as tricky as that. I couldn't understand it, and most of all I didn't wish to! Because in the background there was a new literary magazine in the MAT, it was by then the main Hungarian paper, and that was what made all the statements. And there in Kolozsvár there was another, *Utunk*, that I knew because Lali had persuaded me to subscribe to it, because we had to support one another. Only I never got round to reading it, I didn't have the time. I took it out to Györgyfalva, because there the peasants were so cultivated, they read everything. There was in the MAT a sort of very

Party-line writer—a dogmatic Stalinist, in Lali's words—and he attacked the Kolozsvár journal; it was clearly a personal difference. I was familiar with that Vásárhely–Kolozsvár wing-line, I knew what went on, all that went down it was quarrelling. I was therefore pleased that we had no partner or fraternal institution, as the term was, in the MAT. No *filiala*. The one in Bucharest was enough for me. Was I now to become involved in this quarrel and speak the truth?

'Vásárhely mustn't come out on top!' replied Edgar.

'On top in what?' I asked.

In the textbook dispute. The ideological battle against the textbook was mainly led by *Igaz Szó*, because Kolozsvár had produced the textbook. I said to Edgár that there was no need for Bucharest to silence us, we were cutting our own throat without that. He laughed; 'Oh dear, Vili, you're so prickly. It's just the difference between László Földes and Győző Hajdú.' Well, I didn't know what he was talking about, who they were or what they'd done.

I wasn't interested in Földes, I told him, only *föld*. Both of them had signed the writers' declaration back in November '56, so what were they arguing about now?

In September, I said, I couldn't spare a moment, could I? Do you know what we do at that time of year? We're a research station, that's when we have to carry out measurements of vitamins and various analyses if we are to show any results. If I go away for four days at that time it will at once become a week, as there's sure to be a second session and a dinner I'll have to attend, and I'll be stuck. So if I'm missing from here for a week, everything will be ruined and I'll have to wait a year for the next harvest.

He couldn't release me, mainly because it wasn't he that had put me on, I'd have to go, even though I'd got a broken tooth, I'd have to get it fixed. I looked at Edgár, and saw that he had new teeth. So I asked him whom he went to, because it had been ten years since I'd had to go to a dentist. He did a wide grin to show how nice they were. They were really snowy white. He said I'd better hurry if I wanted nice ones myself because the dentist was leaving. Where was he going, I asked. It turned out the dentist was Jewish, his private practice had been closed as he was emigrating to Israel. He could still work at home, though, and he'd soon fix me up. Géza Neumann was his name, and Edgár wrote down the address. But he couldn't save me from the committee because the nationality question was being taken very seriously at the time.

Then I rushed up to Bucharest to see Fazekas, as it seemed that only somebody in the KB could do anything. I travelled overnight and came back the next day. I handed in my letter explaining my situation and asked to be excused from membership of the committee. Had I a proposal, asked Fazekas. Because perhaps he would keep me on the committee as a name, but I would be absent with permission, and he would put my proposal to the meeting. What could I say? I wasn't even fully familiar with the matter, because, for example, I hadn't yet been given the textbook in which the ideas of Hungarian nationalism were prominent. He believed that it would be pulped, he said. How could I keep out of it? I asked, because one could talk to Fazekas. I'd got exhibition material to see to, a thousand things awaited my attention. Very well, said Fazekas, just this once he would excuse me, but he wouldn't always be able to watch my back.

So, then I had to get ready. Clothes I had, but no carriage!

Towards the end of spring, I'd called on a tailor for him to make me a slightly lighter suit. I couldn't have gone to Paris in one that was so shiny at the elbows and collar! I didn't want anything off the peg that wouldn't do for international rose judging. With great difficulty I chose a nice dark-blue cloth with a thin stripe. I went for three fittings, and when I put it on for the third time, he asked, 'What about shirts?'

So, what kind of shirts would go with it? And then, shoes. And ties. It was just as well I didn't have to buy a gold pocket-watch. It was getting beyond!

When I have anything new made the old one looks like rags in comparison. Therefore I had to buy new. I felt like a circus horse. I had to withdraw money from the CEC to pay for it all. Yet I might be disappointed and not even go.

An invitation came to some special play at the Székely Theatre. I was there are the jubilee, and I thought it would be enough this time to send a telegram of congratulation and a nice bouquet. As if I'd got time to go and sit in a theatre. If I'm going to Paris at all, the train leaves in three weeks' time. Such is our luck, damn it, Comrade Fazekas happens to be coming. He's suffered a little fraternal ticking-off at the university, I didn't know what for. I was so on edge, I didn't even know what he was saying. When we parted, we shook hands, and he said that we'd meet in the capital on Saturday evening, wouldn't we, and winked. To him, 'the capital' means the capital of the MAT, of course. So I excused myself.

'That's impossible!'

I replied that I'd got an international competition to prepare for.

'What preparations will you be making on Saturday evening? Have you no respect for the Magyar Autonomous Territory? If Kolozsvár doesn't respect the achievement of autonomy, what can we expect of you? Do you understand, Vili?'

What was I to say in answer? That I was looking forward to seeing Annush on Saturday? Oh, it had been a week since I'd seen the girl!

He would watch my back about everything, said Fazekas, and he would support me in Paris, but we arrogant types didn't go to the MAT, didn't recognize the achievements. He absolutely appealed to my conscience, as if autonomy depended on whether or not I went to the theatre in Vásárhely on Saturday evening. So I took the official car and told Nicu that I was going home after the celebratory speeches. It was September, a starry night, so he would drive and that was that. He daren't grumble, because I would have had plenty to say about it. I brought a good electric torch and hung it up in the car, and all the way there and back I worked. I wrote out a whole list of what I had to pack, to be typed on Monday so that there should be no mistakes when it went to the Customs. And of the things I had to pack for myself and what to obtain through the Station for myself.

I hadn't expected to, but I worked well and enjoyed myself. At last a play that had something to say. I'd forgotten to look at the title, I'd only just arrived in time for the speeches and hadn't liked to enquire. Tompa, the director—Miklós Tompa, that is, not one of the Kolozsvár Tompas—had produced it, and it was very good. György Kovács, who'd been a prisoner in concentration camp, had returned, and was an up-and-coming actor, a great success! Perhaps it was now the intention for Vásárhely to be the best in everything, including theatre. It was a really forthright play about the life of today, genuine. There were real people on the stage, not second-rate figures. György Kovács could certainly display inner struggle, and at the end gave me hope, raised my spirits greatly. To me, that was real Communist theatre, I could congratulate him heartily. I would have brought a much finer basket of flowers, had I known. I had, however, undertaken to present them to the leading lady, but there really wasn't one, and on the stage in her stead was a sensible, delightful woman. I presented them to Tompa, but if I'd known that he was so talented I'd have brought him some quite different varieties as well. Peaces and Décsis, because then I'd only taken reds; 23 Augusts, they didn't know, of course. Then up came Fazekas and said that we'd had a good evening, hadn't we? And that the next day we were going for a working visit to some village or other, to see the collective farm that had achieved a hundred and fifty per cent. I said to him, Comrade Fazekas, don't be cross, I've got my train going to Paris, I too have got to achieve a hundred and fifty per cent there, I was sure he would understand. I really couldn't stay. So he didn't press me and off I went.

So I wasn't altogether sorry. The Magyar Autonomous Territory was a great thing. I'd been there many times because it had been in existence for six years, but now I could see how important it was. It was just a pity that I had to take the car to get there, because that meant a journey. Kolozsvár wasn't in it, of course. Kolozsvár wasn't anywhere then. The Station was a piece of good fortune, a big one. We might not have been given it all. It was said that Murokország too might have been given it. There was very good land on the Nyárád, as good as in the Hóstát, but of course that kind of horticulture, as it was called, hadn't grown up there. There wasn't much apple growing there or any rose growing at all, just green vegetables. Or it may be that the whole Station had come into existence because of me. Goodness knows. The great thing was, it was here, and couldn't be moved to anywhere else. I was always being given more and more land as it was appropriated.

It was midnight by the time we set off back. I'd had a couple of glasses of wine, and so in the car I was fast asleep. I gave Nicu fifty lei before we left, so he was in a better humour. I also gave him Monday off, which I needn't have done. Not so much as a thank you.

Departure was a fortnight away. Still no carriage. No young Werner. Fortunately, I'd got Annush. Comrade Horváth gave briefings, as if he were leader of the delegation. He went to collect the passports. The vases were not finished. I hadn't seen the pavilion assembled. Those involved with it would go ahead of the rest as it had to be built. There was no news. I hadn't received the railway tickets. Or foreign money. I hadn't seen a Customs clearance.

An interpreter I had been given. Mrs M. was coming with me. Well, that was nice to know. Mogyorós actually commented 'Watch yourself, now, Comrade Décsi.' That he said in Hungarian, though on the phone we—the Station and the Ministry—always spoke Romanian. I said nothing, I knew what he was getting at. Everybody knew about Mrs M. . . .

The suit that I'd had made was ready. I'd had some shoes made in the Old Town that would see me out and do for my grandchildren. Beautiful workmanship, good for ten or twenty years. But were they necessary, I wondered. Because I was going abroad now, but when I'd go again nobody could say. It would all depend on the political situation, said Mogyorós, because now we had to show the world the achievements of the Romanian People's Republic.

I couldn't get a wink of sleep, I was like an aspic, couldn't set for five days. Yesterday my nose started to bleed from stress, I was having to spend all day on my feet. Still no carriage. By that time I was calling the Ministry every day. Either I was going, or let's say that I wasn't.

Meanwhile the phone was ringing all day, everybody was congratulating me. It was in the paper that I was going. By afternoon I was in such a state that I could hardly stay on my feet. I had a sudden thought, telephoned, had all sorts of food brought, got together all that I could, mainly from the Party canteen kitchen. Went out to Kali's, where else, with two big bags. I unloaded them and let Nicu go. The boy was so delighted, he was beside himself. Kali said that he stood at the gate all the time, waiting for me. Why didn't she stop him? Anyway, I hadn't come for an argument, I hadn't the strength. I took the packages inside and put them down. Kali was as pleased as if it were Christmas. So it might have been too, as the year before she'd been given less for Christmas than now. I'd taken everything, hadn't really thought about it. I'd taken a nice lot of tinned food since the factory had been there, and I'd given the boy a wooden train. I think it must have been imported. It was coloured, had wheels and could be pulled along. He went mad over it. I'd brought him some shoes as well, little boots, and that pleased his mother.

Kali quickly got organized, started mixing pancakes, made some tea, she'd got some nice soup and I had that as well, then she began to cook Romanian style, lovage soup. I ate so much, I hadn't had anything so good for a whole a week. She was such a good-hearted woman. I ate about ten tasty pancakes, and my stomach was bulging. I told Kali I'd lie down for a bit. She hushed the boy, told him to be quiet. So carry on. I slept for ten solid hours, and it was six in the morning when I got up. Kali was beside me, still snoring. Then she got up too, didn't want me to go with an empty stomach, I'd better have something. Then she asked when I was coming again. Well, I had no idea when I'd be coming, there was so much going on.

'And will you be coming back from Paris, mister?' she asked.

'You're talking rubbish, Kali.'

But I hadn't said a word. It had been in the paper, and she was always given it by the teacher because she looked after his child.

While I was slurping my tea, Kali said I was the best man she'd ever met. 'There's just two things wrong with you, mister.'

I looked at her and waited.

'Number one, you're very borin'. You never say a bloody word. You don't know 'ow to 'old a proper conversation.'

I looked at her. What would come next?

'Even now you've got your mouth shut, mister.'

'And the second thing?'

'You know that,' and she laughed out loud. 'Yesterday you didn't take your due!'

Well, I could guess. I'm not a statue, I'm a man. Yesterday I'd gone straight off to sleep, hadn't had sex with her.

I was silent. According to Kali. But I talked to myself all day. There was no need for so much talking, in my opinion. I was bored in meetings. All that talk, while outside the roses were opening. I shouldn't have been allowed to become a big man. Big men do nothing but talk, in meetings, at the university, on committees, they propose toasts, open meetings, introduce people, act professionally, give opinions. I would sit there while everybody listened and thought it was amazing what brains the big man had at his disposal. But all he was doing was moving his facial muscles and vocal cords.

There hadn't been a day recently when I could be nice and quiet and just see to the aphids on the roses, because I'd got a real infestation just then. For my mouth to stay shut a bit from all the listening, and the saliva to well up in my mouth and never dry out. Because I had to do so much talking to people all the time.

There at Kali's at least I'd been so quiet that it simply made me happy. I'd organized in my head what I was taking. So as to be able to group things into frames, because of course I'd been given four and a half square metres. That much just for flowers. The rest was fantasy, decoration. What was it all for? The flowers were what mattered. Never mind, I'd got it all on the list that I was taking, if I went. If! Because whose hands was I in? According to Kali, the hands of God. In my opinion it just depended on the whim of authority. The Party leadership, the political situation. In all of this, Vili my boy, you're just a little flea. Annush was always saying that, a flea. Oh, how young Annush cried all the time. Oh, but I love her when she cries. When she cries, she gives in. Completely.

I'd enjoyed such a nice silence that Kali was offended. Once I went out to see her, or rather them, and then too I didn't say a word.

'What am I supposed to say, my dear?' I said. 'I feel that keeping silent is an achievement, not talking. Any fool can talk.' She didn't get the point.

There was no bus, and a cart gave me a lift to the Station. The driver was a carter from the collective, and he flogged the horse like a madman. I was there by eight o'clock. Ten days until we travel. I was calm by that time, wasn't having to direct anything. I'd done all that had to be done, and it just remained to cut the roses, and I was taking about thirty potted hydrangeas and geraniums. I'm not all that keen on those, they're too peasanty for my liking. But I took some, as if a folksy room was being planned they would be in character. Romanian for geranium is *muskáta*. I think they took the name from the Hungarian *muskátli*. So that these days a peasant on the Olt doesn't call them *pelargonia*. Or what the hell, maybe it was the other way round and we got it from them. Everybody thinks they know it all.

There had to be carnations as well. I'd got some lovely ones, but I hadn't developed them. I took some Harvest Moon and some Mammi. People went mad over them because they were two-coloured. Well, carnations aren't roses, but Mogyorós said on the phone that there must be carnations. After all, of he was Minister for Agriculture, he understood, he knew what was required for an international competition, I couldn't say that he didn't. But a minister doesn't know what a carnation's like. A carnation's the way it is. I don't mean to say it's a partisan flower or anything. Nowadays the carnation is the flower of progress, in demand for all festivals. But it's not eternal. The rose is eternal, the carnation's just a flower. There's no explaining that.

The next day there was the silence of the tomb. Was I going? Was I not going? Nobody was saying.

I was perfectly capable of immersing myself in my work. All day I spent out in the greenhouse, and I'd even started off a new crossbreeding shortly before. The previous year I'd tried to produce a fully rounded climber with seventy or eighty petals. The first ten stocks had turned out very weak, and I hadn't expected a second flowering.

Then in the afternoon I got a phone call. Why hadn't I taken over my carriage? What carriage? It had been standing there at the train station for a week and hadn't been signed for as taken over.

I came near to having a stroke. It had been there for a week. When I'd been phoning the Centre to ask what was going on. I was told that it had been out in the marshalling yard. I went and looked at it, and it was quite acceptable. There was a water tank, it could be cooled and the temperature controlled, the many shelves were fitted, could even be fastened up. It wasn't pretty on the outside. It was ordinary. There was nothing festive about it, but it was all right.

It didn't matter to me what kind of sleeping car we were given. I'd have been content with a cattle truck. In fact, the Bucharest part of the delegation was going by air, so thank God I could take the train. I'd said that if I couldn't supervise the train I wouldn't go. I hadn't got a single expert who would know when there had to be ventilation, cooling; I was taking flowers, not rubbish—living organisms.

Everything was worked out to the hour, and I'd made a list of what had to be done when. I was on edge, kept looking at the time, calculating and recalculating, afraid of making a mistake. If I were a day out, that would be it, the end, there would be nothing. I did nothing of the sort. I was aware that it was just my nerves.

We were starting on the fifteenth. The pavilion was being built on the thirteenth, the Saturday, and the special train was running in on the evening of the fourteenth. I'd had to state at what times spraying and ventilation were to take place, as the train would have to stop and that would have to be synchronized with the stations. A special man worked it out by some mathematical system, and I had the schedule of our stops. I was praying for fine weather, that we shouldn't get storms or great heat. It could rain, and that would even be good as it would keep things cool.

In Paris, the embassy had arranged transport from the station for Sunday evening. That was what I'd asked for. If we arrived at midday and caught a heat wave while we were unloading, everything would be ruined. We could keep the flowers cool until ten in the evening, then unload at dawn, so that at six o'clock they would be in the boxes in the pavilion. The show opened at ten, so that was how it had to be.

My green passport arrived. A diplomatic one. That is to say, the train might not be detained, and just then Mogyorós phoned.

'*Satisfacut?*'

Was I satisfied. Well, I said, everything's in order. So we'd meet out there, the pavilion would open on Monday morning, and he'd be staying with the delegation from Bucharest.

There are two schools of thought about everything. Neither guarantees that one will be satisfied if something has to be done in one certain way. For example, flowers are to be cut either early in the night or at dawn. In the night, little white strips of gummed paper on the stems show clearly in artificial light where they are to be cut. At dawn, of course, there's enough natural light. I preferred to cut at dawn.

I went out to do the cutting at half past three. I still needed the lights and we have lights in the greenhouses, but their light is so harsh that it quite distorts the colours of the flowers. The previous day, I'd marked what I was taking with the little tags that Kali used to make. She painted enough to last me forever, slender strips, white at the end so that they're easy to see.

I didn't have to take a lot, but they had to be just the very best. I cut no more than eighty of each variety, and ninety of the Décsi. If fifty remained in good condition, that would be enough. I took them to the cool house in a barrow and out to the train in the evening for departure in the night. They wanted to send me a van with a trailer, but I said, for goodness' sake, we aren't taking manure. A trailer would bounce so in the streets, send something smaller. Mogyorós arranged for me to be sent an ambulance, which was the smoothest ride, it was so well sprung. Well, I'd never ridden in one. The doctor, who was in it as usual, asked whether he might prescribe something to calm me? He could give me some valerian, as he could see that I was on edge. My three cases came with me, as that tailor made me take five shirts when he heard where I was going.

'What if you're invited to a grand ball? Which shirt would you wear?'

One with pearl buttons! It had cost all I had. My plan to order a new motorcycle was shelved. I didn't like being chauffeured; I was thinking of buying a motorcycle, that was what everybody drove those days. But no, because the tailor made me buy a *nécessaire de voyage*. And velvet slippers. Everything was from under the counter, I didn't know where he got them from, didn't argue with him, just let myself be advised. Such is vanity, I suppose. Then I'd fail hideously and be able to laugh at myself. Velvet slippers, I ask you! I'd be able to slink home crestfallen from Paris.

Our special train consisted of only three carriages. The first was the luggage carriage, we slept in the second, and a dining car brought up the rear. We each had separate compartments. If only I could sleep! The last good sleep that I'd had was out at Kali's at Gyurfalu, and if I didn't get some sleep in the two days that we'd be travelling, I'd look a fine sight. There was so much work ahead of me in Paris!

I'd only seen the girl once that whole week. Now she was coming round more often of her own accord. She'd better not come when Kali happened to be there, because she too was dropping in more frequently. I was sorry for poor Annush, she was still a child and hadn't got anybody. But a young girl like her just blew my mind. On Wednesday evening she came round in tears, just ran in through the gate. The dog doesn't like people running and barked at her but she took no notice. She ran straight into my arms, hugged me tight and kissed my face. Then we began to kiss and cuddle as usual. All of a sudden she said very seriously that she needed my help. She'd been looking for her sister for three weeks, because, of course, she didn't live with them. She couldn't find her anywhere. She'd even been to the police, because she'd been told in the hospital where she worked that she hadn't turned up for weeks. She'd had to prove to the police that she was her sister. Then they said that she'd been arrested. Would I help her, because there was nobody more innocent on earth than her sister? And she was sick, she had a bad leg. What could I do to help? She wept, she begged, she'd do anything. I knew she meant anything. Well, I could see that she meant anything, the way she was kissing me, she was losing control. But it was no time for me to lose my head, I had so much to do. I promised that I'd look into it. She had nobody to turn to for help, nobody that could speak to the police. So I said that this was rather a matter of the Securitate than the police, because I thought she hadn't been shoplifting, she wouldn't be arrested for that, it was something political. She sat there on my lap and burst into tears. I didn't want to send her home at ten o'clock, so I went with her just down as far as the corner of Pata utca. I just couldn't stand it. There she was in my arms, crying from time to time.

So I had to swear that I'd find out what had happened to her sister. I asked what her name was, whom should I look for? Rózsa Butyka. Now this was all I needed. The poor girl had got mixed up in something. Well, I wasn't surprised. She was a nun. Or rather, she had been, because there weren't any nuns any longer. I promised that I'd run down to see her in the market and tell her what I'd found out. And if she wasn't there, I was to leave word with her neighbour, old Mária. I promised, I remembered in the morning, and then I thought I'd wait a bit. I didn't want to phone early in the morning, that was when everybody was nervy, I'd do better about midday. I'd only got one friend in the police whom I'd be able to ask. An old footballing friend. He said that he didn't know about any Rosalia Butyka, but he had a pal in the Securitate, he'd find out and give me a ring. He didn't ring back, and with all that I had to do I forgot about it. I even forgot to go to the market,

I wasn't able to say goodbye to Annush. I was on the train and approaching Sztána when I remembered the poor girl. Damn and blast it, I'd meant to help her, and I hadn't been able to. What could the poor girl have done? I didn't know how old she was, she was much older than Annush, a grown woman. Or if she was a nun, not a woman. One was a nun, the other cuddlesome. They were sisters.

Almost nothing went wrong on the journey, and yet I was so on edge. Would the water run out, would I be able to ventilate, would the cooling system break down? I don't understand machinery, roses I do. When I saw that Mrs M. was on the train, I thought that she might have flown from Bucharest, and now she was going to be around me all the way. She was still a lovely woman, and that's a fact. Lovely but tasteless, ostentatious. She had a camisole that couldn't be undone except by some trick, and in the dark I couldn't see a thing. And some silk briefs. Everything was simply designed to drive a man mad. I don't like these professional women. I didn't mind her being there, at least I wasn't thinking about the carriage in front of us for a couple of hours. And if I got tired of her talking, I asked her to translate for me from the French newspaper that she was reading. The sort of things that were in it, film stars, cars, all sorts of women's clothes, hats, even underwear, great costly villas. That was capitalism. Loathsome. I'd have preferred to see a workman. Or a woman using machinery. A woman working on the land.

My luggage was taken from the station to the hotel for me. I'd said I couldn't leave the train, if I wasn't there no one was to move the living organisms. They'd been cut down, but to me they were living beings, period. We didn't arrive late, we were even five minutes early. Three people from the embassy were there to meet us; one stayed with me as interpreter and two went with the others, got into cars and went to bed, because it was three in the morning. Now my work began. Two helpers appeared, to move things by hand to the van. No you don't, said I, nothing by hand. The embassy man, one Gheorghe Gocan, said that he had no instructions with regard to transfer from the train to the van. That didn't interest me, I wanted big hand-barrows brought. He hadn't been issued any money for the purpose. I told him to round up three porters, local ones. He was the diplomatic corps, couldn't have dealings with porters. So I raised my voice and said, 'Comrade, everything here can be ruined in the transfer, and it's not we people that are representing the Romanian People's Republic but our achievements, our results. We're only here to escort them.' At that he fetched three porters with very big hand-barrows, and we made three trips, but I didn't take my eyes off my boxes. When it was all over, the French had the nerve to argue about money, and I sat in the vehicle while agreement was reached. It wasn't a van, it was a bus.

The pavilion was a lovely Romanian room, airy, and it set off the flowers nicely. We surrounded the pedestal with miniature hydrangeas and the vases were ranged on the table. This was cleverly designed so that it sloped upwards to the rear, giving a better view of the flowers; the vases didn't slip because there were little depressions for them to stand in. By half past eight everything was in place and guards were on duty in the hall. I asked for a car, to go for a wash and brush-up in my hotel, and on the way I almost fell asleep, could hardly keep my eyes open, and so I saw nothing of Paris. No sooner were my eyes closed than I thought what our pavilion was like then. Not a soul in it, just the flowers. There wasn't time to look around even a little, to bathe my eyes in it, as Kali had once said. That embassy man urged me on to the hotel and back for the opening. He didn't go a yard from me in case I got lost as I couldn't speak to anyone, could I? Why had we brought Mrs M. then? For all that I had to say, I could have brought the dog to interpret. What was more, I'd managed to lose the big coloured catalogues that I'd been sent. I'm always leaving the most interesting things behind. Hell's teeth!

I did everything mechanically, I was no longer on edge. I went up to the sixth floor, where my room was. Hadn't there been a better one, I asked, but never mind, there was nothing wrong with my legs, but it was the sixth floor. I had to go down the corridor to have a bath. What street was this hotel in, anyway? At least I took a card so that I would know if there was no one with me. But no such luck. I heard *Bonjour, monsieur* constantly. They were so pleased to greet me, they grinned. What were they so cheerful about? I was offered breakfast, and they asked whether I'd like it in my room. Yes please, and it was brought. A chambermaid came, tall, so swarthy, almost a negro but not quite, her lips and nose were much too thin. A white woman, I thought, from the colonies. This country had so many colonies! She was like a statue. But I couldn't sleep with a black woman. So, what she brought wasn't a Parisian speciality, just a croissant and a big breakfast cup of coffee. Curses! And a little jug of milk. She tidied something in the room while I pretended to eat. I picked up the milk, it was something fatty, cream, perhaps. It looked good, but if I drank a jug of cream, I'd spend the opening ceremony in the toilet.

We'd got to be going, the diplomat had knocked three times already. I said, 'Just coming, not quite ready,' but I was sitting on the edge of the bed. I told him I'd still got to go to the lavatory. I heard him go downstairs. I had no strength, I was just too weak to go. If there were a God I'd have had a word with him then. What? God help me, I thought, when I shut myself behind the door of the room: 613. That was my room. Look here, Guillaume Décsi, now you're being selfish! If your father could see you . . .

Never mind, he wouldn't have believed me. He'd be sure to say something coarse. What are you hiding with that tie? That's not your sort of thing. What do you mean to do here? Shake hands with Francis Meilland? Because certainly he'll be the boss, he'll pass judgement on my roses. It was in the invitation.

I was amazed at every step of the way. The ground didn't open and swallow me, the car ran along with me, and then there I was in a vast hall to listen to the opening speeches. And here I was. I myself. I was used to long speeches at home, but this it was somehow different. Somebody played the piano, a lady played the cello, a third sang, wearing a gold-coloured dress. The platform was wonderfully decorated, only from the distance where I was sitting, I couldn't make out what varieties the roses were, because I was in a kind of box. The president of the international association didn't make a long speech, but the way my interpreter translated it, there wasn't much to it. The president at the time was one of the Tantaus. I didn't know whether he was father or son Tantau, he was quite a youngish man. He spoke in French. Then I heard him say *Roumanie*, Romania, that is, and Mrs M. said that I must introduce myself. *Guillaume Décsi de Roumanie*. The country was *la République Populaire de Roumanie*. We'd practised it enough. The interpreter said that Romania and Yugoslavia were being specially mentioned on their first appearance at an international competition. What about the Hungarians? Weren't they there? Then there was a performance of a rose waltz. The girls in their frothy ballet dresses were really lovely. There were more and more of them, and they ended by composing a huge bunch of roses, huge, full flowers, and the petals fell beautifully away. I'd never seen anything so lovely in my life. They each held a white rose, perhaps the ones called Frau Karl Druschki. They were such a dazzling white. If you produced one like that, you could lie down and die, *gata*. Or were they Boule de Neige that they were holding? Weren't they too full? I couldn't be sure. Twenty years previously I knew everything. Everything. But then I wasn't in Paris every week. There were some of the names which I'd written down a hundred times so as to be able to get them right. That Boule de Neige had been one—Snowball, it meant. This time I couldn't remember whether it was Neige or Niege. I no longer knew anything.

Finally, out came a young girl, an actress. The applause was such that I thought it would never stop. And she hadn't done anything yet! Mrs M. told me that she was currently the greatest film star, Brigitte Bardot. She sang. I asked what she was singing, because she seemed rather to be just speaking to a musical backing. Something rather meaningless, evidently. Maybe so, but it was very uninhibited. Exciting. Then there was another explosion on the platform, lights shone, and somehow a rose was outlined in smoke. More loud applause. The whole show was marvellous.

Shortly after that, we went for refreshment and were offered sandwiches as thin as my fingernails. Paper-thin slices of meat. And mayonnaise on them.

I'd have needed to eat a whole tray full to feel satisfied. I was standing with the embassy man, and then along came our people. Mrs M. looking splendid, and the rest. And in the end Mogyorós hadn't come. I was heartily delighted that he wasn't present.

Everything was so free and easy there. People spoke Romanian, nonchalantly. French likewise. I'd learnt some French from Mrs M. en route, and she said that I should try it out, that was the thing to do if I wanted to make a good impression. It wasn't like back home, dour, teeth clenched and unfriendly, but free and easy. I didn't even know what the Hungarian was for *free and easy*. *Löstetni* or something. It was as if people hadn't got anything to do there, were just relaxing. French people. Or perhaps they had, and were merely pretending not to be on edge like I was, trying hard not to shit themselves from stress. The French only pretended to take things easy. Or to sit in the street, drinking coffee half the day. They could afford the time. They'd spend two hours over lunch, five courses. Or perhaps by that time it was dinner, of course. Free and easy. That was the way to live. For one whole day, after which we set to work.

How nice it was that I couldn't talk to anybody! I began making the rounds and looking at things on the second day. Now then, Vilmos, if you'd looked at all that you could have died. Not because I'd have liked to die, I'm not the suicidal type. But there I could see for myself everything I'd ever wanted to see all my life. Every human miracle.

There's nothing to be done about my being born in the wrong place. I don't mean that it had never occurred to me. Long ago, when I'd wanted something very much. To do something great, something enormous, and become the greatest. Now I'd done that. But not in world terms, just at local level. Since 1952 it hadn't crossed my mind that I'd been born in the wrong place. That was when I'd started to be discovered. All the same, however, it crossed my mind after coming to Paris—or rather being sent by the Romanian People's Republic, as I couldn't have come to an international competition on my own initiative—all the same it crossed my mind what would have happened if I'd been, say, the son of a French gardener. Born as that. On the journey Mrs M. translated for me a brochure about the way in which the Meilland family established itself. There's been at least three generations of them. Even when the war set them back, because they had to burn all the rose bushes and plant vegetables instead to have something to eat or sell, because roses were finished. Or the Kordes family, father and sons, in Germany.

I kept looking at the market catalogues. There wasn't a single flower from a Romanian, or Hungarian, or even, so help me, a Soviet grower. I didn't know what improvements the Soviets had achieved, but there was nothing from them in the world market. Perhaps they weren't willing to expose themselves in the West. Anyone born in Romania, whether in Kolozsvár, or worse, in a village or small town, had to be content with what there was. The point was not that we were an ethnic minority or cohabiting nationality, as the term was in those days, I really didn't know what to say, sometimes it was one thing, sometimes another. I understood them all, but I'm a Hungarian. I'd learnt good Romanian, integrated organically into the Romanian state, you see, and by that time I could do everything. A job at the university, the Station, all the books I wanted had been published, prizes, I'd been written about in the papers every week. What more could I achieve? The Minister listened to what I said when I offered advice.

But from there, from Paris, none of this could be seen.

That we were a minority was unimportant. What it was saying in the illustrated catalogues was that our world was small, from there we couldn't aspire to Paris, San Francisco, or anywhere that the other big world competitions were held. Seen from there we would always be the size of dirt in a fingernail. At home we were doing ourselves a bit of good with this and that, popularizing them, if we sold five thousand stocks, even ten or twelve thousand, because Cluj Superior had been a great success.

But I looked at Meilland. There was a big pavilion, and above it a huge advertisement: 'Fifty million stocks in 1958.' Of Peace, that is. A map of the world showed how many had been sold even in Australia. The French firm of Meilland was associated with the American dealer Star Roses. It was all over, then, that was the end, that was world domination. I didn't care where I'd been born and where I was then, I'd got on very well, but my family and my brother knew nothing about it, damn them. I didn't care. I'd achieved all that I could at home. Only there in Paris that meant nothing. Zero. Face the fact, my boy. Mogyorós had said that after Paris, after I'd been to the World Exhibition, I shouldn't have big ideas. 'We've let you go to Paris, Décsi, but then don't let it go to your head.' So much for being stuck up. There I was a great nobody. A nobody with five vases of roses.

And look, there were even English roses! The English were there, but the Romanians and Hungarians weren't, were they? And the English roses had a separate stand. As I understood the term, English rose and Old English rose simply meant old-fashioned. Mrs M. had told me that. I'd never heard the term, so what was it? I got hold of Mrs M., whom everybody was by then calling Klarisz, to look at what it said. *Summa summarum*, it turned out, was an English rose variety. It had only recently been produced, but of course it didn't say that, only that an ancient tradition was being revived. What did that mean? I found such a thing suspicious. What had a man, whether gardener or rose growers, have to do to revive it? Perhaps it was he that discovered it. This Englishman stated that this was now a variety to him: English rose. It blew my mind! I too might create a Romanian variety. A Rose of Romania. A Romanian rose. Well, I couldn't.

This Englishman was exhibiting internationally for the first time. 'David something's rose' it was called. All Englishmen are eccentric, and David too wanted something that no one else did. Everybody worked on hybrids, but he, on the contrary, worked on centifolias, quite thorny varieties, fully filled four-parted ones, and had come bringing the ancient rose varieties. Well, I wasn't working on new things so as all of a sudden to go back in time. What would be the point of developing new varieties?

And the names this Englishman has given them! They were amazing. Either Mrs M. didn't know English or she was making them up. Not ladies' names or celebrities, though all the same one or two Sirs and Ladies, but things like Afternoon Nap, Good Morning, The Merry Gardener, Blushing Maiden, The Poet's Wife, Tea-break, and Pink Settee. When Mrs M. said The Poet's Wife and the other absurdities, I asked her, 'Where did you learn English?' She looked at me and didn't answer.

Tea-break? Poet's Wife? Settee? Things like that don't appeal to people. They want ideals, everlasting beauty, or nowadays the great achievements of the age, things like Victory, Five Collective Farm Girls or Happy Pioneer, as Soviet growers use. We'd had a Soviet brochure in the university, that was where I'd read the names. Or there was Kordes, wasn't there, with Atom Bomb and more. But who would have been interested in piffling everyday stuff like Good Morning and Tea-break? The art of the rose isn't like that!

The next day an 'agent' came to see me. That was now he introduced himself, an agent, *agent* in Romanian, because I already knew several. He asked for me by name in the pavilion. The American dealer who wanted business learnt French, because that was the language of business there. This agent represented Star Roses, and his name card was a real piece of art. Had a gilded edge. There was money there, I thought. We shook hands, I said 'Guilllaume Décsi de Roumanie' and proffered my name card. He wanted to talk to me, and he smiled so widely that I might have been a long-lost relative of his. But it was only me that he wanted to talk to, because the embassy interpreter was there. He said that the Vilmos Décsi rose interested him, and asked whether it was on the market. He would have liked some specimen stocks for his customers, to see how they got on in various climates. It was fortunate that Mrs M. was with me, because the interpreter talked to the American all the time and said not a word to me. Mrs M. told me what was being said, because the embassy man was telling the American to write to the embassy and contact the Station through it. But the businessman said, but look here, I was standing right beside him and it was me that he wanted to talk to. So Mrs M. interpreted no more, because the two of them would do all the explaining.

I took hold of that American's coat and asked Mrs M. to interpret: 'Monsieur, we can't trade with foreign countries, please understand, only the diplomatic people can do that, we're just a research station. None of our flowers are on the international market.'

The interpreter gestured to Mrs M. that he would interpret. I didn't know what he said or didn't say, but he explained for a further ten minutes.

They went on explaining and talking, then they too exchanged cards. Mrs M. told me what was said. The American dealer turned to Mihai Caraman, who was the embassy *chargé* for economic affairs. He was a young man, straight from Moscow University where he'd been studying, and he was able to say what could and could not be done. The agent went away having first taken another look at the competition table and noted something down in a little book.

I didn't have to be back in the pavilion after two, so I could take a walk. I said to the embassy interpreter that Mrs M. would go with me. No, he had to escort me. I replied, 'I'd happily go alone, you know.'

Well, how could I tell him that I'd like to be alone? This was my work. It wasn't even a job. It was like love was to anybody else. I didn't know how to put it to him. He wasn't prepared to understand, wouldn't let me go anywhere by myself.

'I don't mean to talk to anybody, comrade, understand that. I just want to stretch my legs a bit.'

'You can't. You mustn't go alone.'

I told him that first I needed to use the toilet. At least he wouldn't escort me there, into the cubicle. And I didn't go to the snow-white, wondrously perfumed pissoir, but shut myself into a lavatory cubicle. I sat down and thought. Didn't actually think, just was peaceful. I didn't need to go and lowered the lid, which was also wooden and shiny white. How many days had this excitement, this great emotion, been going on, and I hadn't had a moment to sit down and have a talk with everyone. I hadn't even taken a stroll to look at other people's competition flowers. There came a knock on the cubicle door. '*Ocupat*,' I said, which was Romanian, but near enough to the French, so perhaps understood.

But it was my minder—was I unwell? Yes, I said. What was the matter? 'I can't shit,' I replied because by then I was angry, and I said it in Romanian.

He said that I'd been in there for half an hour. 'It takes me this long,' said I irritably. 'I didn't know I had to hurry. And I haven't finished.'

This would be in his report. Let him write in his report that Décsi had spent half an hour in Paris shitting in the loo. I too was going to report on him, he should know. I too had to put in a report, in case he was unaware. I shall state that he wouldn't even let me go to the lavatory, for God's sake. I'd thought that only experienced staff would be sent on this task. He wasn't alarmed at that.

After that, however, he became a bit more accommodating. I was allowed to go for a walk. I had a map in my pocket but I didn't use that. I looked at what I wanted to.

I'd had a dream that left me soaking wet in the morning. Whether I'd gone to bed or not I didn't know, but I was wearing my expensive new shirt. I certainly wasn't drunk. When I got up all I could think of for the next hour was what I'd dreamt about. Sándor—as I was calling Mogyorós—had been asking me to do something. We were at a dinner, celebrating something, but not me, that I did know. Somehow he was seated opposite me and kept clinking glasses, and all the time there was a lot of singing of pop songs. Sándor said to me—in real life I didn't call him that, only Comrade Mogyorós—'Now then, Décsi, it's time for you to ask for something.'

I didn't know what to say to that.

I thought, then I told him that I'd like a new cold store, an entire cold store, because, of course, the best we could do was keep things in storage pits. We couldn't do any artificial testing of frost resistance.

'You shall have it, you shall have it. But don't ask for anything like that. Ask for something for yourself.'

'I am asking for myself,' I replied, 'for the Station.'

'You don't understand, Décsi. Only for yourself. Not for the Station or a colleague or some outpost in the hills. Nothing like that. Just for yourself, do you understand? So, you're a clever chap, just say.'

'Well, what can I ask for?' I asked.

'A state prize, membership of the Academy. Or that you want to go on holiday, but you're entitled to that in any case. A prize, would you like that?'

And he gave me a devilish look, piercing me with his eyes.

'Or a clever little angel. Ask for a clever little angel, one about twelve years old.'

'What sort of angel?' I asked.

He just winked, and I could see little pictures of girls sticking out of his pocket. Young girls in flimsy dresses.

When I woke up, oh dear, the dream was upsetting my innards. And the state I was in, I was completely taken in, so, being a man, completely horny. It was only just five o'clock, why should I get up? I lay hack down, but the bedclothes were cold and I was perspiring. So I went back to sleep, but it all went on. The whole dream.

Sándor spoke again, I should ask for some prize for myself. Never in all my life had I heard of anybody asking for a prize. I began to consider. But by then I was in such a sweat as Sándor kept looking at me, he even gave me his handkerchief as I couldn't find my own. Oh, I thought, why haven't I got anybody at least to iron me a handkerchief.

'Well, I can't go on waiting—speak.'

Actually, I was thinking at the time that I might be awarded a state prize of one sort or another, perhaps even the very highest, for some occasion, such as when I was fifty or the Station was ten. I'd even go in for international competitions if I felt like it. I'd publish books, as many as I liked. I could go and visit the remote Michurinist stations out in Siberia. How was I to know what to ask him for?

'Look here, Sándor,' I said, 'you're such a big man these days . . .'

'You've made a bad start, Vili, old chap. I'm quite a big man because I was rotting in prison while you all were tending roses, doing deals with the king and Miklós Horthy, because you bought a house out of that, didn't you, got yourself well set up. But we've forgiven you all that. Both Dej and I were in prison for a long time, having our nails beaten, but never mind, now our time has come. Now it's we who say what's to be. So speak up, what do you want?'

'Discuss it with your God or with Dej.'

'Leave it to me, trust me to know who to talk to,' he replied.

'Well, in that case ask him stop me wanting to be envious of anybody. Get it? I don't want anything else for myself. Only to become unenvious of anybody in future. Arrange that for me, Alex, if you're such a big man. Because one of these fine days, I'm going to die of envy.'

That's what I told him, I wasn't ashamed at all. He roared with laughter, so much that I could see all his black teeth right at the back. Then the people next to him started to laugh as well, they all laughed, the whole party, everybody laughed at me for what I'd said to the Minister for Agriculture. When they were all laughing at me like that, I woke up.

'You're a right one, my boy,' said I to myself once I was fully awake.

Just at that moment there came a knock on my room door, perhaps that had been what woke me. It was, of course, the man from the embassy, saying I had to hurry because I had to show the ambassador round that day. I'd still got to get something to eat, have a wash and shave. I flung on my clothes and told him through the door to tell them to send up breakfast. There wasn't time for that! I wasn't going anywhere, I shouted to him, I had to have something to eat as my stomach was on fire. That was because the previous day I'd eaten a surprising amount of fish and raw vegetables.

I was able to go round the exhibition to my heart's content. I couldn't see too much of it. There were some things that I went back to look at ten times. To me it was like . . . I don't know what to somebody else, I don't know what other people looked at so often. It was like a valuable old painting. However much I looked at it all I didn't get enough. Because I couldn't take beauty home, could I? I only went back to the pavilion in the intervals between the morning and afternoon sessions, when the water in the vases was changed. I didn't let anybody else do that. They'd break the flowers, arrange the bunches badly or something. That was my job.

I was standing idly in the pavilion looking at the Vilmos Décsis. Stand A3. There wasn't an A4 as yet, there might be one the next day. The A3 displayed the full strength of the flower. Suddenly along came a stocky little man and shook my hand. Mrs M. was standing beside me and he shook hands with her as well. She smiled broadly and said, 'Monsieur le président.' I brought out my card but began to feel that I'd have to sit down, I was so weak at the knees. Father Creator, there in front of me stood Francis Meilland!

He smiled and said that he was pleased to meet me. *Enchanté.* That I had learnt.

There was Francis Meilland, looking at my roses! I just hoped that I wasn't going to have a heart attack. He wanted to talk about what the Décsi came from, even though a description of the variety in two languages was there for all to see. Along came Gheorghe Gocan and at once started to push in and talk in place of Mrs M. But that low-life interpreter couldn't translate Meilland's questions because he didn't understand them. I, however, did understand what Meilland wanted. I told him as best I could, as I usually described roses. I mainly used Romanian words and indicated. In the first generation, there'd been a lot of thorns and I pointed that out; in the second, unfortunately, diseases had broken out, and in the third, the flowers had lost colour and brightness as they aged and so on, following the course of development. And he understood! I could see that it was most of all the Décsi that interested him. Hardly surprising. After all, he'd got eyes. Then he looked at the Cluj Superstar; nice, he said, *Sympathique.* Well, anything that's *sympathique* isn't *fantastique.*

In this conversation we didn't need to speak through an interpreter, it was all securely in a single language, the common language of gardeners. I could see the embassy man becoming anxious as he didn't know what we were talking about. That Gheorghe became agitated if I spoke to someone without him. Unfortunately I couldn't fully understand what Meilland said as he spoke in French, which is written one way and pronounced another. When it's written down, I can make out this and that by comparing it with Romanian. Never mind, I thought, even so I've spoken to him. He would be back, he said, with the committee. What committee, I asked, and I said to the interpreter, ask him. It emerged that a whole committee was judging, and he was the president. On his way out, he asked me to go and see him. I told the interpreter to translate exactly what Monsieur was saying. He'd like to have a talk with me, Meilland said, I should go round and see him after the pavilion was closed and we'd have dinner. The interpreter didn't even translate my reply, but said that it was impossible. Why? I asked, it was important to me, I wanted to go. You can't, he replied, because there's a reception at the Bulgarian embassy. I'm not interested in that, I replied. I'm going to the meeting. We began to argue. Meilland said that he had to be off. The embassy man explained that I had to go to the Bulgarian embassy as a representative of the plant-research fraternity of the Romanian People's Republic's, because Bulgaria was also a people's republic with which we had common economic interests.

Then Gheorghe asked who Charles P. Kilham was that we'd been talking about, as he needed to know. I said that it was a father-plant. *Tata*, in Romanian. I mustn't play jokes on him, because he had to put in his report whom I talked about with a Frenchman. I told him we'd been talking about ancestors, mothers; ancestors, fathers. He gave me a funny look and wrote something down. Charles P. Kilham was a father of American origin. In Romania he had married the Ville de Paris. Who was that? That was the mother that I'd used. Two splendid parents.

Blow you, Gheorghe, I thought, I'm not helping you any more. Get lost.

I told that Gheorghe to say in his report that in Vilmos Décsi's opinion, there was no greater man alive than Francis Meilland, and that he had succeeded in having a ten-minute talk with him, and that, furthermore, *à deux* without an interpreter. There had definitely been a gleam in Meilland's eyes when he'd been looking at my flowers.

And that I immediately howled and shouted for joy. Put that in.

Well, I didn't say that. The hell I did. All that I said was get lost. I'd spoken to Meilland, I didn't need written permission for that.

I'd seen that stocky little man before but hadn't known that he was Meilland, the creator of Peace. He'd been talking with Robert Pyle, in front of whom there'd been name cards on a little table, he owned the American Star Roses, by whose pavilion he was sitting. Pyle wasn't a rose grower but a dealer, and he represented the big European growers on the American continent. They'd been discussing, chatting, laughing. Meilland and Pyle jointly constituted the highest peak in the world. Perhaps they were even then doing the biggest of business. That was greatness, Vilmos. Those two combined. They chatted, drank coffee, and had the world in their pockets.

You, however, will be quietly going back to your Station in your special train, grateful for having been. I didn't weep, not I. I simply felt like a flea when I looked at them.

I took one final stroll round the show. That was what it was always called in English—the show. Mrs M. didn't understand the word, because according to her it meant a performance. She made a clever play on words with *show* and the Hungarian *só*, 'salt'.

There was a sort of collection there. A big collecting box set out, like in a church. There were just six or seven rose stocks in pots on the table, all old-fashioned roses which time had passed by. I asked Mrs M. to translate for me what the sign said. Tell me, dear Mrs M., what are these capitalists collecting for? Because it was a sort of Danish or Dutch affair. It seemed that they wanted to set up a garden of ancient rose varieties, and the collection was for that. To preserve the ancient varieties. The great achievements of the past, one way and another, had disappeared, were no more, and couldn't be identified. They had to be bought from collectors. 'From collectors?' I asked Mrs M. 'Are you sure you understand?' 'Yes,' she replied. I didn't really understand, was this a kind of restoration, people always wanting the old world? Like the Church, like the gentry? Now, when everybody was producing ever more beautiful hybrids, and there was such a beauty competition, with one outdoing the next. It was all bigger, more beautiful, different colours, all sorts of things. Meilland's main concern at that time was for the bush to be beautifully formed. Nobody had ever thought of the bush as a whole before. That the leaves should be beautiful even before the flowers were open. Clearly, Meilland had realized that people have an eye for beauty of shape. Now these people were beginning to collect antiques and to mourn the loss of the past. That nostalgia was such a decadent business. Who was going to be interested? Must we not be looking forward? Doing things that nobody has ever seen for the splendour of mankind? Things which their creator must be the first ever to see? So why tell everybody that the varieties illustrated in some book or other are steadily disappearing and have to be looked for in ancient gardens? Anybody that's in the past all the time isn't going to make any progress. and I call this yearning for the past what it is: lack of taste. But I'd been thinking that if there was some good cause, even if was a capitalist one, I wouldn't mind chipping in with a few francs. But I wasn't contributing to that sort of thing.

Meilland said that in the morning of the day after next, he was taking a party to his place to let them see the Meilland empire, and I was invited. We were to fly to Nice and go on by car. I absolutely must go, he said, he wanted to show me the trial gardens and the way they worked. So that I should know whom I was dealing with in making exchanges. This was planned for the penultimate day of the exhibition, and we would be back by evening.

I had one piece of luck, that I wasn't allowed to go. When I said that I was going to Meilland's place on the Riviera, and that this was very important for the future exports and foreign currency of Romania, and someone should come with me if they wished as I would, of course, require an interpreter,

Gocan almost died of shock. That I meant to travel eight hundred kilometres alone! Well, said I, how would I be alone? I was going with a whole party. I won't permit that, it's not in the itinerary. Well, I said, it's not in the itinerary, but now I'm setting up business with them. I shall be exporting. He didn't believe me. I must wait, he'd have to wire home and ask permission. He must get it into his head that Francis Meilland has invited me, the most important man in the world!

I waited and waited. Meilland came again and asked about the next day. I told him that I hadn't received permission. What permission? Permission to travel. Whom did I have to ask for permission? The Centre. What Centre? The Party Centre, I replied. I should give him the number and he would phone and discuss it all. I asked the consul, as he was right there, to explain what it meant to obtain permission to travel abroad.

It was lucky that I didn't go. If I'd gone and seen Meilland's trial gardens, as he called them, which extended over about a hundred hectares, perhaps there on the spot—what can I say?—my heart would have stopped. I'd have had a cardiac arrest. Or perhaps a stroke. Because impetuous people like me are always at risk of stroke, and are left half-crippled. The trouble, of course, is envy. That's my greatest problem. Once I start envying anybody, I can't breathe. I can't think straight. There's only one thought in my head, and that's envy. Sometimes it takes days for me to get over it. If I'd seen Meilland's garden, I'd never again have set foot in my own!

It was fortunate that I didn't see it. Fortunate.

That afternoon I was given another man by the embassy, a Frenchman, who would show me round the entire exhibition. It was no good my saying that I'd prefer to go by myself, I'd seen roses before, I could tell them from orchids. This Frenchman thought I was a tourist, and that all roses were the same to me. There was a separate pavilion for miniature roses, he said. I told him that I wasn't interested in miniatures! They're the future, said he, for little gardens, balconies, there's not much room in big cities. I wasn't interested, I looked down on miniature roses. But the interpreter didn't interpret that.

He'd like to show me the remontants, the ramblers. It turned out that standard roses were back in fashion! How come, I asked. He didn't know. Of course he didn't know, he knew nothing. He was paid to be a chatterbox. And in particular, who would have thought that standard roses were fashionable? Those had been doomed when big skirts went out. The roses of the bourgeoisie, weren't they? They'd been developed a century or two previously for the benefit of ladies who, because their voluminous skirts got in the way, couldn't bend down to admire roses. That was another world, people didn't understand.

Finally he guided me into a vast hall. Tables everywhere, knick-knacks in showcases, lots of dazzling things, all decorated with roses. Cups, plates, and scarves for ladies, bags, little jars of face cream and masses of perfume. We spent ten minutes there and the Frenchman showed me this and that, shoved them under my nose like a salesman. By that time my stomach was churning at the many painted roses. I turned away and went out. When roses become pieces of merchandise like that, things that one can buy and take home, they have no value.

As I was coming out I saw a big table on which there were an amazing number of books. Oh, I said, I want to look at these. Not books for experts, rather biggish illustrated books for the general public. I couldn't understand any of them, they were all in French and a few in English. So I picked up one, and my heart missed a beat. It was about antique roses that no longer existed. Pictures of them all on every page, painted by a famous artist before photography was invented. A camera can't give the effect that a painting can. Because, of course, a photograph is one thing, but what a painter makes is something else. Redouté was his name, he'd been in the service of some king or emperor in the château of Malmaison. But nowadays nobody paints flowers, do they? I asked the interpreter if he knew how much this cost. I took out the notebook that I always had on me and worked it out. I divided and multiplied, and asked him if I got it right. I'd made it more than one thousand five hundred lei. He checked my figures. Before travelling I'd been given that amount as a bonus by Mogyorós. Out of it I'd pay for the boy for a year. Was I now to buy this book? I didn't. I hadn't the heart. I thought about it for another day, then put it out of my mind.

But I couldn't stop thinking about Malmaison. I saw that one could purchase a day trip there to look at the rose garden. The price was astronomical. And there was a fine Bourbon rose of the same name, wasn't there? The name Malmaison didn't sound too good in Romanian because, Lali told me, there's a prison of some sort in Bucharest called that. I asked Mrs M. what it might mean. Bad house, said she. The correct name for the pretty, pale pink, full rose is Souvenir de la Malmaison. In Romania, of all places, nobody would want a souvenir like that! Especially at that time, when so many people were being locked up, because after the events in Hungary, the authorities were so afraid, scared rigid. Everybody was dangerous. Even Annush's sister. I'd have to find out what had happened to her when I got home. Perhaps she'd be out by then, and it had only been a mistake. All the same, mistakes like that weren't often made.

There was to be another dinner on the final day. The invitation even included details of the menu to be served. So everybody in the delegation read the menu. First of all there would be speeches in the big hall, followed by what Mrs M. called a 'sit-down' dinner. I said that I was used to sitting down, but not to dinners. On that occasion I dug my heels in—I wasn't going to that dinner even if they ate me. Every day I'd been clinking glasses, bowing and scraping, smiling, and I'd even talked to this person and that, and to a journalist—he'd done most of the talking while I didn't say much because the interpreter did it all for me—about the couple of competition roses that I'd brought. So I didn't have to go, I said, I'd had enough, *gata*. Once we were closed I was going for a walk. I'd like to see something of the city as well, because I'd seen my hotel room, and from the embassy car I'd seen the big hall in the suburbs where the competition was held, but nothing more of Paris. The rest of the delegation hardly came there, they all preferred to excuse themselves, wanted to see things, ran about here and there, went shopping, to museums, to the district where there were nightclubs. Let them go then! None of them was interested in the fact that I was in the Universal

Rose Selection. That day I was determined not to go. To eat raw meat again in the evening? 'You can't not go,' the embassy man told me, that Gheorghe, 'because His Excellency Constantin Nicuta will be there as well, and others from the embassy, such as Comrade Caraman.'

I said to him, 'Do you know how many days I was on the journey?'

'How many?'

'If you please, including loading the carriage, seven. Seven days during which I've hardly slept. Now that the exhibition's ending, I'm going to catch up on sleep. Tomorrow I'm going to take a look at the city, and that will be that, I'm going home.' I didn't tell him, but for four days I hadn't been to the lavatory, I'd been so constipated because of my nerves.

'You can't not go. Comrade Décsi must be there this evening.'

'I'm not going, and that's that. The comrade isn't going to fight with me? Take me there by force?'

Before leaving Romania I'd had to sign an undertaking not to talk or meet with any emigré Romanians in Paris. Signing caused me no anxiety, I didn't know a single one. I didn't mean to meet any emigré Romanians, but there were presumably scientists, artists, writers, all sorts of people. And I did want to meet French and German rose growers, and I asked permission. I said their names and put them in writing. I described each of them to the best of my ability, and the family lines which they or their sons were continuing, Meilland, Tantau, Kordes, and the Dane, Poulsen, if he was still alive. Hungarians too, if they presented themselves, and growers from other people's democratic countries, but, of course, they didn't come. Briefly, rose growers.

'Will that be all right?'

'Yes,' they said in the Securitate, 'You may contact rose growers.'

'I also want to get to know international trends. The global situation with regard to rose growing, fashions, developments. Sites, as trial gardens are called these days.'

And did it turn out like that? Did it hell, I was dragged around here and there, had to go to the Bulgarian embassy and the delegation dinner. And when did I get a free day, to see something of the city? And was I taken to a site, to meet growers or see roses in commercial production? A lot they cared!

My precious Gheorghe told me that I had to take to the embassy for Customs clearance the numerous free of charge catalogues and brochures that I'd collected—heavy enough to pull my arm off. They were free, I said, I hadn't paid a bani for them. Didn't matter, they had to go through Customs. You can wait for those, Vilmos Décsi, why were you given them? And what free books! The Tantau catalogue had a shiny cover, silk paper between the sheets, and colour printing on all pages. It was a work of art, though the pictures were photographs. I was given Tantau's, but the Kordes album didn't come in the package. I asked Tantau for a 'test kit', a box of new varieties to try out in our climate. These were only given to professionals; well, that's what I was. I told Gheorghe that I'd put in an order, pointed out that it was free. I hadn't had to pay a single dollar. Well, that didn't arrive. Perhaps the German didn't send it, thought that we wouldn't buy his flowers in any case, so why send it? Or maybe our people misdelivered it.

Well, I thought, it's the last day, I'd pull a fast one on that Gheorghe. Closing was at half past five, and there was sure to be quite a to-do once again. I'd be off like a shot an hour earlier. But, of course, I didn't know where I was. It had been cleverly done. I'd been fetched and carried every day but now I'd be on my own. I didn't speak the language so couldn't ask for directions. Never mind, I'd find the road that led into the city. Then, when I'd had enough walking, I'd take a taxi. I'd got the address of the hotel, 12 Rue Rivoli, and my room number. But that Gheorghe was right behind me all the time.

Ah, but I'd thought it out! I put my hat and coat—I'd had that made as well—down in the pavilion, where he would easily see them from his usual place on the end chair. I told him I was going to the toilet and went without them; in fact I was perspiring, as it was warm. They would be brought back for me. I went out, crossing the whole big hall and turning left at the end. Coming towards me was the president, Francis Meilland. He smiled very broadly, so very pleasantly! I was delighted to bump into him. We shook hands, and he gripped my hand much more warmly than he did that of others. He said something, repeated it, and then said '*Bon?*' And '*Guillaume, Guillaume,*' so clearly with his French accent, '*Guillaume, OK? Très important. Ce soir.*' I didn't understand a word, just grinned so that my face hurt. Mrs M. had taught me that I should say *Je ne comprends pas* if I didn't understand. I said that to him, and repeated it. '*Bon,*' said he, '*bon,*' held my arm and took me with him. '*Le pavilion roumain.*' We were going back to the Romanian pavilion, that I understood. Meilland quickly got hold of the interpreter and said something to him, once more smiling broadly. How could I have smiled as broadly as he? Or be as cheerful?

Meilland waited while the interpreter said that I had to be at the festivities that evening. He would expect me at ten to six. He said I was to sit where it said on the invitation. And at the dinner. Meilland was looking at me intently all the time. *Oké? Oké?* Then they exchanged a few more words. Well, if Francis Meilland was asking me to be there, what could I do? *Bon*, I said to him, *bon*, because I'd learnt that that was the right thing to say. *Bine* in Romanian. Then he said that we would meet there. Meilland asked for a stem of Vilmos Décsi, so I selected one of the A4s with my own hand. It was fully open and marvellous. He had to give it in, he said. I handed him the finest; it had been cut six days before, but was still nice and strong, quite fresh. Well, I said to Gheorghe, so here too one obeys, not just at home. He scowled, hadn't seen the joke.

I no longer felt at all sorry for myself. Francis Meilland was calling me, so I had to go.

Gheorghe asked whether I ought to change my shirt. I looked at it, it was clean, not creased, I'd put it on the day before and been careful. A shirt was brought to me. I said I didn't need someone else's. This dinner was going to be another dull one, I wouldn't have a sensible word with anybody. Firstly, I didn't know any language that I could speak. Secondly, what could one say at a dinner? I wasn't at all seated where I might be able to. Mrs M. interpreted quite well, did her best, didn't know the subject but at least made an effort. That arsehole Gheorghe would want to do all the talking.

When the delegations were taken into the big hall I had to sit apart. Gheorghe gesticulated this way and that, explained things, and was as worried as if he'd lost his wedding ring. But I had to sit apart then too, a chair had my name on it. Well, I'd never seen anything like that. I'd seen my name on a rose, but never on a chair. There were three rows of growers and nobody else. Delegations were in separate groups. First there were some musicians and dancers. Then came a gentleman, as I recall, the president of the international rose growers association, a Frenchman, naturally. He spoke beautifully, but I didn't understand a word. Much applause, then more dancing by ladies in frothy pink dresses. That I understood, and very well. Then up onto the platform came Meilland. He needed no introduction, as everybody knew him. He spoke. I would have liked to understand. He was in a dinner jacket and wore a spotted bowtie. He spoke in a dignified manner, without notes, and smiled. He spoke slowly, and the audience was hushed. In his hand he held a splendid Peace. There was such a feeling of shock in the air. What could he have said? If only I'd known. On one occasion I heard him say his name, Francis Meilland, and then he was silent and the hall became dark. The president said something, and everybody stood up. On the wall at the back, a picture was projected. A man in a rose garden, and beneath the words 'Francis Meilland, 1912–1958'. Good Lord! Francis had died. When did he die? I knew nothing about it. But then, who was the president? The arrangement was that Francis was to be president, that had been in the invitation. He must have died in the meantime.

There was a minute's silence.

Then we sat back down.

There was music, a woman in a silvery dress played the cello surrounded by baskets of Papa Meilland. What a creation that was too! If one created something like that, one could die, because after a Papa Meilland, one would be immortal.

The president resumed the platform. He changed his tone, took a deep breath, and the ceremony began. Perhaps he also told a joke, because everybody laughed. At his side there appeared a beautiful woman in a superb evening dress. She was like a water spirit. A basket of flowers was brought, it was uncovered, and forward came more men in dinner jackets.

Then the little orchestra played a flourish. Right, I thought, the competition prizes are to be presented.

It was all very well for me to sit there and not understand a thing. Though I understood the names.

So it all went in sequence. Pictures too were shown at the back, a film. First came ramblers and climbing roses. The winners stood up from their places, Germans and French, and perhaps an Italian. Then miniature roses. The president took a flower or two from the basket on each occasion and said a few words. Then the winners were named. The beautiful woman presented the prizes. Next came the floribundas, and the variety was shown in the film, then the names of the winners. There were three in every category. Kordes junior won with Kordes und Söhne's floribunda Iceberg, a slender rose with big flowers, shading from white to a pale yellow. I'd seen it being displayed in about ten vases and grafted onto tall stems on both sides, and I'd thought at once that it would be a winner. And so Atom Bomb didn't win, which was also from Kordes. They'd entered three flowers actually. Atom Bomb was a large-flowered, medium-red floribunda. I hadn't thought that it would win, I'd seen something of the kind before. But Iceberg was a masterpiece. Kordes came up onto the platform, bowed, and said a few words in perfect French. Then the hybrid teas were shown. A Frenchman came, then a German, and then I heard my name. I could see the Vilmos Décsi in the president's hand. He spoke and spoke. *Cet hybride de*

Roumanie. That I understood. He spoke for some time, and then I heard my name, only pronounced rather strangely. *Guillaume Déksi de Roumanie.* A lady came from the end of the row and beckoned for me to go onto the stage. She took me by the arm and led me like a child. I went like a sleepwalker. The president shook my hand, smiled broadly, embraced me and said something; the beautiful woman handed me the certificate and a statuette. I said to her and to everybody *Merci, merci,* I didn't know what to say, *merci beaucoup.* I wasn't allowed back to the audience but went off the platform into a small room at the side. All the prizewinners were there, each of them congratulated me, some of them embraced me. Then along came a photographer and the press. The president posed with every winner. I wished I knew who he was! I had to display my diploma separately. *Diplôme d'Or.* And my name. Or the name of the rose. And the statuette. How I'd have liked to know what he'd said about the Vilmos Décsi! The president with the flower, me with the flower, separately and together. And then all the winning growers with their flowers.

Then I had to attend the dinner. Gocan was there at once, as excited as if I'd been kidnapped. I was to sit with the ambassador. I couldn't do that, as the organizers took the prizewinners to a separate long table.

But I had to go to the toilet. I could hardly control myself. At last. After five days of constipation and French food, at last. I hadn't dared to eat anything! Now at last I was to have a good meal, because my inside was empty. And I couldn't engage in conversation at all.

So then I had an excellent dinner without saying a word.

I rather looked at the food and thought about it. I didn't want always to be thinking about my diploma. The gold diploma that the Vilmos Décsi had won. Perhaps I'd be able to see who had signed it. A French dinner takes three hours. One course, then another, then a third and a fourth, and I didn't know which was the main course, perhaps that had already gone by, but I just hadn't eaten well. The cheese was brought. I had nobody to talk to. I looked at my plate, fully absorbed in the food. If I'd looked up, I'd have had to talk to somebody at once, but I couldn't. So little was brought of everything. Once some kind of snails were brought. Real cemetery snails, Roman snails—I knew that they were eaten in France, and there was butter with them. Well, they weren't getting me to eat them! So then fortunately some tiny fillets of fish were served. Then there was another sort of meat pâté, everybody mixed it up for themselves, I saw how the others did it. On top of it was a raw egg, and lots of spices, onions, and toast with it. It was really good, the meat was tasty and sweet. Once again there were a number of printed menus on the table, and I slipped one in with my diploma. Mrs M. told me later what I'd been eating. I tried to spell it out, but I didn't know what course we were on. Soup was served at the end. But who wanted soup by that point?

I hadn't taken a good look at the *Diplôme d'Or*, just a hurried glance. I'd seen that it was signed by *Meilland SA*. Who could that be? But it would have been nice to take a proper look at it, to open it out on the table and look and look at it, until my eyes failed! Instead of that I had to behave like a man who was given such a great international distinction every day of the week. A gold diploma. I mustn't rejoice. I mustn't rejoice enough, as I ought, to jump out of my skin.

But for the time being, I ate that French delicacy. Raw meat, well spiced.

I had to go to the toilet again, but I didn't care. Better go to the lavatory twice or thrice a day than be stopped up for five days. To the 'drawing room', because the toilet was simply a drawing room, gilded mirrors, vases, big bowls of rose petals! And there I encountered Mrs M. She flung her arms round my neck, wept with pleasure, kissed me again and again. It's the drink, I thought. But no, she was simply pleased with my success. I said to her, wait here, I needed her to help me speak with a Frenchman. I asked whether she knew who the president was. She'd heard that he was a writer who'd written a book about the Meilland family.

'A writer?' I said. 'He can't be a writer. A writer wouldn't be in that position, they wouldn't know a thing about roses.'

She didn't know. She took my arm and we went into our private room. There I stopped politely behind the president and spoke to him. *'Monsieur, un moment.'*

He was pleased that at last we were able to talk. We moved into another room, a *separé*. I told Mrs M. to brace herself, because here came a big conversation. She knew her job, she replied. I said to the president that I would like to offer my condolences. I hadn't heard that Francis Meilland had died. The creator of Peace. Yes, he said, he'd died in the early summer.

'But Meilland International SA goes on,' he added.

And he should know, I told him, that Peace had no greater admirer on earth than myself. *'Peace,'* said Mrs M., then in French too, something like *pé*. She repeated, *'Pé.'*

'Ah, oui, oui, Gloria Dei!' the president interjected. It had saved the Meilland family's lives. He would send me a book describing how that happened. A whole book had been written about a flower? I was surprised but said nothing. An Englishwoman had written a novel. Why a woman, particularly, I wondered.

He would help me to patent my flower, he said. He dealt with all Meilland International SA's agency work. One couldn't manage without an agent, one wouldn't be successful. Those days everybody talked only to agents. I should leave it to him. Act quickly, things got stolen. Capitalism was dreadfully corrupt, he said. He wasn't a capitalist but a Communist, like us, and only believed in common ownership. A bud was taken from a stem, stolen, cultivated, rechristened and sold as the thief's own under another name.

'Don't you know what capitalism is? You must buy a patent quickly, and then sell in America. *Comprendre*?' He kept asking that at the end of a statement. Had I understood? He only recommended America. Honest business was done there. Star Roses would produce a million stocks of a *Diplôme d'Or* rose for me in the first year. In five years that would go up to fifteen or twenty, in the third year I would see, all of Europe would be after it.

I told him that I myself was not going to trade. But I knew how to take an alien bud and graft it. I didn't tell him that I too did that. Stole things. Just that I wasn't permitted to trade myself.

'Yes, I know,' he said, 'here things are different. Guillaume, you don't mind my calling you *tu*? But you people want international success, don't you? Surely people don't create roses to keep quiet about them, do they? To say nothing?'

I'd understood, I told him, I'd talk to the Centre and write to him. Might he patent it before then, he asked. Well, I didn't know, I wasn't free to do anything international without the Centre.

'*Quel centre?*' he asked. What centre? I said a ministry, a central committee. The ministry deals with roses? Wonderful! said he enthusiastically. Here in France no flower interests a minister, no chance!

Perhaps he misunderstood. They didn't so much deal with things as license our activity and connections with abroad. The Station's link with the Station de la Revère du Plant. That I'd learnt. Yes, he nodded, I should talk to the ministry. I should sent him the request, commission, official letter, so that he could institute world patent proceedings on my behalf. He would patent my name! Was that in order? We shook hands.

He trusted me, he would send plants for testing. You people won't steal anything. I would report in writing.

So that agent slapped me on the back and talked the hind leg off a donkey. He embraced me as a man never had in my life. He looked me in the eye and called me *mon ami*. I didn't think he was a queer or anything. Though you do see things in Paris that you don't see elsewhere.

'See you next year, Vilmos, do you hear?'—he made my name into Guillaume—'Bring what you're working on. Never mind if it doesn't prove suitable for commercial production. But show something new. You must always be here. Winning isn't what matters, it's being here, being with us. *Comprendre?* Together. *Fraternité de la rose.* Let's stick together.'

I'd got the message. A final embrace and I left. For ever. I'm with you, brother. *Mon frère*. Because that's what he called me. Mrs M. translated it: brother.

The next day, lunch at the embassy, I had hardly three hours to see something of that famous city. And I had two escorts. Gocan and a new man from the embassy who'd just come out. I told them to show me what I ought to see. A big straight avenue, then the famous iron tower, I didn't go up it, there wasn't time, they rushed me along. Then the Arc de Triomphe, like that in Bucharest. Exactly the same, only bigger. Then in the evening a stroll on the Champs Elysées. Well, there they kept looking in the shop windows, there was no more need to hurry. Everything was dazzling, there was terribly bright light, and extravagance. And the women, the women. It's a good thing I don't have to live there. I wouldn't be able to talk to a woman in Paris. Not because she'd be French, but they're all such great ladies. Their lovely, slender, stockinged legs rise like reed stems from beautiful shoes. But that I might stop and speak to one . . . Women there are a different breed. Not my type. Then all of a sudden I caught sight of a florist's. I said to Gocan, look here, I must go in.

Well, in the end they stayed outside. Inside, the shop was as big as a ballroom, and every big vase was illuminated. There were some so big that they stood, tall and slender, on the ground, and smaller ones were on a variety of shelves. There were twenty, thirty, fifty stems in a vase. There were roses and other flowers, tulips, carnations, delphiniums, daisies. More than twenty sorts of roses. There were readymade bunches, bouquets, table decorations, stove decorations! Because there was an enormous stove with bunches tied on at both sides. I just strolled among the rows, but I didn't mean to buy anything there. When the shopkeeper couldn't see me, I bent and sniffed. There wasn't much scent, but there are flowers with big, full blooms that have a strong scent. Gocan came in, wanting us to move on. I said, I haven't finished.

'Don't buy anything in here, Comrade Décsi,' said Gocan. 'This is the most expensive shop.'

To hell with you, Gocan.

In came a man, found fault with everything, nothing pleased him, and then he bought about twenty pistachio-coloured roses. There used to be a Tantau variety like that, but these were stronger and the flowers bigger. They were wrapped up in pale purple silk paper and tied with silk ribbon. A woman ran in, her car waited outside for her. A big bunch was put together for her, almost all the flowers were of different colours. A bunch like a . . . I didn't know what. A still-life. Such things used to be painted ages ago.

I just strolled, there was a feeling of warmth in my chest and tears came to my eyes. I was about to fall over and didn't go another step. Or I'd have collapsed.

I said to Gocan that I was going home, I was worn out. 'You've still got to have dinner,' he said. I told him that I didn't want any. By that time I could scarcely stay on my feet. Outside in the street, there were girls of easy virtue. There was shame in them, they approached me as if they were selling flowers. I looked at the women, that at least relaxed me. One was flirting with her boy, chasing him. Then as she ran past me I saw what she was. A man dressed as a woman. Disgusting. In Romania that sort of thing isn't even mentioned in the papers. A lot is written about the imperialist countries, but who would believe it? Such a thing happening in the public street. I said to Gocan, let's get away from here.

I'd wanted to do some shopping, he told me. There was nothing at all that I wanted. Just to die. We went into a shop and I bought some bread and salami to eat in my room. I couldn't see anything else. Nothing at all. There were twenty kinds of croissants and as many of salami. I just bought one of each. And half a litre of wine. I was hardly able to get up the stairs to my room. I was utterly worn out.

But was it possible? Was there such a florist's in the world as the one you saw? Vilmos Ottó Décsi, how can you want to go on living after this?

That I didn't know. Only a day had gone by since I'd been given the *Diplôme d'Or*, and I was miserable enough to die straight away. The next morning I could hardly get up, I'd been so upset that I'd slept very badly.

I had to be going home the next day, and I hadn't bought a thing. What could I buy there for that Szék woman and the other girl? And for my mother! In the morning Gocan took me to a shop where there were all kinds of kitchen utensils. Such gleaming pots and pans. Neither of them would use them for cooking, they'd hang them on the wall. What was I to buy there? Gocan told me not to buy anything heavy, because I wasn't going by train.

'What do you mean? I'm going by farm cart?'

'By air. Flying to Bucharest.'

'What about my carriage?'

'It'll be returned, we'll see to it.'

'Why should I go to Bucharest when I've got my train, and I can get off in Kolozsvár? I'm not going to fly.'

'There'll be a delegation to welcome you at Bucharest airport tomorrow evening. The great news has been received, they'll be coming out to meet the comrade.'

'What news?'

'You cannot be serious,' he said.

He wanted me to make light of it, I thought. The *Diplôme d'Or*. I understood. In Bucharest it would all begin again. A dinner, speeches, a hotel, the press. Let's go to a shop for toiletries then, I said to him. Help me to get straight. What can I buy for women? So I bought three of everything. Sweets, soaps, creams, sponge bags, little bottles of perfume. Perfume for my mother? It'd do. It was from Paris, so she'd keep it. Then a scarf, a towel, that too Gocan handed to me. A little bottle of liqueur, some chocolate. For Kali? It'd do. For once at least that man was of use to me. I didn't know how to shop in places like that. They were as big as stadia. How could I have found what I wanted in there? And for the boy I bought a bag of toys and something to wear. Roller skates not to go on the ice but on a smooth sur-face. A tin top, a flexible toy that jumped by itself, some coloured plasticine, and a set of garden tools. Kali would go mad with delight.

I didn't tell anybody that I could live without that Paris. Nobody, because there was nobody that would have understood. I didn't want to know, and that was final. I didn't mean the *Diplôme d'or*, but the whole place. What could I do after that? What could I aim for? I didn't mean that nobody would have believed it. One wouldn't have because they'd think me conceited, just showing off. Another wouldn't have understood at all because they'd never seen anything like it. As if there'd ever been a big florist's anywhere, brightly lit up at ten in the evening for you to buy roses with stems as tall as a ten-year-old child, and so many of the latest Meillands and Tantaus that how could I want to go on living?

I had to be on the plane the next day. I wasn't frightened of flying. Only of Paris, that was all. What would happen to me next?

The flight wasn't exactly pleasant, but I made Mrs M. translate for me a prospectus that I'd put in my pocket, hadn't put it into the bundle to go through Customs. Nor had I put in the great mass of name cards that I'd been given. Was I going to correspond with those people? Or exchange things? Would that lead to anything? Of course, they were all in imperialist countries, hardly anybody from the people's democracies. Yugoslavians, but we had nothing to do with them. I'd see, I'd have to talk to Mogyorós and the Centre about the possibility of initiating exchanges and test results.

We were just overflying the Carpathians when I took out the menu and asked Mrs M. what we'd had at the final dinner. It didn't really interest me, but so that I could tell people if I had to say something about Paris. After all, I'd really seen very little of it. More or less nothing.

She began with something stuffed, then some fish, pâtés, spiced buttered snails. 'Yes, I'd noticed those,' I said. Quail soup. Beefsteak. 'Well, I could have eaten a nice steak, but that had been kept in the kitchen.'

'Here it is,' said Mrs M. 'It was horse meat, beefsteak of horse meat.'

'That was never beefsteak,' I said. 'I wish I had seen an actual piece of meat.'

'It wasn't a piece of meat, but minced, spiced minced meat, eaten raw,' said Mrs M. Devil take it, I'd been fed horse meat. But what poor people, that they should serve horse meat. Even during the war I never ate horse meat. Now my stomach really began to churn. With horse meat and flying alike. Then we were descending, and the great Romanian puszta was soon there.

In Bucharest there wasn't just a delegation, everybody had turned out! The Principal Secretary of the Party, Gheorghiu-Dej, Mogyorós, members of the central executive, Lajos Csupor from the MAT representing the Hungarians. Photographers, reporters. I was sweating. And the way the wind of the puszta was blowing from the south I was bound to be ill, in a sweat as I was.

Dej made a speech there at the airport. He had a single rose in his hand, an achievement of the Romanian People's Republic, he said, which the world had acknowledged. Photographs were taken from all angles. When they wanted to take me with the flower I was evasive until I'd put it down. Then I said that until then I hadn't been afraid, but now I was afraid that there'd be a scandal. Even if it wasn't my fault. I wouldn't have the flower in my hand. I told the reporter to come up to Kolozsvár and photograph the flowers where they were grown, not cut like this. Then I'd pose with flowers as much as he wanted. With difficulty we agreed that that was what the paper would say.

Then I asked who at the Station had cut the flowers and brought them to Bucharest. Because, of course, as I was getting off the plane, going down the steps, a band played the national anthem, I could see the delegation and all the members had flowers in their hands. Then the formalities began and there were speeches, so when was I to speak? There just hadn't been a moment for me to bend to the microphone and ask, 'Who the hell had them brought from the Station? There wasn't anybody there that could recognize the Vilmos Décsi.'

When the rose was in Dej's hand and he was speaking, there were at least ninety present. I couldn't send whoever had done this to hell for fear of ruining the occasion.

Was there to be a fuss or not?

Because Francis Meilland's world-famous rose Peace had been sent. Number 3-35-40, everybody was holding one. Absolutely beautiful roses, and not one fully opened and displaying itself.

Otherwise known as Gloria Dei.

Aka Gloria.

Yet a third name, Madame A. Meilland.

All three were the same: Peace. The Glory of God. Glory. A. Meilland was obviously a woman. Then it had been introduced to so many countries. In its creator's eyes, it was just number 3-35-40. If anybody understands mysticism, let them make something of the number. There stood all the comrades, the entire central bureau, people from the Academy, even Csupor from the MAT, with Francis Milland's Peace in their hands.

That was what we were now celebrating, glorifying.

But they were not holding the Vilmos Décsi. The one with the *Diplôme d'Or* or what the hell. There was just no comparison! Peace had a much bigger flower, its stem was stronger and thicker, it was inward-curling, had 40 to 43 petals whereas mine had 32 and they spread outwards.

The whole thing was completely different. It was like mistaking one woman for another.

One was placed in my hand too. Fortunately I didn't have to make a long speech; for one thing I hadn't been expecting to, one wasn't called for, and I hadn't written anything down—I can't speak without notes and I haven't got a speechwriter. I just had to thank my fatherland, the RNK, and the Party for the trust. When I went to the microphone I told someone standing beside me to take my flower and put it to his nose. So then I went up onto the platform without a flower.

So the person who'd cut the wrong flowers in the Station and sent them down to the reception was going to get his backside kicked if I found out who it was.

And who had realized what was being fêted? Nobody. We weren't celebrating the one that had won the *Diplôme d'Or*. Everybody had got onto the bandwagon and glorified it. It was just lucky that it wasn't actually me that was being celebrated. I didn't care for that sort of personality cult. Especially at that time!

But when I first caught sight of the flowers, I was so overcome by rage that I lost my voice, couldn't get my breath, kept choking and was scarcely able to say hello to the comrades. Then I calmed down during the speeches and music. Afterwards there remained only the great regret.

My report ran to forty-five typed pages. I also had it bound, as I made six copies. One I kept at the Station, while the rest went to the Centre. There was a section on how we ought to develop internationally, the contacts that I'd made, and proposals for exporting and reciprocal activity. Another section was on Vilmos Décsi and its international patenting and propagation worldwide. Possibly a new name was needed for the variety; President Meilland himself had said that it had to be brought into commercial production under a different name. He hadn't thought trade conceivable under the name Vilmos Décsi. He was quite outspoken: didn't think it conceivable, and so Mrs M. said.

I would be sorry if I had to take it to America under a different name. I wanted to see my own name, after all. Well, I had enough to say about considering the name by which to introduce it, because after all, Peace too had four names. At least. The thieves too who took buds and cultivated them also traded it under other names, didn't they?

It was a great victory, I was awarded two prizes at home, and had great plans for a million stocks. Then all went quiet. There was silence in late autumn, silence in winter. Silence and wild rumours.

But poor Annush was going mad since her sister had been imprisoned.

Lali too brought wild rumours. I didn't understand Lali at all. Could a man who had no land at all rave like that over a flower? Want twenty or thirty stocks for his own gratification? Lali was a university lecturer, and they were so poverty-stricken. All that time in prison and everything meant that he hadn't been able to get anything. When he was at liberty once more, he asked if I minded him coming to see the flowers, and to see me. I'd said, why should I mind? What was wrong with somebody admiring flowers? Was it wrong for a writer to read his books, for a painter to admire his pictures? In fact, I was honoured. But did I realize, and he lowered his voice, he didn't want to get me into trouble. I didn't mind, just let's keep off politics. Well, we hadn't usually, and I simply couldn't. Lali had even had to tell me off in the summer of 1956, when there had been such high expectations. We'd been sitting with friends, he'd taken me into town for a drink at the Darvas, and there had been some poets and writers from Hungary present. Lali had inquired of them all what was happening to the Petőfi Circle. They had a lot to say and tales to tell, while I just sat there like a sack of potatoes, not knowing a thing. Then when Lali came up to see me again I asked, tell me, what is the Petőfi Circle?

'Honestly, Vili, the way you live is just impossible. You're a serious man, a scientist, you write in the papers, yet you bury your head in the sand. It's ridiculous. You must listen to the radio like everybody else, you can't go on living like a hermit.'

So I too acquired the habit, and from autumn onwards I was listening all the time.

Then Lali came up, by that time he'd been dismissed from the university, had only a sort of little job in some organization, and wanted to note down a few book titles and the like. Then he said that executions had started again, a dozen or so had been executed. Executions? He was seeing spooks, I said, always fearful of being imprisoned again. But he was a great Communist and a very law-abiding man, never opened his mouth. He'd been a social democrat, but I could see that he'd become a staunch Communist. He just hadn't been allowed into the Party, which always remained painful to him. Executions, I said, we'd know for sure if there were any. And he said that a subversive group had petitioned the ENSZ for Transylvania to be separated from Romania. Or made independent, autonomous. I didn't know what he was talking about, it came as a surprise. Firstly, I had to remember what the ENSZ was, it must be an organ of some sort. Ah yes, I'd got it. It was the UNO. That was we usually called it in meetings. UNO. An organization. Well, I couldn't believe such rumours, Lali was exaggerating. Executions, and a plot for the independence or secession of Transylvania!

He also said that there had been ten death sentences passed in public proceedings in Kolozsvár military court. A priest, Szoboszlay by name, had been plotting. How greatly must a priest have offended to warrant execution? I had no time for the clergy, but executing them . . . They'd wanted to break Transylvania away, said Lali, that had been the gist of their petition. The evidence was there. A clergyman wanted Transylvania to secede and wrote to the United Nations? Another three priests had been executed in October, Reformed Church this time.

'Look here, Lali, this sounds like a fairy story.'

'No, no, it really happened.' I didn't want an argument with my friend, he was a very clever man, terribly clever, he's read all the books, and think of the books he might write—if he were allowed to, of course. But he's excessively pessimistic. Forever seeing dramas everywhere. I couldn't imagine that there was any such person in the country that would write a petition like that. They might think about it, people did, but to actually write it? And take it seriously? And a plot to go with it! I really didn't think so. Everybody knew what country this was. Do that sort of thing and you'd only end up on the gallows, not improving things for everybody.

All the same, I had to listen to the radio again. So I thought, Free Europe would at least announce it all. I listened to Romanian and Hungarian radios and neither said a word. I didn't know whether Free Europe Hungarian or Romanian service would deal with our affairs better.

People were crazy to write stuff like that about the secession of Transylvania. So were those in authority as well, if they really had sentenced a priest to death. That was going too far, abuse of power.

I told Lali to come into the greenhouse because the new hybrids were opening, but he didn't care for greenhouses, thought them too artificial. Why? Weren't hybrids artificial? I didn't argue. If you don't like them, Lali my boy, you'll have to wait!

'Do you know which isn't artificial? The wild rose, of course. Can that be compared with a hybrid?'

It seemed that there was rather a cooling-down by then. I heard that Budapest had enacted for travel to be easier and the authorities said that two thousand might go. Meritorious Romanians and Hungarians could be given permission. Tongue in cheek, I asked Mogyorós if I was meritorious. Because I hadn't yet been awarded a prize in the 'Meritorious Artist' category, because there was such a thing, it had been defined by a recent decree, but I, of course, had only a State Prize. 'Where do you want to go, then, Vili?' he asked. 'Go back to Paris or somewhere, to a competition in the West.' I said, 'I'd like to meet the Hungarian rose ambassador, Gergely Márk. I've heard about him, and I'd like to pay him a working visit.' That was different, if it was a working visit he would arrange it for me.

Then again there was some excitement. But not exactly rose-excitement. The university was shut down. Or rather, the amalgamation of the two, Hungarian and Romanian, was scheduled. 'Like when Transylvania and Romania were amalgamated on 1 December,' said Lali.

Everybody began questioning me about the university. Those that dared ask, that is, because even over a beer on Saturday evening, the company was very subdued. Everybody was so cautious, hardly a word was said. It had happened, but how, who'd done it, who'd started it, who'd allowed it, who hadn't spoken against it. On this occasion I hadn't been there, I didn't know. That is to say, from the end of February I'd been present, because I'd had to be, at the whole mass meeting in the University Staff House. I was there, but we did nothing. The mass meeting wasn't for holding conversation and discussion. One could tell from the outset that amalgamation was intended. Although Lali told me that he wasn't there on the first day but in Bucharest, at the meeting of student representatives. The students had acted as if they wanted amalgamation.

My friend Lali, however, was no longer in the university. He hadn't signed in 1956 so he was out and couldn't teach. He was carried round the city like a bloody rag and had to deliver a self-criticism. Everybody called him Bubi rather than Lali. I didn't like such names as Bubi or Kocka because there was no telling whether they meant a man or a woman. I preferred to call him Lali.

But when it was the tenth anniversary of the Bolyai University, what a fuss there was. A kind of album or memorial book was published, there was a conference with the Babeş University, learned sessions, foreign delegations, dinners. Hungarians too came from Budapest, Szeged and Debrecen. All the MAT had been there in 1955. The Hungarian university had opened in 1945. There were great celebrations in May. At the time Lali had asked me to intervene with the State Library because my books were there and he, as one with a prison record, was not allowed to go. He proposed that if the university was named after János Bolyai because he was a local mathematician, and belonged to us and to Kolozsvár, his book *The Doctrine of Salvation* should be printed for the occasion; what a great thing that would be, and would I try to speak to someone in authority on the subject. I'd told him to leave it with me, I'd see what I could do. But, I said, the title wasn't suitable, let's give it another title, if we put it forward like this it wouldn't be accepted. This entirely churchy work wouldn't be wanted at that time, because it alluded to religious salvation. Lali was, I think, a bit religious, not in the sense that he went to church, but he believed in some great super-terrestrial beings. But he kept it to himself. Lali said that he wasn't religious and wouldn't even commend it, but Bolyai had just written simple things such as made one happy and brought salvation on earth, or rather public happiness. Public happiness, because that was what he strove for, as did the current regime. Because we too happened to be living in an age of public happiness, in Lali's opinion.

'Let's publish it!' I said.

'The only happy man,' said Lali, 'is one that lives in a happy society, and becomes keen. I imagine,' he said, 'that the people around Bolyai had no names, and no passions either!' 'Well, I like that,' said I. Names were always the hot-bed of personality cults. 'In Bolyai, there are numbers instead of people's names.' 'Marvellous,' I replied, 'we must publish it!' And didn't roses have numbers?! My rose Annushka only had numbers. It was number 3-35-40. Was that because it was the biggest in the world?

'So tell me, Lali, what's in this book?'

'That there should not be love,' he replied. 'That's good,' I said. 'But is procreation still possible?' I asked. 'Sexual life has to be regulated,' said Lali, 'that's what Bolyai says.' 'Can it be regulated?' I asked. It interested me as a biologist too. I was always trying to tie a knot in it, as Kali said, but I really couldn't regulate it. Lali had a wife, and he was a quiet type, not such a lecher as others. Lali said that Bolyai's ideal was a man in ancient times who'd castrated himself. Then this János Bolyai too had wanted to castrate himself, because it hindered him in his work, in creation. Bolyai had a powerful intellect, we still didn't know how great. Bolyai wrote that he couldn't find a surgeon that would operate on him, and he daren't do it himself because he was afraid of bleeding to death. And if he'd bled to death, *The Doctrine* couldn't have spread in the world. *The Doctrine*.

'In that case,' I said, 'it ought rather not to be published. It's foolishness.' But I liked that asexual property. Hybrids are asexual.

Lali continued to explain: 'That's philosophy. There's no need to fully understand it, in order to practise it.' He said that, on the other hand, because he was describing his own life in the book, he'd had a Wallachian wet-nurse, a Romanian woman, who was his father's lover—his father was Farkas Bolyai—and she'd suckled him in his infancy. He imbibed amorous passion with the milk from the Wallachian woman.

'Not with the milk exactly,' I replied. 'As a biologist, even I know that much. That's the sort of thing you learn.'

Lali told me that our mathematician János frequently abstained throughout his life, so as to be able to advance in his science, but then sank more deeply into desire because of his great abstinence. He did abominable things, was constantly in heat, and then overcome with remorse. According to Lali, such was the purpose of married life—the sexual element in it was neither much nor little, just right. He winked. He wondered why I'd never married. Because, of course, there is no living organism in the animal or plant world that has no sexual urge.

I liked philosophers, liked them a lot, but unfortunately they knew nothing about nature. They talk of generalities.

'As you say, Lali, my boy. But rose hybrids are asexual. They can't propagate themselves. Hybrids are often asexual. They're near crosses, if you know the term.'

I explained, as he didn't understand.

Never mind, neither could I understand *The Doctrine of Salvation*.

A couple of pages from it had been typed out. The entire manuscript was in Marosvásárhely. The writing was difficult, typical of a philosopher, and I had no patience with it, but when Lali talked about it, it was interesting. That's how I've always been with philosophy. Lali said that the title couldn't be *The Doctrine of Salvation*, it should be just *Doctrine*, but let it come into the light.

According to Bolyai's *Doctrine,* money doesn't exist, only barter, and everybody who is healthy must spend two hours a day tilling the soil. Then they'll be happy. Lali read aloud nicely: It is stipulated without reservation that such as are not confined to their beds by illness shall spend a minimum of two hours daily working on the soil, in the open air and among Nature, since the life force which breathes from freshly turned soil and pours into the nerves neither chemist nor way of life provides.'

'Nicely put, don't you think, Vilmos? Man is to spend his time "working on the soil". Working on earth! Perhaps he can also work on heaven?'

Well, in that he was quite right, Man should spend his time 'tilling the soil' and working. 'At such times I too am happy,' I replied. Though just then I was having to attend meetings all the time, and wasn't allowed to get on with my work on the land. My hands were too clean as well, which didn't look good for me. That was what my Annush told me, 'Your hands are too clean, Vili.' We weren't suited to one another. But we'd come from the same place. Weren't in harmony yet.

I'd had no success at all in publishing *The Doctrine of Salvation*. I'd made a bit of an effort, submitted a few pages, and been told viva voce that this wasn't the time for the society of the day to be blessed with such theories. The doctrine of salvation was right there, and we were the ones to put it into effect. We didn't succeed in publishing it, indeed, nor had I been all that enthusiastic about it. Its time would come. If the manuscript had been lying there for a hundred years it could be patient a little longer.

And so *The Doctrine of Salvation* was not required just then. Nor was Bolyai. Bolyai was finished, as was the Hungarian university. *Gata*

Well, at that general meeting in the University Staff House in February, when the whole thing began, there was so much to be anxious about. At the meeting one man spoke—Szabédi, the Hungarian poet and university lecturer who'd been recommended to me for the Naming Committee—and raised an objection. The other speaker overruled him on behalf of the Party. This was the new secretary, Nicu Ceaușescu, and he put him down in such a fashion that I was quite alarmed. So then there was a bit more conversation. But by conversation I don't mean the sort in which I speak, you consider what I say, then you speak, and then we try to get the best for both of us. This was the sort of conversation in which they spoke and you kept quiet.

As they usually did in a synthesis. If you can find something to say you're overruled.

But that could have been seen coming, anyway. Not that I meant to be a prophet, but everything was then only the MAT, the Autonomous Territory. Kolozsvár meant nothing. All that mattered was the Magyar Autonomous Territory, nothing else. Everything had been removed bit by bit to Marosvásárhely, the medical school, the actors. I'm really not a psychic and didn't understand politics, but even I could see that the Hungarian university as such wasn't wanted. It didn't matter that it had been proclaimed in 1949 or thereabouts, just after the war, when Transylvania was still Hungarian. All sorts of things had been proclaimed. But I'd seen that when the Agronomia, the Agricultural Academy, had almost been shut down, there'd been a scare and it had stayed open, the Psychology, Philosophy and Engineering faculties had all been closed too. This time the university had been closed, but this time there was no scare. It hadn't actually been closed down, but there was an amalgamation.

So there.

An amalgamation.

'Aren't we amalgamating a bit too much of our own accord?' asked Lali. He was familiar with conclusions. Dramatic conclusions, as he called them, because of the theatre, as that was all he ever thought of.

'Endgame,' said Lali.

Because the university was being checkmated.

The whole thing had so innocent an appearance and was so smoothly organized. When one was in the middle of it one couldn't see, couldn't understand, wasn't even afraid. Then afterwards, when it was over, one kept thinking that it was over, so it must have happened. By then, of course, there were dead bodies too. Not just the university, but men as well. As Lali said— he was a great chess player—checkmate in five moves. Six months later, of course, I could see that the amalgamation of the university had proceeded in five stages, but in February I didn't seriously think that it could happen. That was when we ought to have been clever, when events were stirring and we might still have been able to intervene, but not afterwards.

First of all there'd been the meeting of student delegates in Bucharest. At which our students had declared that they wanted union. Harmless talk, and when it appeared in the paper, nobody took any notice. It was STAS talk, we were always hearing that sort of thing. Who wouldn't have wanted union at all times?

Second came the university student assembly, but I couldn't understand why so many top men were there, because even Dej was present, together with the whole Central Committee, Iliescu (the president of the students' union), Ceaușescu, everybody. It was said that there was grave danger of nationalism in the university ranks. If nationalism was mentioned, it was always Hungarian nationalism, because Romanian nationalism was never discussed. Purity of the principles of education was demanded. So that, I thought when I heard it, was just the usual talk, a dressing down would follow, and in the end somebody would be made to suffer and put out in the cold. Then that person would deliver a self-criticism, be forgiven to some extent, and reinstated at lower level.

Then came the congress and the declarations, so that was the third stage, in which the ex-rector, Pista Nagy, Edgár and Szabédi delivered self-criticisms, but everything was organized, I could see, the debate was already rigged, not just beginning as in an active meeting. After the self-criticisms, I thought that it was settled.

After that came the celebratory part, which was the fourth stage. Telegrams of loyalty appeared in the papers, and everybody that had a name had to sign. The most important people frequently made speeches—Dej, Ceaușescu, Iliescu, and the Hungarian university people, the rector and leading intelligentsia. What they said established a pattern, principally that it was only an administrative matter. Ceaușescu actually said plainly that Romanian and Hungarian cultures were no different, but there was only socialist culture, socialist or bourgeois. I sat through all the speeches, what could I have done?

Then came the fifth stage. A joint dinner was held, Romanian and Hungarian students together, and there were guests. The intention was to bring everybody together, I couldn't go and excused myself, I'd been to quite enough dinners.

When next we met, Lali said, 'I don't like final dinners. No good has ever come of a dinner being final.'

At the end everybody delivered self-criticisms, acts of confession before the assembled company. May fate spare me from that. That could have been the sixth stage, we were completely checkmated, everything was settled, but it wasn't yet obvious. One speaker said that he'd erroneously served isolation, a second that he'd strayed on the path of nationalism, a third that he'd been a separatist. Each of them had his word for something of the kind. I thought there'd been discussion in advance of what they would say, helped by authority, as that was usual.

While there were still talks, negotiations, conversations, we couldn't see that things had been settled and how. At which stage it should have gone differently. It wasn't we that had done it, we only confirmed it *post factum* in the celebrations. We took it as a given that separatism wasn't good, that insulation, doing everything separately from the Romanians, wasn't good, and that nationalism should be nipped in the bud, because that wasn't good either. Period. Amalgamation was achieved.

'The Hungarian university has ceased to be,' said Lali.

It was a huge tragedy. Huge, but that couldn't yet be seen. It required time for that to become visible.

They said it was just an administrative matter. The administration would be unified and everything would just carry on, everybody would be able to study in Hungarian to their heart's content. According to Lali, the Fine Arts Institute, together with Philosophy and Psychology, were all closed. The Medical and Pharmaceutical Departments had been moved to the Romanian branch. I hadn't been aware that the Fine Arts Institute had been closed. Or rather, amalgamated. Lali said that all the Psychology Departments were being closed, that subject was now too bourgeois, but he thought that that was a mistake. The best Romanian brain, an academic psychologist named Mărginenau, who had been educated at the best universities, had been imprisoned in 1949, even before Lali, but he hadn't been released because they were frightened of him. He'd been given twenty-five years! It certainly took some psychological expertise for a man to endure twenty-five years in prison.

The amalgamating really made no difference to Lali, because he wasn't likely to be reappointed to the university. But now he did his utmost, even attended Party meetings with us, delivered his self-criticism, and then was taken around to every town in the MAT and had to repeat it. If he hadn't, he'd have been destroyed. Why had he had to be so obstinate about the business in Hungary? What would have happened if he'd signed in '56 and condemned it? By that time he'd have been lecturing happily at the university, readmitted to the Party, possibly given a better flat, as the one where he lived with his wife and child was so small. And everybody would soon have forgotten. Two years later it would have been forgotten who'd signed and who hadn't. Perhaps he'd even be allowed a trip abroad one day. I certainly didn't talk to him about that because we didn't agree. Not on that subject. We did on roses. Why risk the valuable friendship of the rose? I've always said that one shouldn't struggle, be a hothead. In our situation there's nothing to be achieved except a standard compromise. Or everybody should just up and commit suicide.

On that point too we always differed.

Then in the months of April and May, lo and behold, three did commit suicide.

First was Szabédi, the poet, man of letters and linguist. He'd supposedly done it because his book hadn't been published. But he'd spoken his mind in the congress! There was a tremendous fuss which even reached Bucharest, because he'd thrown himself under a train because of the university, not at all because of his book—that was only some linguistic point about the origin of Hungarian and its relation to Turkish. I don't think people commit suicide over stuff like that. Because of the university, that was plain. Then there were two more lecturers from the university, one a statistician and the other Jewish, an economist by the name of Löwinger. Löwinger Molnár. I heard that his parents had been deported and had not returned. Their son had now taken his own life just two days after Szabédi. 'I imagine,' said Lali, that Szabédi wasn't allowed a Church funeral because they were afraid.' The clergy came—actually he was a Unitarian—and stood there mute in their robes, several of them in the gowns or cloaks that they wear. Clergy standing in silence at a funeral! Not a prayer, not a hymn, not a committal. They weren't even allowed to perform funeral rites. 'It was quite something for clergy to come to a suicide's grave,' said Lali. Would the Church have permitted a priest to speak? Was the Church that brave in those days? Lali didn't know who ordered all those clergy to remain silent. Either the Church, or, of course—we know who, or perhaps both! Lali thought the Churches were weak. With the exception of the Catholic, the rest were feeble.

'I could be suicidal every day,' I said. 'Well, not every day, but a couple of times a year. When the roses are opening and in November, when the flowering is over. Not when they're opening exactly, but when there's a month to go and I can see that it's not what I was after or imagined, and I'm disappointed. When the first couple of flowers of the new development are finished. And I can see that I haven't got the real thing that I've always dreamed of. You know, a bit like the Annushka. Then I could certainly string myself up.'

'Vili, you're heartless. Here am I telling you about a tragedy, and you just shrug and say that you could easily kill yourself. You and your roses. You're a cold, egotistic man. All you care about is flowers, the things you've made.'

Nobody had ever said such a thing to me. That I was always thinking only of myself. So who was I to be concerned with? We had a bit of a row and he went off in a huff. He'd come to look at the early flowers, as they were in the hothouse by then. The first suicide was in mid-April. Did he think that I felt no pain? I did, but it didn't show! And I couldn't take him to see the early openings because they weren't at the Station but at home. At the Station I'd told him that I wasn't going to talk university business or anything else.

It was no good my telling Lali that when I was searching for a new rose it was just like the university. I didn't say the name of the rose that I was after, because they had only numbers, and I had about ten numbers before I hit upon Annushka. Ten numbers or more, as many as I'd selected from siblings. I searched and experimented, and only had to name the final rose. It was like that at the university. A compromise. The only thing we could do was make a deal. We had to strike a bargain with the life we lived, just as with flowers. Anybody that was fanatical, didn't reach agreement, came to a bad end. We did the best we could, but how great a compromise was that best.

Lali didn't understand. I didn't want to talk about suicide so much. But I could have.

The vice-rector Zoltán Csendes and his wife had both committed suicide. He'd been younger than me and I hadn't known him very well, only his wife, who had been a regular customer of mine. He'd been made to draw up the deed of amalgamation between the two universities because he had perfect Romanian and had worked in some institute in Bucharest. Lali said that he'd had to take the filthy job on as nobody else would do it. There was blood on his hands, said Lali. But that his wife should commit suicide as well! What wrong had she done? I wouldn't have thought that a woman would do such a thing. It was said that when it turned out that the whole ceremony of signing and amalgamation was made his responsibility, she criticized him severely, argued with him and called him a traitor. Because she was like that, argumentative. Then a couple of days after her husband had killed himself she did the same. 'How did they commit suicide?' I asked Lali.

Csendes had been at the valedictory speech to the other poet, where there'd been hundreds of people. Perhaps that was where he got the idea from.

On 18 April, the same day that Szabédi committed suicide, I'd been at the name-day party of a Romanian woman. Andrea worked in the Botanical Garden as a chemist, and staff were there from both universities. Somebody told me there, because by evening the news had got around. But I didn't go to the funeral. I don't like funerals, I've got enough trouble. Then Csendes followed his example. He'd had to do it as the man who'd put his name to such a thing. That young professor had gone about the whole thing in a really scholarly way. He left a letter saying where he'd obtained the poison, he'd thought it all out. He stated in it that he'd inherited a disease that ran in the family, and therefore . . . Even before the funeral a party activist read the letter aloud publicly to the student body so that it should not be thought that his suicide had been political. Such a thing would have had to be formally censured. So that the student body should know. Vice-rector Csendes had developed a deadly disease and hadn't wished to be a burden on his family. When the letter was read out, the bit about where he'd obtained the poison etc. was omitted. In case the students got the idea, of course. It was read out and silence fell. What were the students to say to that? Silence fell, there wasn't a sound.

The same was done in the case of Szabédi too. It was said that he'd thrown himself under the train at Szamosfalva because his book hadn't been published, and the letter in which it was rejected was read publicly too; it said that the book on the ancient history of the Hungarian language was not sufficiently scientific. Did the students believe that he'd done it because of the book? I didn't know.

Then it was Csendes's turn. Then the third, Lajos Nagy, also a vice-rector. It was alleged that the two of them had petitioned in writing for the amalgamation.

Why did that have to be read to the student body? Examples are infectious. This time, that of being suicidal. The idea that if you were in difficulties you just ended it all. What did I know, there were so many ways of doing it. Csendes had taken poison, the second went under a train, the third, I don't know, may have hanged himself.

And on top of that, the young Jew Löwinger, the economist. That made four.

They were all men. Now, do you see, the university was the poorer by four great brains. Was that called for? But it wasn't the university's fault. It was the whim of higher authority.

But I also heard something to the effect that the female student Magda or Márta (I forget which), who had been the first to bring up amalgamation as a student proposal at the delegate conference in Bucharest, had afterwards been reported as having committed suicide. She was a young woman, twenty or twenty-two perhaps. That was terrible. Perhaps it was just a bad dream. The others had at least achieved something, books or marriage or a professorship. I too, for example. They'd made their names and taught the world something. If I too were to do something of the sort, suicide for instance— what would I have accomplished? A whole book could be written about my results and all my experiments. Even if they were only experiments—many of my hybrids came to nothing—and even if I died (of natural causes, not by suicide), it might be that others would carry on my work, and that too is a result.

And that girl? That Magda or Márta let herself down. As a student she'd shown great promise, and then been a failure. Perhaps it wasn't true. I rather hoped that she hadn't killed herself. There was so much gossip about at the time. Everybody was going mad and malicious rumours were circulating.

Since amalgamation took place, there's been a meeting every month for us to consolidate feeling. In June I walked out of a meeting. I said that I'd got a little delegation coming from the south to see me, and ran off to my garden. In fact, the sun was shining beautifully and my Annushka was opening. Or rather, not quite yet, and I had to do some selecting. I wanted to smell it, see it open. It was like watching the birth of a child. Only there was no blood or cries of pain, that I couldn't have stood. But there was a great silence in mid-afternoon, and I sent everybody away. I just watched in solitary silence as my creation opened.

It was Annushka's first year. You can't really see a rose the first time it flowers, you have to give it time. Because, of course, what is weak in the first year may be as strong as an oak two years later. I've known it happen that a specimen has been so weak that I've felt like uprooting it straight away. Then a year has gone by and it's matured, like a young girl. Nothing at all last year, and now she's got a bust. You just stand and feast your eyes. Where were you last year then, eh, girl? Because now its habitus is wonderful. I made a careful selection every summer so as to achieve the ultimate Annushka. I didn't care for the lilac-coloured variety that I'd been testing. It hadn't been successful, even though I'd persisted with it for five years. After all, lilac was only an experimental colour, I'd been after a pure violet. It was like a blue rose. It was weak, sickly, tended one way and another, never quite the real thing. Too bad. I'd got to accept it: the blue rose didn't exist. Neither blue, nor black. Anybody that said they'd achieved it was lying. Meilland, if you please, hadn't even tried! Or maybe he had but kept quiet about it, and he did right. That was prudent. He produced red ones, yellow ones, pinks and whites, that could be done. One summer I'd been thinking of actually writing a scientific article about the blue rose, but I gave up on the second page. Why write about what couldn't be achieved? That's decadence!

I was sure in advance what its name was to be. It had a name but the flower itself didn't yet exist. If a serious rose grower—a Poulsen or a Tantau—were to see such a thing, he'd absolutely despise me! What an amateurish thing to do, giving it a name before seeing the flower itself. But I could see it, there it was before my eyes, every part of it! I could see the foliage, the stem, its strength, the shape of the buds, the sepals around them. I couldn't quite envisage the colour fully. I'd kept thirty-two flowers from what I'd produced, thirty-two of the same generation.

So, Annushka my dear. How was I to reach you? You were for ever slipping from my grasp.

I didn't care at all about the university. It was all over. Then came autumn. How foul! It rained, and would have destroyed everything had it not been for the greenhouses. But the spiritual mud there was in the university! Everybody was so subdued by autumn. I didn't even talk about it. All that interested me was whether or not I was going to a rose competition. At the time it would have been better not to go. I just didn't feel like it. After the peak that I'd reached the previous year there was nowhere to go. I could only have done badly.

The Hungarians too had been so quiet when the amalgamation—or rather abolition—was taking place. But they were always so quiet. That's the kind of people they are.

Then I had to write my autobiography. To be exact, it wasn't I who wrote it. The journalist expressly meant to write a book.

'A book? About a living organism?' I asked.

Couldn't he wait until I was dead? He wanted to know everything, said this journalist type, from the very first beginning. He even wanted to know about my dear mother, who'd brought up her naughty children by herself. I had to bring out the files in which I always put my curriculum vitae. He too asked me for a CV if I had one. Well, who hasn't? Anybody that hasn't got a CV has been a nobody.

Of course I'd got one. When I've written a new one I've always put it on top. So, if you please, I had to count how many I'd written since 1950. There'd always been something that made me do it. I had to write a new CV because of the award, as I'd been given a State Prize after Paris. And before that I'd had to for the benefit of the university and when I'd been admitted to the Party. Then because of the books, when one had gone for scrutiny it had to be stated who'd written it and all about me. So the devil alone knew how many there were. And of course! In 1952, when the Station was opened, I'd had to write a veritable book about myself. The longer one was, the more there was in it that I had to explain. For example, because of Paris, when the world exhibition had been held in 1958. And then a new one for every exhibition. In the old days I'd even written confirmations, duplicate CVs. More recently there were no such verifications, as everything about me was known. And in the beginning, when I'd been grilled by the Securitate, that was the first I did—was that in 1950 or '51? I'd had to tell them how my first sales were to the Dutch, then to the king of Romania and to Horthy. I'd even had to tell them what I knew about 1941, when the National Royal Hungarian Plant Research Department was established. So really, I told them nothing. I was nobody in those days. I'd been a junior firefighter, that's what my work was, of course, and there was no need of any CV at all in those days. By this time I'd got three fair-sized boxes full. And some were actually more than one page.

And I had some CVs in which there wasn't a word about me! Because what mattered wasn't me but the improvement of a variety, the result, what I had created. For example, there was the description of hybrid 11-16-45. I'd forgotten why I wrote that. Perhaps I'd meant to mass-produce it. It had found its way into the box of CVs. Employment, what I'd done, was what mattered. What use was the sort of CV that said where I was born, that my father was a painter and decorator, and where my brother lived? That didn't interest me.

There was nothing in any of them about little Vili. No secret or anything for me to be ashamed of. By the time the paternity process was starting, I thought, I was giving him my name. I'd taken him boating as well, and out down the village. We'd been to Magyarbecs. So I wasn't ashamed of him. But I hadn't had to put that down. Poor Kali didn't appear there either. It always just said that I was single. It even said in the Party report on me that my private life was unregulated.

And I had, if you please, a CV dated 1958. It had been requested and so I complied. It was, of course, for when the delegation came from Hungary. The first big visit by the Hungarians. We that went on the special train to escort them had had to write who we were so that it could be sent to the other side. So that they should know who they'd be talking to. So on that occasion I wrote in my best Romanian and handed it in to the Ministry, where it was approved and translated into Hungarian and passed to the Hungarian mission. The embassy, that is. It covered my career to date and my plans. So that was what I could give the journalist, but, of course, nothing had come of it. Because then I'd meant to highlight what great connections I'd had in the past, and that now I had good connections, post-1949, democratic ones, on a reciprocal basis with rose growers in Hungary. There'd been no to-ing and fro-ing, though there must have been just a little in 1956 when the frontier was open, and then it was soon closed again. So this time I highlighted what I'd previously tried to keep secret. When the delegation came it was so that they should see that I had a flourishing technical connection with the people in Hungary.

Anybody not familiar with my life, who only read those documents, couldn't know that the plans that I'd listed had mostly not come off. I could now hand over those tidy boxes but they didn't constitute a life.

My CVs filled several files. I'd obtained from the stationery department some nice boxes, the front of which pulled down to open, so that I didn't have to open the lid and put things on top of each other. In fact I'd got three such splendid boxes containing the files which held the CVs. Some were handwritten, some typed. And some were photocopies. The journalist told me not to bother, I should just give him everything and he would disentangle the essentials of my life, dates, achievements and all.

Then I thought that it would be a good idea neatly to interweave Peace into the book. After all, I hadn't yet been able to tell anybody about it, there'd been nobody to listen. I'd have told Mrs M., but she wasn't interested. To her, flowers were just something in vases in her sitting room. She hadn't worked on them, didn't even have to put them in water, avoid the thorns. Kali—well, she was a dear wildflower, absolutely a remontant wildflower, a contradiction in terms. She didn't even know what the ENSZ was when I mentioned it. Because, of course, a stem of Peace was placed on everybody's desk at the ENSZ, the UNO, in the congress at the end of the war.

How was I to tell her the enormous history that Peace had written! I hadn't been able to talk to Annush about anything of the sort. She was a very good listener, clever too, she'd have understood, and she had such a feeling for the soil and for flowers. But once I'd begun grafting Annushka from it, I couldn't give myself a rival by telling her 'This is Peace, Gloria Dei,' or all the other names that it had, and that it was the greatest rose in the world! Lali would have understood. It was his kind of story. He'd even have been able to write it up, he had that kind of mind. Only he and I had drifted apart by that time. He'd become distrustful, complained that he hadn't got a real friend. Complained to me, didn't he. So, I thought, even I wasn't that to him. He was always submitting proposals to the Party. I didn't read them but he told me, and was forever pushing, putting ideas forward or making recommendations. But we couldn't even talk about roses any more. Though he hadn't run out of steam. Raw energy. Well, I did acquire that from him. Let the world not forget Peace, then. No chance of writing in the papers about it, naturally. It was an imperialist flower! Even if it had brought peace. But I couldn't swallow poor Francis's name for it—Glory of God, Gloria Dei. Perhaps it hadn't been he that gave it that name, he may have had a Naming Committee like I did. Or the boss had named it. All I could do was to insert the great story of Peace into the book. Or rather, have it inserted, because I wasn't the one writing it.

Before I depart this life and go into the Házsongárd, I must see to it that these fine boxes with all the CVs are well and truly purged. Because if anyone were to find them they wouldn't understand a thing and would string together all sorts of stuff and nonsense, which would be untrue. There was a great problem with all these CVs, of course, that for every one of them there was a copy somewhere. I hadn't written them of my own accord, that's for sure. I hadn't been interested in myself. I wrote them when they were required, when I was made to sit and write, and I sent them in. And the number of places I'd sent them to! They were in the Securitate, the university, a couple in the Station, the Ministry, the Party records, and I had to give at least four copies for checking to publishers and to the papers when they got me to write articles. I'd been quite anatomized!

My father's mother, Granny Mari, used to collect her hair and nail clippings in a pillowcase, because she had the superstition that when she died she would have to come back and gather up what she'd left lying about. Poor Granny Mari, she was one of the old school with all her superstitions. She didn't leave anything, had to pick it all up, or the devil would be on her heels and she'd have no peace until she'd got everything, wouldn't be resurrected and go into eternity. She was always on about such things.

So, I too have got everything scattered about, haven't I, my whole life, my autobiography? I don't mean my roses being scattered about, my Michurin hybrids, but rather the way I've lived.

The person who'd recommended this journalist to me for writing my life said that Sütő was a clever man, a writer and editor, and he knew because he'd worked with him on the MAT newspaper. And he would become a talented writer. His name was István Szabó—or was it József, I can't remember. Anyway, quite an ordinary name. I said, if he was going to be a writer why should he study me, a living organism, he ought rather to be clever and invent something. Sütő's answer was that I ought not to be difficult, I too was well aware that a writer's most important source of inspiration was the truth. Sütő even called me personally, to persuade me over the phone. Well, I didn't intend anything of the sort! So he'd better come round: We talked, and he noted everything down in shorthand so that I couldn't read it. That was the way he worked, said Sütő, writiing everything down word for word. Perhaps he'd do that, then make something up, not show it to me, and print it. Though I didn't think that he'd treat a State Prize holder in such a fashion. It would have to be approved. A good thing too! Things were still checked! Sütő said that the title had already been chosen. That was pretty quick. The man had never before set eyes on me, sat down and talked to me, and the title of the book was there already. *A Life in Flower.* Evidently that was what Sütő proposed.

So that would do for a title. But I was not to be in it, only my achievements. Sütő tried hard to persuade me to agree. The youth needed real-life role models. Real events.

Lives in flower.

At the time he wrote *in flower*, of course, and then—because he was younger, and would survive me—he'd write *faded*. Or *dried up. A Life that dried up*. That was quite right. At the time I was in flower, wasn't I, but then I would depart this life and it would turn out that it had all been a life *that dried up*, not worth a tinker's cuss, not a bani, there was nothing left anywhere, neither in the world of men, nor their memory to show that I'd ever trodden the earth. Meilland would live on. Décsi would cease to be.

I was in flower, but then I would vanish. Yes, but most of all so would the flower. That was what really hurt me. Not Vilmos Ottó Décsi, old man with a moustache. What did he mean, old? I wasn't even fifty. Just a minute! But the hybrid Vilmos Décsi.

I took down the four boxes. I looked in this one and that to see what to give him from them, so that there wouldn't be a lot to explain, because I'd always had to make myself clear. I hadn't written my CV without good reason. I didn't want to give him my plans either, as they hadn't come to fruition. And then all the bits and pieces about my being outstanding, my awards for this and that, what I'd developed and produced. In bad taste. All reports are like that. A report is another CV. As are check submissions. And self-criticism, and the making of plans, the lot. I'd always been putting on the style.

A Life in Flower? Was that to be the title? Just *a* life? I looked at the boxes. So, was that your one? Blessed is he that has had one life.

One life and one death.

If anybody has wanted more lives for himself, as I have, if anybody has multiplied his life like me, what have they really been after? If I name my rose after myself and disseminate other roses which are my work, I shall have many more lives. And many more deaths. The first time, when I die, and another time, when my flower dies and is with me. When the registered Vilmos Décsi is not for sale in a single nursery and has vanished from floristry. When Décsi can no longer be obtained but will still open somewhere in a garden in May, and the amateur will look at it and say, 'A yellow rose.' In fact, the rose will no longer have a name. And anybody who sees it will only say, 'Now, this is a yellow tea rose.' Because, of course, the rose won't be able to say what its name is. It will be silent. Such is life. I've been here, broken my back bending low, and nobody's going to know.

'Is this *A Life in Flower* necessary?' I asked András Sütő, as I had to speak to him on the phone.

'Yes,' he said. 'It is we that shape our lives, no one else. We're in our own hands. You're in flower, Comrade Décsi.'

'Yes,' I replied, and laughed aloud. 'Both you and I are in flower, my boy.' He was scarcely younger than me, but I called him 'my boy'. 'We're in flower.' But it was December 1959, wasn't it? A new decade was about to begin. I was in flower, and Annushka had flowered that autumn. I would do no further selecting. It was perfect. Perfect, and nobody had noticed it. And above all, nobody ever would. Why? Because now it was all up with me. I'd trodden the heights and could rise no higher. All that was needed now was this *A Life in Flower* book. And that it be written. It will be, when one day somebody takes it into their head. If there was ever a big Meilland book, and surely Tantau had one written about him, then let there be one about Vilmos Décsi. Or rather about 'Vilmos Décsi'. Because, either way, I shall be the one to go.

PART III

Annush's Tale

Dear Father, forgive me, I have sinned, and not only in my thoughts, because I haven't been able to control my thoughts or my heart. Forgive me, dear mother, your orphaned daughter. I promise never again to set foot in Vili's garden. Don't judge me, don't punish me, I've got enough trouble as it is. It was precisely on the day of your death that I did it all. Oh, do help me to get back on the right way, you're the only one that can help a girl in love now you're so pure, because you're dead. And of course, because the Virgin Mary died a virgin, we too must likewise be vigilant here on earth, especially we girls. What would you say, dear Mother, that have lain in the cold grave these fourteen years? But since I did that deed, my tears have flowed, but I really don't know whether from happiness or shame, because now I'm experiencing both. Dear Vili, I don't know what to say, perhaps it would be better for you to die soon, and then all would be over between us. Nobody in all the world loves poor Annush, but Vili's always kind to me, as is poor Aunty Mária, Mária Zidaru, who suckled me all those years ago after my mother died. Because poor Mummy had no sooner given birth to me than she abandoned me in this wicked world. Nobody loves Annush, only Vili. And the animals. And there's that stupid little Mihály as well, but he was so simple, even at the dance, and anyway he's too little, hardly comes up to my shoulder. Dear Mummy, enlighten my mind, tell me what to do so that I don't come to a bad end. Can't you say anything now? You're as lonely as I am here. And nobody talks to the dead.

I was so full of grief. But Vilmos told me that he'd wait.

'What will you wait for, Vilmos?'

'For you to grow up, Annushka.'

I told him, 'I'm already grown up. You can see I drive the horse by myself.'

Why did I have to talk like that? That I'm grown up. It was like making up to him. Offering myself.

It was like this, I had an accident with Puju. I'd been lifting the carrots, cos we'd got quite a big piece of land over Békás way, it was all that was left cos all the rest had been taken into the collective farm. Daddy had sent me out and he stayed at the milk collection point. I'd been all day digging and loading. I'd put so much on that narrow cart that the poor little horse could hardly move it. The carrots couldn't stay in the soil any longer cos all the autumn rain would be starting, and I wasn't going out there twice, I said to Puju, and they'd got to be put in the cellar. We put them in sand, in a semicircle, and there they stayed until spring until the new ones were ready. So I'd piled up the cart and set off down with it nice and steady, I wasn't hurrying, going carefully and holding the brake, cos our cart's got a brake, so when we began to pick up speed I said to Puju, 'Whoa, my boy, where are you off to like that? We're not in a hurry,' but he couldn't say anything back, of course.

By then I couldn't see the road all that well as it was getting dark. And then, wallop, one wheel went into the ditch, the cart pulled to the right and collapsed. Luckily I was able to jump off and I let go of the harness, and it broke as the cart turned over, I suppose. The poor horse fell over sideways. All the carrots went into the ditch. I looked to see if the horse was all right, whether he was hurt, and he was trying to get up. So I helped him up, and said, 'Stand up, my boy, let's look at you, are you hurt?'

He stamped a bit, I held him, felt his ribs, checked all four legs, made them bend. No harm done.

'Well, come on,' I said to him, 'I'll have to get on your back and go for somebody, come on, help me. We can't leave the carrots on the ground.'

I stepped onto the shaft to get onto the horse from there. He didn't like it. I didn't know what to do, because of course Puju could pull a cart, but he wasn't a riding horse. I had an idea, put half a dozen carrots in my apron pocket, and then spoke into his ear like I usually did.

'Look here, my boy, now you be a good horse. Here you are,' and I gave him half a carrot. 'So come on, gee up, into town,' and I tapped his ribs.

He just stood there. He could pull, but we didn't usually ride that little horse.

I said to him, 'Look here. Please ever so nicely. If you don't get moving straight away, I'll give you such a kick in the ribs that you'll know all about it,' and I gave him a poke. The way I was sitting on him, his hair was sticking into my backside. It wasn't cold enough yet for me to wear briefs, I can't get used to 'em, they're always too tight. Bloody hell, who'd have thought I'd need to go on horseback that day.

So I got on, took a firm hold with my knees and hung on to his mane so that he'd be aware that the boss was on his back. And I told him to giddy up. But I was nervous. The last time I'd been on a horse was when I was little, I wasn't used to riding.

When he felt the pressure, he eventually set off. Then he could tell what a light load he'd got, and there wasn't a cart, was there, and he started running downhill like the wind. I had to lean forward and put my arms round his neck, or I'd have come off at once, the way he was running. And my headscarf came off. Damn! Never mind, it wasn't a nice one, hadn't been hemmed.

The Békás Wizard's garden was the first place we came to. Vilmos Décsi was called that because he'd got such a great big flower garden, and the Station had been built next to it on the land that had belonged to Hóstát farmers. We'd been very lucky, we hadn't had that much land up there, but ever so many farmers' land had gone to make the Station. Good Hóstát gardeners' land, there used to be about eighty families. Only a little bit of ours had been taken, and I didn't care cos it was a good distance away. The Station was shut, it was night by then and quite dark. I started to shout at the gate but nobody heard, just two nasty Romanian dogs began barking, great big mountain dogs that were kept as watchdogs. I wanted to tie the horse up but there was nothing to do it with, so I had to leave him there, told him to stand still, not to wander off and disgrace me. He's a good horse, a quiet horse, is Puju, but when he gets an idea in his head, you have to watch him.

I ran in, and that big spotted dog came and barked, the one that belonged to Vilmos, and I threw at it to make it go away. The servant came, but she isn't a servant, she's had a child by Vilmos, and we've always taken them vegetables, and I ran inside and said would they come and help. 'What's the matter?' asked the master, and I explained quickly that my cart had overturned, would they come and help me. He said, 'Kali, run and fetch help from the neighbours down below.'

'Come in,' said Vilmos, 'and have a glass of soda water,' as he could see that I was very warm. I went into the kitchen and sat down on a stool. My legs were trembling, I was worn out with the riding, after all, I'm not a countess, to go everywhere on horseback, and I'd had to be careful that I wasn't thrown. He gave me the water.

'Take it easy, girl. You aren't hurt, nor your horse.'

'All the carrots have gone in the ditch,' I said, and I shed a tear. 'I've been unlucky. I worked so hard, and now my cart's crashed.'

'That's only carrots, don't worry, you'll soon pick them up.'

'My father'll find out,' I said.

Then I began to weep. Goodness knows what for, it just came over me. Vilmos came over, sat by me and stroked my head.

'Don't cry, you're only young. Don't cry. We'll pick them up for you.'

He put his arm round me. I just flung my arms round his neck and cried. I was crying for my whole life. He just gave me a hug. He put his mouth against my neck. I didn't try to get away. I just clung to him. I knew that it was wrong. All the same. But then I was sitting on his lap. It was so nice. And he was kissing me. Covered in muck as I was after working all day.

Then a cart was brought up from down the hill and we loaded up the carrots. Vilmos put his arm round my waist, and Puju was tied on behind the cart. I was trembling so all over, I couldn't even think about the carrots. He was such a nice, gentle man. I didn't have far to go, we live just in Borháncs utca. He saw me home. My father was bound to be asleep by that time.

Since then that's how we'd been.

Sometimes he'd know that I was selling in the market and would drop in. The car would bring him down, turn round, and take him back. He'd hurry to my stall, say this miss, that miss, buy a bunch of parsley or some small thing and count out the lei into my hand and give it a tickle. That was really all he'd come for. He'd whisper that he'd come that evening, I was to get the milking done quickly and he'd be there by dusk. I'd whisper back, 'Vilmos, you don't come first with me, I have to see to Csinos.' That was the cow's name.

How nervous I always was when he was coming. I waited for him. And I was so afraid. I was being driven mad. Everybody could see him come in and not leave. He wasn't ashamed of himself, he said.

He asked how I was able to attend to everything by myself—all the garden, the cow, the house and the selling. In autumn he'd bring me a decent tractor from the Station and do the ploughing. But I wouldn't let a machine into the garden. God forbid!

He said he was so young when he was with me. He was full of strength, could do as much as when he was twenty. When he'd been with me, he said, the next day he was always sleepy, but all the same, he could work like a machine. He wrote so much, did so much research, discovered such new things. He was simply bursting with energy. He was the young one. I was just getting older, though I still wasn't even sixteen. But all the work was ageing me.

I hadn't even been able to pick all the tomatoes on the land, there were so many, I didn't know when there'd been such a crop. And lots of them were split, there'd been so much rain, you'd have thought God had meant to destroy the world, only hadn't succeeded. I couldn't get to market and sell everything and do the garden as well, it was more than one person could manage. But there I was, a girl all by myself. I picked out the softer tomatoes and threw them to the chickens as we hadn't got a pig. There hadn't been a pig in the sty since the last one was killed, I hadn't got a new one, some people are good at keeping them, but there's such a lot to do with them that I'd rather not. So we didn't keep a pig, it was too much trouble for us. But it wasn't the case that I threw the tomatoes to the chickens cos I couldn't sell them. If I was out all day at market, I didn't work in the garden, and if I didn't go selling there was nothing I could do with all the vegetables. And it seemed as if God could see the state I was in and kept sending more and more to the garden, and it all grew like mad. So when I looked, the tomatoes were falling on the ground, and those were what I liked most of all, I loved them as if every red fruit was my own child. And they were as big as a little child's head. When was I to cook them, I asked, if I couldn't sell them any more? Cos I'd have been able to store them all right, there were jars that had been my mother's, we'd still kept them, glass jars with airtight tops, in case we ever had anything to store because it would be very good to sell in winter, when there wasn't much. But there was never anything left cos we sold the lot. I'd pick a big bucketful in the evening when there was scarcely light to see by. I'd put the nice firm ones and those that could go to market in a basket, and I could take them two days later, cos if I didn't pick the beans the next day, there'd be nothing left of them. The heavy rain splashed them all with mud, and I had to wash them and see that the water didn't soften them. I had to get the first-crop carrots and celery and store them, the second crop was already too big in the clay soil. If I didn't bring them in, they'd come to nothing. They wouldn't grow in the clay, it was no good for them.

I'd give the chickens two good buckets of tomatoes, one then and keep the other for the next day. Then I saw them eating well, the eggs would have good yolks and people would think they'd been coloured with paprika. In fact, there was one farmer's wife who did feed her chickens paprika to make the yolks yellow. When she sold them she would have one broken in two so that it could be seen what they were like. They were nearly red! I'd never do a thing like that. My mother would rise from the grave and box my ears.

'Now, Annush, is that what I taught you? To deceive people? God strikes people that cheat like that all the time.'

I daren't say anything to Vilmos then. What could I have told him? He could tell how hard I worked. He was always saying when he saw me that I should give it up. How could I? I asked. Did he know that it was the same as having blue eyes? There's nothing to be done about it. You can't change them either. He's certainly got such lovely blue eyes, I've never seen a man look the way he does with them, it'll be the death of me. He can't help it, they'd have to take his eyes out. So I asked him if he'd be able to give up his roses. He said, he already had. So I said, that wasn't what I'd read in the paper.

'What paper do you read, Annush?'

'Well, that's what it said in *Igazság*, one of the Station flowers was going to be in some great international competition.'

But it wasn't he that was doing that, he said, not all by himself, he'd got the whole Station, lots of people.

He said he could get me a job in the shoe factory. I could go to Dermata, or János Herbák, as it's called now, learn a trade, not wear myself out on the land. When I heard him talk such rubbish I laughed out loud like somebody being tickled. He liked it when I laughed. And I said, 'Are you trying to make me laugh, saying a thing like that? That I should go to the Dermata works and make shoes?'

Why didn't I want to have a monthly pay packet? he replied. He could have given me a job in the Station as well, if I preferred, working with trees there. Though he preferred employing men for work on trees, as they had to climb ladders.

'Well,' I said, 'I don't know, why wouldn't I be able to climb a ladder?'

'Women aren't cut out for it,' he replied.

'You should see me loading a cart with manure and taking it out to the land. Perhaps you're saying I don't do it properly?'

Oh, he said, that was just what he liked about me, my arms were so strong, and I was small and not stocky. He didn't put it quite like that, but how nice my arms were with that bit of red hair under my armpits. Oh, was I embarrassed when he was so keen on that red hair. Well, it's not really red, but a kind of light brown, blonde or, well, reddish. When I knew he was coming I would always have a good wash with soap cos he'd always take a sniff there, wouldn't go without it. I had some special soap, not the sort I washed my feet with in a bowl in the evening. I'd bought this other sort for under my arms and my face and other places. It was expensive, perfumed with lavender. And he would kiss my armpits. Oh my God, the way we carried on, he always had to come in secret. And the life that orphaned girl lived, she'd nobody to take care of her, she was out on a branch like a leaf, any wind that wanted would carry her off. Well, I couldn't tell Vilmos not to come, I didn't know how. I always got so worked up when I knew he was coming, not that I always knew he was coming, but oh, when I did know I could hardly catch my breath. Such is nature, there's nothing to be done. That's how man and woman were created, for one another. Nature has no regard for how big one is or how small the other, cos Vilmos is much older than me. He could obviously be my father.

Then he'd come by car as well, and it always waited for him at the corner of Pata utca by Samu Téglás's pub and picked him up. Everybody could see him come through the gate. My poor mother's brother-in-law, who had helped me previously, actually sent word that he wasn't coming to work at such a whore's place. He'd work on the land for somebody that paid him. Only Aunty Mária called, and she's a Romanian, Mária Zidaru, and told me that she'd pray for me. She's a clever woman, it was so nice to be able to talk to her, and I'd learnt Romanian from her since I'd been ever so little, and better than in school. She was always talking about the saints, always knew whose day it was and told me, and then about the miracles that the Romanian saints had performed. There are lots, we've got some as well, but theirs aren't like us Calvninsts' ones but the Catholic Hungarians'.

But Vilmos wasn't paying me, not a lei. Nor was our relationship like that. You have to give a woman money, said he, a wife or the other. Meaning a whore. If I love someone with a pure heart, I don't have to give them money. It was only when I gave him something, like in the old days when I brought up the vegetables, and there wasn't even anybody to cook for him, cos Kali was living in the country with the child, then he asked, 'And how much would this cost in the market, please, my dear Hóstát girl?'

'Well,' I said, 'a kilo of cucumbers, tomatoes,and paprika, ten eggs, wasn't it, a little jar of sour cream, well now, that'll be nineteen lei, please.'

We did business properly. I didn't ask him for more or less than anybody else. He ate it all raw, just like that, with sausage or salami, whatever he got from the shop. He'd even buy a handful of spinach, and so I enquired whether he could cook it. He said he'd eat it raw with bacon. He'd read in an American paper that you could eat spinach raw like lettuce, it was very rich in iron. So I said, was it good for him raw, like for a cow? And he could have got it from the Station, because there were thousands of experimental things there, especially tomatoes and paprika.

He said, 'I've got to have real Hóstát tomatoes and greens.'

'Look, why do you tell me not to do it if only Hóstát stuff is good enough for you?'

'Well, aren't there enough Hóstát people to do it, you little ladybird? You'd be off to the factory for six o'clock, or two o'clock for the afternoon shift, finish work by eight, and take half an hour for lunch in the canteen, there's cooked food there, you wouldn't have to go shopping, you'd come home, take it easy, read the paper, go to the cinema with your girl friends. And you'd get your wages on the tenth of every month. It might not be a fortune but you could depend on it. Then you could go to bed, we'd go to the cinema, or I'd take you for a trip. If you like you could look at the sea with me.'

Oh, I heard so much about the sea. Way back too he was always saying. He'd get a pass and be able to go, cos they were building sanatoria there at the time. I must go one day, he said. And what would I do about the animals? Where can I put them, I asked. He'd send somebody over from the Station cos I hadn't got any relatives that I could ask. I didn't like the idea of somebody else going messing about in my garden. They wouldn't know what to do, where I'd put things, and I wouldn't let anybody else harvest them.

Why should I be the one to work on the soil, he said, when land outside the city limits had all actually been expropriated and inside there were only a couple of pieces left in the Borháncs and the Békás, and the garden, and perhaps we too would join the collective farm with that bit? There was quite enough Hóstát produce there. Well, I said, there wasn't enough at all. There could be more still, cos we could sell what we produced. It was ever so much nicer than *aprozár* stuff, wasn't it, the vegetable collective farm? We were superior. But Vilmos didn't push all that much. He never raised his voice or shouted like a lot of men do all the time. He had rather a cool nature, he gave orders like a father figure. I never even for a moment saw him being as kind to me as that first day when he took me into the kitchen. If he was always so good to me, I couldn't have left him. How could I? When I consider the young lads of my age, they're all so stupid. None of them knows how to be nice. There used to be some, but now I needn't even look, there aren't any. What was I supposed to do if they're so boring? I'd wait for a kind word, but they'd just ask how much land I'd got, how many cows. And they just wouldn't leave me alone once it was dark. Vilmos wasn't like that. Rather he said I should pack it in, go for an easy life.

'I've never seen such a thing,' I'd say, 'as anybody's life being easy. Not even for a big farmer. Because the more land he's got, the more work there is to be done. Makes no difference if he takes on a Szék girl or even two, if he's got a family. They work as well, dawn to dusk. There's no such thing as an easy life. Why, is yours easy, Vilmos?'

And Vilmos said that a farmer's children shouldn't be on the land all the time but should rather be in school. 'That's good,' I said, 'I'd have gone to school as well, but now it's too late, I haven't got the head for it now. And I'm too old now to be admitted, I'm off the floor, I'm nearly sixteen. Where would I go to school now? I've done my six classes. You did seven, I know, you didn't say, but it was in the paper.' It said that in the old days a clever person like him, coming from the common people, hadn't been able to stay in school because of his working-class origins. Now he'd been made a member of the Academy. He was a member, it said in the paper, because the city was proud of him. So how many academicians have we, especially

Hungarians! Of course the city's proud. Seven years of school, and he's risen to the Academy. I did six, and the highest I've been is the stage in a bit of a play. And he's an inventor. I don't compare myself to him, cos all I can do is what a Hóstát girl does on the land, and the highest thing I consider is when and what will go better at market, and to put more of it on the stall. But even that I've got wrong. In spring there was a big demand for salads, and when I took more they weren't required. When the first greens began to appear, which we sold from the greenhouse, they'd been under glass, goodness, were they wanted, people would give their last bani for them. Then in June, when everything was coming up, we could hardly sell them. That's what people are like. They can't wait for the sun to shine so that we can get onto the land. Everything's wanted when there isn't any yet.

Vilmos had got the Station, he didn't have to sell anything, he wasn't dependent on anybody, a free agent. That's why he was always telling me about the factory. The land is fine, but the factory is finer. You get there for 6 a.m. and finish in the afternoon. Who should I ask what to do? My mother. Only she could advise me. So I went to see her, cos she'd put me straight at once.

Just at the time, however, Vilmos was all worked up. He was listening to the radio all the time, there'd been a revolution in Hungary, hadn't there, but then it had been well and truly defeated and the Russians had gone in. But this time he was worked up in case something happened at the Station. He couldn't even come and see me. All he did was listen to the radio.

I went out to see Mummy in the cemetery. Evening was falling, cos I'd been in the market all day, just ran home and had a wash. There were a lot of people. The cemetery's lovely at times like that. It was a feast day, a great festival, and there were lights on the graves, and Hungary had chucked out the Communists and there was freedom. Daddy came home drunk in the afternoon. He couldn't walk straight, so he went and lay down. When I'd finished my work, cos there was a big market that day and I couldn't miss out on it even if it wasn't my day, so out I went. There were so many chrysanthemums, you couldn't move for them. There were a lot of people, everything was bought up, and I sold out of Brussels sprouts. Why those in particular I didn't know, there was no telling beforehand what would sell well. The world had gone completely mad! The city was full of uniformed police.

I went home at three o'clock. I hadn't taken any flowers to the market, we hadn't got many, we weren't flower people. We had just enough to please Mummy. I like chrysanthemums that nice brick colour, not those with big flowers. Rich people are always buying those. They think that big means beautiful. I like tiny little ones. The sort you find in the field. I stick their stems into the grave so that it looks as if they're growing there. Perhaps I might have met Rózika there? Would she have come out? That day was a big festival for them, she was sure to go back to church. Or perhaps she'd have been out early in the morning. I had to go a long way up, we Calvinists have our graves at the top, where the poorer people are. It would have been cheaper in the Monostor cemetery. And Hóstát people are quite often buried in the Kismező. But Daddy wanted us to put her in the Házsongárd. It was nearer to home. He had to sell a bit of land, let three strips go to old Pityu Butyka, and that covered the cost of the funeral. I couldn't remember her, Daddy said, when we talked about her later. I do, either coming and going or working in the garden, but I can't visualize her. I only remember her from photographs. I took her a nice candle. Then as I was leaving the cemetery, I bought a few chestnuts. They were really tasty. We've got no trees. I don't know what tree they're from. Cos there are only wild ones on the Sétatér.

I'd had a bit of a wash and put on my blue-spotted dress and a clean headscarf. I hadn't got a black one to wear there, only my black sweater. I was really perspiring by the time I got there. I said hello to Mummy. I sat down for a bit on the neighbour's grave, cos that's got a stone surround. Ours hasn't, it's just earth. I made the grave nice, tidied it up and all that. Somebody had been already and brought a little pine branch and a flower. I ought to plant it with something so that Mummy can always have flowers. I sat there and went on talking to Mummy. I told her my trouble and she heard me out. The candle was burning and there wasn't any wind, so it burned nicely. I didn't look at the other graves to see who was there, or what they were doing, I'd come to visit Mummy and talk to her. I don't complain about Daddy any longer. She knows. I'd said so much, cried so much for her under the picture in the room. This time too, Daddy was asleep there, fully dressed on his bed. In the morning he'd get up, feel ashamed of himself, say some bad words, perhaps, and hit me, but he'd be doing it to himself for not coming today. He neglects his duty, but I get told off.

'Dear Mummy, why have you left me here? You're lying there in the cold ground, and I've got to live here and work. Nobody at all loves me, only Vili. And my sister. But she's given her heart to God, and she doesn't bother about people any more.

'I'm embarrassed to mention Vili to you, Mummy, I know what you'll think. Annus, why are you getting mixed up with this great man? He's not your type, he won't marry you. What happened to my cousin's neighbour, that clever Alex? Who you always used to play horses with, when you went out to the Brétfü? Well, Mummy, that Alex is possibly married by now. He was with somebody called Évike at the vintage ball. And that classmate of yours who you were always coming home with? Oh, Mummy, they've all vanished now, I don't know what's become of him, perhaps he's gone into the factory. Now there's only that bonehead Mihály, and I haven't got the least liking for him. Always got his nose in the air, when he comes, he's so conceited. He actually took me to the vintage ball, oh dear, he smelled awful. He didn't smell nice, Mummy, that's a fact. I don't mean unwashed, cos he does wash. The way he always goes up the street, he runs in front, can't walk at your side like a couple. I don't want him. I'd rather be like Rózsa, give myself to Christ. But I say that more as a joke, I'm not the sort to go to Christ. We Calvinists don't go in for nuns. Our faith is in the right place, in church on Sunday. The only Catholic saint I like is St Mary. She's got such a lovely face! More like a girl than a married woman, in the big church in the Főtér.'

'That one's not right for you, Annus, that great man, give him up while you still can. Otherwise you'll get caught in the weeds and they'll drag you down to the bottom of the pond and you'll end up like Sári Juhos. And he's well off, he's a great man. Teaches at the university and all.'

I didn't know what to say to that.

'But he really loves me, does Vili, from the heart. And he smells nice, and I'm fond of him, so. Oh, Mummy,' and I began to cry.

I'd like to tell Rózsa about it, but what does that poor girl know about such things? About being in love. She's left the world, knows nothing about human affairs any more. It makes no difference that she's older than me, that she's seen all sorts, she doesn't understand this kind of thing.

Cos once I'd brought out my notebook. The one I'd got to go into the seventh class. Which I then didn't go into. I'd really have liked to. Oh, I did love school! It was my whole life. I wanted to learn, arithmetic and reading. I even learnt a bit of Romanian. But Daddy said I'd done enough, no more school, I was grown up, I'd got to help him, he couldn't keep me. Cos Rózsa had already left home. So, no more school for me. Along came dear Aunty Patócs, the teacher, such a lovely little old lady she was, such a sweet face. They said she'd been a nun in the old days, and in fact she always wore black with little white collars. Then the nuns were stopped. She came and had a long talk with Daddy, talked and talked, but it did no good. So I'd got two notebooks to remind me of that autumn. I'd written everything down in them. All the clever things I'd heard from grown-ups. Words of wisdom, so to speak. Things that were posted up in the classroom in big printed letters, and all that. The way Man had come from monkeys by means of work. That I remembered from the classroom. The victory of the workers and peasants. So, we'd won. Only we weren't workers, nor peasants either. Hóstát people weren't peasants. That made no sense. Peasants lived in the country.

Well, even if that's so we're people twice over cos we work so hard. Like horses.

I'd put Vili down in the notebook. But not just like that in Hungarian. Not just like that, cos I was afraid to. Ages ago Rózsa and I invented a kind of writing. It wasn't actually we that invented it, but we came across it in a book. Hieroglyphics or something. A secret writing that just the two of us knew. Or rather, I don't know whether Rózsa still remembers it, but I do. Why we wrote it, what it meant, I don't know, it was ages ago and we lost the paper. And I can't remember all the symbols that well, cos since Rózsa's been gone I haven't practised and I've forgotten. We wrote each other messages in that notebook when we were unhappy. But now I can't make them out. She said that when she'd gone I was to burn the notebook. There were all sinful things in it. People only wrote down sinful things, she said.

'Why are they sinful?'

'Well, if they weren't sinful, we wouldn't have needed to write in secret.'

Then she asked whether I'd brought the notebook out to burn it. I said yes. But that was a lie.

All the same, I wrote as best I could, and I put Vili down.

Mummy doesn't understand me either now in the way that notebook does. Cos Mummy's died, and she only exists in my heart.

I didn't know whether to wait in the cemetery any longer in case Rózsa came. I'd been there a long time. I said hello to people I knew, all in Hóstát costume as was correct. Then I set off down the hill. Then all of a sudden there was my sister limping up! I was so pleased, my heart gave a leap. Oh, my God, did I give her a hug! Rózsa is very like the picture of Mummy out there. Except that she wears her headscarf differently. She hasn't worn Hóstát dress for ages. She used to, but then she put on the religious habit and then had to take it off, because people dressed as nuns were given a hard time in the street. Being a nun wasn't allowed. After that she hasn't worn anything distinctive, neither town, not Hóstát. nor religious. You can't tell, there's no sign of anything. Her skirt's on the long side, she ties her headscarf down flat, not in a bit of a point as we do. And hers is grey, like a dishcloth. But her face is so dear to me.

We hugged. She'd brought a little flower and laid it on the grave, then knelt and said a prayer. You couldn't see that she was a nun. I waited for her, knelt beside her, and Mummy must've been so happy at her two little girls being there and praying like that. I'd prayed to Mummy enough, this time I was praying for Rózsa.

Dear Mummy, help my poor sister, watch over her in her ways, don't let her have any trouble, because the poor thing's given her heart to God, only she doesn't quite know where to go, cos she too is an orphan, her father used to beat her and her mother died just when she was becoming a girl, and she's got nobody. I'm here for her but I'm the younger, and she can't come and see me at home cos she's left home and can only come when Daddy's out. Dear Mummy, I don't ask anything for myself, nor that you'll look after our cellar, cos it's so soaking wet at Uncle Mikhály's next door that I'm afraid the water's going to get in and ruin what we've stored for winter, everything's really so nice now, all the carrots, and the celery's as big as a baby's head. I'm not asking you for anything, not even to make Puju's eye better, cos nature will take its course, and if not I'll take him to the vet at the slaughterhouse, cos his left eye's weeping badly, it's all white and there's inflammation. But do look after Rózsika, lead her in the right way so that she shan't have trouble, cos she's the sort of girl that's made of such hard wood, I don't know what tree it comes from, it's so hard. Cos if you have to split it the axe will just bounce off. It's like her name. Rosewood, that's very hard, but I don't know, I've only ever seen it in flowers. Dear Vili, don't be cross if I've just thought of Vili when I'm really praying for Rózsa.

Rózsa was saying, '. . . for ever and ever. Amen.'

Cos she was just finishing her prayer. Oh, dear sister, I overheard your prayer too, but of course it was said in secret, I know that nobody else's ear is supposed to listen, only the person's that it's meant for.

Then we said goodbye to Mummy. Rózsa said that anybody that prays every day from today on can win complete remission. What 'complete remission' means I don't know. That's the sort of other world that she's in now.

We went down the hill. There were so many people there, masses. Wreaths were being placed on the graves of all sorts of famous people. There was a Hungarian flag, and speeches and singing. I didn't know that the

Hungarian flag was allowed. Anyway, this is a Hungarian cemetery. People were even taking photographs at the graves, I'd never seen anything like that, embarrassing the dead by taking photos. Fancy, taking photos when the street lights were lit. Flash as well. Very odd, that sort of thing. It's not usual to photograph the crowds in the cemetery. It's not right, so there.

I said to Rózsa, let's go for a walk. We went up the street arm in arm. I kept on kissing her cheek. She said, stop it, now, don't kiss me so much. Well, why shouldn't I? Who else will? Have you got a boyfriend now, Rózsa? Stop that horrid talk, let go my arm. At least I mustn't shame her vow. Kissing doesn't wear people's faces out, does it, I asked. I see the poor girl so seldom.

I asked Rózsa to come to the house.

'Will he be there?' she asked.

'It's a holiday,' I replied, 'He might be. Have a word with him.'

Daddy was in a bad way. He'd taken to his bed. Couldn't do anything, just lay there. I asked Rózsa, might somebody have a word with him? Who would he listen to, I wondered? His family all despised him now, didn't want to hear about him. I'd been to see my aunt and my uncle, and they both said that I should go and live with them. They'd feed me, I could work and share the takings if I sold things. They'd got a garden, cos there was still a bit left here and there in the Hóstát, though the bigger holdings had all been given up, but I could still have done as much as I wanted. My Aunty Julia was fond of me, and Daddy's little brother Samu was always inviting me. But they didn't want to hear a single word about Daddy. They all lived close together in Téglás utca while we were out here in the Borháncs, the poorer area. Well, how could I desert Daddy? I couldn't do such a thing. Rózsa's left home now, I'm doing the garden by myself, cos Daddy hardly does a thing. He goes to the milk collection point when he's in a fit state, but more often than not, he isn't.

I always go and meet Aunty Julia at the market, Uncle Mihály as well, in case they need help, they don't mind, we're all one family, they say. But they no longer regard Daddy as family. Cos when Mummy died, said Aunty

Julia, Daddy looked after us ever so well, we were nicely dressed on Sundays, and he was proud of having two fine children, worked like a horse, took it out of himself. Kept us well dressed and clean, took us around, showed us off, had us photographed. As time went by, he treated us better and better. But then at first it was only on a Saturday evening, when the milking and everything was finished. He'd leave us with Aunty Mária, Mária Zidaru, and go down the pub. Then things began to get worse, but at first he was quiet, didn't appear drunk. Even when he was drunk on the Lord's Day. Then he started missing two, three, four days of work and just drank and drank, he couldn't leave it alone. Then another couple of weeks would pass and his head would clear. Then he'd start again. By this time he was always that way. You could never tell when he was drunk, it seemed he was all the time. He lay in bed a lot. He hardly had anything to eat yesterday. And I had to wash him down. And you should have seen his belly, it was all swollen, it was as if he'd run to fat, his trousers wouldn't do up. His legs and arms ha gone so thin, but his belly was like a sick cow's, when it's full of gas. And his skin was so pale. But he won't let me take him to the doctor. Aunty Mária kept saying that he was a poor bereaved man, we mustn't be angry with him, it's because his wife's died. She'd seen him when Mummy was still alive. There'd been such pure, innocent love that everybody had been envious. By that time they didn't even care that he wasn't from these parts but from higher up, cos Daddy had married beneath him, into Téglás utca, while she was from Kerekdomb, the other side of the tracks, a poorer family, not much land. Oh, they were cross with him at first. Because one of them was from the right bank of the Szamos, the other from the left. Down our way, the left and right banks are always falling out, but they're both in the Hóstát. It still happens that a suitor is met with a knife. Later they made it up. Then they moved out to the Borháncs, cos at the time there still weren't even any streets there, just a piece of land on which the little house had been built. By the time I was born, there was a street. They'd moved out so that neither of their parents should be close. Cos at the time there was always bickering. But it was when Mummy died that he started drinking. Then when the land had to be given up as well, more and more so.

'Other people's wives have died, and they haven't turned to drink,' I said to Aunty Mária, cos she was the only one I could talk to, that dear churchy old lady. She was a sectarian, but she was a very nice woman. 'Other people have given up their land and worked for wages in the collective, and they don't have to be like this. Perhaps we ought to look for a good woman for him. Doesn't matter that he's a bit older now. There are some that have got no house, no land, nothing. But I really don't think a good woman would have him, of course, the state he's in. You've only got to look at him, nobody needs that.'

'Hush now, Ankutsa,' Aunty Mária's a Romanian, so that's what she always called me, Ankutsa, 'just you pray, nothing on earth will help,' she said. That was her name for me, Ankutsa, it was a name she loved. If she'd had a daughter, that's what she'd have christened her. But she didn't, she just had a son and he died when he was poor little thing. Then Aunty Mária joined the sect. But unfortunately I couldn't talk to her about any grown-up business cos with her it was always God and more God. I was sure that it was her doing that Rózsa was the way she was. When we were little we were with poor Aunty Mária so much, cos Daddy left us with her such a lot. That was when she'd been led astray.

But even if I'd had a foster mother, and she'd slept in Mummy's bed and on her pillow, I wouldn't really have minded as long as Daddy could get better and be like he used to be. Perhaps Daddy would have cheered up if he'd had a new wife. It wouldn't have mattered even if she was a relation. Cos I was angry with him, really, deeply angry when I saw the state he was in. But I couldn't hit him, I hadn't got it in me. I'd wait until he had his sleep out, then I'd take him some tea. And he'd push it away and want wine.'

'I'm not bringing any,' I'd tell him. 'Get up, take some water from the wash-tub and have a wash. I'll give you a clean towel. Come on, Daddy, have something to eat,' I say, 'Please come, we've got to go out and dig things up.'

'You damn girl, I wish I'd got got a son who would do as he was told. If you don't go this minute and bring a litre of wine I'll give you one with the iron.' That's how my father speak to me, that was so pleased with us when we were little. A woman washed our clothes so that we'd look nice on the Lord's Day. And he plaited our hair, and held our hands on the way to church, the Kétágú, cos that's the Hóstát church. After church we'd go into the town to be shown off in the main square. He was such a good father to me. I remember. And he kept the Lord's Day. And now . . . I'd go to the pub at the corner in tears and get the wine. I'd ask the publican to make it half water, never mind, I'll pay for the litre, just water it down. He wouldn't do it, because my father had threatened him in the past that he'd beat him up. So I'd pour some out and top it up with water myself. That's the way he'd drink it, watered down, all day long, drinking it slowly, not getting out of bed. There'd be silence in the room all day. I didn't sit with him to see it. I thought once that he'd be dead when I got home. Oh, my God, what can I do with him. Vili knows about him. He knows, but we never say anything. Vili doesn't drink. Not a drop. That's why I love him so much.

Then he'd sometimes brighten up a bit. Come and beg my pardon. Cry to me nonstop, he'll never drink again, he'll give it up, I'll see. He'll stop me working so much, cos I'm doing all the heavy work. He makes a start, but he hasn't got the strength. I have, even though I'm a girl. I say, 'Leave it, Father,' cos I can put a good basket of cabbages onto the cart, and he can't any longer. Then he gets angry, says I'm making fun of him, starts crying, lays his head on poor Puju's flank. So I forgive him, what else can I do. He's the father that begat me, so I can't go as well. Go to the next world. like Mummy, poor thing. Or leave home, like Rózsa. Here I was, I was all he'd got. Come on, girl, this and that, he'd buy me some material for a dress, I can get it made up. What will he buy with, I asked. He'd got something put away. He promised, next day we'd go up to the centre and buy something. Then the whole day passed quietly, we just dug and stored things in the cellar for winter. In the evening he said 'I'm going for a walk.' Well, by that time I feared walks. When he said that I was very cross. Then he was completely drunk again. He came home. This time he'd left his knife in the pub as a pledge.

Anyway, he's been like this since he's had to see to his children. He's felt sorry for himself and started to do nothing but drink. How could a man wash and cook for his children, cos I couldn't even walk when Mummy died. His children are such a burden for a bereaved man. so he broke down completely. And in addition there was all the work and no one to help. Rózsa was a bit of help, cos she was bigger, but in any case a child was a lot of trouble. Rózsa didn't even know how to feed the chickens, cos when she did they fought until they bled. Or if Daddy set her to thinning out seedlings she'd pull the lot up, because, of course, she was just a child. The way Daddy beat Rózsa made her ill, just cos she didn't know how to thin out. There are grown-ups that don't know, never mind children.

When I'm out in the market, selling, I think of Mummy all the time. What am I to do, I'm so sorry, my heart is breaking. I go to the milk-collecting point at dawn and the milk is delivered, I test the gravity, measure it for fat content, as there are those that water it down to make it more. So I don't accept it. I do that as well in Daddy's stead. He gets money for that, four hundred lei a month, which really isn't very much.

When he's sober I'm cross. When he's drunk, then too I'm cross, but even more I feel sorry for him. There's nobody that he can talk to. These days everybody tries to avoid him. As they do poor old Romitán as well. And yet people like them don't get together. The drunkards, I mean. They just do it all by themselves in their misery. I at least talk a lot, both to myself and to Puju, cos he's a good listener, and I talk to him cos he's the cleverest animal. I talk to Piros as well when I'm milking her. I don't talk to Csipész, only when he starts getting excited and barking, but he's an animal and likes to be spoken to, and he listens as if he can understand. I only talk to Foltika, though, when she's pregnant, and then I tell her off, cos she's always giving birth, poor animal, it's she knows. And in the market I talk to everybody, I go and see my aunt and her family, and I talk all the time all day. I even say to the carrots, when I'm lifting them: 'Hey, you're a beauty, you're a perfect picture! I'll tie you tight together, five of you, five brothers, all different but you're lovely, all five of you, and I'll ask four lei for you. In the Aprózár they'd give two for the money, but theirs are such nasty-looking, dull, shrunken things. This carrot, my boy, just look at this,' I show it to Puju, or I lift a less good one with two roots, 'Well, couldn't you have grown one root? Don't you know that in the market the women don't care for carrots with two roots, cos they're hard to scrape? Why are you giving me trouble, having all these roots so I shan't be able to sell you? Look here, Puju my boy, behave yourself and you'll get a carrot.' Or one's split, and I tick it off: 'Look here, when did I teach you to grow cock-eyed? Can't you grow nice and straight? What have I not given you, if you can't do that? I've brought manure, carried water all summer long, watered you with it all, nearly pulled my arms off. And you go and grow like this.' And I'd say to another that was on the thin side, 'Look here, who's going to buy you, eh? You're as thin as a rake, that's what. No good to anybody. Young you may be, but you're so skinny. You've grown all this greenery, but there's nothing underneath. You're like a girl with as much hair as a horse's mane, and not a scrap of flesh, that has to wear about three skirts to give her backside some shape when she goes to the vintage ball. So who needs you, you scruffy object? Do you think you're Hőstát parsley or something? Go to the Aprózár collective, that's where you belong! So look out, cos even if I pick you I shan't take you to market in case I blush the skin off my face because of you. Stay where you are, I'll give you to the chickens. So look here, you lovely horse, I'll give it to you.' And I take it to Puju, but he doesn't like parsley, only a tasty carrot. I give him the misshapen one. I don't regret it. I've sowed it, hoed it, broken my back for it, by damn, and I'll give it to the one that deserves it, right, my boy? Here you are.

That's how I talk to all the animals and living things that I work with.

When I've got nobody to talk to, I talk to Mummy. Perhaps I shouldn't, I know the church forbids it, but it's all right for me. The Reverend said so. If somebody's dead, then they're dead, so you must pray for them and respect them in death. All that superstitious mysticism is spreading more and more, it comes from the Romanians, that's what the Reverend said. We'd got to uphold our pure Reformed religion. We weren't mystics, our religion was founded on reality, the reality of the Kingdom of God. That's what he said.

But I do nobody any harm by cheering myself up and giving dear Mummy some company up there in Heaven, as she must miss her children. Perhaps she's right there among the saints. Aunty Mária has so many saints, and I like them. Nobody needs to know who I talk to. I tell her everything that's going on. And I tell her that I love Daddy dearly, and that I'm sorry for him. I've asked her before whether she'd be cross if I looked for a new wife for Daddy. She said she wouldn't be cross with anybody. Not even with Daddy? Oh no, let him be cheered up if it's possible. I only talk to her when Daddy can't hear. Either he's out or he's drunk. Or asleep. I was still quite little when Daddy caught me talking to an angel one evening. I was already in bed, Rózsa was still out at work, and he came in and heard me talking.

'Who are you talking to, child? Who is there here in the dark?'

Cos there wasn't a candle burning, so as not to waste it. I said I was talking to Mummy.

'What are you talking about, don't say such things.'

I told him I often spoke to Mummy and she answered when I asked her things. She told me lovely stories about orphans and wicked stepmothers.

'Now look,' said Daddy, 'if I ever catch you again talking to your dead mother I'll give you a hiding you won't forget. I won't have you casting spells in here about talking with the dead, do you hear me?! I'll thrash you so that you'll forget how to talk.'

Well, he didn't beat me that time. I said to him, 'Daddy, tell me a fairy story to help me get to sleep.'

'I can't, girl, I don't know any fairy stories, now shut your eyes and go to sleep.'

'Then tell me about something true, doesn't have to be a fairy story, something that really happened.'

'I'm not telling you anything. I've got to go out while there's still light to see by. I can't sit here telling you stories.'

So he didn't beat me. But I've never again told him what Mummy says to me when I'm by myself. But after that I haven't spoken aloud, just inside my head. Anyway, a little child had to talk to her mother.

Most of all, Mummy's always been ever so good to me. She's worked miracles. All the time since I was little. But I don't tell anybody. I told Rózsa a long time ago, before she was so churchified, but she contradicted me. She said it wasn't Mummy doing it but the lord Jesus, so she said. But in my view it was Mummy. When there was a little purse in the street, and Mummy knew that I'd been crying so much and I'd told her that I wanted to go to the vintage ball but hadn't got a dress to wear. So who put that purse in my way if not Mummy, so as to help her orphan? There was so much small change in it that I could hardly count it up. And the time when my nice shoes with straps broke, and I went to Aunty Julia's and couldn't take her anything for her name-day but a few flowers and a pastry. Didn't she say there and then that her old shoes had got too small for her, and give them to me? Well, only a mother could think of her children, the way all those good things have happened to me.

I wasn't upset like Daddy at the land being given up. Two pieces went to the collective farm—one was seized for national purposes, the other went to Vili for the Station. I've never told anybody that I don't miss the land, I don't, cos it would be shameful for a girl who owned land to think like that. But I wasn't cross. Rather it was to my advantage. Cos that up in the Borháncs had been Mummy's, and so didn't have to be surrendered, cos it was seized. The national institute was established on it, and now it's covered with apple trees. Vili's Station has expanded. Every apple tree is dear to my heart. But I don't tell anybody at all that, I can only tell Puju.

Other people were dispossessed as kulaks but not us, we didn't have enough land but others did. For instance, the other Butyka family and farmer Kilin, and the Diószegis, they were all together up there. They owned so much land that it was taken off them. In particular farmer Butyka's. The name's the same but we aren't related. Ten hold he had. The state just took ours and gave us in exchange a bit of poor land out there beyond the Strekk, next to the forest at the bottom of Szentgyörgy Hill. Anyway, we don't go there cos it's very stony, poor soil that's never been cultivated. The word is that we'll complain when somebody from the Party or the council or somewhere comes round, I'm not sure where from. But I mean, I know nothing about it, I can't do it. It's a long way away for me, and it's such poor soil. We gave up good soil and got back stony rubbish like that.

But I don't regret that it was given up to the collective, or that it was lost, cos there'd also been a bit in Szopor and in Eperjes. Small plots, close to one another, and those were both given up. Cos Daddy gave them up, there was no way that he could have kept them. Now I'd have had those to do as well. Cos he couldn't really go there and work. He's in such a state, poor thing. His strength has run out. Well, he's drunk it away, but most of all he's become so depressed. Rózsa too has left the land and she can't do anything, she spends all her time around the sick.

So now all that's left is the garden and a little patch up on the top, where the carrots were. That can't be given up to the collective, of course, cos it's here by the house, so it can't be. The house can't be taken away. There are also two tiny plots on Kerek Hill, and I have to go there by cart, and I do, but I seem to be spending my life in the cart. As for the grandparents' land, it's not so good and I'm neglecting it. I tell dear Puju about all this on the way, but he never says anything back. He doesn't answer, but he's a good listener. So out there I've just been doing the little jobs and things that aren't needed every day. It's under cabbage at the moment, but even that's very bad as the snails have got to it and I wasn't able to spray. Vili said that he'd let me have some sort of chemical that would keep snails off the soil for ten years, but then it wouldn't be possible to plant tomatoes, beans or peppers. I've planted carrots, cabbages, and a long time ago potatoes as well, but only enough to keep us going over winter. Leaf crops have to be thinned out a bit, and I've been out in summer and watered. It's not far, and there's water available there. And you have to hoe. The cabbages are always covered with butterflies and they eat the hell out of them. But the things that have to be constantly tied up as they grow, and of course the peppers and beans and spinach, have to be looked after all the time like children. Things like that can't be planted up there cos I can't go that often. I'm doing well if I get away with spending a couple of hours on the milk in the morning. I go to sleep in the cart on the way. Fortunately, good old Puju is clever and takes me there. The only problem is then that we have to cross the railway, and there are all the lorries and buses, so I have to watch out. There are a lot of factories up that way, and there's a terrible smell that makes poor Puju sneeze.

So it's not permitted for a girl to go elsewhere to marry, or for a boy to take a wife from anywhere else. Cos then the pieces of land are so far away, and little bits are scattered all over the place as they're divided among the children when they marry, far enough apart to need a cart, and they're never going to be properly worked. If a plot is at such a distance that it can be well tended, produce from it can be sold.

In the old days, said Aunty Julia, there were servants. Servants from Szék. But that was ages ago. These days not many people have servants. How proud the Hóstát people were at never having been the servants of others! They'd never served other masters, like the peasants that came into town did, had to work for somebody else for a mere pittance, and had to be a long way from their families. So they were all their own servants after all.

Aunty Julia was always saying how big I was getting. I ought to have a young man to court me. Ought to have, I said, didn't have to have. Or if I ought to, then just so that he came hoeing, cos two would get it done faster. But I didn't tell her anything, I didn't tell Aunty Julia how things were. Well, perhaps she'd have hit me fit to break my back. But she's never bothered me. Uncle Mihály, now, has had sneaking suspicions. But he hasn't hit me. Not his child, he said, not his to hit. But I had no intention of saying that it was Vili.

The only good thing about our good land being up on the Borháncs was cos of Vili.

For me to be able to see him and he me. When I wanted. Not just stealthily. Aunty Kali was always going to his place, and we had to be careful. It wasn't right, not at all, of course, I knew that it would be nice to go nicely dressed on a Sunday, take a turn arm in arm on the main square and then go up to the lookout. But it couldn't. He came down to see me, but only just looked in. If Daddy was out he'd come in and stay. But I've told him not to stop the car outside the house. No official car comes to a respectable house on that street. It's a great big car with a chauffeur.

Vilmos said recently that he'd take me for a trip. I should dress up. Wear a towny dress. Well, I'd got such things, cos we were town people, not peasants. But I only went about in Hóstát costume, though it wasn't what you'd call a costume, it wasn't all embroidered or anything, just a skirt and an apron to keep me from getting dirty. Not a lacy apron, just the sort for the market, covering above and below the waist. I could just turn it down, but I hadn't got anything else. That'll be all right, said he. I told Daddy when I knew he wasn't drunk and would be angry. I said I was going out with a girl friend. So who with? Gosh, I had to make something up, I nearly got it all mixed up. I could go, only I'd got to see to the animals first, cos they couldn't wait.

I told Puju I'd have to be up nice and early on Sunday morning, but even the day before I got everything ready and cleaned by lamplight to take on Monday, cos there isn't much of a market on Mondays, people just don't come. That bit of cash is needed, though, tax has to be paid, cos these days you're jailed if you don't pay. Daddy would be punished. I made some puliszka but he didn't eat cos he was drunk. I offered him a bit of light vegetable soup, that might be good for his stomach, cos it was in a bad way, all blown up like a ball. Didn't want that. I asked, would he like some sour milk soup? Couldn't eat a thing. He was going to bed. And he shouted that all I could ever think of was enjoying myself, I was always off out with somebody. Not a single decent young man ever set foot in our house. Just one slut after another, wasters the lot of them. That day as well I was off out having fun like the gentry. Who'd ever heard of such a thing, going for an outing in May, with all that work to be done.

I said to Puju: 'Listen here, you lovely horse. I'm going to put you all this hay, so you'll have a nice day. Cos I'm going to have a nicer day than I've ever had Mummy to thank for. And I'm putting all the carrot tops for you that I cleaned yesterday. Women buy them like that in the market, they don't want the green part, so I don't take them down and they don't take them home. So have a good look. I'll be home to see to you in the evening. You won't have to work today, it's the Lord's Day. I'll be home later. One day perhaps I'll make up my mind and won't come. I'll go straight into the Szamos for sure, with a big back-pack of stones, just above the Germans' footbridge, where the water's dark and deep, cos what kind of life has a poor orphan got when all her father does is treat her badly, and she works all the hours God sends. Her hands are like two great bricks, the way she knocks them about. First thing in the morning, I can hardly move them, they're so swollen. Aunty Mária tells me that I should bathe them in cow's piss as that will do a lot to reduce the swelling. So I've taken a bucket and kept an eye on Piros, but she simply hasn't needed to pee. I told Aunty Mária that I hadn't been able to collect pee from her, I'd stayed standing there but I couldn't. When she came round, she tickled Piros under the armpits until she peed for her. So I put my hands in while it was still warm and it really stung, but nothing happened. But Aunty Mária said they were looking better, not so red any longer. After all, I'm young and strong, but the work I do isn't girls' work. I preferred to buy some milky cream from the chemist. He told me to rub them with butter. I didn't tell him about the cow's pee, I was too embarrassed. But how can I waste butter on my hands? Listen here, Puju, if I never come back home, you be a good horse and work, but I don't know who'll work with you, cos Daddy can't any longer. Now look, perhaps I'll ask dear Vili to take me in, he could do with a girl in the house. How can I go on living like this, I never have a bit of fun. The only pleasure I get is when I see that the little thing that I've planted as seed is growing in the soil, the seeds are so tiny that a thimble-full is enough for a whole long bed. When I watch I think all the time of the nice bit of money that I'll get for it. It was said in church that it says in the Bible: what grows in the soil belongs to everybody. That's what the Reverend László said. Well, this is our land and it produces for us, it's not everybody's. If what grows on it is everybody's, let them buy it! But then, I've got no other pleasure, I just watch the lovely spinach and sorrel coming up. Ours comes up so early cos we start it under glass, and when the one sowing's planted out, the second's coming along.

You're mine, you lovely, and dear Piros is, it's lucky we've still got Piros but she doesn't yield much milk any longer. You don't say anything to me, you just look at me exactly the same whatever I say, whether I'm having pleasure or sorrow, you're always just the same. You're boring, you know, Puju. You might at least look as if you understand, like Csipész. When I speak to him he always looks at me. He sits on his backside, wags his tail, and looks into my eyes. But what if I don't come home, and Vili takes me in? What's going to become of you animals and the land? Not to mention Daddy. What will happen to you? Where will you be able to go, my lovely? You'll be taken into the collective, you and Piroska, and then slaughtered. Cos I hear that if anyone joins the collective, their stock is slaughtered. And all my lovely plants here, cos whoever comes into the garden won't say that a girl did this, rather than a farmer, for it to be so nice. There's no month as splendid as May, you can just sit by the land and admire, cos the way it does its duty, it's as if it regretted nothing.'

I was excited at going for a trip and my pleasure was all the greater, and as I was getting ready I hardly slept for three days. But I was hoping Daddy wouldn't go up Méhes utca to the school and enquire whether I really had gone for a trip with the girls I went to school with. Meanwhile my new blouse was finished as well, ever so pretty, white and pink, and the day before I sewed on the fastenings and everything was ready. But I wasn't able to buy Indian material for a skirt, I couldn't afford it. I'd baked a nice apple doughnut, the sort Vili likes, with caster sugar and cinnamon, and put it in my basket under a nice cloth.

'Puju, my lovely, you see, only people cry like this, cos God made even horses better, cos at least they can't shed tears.'

He just stood there and looked at me, same as ever. Understandingly. Silent. He doesn't complain all the time and want sympathy like people do. But how happy I was when I got up today nice and early, even the chickens were still asleep. I was going for a trip with Vili. Then I wished the devil would take the whole trip, cos I didn't feel at all like going. But I'd promised to meet Vili at the station at nine o'clock. What was he going to say if I let him down and didn't go? Even the weather was that way. The sun was shining first thing, then it's clouded over, as if the light too had lost interest in being in the world.

But I'd been looking forward to going for a trip so much. To being invited to go. I didn't even ask where the train would b to, or how long it would take. I'd got no idea about this trip! I was so happy and there was nobody I can tell. Even that we'd been by train!

But I hadn't seen anything. I'd only once been down to Murokország, as it's called. There was a widow woman there, and Daddy and I had had to go and see her cos he wanted to bring her in as stepmother for me. Rózsa had left home by that time. So, we dressed up and Daddy spread blankets in the cart and took a nice basket of apples. We'd had to make a whole pot of plum jam, he'd called Aunty Mária to come over, and I put the fruit in while she stirred. And I saw Daddy take one of Mummy's headscarves out of the chest, cos we were still keeping her things, turning them over and airing them, and taking everything out once a year and freshening it. That was all going to be for our dowries. Not for Rózsa by then, actually, but when we were little we weren't to know that. Daddy took out a lovely tablecloth with stripes and lace in the middle and said that we'd take that to Aunty Eszter as an engagement present. He told me to wrap it up in tissue paper. Well, I started screaming, I remember, I howled like a little pig, and hurt my throat. I said he couldn't give Mummy's things away to anybody cos they were Mummy's, and she'd be so cross she'd come back and haunt! That's what I told Daddy.

Well, he hadn't beaten me much since he saw the effect on Rózsa, but he came at me then and took a tight hold on my neck, so tight that I passed out. He'd caught the vein in my neck, and I collapsed. When I came round, I started screaming again that he couldn't take Mummy's things. But I'd never seen Mummy, had I, except in pictures, cos I'd still been an infant when she died, poor thing. But she'd always been caressing me, talking to me, so she hadn't been such a stranger to me. So we had to go and see Aunty Eszter, for Daddy to marry her and for her to become my stepmother. But it didn't come off. Cos she was so poor, she'd got an awful little house a long way away, one room, a dirt floor, and we went down to Aranyosvölgy and then up towards Vásárhely. Daddy saw that and everything, how Gypsy-looking she was, could hardly bring so much as a cart-load of furniture and a rotten son who wouldn't work and wouldn't obey her. Cos Aunty Eszter had one son, she was a widow, and the boy was the same age as Rózsa. He would have been able to work but just wouldn't.

While we were at their place the two of us went out to play finders in the shed. Well, that was all right, but we were afraid that Daddy might catch us. Cos what the game consisted of was that one hid a chopper, and to find out where it was the other had five questions, which had to be answered yes or no. If the other person failed to find it, then the one that had hidden the chopper might ask for a forfeit. So the first time Pityu asked for a kiss, then I had to show him my nipple, then to lift my skirt, and in the end he touched me up and took hold of my breast.

So, how old was I at the time? Twelve or thirteen. And my breasts were about as big as they are now. Maybe a bit less, but it was clear that I wasn't a boy. I'm not as big as Aunty Mária, but then she suckled me, and she's quite stout. I'm just big enough to wear Mummy's blouses, They're a bit big for me, but if I fasten them tight I can wear them. Daddy doesn't let me, but when he's not at home I get them out and look at myself in them.

Well, I was too young to know what that was all about. Thought it was all right when Pityu took hold of my breast. And both together. That was all right. By then I didn't really want to find the chopper. Daddy and Aunty Eszter were holding a discussion in the room and we weren't allowed in. Pityu and I just went on playing. Suddenly he said that there was a boy next door, he'd ask him round. Sanyi came round, he was younger than Pityu. He didn't have much to say for himself, and he was fair-haired. Pityu said to him, 'Ever had a kiss, Sanyi?'

'Yes. All I've wanted.'

'And held a wotnot? A cunt?'

'In my time,' and he blushed all over his face.

Pityu burst out laughing. 'You're lying, you dirty dog. You've never even touched a cow's udder.'

So then all three of us played. But that Sanyi was such a *papalaptye*, as Aunty Mária says, butter wouldn't melt in his mouth. He was stupid. Didn't even know to touch me. I only ever asked for a kiss from Pityu. Nothing more. It wasn't right, I knew. Pityu went under my skirt. At first I didn't like it, then I didn't care. Nobody'd ever done that before Pityu. But suddenly I thought of poor Rózsa, she'd have been upset if she'd known. Cos she'd taken her vow of purity by that time.

Daddy and I went to see Aunty Eszter once again. this time not in the cart but a lorry took us that was going that way. The village was called Nyárád something. This time Pityu played no more games but was more grown-up and conceited, and Daddy had cooled towards Aunty Eszter. She cooked so meanly. But in her house Daddy didn't drink but controlled himself so as not to show what he was like. Only Aunty Eszter had been so universally commended as an industrious woman from there in Murokország, cos there are big vegetable farms in those parts, and she knew how to cultivate them. Well, perhaps she did know, but she had hardly any land, just a tiny garden. She was something of a rag-and-bone woman, went round jumble sales all the time. Once she came up our way, a neighbour brought her and Pityu in his cart. She took a good look at all that we had, went into the shed and climbed up everywhere to see what we'd got. She opened a cupboard. I was standing there and I said that those were all things that had been Mummy's, they were my dowry.

'I'll tell you what your dowry is,' she replied arrogantly.

She was going to be a real stepmother, I could see that. I'd be sleeping in the shed with Puju if she moved in.

There was nothing on earth dearer to me than Mummy's cupboard. There were all her lovely headscarves, table cloths, pillow slips, all starched and ironed. She'd made everything so carefully and got pairs. Once a year I make sure I'd take them out, wash them thoroughly and iron them. The cloth embroidered with cocks, which had ten matching napkins. I'd leave them hanging up for a day and look at them. There's a wall protector with four peacocks on it in cross-stitch, but so tiny that I can't do such work. I'd lay it out on a damp cloth and leave it like that. I 'd ask Mummy, 'Do you like to see that I've been looking after everything, Mummy?'

But I didn't speak formally like that, but rather I said something like 'Dear Mummy, come round and have a look.'

'Now, what are you hanging on to all these things for, girl? We didn't bury them with her, did we? We don't put them on the table even for a celebration. They just sit there in the cupboard, wrapped in tissue paper. I collected them one by one, sewed until my eyes hurt, and what for?'

Well, that's right. What's it all for? Cos I've worked on it and seen to it that it's always clean. But it isn't even that now. I can't have a bit of beauty. If Aunty Eszter lays a hand on it I'll scream loud enough to make her deaf. She wasn't going to paw that. I told her those things were mine, she could bring her own when she moved in. So off she went to her stinking slum.

I told Daddy, 'I'll do everything, Daddy, I'll work harder, go to market, if I've got to. Don't bring that Aunty Eszter here, she's a wicked woman, she just wants our belongings.'

I didn't realize that he needed a woman, and what for. Well, I did know what for. I almost came out with 'Just take yourself down the street, the famous Aunty Julianna lives there, everybody knows that men go having it off with her.'

So that was the last we saw of Aunty Eszter. And of that Pityu, and I wasn't sorry.

I was always thinking of Vili. When I was feeling down, I wished he'd come so that I could see him. When I was cheerful as well, cos I knew he'd come and call. Or I'd go over and see him. What did I want with such an old man, forty-five or even fifty? But to me he didn't seem old at all. He wasn't even my type. And yet he was, everything was just right between us, we spoke the same language. We just hadn't tried living together as man and wife. Perhaps we'd even get on well at that. But, of course, it didn't seem like that to others. But Mummy can see my heart, and she's not cross. She can see clearly what's inside me, and she can't be cross any longer. Cos she's up there in Heaven and can forgive everything that's wicked. It's no matter that Rózsa has become such a great churchwoman, I don't believe she has the power of forgiveness. A little while ago Vili came over in secret. Well, he can't come to our house secretly. I've told him that. Everybody in the street can see him and they know. But fortunately Daddy wasn't at home. He'd picked a big bunch of laburnum in the road, and it was beautiful! I put it in a bucket and crushed the ends so that it would keep, and it flowered for a week! Cos Vili said to change the water every day. Same as for the horse, isn't it? And I like clean water, same as the animals. Oh it was lovely! Daddy gave it a look and said nothing. Then when it had faded, I took it outside onto the side of the garden, where we put the potatoes and tomatoes, cos we don't give those to the animals, they make them all bloated. And I stuck the bunch firmly into the ground, same as I did with that beautiful rose that I got from Vili. He brought such a marvellous rose, it was as long as a walking stick, and the flower was the size of a sunflower.

When Vili gave it to me he'd just dashed out to the market on a Friday. He knew that I'd be there, and put it on the stall. He bought a few things for making soup, not costing very much but I had to take the money, it was so hard to make ends meet then. So he didn't stay and left his flower there. It was wrapped up in paper and tied with a silk ribbon.

I didn't want to undo it there and then. I just remarked to Aunty Piroshka, who always had the next stall, goodness, look, that gentleman has left his flower. Let me see what it's like, said Piroshka. So I undid it a bit from the paper. I didn't like letting anybody else see it. I'd have liked to be the only one. But I couldn't run after Vili cos another lady had come to buy something and I couldn't leave the stall. It would have been nice to fling my arms round dear Vili's neck, and to smell the nice smell of his shirt, cos he always wore a smart checked shirt, a fresh one every day, and the cap on his head smelled nice as well. Not that he wore perfume, just that the scent was nice. There must have been a bit of lavender in his aftershave when he shaved and sprinkled his moustache, but that used to have a sharp tang of tobacco. When I caught that nice sharp tobacco scent and the lavender and the soap, I couldn't help being carried away, it was so good. But I'd just reach across the stall to put things in his briefcase, cos he never brought a basket. So I'd wrap the carrots and whatever in newspaper and put them in his leather briefcase, and catch his scent as I did so. Oh, I was looking forward to Sunday, when I'd run across and see him. And Piroshka asked when I was going to unwrap the flower.

'Look here, Annus, you should sell that flower. I don't know what you'll get for it—ask four lei.'

'Four lei? How could I ask four lei when I only ask two for a bunch of zinnia?'

'Well, it's so enormous and special. Nobody's going to believe things like that grow in your garden.'

'I'm not going to sell it.'

'Why ever not? Don't you need the money?'

'An' what if he came back for it?'

'He was going to see his girlfriend, he'll get her another. By the time he remembers where he's left it he'll have bought another one. You sell it.'

'I'll wait a bit,' I said. 'I'll hang on, he may come back. And if he doesn't, I've got to go and greet a neighbour on her name-day, and I'll have something to take her.'

So then I took that gorgeous flower home. I wondered where to put it. Cos obviously it would attract attention, it was so enormous. Daddy would spot it. I thought and thought, and I even asked Puju. Now then, dear horse, what am I to do with this gorgeous flower? It would be like putting a gold earring. Everybody would see it and know. And dear old Puju hadn't got a word to say. As I was on the way home with it, I said, 'Here, Puju, I'll fan you. Can you smell it?' There wasn't all that much scent, but what a colour!

It was like fine powder, such a clear, whitish pink. Like a baby, still at the breast. So I held it to Puju's nose, and he turned his face towards it as if to eat it. I said, 'You're not to eat it, you cheeky horse, cos it's been given to me. And roses mightn't be good for you. Might bloat your stomach. No good it being beautiful if it makes you fart, is it?' It had been given to me, that was a fact. Nobody'd left it there, it had been meant for me. Only I didn't know what to do with it. How could I keep it without getting into trouble? I put it down carefully in the cart and wrapped it up again in the paper. I was just doing that when it came to me: I must ask Mummy. One woman's heart will suggest to another what to do. When I'd finished everything at home— didn't have to do the milking cos Daddy'd done it, I fed Puju and changed his water, and then sat outside for a bit, I wasn't cold.

I said to Mummy, 'Dear Mummy, look at me and sympathize! Where ever am I to put this rose? Cos Daddy'll kill me.'

Mummy said, 'He won't kill you. He isn't a bad man, just can't control himself.'

'Well, he's not killed me yet, I don't really mean it. But even so, where am I to put it?'

Mummy said, 'Go down the garden, darling, get a basket and produce it from that.'

'We haven't got a basket as big as this flower,' I replied. 'It reaches half-way up my leg..'

'Take it and put it in your bosom, and mind the thorns.'

'There aren't any thorns, Mummy, not one.'

'What do you mean, girl, no thorns? It's a rose, isn't it?'

'All the thorns have been taken off so as not to prick me.'

'So, these days you have to take the thorns off a rose so that it doesn't prick the customer, is that right?'

'That's what they do with roses. Vili knows all about roses. He's got people who do nothing else but break off the thorns. Cos there that's how they're sold.'

'In that case, stick it into your bosom and pull the end down under your skirt, and take it down the garden like that. Plant it there, where you've put the laburnum, push it in to at least a third of its length so that there are two or three leaves left. That way it'll stay nice for a week, and then you'll see, perhaps it'll grow and flower again.'

'Mummy, how can it flower again when it's got no root?'

'You'll see, my dear, it will.'

Oh, how good Mummy was to me to tell me where to put it. There by the fence, where only I shall see it. I planted it and watered it, and she was quite right, it was lovely there for a week. As if it had gone straight into a vase.

But when I was talking to Mummy there I sat outside for a bit, leaning on Puju's legs, and he was letting me do that. I'd got my back to the door, and although I was speaking softly Daddy overheard me. 'Are you talking to yourself again now? Won't you stop nonsense like that? You're a grown-up girl now, to be doing such a thing. Who are you talking to?' Daddy was quite drunk then, but not so much that he couldn't speak. That's when I have to be afraid of him. Cos he's very strong even then.

'I was talking to Puju.'

'What are you saying to a dumb animal? He can't answer you.'

'He doesn't have to, I don't ask him anything, all he has to do is listen to me,' I said.

And I'd have liked to talk to Daddy, or to have given him a little hug. I was so happy. He'd done the milking, even taken it where it has to go in the little cart, and I knew that he'd be going for a snooze before long. He was doing well that day, hadn't had much to drink, just half a litre. I asked him what I should cook so as to be in his good books. But I can't give him a hug, he's not that kind of man.

Daddy was very cross when he realized that I was talking to Mummy. I never said a word to him so as not to irritate him. He'd got enough to worry about. We've got a little book about the departed, and how the Hóstát people bury the dead. There's a description of us in it. When he saw me reading it,

Daddy said that it wasn't correct. It had been written by a Hungarian from Debrecen or somewhere; he'd been to see him as well and kept asking questions. It was printed in the second Hungarian period. Cos it was Hungarian time again during the war. Just when I was born, and then Daddy wasn't called up cos we children had become orphans as Mummy had died. But according to him it wasn't so. Not as it said in the book. Cos that well-meaning man had come here, a clever man, and spoken to all sorts of people, Hóstátis and others, but in Daddy's opinion he didn't even know what our people were like. He'd written this little book about how we bury the dead. Well, I don't know if it's quite like that. Cos I've been to enough funerals and there's never been such a performance as he describes. But in the book he says all the time that we treat the deceased properly, that we don't only see what there is in the world, we're a sort of vegetable people, aren't we, that's what we're known for, we work on the land. Tillers of the soil. And that we also see what isn't there, we're strong on religion and superstitions and beliefs. I neither know nor see anybody else's business. Here I can only see Aunty María, but she's not a Hóstát person, nor a Hungarian, but a Wallachian, belongs to the Pentecostal sect. She's a crazy sectarian. Those of us who can, go to church, but sometimes we can't cos we have to work even on the Lord's Day. I go once a month, if that. These days even less often. The churches aren't what they used to be. If anybody goes it's taken amiss in school as well. I remember that once it happened that in the fifth year, Miklós Hatházi was being tested on his homework—he was a tubby boy, couldn't run very fast when we played football. His family lived in Pata utca. It was a Monday, and we'd been made to learn a poem for the occasion. Mayday or some such official holiday. Miklós didn't know the first thing. So comrade teacher asked, 'What were you up to yesterday, that you don't know a single line?'

'I was in church!' he exclaimed. So he got such a caning that he couldn't sit down.

Aunty María goes every evening. She puts on her headscarf and ties it up, and they've got a secret house here on the Kövespad. How can it be secret, when everybody can see all the women in headscarves going in there with their husbands at seven in the evening? Then she talks freely with the dead. With us Hungarians it's not allowed. It wasn't in the old days and it certainly isn't now. There used to be table dancing at Aunty Julia's, and then that was forbidden, and Uncle Mihály was involved in that as well. But the Reverend found out, and he was furious. A special little table had been made as well, and that had to be burnt, but the ashes were stolen and used to rub into another, and table dancing could continue using that. I think it's done in secret. It's mostly done in winter, when there isn't so much work to do.

But the book is somehow different. It's all about the Hóstát. I'd never heard of such a thing as a book being written about us. Who we are and where we're from. It's so strange, it's as if this Hungarian book wasn't about us at all. I can't even recognize us in it, or the relatives. According to Daddy, a long time ago, in Hungarian times, there was a strong move for us to become a separate people. We were supposed to be a separate people and hadn't yet been discovered. Then interesting books like that were written. About burial and how things were delivered. Produce. I don't know. There was a picture in it of women carrying buckets on their heads. I'd never seen anything like that, though I've been going in the fields since I was a child. It's not done now, cos nobody's got any fields, they've been impounded. But not previously. and it showed horses pulling a kind of sledge, and carrying hay on it. Well, we've got a cart. Like all the houses. The saying was that there was half a cart in every barn. Well, that's true. And some useless old tools, that nobody knows what they were for or how to mend them, and they keep them in case they come in handy. We've got some old stuff like that as well. A harrow. When we had a field we used to harrow it. I didn't do it, it was a man's job. We've got nothing else up in the loft. I don't think we've got anything unusual that a book could be written about. We're not that special.

In my opinion the great distinguishing feature of us Hóstát people is that we have to work so hard. I don't know of anybody else who breaks their backs all day long from childhood. They used to say that servants from Szék avoided Hóstát employers cos they worked people to death. They fed them well, were kindly disposed to them, but worked them until they dropped. So that one thing, the amount that we have to work, is very unusual. Certainly there are plenty of Hóstát people who have left the land, especially these days when there are such outside opportunities as employment in a factory or a state Station like Vili's. They often go cos they've been given bad land in exchange for good and can't work it and produce enough to sell and live on. Or they've gone into the collective farm to work. Some of us have gone into factories or to learn a trade, and that used to be the case as well. There's getting to be fewer and fewer of us, says Daddy. People aren't prepared to go on tilling the soil, it's a lot of work for so little money. They'd rather go where they get paid. Perhaps that's what's in store for me. I just don't know.

On the other hand, I can't imagine us not having a bit of land and an animal. Everybody needs a bit to make them happy. The way we emerge from winter when spring comes, start planting seed under glass in February. Your hands get frozen but you just get on with it, cos that's what we do. The trouble with work like that is that it takes two. When Daddy's drunk he just takes to his bed and can't do a thing. I have to call in somebody to help me, and I have to pay them. Nobody comes for nothing. I can't see any other way of managing. And of having the pleasure of planting out the nice little seedlings at the end of April, or perhaps having to wait until May if the soil hasn't warmed up. The whole of communist mankind isn't going to pave over their gardens so as not to grow things in them. Here we've got about thirty ares of garden. I can't see that being lost! Taking away the gardens is unheard of. Don't even think it!

Neither should I! Especially just then!

I was so happy then, I was just bursting with it.

Daddy'd gone back to normal again. He'd been sober the past three days. He'd been working and doing the heavy jobs. Yesterday he even took me down to sell stuff in the market, but now that the holiday's over there wasn't much business. It's always the same. People spend out for the holiday, then look at their empty purses and eat up the leftovers. Or they live on caraway seed soup, so there's no need to go to market. Daddy had been seeing to the milk in the morning as well, except that he's not too good at writing so I had to help him, but he did the measuring. Then he was out hoeing, and mended the fence, cos naughty children had damaged it by the garden. As long as it lasts well and good. Daddy, I mean, not the fence.

All the same, I mustn't be so happy that I skipped about and sang all the time. He doesn't like that sort of thing. When he remembers how things were before he gets cross. I have to behave as if nothing new is happening between us, that this is how we've always been. But Daddy hadn't touched a hoe in a long time. I've been thinking that if he can go on like this I might get out to the cinema occasionally, have a bit of pleasure myself, live like a girl. Only I daren't say anything. Vili was always asking me to the cinema cos he was always talking about it. The sort of films are on that he understands. I'd like to see them. In colour! Colour, just like real life. I've never seen such a film. Coloured films from the USSR. I'm still waiting, but now I might get to see one in what used to be the Selekt, in Egyetem utca next to the Piarist church. I don't know what it's called now that it's a cinema.

I'd have liked to give Daddy a big hug, and kiss him, so as to catch the nice Daddy-smell. But I couldn't. I'd have run and told Rózsa! But they weren't on speaking terms. Neither of them wanted to be. Nobody could reconcile them. Not even the Reverend. He did come once, though, and had a long talk with Daddy. Daddy doesn't even go to church much cos he's not too steady on his feet. The Reverend came round for a pastoral visit, as he used to call it, cos he visits the faithful who don't go to church. These days it's forbidden, he's not allowed to go pastoral visiting. Officially the priest's place is in church, period. So he can't even go to the cemetery. But our priest's a brave man, Adorjáni he's called, and he comes to see the sick, the invalids, even the backward children, everybody, cos Aunty Kujbusz has a backward child. When he was little it didn't show, but he was just a bit slitty-eyed, like a Chinese child. I used to play with him ages ago, then when we started school he began to be very odd. He couldn't learn anything. He wasn't naughty at all, just backward. And he stayed like that. The Reverend visits him as well. Aunty Kujbusz doesn't take him to church, he embarrasses her by being crazy and shouting out or misbehaving during the sermon. Christ our Lord took crazy people, the weaker and sinners too into his church. Only he told them not to shout out. And the poor boy doesn't do it all the time, just suddenly. He claps his hands, sings, says things like gaga. But Aunty Kujbusz is embarrassed to take him with her on a Sunday, although everybody understands. Her husband left her as well when he saw what the boy was going to be like when he grew up.

Anyway, the Reverend came to see Daddy as well. Daddy was drunk, just a bit, and the Reverend asked if he might come in. Daddy said yes. The Reverend talked and talked to him. Daddy just said nothing. Then he said that he'd got one daughter, Annus. He knew no other. The other one had cheated him, deserted him, rejected her family. The Reverend said, 'We're all born children of wrath.'

Since I heard that I've kept wondering why it is that God created Man so cross. Cos I too am well aware that he is. And how cross I get myself. My feet hurt cos I'm on them so much, and I'm cross. I get tired, and I'm cross. Piros doesn't yield enough milk, and I'm cross. The cat fools about, and I'm cross about that as well. I run out of soap, I'm cross. And I'm always cross with Daddy. Cos I always shall be.

But I daren't ask the Reverend. He's not so reverend that he'll talk about such a thing. He's a nice man, goes around calling on people, but I couldn't ask him if, say, I didn't understand something in the Bible, what did it mean. That's what the church is for, go in there and the priest will tell you. He only attends to business. He wants to have a lot of believers in the church, for it to be nice and black. Cos when it's full, the church is so dark with people and black clothes. So that's what he likes.

The Reverend was cross with Rózsa as well, cos he knew that she'd changed her religion.

When he'd finished talking to Daddy and was leaving, he asked me to go with him to the corner. I got my headscarf as it was a bit chilly and ran along. Adorjáni asked me, 'Listen here, young Anna. What's this I hear about you and the Romanian witch doctor?'

It took my breath away when he said that.

'How does your reverence know that I'm anything to with her?'

'Just you have nothing to do with her, young Anna. You're not to go in for incantations or anything, to get you a husband or whatever. What the witch doctor does is sinful, and you know it.'

'Well,' I said, 'I only want what's good for Daddy.'

'Then say your prayers, my dear, behave yourself properly and you'll get your reward. Be modest, obedient, and pure. That's all you need, those three things. Pray for your father.'

What could I say? That I already did pray a lot?

'Do you promise, my dear?'

'Yes.' Well, what is one supposed to say? To a priest. When he asks something like that.

When he'd gone I just watched him go, struck dumb. Why aren't there the kind of priests that can help with people's troubles? The sort that asks what's wrong, so that he can help? Nothing but little Jesus, little Jesus all the time. And that you must pray and go to church all the time.

But as for saying a kind word to anybody, cheering them up, helping them, giving advice, well, that the priest can't do. Neither an old priest nor a young one. An old priest might have acquired a better understanding of life and know that he has to help. But perhaps he's that much more tired. A young one wants nothing but to show how black his church is, how many faithful he's got. He knows nothing about the woes of mankind.

So I'd have asked the Reverend gentleman what made people so cross. If indeed God had created Man so well, why had He given him such a bad temper? And in particular, why had He given him a drink? Clearly so that the drunkard should wet himself and his daughter would have to clean him up. Like Daddy.

I so yearn for a clergyman with whom I could talk things over. You go to a Bible class or the like cos you can't ask questions in church, nor is that great big church there for us to play question-and-answer, like in playtime at school. But there are such classes for children even younger than me, who know nothing, and they're given answers. Then perhaps believers would go to church more, cos now, of course, they don't like it so cos it's such an out-dated thing to do, and nowadays there's so much talk about creation as well. Vili too made that exhibition *The Origin of Man*. In it Man had to work and display. A scientific exhibition of how Man developed, how the whole of human life came into being. In science, of course, the origin is different. Well, there's no talking to Reverend gentlemen about that.

I would go to church, especially if I were alone, and there's not so much to do in winter. Only the priests aren't such that I can understand the sermon. They state this and that but there's no opportunity for conversation. They like to talk, but we don't care to be asking questions and prefer to remain silent. They certainly enjoy preaching. All the same I go along when I can, and just now I went to Whitsun—I go to major festivals cos one's supposed to, but it wasn't so very good. I can't enjoy being preached at in that fashion. I don't learn from it how I should deal with what's in store for me.

The Hóstát people ought to have built themselves a smaller church here. The Kétágú's such a great big church, obviously intended to compete with the Catholics in the main square. It's so impressive cos it has two towers. Not one, like the church in the main square, but two! When I was little and sang in the choir I used to be quite scared up there when I saw how big it was. Why does God's house have to be so enormous? That church was obviously not built to encourage conversation. All the good Hóstát farmers had it built. In the old days, of course, when there were still rich people.

As the Reverend was leaving Daddy he said, 'We forgive you in Jesus. So you too must forgive your daughter.'

That's what the Reverend told Daddy as he was leaving him. Well, Daddy still couldn't forgive as a result. Cos he was referring to Rózsa. That was for sure.

I'd given up talking to her about becoming reconciled with Daddy. It was nothing to do with me. I'd tried but I couldn't manage it at all. Was I supposed to bring them together? To hell with it.

Daddy changed a lot, unfortunately. He sobered up, but he was so gloomy. He hardly said a word, just worked, drove himself. It was no good him sobering up if I'd got nobody to talk to. Couldn't he feel a bit pleased at not being drunk? Not under the influence but acting normally, like a decent person? He'd got over it. At the time I thought that anybody that had sobered up was purged of drink and could be happy. But he wasn't at all, he was worse than before. He'd been able to enjoy the drink when he started, and at first he was always pleasant. For an hour or two. But not after that, cos the drink began to take effect. Now, however, he was just dull, and if I said anything he'd just spit out a reply. When I said 'Let's have dinner,' he'd ask if I couldn't see that he was busy. He'd got to get on while the daylight lasted.

Now that Daddy was doing the heavy jobs. I'd take myself off down the garden where there was a big pile of wood, and I was chopping it up for kindling. Foltika the cat would come along, nice and pregnant again. Why the hell did she bring so many kittens into the world? Couldn't she see that nobody wanted them? In the old days people would give a lei for them. For the big cat. What became of a cat that was handed over like that? A fur hat, perhaps. I wouldn't get rid of a cat, that's for sure, however hard up I was getting.

'You mustn't have so many kittens, do you hear, Folti? Do you understand? Mind how you behave with the tomcats. You mustn't make yourself available all the time.'

There's no talking to her, it's just in a cat's blood. They have two litters a year. Daddy found them not long ago. The little ones were well developed, four of them. One was black, another snow white, the other two piebald. I looked at them, had they all got different fathers, to be so different? No two were alike. But people pass on their parents' colour. A really swarthy Gypsy doesn't have white children. Daddy picked them up and said, 'Look here, are you keeping cats again? Haven't I told you what to do with them?'

Cos kittens had to be done away with.

I replied, 'I couldn't do it. Foltika knows when she's like that and takes her kittens away. We don't see any more of them.'

That wasn't true at all, of course. But when was the last time that Daddy had been into the sty, where there was a pig ages ago?

Then he'd come out with the kittens.

I said, 'Don't take them away, cos Aunty wants one, her cat's died, and they need one for the hospital kitchen to deal with the mice.'

'You're not telling fibs are you, Annus? Who on earth needs a cat?'

'An' who's going to catch mice? Only a cat. So they are needed.'

Well, of course I was fibbing. I had to go and see Rózsa, as in the past she'd been very clever at disposing of kittens. But she'd said not to take her any more as nobody wanted any. So I took her these further four. It turned out that Aunty Julia's cat had been resurrected, as it hadn't died. I was only saying that.

I used to sit there in the evening, chopping the kindling, as I liked always to have plenty. I took the hand-axe to chop with, as a big pear tree had been cut down. The root should have been dug out so that we'd be able to plant there, but there was nobody to do the digging. I couldn't dig up the root of a tree, that's for sure. That's an awful hard job. I liked kindling and had four baskets full.

Making a fire is nice.

Daddy was fine then for four days. Only he was dull and gloomy, and wasn't eating. Little or nothing. Perhaps there was something wrong with his stomach and he couldn't eat anything strongly flavoured. Eating little bits all the time, and now and then fetching up. He'd run out to the yard, just get there in time, and the dog would lick it up.

When I washed the carrots to take them out, it was really painful. Carrots, celery, parsley, parsnips, because this year had been the first time I'd tried them, and people had been asking for them. They had to be washed, I couldn't just take them covered with mud. But it wasn't summer, not even September now, and I'd just lifted the last of them. You'd think that washing all the vegetables in the yard in a bucket would be the last thing to hurt me. My hands were all red and the cold water made them hurt all the time. I couldn't take things to sell just as they came, all dirty, and the better they were washed the more I could get for them. And the roots had to be cut off as well, and my hands were so painful I'd rather not think about it. I got it done, and that was that. If I'd thought that I'd got another two baskets of vegetables to wash, and my hands were already hurting enough to kill me, I just couldn't have done it. If I'd let the soil dry on them so as to do it next day or the day after, it would get so dry that I'd have had to scrape it off with a knife. Then the vegetables wouldn't have looked so nice, cos the skin would be scratched. Aunty Mária came last year and helped, she sat in the yard and worked with me, and I gave her a basketful. But now, poor thing, she mustn't be out in the cold, she's got something the matter with her kidneys and they're hurting her.

But on the fifth day, Daddy started again. It's a good thing that we've got such a big gate, and people can't see in. It's not like the ones that are made of wire these days, cos it's cheap. We've got a lovely big tree, and the side gate is let directly into it. What if people could see in and watch the poor girl doing the heavy work by herself, while her father just lay in bed drunk, or was so weakened by drink that he couldn't stay on his feet. He got so drunk that he went to sleep on his feet, tried to pick up the bucket, then just stood there over it, swaying this way and that, not in control of himself.

'Dear Mummy, help me,' I said when I saw him like that. But I couldn't pray for Daddy any longer. Now I was used to his always being like that.

It was then that Aunty Mária cast a spell on him. She went to see the *papné*, the Romanian priestess, cos she knows things that nobody else does. She can send away the dead. When somebody can't die, only weeps and moans all the time, is bedridden and can't even get up any more, is just waiting for death which doesn't come, the Romanian *papné* is called to them. She can talk to death. She summoned him, and then the old woman died. I don't know who the old woman was, she lived somewhere in the Tököz. She went to her house, prayed, cast a spell, whatever. She said that nobody should go to the dying woman's house for a couple of hours, so that she might pass away.

So, I asked Aunty Mária now to do something, anything, just to bring Daddy to his senses, so that he might become more normal again. By then everybody had spoken to him so much, all the relations, even my uncles, who hadn't spoken to him for a very long time.

Aunty Mária went to see the *papné*, who asked her to take three little things from Daddy that he had held in his hand. And I had to give her some of his hair. So I gave her a little glass, a cigarette holder which he'd mislaid, and a little flannel with which he'd wiped his face when he washed, and it was still wet. But oh dear, the hair! I was really frightened! I had to wait for him to be asleep, then I took the smallest scissors. I sat down level with his head, at first so that he would be used to having someone beside him. If he'd woken up and caught me with the scissors he'd even have thought I meant to do him harm. But I never ever have. I just wished that evil and the demon drink would come out of him. Then I managed to snip a little hair and I put it in a paper bag. Aunty Mária had instructed me to have a good wash that evening once the moon had risen. To wash myself all over. So I waited and waited for the moon to rise, but the sky was overcast. But then it showed through, and I warmed up the kitchen and started to take a bath in the big tub. But it wasn't Saturday. Even then I was afraid. What if Daddy woke up and found me, what was I to say, why was I taking a bath on a Wednesday?

That wasn't all I was afraid of.

When once he saw me naked, and he was drunk, completely sozzled, he grabbed my breasts. All he could think of was fondling his daughter. I pushed him away and screamed. In ran the dog and Daddy was alarmed cos it jumped at him from behind. It wasn't a very big dog. He gave poor Csipész a good kick, and I managed to run out. The dog howled and howled. Since then I hadn't washed except in the pantry, and I bolted the door well and truly. There wasn't room for the big tub in there, only for a basin, and I set it up on a stool, but I really liked to soak for an hour in the big one. Now I only wash in a basin, and I undress and dress in the pantry. Or in the barn. Cos when it isn't cold I go outside and sleep on a big old chest that's out there. Dear Puju doesn't bother me. Like that I can sleep like a child, without any anxiety, not wake up for anything. The horse just paws the ground in the night and can't stop chewing. I used to put cotton wool in my ears, but I was afraid that I wouldn't wake up if something happened. If Daddy came in or anything. So that I'd have to get up.

What the *papné* did or didn't do I don't know, but then Daddy was all right again.

He'd been fine for three days, and now he was only drinking half a litre. He began first thing with a little cup, but wasn't getting drunk. It was only when he started to tremble that he filled it up. Perhaps he wouldn't have been able to work if he didn't drink anything.

A while ago I talked to a woman who sells herbs at the market. She was always there selling roots and things that she gathered in the fields, and teas, and she knew which were good for problems. I asked her for something when my breasts were painful and she certainly helped me, gave me a root of some sort that I had to drink. Well, once she came to me and asked if I could spare some vegetables. Of course I could. She asked whether she might give me a few herbs in exchange, as she hadn't sold anything yet and hadn't got a single lei. I said that I was very short of cash as well, let's wait until she'd made a sale. But she wasn't going to be allowed to any longer, she'd got to join the herbalist collective. Was there a collective for herbs now, I asked. It had been set up on a national basis, and shops were being opened that sold only medicinal herbs. It was the end for her, then, cos she wasn't a member. Hadn't I got some trouble, she asked, or perhaps some relation had, that she could give me a herb to treat? If I'd caught a cold she would give me something. There was nothing wrong with me, I said, but my father wasn't well.

What was his trouble, she asked. Well, I said, he couldn't eat anything. Why was that? she asked. Cos his stomach won't take it, he sicks it up. He doesn't drink? asked the old lady.

Oh dear, that brought tears to my eyes! Everybody could see them running down my face. All he does is drink, I said, and I cried like a child. Cos he hadn't been able to go to work the day before. Fortunately he'd slept on the bench and I hadn't had to wash up after him, only his trousers. When he got up he saw them and threw them into the pantry. Well, Daddy was a grown man, just imagine, going in his trousers.

I told Aunty Rozália—that was her name—that Daddy has been living on nothing but drink for a long time. If she could give me something for that I'd give her a cart load of vegetables. I promised her everything, and she brought me some kind of root. She told me to crush it in a mortar and give Daddy a teaspoonful of it. So how was I to get it into his mouth so that he would swallow it?

I should tell him it was a powder to give him strength. Not to discuss it, just say that it would give him strength.

So, that I did. No, no way, Daddy wouldn't take it. I begged him on and on, and he went to bed. When he called for me to take him water I said I was putting my foot down, he must drink it.

'Daddy, you've got to drink this. Please get better.'

By that time he was very weak, didn't refuse and drank it.

Next day he didn't touch drink, got up early and lit the fire, then went back to bed. In the evening he asked for some soup. There, I thought, it's working. So I put some more of the powder into the soup for him. Rozália had said that that was the thing to do. It tasted slightly bitter, but I put plenty of salt in and he ate some. And he began to get better. But when, on the fifth day, the powder was all gone and Daddy was completely cured, in the evening he only went down to the pub. He stayed there for a while and then came home—he didn't like to be seen drinking. He'd brought two litres home.

I begged him to have a drop of soup, and at that he slammed the door, threw the spoon at me, and told me to shut my face.

I asked Aunty Rozália for more powder, she gave me some and I began again. I still had to be careful so that he shouldn't see what I was doing. Rozália said that the root would reject the drink in him, and when he drank it he wouldn't be able to drink wine. Only his body would get used to it if I gave him a lot. And I thought, that was beginning to happen. Cos on the third day he was drinking a bit once more.

Aunt Rozália asked whether his belly was very swollen. She just asked quietly, when she saw that there was nobody near me, So I said, yes, very, and he wasn't farting. And the day before he hadn't eaten a thing. Perhaps he should eat something first. He ought to take some herb or powder.

She gave me something that was good for the appetite. I tried everything. From the previous autumn until spring, I tried all sorts of things that she recommended and gave me. She wouldn't take any money. I gave her vegetables, and at Christmas, shredded cabbage and cabbage leaves, everything.

Then when she caught sight of me at the household stall, cos I'd gone to get some string, she said, 'I've been thinking about your problem, my dear. Let me tell you, in the past I've even cured cancer with a tea. I had somebody that came to me with leukaemia, and he was on his feet a month later. There was a child that was crazy, and I cured him. But never in my life have I been able to cure an alcoholic. A doctor came to see me once, he'd heard about me and wanted to see how I did it. He was there half a day, because I had to show him everything, and he even enquired about my grandmother. Because it was through her that I'd started to gather herbs. He wrote it all down. I told him when to gather them, for example, you have to go at dawn when the dew's still on it to gather lungwort. But I didn't tell him to go at the full moon, or when the fox turns round three times, because that's witchcraft, and he wouldn't believe it. I tell you, I didn't mention the fox or the moon, but certainly you have to gather them at dawn. It does make a difference to the plant. I asked him whether it mattered to a patient when he operated on him? At night or in the evening or early in the morning? If it made no difference to the patient, early morning was best, because their stomach had to be empty and their blood clear. So you see, doctor, plants are the same. By evening they're tired, their strength has gone, they need to sleep. When they've had their sleep out and absorbed some moisture, that's when they're full of strength. Then I taught him how to dry them. Some in full sunlight, others in the shade so that the sun doesn't take away the goodness in them, some in the dark because the light spoils them. He took a big bag of all sorts of things that he asked for. I was given so many lei that I could have bought sugar, oil, and a little fat, but I just didn't get anything in the shops, they said that I had to go early in the morning when they'd be opening. So that's how it is, the same goes for patients as for plants, they're at their best in the early morning. He asked about all my cases, and I told him about all the healing I'd done. It was all written down, ever since I'd been working. I even told him about the old man with gout, go and look at him, I said, here he comes running, he's my neighbour. But his wife wouldn't let him, because, in my opinion, I meant to cure him with my what's-it. But the trouble is, my dear, I've not succeeded in curing a drunkard of his problem. There was one whose heart was beating like an engine. And I told him as well what he should do. Another had a brick fall off the roof onto his head, and he saw angels all the time. I told his son how to treat him—if ever he saw an angel, leave him alone, that wouldn't hurt anybody. But drunkards are beyond my powers.'

So if even Rozália said that, there was nothing more that anybody could do to help.

'My dear,' said she, and tears poured from her eyes, cos she was the sort of old lady who is always a little weepy, 'I won't accept another carrot from you, because I've treated your father shamefully. I've failed to cure him of his drinking, because he's so thoroughly committed to it that the good Lord alone will be able to break him of the habit. So forgive me, poor ignorant old woman that I am, who thought of myself that I could exceed the devil in cunning. When you come with your own problems I'll cure you of everything with an infusion, give you everything for nothing, won't take a single lei or bani from you. But I can't do anything for your father, I've tried everything that God has created in field, forest or flood, and as you see, I've failed. I'm so ashamed of myself, my dear, I've accepted all sorts of things from you that you've produced by the work of your hands, and I know the way you've bent your back, I've done it myself, almost broken in two. Forgive me, my dear, and don't go telling anyone that old Rozália couldn't help you. Don't tell anyone that, my dear.'

The old lady sobbed bitterly, and it was for me to console her.

When Aunty Rozália told me that, I was so very, very embittered that even Vilmos couldn't raise my spirits. He was always saying that I should go to the Station, leave the land, take a paid job with him, I'd have to work, of course, as nothing there was free, it was public money. But how could I leave it? He'd better not say anything more like that, cos I'd got enough trouble. I should go and work for him, and see to the garden when I liked. Just as much as I had to. I was there until late in the evening. He really made me happy, caressed me, I was in his arms, and he would hardly let me go. And I really didn't want to go home, that was for sure.

Then I had to tell a big lie when Daddy asked me where I'd been, because towards evening he'd come to himself a bit. I can lie with the great actresses. So what was I to do? I said that I'd been out selling, cos I had a customer that I delivered to. I'd taken five kilos of beans. I'll show you the money, and I did. I'd had it from Vili, cos he always paid me. And Daddy took it off me. Didn't ask for it, just took it out of my hand. I let him take it. Fortunately I'd only shown him half of it. I've got a pocket in my apron in a place where no respectable man will get it. I gave him just enough for him to buy wine, two litres.

But then he couldn't go himself, he was that weak. I had to go, I was so embarrassed. What could I do? I went. Like anyone else goes every day for bread. I went to the yellow pub for wine. Well, those that knew, knew, and those that didn't, didn't. What was I to say?

It had happened about three days before that.

Aunty Mária had made another attempt. And goodness, she and the *papné* succeeded. They cast a spell and Daddy came to. He was in his right mind, he was purged. Over three days he drank half a litre. He was working and eating. Just the first time he was sick afterwards, but after that he kept it down. So that made me happy. I didn't even think that it might all end. He couldn't work quite as he had in the old days, but I couldn't remember what he'd been like then.

On Sunday, I thought I'd just kill a chicken. That I did first thing. When Daddy saw he shouted at me so that I dropped the knife. What was I thinking of, what day was it? Christmas? To go killing a chicken? I said that it hadn't been doing any good, its back had all been pecked. It was a new one that I'd bought the week before to see how it got on, I'd been told it was a new variety, bigger, good layer, had feathers on its legs. But we'd already got eight or nine, hadn't we, and this had meant introducing a new one, and a different kind. The others had all pecked it, its back and breast were bleeding. It had to be killed.

'All right, you've done the right thing. You're a clever girl.' said Daddy, reassured.

Clever. So clever at lying, you wouldn't credit. I hadn't had a new chicken, I couldn't afford to buy new varieties and try them out. Clever. He'd never said such a thing. I'd never heard him.

I'd just killed one of the old ones, from spring. It didn't taste so good, I must admit. He hardly ate any of it. He couldn't eat, and when he tried to swallow he kept burping and couldn't. He had to put his hand to his mouth so as not to fetch it up. His stomach kept soup down better. I'd also thought of baking a pastry of some sort as I'd got a little basket of plums from Vili, a special sort, with big fruit, reddish. But I didn't really think that Daddy's stomach would stand plums. Plums take a bit of digesting.

When I asked on Sunday whether we were going to church, he replied, 'People with nothing to do can go.'

So I daren't go. He even thought I'd got nothing to do. But I did sing a psalm, a short one that I could remember. It might have had some effect on him. It was so cheerful, went so quickly, but I didn't know it all. It wasn't as sorrowful as the rest. That was while I washed Puju and Piros down. It was Sunday, so they had to be washed as well. And I brushed Csipész's head. When Daddy couldn't see. Little Csipkész likes being brushed.

But the last time I went to church, the Reverend explained the psalm, saying that God had created Man to have dominion over the earth and animals and plants and everything. And not so as to hug his animals. That was not nice. The Reverend said that it wasn't nice for anybody to hug animals rather than other people and to kiss them and have them on their beds. That was degenerate. Man should embrace and kiss his enemies and fellow men. Not his animals. He was there to have dominion over them. All that came to my mind when I was singing to them and washing Piros's backside. Animals have to be cared for and that's all. I told him that when I slept out in the barn, the cat kept me so nice and warm. One of Folti's kittens, a three-coloured one. I ought to give it a name, cos it hadn't got one. It kept me so warm, that I did. Not just puss, but a real one. Claws or something. Cos it was always scratching and kneading with its paws. Dear old Puju as well, he was so warm. Only there was no way I could sleep with him, he was very big. Or with Piros. She didn't understand. Cats and dogs understand, but not cows and horses. So it wasn't out of order for the cat to keep me warm, Anyway, God created cats to catch mice for Man and to provide a bit of warmth when he's in bed. When I heard what the Reverend said, I stopped talking to Puju. Didn't tell him any of my secrets for a week. It'd really bothered me. Where was I going to find a fellow man to give a hug to? I wasn't supposed to give Daddy a hug, was I, when he was out of his mind? Cos he was my fellow being, perhaps, and my greatest enemy.

Then I asked him how he'd liked his lunch, was he going to have a lie down. He replied that he wasn't so weak that he had to lie down after lunch, there was enough to do. That was certainly so. The potato clamp needed clearing out. But I could see that he was sweating all the time. If he hadn't been weak he wouldn't have sweated like that.

How was I to ask him, now that he was more himself, whether he meant to go and see the doctor about his stomach? How can you ask a man whether he's going to the doctor? I don't know. I've never yet seen a man go of his own accord. Or have the doctor called to him, it makes no difference. Both my grandfathers were like that. One's bollocks swelled up and the other's lungs rotted away. When poor Granny succeeded in taking Grandad Miklós to the hospital, they X-rayed him, but it was too late for them to do anything. His lungs were completely cancerous. My other grandfather was embarrassed about his balls and we little children didn't even know. Grandma saw to it that we shouldn't. She made him trousers like *gatya*, very ample in the crotch, so that it didn't show. All he drank was a kind of tea that Grandma made him. But he wouldn't see the doctor though he knew that something was wrong if his balls were so big. Pigs get castrated, as do horses, they squeal a bit, they're daubed with something, then they're all right and get over it. If only the same could be done for people, I thought. Women prefer to go to the doctor, but men are embarrassed if they've got a problem, you'd think it was the end of the world.

I said to Daddy, 'The doctor will be coming to the street on Monday, cos he's got to look at the children. I'll have a word with Aunty Zágoni-Szabó, our next-door neighbour, and get her to send him round to have a look at you and your stomach. Cos she's got two little grandchildren, it's them he's coming to see.'

That's what I told him. Cos there was no way he'd have gone to the surgery and waited his turn. And it's true, in the surgery you have to take your turn. I had to as well when I had a bad tooth. I had it filled, and the way it was drilled, it hurt the soles of my feet.

The way he shouted at me when I said I'd call the doctor, I nearly shit myself. He'd been to the doctor already, nothing could be done to help his trouble, he'd got a nervous stomach. I wasn't to call him round or he'd hit me. He was a children's doctor. Why call a children's doctor to him?

But Daddy couldn't eat properly. All he could eat was hominy, if it was soft enough. And he couldn't have milk on it. A bit of buttermilk was all right, but nothing containing onions or cabbage. Potatoes if they were boiled, or greens if they were well cooked. Nothing raw, not even an apple.

Nothing at all fried. I made a little *túró*, and that he could manage. Not enough to keep a sparrow.

Vilmos knew nothing about Daddy. Not from me, anyway. I never said a word. I didn't complain to him. Then it turned out he did know. He's the sort that senses everything. He only looked at me and he knew. He'd got an instrument that sensed earthquakes—there is such a thing. And it's needed, cos down in south Romania they're always having them. We feel them as well when they occur. The lamps swing about. Vili had something of the sort in his heart. He knew somebody else's troubles, he could see them, there was no need to whisper in his ear, like to a rotten Catholic priest. I'd just go to his place, he'd see me and give me such a hug! Gosh, such a hug, he'd pick me up and sit me on his lap, wouldn't let me go. Nor did I want him to.

Now that Daddy was better I didn't want to go to Vili's. I'd rather attend to Daddy. I was happy that he's come to his senses and overcome the drink. Mummy, dear Mummy, help Daddy to be able to stay like this.

The work at the time wasn't very nice, but never mind. The main thing was that Daddy had been himself for five days. Now the garden had to be cleared. I didn't like that kind of work, it wasn't nice. Any unripe tomatoes that were left I put into sweetened dilute vinegar, but there were some that had nasty-looking blotches. We had to pull up the stems as well, and the roots, and put the stakes away for next year. The roots were just rubbish, the animals wouldn't eat them, they'd give them wind. But the result is nice, when the garden's been cleared and dug over, It's lovely. Just like a made bed. I don't like the pulling up, I prefer the digging. At that season we had to turn the soil over thoroughly so as to let the water get into it. And spread the good manure from Piros and Puju. That was hard work. Good manure is wet and heavy, and it mustn't be used fresh. It has to be piled up, matured and spread around. Even by the spadeful it's heavy. I didn't even fill the barrow full, I couldn't handle it, strong though I was.

When Vili took hold of my arms, he said, 'I've never seen such a strong girl!' Then he looked at my back. I wasn't heavily built or tall. 'You'd make a weight-lifting champion, my girl,' he said, 'Pick up those weights.' Cos he'd got some that wrestlers use for training.

But I've got such skinny arms that when I've had a blouse made, I have the sleeves made ample and pleated, so that my ugly, thin, sinewy arms don't show. Vili said they were very beautiful. Strong and smooth.

Smooth?

Well, thought I, what's that supposed to mean? But they're not hairy, like a man's, But his are really nice and smooth, and always well tanned cos he works out of doors.

I'm strong all right, but when the barrow is completely full of manure I can't push it. Well, just about, but I prefer not to fill it full, take it like that and make another trip. I like it when it's all nicely tipped onto the garden for me to smooth round and dig in. The good manure has to go into the soil. It's good for the soil. Like meat is to us, it gives us strength.

But Daddy couldn't take meat, nor bacon nor the tenderest chicken. Nor sucking pig. He could take puréed things, things that were semi-liquid. I put mashed potato in front of him, that he could eat. He said that I ought to make it thinner. And he could eat hominy only if it was thin.

He had to drink a lot of water when he ate anything, otherwise he brought it up. He had to water wine likewise, as his insides would reject it. So I was very much afraid that Daddy had something terminally wrong with his stomach.

One evening he asked where I kept the money. I'd always been afraid of a question of the kind. In our house money was the devil, and I always had to hide it away. It was better if there were no money in the house at all. I told him the situation. 'We've only got seventy lei at present.'

What was I putting money away for, he asked. When I went selling three times a week.

I went and did all the selling. But then I had to pay some in tax. They'd been round and collected it. It was all down on paper. Daddy had evidently not been at home, so I'd had to go out and pay it.

Cos we didn't just have to pay tax on the land, but also on the produce. Goodness knows how that was worked out. The land wasn't much, but there were animals as well. One horse, one cow. And, I said, the things I'd had to buy.

'I bought soap, sugar, two kilos of flour. cos there hadn't been any, then one day it came in and I bought some. And two one-kilo loaves a week.'

Then I even listed everything, but I didn't mention the whip, cos I'd bought a nice new whip for Puju, decorated with red.

'You know, Daddy, everything's so dear. Here, you can see, I've written down how much I spent,' and I showed him the list.

'Well, if things are such a price, how much do you take?'

'I sell as much as I can, but there was only one market last week cos everything had to be brought in, there was going to be a frost, they said. I had to pay a man for a day to get things in. There's only been money from people who came for milk until today. But now there's none of that, cos now everybody's on tick, cos there's no money about. Not a lei. And I bought two bags of maize as well, I got it cheap.'

I can't, of course, have said that Daddy had done nothing for me, just lain in bed the whole previous week, and when he got up he took the money, fetched wine, and how much it cost.

Nor did I say that that I'd bought a nice cream mug from a Gypsy woman, cos I'd dropped the old one. Was I to do without a cream mug? Bugger that!

At least Daddy could see how the poor girl lived, that nobody helped. He said, 'Go down the market tomorrow, and in future go every day, we need the money.'

'Well, I'll go, dear Daddy, but in that case please see to what has to be done here.'

So now we wanted to sell in a big way, now that summer was over? In October? When we had plenty of everything I could hardly get away. This and that had to be hoed, this picked, that stored. And I had to go to market! All that had been squandered! Either I couldn't pick things, or I couldn't sell at market. I couldn't be in two places at once.

I couldn't even say to Daddy where's the money gone? Cos he never kept account of anything, of my buying this and that, hay for the chickens and the horse. If he'd found out that Vilmos was always giving me money. Always.

The way I felt when he first gave me money was that I wouldn't take it. What a thing, me taking money from a stranger just cos he was giving it to me. And cos he'd kissed me, of course. He'd suddenly kissed me. The time when I'd had that stupid crash with the load of carrots. At first he'd given it to me only cos I took him vegetables. I did that once a week. I'd go up to his place in the Borháncs and stay there an hour or two. I took money for vegetables. Then he wanted to keep buying me things, soap, cream, dress material. He gave me a little porcelain deer, a sweet little thing. I told him, don't keep giving me things, Daddy will see, I don't want any trouble. I've got to be very careful. Then he said, if I kept going to his place, I couldn't be selling in the market. I'd be short, not achieving my norm. I don't even remember how it happened, the first time I put money away. I was quite desperate, and Vili was the kindest person in the world that I could go to. He put it into my hand so nicely and kissed me over and over. Higher up and lower down, and he put something wrapped in tissue paper into my hand. He kissed me so much that my arms were getting sore, cos his moustache was so bristly, it was like a brush on his face. He said I should take this little thing and not worry at all. It wasn't as if it were money. And I shouldn't unwrap it, cos it was wrapped up, you couldn't see it, so I put it in my skirt, the front pocket that I'd sewn on, so that nobody could see it. I didn't even look to see what was in it. I went home, and I saw. Six lovely brown ten-lei notes, as new as if they'd just been printed.

I was so pleased, though I didn't like it being so much. But I was pleased.

Cos it was still cold then I was sleeping in the kitchen. I'd moved out of the room a long time before, away from Daddy. He tossed and turned so much that I couldn't get to sleep. I was cold, perhaps for that reason, but I'd got nice thick wristlets. I gave my nose a good rub. I can't sleep when my nose is cold. Or my feet. But most of all my nose feels the cold, and if I keep rubbing it nothing is wrong.

Then along came Mummy, and hugged me. I thought she was going to sing. She used to in the old days. I said to her, 'Mummy dear, ought I to not have taken Vili's money? It wasn't a nice thing to do. Taking money for doing nothing. Is that right, Mummy, I shouldn't have?'

'Well, my dear, you've taken it and that's that. Too late to worry now. It's all right. Only spend it on something sensible,' she replied.

'I'll get some nice warm stockings. That'll be sensible, won't it, Mummy?'

'Very sensible. Now, off to sleep.'

'An' I'll get a bit of maize as well.'

'That's sensible, my dear, very sensible.'

'What about a load of firewood as well?

'Why not pick it up in the forest, my dear?'

'You get punished for picking it up in the forest.'

'Fallen wood? Punished for that?'

'What the wind's blown down. You get punished for that.'

'What a thing! Poor people get punished even for that, for taking a little stick away. Where will you get a load of wood from?'

'From the state, Mummy. It belongs to the state. But Aunty told me, she knows a place out in the Bács Forest where you can take wood cos the forester doesn't mind.'

'You do that, then, my dear.'

'An' when am I to do that, Mummy? If I'm fetching wood, when shall I be in the market? I've worked it out on paper, look here, cos I add up every bani. If I go out selling and make moderate sales, not very good but not very bad. Then half of that will be worth half a load of wood. And I shan't fetch a load of wood for another week. So I've worked it out carefully. And then it won't matter, you think, that I've taken the money from Vilmos?'

'No, dear.'

'Shall I accept it another time if he gives me any? What do you say, Mummy?'

'You take it, dear. You're an orphan, your mother's died, your father's a sick man. There's nobody to help you. Rózsa's a poor thing, she's lost touch with everyday life. Now off you go to sleep, because it's struck midnight. I must be going.'

Cos spirits can't hang about after midnight. I slept so well after having a talk with Mummy. When I've opened my heart to her, I always sleep like a newborn animal.

So, I talked to Mummy. I'd accept Vili's money if he gave me any. I'd never ask for any, I'd rather my tongue withered away. Never.

Then he began to give me money all the time. Who would think that? Money has no smell, so that anybody could tell. Vili gives it to me out of the kindness of his heart. I know and Vili knows. And Mummy, cos she knows everything. So why should I feel embarrassed now? I've got to live. I'm living on my orphaned state, and from the work I do.

When I went to bed this evening the dog growled. Not a lot, but he did. I couldn't see whether he had his head up or down, I could only hear him. If it was down, that's a sign of death. If it's up, I can't remember what it means. Aunty Mária knows all about signs like that. If he digs a hole by the gate, somebody must dig a grave. That kind of thing's a sign of death. He can't dig by our gate, it's all paved. And he can't get there, he's not let out at night. I wish I knew who was going to die. That drunkard. He's at it again, he was clear for five days, sorted himself out, now that's finished.

So in the end I had to say to Vili, please. Do it. I don't mean to say that he'd never laid a finger on me before. Cos he'd always kissed me, undone the front of my lékri and sat me on his knee. I know that he's a man. I could feel it, cos I'd been on his lap. I've smelt him, he puts such fine cologne on his face, his whole house is sprayed with lavender. He said, 'You're still a child.'

'That I'm not,' I said. 'Have you ever known a child to show off by asking for such a thing?'

An' did he think that a girl had it in her to so desire anything of the sort? I didn't ask.

I'm not saying that I was his lover, But I knew that I was by then. Ever since the carrots overturned. I felt such a thrill when I was there. When Vili came in the past or I'd been to see him, cos then I was always going all the time cos his shoulder was hurting. It was so painful, he said, that he couldn't raise his hand. He'd been in Bucharest for a week, had to work in the office all the time, spent all day in meetings, people writing, talking, sitting in the smoke. His shoulder was hurting so that he couldn't lift his arm. He'd take his shirt off, he said, and get me to massage his shoulder.

I'd never before seen Vili stripped to the waist. I didn't touch his shoulder, or his back. He lay on the bench, cos he'd got a painted bench big enough for six to sit. We didn't go into the living room, he'd got so much stuff in there that there was nowhere to sit. He'd bought the chest in a village, cos he liked peasant furniture. It was a nice wide seat, covered with a patchwork cloth that Aunty Julia had made herself with a crochet hook. When you could get rags, before the war. He took his shirt off, brought the lavender cologne, and I was to rub it into his back.

Then he took me back onto his lap and hugged and kissed me. I let him, of course I would. I wanted him to do even more. He unbuttoned my lékri, and the shirt underneath, cos there was a strap above my breast and a little button. His hand was clever. I was sitting on his lap and feeling how it was. Oh my God. I would so have liked him to take everything off me. What was he waiting for? I didn't ask him to. I was going mad with the waiting. I simply couldn't say I'd take my skirt off and my briefs, come on, Vili, oh my God, but I didn't want to be anybody else's. He took his shirt off and said I was to massage him and rub him. His shoulder was hurting. He said I was to knead him like the best pastry. Then he didn't talk at all. You mustn't talk when you're undressed. His soul was undressed, cos it wasn't possible that Vili didn't know what was in mine. But he'd always said, what small hands I have. And indeed I haven't got big hands. He said that they were lovely and kissed my palms. I've looked to see what's lovely about them. I've always taken care that my hands and ears were clean. I've washed so much since the cart overturned with the carrots. So as always to be clean for him.

So I stirred myself, filled my hands with the expensive perfumed water and began to knead. My lékri stayed unfastened. It wasn't cold, but my nipples were all tense and actually painful. They're bright red when they're like that. The blood collects in them. Then my clothes brush against them as I pull them over. I didn't even look at his back. I couldn't look, as if I didn't know what I was doing. But it was so brown. Oily and smooth. Youthful. His back was youthful.

I wasn't kneading, rather I was spreading myself on, my whole attention, just embracing that lovely smooth skin, the fine smell, such a strong man he was. When I was with him, nothing bad ever came to mind. That I should be afraid, or all the worries I had. But I could always see how late it was, and that I had to go.

An' so I rubbed the liquid into his back. I became totally absorbed, like butter into pastry. I no longer even seemed to want to be Annush, but to plunge into Vili and be no more. Vili turned over, and there too he was so lovely, so brown, I'd never in all my life seen so handsome a man. He liked to work all summer in his garden stripped to the waist, and he was scratched by thorns and bloodied. But still so handsome. His chest wasn't hairy. Other people are as hairy as apes, which I find disgusting, but Vili was as smooth as if he'd been shaved. He lay on his back and I stroked him. I didn't knead at all. He drew my head to his chest for me to put my face to it. To me that was such great pleasure. I did so and kissed it. The first time he'd kissed me— or rather the second time, as the first time he didn't speak—he said that he'd never seen such strong little lips. My lips were sturdy and desirable, he said. I didn't know what desirable meant or didn't mean, but I could see in the mirror that my lips were rather thin. So I kissed him with those desirable lips. And I kissed his nipples. I was completely out of my mind by then. When I kissed his chest, I thought he was another man, relaxed. I kissed his nipples again and licked them. He had his eyes closed, held my head and caressed it. Oh God! I just kissed his chest and he stroked my neck and my ears and held my breasts, his hands were so gentle, I'd never known such a thing in a man. I was thinking to myself, now we're here, we must go the whole way. The way of lovers. I was nervous, but I was so looking forward to it, to my happiness.

But it didn't happen.

We'd only put the nice hot soup on the table. And looked at it, left it to cool down. That's how it felt. We didn't do it. And I'd turned seventeen.

So we moved apart, and Vili said that I'd better go home, not let Daddy catch me. Go home now? There were times when I wished that on the devil. Or perhaps it was the devil keeping me there. I didn't want to move a step. I wanted to sleep there on that bench. I didn't say such a thing, I didn't want Vili to be cross. Or put me out and never let me come again. I didn't want to be his wife. Nor anybody else's at all. And just to have children and do the washing all my life. I wanted to feel good a bit, and there on the chest he gave me that. Everybody's desperate to get married. Well, I'm like Rózsa. Only the other way round.

Early the next morning, Daddy took the cart to market. He was himself again. He'd been saying, let's try the little market, but I very much like the big one. The little one is the nearer, but the big one is the real thing. He'd loaded up in the evening, covered everything up so that it shouldn't get wet, and put the cart into the stable. In the morning we only had to get Puju going once we were up. I was outside by half past six. He said he wouldn't come for me, I'd drive home. Today the sale went so well, I've been really happy about it, though there wasn't a holiday and it was only Wednesday. Daddy came out at midday. It wasn't yet noon, the bell hadn't yet rung. When I saw him in the distance, I ought to have been pleased, but it was such a shock when I saw him. He was walking straight ahead, as he did what he'd been drinking. I'd only got to look at him out of the corner of my eye, and I could see at once. From the way he was putting his feet down you could see that he had to keep control of them so as to be able to walk straight. He was drunk. He came up and asked for the money. He said he was going to buy maize, cos he would get some cheap. I said, 'Daddy, we can go together when I've done with selling, and take it home in the cart.' That way I tried to avoid giving him any money. He began shouting. What could I do? People were looking at us. They pretended not to, but I could see that they were. I said, 'Daddy, come and let's have some lunch, I'll get Aunty Ili to attend to the stall. There's a place here where you can get warm cabbage soup.' No, I was to give him some money straight away, or he'd smash this glass bottle on the floor. Cos I'd got bottles of tomato soup for sale, I'd made about eighty when we'd had all the tomatoes, and hadn't sold them all. I bent down and took money from my pocket under the counter, turning away so that he couldn't see anything. So I handed over some coins, a three-lei and a five-lei coin. I didn't give him a tenner. He looked at them, turned them over, said I was trying to have him on. 'Daddy,' I said, 'it's Wednesday, business isn't brisk.' So he took them, put them in his pocket, didn't say a word of thanks and went off. When he'd gone Aunty Ili looked me in the eye as if to say she'd seen everything. What could I have done? There I stood, like a sack, hardly sold a thing. Well, I thought, shall I go home or shan't I? Where the hell am I to go?

At three o'clock I loaded all the baskets onto the cart. Aunty Ili's husband gave me a hand, they were very sorry for me. And we went home so slowly, it was as if we didn't want to get there. I went along Pata utca but in one place and another I stopped, had a chat or drank a soda. Then I arrived home. It was getting dark by then. The time had gone by.

I could see that the door was open and all my chickens were in the street. It was just as well that the dog hadn't caught them. Daddy was inside on the floor, sitting, not lying. He merely looked up at me but was out of his mind. He said something, dribbled saliva, but I couldn't understand anything, and he lowered his head again. I stood in the doorway to the room, everything was wide open, and I was as rigid as a hoe blade. He was half lying and sitting, not doing anything, sometimes asleep, sometimes trying to speak, raising a hand, trying to take hold of something. On the side of his coat was a big white patch of vomit. When he turned onto his side, I got a tatty blanket off the bench, a thick one. I laid it over him and said go to sleep. He would sleep it off and see to himself in the morning. I couldn't have lifted him onto the bed nor would he have let me. I backed out of the room and saw what he wanted. He was trying to stand up, but couldn't control his legs. Then I pretended not to have been in the room and left him to himself. He sat there, his head hanging.

I unharnessed the horse and put him inside, as he'd been out in the yard all this time. Fed him and the other animals, drove the chickens back in and gave them their seed as it was, didn't grind any more, let the dog out, bolted the gate and shut the door. Shut the outside door as well. I put on my big headscarf, didn't even wash cos the water was cold, it wouldn't have got the dirt off, and I didn't want to heat it and make a noise so that he would wake up. I'd never been up to Vili's before like that. This time I was going. But my legs were buckling under me, I was so worn out. I'd been on my feet all day long. I could hardly walk, I had no strength left.

I was scarcely able to go up to Vili's now. I couldn't go on foot. I had to go by bus, and it was an awkward journey from my place to his, not a long way but awkward. There wasn't a bus from the one suburb to the other. I could have done with a bicycle, cos that was how he always came. I prayed that I'd find him in, cos we hadn't made an arrangement that I'd go that day. I'd been up there the day before as well. I'd never gone without our having made an arrangement. This time he'd have to forgive me. You won't be angry, Vili? Oh, I was so nervous. Vili, there's such big trouble, dear Vili, please don't be cross, only today, I'll just stay today, dear Vili, don't be cross, do what you like with me, only please let me stay.

It was pitch dark when I got there. The gate was shut, but the dog didn't bark, it knew me. I had no key to there, we didn't have that kind of relationship. Should I go to the Station? What if he was there? Oh, I didn't want to cause any trouble. I went as far as the gate, but the big building was in total darkness. So there was nobody there. Only the porter and his dogs. He was sitting there drinking from a mug. I went back to the house. Now I was in tears. What was I to do? Wait for him? Can't you see, Vili, I'm here waiting, my heart needs to talk to you. Where can he be if he's not at home? I walked up and down, cos I was really freezing. Fortunately nobody came by, nobody had any land that way, there was only the Station and Vili's big garden. My tears were pouring, streaming down, my face was cold and the salt stung my eyes. I heard it strike seven in the main square, so how long should I wait? I thought I'd get the bus down and come back later. I was ever so cold. Then I'd go into the church in the main square. It wouldn't be all that warm, but I'd be able to sit down. Was there a God, when He was tormenting me with Daddy all the time?

In the church in the main square, I had such thoughts all the time as I sat there, it was a wonder the cross didn't fall off the roof. Cos there's a cross on the Catholic church as well. I was thinking such thoughts. Not that I meant to, I didn't for a moment, but they came by themselves. I'd gone into the church to get warm, but I neither prayed nor got warm, and my feet were so cold I couldn't feel them in those light shoes. If I were to choose between God hearing my prayer and doing what I said with Daddy, rather than me warming up, at that moment I'd have said let me get nice and warm. But I'd been saying bad things about God, and very bad things about my father. For a long time about Daddy.

I was always thinking such things. Such as, how nice life would be for me when he was dead. I'd sell that little patch of land out there, and if it couldn't be sold, then too bad, it could go to the collective. I'd whitewash the room and the stable. If I got a bit of money and it was building up, I'd buy another little horse so that Puju wouldn't be alone. Cos I wouldn't give Puju to the collective, I'd rather die. There I could only think how nice life would be when Daddy wasn't there. Then Rózsa would come back to the house where she was born. No more living in a nunnery. We'd have a nice life and work just enough for us and the animals to be able to eat. And we'd forget all the nasty things that had happened to us.

An' she and I would plant red onions together in the spring again! When the sun started to warm the soil. And we'd sit out in the sunshine, enjoy our lunch out of a pan when we felt like it. Nobody would tell us any more what time to have meals. We'd live together like birds. She wouldn't want to get married. Neither would I, cos Vili's enough for me. So we'd have a nice life together one day. When Daddy was cured completely and for ever, and God had pardoned him.

I wasn't ashamed of myself. I was not. Daddy's the one that should have been ashamed. I'd done nothing to be ashamed of. If I could think such a thought in the house of God, it was God that should be ashamed of Himself.

There in the church I thought up a very nice life for myself. Only I'd have to go home to Borháncs utca. I liked the Catholic religion, the way their church was always open. God's time isn't so apportioned that one can go at any time at all. Only even this was shutting, half past seven and time for sweeping out. I went along Magyar utca, all along by St Peter's Church and turned up just there. Then along the Kövespad and through the Pillangó estate. So I didn't go back up to Vili's. And I was glad that he hadn't seen me like this, all dirty and crying. And pleading to be taken in.

Where was I to go but home?

The room door was shut and I didn't care what was in here. If he was there that was fine, if he wasn't, that too was fine. I lit the fire and had a wash. Bathed my feet in nice warm water and made a nice big fire. I washed as much as if I were going to my wedding. In those days I was sleeping in the kitchen, I wasn't afraid any more, I'd strengthened myself. I took the spade in and put it beside the bench, so that if anything happened it would be to hand.

'A child shall not lift up his hand against his father and mother.' That's what the Reverend said. Quite so. He was quoting that, perhaps, to show that he'd seen how much anger there was in me when he referred to Daddy. But he didn't exactly say that if a parent didn't trouble the child but respected him like he did his horse and cow, and caressed him like he did his pig, that child would respect him in return.

When I was nicely tucked up in the blanket and had placed the spade by my head, I wondered where my hymn book was. In the room, perhaps. Cos I thought I'd read a hymn by the light of the stove. That would send me off to sleep if I calmed down. But it didn't. I couldn't think of a single one, just things all jumbled up, but not a line correct. I began 'Judge me, oh God, for I have walked in faith and innocence'. I said it as far as I could remember. I spoke to Mummy, kept calling her, but she didn't come. Perhaps she was afraid. Of the spade or of what I was thinking. When I was no longer afraid I'd be able to go to sleep. Nothing had been put ready for next day, and it was a Thursday, my market day. Well, too bad.

It was true, I didn't feel at all like getting up. When I did, the stove was already warm, the water had been filled up, and Daddy was outside in the stable. He wasn't pleasant, but neither was he offhand towards me. But he was working as if he'd never done anything else. Perhaps he'd just come back from the milk collection point. And I was sitting there on the bench under the nice warm blanket! And it was very warm indoors by then. There I sat, didn't feel at all like getting up. There's never any telling how a drunken man will be the next day. So I got dressed and put the puliszka on.

It was nine o'clock already, I couldn't remember getting up so late. He asked what I was going to do, as I hadn't gone to market.

'Mummy said I should have a good rest, cos if I don't I'll be ill,' I replied. I only mentioned Mummy to annoy him. He said nothing but was very gloomy. He was spooning up the puliszka very slowly, cos I'd made it soft. And he was putting cold buttermilk on it. He was able to eat a little bit, a little bowl.

'You're a poor child, you know,' said he.

Daddy meant that I was gloomy as well. We just sat there gloomily, as if we'd just buried Mummy.

So I said, 'I'll see to the animals today.'

Cos the animals could take all day. I ground maize for the chickens, swept up the yard for them, sprinkled a bit of ash in the pen. When I was

cold or tired, I went in and sat down. I washed my hands in nice warm
water. Daddy kept the fire going all day. It hadn't been like that, I couldn't
remember the last time we'd had a fire going all day. Not even on a Sunday
or a holiday. I made a bit of potato soup, there was some sour cream, and
some bacon on top, but only for myself, Daddy couldn't eat anything fatty.
I didn't cook so as to please him, didn't really enjoy doing it, just so that
there'd be something to eat. And I went and got some bread. I let Puju out,
took him into the street as he had to have a walk. So I went right down the
street, all along Pata utca, towards Eperjes a bit, and turned by the chemist's.
We used to have a bit of land Eperjes way, but no longer. Puju walked nicely
at my side, I just held the bridle, that was all. We strolled for a couple of hours
like gentry. I looked into the yards, people were beginning to come home and
move about, returning from market, from the land and from their other
affairs, and settle down. Such a lot of people, and all happy. Lamps were being
lit, and it was nice and light in the houses. It really pained me to see how many
people were living pleasantly in their houses and doing their things.

Walking was hard going, and my legs would hardly carry me. When we
got home I cleaned out Puju's water bucket once again, as it was as green as
the bottom of the pond. Then I also washed Piroska down with a damp
brush. We never take Piroska out any more, as there's nowhere for her to go.
We've got no grazing now, it's all the state's. She's always cooped up. She
doesn't like it. She's used to being in the open, doesn't care for being inside.

'Well, my dear, if you don't like it there's nothing for it, you'll have to
get used to it.' Cos we'd had no grazing for a couple of years by then, and
the poor animal was only yielding half as much milk.

In the afternoon I picked up the paper and read it. I always used to get
a copy in the market as people who'd finished it would give it me, and I'd
pass it on as well, just keep it for a day or two. I read it but it wasn't all that
interesting.

I wouldn't go up to Vili's that day, I thought. We'd arranged for sometime in the afternoon. But not for me to look after Daddy, his guardian angel

could do that. Nor cos I was worried about of what to say. By then I could make things up like a poet.

But I didn't believe in happiness any more. It wasn't coming my way. To hell with life as a whole. My life wouldn't improve whether I went out to the Békás or not. I hadn't got the slightest hope, just that rotten life that was always disappointing me.

The same had happened with the wood as well. I'd been given wet wood. It had been correctly weighed out and checked over twice. Then when I tried to light the fire it drove me mad, I just couldn't. I simply hated lighting the stove. I got so much smoke that I had to let go of even the little heat that there was. I'd been diddled, they'd seen me coming, stupid girl, wouldn't see whether the wood was wet or not. If I ever got married, it'd be simply so as not to have to light the fire. I'd set my husband to it and say that it was a man's job. I'd dig the garden for him, do the ploughing and scything, load the cart with hay, cos I'd have the strength in my arms. Though in those days we didn't have any scything to do. But so that I'd have somebody to light the fire when it was cold, or when I wanted to cook a hot meal or have some hot water—that was the only thing that I'd have married for.

But I didn't go up to Vili's that day. I didn't go, didn't feel like it. Happiness wasn't for me.

As evening came on I told Daddy that I was going round to Aunty Julia's. Why should I just sit about the house, I thought. I'd seen to the animals and didn't feel like working that day. I had washing to see to, but I didn't feel like it. I never do. I said to him, 'If they play rummy at Julia's, I'll stay a while.'

'You do that. You're young, have some fun.'

Well, I'd never heard him say anything of the sort. Cos playing rummy at Julia's was something I enjoyed.

'Only don't stay there until midnight, you're going to market first thing. I'll load up.'

Next morning I could see that Daddy'd had a bit to drink. Two glasses, not such a lot. He said, 'A man called to see you yesterday. A teacher or something. You'd promised to take him round what he'd ordered. Why didn't you go, then? Don't we need the cash? He left a message for you to take it round, cos they've got to be cooked.'

'Why didn't you give him what he wanted, Daddy?'

'I would have, but he said he wasn't going straight home, he'd got a meeting, and he was on a bike, couldn't manage the basket.'

'I'm not going round,' I replied. 'I've promised somebody else for today.'

'Look here, you're going to be in hot water if you don't take his stuff. Go up there when the market closes. I told him you'd be there at four o'clock. If you don't he'll go to somebody else.'

He'd be going to somebody else in any case. He didn't need my cabbage. To hell with him. Now Daddy was sticking his nose in. Wanting me to be somebody's girlfriend.

'An' why did you tell him I hadn't been?' I asked, 'Just so I needn't tell any fibs.'

'I said you hadn't been well, you'd gone to the doctor's.'

'Well, that's just what you shouldn't have said. To the doctor's. If I go to the doctor's, I'm really ill. I'll tell him I'd been to the chemist's for some ointment for my leg.'

'You can certainly tell a lie. You could tell a whole book full of lies. Your mother was the same. Always making things up.'

When he mentioned Mummy his face turned quite black. He went into the room for a bit and I heard him fill a glass.

Just one thing was worrying me. Mummy wasn't coming any more. I didn't go to Vili's the next day either. I certainly didn't. I hadn't got anyone to take a message either, saying that I wasn't going. I hadn't got a friend that I could send. I'd say that my father had got suspicious, so I couldn't go to his place. Instead I spent the whole day selling in the market, offering things, talking so much that it gave me a sore throat, and I sold so much that I didn't have a single cabbage left, nor a jar of tomatoes. So there you are, dear father, here's the money. There you are, have a drink.

One day just went by after another, sometimes I went out to market, sometimes I didn't. We did all the autumn jobs, and it was November. Autumn work is boring, there's nothing beautiful about. The weather was so dull, I didn't feel like getting out of bed. I was so bored with life then, and I was only sixteen. How much longer was I going to have to live? A very long time, presumably. If I only lived as long as Mummy had there was a long time to go. And, if you please, Daddy was ever so well, though he was doing his best not to live for long.

There was another girl called Annush. She lived up above, next door but one to Aunty Julia, and she was a bit older than me and had a sister called Olga, a plain girl. Annush was the elder, Olga the younger, and she had such a flat face. This Annush just didn't mean to get married. Whether anyone asked for her or not, she didn't want to. She was always so unhappy, but I never knew a nicer-looking girl in the street. When occasionally we'd played together, she'd always been like that. What's the word I want? A spoilsport. If we were playing she'd trip me up so that I fell, if we were hiding she'd kick and pinch. She had a foul mouth, oh, I'd never heard such language as she used. If somebody wore glasses and a headscarf she would pull their hair. Oh, I loathed her. And she was a bit of a whore. That's what was said, cos she did what she liked with the boys as well, twisted herself this way and that, let herself be felt. They had no father, cos he hadn't come back from the war. Then she began to quiet down when she became older. She didn't play any longer, didn't talk like that, became quiet, didn't speak but worked, that was all. Her mother kept trying to marry her off to this one and that, and even Aunty Julia had to invite some nephew round in case she liked him. That Annush kept saying that she was waiting. What she was waiting for goodness only knows. Then she threw herself under a train. One day she just got up, went down to the station, and threw herself under the Apahída train. Oh my God. She was beautifully dressed, as if she'd been going to a dance. The train cut her clean in two. At her funeral the coffin wasn't left open. We went along, though we hadn't been fond of her, just wanted to see her. It was quite something for somebody to throw themselves under a train. It's not common. Especially a young girl. Nobody knew why she did it. There was no secret that emerged later. Her mother had told the pathologist to take a good look at her. Down below, her cunt and that. Wasn't she in the family way or anything? She was examined, opened up down there, but there was nothing. Whether she'd been a virgin or not I can't say, surely not, cos she was a big girl, had messed about in the past. But nobody could say why that Annush had done herself in. Much as I asked I didn't find out. I couldn't stop thinking about somebody doing such a thing. She'd left no message, just went out one evening and under the train. Maybe it had been on her mind, how long she was going to have to live, all the work she'd have to do. Perhaps she'd been tired of life. Hope that doesn't happen to me.

I didn't go up to see Vilmos all that week. Not that I wanted to finish with him, nothing like that entered my head one way or the other. I was up to the eyes in work, just grinding away. I certainly wasn't shaping my destiny. Not a bit. I was just being careful not to upset Daddy. He was all right at the time, drinking, but a lot calmer. Not drinking so much at one go so as to lose control, but slowly, rather, spread over the whole day. Getting really tight. I was there all the time, keeping an eye on him. What was I to do?

But Mummy didn't come any more. I was really down in the dumps, I didn't go to see Vili, nor Aunty Julia, there was nothing but the house and the garden and the market. I forgot about Mummy. I stopped calling for her. I didn't call, she didn't come. Perhaps she could see that I was all right. But I wasn't really. Just by myself. Vili didn't come all week. Well, never mind. When I'd been to see him, he'd had to hug me and cheer me up, it hadn't been like his lover but like a feeble little girlchild, always being knocked about by fate. This time he hadn't been there. Then we'd arranged for the next day, but I hadn't gone, goodness knows why. Just didn't. I was fed up. Then when Vili came down to our place and spoke to Daddy, asked me to go, he was expecting me, I thought then that I wouldn't go, he could wait for me a bit. I wasn't a puppet, to dance all the time at his lordship's pleasure. He could wait. Then a week went by, and I hadn't gone. Daddy got himself plastered again on Friday, kept shouting, 'God damn this cow, she won't let herself be milked,' and horrible things as well. She won't let herself be milked cos she won't let just anybody milk her. He kept tugging roughly at her udder, kicked her rear, and she danced but wouldn't let him. She's an animal, you can't treat that like a human being. When I saw him kick her, it reminded me of the time that Rózsa knocked the milk bucket over. She'd finished milking, but when she stood up, she lost her balance and bumped into it, and all the milk was spilt on the floor. Then Daddy gave her a terrible hiding.

I didn't care any more. I didn't care about Vili. I wasn't ever going to be happy. There was no happiness in store for me.

When I went past Annush's family's house, she always came to mind. How many more times would I have to light the stove in my life? How many briefs would I wear out? How many baskets of cabbages would I load onto the cart? How many shoelaces would I buy?

My gloomy mood had lasted several days by that time. I did my work mechanically, with no enthusiasm. Daddy was this way and that, had his good days, sometimes lay in bed like a piece of wood, then got up and staggered about. One day he fell and hit his head on the doorpost so that it bled and his forehead was all swollen. I was out at the back, thinking that I'd mend the fence cos it was broken, dogs would sneak in and get hold of the chickens. I went, but couldn't manage it. My heart was pounding, I didn't know how badly he was hurt, well, he might have lain there and bled to death. I watched to see if he was moving. By then my hands were shaking. What was I to do? You must run and pick him up, call the doctor, and while he's coming bathe the wound on his head. I just sat there, doing nothing, just waiting. I'd taken out the little chair to stand on to fix the wire. My back was hurting and my foot was all swollen. Perhaps he was dead. I hadn't seen him fall, only found him when I came in, and I could see a lot of blood on the floor by his head. So I ran out. I wasn't afraid of dead people. Nor of Mummy, when she came.

Cos Mummy was very pretty, as pretty as when she died. I ran out to the back, right to the end of the garden, I wouldn't hear anything down there. I couldn't do any more wiring or knocking in nails, my hands were shaking so much.

I said to myself, 'Dear Mummy, call Daddy to you, take him away, nobody needs him any more, he doesn't need life, he wouldn't live like this, like a pig, if he could help it, wouldn't do it all the time. Take him away, Mummy dear, you're the only one that can make him better now. He won't listen to what anybody says, Nor to you either, take him away, see if you can make him better.'

I didn't actually say that. Cos I wasn't praying for Daddy any longer. I just sat there, and it was completely dark. My hands weren't shaking much by that time, my heart wasn't thumping. And then I heard more sounds from the house. I thought, he'd got up, come to, but he wasn't shouting so he wasn't that badly hurt.

He hadn't died. No.

He came out into the garden and called for me, 'Annush, where are you?'

I said, 'I'm doing the wire on the fence.'

'Come in,' he said, 'you can't see what you're doing.'

There was a bit of moonlight, but I couldn't see, that was true. He'd bathed his head and wiped up the blood off the floor as well. There it was paved with stone. But there was a great big gash on his head. I didn't ask him anything, I was afraid of getting a sharp answer, it wasn't any of my business. And he'd put some potatoes on to cook. I roasted some onions to go with them and we had dinner. I did the milking and put the vegetables from the cellar into the baskets, as I'd got to go to market in the morning. Then I went to bed.

Mummy didn't come to say, 'Annush, be ashamed of yourself, praying to me for a thing like that.'

I remember her once saying, 'Look, Annush, you can be anything you like. If you fool about I shan't care, one has to have some pleasure. And a young girl especially. Marry whom you like, don't bother me,'—so she said when I started going out with Vili—'go where your heart takes you. Only may your heart never dry up, because then you'll know no rest. If it does, it'll never be at peace even in the grave.'

I went to bed, and I was nice and warm under the duvet, cos Daddy had brought them out, but my feet stayed cold, couldn't get warm even though I was wearing woollen stockings. I tossed and turned until I dropped off. I couldn't warm up, even my heart was chilled. I tried to pray, cos I knew I'd done something wrong. Mummy still didn't come. Well, how could I have such thoughts about my parent? How could I wish for such a thing? Cos I'd really, truly, wanted him to die. With all my heart.

But there'd never be an end to this life.

One of Mummy's things that I had was a photograph, all three of us had been taken, Daddy, Rózsa and I. How old must I have been? Four? Or five? Rózsa was already quite a big girl, cos she was much older. We were dressed in our best for the picture. I can't remember where it was taken. I can't remember anything about my childhood. There's a great black hole where it should be. It's a good thing children forget all about their child-hood, cos if it were to come to mind, they'd go quite mad. So much that's bad happens to them that they have to forget. When they've grown used to what's bad, you see, they can remember better. They know that life is hard, and that's that. Daddy was standing proudly there holding hands with us, you could see he was proud of his children. The picture always used to be on show, but when Rózsa finally left Daddy knocked it off the wall. With a stick! The glass was completely smashed. I picked it up afterwards and put it away between Mummy's headscarves, and he hasn't been there, hasn't found it. At one time I used to look at it a lot, always thinking. Daddy used to treat his little girls so nicely—Aunty Julia, the market people, everybody says that he used to take us out, dress us up, even do our ironing when he could. That was how we were in church, they say. I don't remember. Thank God, I don't remember.

The next day when I saw Daddy he'd got two lovely black eyes. And they got blacker still later on, he was like somebody that had painted themselves as the devil at Carnival. But Jesus and Mary, what did he look like? It was as if he'd just risen from the grave. I asked him, cos I couldn't stop myself, 'What's happened to you, Daddy?'

He didn't answer.

'What's happened to your eyes?'

He went into the pantry, where the washing tub was and the little mirror that he used for shaving. He took a look and still said nothing. I said, 'Please go and see the doctor, you can't go about like that. Perhaps there's something the matter with you, that's causing it.'

He certainly wasn't going to see any thieving doctors.

'Well, just go to the chemist's, then. There's such a kind assistant there. Do go along. She used to be a nun,' I said. Oh dear, that was a mistake. Daddy was as angry with nuns as he was with the devil.

With all that black on his face, he looked like something straight out of Hell. Whatever was causing it? Perhaps his liver was now failing and bile was coming out of his eyes. I had no idea.

He said that the damage had spread down from his forehead, that was causing it. But it would have been better if that were not so, cos the injury would heal. But if the trouble was something internal it wouldn't. Now then, Annush, I thought, what are you saying again? What do you really feel, eh?

When he called again on Friday, the Reverend told me to have a word with Daddy because he hadn't paid his church tax, and when he was leaving he asked me to go with him again. Daddy was reluctant to let the Reverend in cos of the mess below his eyes. It wasn't so black now, rather turning green. It looked as if he'd been struck by something. I had to go with the Reverend, and I asked him if I might give him something, would he accept a little pack of greens. He wouldn't take anything as he was on his bike. One thing he did ask: 'The Fourth Commandment. You keep it, my girl. Always have it in mind. Will you promise?'

'Yes,' I said.

Well, what was I to say to a clergyman? I had to promise. But coming like that, on the spur of the moment, I didn't know what the Fourth Commandment was. And I was so taken aback I couldn't have thought of the first or the second. So as the Reverend turned away he asked again, 'Now, my girl, what have you promised?'

'To keep the Commandment.'

'And which one, my dear?'

'The fourth.'

'The fourth. And all of them. Especially the fourth, with all your heart. Do you agree?'

'Yes.'

I was so completely confused that the Reverend had been gone for some time before I could think which was the Fourth Commandment. Poor Rózsa would have known straight away, she wouldn't have had to go through the list.

Why did the Reverend say that to me? Perhaps he thought that I'd blacked Daddy's eyes.

Ah . . . Honour thy father and thy mother . . . That was the Fourth Commandment.

On Sunday I went to church. Daddy didn't get up, he'd been very drunk the previous evening. At least I didn't have to stay in. I sang the psalm, number 150. I sang it, but my heart was empty. I was sinful. That I knew. So what was I to do? Wasn't he sinful? Why didn't Daddy come here as well? He should get up, pull himself together, get on with his work. How was I to honour him? The Reverend was always on about submissiveness. So if Daddy came at me and went for my breasts, was I to be submissive then as well? The Reverend should come round when Daddy was in a state and look at him. Then let him preach submissiveness to me. And that parents always know what's best for a child.

I didn't receive communion. No way. God can see what's in a heart, so I'd better not pretend to Him about being pure. I'd thought that Aunty Julia would invite me after church to have lunch with them, but neither she nor her husband were there. Perhaps they were having to work. Whatever could they do in town? In town, where nobody certainly needed me. I walked through the streets, but it was as if it wasn't me walking, just my empty dress. And I looked at the streets as if they were only a film in which I didn't appear. There now, Annush, such is life for you. This film. It's running without you.

I went into a beer garden somewhere and ate some cabbage dish. Not cos I was hungry, but it was one o'clock, of course, and I usually had something to eat about that time. It was a bit watery, but it didn't cost much. I had three good slices of bread with it. I stuffed myself as if I hadn't eaten the day before. And I had a coffee. Like a countess! Then I went for a good walk. I hadn't arranged to meet Rózsa that day, but all the same I looked in at the hospital on the chance of finding her there. There's no visiting after lunch so that the patients can rest, but the porter let me in and I went in behind another man who'd given him a tip. Rózsa wasn't there that afternoon.

Then I walked on, and found myself at the theatre. Well, I might as well go in, there was a performance at three o'clock. So I'd see that, and at least I'd be in the warm for the time being. If I wasn't interested I'd just shut my eyes. I sat in the gods, which was full of Hóstát people, all nicely dressed. I hoped it wasn't going to be a gloomy play. Things like that were on all the time, I'd heard from a Hóstát girl in the market, the Jakabs' daughter from Honvéd utca, and she was very keen on the theatre, though she got beaten because of it. But she told me there were plays set in factories, nothing but working-class people going to factories and building things, working. And the ending was always very happy. Well, work was the last thing I wanted to see on stage, I did enough and wasn't going to watch it. I was alarmed when I went in that I was to see a play titled *Happiness*. Not cos it was by some foreign dramatist called Maximov, but I didn't want happiness, not even on the stage. I wasn't the least bit interested in other people's happiness, and I was never going to see my own. So what was I to watch? They needn't put on plays about happiness for me, cos I'd go up onto the stage and say that they were lying cos happiness didn't exist. It was only advertised in order to deceive people. What they ought to put on was the wretched life that God inflicted on mankind.

I looked at the titles that were given. *Working Days*. I wasn't going to watch that even if they paid me. I'd got enough working days, that was the only sort I did have. I didn't need any such serious or heavy-going play, any-thing so depressing. Then, with great difficulty, I made out that that wasn't what was on, but *Zsuzsi*. So I'd landed a nice piece of nonsense, slapstick that made the whole theatre roar with laughter, fall about, applaud nonstop. I'd bought the cheapest seat, three lei. What did that mean? I used to give customers two bundles of carrots for that amount. The audience laughed and laughed, I just watched, and I said, 'Good for you, Zsuzsi, the effect you've had on me.' Cos from there I had to go home.

Then up there I met my dear ex-classmate Zsuzsi. She'd gone simply cos the play and she had the same name. She was with her married sister Ibolya and her husband, a big, good-looking man. In the interval they said that I should go with them to a cafe in town. I said that I couldn't, I had to go home and milk the cow. Never mind that, your father will do the milking! What was I to say? They knew nothing about Daddy. When we left the theatre I was at least nice and warm, Zsuzsi came and took my arm, I was to go with them and say no more. But I didn't want to go, cos all I'd got left were fifty bani. How could I have gone? I said to her, 'Look, Zsuzsi, I haven't got any money on me to go to a cafe.' I spoke nice and quietly. What was I to say?

'You're coming, and that's that!'

So, they wouldn't let me go The cafe wasn't really all that nice, cos we bought some sort of creamy gateau, coloured meringue, terribly sticky, tasted of nothing but sugar. I didn't care for it at all. And they bought me a rum.

That'll be nice, I thought, what if I get drunk as well as Daddy, that both of us will be happy!

Zsuzsi wasn't a very pretty girl, she was on the short side and quite fat, and her nose was piggy, in fact she had quite a flat face. But she was always laughing, always in such a good mood! What was she laughing at? What was she so pleased about? Such are God's gifts: one was really pretty but unhappy, and killed herself; the other was rather plain but hadn't got a care in the world. How did that leave me? Cos I was neither very pretty nor all that plain, so what have you given me, Lord?

Zsuzsi was at the time in class ten. I'd have been very pleased as well to go to school. Or rather, I always wanted to, but too bad. Zsuzsi's father told her that if she left school she'd be hoeing. Didn't she even want to pass her matriculation? Cos when a child was asked which it wanted, a garden hoe or school, everybody replied a garden hoe! Zsuzsi had chosen school, she preferred to study, there was no future on the land. Ibolya had preferred to go into the shoe factory so as not to have to work so hard. It was shift work and she had to achieve a monthly norm, but when work stopped, it stopped. Didn't have to spend all day long tilling the soil. They'd still got a couple of animals and the little garden, and the parents saw to that. They had a good life, those girls. Went to the cinema and the theatre, tickets were so cheap, they did the rounds, as they said. So she could until she had a child, and she winked at her husband.

Zsuzsi too had a young man, cos she said she had a partner for the vintage ball. 'Why didn't you come to the ball this year, Annus? Have you got a boyfriend?' Cos that was the only reason people went to the ball. I replied, 'I'd split up with my boyfriend before the ball. Then I'd got nobody to go with, and I couldn't get another in the time.' So, again I was telling a lie. What for? That's the way I was, a liar. Zsuzsi was well off, none of their land had been taken off them, their father had just surrendered a little bit and retained the garden. Her father had both joined the Party and had enough to spare. He did all the right things. Mihály wasn't very much liked, because he'd gone from house to house getting people to surrender their land, explaining how things were in the collective, how much monthly wages could be. When people saw him coming, they went inside and wouldn't open the door to him. He'd been the making of the Petőfi Sándor, as the local collective was called. He'd been clever and explained to the wives, cos they were the ones to convince, and in many places it was the wife who'd agreed to join. He'd been to see us but didn't catch Daddy, I'd said he was asleep or ill, mustn't be disturbed, the doctor had said, he had to rest. I'd only have been thirteen at the time. He even started to talk to me, but I said I didn't know, he'd have to talk to Daddy. We've discussed it since then as well. He'd said that perhaps I'd be given wages as well. But of course, we'd have to surrender everything—land, tools, cart, horse, cow.

'An' the pig,' I asked, 'and the chickens? And the garden, we couldn't surrender that, it's right by the house, the house wouldn't be taken off us, would it?'

I mustn't talk rubbish, of course it wouldn't be taken. And things wouldn't be taken, we'd surrender them. Of our own accord. It'd got to be voluntary. 'An' we'd not have to surrender the house? And how would we do the garden if we had to work in the collective all day long?'

'That's what you'd get wages for,' he replied.

I asked how I'd manage to sell in the market. He replied, 'You won't have to, Annush. The market'll be done away with.'

'What do you mean, done away with, Uncle Mihály?'

'Everybody will go into the collective, they'll work there, they won't go selling in the market.'

'Then where will vegetables and everything come from? Where will people buy their stuff?'

'Well, at the Aprozár,' he said.

'Will you go to the Aprozár as well, Uncle Mihály?'

He wouldn't have to, he'd still have a garden. But the Aprozár stuff was poor quality.

'An' won't Aunty Babi be going to the market any more?' I asked, cos Aunty Babi was Zsuzsi's mother, and she went to the market, but not the big market, the small one in what used to be Széna square.

'Yes, she'll still go now and then. And you must go to school, Annush, and go into the factory like a good girl.'

I was very surprised that everybody would go shopping at Aprozár. Well, I'd been in there, but the vegetables there . . . they were nothing like ours. I didn't sell dried-up spinach like that. I rather gave it to the chickens, or made soup of it. You'd only got to look at the tops on the carrots to see how long ago they'd been lifted. Easily a week. They didn't keep them correctly. They'd all gone soft. Not been looked after. They have to be properly stored in sand in the cellar, then they stay fresh.

Then, as we were leaving the cafe, Ibolya said, 'You're doing nicely, Annush. Everybody says so. You're doing a great job, helping your father, you're a really kind daughter. So keep up the good work. You're a good daughter to your father. Oh, everybody used to look at you when you and Rózsa went on the main square in those frilly dresses, hand in hand with your father. But Rózsa, of course . . .' Ibolya was trying to cheer me up. She'd seen that I was like a piece of wood. Not laughing, not enjoying myself. And I'd had that rum as well. It had gone to my head a bit.

An' she kept on and on about what a lovely, good girl I was, how hard I worked for my father, everybody complimented me, envied Daddy for having brought up such a good Hóstát girl.

I listened to her, and it completely stopped hurting me. Was that really what people thought of us? Could nobody see our hearts? They were really like those porcelain Mary's in the Catholic church. Cos there she was with her heart fully visible through her dress, all broken and bleeding. That was how we were, our hearts were broken. The blood had drained out of them. I was no longer shedding a single tear. I'd been accustomed to my pain for a long time. The face that I'd put on every day had now set hard. I was looking at the rest of the world as if from a distance. I was no longer part of it.

Ibolya said, 'Why are you blushing, Annush? Don't you like being complimented? You've got to be complimented now, because one day you'll get married and your husband won't pay you any compliments, will he?'—and she looked at her husband, and he had so little to say, he was a real *papalaptye*. He was a well-built man, but so silent, never said anything of interest—'Well, there aren't many Hóstát girls like you. They all prefer to go to school or to the factory. They'd rather work there, same as me. There aren't many on the land, what there is of it. Cos it may be that the Hóstát's finished.'

'Stop the eternal moaning,' said her husband. 'You're forever moaning. How can the Hóstát be finished?'

'Don't you listen to anybody that says this and that can't happen to the land, you just mind your own business,' said Ibolya. 'You stay a nice Hóstát girl as you are.'

Cos Ibolya had given up Hóstát dress a long time before. She'd shaken off her Hóstát ways, gone into the factory. Why wear Hóstát dress in the factory? She wore a skirt and top town fashion, end of story. And she didn't wear a headscarf any longer. So I was supposed to remain an ignorant carrot-girl. Wear the local dress, work on the land even in November, sell at the market while my feet froze.

I'd do it, I didn't care. It was as if that wouldn't be my life.

But that rum did something to me, and the words came out of my mouth straight away. So, Zsuzsi and Ibolya, just you look out! Cos if I started talking the cross would fall off the main square church.

What sort of Hóstát girl was I? Not what I appeared to be. It was all right for them to talk about how nicely I lived and worked, while they took it easy. It was a fine life, true enough. I'd be going straight back to Daddy to see that fine life.

I caught hold of Zsuzsi when we were saying goodbye outside the cafe, and we all stood there for another half hour, and my feet were freezing cos I'd only got my light shoes on. The cafe closed at seven o'clock and we'd had to leave. I gave them all a hug, but I didn't want to let Zsuzsi go. My God, somebody take me home. I wouldn't need anything, just a bit of straw like the animals. I'd work as much as need be, just let somebody take me away from all this. Oh my God, I'd run away to him at once. To Vili. I hadn't been to see him for a whole week, I hadn't even been when we'd arranged. What did I want with him? He wasn't going to take me in. He'd just caress me and caress me, he was good at that. So what was I to do about Vili? He'd got a grown child, a nice big one, even running around.

There I stood, and the church clock struck half past seven. What was I to do, where was I to go? I walked round the church, thinking and thinking. My head was beginning to clear of the rum. Drink is what drives people mad. Then I stood at the bus stop, but nothing came, only a yellow van going out into the country. Vans came and lorries. So I walked home. There was nothing for it.

At home I went to see Puju. The poor dear was just standing there chewing, waiting patiently for something. Goodness knows what horses are always waiting for. I said to him, 'I'm selling you, I'll get some cash for you and I'll have to work in the collective.' I tickled his ears a bit, cos he liked that. 'I was joking, listen, didn't you get the joke? Of course I'm not going to sell you! What kind of a house is it, where there isn't even a single horse? You know the expression of ill will, "May the grass grow in your yard". Aunty Mária told me that charm, it's what people say to put an evil spell on somebody. May you have grass growing in your yard. Cos who'd trample it, get it? Not the chickens or the dog, only the cow and the horse. I've never yet been in a Hóstát house where there hasn't been a single horse. But two is more than you really need. We haven't got enough land to need two. Now, of course, we haven't got any land at all, only the garden. And you only go to the market, my boy. But the garden's enough! The Hóstát man gets a lot done on little land. Anybody that's not clever needs a lot of land. We don't need a lot. But out there we have to work like machines. One small horse is enough for that. And to take me to market, that's all. So I'm not selling you, certainly not, I'd rather cut off my right arm.'

It's not right to tell a horse jokes. I could see he didn't get the point.

Daddy had tidied everything up while I was out. He'd got up, milked the cow, seen to the animals, I could see, even hoed the chicken run. He'd even got the things for market the next day ready on the porch. So, Annush, now you're for it.

'Where've you been?' he asked. Where indeed. I thought to myself, 'I'll say to him, please beat me to death, Daddy, at least that will mean I won't have to get up any more.'

'I went to church early. You must have been asleep and I didn't wake you. Then I got something to eat at a restaurant in the main square, then I went to the theatre. There I met Zsuzsi, that I used to be at school with, Mihály Diószegi's daughter, and her sister Ibolya and her husband, he's not from the Hóstát, I don't know his name, Pál something. We went to a cafe, I had a couple of cream cakes and two tots of rum. I didn't pay cos I didn't have enough on me. I'd spent five lei in the restaurant and the theatre was two. And I put fifty bani in the collection in church.'

So I told him everything the way it was. Even about the rum, the two tots. Actually, I'd only had one. I couldn't have managed a second. Let him see, the drunken daughter of a drunken father. One daughter's taken to drink, the other's wandered off. I was just in the mood that day for telling him everything. If he beat me to death so much the better.

Then he didn't say anything. He didn't hit me, he hadn't for a long time, Perhaps he never had, it was only Rózsa that he'd beaten all the time.

'Want something to eat?' he asked.

Such a question too he hadn't asked for ages. What's happening, I thought, has he recovered completely?

Next morning I was early up as I'd set my alarm clock. I'd got a splitting headache. That was the rum, I thought. Oh, my stomach was in such a state I couldn't manage a drop of buttermilk. Well, you look good, you drunkard, said I to myself. I'll be nice and late for the market, it was seven o'clock. There I stood like a chicken that had been given bread soaked in spirit before being slaughtered. It wasn't quite ten when I saw Vili coming. I saw him in the distance. I couldn't actually see his face but the way he was striding, always walking fast. I'd have spotted him among a hundred. My God, oh help me, I was all a-tremble. When I saw him I wanted to run straight away and fling my arms round his neck. Oh Vilmos, forgive me, oh my God, don't let him be angry with me, I'm not such a bad girl, don't let him be angry.

He came up and said good morning quietly.

I said to Aunty Mária, 'I'm not feeling too good, I'm terribly sleepy. Would you keep an eye on my stuff, I must go and have a coffee, I've got a terrible head.'

She said, 'You were at the dance, I suppose? Everybody was there, and now they can't get up. My Sándor couldn't this morning.'

'I certainly wasn't dancing, Aunty Mária. I'll be straight back.'

Vili led the way behind the market, where there's a sort of coffee bar, and we sat down. It was hot, and the coffee was made on sand under the counter.

We couldn't speak, just drank the coffee.

Was I still going to see him, asked Vili. Yes, yes. I replied. My tears began to flow, and I had to keep wiping them with my headscarf. Yes, I said, I'll come today. I shouldn't go that day, he'd got to go to a meeting. Perhaps Kali might call. Would tomorrow be all right?

'Don't cry, my girl. Don't cry.'

The more he told me not to cry, the more my tears gushed forth. I didn't mean them to, not at all, I just said 'Vili, forgive me, I meant no harm.' What was he to forgive me? I should be forgiving him.

For not going on Thursday.

He hadn't even been there, he'd had to be down in Bucharest a lot, hadn't been in. Had to leave on Wednesday. Well, I said, I hadn't gone on Thursday. I didn't go cos I thought I didn't want to go again. I couldn't lie to him. And did I want to go now, he asked. Yes. But all I could do was cry and cry. I couldn't cheer up. I so wanted him to give me a hug, but he couldn't, there in the coffee bar, everybody would see us. So he'd wait outside in the car and we'd go up. What about my market stuff, I asked. Never mind that. Couldn't I get somebody to sell for me? Give them a third of the takings? I could ask Aunty Mária, cos she loved money. When I was feeling a bit better I'd go back and ask her if she'd agree. I'd got to go to the doctor cos my stomach was hurting so much, I couldn't stay on my feet. He said, she'd see I'd been crying. I said, yes, it really does hurt, I didn't get a wink of sleep. So, I'd go and take care of myself.

I told Vili to go a bit farther out, if the car was waiting at the corner of Pap utca I'd get in there.

He'd got a driver. Drivers know everything. See everything, realize everything. His knowing didn't concern me. Even in the car I wept and wept, wept for a life. I stayed up in the garden for two hours, then by two I was back in the market. Those two hours up there at Vili's place were such that at least I knew that it had been good to come into the world. If it was over, I could die. Vili just sat on the bench in the kitchen, didn't even want to go into the living room. I sat in his arms and stopped crying. He gave me a lovely cuddle—it was just as well I'd had a good wash that morning!—and spent an hour kissing me, and I him. His face was so handsome, I'd never seen the like in a man. I held his whole face in my hands and looked at it. I could see no sign of age, only niceness and kindness. He had very kind eyes.

I'd never looked into anybody's eyes the way I did his that day. We looked and looked into one another's eyes and couldn't stop. People can't look at each other like that. There was only Puju that I could do it with. He would let me, but nobody else would.

We'd taken our shirts off and sat there like that. It was nice and warm in his kitchen, he just lit the gas and it was warm straight away. There was no dirt, no need to go raking the fire—I really deeply loathed making a fire! We were just sitting there, half-naked. I wasn't at all cold, that was for certain. And we kissed each other all over. We didn't do it . . . that one thing. He said we'd wait. How long? I didn't care. Why should I wait?

I told Vili, I told him then, to do what he wanted. He could do it with me there and then. Take me completely. And I even started unfastening my skirt cos I could see that he wanted to, I wasn't blind, I could see! Come on, I said, come on, do it.

'When you grow up,' he replied.

He just wouldn't. So when would he?

When I had to go I started to cry again. I simply couldn't stop. He made some raspberry tea in a pot with roses on it, a lovely rose teapot that was kept in the glass cupboard. He turned on the radio to help me relax. Such lovely music came out of it, people singing in Italian, he said. Vili knew so many languages. He'd had to learn cos of the roses. they're an international thing, so he had to know lots of foreign languages cos of them. It was a good thing I couldn't tell what the words of that aria were, I'm sure I'd have cried even more. Cos it sounded to me like a man yearning for love. He suggested we might go to the opera, cos it had been open for a long time. Ten years at the time, cos plans were being made for the ten-year celebration, and he was going to provide the flowers for the occasion.

'You certainly like to sing, little Anna-bird, why don't you go to the opera?'

'I do, I went to the theatre only yesterday, and I saw ever such an amusing play.'

'But in this there's only singing.'

'I know, I'm not quite so dim, I know that everything's sung in an opera, no speaking.'

Then Vili said that the opera that had been on the radio was actually being staged at present. But in Hungarian! Everybody would be singing in Hungarian, so that people could understand it. The woman that was singing just now so sadly about breathing her last because she was having a secret affair with a rich man, was on the point of killing herself. Or did she commit suicide, he couldn't remember, but he had seen the opera.

'Well,' said I, 'I can happily die here and now, Vili. Anybody can! Why don't they show a poor Hóstát woman working all day long? Why not? One who's got no land outside the Hóstát any more, and had to sell her horse. That's what I'd go to see.'

Vili said that in the old days the people had been greatly falsified on stage. They were only shown as forever singing and merry, but they were suppressed. Nowadays they were being shown as they were, especially the factory workers, and the way that the workers had taken over power from the gentry. That was what every writer was writing nowadays, and what was being shown on stage. Things were being written that previously had been impossible. He gave me a book to read.

Vili was always teaching me things. He knew everything. I told him, 'I don't read anything, only the paper if the woman next door gives it to me. I don't know when I'll find the time.'

Fortunately, he didn't start again about my going to work in the factory, or to work for him in the Station, and getting a decent wage and not being worn out all the time. He said that when I had to go he'd take me down to the market in the car. I said to him, 'Don't bother, Vili. The walk will relax me.'

When I'd gone through the gate I started crying again. It wouldn't stop. I didn't want to go anywhere in the world. Last of all to Daddy's house. What on earth was I to do, to stop crying all the time? Why couldn't I stay in that house? Where was I to go? Whose was I to be? Nobody at all wanted me, nobody, except Vili. And he only wanted me on Mondays and Thursdays. How much longer would I have to live, I thought, cos I was young and healthy. Nothing wrong with me to make me die.

When Vili saw how I was he put me in the car and told Nicu to take me to the Catholic church. He said he'd come again.

I was back on the market and Aunty Mária gave me the money from sales, but I didn't look to see how much she'd taken. She said she's seen from the look of me that I wasn't very well, she could tell from my eyes. Which was true, cos I'd been crying so much. I hadn't got a temperature, had I? Cos there was typhus in the town, carrying people off all the time, you had to be careful. That would be nice, typhus. It'd carried Mummy off as well, she'd caught typhoid fever. I might die of that.

I was last to leave the market that day. Another woman came along, was rude about everything, wouldn't buy. I took no notice of her, and waited while she made her mind up to buy a bunch of parsley. Then a man came, running, in such a hurry, took some beans and other greens. I was packing everything up, starting to load the cart, when a woman came running, a great lady, wanted me to stop cos she still wanted all sorts of stuff. I said I was closed, cos I'd taken my baskets off. She needed things, she'd got people coming the next evening and she'd have to cook, she'd give me a good price. Would I tell her what she could cook really quickly. I got everything out again. A clever peasant girl like me surely knows what would be quick to cook. We weren't peasants. I was born in town, my father and mother likewise, both my grandfathers and grandmothers as well. Hers certainly hadn't been, I'd bet. She'd pay, she said, only please hurry. What was she to cook, she asked. Soup. Substantial, let it simmer, wouldn't take an hour. Then I got her some vegetables. I took another eighteen lei. Then she thought, when I was putting things away again, had I any tomato juice? Yes, I had, that day too I'd taken three jars along and hadn't sold them. Please let her have one. How much was that? I said I usually asked eight lei. A jar contained a kilo and a half of tomatoes. So would I let her have two, she needed that for the vodka. She was such a great lady, all made up. So what else have you got, my dear? She took some onions, you need onions to go with drinks, right? So she took some. Red onions. And shredded cabbage, that was good as well when there was a lot of drinking. What did she have to do with it? Just put it on the table, and some bread to go with it. That was what people usually did. It acidified the stomach when there was a lot of drinking. How do you know all this, young lady? Well, you know such things when you sell stuff, I replied. What could I say? Daddy used to eat some. Now he wasn't eating anything. I'd make some puliszka to go with it, I said. Where was she to get polenta? From me, I always took some. We hadn't got all that much. In the old days we'd had our own land. Now all we get is a couple of baskets of maize, pick and grind it, but it's not off our land. But people didn't need to know that. That maize had been stolen, so it was going cheap. Stolen from the collective.

When she'd got everything she wanted she said would I help her, she couldn't manage with all her things. Her car was over there. She'd give me another five lei. I agreed and packed it up for her. By that time the gateman was shutting the market, and he shouted for me to hurry up, he'd got a family as well, and children, wanted to go home. Good for you, I thought. I loaded up my cart and took what was left home. I couldn't take the horse any longer, and everything had to be tied down so as not to fall off. It was pitch dark by the time I got home with the cart. I couldn't use Puju any more to take the cart to market. Cos Daddy had been registered as a carter to give him a job, and somebody else had been put in the milk collecting point, but Daddy didn't do any carting. He'd only been allowed to keep the horse by saying that he was a carter, that was his work. We couldn't keep the horse to go with the land any longer, cos we hadn't got any that required it, had we? Either the animal would have to be sold, or I'd have become a carter. And if I took things to market with the horse and the poor creature stood there all day while I was selling, he'd be confiscated, I'd be punished, and we'd lose the horse into the bargain. So what happened then about the use of horses was that the farmers in the street would get together, take a cart, four or five Hóstát farmers would all load it up and take it jointly to the market. When the baskets were all unloaded and taken to be sold, the farmer would take the horse away. And it had to be paid for as well. We preferred to take things in the small cart, cos that was free of charge. I was the horse, of course. Daddy only drove the cart. He was able to take me and a few other farmers to market and then drive around the town, out to the station, taking people. But he sat on his bed in his muddy shoes. That day it took me an hour to get home from the market.

When I reached home it was so quiet there.

The chickens were in the coop, perhaps they hadn't been let out all day. What were they to peck? There was nothing in the yard. The dog too was chained up, didn't bark as he usually did. Perhaps there was something wrong with him too.

There was such a silence; had the world died?

The kitchen was in darkness and the door to the living room was open. There was no sound from inside. Daddy had gone out, I thought. I put the light on, and saw one of his footcloths on the floor. It was filthy. I pushed it with my foot, didn't like to pick it up in my hand. Oh, how I loathed having to wash his clothes. I preferred to pour hot water over them, sprinkle in plenty of soda and leave them to soak. When they'd had a good soaking I was able to touch them.

Aunty Mária came over when she saw the light on. She said I should go round to her place, she had some hot soup. I didn't feel like going round to the neighbours', but it was kind of her to ask me. There one had to do so much praying over a bowl of soup. But round I went and had the soup, She made such nice soup, plenty of lovage in it, sour cream, a tart flavour, Romanian fashion. That was good. Then she began to talk and tell stories about some priest, a holy man, a Catholic priest, who'd been in prison for a long time, and so became an even greater holy man. Now he was freed and everybody flocked to him, asking him to lay hands on them cos that would cure them. But the police drove the people off when they came to his house. They didn't want there to be a crowd. That holy man was moved to another village, where he wasn't known. But there again, sick animals gathered around him of their own accord. If any peasants were sick, he went to their houses, laid his hands on them, and they were cured. I said to her, 'Aunty Mária, *nu kred jo aşa ceva*, I don't really believe that. How could animals know where to go?'

'Animals are all pious, God created them all, and they're not sinful like people.'

'An' what did the police do about the animals?'

'Drove them all home.'

'An' where's that holy man now?'

'He's going about the country. All the sick birds fly to him and are cured.'

'An' what do the police do?'

'When they see him wandering about, they lock him up for hooliganism. You're not allowed to wander about. You've got to stay in your place.'

'An' does he preach or something? You can't be jailed for just going down the street.'

'They took the monk's habit off him, he couldn't go about dressed like that. They gave him some shoes and told him to go and live in a house. Only he hadn't got one. So he was put in the old people's home. Put in there. In Vásárhely. Then he was removed from there and put in with the lunatics, and tied up. So, he couldn't get away from there. But he went on healing the lunatics. They kept giving him electric shock treatment but it didn't work. Others were cured, but they couldn't cure him cos Jesus Christ was in him. Then the icon of the Virgin was taken from his breast, because he had a little icon. Then his cross was taken off him. When they saw that they couldn't cure him he was put out of the hospital. He began wandering again. Then St Nicolae said to them, because he answered to that name, that was what the Romanian people called him, that he could make two fingers into a cross, he'd always got a cross when he wanted one. Then the police told him that if he ever did that again, they'd bring an axe and cut off his fingers. And when they came, he just made a cross with his arms, like this, because they were sent by Satan. Then the police said he'd have everything cut off. First they cut off all his fingers. But he made a cross with his arms. Then the police cut off his arms. So he made a cross with his legs. So they cut off both his legs. And there he was with no arms or legs. Then he made a cross with his eyes. Because he could cross his eyes. He wouldn't abandon Jesus while he'd got anything that moved. So the police tore out his eyes. So St Nicolae said that he'd make a cross with his tongue, because he could do that as well, twist it like this. So they cut out his tongue. And when they threw his tongue away, along came a white dove and picked it up. It flew up into a tree and called that it was taking it to Golgotha for him. St Nicolae was lying on the ground, because he'd only got his body left, couldn't see or speak. So what became of him then I don't know. They say that he christened a policeman and cured him of being a policeman and beating people with a truncheon. And that policeman was arrested for wearing a cross. He was thrown out of the police, cos they aren't allowed to wear symbols of Jesus Christ.'

Aunty Mária went on like that, didn't want me to go home. It was like rum or drink affecting her, so that I shouldn't be in this world.

'All St Nikulaj's fingers, arms and legs were taken away and scattered all over. And everywhere that they were buried in the ground there grew great big walnut trees. And their leaves worked miracles. If anybody rested underneath one and listened to what it whispered, they realized that they'd go to the Kingdom of Heaven. Because the walnut told them what their sins were and what to cleanse themselves of.'

'An' where are these walnut trees, Aunty Mária? So that I can find out what sins I've got.'

'You haven't got any sins, my dear, you're still a child. Children don't have sins. But when you grow up you will have. But if I find out where those places are I'll tell you. You could take your father there. He could be told his sins and so be cured of them. Because then he'd have to be so frightened of God he'd never drink another drop.'

'An' if he wouldn't go?'

'Then we'd take his footcloths off him. When he was going to put his footcloth on he wouldn't be able to drink any more.'

When she mentioned footcloths, something caught in my throat. My life was waiting for me at home but I didn't know how I was to live there. Daddy's footcloth was on the floor. I'd picked it up with the poker and put it in the bucket to soak. I loathed his footcloths so heartily, I couldn't touch them. But Aunty Mária thought there was no sin in me. Oh yes there was!

The first time Vili took off his smart shoes—he always went about in lovely brown suede shoes—and put his feet up on a chair to take me on his lap I looked at his feet. They were nice and smooth, and he didn't wear foot-cloths but a sort of socks, of thin, silky material. They were so thin. Things like that are factory-made, not hand-made. They're too delicate. I kissed his feet for him and he kissed mine, but oh! I was worried, ashamed of myself. But I'd given them a good wash in the morning. I always wash on Monday morning. But in any case. My feet are my concern.

Now what is Vili waiting for? We've been carrying on for two years now.

When I wasn't selling, cos it wasn't my day at market, I went out with the cart. Daddy seldom went. At that time he wasn't in a bad way. I'd go out, smarten up the horse, brush him down to begin with. Daddy can't do anything now. He just lies in bed, very weak. It was up to him, he's done it to himself, being like that.

At least it would have been nice to see Rózsa that day, cos it was a Thursday, but no luck. She must have gone up to the emergency department, cos she'd asked Aunty Albert at the market for me to run up and take her sister a jar of jam and a warm scarf. I did that, but she wasn't on duty, so perhaps she's on nights.

I'd arranged to meet with Rózsa on Sunday afternoon in the main square, as we always did in the afternoon of the first Sunday of the month, before Mass. But anybody who's gone the same way as Rózsa can't keep meeting their relations, they're not allowed to. So she and I used to meet in secret, as she wasn't allowed to meet me every month. She had mass at that hour, I had divine worship, but I didn't go as I had to load up for market the next day. She hadn't said which church she'd be going to cos there's more than one Catholic church, but they preferred to go to the Monks' church. I'd have liked us to go to a restaurant together and have something to eat. I knew she wasn't allowed in restaurants, but I meant to persuade her, say that I'd die of hunger if I didn't eat something. I waited an hour but she didn't come. She'd never before done that. I went for a bit of a walk, thought of going up to Mummy's grave in the cemetery, but it was shut by that time. I hadn't spoken to Mummy for a long time. Then I went back to the main square in case Rózsa'd turned up in the meantime. Perhaps she was ill. I never said anything to Daddy. I thought that the next day or Tuesday I'd go up to the hospital where she worked, I'd more likely catch her there than at the flat. They lived together just where the street joined Mócok útja. They didn't like outsiders going to the flat. The convent, as they called it. Perhaps I could have phoned the hospital, but I'd have had to wait so long at the post office for the public telephone that I'd rather go up and try to find her. But then I couldn't get away for a whole week and she hadn't come. So on Saturday I went along, she was sure to be there. After the market I quickly closed up and Aunty Ili's husband loaded my baskets and took them away for me to collect from their place. But I didn't find Rózsa. They had a room where only the nurses went, and she wasn't there. I asked where Rózsa Butyka might be, cos the woman that acted as porter in the corridor was a Romanian. She was there to see that people only visited the patients when allowed. She said that Rózsa wasn't in. So I asked when she would be at work. She didn't know. Whom could I ask, I wondered. I waited, thought, and along came somebody in a white gown. I was hoping to catch a Hungarian sister to whom I'd be able to speak. There were various sisters working in the hospital, people like Rózsa, but all in different departments, they weren't allowed all to be in the one.

I sat and waited, and then there was a big diabetes doctor, an inspection was taking place, and I had to wait for it to be finished. So after that I got hold of one of the younger nurses and told her why I was there. She didn't know anything, but she hadn't seen Rózsa all week. She told me to ask for Dr Muntyán. Where could I find him? She didn't know, but I'd catch him on Monday. Well, I certainly wasn't waiting until Monday.

But then I did have to wait until the following week. I went up to their flat, but that was no use, it was all shut up, there wasn't a soul in the yard, and I didn't know who to ask for. On Sunday I was down in the main square again after mass, but Rózsa didn't come though I waited and waited.

I couldn't go on Monday, so I went on Tuesday afternoon again after my day in the market, sometime after four o'clock. The earth hadn't swallowed my sister up, I had to find her. In the doorway I found the old lady in charge. Rózsa had pointed her out to me, a Dr Neumann, who had a limp like Rózsa. I suddenly felt brave and said to her, 'Doctor, please help me, my dear.' Cos she was only a little old lady. I found it easier to ask a little old lady than a hulking great man. She was little, but she was in charge of that great big hospital. 'Please help me, if you'd be so kind.' And I began to cry. That was the way I was, I opened my mouth to speak and straight away I was in tears. And I hadn't even asked for anything. Well, she stopped and asked what the problem was. Close to she didn't look so kindly, rather stern. I said, I can't find my sister.

'What's wrong with her, is she a patient?' she asked. 'What department?'

I said she wasn't a patient, just serving there.

'Nobody serves here, they all work,' she said sharply.

'She's a nursing sister. Rózsa Butyka.'

'Is there something wrong, my dear?' she asked

'I can't find her. I've looked everywhere, but I can't find her.'

'Perhaps she's not on the afternoon shift.'

'I've been told she hasn't been in all week.'

'Then she must be ill, my dear. Go to her house.'

I began to cry again, I didn't know why.

She said, 'My dear, what are you crying for, you don't even know what's wrong with her. The time to cry is when there's something the matter.' I hadn't got a handkerchief, and she took out a sort of paper handkerchief that they used in the hospital and gave it to me.

She said something to the porter as I was going through the door, and called after me, 'You don't mean one of those nuns?'

I ran back. 'Yes, yes, she's a nun.'

She hadn't known that they'd all resigned from the hospital, but their letter of resignation had just been received.

I went back up to the flat. Strangers weren't welcome, weren't allowed in. Such was convent life that no one who wasn't a relative was allowed in. Well, they won't throw me out, I thought.

I had to go up Monostori út, past the salt works, not right up to the Calvary, and at number 11 Fogadó utca, in a long yard at the back, there was a little flat, two rooms and a pantry. I knocked, nothing, just silence. I tapped on the window as well. I wasn't leaving there until the earth gave me back Rózsa. Then out came a man, quietly. I asked whether they were in, but didn't know what to call them. They couldn't be called nuns. So I said I was looking for my sister, Rózsa Butyka. He didn't know, but I wasn't to shout. I stood a while, waiting, then I left. As I was going through the gate, a little old woman appeared from a door, caught my arm, pulled me inside and said, 'Don't come here again, young lady.'

'I'm looking for my sister,' I said, 'Rózsa Butyka.'

'She's not at home. And don't you come here again. They've all gone away, don't live here any more.'

'What do you mean, don't live here?' I asked, cos my sister would certainly have told me if she didn't live there any more, 'Where've they gone?'

'They were all taken away to the police station. Go away, don't come here, you'll bring us trouble. They've gone.'

'What do you mean?' I'd not had word, so I was alarmed.

The old woman only said that they'd all been taken away a good three weeks before, they'd all been rounded up and not one had been seen since. But I wasn't to go there again and I wasn't to say a word. And then she said, 'God bless you.'

Rózsa was in police custody. Arrested three weeks ago. So what had she done? And what about the others? The old woman as well, what was her name? Aunty Jusztina. In the hospital she was called Aunty Márta, cos the other name wasn't allowed. Had she been arrested as well?

Where was I to go? To my aunt's? That would really scare her, and what could she do? Should I go to the police? If she'd not been jailed yet they must suspect that she'd done something bad, and she'd be jailed later. I'd wait. Better wait, and keep my mouth shut.

I thought, wouldn't the police say something to the family? Or send a document saying what had happened? Perhaps there'd been something in the paper. Like when people committed big crimes, robbed or killed, or damaged property, or acted against the state. Those days people went to jail for the slightest theft, even something like a bit of wood from the forest. Good Lord, what had poor Rózsa done? It must be something religious, like before, when the convent was closed. That sort of thing was forbidden then. Had they not understood that it was forbidden? That being a nun was not permitted? I didn't think it was good at all for anybody to be so alienated from the world that it was nothing but God, God all the time. God had his place and we had ours, and had to work. Why did people have to make such a fuss to become nuns? If it was forbidden, all right, let them do it in their own homes. Life was created for people to live. It wasn't right for people to escape from life into religion. Cross-bearing wasn't right.

I was so angry. But I shouldn't have been. She was a silly girl, my dear Rózsa, and she'd had no mother to tell her what was and was not permitted.

I could hardly keep it bottled up. I would so much have liked to tell somebody. But who could I tell? I told Puju, he was such a good listener. I had to go and groom him anyway, and take him for a walk, cos the poor thing hadn't been out for a couple of days. I spent all evening washing. After that I tidied up Piros and Puju. I told him all about it. I knew that when I'd got so much grief I had to talk. Put it into words to somebody. Never mind to whom, just let it out. I could have told a wooden spoon. I've always seen that anybody who has an animal talks to it. It's better than nothing. An animal is a living thing. Some can look so knowingly at you. Well, not Puju, but some can.

I whispered into his ear: 'Listen here, my boy. Great misfortune has come our way, as great as when Mummy died. But then I was little and knew nothing. I could only see that she'd stopped coming. But this time it's Rózsa that isn't coming. She's been arrested by the police. She must have done something wrong. They don't arrest people for nothing. Only I hope the poor thing doesn't get beaten up. A poor lame girl like her, and to get beaten up just the same. What can we do, we? Say a prayer, perhaps. I don't know. That would be good, cos it means at least I'd be speaking. Listen, Puju my dear, I can't pray that much any more. I've prayed in the past and nothing's come of it. I've prayed for Daddy ever so much.'

An' so I kept talking to Puju while I was giving him a good brush. And Pirosa as well, and the other cat with the little brush, the one that hadn't got a name.

Daddy was drunk again, working a bit, but I said nothing to him. She wasn't his daughter any more, what should I have told him?

I said nothing and waited. I asked the old woman next door for all the papers. She asked if I was cleaning the windows, she'd give me some old ones. I said no, I wanted recent ones, the last couple of weeks. I read and read, but there was nothing of the sort in them, nothing about Rózsa and her companions in crime. Fortunately there was a good moon. I can't sleep when that happens.

I was still waiting, selling, doing my work. Then on Saturday, I don't know why, I was afraid, but I daren't go to the police station for fear of making things worse. Vili wasn't coming at the time cos he had to go abroad. I phoned the Station. I'd never done such a thing as phone him. The secretary asked what it was about. So I said it was nothing important, and rang off. Now what was I to say? I went up to see him that afternoon. I didn't want him to snog cos I hadn't gone for that, but I was crying all the time. I asked him to do something, find out what was happening to Rózsa. He promised he would, but didn't telephone there and then, and said that such a thing couldn't be done on the phone but had to be in person. Then he'd have given me a hug, but I didn't feel like it then. I didn't enjoy him kissing me. His face was quite rough, and his moustache smelled of tobacco, not nicely, but sour. It quite upset my stomach. When he kissed me I felt I was going to be sick, and I really had to hold it back. Being sick, I mean. So I let him, what could I have done? I couldn't have said don't, cos he might not have helped me. He even tried to touch me up. And he'd always said he wouldn't, so why did he then? A few more days, he said, and he was leaving. But would he find out what had happened to my sister by then, I asked. He promised for sure! Even on his mother's life.

Then he went off and travelled.

Two weeks went by and nothing. I went up to the hospital once, and was told not to go again. I'd have to look for her at home or somewhere else. It was no use my reading the paper, and I even got the national daily, *Elōre*, in case there was something more in that. Not a word. Nothing about Rózsa. By then Vili was over in Paris, but hadn't spoken, hadn't sent word, hadn't been to the market, hadn't come home. He was bound to come when he needed a big snog! That used to be every day.

Then I could no longer contain myself. When Vili didn't come and had gone off abroad I could stand it no longer. I went to my aunt's place and just sat there, not knowing what to do. When my uncle had gone out to do the milking I spoke to Aunty Julia.

'Our Rózsa? Arrested? Where's she been taken? A nun? She must have been locked up.'

I told her what I knew. I wasn't crying at all by that time. I'd cried so much I couldn't any more.

Aunty was alarmed, she'd never seen me like that. In came Uncle Mihály and found me in that state and my aunt the same. We couldn't deny it. I had to tell him as well. I said to them, 'Help me, what am I to do? Should I go to the police?'

'Or perhaps the Securitate,' said Uncle.

'Oh, Uncle Mihály, don't say such a thing. But I don't even know which is which. Nor do I know where they are.'

My aunt said she'd come with me. At the police station they wouldn't tell me anything. They asked who I was. I said I was her sister. And this lady?

Her aunt. We were asked for our identity cards. I hadn't got one cos I was a minor. So where were this girl's parents, since they weren't the people that had come. I said that her mother was deceased and her father seriously ill in hospital. I was having to lie again. In that case, oughtn't I to be in the care of a guardian? *Tutela* in Romanian. I'd never even heard the word. The policeman said that the Hungarian word was *gyám*. Well, what was I to say, so I said that Daddy would be coming out of hospital and there was no need of a guardian. In that case, tell him to come in. Then my aunt began to join in, trying to help, but her Romanian was very bad. So the policeman spoke in Hungarian. He might only give information to immediate relatives. So wasn't an aunt that? She'd been the one that had brought me up. Did that make her my *tutela*? So in the end he asked us to leave the name and come back next day. We were to leave the name and come at three o'clock next afternoon. 'Aunty,' I said, 'come with me, what if they won't talk to me cos I've got no ID?'

The next day we were told that we shouldn't inquire there but up at Republici utca. 'Which is that?' asked Aunty Julia. That was Majális utca, the Securitate office, cos there in the police station they knew nothing and perhaps they would there. But possibly they wouldn't give out information cos we weren't immediate relatives. I wasn't 'of age'. Daddy would have to be told to come, Aunty said she'd come round and have a word with him if we could catch him sober. And if he threw her out? He couldn't, she was a relative. He wouldn't throw her out. Let's ask Uncle Mihály, I said. Oh, we mustn't do that! Once they'd nearly come to blows. That had been ages ago, when he'd happened to find him drunk. So we didn't, cos Uncle Mihály was a very impulsive man. We didn't want any trouble.

Luckily, that afternoon Daddy was normal in himself, a bit silly all the same, cos he'd been drinking earlier but he'd had a sleep and hadn't drunk any more. He'd gone out into the garden digging. What for, when I'd already dug it over? Well, I didn't say anything to him. But it was lucky he'd brought the manure out so I wouldn't have to, cos it was so heavy, I could hardly have done it.

'Hello, Feri. I've come because we have to talk,' said my aunt.

'Hello. What's the matter?' answered Daddy. He looked us up and down, arrogantly, what the hell did Aunty Julia want?

'Let's go inside,' I said, so that we shouldn't talk in the yard. Walls have ears.

We went into the living room, Aunty sat down and came straight out with it.

'Look here, Feri. Rózsa's in trouble.'

'What Rózsa?' asked Daddy.

'Don't start that now, Feri. Cos you've got a daughter called Rózsa. She's just been picked up by the police.'

'They've done the right thing,' replied Daddy. What could I think? I wished Hell would swallow him, that was my thought. That the devil would take him away for good. I could see the hand-axe by the stove. Oh, I thought, I'll grab it and crack his head this minute. May God strike him.

'Come to your senses, Feri. The girl's left home but there's no need for you to talk about her like that. She's as pure as a flower. Now the police have locked her up. Interned her in some camp. Or the Securitate have. We've been to the police, and they know nothing about her.'

Daddy was silent for a moment.

'This what you've come about?'

'Look, Feri, go up to Majális utca, to the Securitate place. Cos you're the only one they'll talk to. The poor girl's mother's died, she can't go and speak to them. They won't tell this child anything. They won't tell us relatives anything cos we aren't her close relatives. You're the one that's got to go. Do you understand?'

You could tell from looking at Daddy that all that drink had left him unable to think clearly. He could hear what Aunty was telling him but he couldn't understand. He didn't get it. His head had gone wrong, he'd lost his marbles. There was a silence, then he asked 'What do you mean? Where've I got to go?'

'Up to the Securitate, ask them what's happened to your daughter.'

'I haven't got a daughter.'

'Daddy!' I shouted at him.

'Look here, Feri. I'll go with you, Anna will come as well. And we'll wait outside while you go in. Understand?'

'An' what am I supposed to ask?'

'What do they know about Rózsa Butyka. That's what. Understand?'

'What do they know?'

'Feri, your daughter's disappeared. It's been three weeks. Almost a month. Been locked up. Arrested by mistake and held in custody.'

'How do you know?' Daddy was beginning to catch on.

'We've been and found out.'

'We'll meet in the main square at two o'clock tomorrow and go along. Understand?'

'Go where?'

'To Majális utca, the Securitate.'

'What do we want to go there for?'

By now Aunty Julia had realized what was wrong with Daddy. She'd known all along, but only now had she seen what he was like. And at that moment he wasn't drunk at all, he was just beginning to sober up.

'Feri, just be careful not to . . . have anything to drink. Otherwise, if you smell of it, they won't talk to you. Understand?

'Stop giving me orders,' Daddy started.

'I'm not giving orders, but I needn't tell you how bad it'll look there if you're drunk. Understand? We'll have wasted our time going. Now do you understand?'

He didn't reply.

'Do you understand?' Aunty repeated.

This time he said 'Leave me alone. Very well. I'll go.'

After that I watched Daddy all the time. I was anxious he might go and drink. That evening he only had half a glass and slept until morning. I didn't go to market that day. No way. At about eleven o'clock I made him some puliszka and sour cream. He ate a bit, then went out to work. When he came in he asked for warm water, he was going to have a wash. That was saying something, cos he never washed. And in fact we set off at one o'clock, though we'd only said two. We caught the bus and went that way. Daddy wasn't very strong, couldn't walk far. Aunty was there first. We didn't talk. She just asked whether Daddy had brought his ID. He had, he said. Hadn't gone out of date, had it? We looked at it and fortunately it hadn't.

Daddy was in that grey building in Majális utca for about an hour and a half. Aunty wasn't allowed in, as she wasn't a relative, and I was still a minor. We had to wait in the street as we were also turned out of the yard. The porter told us to go to the other side of the street. They didn't like people hanging about outside the Securitate. So we had to wait.

Then out came Daddy, very grey in the face. He said that they'd had to check up to see whom it was all about. Rózsa had been detained early in September at the flat. Similar places had all been raided that night. She wasn't in Kolozsvár, and they didn't say where she was. It wasn't permitted to speak to her until the preliminary hearing. Until then they wouldn't know what she'd done wrong. They'd said nothing about the others. A document would be sent about the hearing. One person might attend, a member of the family.

Daddy related it all in one fell swoop. That was all he'd been told. Was he sure he'd understood everything, asked Aunty. Yes, cos they'd actually spoken Hungarian. The man had been a Hungarian, in plain clothes. First he'd spoken in Romanian, then in Hungarian. We set off for home. Aunty Julia said we were to go to her place for dinner. We didn't go. Daddy was exhausted. Now, I thought, he'll really put it away. He won't get up. And, of course, at Aunty Julia's he'd have got nothing to drink. And he'd never be himself again.

No, he didn't drink a drop. Not half a glass, even with soda. Daddy was now stopping his drinking. But something was causing him real pain. He was ill, liver trouble perhaps. He couldn't eat much, I made him some tea, and that he drank. And he worked indoors, and the previous day he'd washed. I'd never before seen him do that, wash. Or maybe I had when I was a child, I just couldn't remember. I can't remember my childhood. That's my great good fortune.

I kept taking the papers, but didn't see anything at all. Then Jesus! That day! On the front page! Vilmos Décsi! Celebrations. He'd won some great prize, a gold medal, with a flower. I looked and looked at the photo of him. Read the caption over three times. Well, not a good likeness . . . but I could tell it was Vili. But he was so strange, as I'd never seen him. My mind wouldn't accept that it was Vili. We'd been going together for two years now. Two years or even longer perhaps. I hadn't even been sixteen when he first took me in his arms, and now I was very nearly an adult. I couldn't wait. My God! Why should I wait to get my ID? Why indeed? I'd certainly have to marry a nice Hóstát boy. I wasn't going into the factory, that was for sure. Certainly not. I'd rather get married, and be my own boss. And I wasn't going to leave the garden. I didn't fancy being indoors, in the factory or an office. I liked outdoor work.

As did Vili.

I kept looking at that picture of Vili in the paper. Never mind his telling me that he was a man of the people, cos he came from a factory-worker family, and according to the paper his father had been a painter, a painter and decorator. We were the same sort of people, he said. The difference was that we had land and vegetables. But we weren't. There was he in the paper, a big man, he'd got a reputation. His destiny was to be a famous man. And did it affect me? It didn't count that Vili was 'of the people'. He wasn't any longer. He wasn't as nicely tanned as a working man either. He was getting paler with all the meetings he went to.

Daddy wasn't strong but he was working, even driving the cart, and I was going to market. When he came home he said that I should sleep indoors, in the living room, and he'd go out on the bench. He heard me coughing and was sure my lungs were bad. My sister as well had always been sickly, he said. I'd never heard him mention her in a long time. He said I ought to eat salted cabbage, shredded cabbage, cos it was full of vitamins. I said there wasn't any yet. And onions, lots of onions. He'd read in some book that during the war, when there'd been such hardship, that had saved lives. Salted cabbage and onions. So I ate and ate, and all that cabbage gave me indigestion. I had to eat bread and boiled potatoes. Or a bit of vakarék. When I hadn't bought any bread I made vakarék in the stove, just scraped the burnt part off it. It worked, I was soon all right.

I didn't tell anybody about Rózsa. Not even Aunty Mária. How could I have talked about such a thing? I'd only got one hope left. One. When I went to bed in the living room, cos it as nice and warm, I was really perspiring, perhaps I was ill. My back was very painful. I had one more conversation. I really didn't know how to begin it. One evening I just did. Daddy had already gone to bed, cos he was more orderly then, early to bed and early to rise, like a decent person. He was asleep, snoring. I'd got a nice quilt, and under it my forehead was dripping wet, sweat pouring off me. Daddy was afraid I might be getting consumption. He was always wanting me to call the doctor, or go with him to the chemist's. But I didn't want to. I wouldn't. I took off my other underwear cos I was perspiring so much, then I got up and changed. Since this has been going on with Rózsa, I've been reading the psalter more. The newspaper and the psalter. Which would help me? Then I put the book down and lay in the dark. Well, I thought, I'll have a word with her. I called up my mother. I told her that this was the last time she'd have to come, cos there was big trouble. Her heart must have known. Only would she please tell me what to do, and what wrong Rózsa had done.

It had been more than three months now, and they'd said nothing. No letter had come, no notification. About a hearing taking place and sentence being pronounced. What the crime had been, and the punishment. I said to Aunty Julia let's go again, we simply must find out what's happening. Let's not keep going, said she, we'll make them cross with us. We'll spoil things if we keep nagging. Daddy was almost completely off the drink by then. He hadn't stopped altogether, was drinking a little bit, not so much as to be incapable. He was working a bit, driving the cart a bit, and I was going out to market as much as I could. Cos we'd got so little money we couldn't even pay the taxes. Previously I'd saved a bit up to get some lovely Hóstát earrings set with three stones, but that had all gone now.

Then the document came, brought by the postman. He wouldn't give it to me even though he knew me, even though I begged him, but he said, quoting Romanian, I wasn't of age so he couldn't give it to me. And Daddy was out. I told him to give it to Aunty Mária, he'd find her at home. He wouldn't be able to give it to her, the sort of letter it was. So what were we to do? I began crying, cos Daddy might come in the evening and not catch the postman. So he'd have to go to the post office the next day. We went, queued up, they looked for it everywhere, we stood there half an hour and they still couldn't find it. Then it was found in a cupboard, cos it was a sort of letter that couldn't be given to anybody but the addressee.

We opened it and read it. I read it, cos Daddy couldn't read very well. Perhaps he needed glasses.

Verdict was to be announced, we had to go to the tribunal. The Kolozsvár county military tribunal, the hearing was to take place in Várad. I didn't know whether we'd made it out correctly. We went quickly up to Aunty's for them to read it in case we were getting it wrong. It said that one person might go to the tribunal, a family member, must be of age, must take their ID, and the case was to be heard in Várad. Next Tuesday, beginning at 8 a.m.

Daddy said that I couldn't go with him. 'I'm coming,' I told him. 'Who's going to look after you if you're unwell?'

'All right,' he replied, 'and what about the house? Who'll look after the house?'

'I'm not interested,' I said. Always that imprisonment, always, so that I couldn't be away for two days when my sister was held in custody. I told Daddy that we'd ask Aunty Mária, and she could have whatever there was, eggs, milk, everything. Then we'd have to take twice as much money. I was going, I said, I wasn't prepared to go mad not knowing anything.

How many days the hearing would last they didn't say. We'd have to take money to pay for accommodation as we didn't know anybody in Várad. Aunty Mária said—cos we'd had to tell her that we were going cos something was wrong with Rózsa—that she'd got a friend, a non-conformist woman, she'd write a note and we could sleep at her place. We'd have to take her something if we slept there, I thought. Best take her some produce, said Mária, cos she'd got no land, just a little yard hardly the size of a tablecloth. A chicken or something. So we packed our things and I put two chickens in.

I'd been thinking all the time about how we could make money, what we could sell. We were going without any money and didn't know how long we'd have to stay.

So I screwed up my courage, took the bit between my teeth, and asked Vili. He'd given me money previously, when I hadn't asked for it. Please let me have some now, when I needed it. I said I'd give it back. At the end of spring, when business would pick up. And in summer. No need to give it back, he said, no need.

Only then Vili didn't like my going to see him at home. Or at the Station. He told me straight that he'd been made a major State Award, and so was then in a position in the public eye. He'd been given a great distinction and had to be careful. We went to a sort of beer cellar in the main square. Not there in Pata utca, where all the farmers would see us but where there were tables in alcoves, and even little swinging doors so that nobody could come in when two people were holding a discussion. Vili ordered a delicious dinner, cos he was brought the sort of things that weren't given to other people. Since he'd been back from Paris, we'd always had to meet in places like that. I drank a glass of beer, and then another, and only after that did I say that there was going to be this hearing and we'd got to go to Várad. And would Vili please be ever so kind and lend me some money? When I said that I was already in his arms and kissing him, Not so that he'd do that, but from the heart, out of pure feeling. And I'd got a little Dutch courage. He would, he said, but I must be careful. Very careful, whom I spoke to and what I said about my sister. Nobody was to be trusted. I didn't have to return the money. But I didn't want to be in debt, I would give it back. And then he kissed me, well and truly. We'd had two beers, both of us. It had gone to my head. And my legs. I nearly fell off my chair. Just then he could only let me have two hundred and sixty lei, but he'd give me more if I needed it. What could I say, I would. He'd send somebody down to the market and give it to him, the driver, I knew him. It would be in an envelope, and the envelope would be inside a book. Vili gave me a big hug, well and truly, but as we weren't at home . . . But it was that kind of a hug.

But then I felt ashamed when I left the restaurant—The Huntsman, or whatever it was called. I was ashamed because I wasn't only doing it for my sister. And I'd accepted money. And in exchange I'd give him I wasn't saying what. I'd do it because I loved him.

We stayed in Várad for four days. Daddy came in late every evening. I didn't dare wait outside the building where the tribunal was sitting, not in the town but away from the centre in a cultural place of some sort. When the sentry saw me on the first day he sent me away. I stayed in Aunty Rodica's house and went for walks in the town. I went into the church as well if I was cold, cos the weather was chilly. Aunty Rodica wasn't very nice after the second day, so I gave her another ten lei. The members of her sect came every evening, closed the door and said prayers.

There were five in the group in Rózsa's case. The five nuns who'd been living together. They read out their confessions and said that they admitted the charge. Daddy didn't really understand. He didn't speak Romanian all that well, and didn't know about such official matters. And nobody was allowed to speak in the room. If they tried they'd be ejected. The accused were addressed a bit in Hungarian too, said Daddy. He was asked if he'd understood and he answered in Hungarian that he had. Not everything was interpreted.

Daddy said that Rózsa was in good health. But he hadn't seen her for a long time. He couldn't remember the last occasion.

'There's nothing wrong with that one!' he said.

Nor with the other nuns. They were just very afraid. They were before a court, about to be sentenced.

'An' the way she limps! Even more than before,' said Daddy. 'She puts it on, to gain sympathy.'

Daddy didn't understand what Rózsa was being accused of. *Uneltire*, What did that mean? Then we found out that the charge was treason. Conspiracy. What they'd done, what crimes they'd committed, that he didn't understand. Rózsa had a lawyer appointed, the same one that acted for the whole group, but Daddy wasn't allowed to speak to him. And they were all in handcuffs.

It was all read out about how they'd been organized since 1949, when they'd been prohibited. Cos after that, being a nun wasn't allowed. Such convents were closed down. The principal accused had been the head of Rózsa's order, as she had been then too, Aunty Jusztina. Aunty Márta, by her ordinary name, Márta Balázs. Rózsa too had a name as a nun.

Next morning we were going out there on foot, cos we didn't catch a bus, we didn't know where it went from. A car stopped and called Daddy over. I went with him. A gentleman got out. He said he was the appointed lawyer. He gave his name, Ioan Toma, a Romanian gentleman, and he spoke quite good Hungarian. Did Daddy understand what his daughter's offence was? They weren't permitted to talk, but he told him. They were accused of conspiracy. The whole Society of the Rosary. I hadn't even known that that was what they were called, cos Rózsa had never said. How was it possible for me not to know about my sister that she was in some society? The most guilty was a certain Mária. We didn't know the names, because we didn't know them personally, did we, only by their religious names. I didn't know which was which, just the names Márta and Évi. But it was mainly action against the community. And changing the frontier of the Romanian People's Republic, annexing Transylvania to Hungary. How was Rózsa accused of such a big thing? Daddy asked whether this crime was proven. Yes, replied the lawyer. They'd confessed. The confession was signed, all of them had signed it. And had she confessed? Rózsa. Rózsa Butyka. Yes, said the lawyer. She'd told him, the lawyer, that she'd done that? He hadn't spoken to her, said the lawyer, he hadn't spoken to any of them, he'd only been appointed to defend them. Only there was no defence against treason. Rózsa Butyka wasn't a principal defendant, only in the third category. The verdict would be pronounced the next day. Daddy wanted to speak to Rózsa, but the lawyer said that would only be possible after the verdict had been pronounced. And in the case of traitors, if such were the verdict, not even then.

So then I asked, cos Daddy'd dried up, 'What had Rózsa done? What had been her offence?'

'She'd been inciting, agitating against the power of the workers.'

'But they won't want to put her in prison?' I asked.

'The verdict will be pronounced tomorrow,' said the lawyer. 'And an appeal will be possible. Only . . . Well, I must be going.'

I even forgot to thank him. Cos he'd been kind, he'd stopped and spoken to us even though he wasn't supposed to.

Daddy and I didn't understand a thing. What were we to say if we didn't understand and weren't likely to? In fact, Daddy was quite stupefied by all the drinking, in my view, and wasn't as bright as he used to be. We went down the street, dragged ourselves along, and I could hardly walk. And I'd got such a high temperature, perspiration was pouring off me. I just went with Daddy to the culture place where the hearing was being held, and went back to where we were living. I just slept all day cos of the fever and drank only water.

Daddy was a long time coming that evening. And when he did, he'd been drinking. He had a sour smell and it turned my stomach when he slept in the same room as me. It was a good thing he was steady on his feet, or Aunty Rodica might have turned him out. I was afraid of that happening, and that I wouldn't be able to get him up in the morning. He simply had to get there, they wouldn't have let me in cos I was a minor. The next day I even took him across the road so as to see him in. I looked in every direction to catch a glimpse of Rózsa, but I didn't see her being brought; maybe they came in a back way. So that people shouldn't see. I told the sentry that Daddy wasn't very well, might I go in with him. That wasn't allowed, one person went in, the one with the pass admitting them. I asked Daddy whether he'd brought any paper with him to make notes of what was said, so that I could know as well. That wasn't allowed, one woman had been writing and was thrown out for it. Writing wasn't allowed.

I took a firm hold of Daddy's hand, squeezed it quite hard. When he was drinking and was weak I wasn't afraid of him at all.

'Now look here, Daddy,' I said. 'If you come in this evening drunk and can't tell me what's happened here to my sister, then mark my words, I'll get a knife. Do you hear? I'll get a knife and kill somebody. Either you or myself. Understand? Do you hear what I say? Don't you dare go drinking and come in drunk when my sister's blood is being shed, do you hear? Cos they intend to kill her, do you hear? As a traitor.'

That's how I spoke to him before taking him over the road. I gripped his hand so tight that it went blue and hurt him.

'Promise. Promise here and now that you won't go drinking.'

I was sorry to have said that. A drunken man is like a child. You shouldn't hurt him, he'll do that to himself. He came along like a guilty man. He was the one who should have been judged there and put inside.

That day Rózsa's crimes were read out. Her statement was made. Daddy said that she'd confessed to everything, said yes to everything. She'd said in Hungarian that she was guilty, as it was interpreted into Romanian. All men are sinful. That was what she'd said.

As Daddy understood it, the sort of thing that she'd done was that the five of them, the Society of the Rosary, had proclaimed the kingdom of Mary. And by so doing had rejected the people's Romania. They'd said all sort of religious things like that. So Mary was Queen of Hungary, and therefore a prosecution for treason was brought against Rózsa and the other four. Five in total. They'd gone about the town proclaiming the land of Mary, and had sung religious songs for money. And they'd incited the people against the power of the workers and the people's democracy, saying that the kingdom of God was at hand. They'd received money from abroad. The society had had fifty dollars in their possession when they were arrested. And sundry forbidden books, which had been confiscated.

The main thing was that, as Daddy had understood it, they had conspired. That was the principal crime. Cos even if they'd wanted to in themselves, as individuals, they couldn't have committed treason. But as it was, they meant as a group to subvert the authority of the state.

At dinner Daddy was given just a single pálinka by Aunty Rodica. And I'd told her that he mustn't. I'd told her that he was sick, said it in Romanian. *Nu se poate. Nu e voie.*

The next day the verdict was delivered. Márta, that is Sister Jusztina, was given twenty-five years. I don't know which was which of the others. Sisters Melánia, otherwise Évi, and Paula got fifteen years, Rózsa and Sister Leona ten years. Rózsa because she was lame, said the lawyer, and Leona because she was young, still a minor like me. An appeal would be heard on the spot. Since they were traitors, we were not permitted to speak to them. We didn't know where they were taken. The charge was *uneltire.* Conspiracy. So, we were no longer sure whether it was conspiracy or treason. Or whether the two were one and the same.

Daddy took what money I had left. He came close to hitting me. So I gave it to him before he punched me in the face. There were so many on the train that we couldn't sit down. By the time we reached home, my feet were freezing. Daddy drank a bottle of Monopol with another drunken passenger, who gave him some rum in return. He all but fell off the train at Élesd. Well, I thought, I'm not going to pick you up. Then the other drunk got off at Csucsa. I had a job getting Daddy off the train cos he was out of his mind. And asleep on his feet.

Well, Rózsa my dear, now what has your God got to say when He looks at what you've done? And looks at the father that beat you? Now where was that Jesus Christ, to whom you're well and truly married? Even when he was blind drunk, couldn't stand on his feet and all but fell off the train onto the tracks, He brought Daddy home. But my poor sister's had her life ruined.

Then, even so late in the evening, I went round to my aunt's, and though they were already in bed I knocked and woke them. She told me that I mustn't say a word to anybody. Keep my mouth shut, mustn't utter, It was enough for us to know. Daddy, you, and us. That's enough. Don't say a word at the market. Tell people that Rózsa's gone away, that's all. I hadn't known, I told Aunty, that Rózsa was involved in politics like that, and was accused of trying to subvert the power of the people, a traitor. Aunty said that a while ago lots of nuns, priests, and such as Baptists, Jehovah's Witnesses, Pentecostals, Adventists, Greek Catholics and the like had been picked up, they'd all been prohibited. Shouldn't have been provocative. Romanians and Hungarians alike, no distinction made. Hungarians especially had to be very careful, keep their mouths shut.

I went home, and wanted to give such a great shout that the moon would fall from the sky. And to go on shouting until I had no voice left and wouldn't be able to say another word. Cos I certainly wasn't going to talk to anybody. A long time before, I don't know when, can't remember, but once Rózsa had said to me that the fact was that Daddy hadn't meant any harm when he beat her. But beat her he had, beat Rózsa, and it came to me that he'd beaten me as well. What we'd done Rózsa didn't know either. It had been enough for me to shout at the top of my voice, as loud as I could, for him not to beat me afterwards, cos Uncle Török next door had stopped at the gate and asked, 'Hey, Feri, you aren't hurting that child, are you?' But I'd gone on and on howling till I had no voice left. They were afraid I'd gone completely dumb, cos I didn't speak for the next three days or so. So after that Daddy didn't beat me any more. Well, Mummy, what do you say to that? Have you been struck dumb as well? You've fallen silent forever, I think. I'm certainly not going to call you if you haven't come by this time. If you can't see that you've left me completely alone, abandoned me and my sister, and aren't saying anything. I'm certainly not going to make the table dance, cos Zsuzsi invited me and that was what they do and they're able to talk to the dead. Certainly not. Come of your own accord, if you want to. I can't even talk to the living, let alone the dead.

Aunty told me that I was a good girl. A very good girl, cos I didn't cry. Neither did I, that was true.

But I did tell Vili. And it had been a month since I'd been round, but then he'd been down to the market and said over and over, whispered 'Annush' in my ear, so then I went and stayed half the day at his place. But previously he'd told me not to go cos he had to be careful. I even slept in his bed. Then I washed, he ran a nice warm bath. And when I got there, I told him. Perhaps he'd already forgotten. Cos even when I asked him in September to find out where Rózsa had been put, he didn't do anything. Just went to Paris. And how long had gone by? Four months? Five. And now the sentence had been pronounced. Ten years. Ten years in Gherla Prison, I told him. In Szamosújvár. I'd gone and inquired, cos they used to go to church there, and a theology student told me. They've been sent to Szamosújvár. All the great villains have been put away there as well. That was where the worst are sent, murderers and traitors. Sándor Rózsa as well, there was a book about him. He's buried in the prison graveyard. But maybe they'll be taken somewhere else, said the student. And anybody that's a traitor is taken to the Danube delta, to work on the drainage. But I wasn't to ask him any more, that was all he knew.

I only told Vili that much so that he wouldn't try to find out anything, cos I knew where my sister was. And how long she was going to be there.

Well, he was apologetic when I said to him, 'Do you remember, Vili, last September I asked you to do something?'

'I know, I know, you don't have to give it back.'

'I don't mean the money, Vili, cos I can't give that back yet. It's only January, and I haven't sold anything. It was to enquire about Rózsa.'

'What?'

'My sister, Rózsa. She'd been arrested.'

'Yes, I know.'

'There's no need for you to inquire. I've found out myself. She's gone to work on the drainage for ten years.'

Just so that Vili knew that when he ought to have done something, he hadn't. But he was a big man. I was no longer even thinking that he would get her out. Nobody could do that if somebody was arrested. It didn't matter that I was cross with Vili. I couldn't just be his lover all the time. What would that amount to? When he asked and asked me to go up to his place, and he'd be so nice to me, well, I couldn't say no. He was always whispering about how he loved me, whether he meant it or not. And that he couldn't do without me. I should go up, I'd see what would happen.

Well, what did happen? I was thinking, now he's going to want something. Perhaps he's going to propose to me. But Vili said that he was an inveterate bachelor. So if that's the case, too bad. A bachelor. And then he'd got Kali and the child, as well as I knew. He couldn't change so quickly, he said, and submit to the bourgeois yoke. I didn't even understand what he meant. What yoke? Did he want me to propose to him? He'd need time, lots of time, to accept it. A long road had led to that Annush. What Annush? What was he always on about? Well, until he'd developed the flower that he was to name after me. He'd actually spent two years on it. Same as with me, I thought. Two and a bit. Vili's in a world of his own. Just like Rózsa, when she went off to be a nun. Everybody's got one but me.

I've sworn that I'll think of Rózsa every day and pray for her. Not a Lord's Day may go by without my praying. On the wall I've hung a little crucifix that she'd given me. I couldn't be there when she took her vows cos I was too little, and she gave it me later. I've hung it up so that when I look at the crucifix, I'll know I must pray. On it is Christ's crucified body. I don't like that body when it's dead and stretched out there. I know that he died for me, but I don't like it. I prefer him when he's going into Heaven or going about among the saints. I pray that my Rózsa will one day stand behind me in the main square and cover my eyes. Cos that was what she always used to do! And I'd be so startled I'd actually scream. Oh Rózsa, get off me! And she'd say, 'Guess who.' And give me a kiss. Oh, just to hear her voice once again.

Daddy went up to the court to disown his daughter that's in prison. He was told that if he wanted to remain in the collective—cos now he's in the collective as a driver, one of the transport section, receives a wage even if it's not very much, but he does—if he wanted to go on being paid, he'd better go along and say that she wasn't his daughter any more. She was of age, of course. Others have had to do the same. Anybody whose husband's put in prison gets a divorce. Then the wife can remain in her job, the children can go to school and so on. Or vice versa, cos there are wives that also go to prison.

After Rózsa was sentenced, I started to break up with Vili. Not that I didn't love him, cos I always will. But he rather drifted away from me more and more. Everything had gone well for him, he'd risen to as high a position as a Hungarian could, almost become a minister. He was given such a great state award that the paper was full of it. So what would he want with a Hóstát girl, I thought. A landless peasant. That was what they said in school, and I was always embarrassed. A town girl and a peasant. But peasants we never were, we Hóstát people. In Méhes utca School, nearly the whole class were Hóstát children, only two or three weren't. Everybody that lives up here and goes to the market is a Hóstáti. If only there was plenty of land, so that I could be proud. But what is there now? Only the garden, no field any longer. We surrendered that, and the land outside the town. And the tools. There's only the cart now, and the horse and the cow.

Vili was always saying that I should study. Some trade school or something, and go into industry, not have such a hard life.

But that's the way it is. And Vili only took what was his due. So quickly, hurriedly. He couldn't even enjoy it to the full, cos he pulled something or other onto himself, to be on the safe side. So that there shouldn't be a child.

But I must settle down. I'll have to get married—best would be to some nice Hóstát lad. He'll have to live here, not miles away, so that we can go round everything, and have the garden here and so on. I shan't go into the factory, no way, that's not for me. Daddy won't be working very much, in fact, and I shan't be able to manage alone.

But I'd like once again just to hear Rózsa's voice saying 'Hey, Anni', cos that's what she always called me, Anni. Or as she always said as we were saying goodbye, let us pray.

But I can't always be praying for her. There's so much to do now in springtime, I can't always. Aunty has told me that Mihály will be coming home from his army service. He's always liked you, so go and marry him. He lives up above my aunt on the Pillangó estate on the corner of Orbán Balázs utca and the Kövespád. Go and marry him, she said. How can I, I said, if he doesn't propose? He will, she replied.

Aunty was right. I'm getting married, and it's settled. Life is settled.

PART IV

Eleanóra's Tale

I'm only telling this for my sister's sake. And for her sake, because she's asked me so often. And I've told her that anybody that gets the sort of requests that I've had doesn't talk about themselves. We're not used to talking about ourselves. It's not right. And she must understand this, the person doesn't matter. Anybody that talks discriminates, because they choose themselves. But then, we don't choose ourselves, we're chosen. And I haven't even got any words to speak. I didn't embark on this path in order to speak in my own words. That's what prayer is for. Actually, I very much prefer set prayers, there's no need to make them up, every word's ready laid down, comes from the Lord, you just have to put your heart into it. These days I don't like praying in my own words. Because we pray differently, don't we, every word we say is not from ourselves.

My sister wants to know all the time what happened in there. Well, how am I to be able to tell her? She must understand that I'm forbidden to do that. I told her so. I've signed the omerta. But she even brought an exercise book so that if I can't speak, I should write it down, because that would be easier for me. If I described in writing, it would help me to forget, she says. I'd recover from it, because in her view I'm sick. But look here, the Lord's preserved me, I'm not sick. When she writes something down it's no longer in her head but on paper, she says. That's why mankind write so many books and newspapers, all those letters, so as not to keep things in their heads. Write it down and it's forgotten. That's true too, our Lord just once wrote something in the dust with his staff. Not even the holy scriptures remember that, but we remember every day in transubstantiated bread and wine.

My sister's become a great philosopher. A cabbage philosopher. Because these days she's working with cabbages all the time. And salads. A salad

569

philosopher, because she worships salads, and even though it's autumn she's still got some.

But I told her I'm only going to tell her about release. And clemency. *Graciere*. Nothing else. Especially clemency. Because they believe that it is they that have granted it. They're going to be proved wrong. That came not from them but from the Lord. And I'm not going to give a full account from the beginning. If I told her everything like that, the poor girl would go mad. She doesn't need to know. She cries enough as it is. But now I'm out, the Lord has preserved me. Why should she cry now?

Let's begin with us being the last to leave. The ones that worked in the kitchen. And we could see that there were fewer and fewer of us, because less and less stuff had to be given out for the *efektív*. That was the word they used: *efektív*, staff, or whatever. How many of us still were up there.

When they first came in and told three women to pack their things they were alarmed and asked where they were being taken. The answer they got from the guard was 'Back where you came from!'

'Then we're being taken into the presence of the Lord!' said one of the Romanian *pokaita* women, though we no longer used the term *pokaita*, it was just them inside that did. Other people, the guards, and those who didn't respect the Lord but just cursed him. She was very pious, that Romanian woman, a Seventh Day Adventist, but they walk in Jesus as well.

And we weren't being taken into the presence of the Lord, we were being sent home.

I was called in twice to the mansion, as everybody called it, but it wasn't gentry that lived there. The Martinucci mansion. Who had that Martinucci been? Nobody knew, he hadn't been a Hungarian. The first time it was for me to sign the document, but first I was given a good talking to. *Eliberare papir*. A discharge. I was told what I'd got to do when I was out. The Romanian People's Republic was exercising clemency on me, and from then on I must be grateful, because if I did wrong I'd be taken back and have to serve the rest of my sentence. Another five years, in that case. Another five years and a month. Did I swear to express gratitude? they asked. I did. If I knew of anything of the sort in church circles, would I tell them? I promised. I would inform in writing. And they'd be keeping an eye on my sincerity. At times when I wasn't expecting it.

I had to write down the names of people that I'd look up when I was out, and where they were, what town, postal addresses. I found it hard to write, couldn't hold the pencil. My hand had gone all stiff. Anna, my father Francisc Butyka, his sister, his brother, mother's sibling, and also which of my relatives, the boss where I used to work, Dr Constantinescu, who was a Hungarian, a Jewish Hungarian. Clergy. My confessor, Father Fidel at the Franciscan church. I didn't put the nurses and other relatives down because I didn't know where to find them.

'Is that all?' asked Ferenc Páll. He was on duty to question me, as he introduced himself. I'd never seen him before.

Well, I said, and people from the church, but I didn't know anybody's addresses. Put the names down. So I put another couple of names, but didn't know addresses for them. Not lay people that I'd been to see. I put the names of other nurses, not the five of us, not them. Those who had lived together in other tied flats, like us. Sister Angela, Sister Cemetria, Sister Febronia, and Brother Pál, Brother János, and another couple of names from other orders as well. Perhaps I oughtn't to have put them down, I was only making trouble for them. Ferenc Páll asked, 'Who are these?'

I said that they were people that belonged to the church, just lived the same we way as we did. I didn't actually say that, he wouldn't have understood. So my brethren. Who are they, then? 'How many brothers and sisters had I?'

'Everybody that walks in Christ.'

'Now, don't give me that,' said he crossly. 'But put down their regular names.'

'I don't know their lay names. So what should I put?'

'Is that how they roam about the world?' asked Páll. 'No names or addresses? We aren't going to be able to get on like this. Make an effort. Names, addresses, places of work.'

It was no use saying I didn't know. We had no other names for one another. We'd never been to their homes, always met in church. And if not in church, then in the Sub Rosa hall. Where was that? On the side of the Franciscan church. What town? Kolozsvár. What did we do there? Confession, spiritual hours, Bible reading, rosary hour, singing psalms. Or just keep silence together, say our prayers or just say the rosary together. And organize church affairs. He made notes in a notebook. Sub Rózsa.

'What church duties do you have?'

'We have none at all, only the spiritual hour, confession and rosary, adorations, vespers, punkta, and lauds in the morning. And readings.'

'Whatever is that? What's this hall you mentioned?'

'Sub Rosa, that's what it's called.'

'What sort of rose?' he asked.

'Well, I don't know,' I replied. 'That's not Hungarian, it's Latin. That's what it's always been called, it's not a recent name. We know the whole Mass in Latin, all the prayers, all the rosary, but the individual words we don't understand. But perhaps the music school's taken over that hall as well. Now that the convent's been taken away.'

'Which priest did you go to?' he asked.

'Father Fidel. He's a monk,' I said. Then I thought and corrected myself. 'Was a monk. Now he just helps out,' I added. 'But he's gone to prison as well. We haven't heard anything about him since.'

I was dismissed to think for another day whom I would look up when I was out. And their names. They didn't want to be told their religious names. It was no use my saying that we didn't know them. If I'd told Father Fidel that my name was Rózsa Butyka, he'd have been shocked. That wasn't how we knew each other. But I was Rózsa Butyka Eleanóra OFM. Only that's not how the world knew me.

I thought until the next day. I couldn't say such a name. The sort that he wanted. Ferenc Páll gave me a ticking off, because he'd thought he could rely on me, I'd be grateful to the country for showing me clemency. *Graciál*. And he hoped that when I got out, I wouldn't start religionizing again. Being a nun. Surely I didn't want to be forever in a church that wasn't even officially recognized? Because I knew that it wasn't recognized, didn't I? The Reform Church was, but not the Catholic, I should get that into my head.

I didn't answer, because I hadn't known. Anybody who walked in Christ had no regard for the law of the world. But we weren't in agreement on that point. We didn't consider whether our Lord Jesus Christ and his Mother the Virgin Mary were officially recognized or not. How many people hadn't known their faces even before religion had been banned. Because even if it wasn't recognized, even then it was the only one in the hearts and minds of us that had stepped onto that way. I'd never heard of such a thing, the Roman Catholic Church not being officially recognized. That's what Ferenc Páll said; for fifteen years past the Catholic church hadn't been officially recognized. Because 'your bishop' had until then persistently dragged negotiations out until he'd got nothing for it. Was he talking about Bishop Áron? I didn't dare ask.

Had I thought of anything else? Páll asked again when I was taken up to the mansion a second time. He would have liked me to serve my fatherland, he repeated.

I couldn't work out what he was thinking, what I was supposed to tell him. What would he like? I didn't know any important people, didn't have much to do with the priests, we just lived together. But I saw that he was trying to get me to tell him something about Bishop Áron and the other secret authorities, but I'd only received his blessing twice. Bishop Áron's, that is. And a lovely green rosary.

By then I'd made my mind up not to tell officialdom anything about whom I associated with. And that nobody was going to be able to put me off even if it cost me my life.

But I would say who I'd be contacting because of my social origins.

Again the file was brought out, my personal file. Once more I had to write everything down. I was questioned, I answered, and then I had to write, that was how it was done. But this time I could only write the answer down if it was pleasing. We had to talk until my answer pleased them. Now they wanted to know about my social origin for the first time. I thought, I'll put Hóstáti. But only that I had been. I no longer was a Hóstát girl.

'What's that exactly?' asked Páll. 'A religion? A sect?'

If that Ferenc Páll didn't know what Hóstát meant, he certainly wasn't from Kolozsvár. Even the Romanians knew the word *hostázeny*. That was Romanian for Hóstáti. *Hostazence.* Hóstáti girls.

'You know, a community in Kolozsvár, a big community. They work on the land,' I replied.

'Then put country peasant origin.'

'We aren't peasants, we're townspeople. Hóstát people have never lived in the country.'

'Hóstáti, there's no such thing, I've never heard of it. Put that you're a Hungarian, class peasant.'

I was surprised that there was no such thing. I'd been aware that nuns didn't exist, monks and deaconesses likewise, all were banned. But I hadn't known that there were no Hóstátis.

Had I considered, asked Captain Páll, where I wanted to work? Will you go back to the land? No, I said, I've never worked on the land. I left at the age of fourteen. I've been a nun. If I'd help him, he'd help me, he said. I was silenced for a moment. Then I thought he was only saying that, what could he do to help me once I was out of there?

For example, he said, to find a job. Would I like to go back into the hospital, to the sick, or to an old people's home? The hospital for choice, I said, because I'm a trained nurse.

Yes, I answered, I had been thinking, and I started to think of the names of the Fathers that I knew who had been monks and those from deaconess training, who had become hospital staff, some of them nurses. I didn't know anybody's address, we never went to their homes. As for priests, I only knew Father Árpád and brother Zoltán, and deaconesses Clarissa and Cecilia.

Then Páll said, as he'd had my dossier in front of him all the time and was looking at it, I lived in a kind of world of shadows. What are all these, cover names? He hoped that I'd become serious, we wouldn't be able to work together like that.

What was my opinion of priests that had democratic sympathies? he asked. Because, he said, democratic priests criticized the running of the Church and the Pope in the papers.

The Holy Father? I'd never heard of an ordained priest pronouncing judgement on the Holy Father. I was shocked. I didn't know what answer to give. I didn't know who the democratic priests were, we didn't examine the Church like that. We were its servants. We didn't read the papers. I said nothing, I was alarmed. I tore at my right thumb under the seat until blood showed. If I'd been able to guide my thoughts towards prayer, I'd have said at least a line or two in the hope of hearing the right answer to give. But even prison hadn't broken me of the habit of picking at the skin on my fingers. And my nails, when they grew a bit. I did that with my teeth, because we weren't allowed scissors to trim them with when they broke. They were cut once a fortnight. I only had a half rusty razor blade that I'd obtained in exchange. Now blood was spotting onto my dress. So I said, 'I have a good opinion of democratic priests. They serve the Church and they serve the people.'

'And reactionaries? What do you think about them?'

My God, enlighten me, dear Virgin Mother Mary, dear Christ, who died for me, help me now. What does that mean, reactionary?

'I don't approve of them. They rebel against the word of God.' Because, I thought, if they're reactionaries, then they're rebels. I was talking like a child in an exam. Saying something I shouldn't. Talking rubbish. I didn't know what I was talking about.

'They rebel?' he asked. What reactionary priests did I know? Whereabouts were they from? Gyulafehérvár? Alba Iulia? Because he knew I'd been there.

It was lucky that I didn't have to write anything then, there was no paper in front of me, we were just talking, and I had my hands under the bench. Like I used to do in school. It was a table, but more a kind of bench. My one hand was holding the other really tight, I was hanging onto it. The way that our Lord Christ holds our weak hands all our lives, so that we don't lose our way. So that we don't stumble, don't spill our oil. Because in one hand I carry the jug of oil and in the other the lamp to light my way. At the end of the road, I shall glimpse my Creator's face as long as I don't stumble and spill my oil. That's how we are to go on the way, with our hands full. If we have to climb a mountain, we have nothing to hang on with, and we don't get to the summit. If we have to go down another hillside, then too we can't hold on and we roll downhill, our oil is spilt, and then we can't go in the dark. But the Lord commands us religious to take the flickering lamp in one hand and the jug full of oil in the other, and so to proceed in our lives. The foolish will spill the oil and won't see the Lord's face. And what is my God's plan for me? Shall I spill it like a foolish virgin or shall I reach the face of my Creator with my lamp alight? Because I'm more like a foolish one. And lame. How am I going to be able to go up and down the mountain if I've got both my hands full?

So I was going to spill my oil in this conversation with Ferenc Páll of the Securitate. Not all of it, but some.

I didn't really know what answer to give him. I dug my nails in until it was painful. If only I could have said a prayer, but praying requires one's heart and mind to be with the Lord. But I'd got to talk to Ferenc Páll. My heart too was dry then. Ferenc Páll. Who had taken his name from our order, that of our greatest saint, without whom our Holy Mother Church wouldn't have taken shape. But I didn't, so to speak, see in him the likeness of my Creator. He was both Páll and Ferenc, and yet he turned his back on our Lord Jesus Christ. Yet I had to see the deserted Jesus in every man. But I couldn't in him. I was so sinful. Try though I might, I couldn't see him. Perhaps that wasn't his real name? Why should he give the real one?

Now I looked up for the first time. I looked at him, and though I could see his face I couldn't see the man. I looked at him pleadingly, let his heart soften towards me, what did he want from a foolish virgin of a girl, I hadn't been born to pass judgement on the fathers of the church and to know about the sin of reactionary priests. I looked at him pleadingly, might he soften up.

'We can't judge the fathers,' I replied. 'It's not our job.'

'Just now you were saying that you didn't understand a thing.'

You see, Lord. We make a mistake, and your goodness shows us our error at once. Because I'd stumbled at once, and drop of my oil had been spilt.

'Who do you mean by "we"?' he asked, and the way he was looking at me, I couldn't so much as blink.

'Well, the . . . people we used to be.'

'Who recruited you?'

I didn't pretend, everybody knew that we were recruited. They knew who my fellow criminals were, everything had been wrapped up. How it should have been possible, ten years after every order had been banned, for you to have organized, conspired, wanted to live in a convent. But that was old news, we'd confessed to everything, all our sins, when we'd made our statements, been imprisoned five years before. Why go over it all again, God? It's all there in the dossier, because I'd got such a big dossier, in all my life not so much had happened to me as was written in that dossier. If anybody had asked for it, my whole life would have gone on half a page because that was all that had happened. And here was that great big dossier, like an evangelist's, some great man's. Every record of this and that was in it, I'd been taken here, then there, my clothes were listed, my books, all my offences, all the punishments, the spells in solitary, that I'd been given. That was true, by then the catalogue of my offences was a long one.

'Who recruited you?' he repeated.

'Jesus himself called me,' I replied.

'How did he call you?'

'He called me by name.'

'He said to you, Rózsa Butyka . . .'

'Rózsa . . .'

'Come and follow me.'

'Yes.'

'By name?'

'Yes.'

'You were going down the street and he spoke to you?'

'That's right.'

'Do you take me for an idiot?'

What should I say to that? I said nothing. God summons by name the person that He loves. Because He said what He has always said since ancient times: 'I am here.' The person that He loves, He summons Himself. This always happens in the same way. But it's always different in that He summons you personally.

'And why you in particular? Such a . . .'

I didn't know the answer to that. It was God's mystery.

'When did all this happen? And where?'

On the most sorrowful of feast days. When Our Lord rose into Heaven. It was sorrowful, but I didn't tell Ferenc Páll that, because he'd just have been derisive. We hadn't been allowed to process round the church.

'What year, what was the date?' he asked, and stood, pencil in hand, to write it down.

'I don't know. I'd hardly started school. I was eight or nine when the Lord called me. It was years ago now. It was worked out when I made my first statement.'

There I sat again for three or four hours. I don't know how long. Perhaps it was five hours or even longer. It was the Lord's plan for me to lose track of time. So there I said everything, told him everything, but nothing pleased him, he was vulgar, angry, abusive, said that he was wasting his time on me, as if I'd been giving wrong answers all the time.

'And where did all this happen?'

'I was going down Bod Péter utca, or Gyarmathy utca, because I'd turned the corner, and He was with me. That's where He spoke to me.'

He turned over the pages of the dossier.

'You're lying again. Here it says, and it's signed, it's in your statement, it was in Artelor utca. Who recruited you?'

Then I was taken away. Perhaps they could see how stupid I was. I couldn't talk sense. I couldn't redeem myself. Try though I might, I said what they wanted from me, if ever I didn't know something. I promised to behave myself well. Not to join any groups. Not to proselytize. If I was caught I'd have to serve the remainder of my sentence. Had I understood? Yes. That wasn't sufficient answer. I'd understood and I wasn't going to form a group or proselytize. I was to sign. Perhaps I'd still be called, they said.

Then I had to sign the agreement to remain silent. Omerta. I had to write in my own handwriting a statement that was dictated in Hungarian.

It was said in the final conversation that I had to go to somewhere else. I might not go to Kolozsvár, Arad or Vásárhely. I asked what about Gyulafehérvár? Not there either. That wasn't a suitable town. There I'd be able to go and work for the diocese. Perhaps Bishop Áron was still in prison.

In that case, might I go to Csíksomlyó? There I'd had fellow Franciscans, perhaps they'd returned from prison in Dés. I might be able to find a job there. No, I might not go there.

Then I dug my heels in. I said that Kolozsvár was where I came from, I certainly wasn't going to any other town. It was either Gyulafehérvár or Kolozsvár. Then I was put in the cellar for four days to reconsider. I just slept and slept, paced up and down, said my prayers. Said the rosary three times a day. If I was taken down to the cellar, I would soon be set free.

I'd signed, I thought, everybody did. That we wouldn't say anything about what had happened to us there in prison. Nothing. Omerta. Ordered to keep out mouths shut.

'*Ti-ai semnat* omerta?' the girl asked me in the prison kitchen. Have you signed your order not to talk? she was asking, because in that case you'll soon be released.

Omerta. I'd never heard the word. I couldn't even comment on it. I had to write it down. When your clothes were taken away to be exchanged, because now you could be released, you were given the document on which it said omerta.

Then I was given a further week of solitary, in the cellars, because I'd scribbled something. Another interrogation, about what else I'd written and to whom. Nothing, I replied. I'd written for that girl who'd been learning from me how to pray the rosary. I'd drawn the rosary beads for her, and I'd described how to do it and how often. It wasn't so easy for anybody to learn that was only beginning. You have to do a lot of counting at first, and to know the prayers and the mysteries, the mysteries of Christ. So I'd written the rosary out for her and how to pray it.

I wrote on linen stolen from the furniture factory. Did time for that as well.

Only I just wasn't beaten this time. In fact I hadn't been beaten for a long time. But in the early days I was struck once or twice in the face until

I'd written my statement, and after that I was left alone. Perhaps it was because I was lame and they felt sorry for me. Or they'd received orders to behave humanely, I don't know. I wrote down just one word, omerta. So that I should know it. I'd learnt so much there, I'd become quite a different person, that I'd learnt.

So it had been no use my agreeing with the brethren that we'd meet on Monday in the main square, because I couldn't go. Before we parted, before the court hearing, on the last occasion that we saw one another, we'd agreed to meet on the first Monday of the month at six in the evening, by the statue in the main square. And that would have meant the first Monday of September. So I calculated! Every first Monday in the month. But I had to stay there in prison. I was no longer in any hurry. I'd been waiting a good six months or even longer, because it had been autumn last year when they'd started getting rid of us, so by this time we'd all have been released.

The Party Congress took place as well before we were released, and we had to go to the mansion. We had to watch an ideological film so that we should see the harm that traitors did to the country, how they undermined the achievements of socialism. The walls were covered with pictures of the crimes of enemies of the people. And we had to take an oath in unison. Because now we were being shown clemency.

State clemency.

There was a decree about it, about clemency.

Several people stood up and said thank you, expressed gratitude for being granted clemency. And confessed to their crimes, in public. Performed self-criticism, as they say. *Face autokritika.*

One Jehovah's Witness woman, who was said to be their gang leader because it was she that had introduced those present to the Jehovah's Witnesses, had actually been a deaconess and converted. She too stood up and said politely that she thanked the Romanian People's Republic, the Party, and Comrade Gheorghiu-Dej for clemency. It was decree number 411. There had been another last year, but we hadn't qualified for release under that, so here was number 411/1964. That we engraved in our minds. That was the one by which we were set free.

Then we were once more taken off in small groups to receive ideological instruction. So that we should understand what was meant by state clemency, that the remaining sentence was annulled. But it wasn't an amnesty, that was different. That meant that the crime was wiped out. Our sin was not, we must be quite clear. Sister Melánia actually whispered, as we were gathered in the big hall, and she was in another part some distance away, that man might not forgive sin. That was not for man to do.

At that point those in the smaller group too were asked if anyone would like to express their gratitude. There was silence, and an older woman stood up, not a religious but a farmer's wife of some sort who had stolen from the collective or something. She ground out her gratitude. It seemed that she'd memorized it, she wasn't speaking from the heart. Then she delivered an *autokritika*, as did several more too, confessing what offences they had committed.

Graciere. We were now to receive clemency.

The church too makes a distinction between sin being purged for ever and forgiven, or only being condoned. In my view, the good thing in our religion is that we have forgiveness. Eternal, infinite. Oh, not quite. Because there are mortal sins, that can't be forgiven. Dear God, where's Father Fidel to tell us everything?

None of us that walk in Christ dared stand up and say that it wasn't the Romanian People's Republic that was showing clemency but the Lord, who was gracious to all. As we said in our prayers next day too. Thus we betrayed the Lord. He was gracious to us, set us free, but we were silent and didn't speak his name and give thanks openly for all to hear. We daren't thank him with our voices. Every sinner was silent.

Or did actually speak, because then next day we all had to stand up and say together out loud: I, Rózsa Butyka, aka Roza Butyka, *mulcumesc Partidului Muncitorese Roman*, thank the Romanian Workers' Party and

the Romanian People's Republic for the granting me clemency and I swear
. . . I preferred to say silently to myself: I, Sister Eleanóra.

My God. This was my second oath. I'd already sworn the first, the oath
for life, but to a much mightier Lord. And there I was doing it again. Was I
breaking my great oath if I repeated it now?

I was swearing to my fatherland, *patrici mele,* and to the Party.

The mouth of man is filth. How did old Miki Weissz put it, our teacher,
the professor of dentistry?

'There's nothing that stinks worse than the human mouth.'

That's true. All our sins are in our mouths.

Old Miki had emigrated to Israel when he could no longer practise.

Sister Zenóvia suggested that we should say two rosaries for pleasure
that evening. She wasn't a sister of mine, she was a Romanian, had originally
been a Pentecostal and had converted to Greek Catholic in prison. And she'd
learnt the holy rosary from the Roman Catholics. We didn't speak, just made
signs at a distance to show which rosary it was that day and how many. We
had four signs for the four rosaries. We prayed together but separately. She'd
even learnt from the Romanian sisters the five hundred names of the Virgin.
They have five hundred names for her, each with its embodiment. I don't
know them, we too adore the Virgin and give her some very lovely names,
but we haven't got five hundred. Or rather, I'd have to count how many
there are in my Loretto litany.

Just the four of us prayed the rosary in the big room, that was our garland. Sister Euphrasia hadn't made herself a rosary for a long time. Hers had
always been taken from her. So she'd decided to pray inwardly, and she
always pulled out a hair instead of a bead. That was how she counted and
never made a mistake. It was fortunate that she had so much hair, and so
long. She was a Greek Catholic and she too had been a nun, but now was
nothing special, unattached. People said that she was mad, the way she tore
her hair out. She'd lost her marbles. But we knew that she was only praying.

Then when more were released in spring, every week there was ideological purification, so that when we were free, we should know how to behave ideologically, be able to fit back into society and be useful. Films were shown, followed by discussion. We in particular had to recover from religious backwardness. We saw the film about the Huguenots. We watched the film, and then there were declarations.

There was still confrontation. There had been none for a long time, and perhaps people had forgotten. At times we, the religious reactionaries, nationalist bourgeois intellectuals, and the oppressive landowner class, not to mention the reactionary farmers who refused to join collective farms, were pitted against the workers and peasants. Now it was mainly against the farmers' wives, who had realized that they had been wrong. They too were political prisoners, of course, they too were to be released. Farmers' wives had gone and lain down in front of the tractors when attempts were made to collectivize them. They'd organized demonstrations! Three ringleaders were there, but those that had been given more than twenty years had been taken away at the outset to the drainage. They were very brave women. The men had discovered that the women would lie down in front of the tractors, and then they too made trouble. In prison they were fearless and fought if they had to. One bit the ear of a guard who was trying to do something swinish to her, and tore it off. For that the woman got a month in solitary. Their husbands had spurred these brave women on. Perhaps they were rid of them and had long since divorced them, because that was usual. If anybody didn't divorce, their entire family was marked out, couldn't find work, go to university or draw a retirement pension. The farmers' wives were now told by the agitator, a man from the Party who was in charge of purification, that they were suffering because of us, the rapacious class, and he pointed to all us women sitting there in silence in the room, who had suppressed them, defrauded them, and they had been mistaken because they were poor and hadn't realized that the collective farm would be good for them. Several women were asked to perform *autokritika*. Farmers' wives were religious, intelligent women. There was a teacher from Bucharest, a teacher of French and Spanish, a Jew, who was also a traitor like us, as we were all traitors that were political prisoners.

I asked Sister Melánia what kind of landowner she'd been. What had she owned? Because, of course, we politicals had had all our property confiscated and were only being given clemency, not amnesty, so that we wouldn't get anything back. She'd been part-owner of a house, out in Lóna, Magyarlóna, which was where she came from. She'd had a sixteenth part. So, I asked, how could a sixteenth be confiscated? 'I don't know, I haven't even been allowed to correspond with anybody. They've written in secret but not about things like that. I had a little field, inherited from my mother, between Szopor and Borháncs, nearer to Borháncs, That was fifty ares or so, I can't remember exactly. I haven't set foot on it since I left home. It used to be under cabbage, carrots, and red onions, it wasn't a house garden. I think it's in the collective farm now. I don't know.'

Well, so great was the effort at re-education that those days even television was shown in the kindergarten, as we called it. I too once had the chance to see television. We were looking at the latest achievements of the Romanian People's Republic that had been realized while we'd been in there. Factories everywhere, huge factories. Gosh! That's Kolozsvár, said one of us. In fact, there was the *strekk*, and next it the new factories. And a great procession for peace. The film had been shot from the Kerekdomb and from a height, very likely from an aircraft. In there we didn't even know that there was a war on. War with whom? We were told there was a peace-struggle taking place. People were marching for world peace. I didn't quite understand, because at the time there was no war on in Romania, I thought. The Party had brought peace.

Then there was a film of blocks of flats taken from an aircraft. New blocks of flats in Kolozsvár itself, possibly at the bottom of Bornyúmál or the Dónáti area. And mostly in Hunyad. Hunedoara, in Romanian. The new industrial centre of the country was displayed. The aircraft flew over the new buildings, and as I watched, the rushing pictures quite upset my stomach. I began to feel sick. I shut my eyes, but I was prodded in the ribs to open them because the guard was watching, and I felt the cane at once to keep me awake. I looked this way and that for another half an hour, the rapid change of images made me so nauseous.

Then I was taken to the cellar. I wasn't told how long I'd be there. Four days? Five? I lost count, but I was always so careful. Previously, in the beginning, I'd been so good at calculating time. Having to be there in the silence didn't bother me, at least I could say my prayers undisturbed and live my whole day completely in accordance with the Rule. I was confined to the cellar because I hadn't given the names of people that I'd want to make contact with. Names and addresses.

'*Fa-ti bagajul*,' said the guard one morning. When I heard that, I knew it was time to go. I had to pack my things. In the past anybody who was told that meant they were being taken somewhere else, put on a train or a lorry, perhaps going to a different prison. This time it was clemency.

I was given my clothes, the old ones included. Everything, just not my headscarf or my rosary. I looked but couldn't find them. My rosary that had been blessed in Gyulafehérvár. I'd received it from the hand of Bishop Áron in 1955. It had been in the pocket of my grey dress. There was a pocket specially sewn into the breast of that dress, so that I'd have somewhere to keep it. Oh, that did hurt, and I could have wept, I was so cross. It was all that I'd had from him. A sister consoled me saying never mind, you made a new one last week. I had indeed, and stained it a strong colour because we had some beetroot delivered to the kitchen. Some people in the kitchen dealt in such things and asked for cloth or razor blades in return. I never took anything for a rosary. I made them for anyone that asked.

We were given fifty lei for the journey, and next morning the lorry was waiting and took us to the station. Anybody that received parcels from home wasn't given money because it was sent to them. Anybody that worked might receive parcels. There everybody worked in the furniture factory. I didn't, only in the kitchen, so I wasn't sent parcels. Politicals weren't allowed parcels or letters. Most of those being shown clemency at that time were politicals.

And depending on where they were going.

I couldn't find my old headscarf, the blue one. We'd worn blue headscarves. We wore them after we'd been forbidden. A secret habit.

'My headscarf, please,' I said to the guard.

He told me to clear off while I was all right.

'I can't leave prison without something to wear on my head,' I said.

Then I could stay and finish my sentence, he spat at me.

I tried to keep my prison headscarf but they wouldn't let me, and it was torn from my hand. It wasn't allowed, everybody would see where I'd been. Everybody that had previously worn one as a nun had it taken from them. Headscarf, cross, rosary, the lot. So we had to go bare-headed. So that we should be so ashamed that it hurt. Some people came across big handkerchiefs and put those on. I kept wondering what to put on my head. I couldn't use my skirt. There'd have been enough material, because I'd been fatter when I went inside. One of the older girls, Lucsika, who had supposedly been inside for prostitution, had a razor blade. In the lorry on the way to the station, she gave me her skirt for me to cut a strip off the edge to cover my head with. It was too long, anyway, almost to the ground, she said, and she laughed. It didn't bother her that it was above her knees, that showed her legs better. I covered my head with that strip of grey cloth. What could I give her, I asked Lucsika, because in the prison nothing was for free? She said that I should pray for her, that she might find her fiancé, as she hadn't heard from him for three years.

That poor lesbian woman Magdó was the only one to go to Kolozsvár with me. Everybody so avoided her, not a single one gave her a hug when we said goodbye. She disgusted them. The rest went their ways as their trains left. I even gave her a kiss. Christ our Lord didn't shun lepers, and I told the rest so. Then it turned out that she was going to Kolozsvár as well, and we were to go together. Those for Kolozsvár and Várad were escorted to the train so that we shouldn't cluster in the waiting room, and be conspicuous as ex-prisoners.

The train for Dés pulled out, then one for Temesvár, but we had to go on waiting. We had nothing to talk about. I dozed off. If it hadn't been for that Magdó I'd have slept until next day. The moment I sat down I went to sleep. She woke me up to go—look, here comes our train!

Just the blinking of an eye and we were in Kolozsvár. Either I went to sleep again or time passes more quickly outside. At the station a carter said that he would take me anywhere I wanted for five lei. Magdó gave me a hug and kissed me on the cheek, and I let her as nobody was watching. The poor wretched girl hadn't got over her trouble even in prison. You certainly should hear what the guards and other women did to her. She was on her way to Bács, in Serbia, where she was from. Would she see me again? she asked. We've seen quite enough of one another, I replied. Though we never would have. I was going a different way, I told her. What was I to do out in the world with a wicked girl like her? If somebody wasn't cured even in prison, I wouldn't be able to do any more for her. Except pray. We gave each other hugs, and I didn't loathe her any more. She kissed my cheek and she was in tears. And she clung to me as if she wasn't saying goodbye to a sister but to a lover. That Magdó wasn't even a particularly good-looking girl. Even if she had been, so that other women would fall for her, but she wasn't, and sort of . . . gawky. So not an attractive girl. Especially not in that old horrid dress.

I said, 'Look here, Magdó, stop kissing me, I'm not your wife. I've given myself body and soul to another, and He's accepted. And I haven't become the wife of Mary, because that's sinful. I'm the wife of Christ because in Him, our Lord, I'll never be disappointed. So you take the right road, and don't persist in your bad ways out here in the world as well.'

Because, of course, in prison I even understood her. Anyone that became uncertain was open to all kinds of sin. Other religious too had lost their faith in there and done things that were permissible in the world outside but they'd think better of it. But there was no leading Magdó onto another road. It was her nature.

I accepted the carter's offer, I was so shaky. A taxi would have cost ten lei, he said. He asked me where to go. To Magyar utca, I said, then up onto the Kövespad, and drop me there.

I didn't know where I was going. Perhaps my father was living alone in the house now. I thought Annush had moved out, got married, because she had a child now. She'd only written secretly to me twice and said that she had a husband and a child, but not where she was living. And I hadn't been able to reply to her message. Perhaps she'd forgotten to put the address. Or been afraid to. So I'd got to go up to my father's place in Borháncs utca.

I thought I'd get off at the end of the Kövespad and go up Patak utca. I'd walk from there to get a bit used to being back. I didn't think that anybody would recognize me.

I had to find some place to live so as to be able to report to the police. My documents were valid for forty-eight hours, so I had to find somewhere by that time and say where I was living. If I didn't report in, they told me, I could go back inside. I'd been told I was still a criminal, my crime was just being tolerated. I'd be watched, and therefore would have to report. If I didn't, I'd be found and punished, possibly even taken back to prison.

I realized that I was exhausted, and I asked the carter to take me out towards the fields. That way I would walk into Borháncs from the direction of Szopor. He said that he could hardly get into the fields because of the mud. It had rained the day before and there were a lot of heavy machines working there, so he couldn't take the cart. There was a lot of work going on in the fields, something being built. He wouldn't take me any farther because I'd said to the Kövespad and that was what he'd reckoned five lei for. Oh, what an awkward man. I got off and was cross, though it was just the sort of time when I should have been able to pray for him.

I looked all around: surely they weren't building on our land, were they? And which was our land? I couldn't tell any longer which of the fields was which. It had been at least ten years since I'd last been that way. Perhaps even fifteen. Not because I hadn't gone to work on the land any more, but it was all that my poor sister had. She so loved it, she was a real Hóstát girl and proud of it. But now the land looked so beautiful to me. It had never been so lovely before. As I was going down Patak utca, I kept taking a look to see a little garden. Because the gardens were there all right, the street and the houses couldn't be collectivized.

I was hoping to catch somebody at home and that I'd be allowed in, that I'd be able to have an address. We'd only been able to live in a private house previously. There wasn't a house that the Order owned, and if I were caught again with the brethren in the Order, I'd be put back in prison. It would count as assembly. And our past would never be blameless. We were told they'd be watching us, they'd know everything that we do.

I reached the end of Patak utca. Lord Creator! What huge blocks of flats over there, over Tököz utca, I didn't know what the suburb was called. They were just like what was shown on television. Big machines going about, people working, putting up a block of flats bigger than I'd seen in my life. How many stories were there? I had to count. Eleven! It was almost higher than the church in the main square, St Mihály's. That was impudence if it was any higher. It was decorated with coloured tiles. In the old days it was all fields, we had some land and Mummy had a little bit there. And what was that? The road was lined with crosses, on both sides, as if dead people had been buried there after a war or something, with no names. What could all those crosses be for?

At the corner of Borháncs utca, where it joined Patak utca, there was a stone with a flat top. It had been there in the old days. I sat down on it, because I was worn out. At one time there had been a cross there, on the corner where the road turns into the fields, there was a bright blue roof over our Lord Christ's head, and the figure was nicely painted. Not even the footing of the cross was left, only the stone.

The sun was powerful, it seized me, held me tight to itself, my face needed it so because it had been ever such a long time since I'd sat like that. Six years. Just about six years now. My rosary was tucked into my blouse, because I'd brought it out. I'd made it, but wasn't allowed to wear it openly. If it had been seen it would have been confiscated. I had to wear it under my clothes so that nobody should see it. I just used to say a rosary using my fingernails. When I counted on my nails, I had to be very attentive. It was really difficult to immerse myself in prayer when I was counting on my fingers. My head was . . . not what it used to be. Nothing would stay in it. If you concentrate it's easy to say it right through. But counting on my fingers it took me five tries. Whoever invented the rosary did it so cleverly that you can pray it even when you haven't got one available. You've got fingernails to count on. The heart is the cross, that's how we do it. You put your hand on the heart to say the Apostles' Creed. Five times on each nail all the way through. Today I said the Mysteries of Light, as these are set for today. Not because of the day, but because I shall commemorate this day, that of the Lord's shining mercy. It's September. It'll be St Michael's Day soon, on the 29th. What's today, the day of my holy liberty? Oh, I don't know, but a martyr. A famous martyr. Or perhaps today's the day of all martyrs, those whose names aren't known. Those who aren't remembered by name in the church, but even so we commemorate them.

I slept on in the sunshine. I woke up to hear a man driving a horse that wouldn't go. It was standing there, not going anywhere, and he was shouting at it. When I opened my eyes, the sun so dazzled me that for some time I couldn't see a thing. Oh dear, I was alarmed in case I'd gone blind, just when the Lord had shown me mercy. Then I saw that it wasn't a horse, it was a donkey. It was harnessed to a cart. The driver was a Hóstát man in a blue apron and wide-brimmed straw hat. I recognized him. He was one of us, one of those I belonged to. It was disgraceful. A Hóstát man with a donkey, they were reduced to that. Then he got down from the cart and began to lead the donkey, and so it walked. The man got back into the cart and the donkey stopped. A little cart of cabbages, only half full, and they were all muddy underneath.

I thought I'd say another rosary. Before I went to look for the house, because I was going to have to go to my father's house, wasn't I? To purge my heart in his regard, because there was surely darkness in it. I began the Mysteries of Light again, because there we can ask, in the Introductory Mysteries, for it to cleanse us and preserve our spiritual peace. The Introductory Mysteries came on the index and middle fingers. I held my index finger pointing at myself.

I closed my eyes again. I was still only at the Fatima prayer for the forgiveness of sins. How many Fatima prayers would I have to say to be forgiven and granted spiritual peace with my father, like I was with those that tore the veil from our heads and scattered the religious, put us in prison? We understood that it was for sinners that we had to pray most. How otherwise might the Lord reveal His merciful face and grant us His wondrous forgiveness? He had taken us in and preserved us. Performed a miracle on us.

Then suddenly I couldn't remember where I'd been. My God, had my brain gone so addled? Or was I thinking too much instead of saying the fine things in the prayer. But I'd been careful, always revised everything that I knew, taken care of my mind so as not to become stupid in prison. I'd learnt all the rosary prayers in Romanian, and we'd always said them in the language of choice, but all together in a garland. There in prison we'd held as many garlands as we liked! Said the prayers in our own languages, because what mattered wasn't the language but the prayerfulness, and that was the same in all languages. And now my head, my memory, was all in such a state that I didn't know where I'd been. Forgive me, God. My eyes were watering in the strong light, it was dazzling me, I wasn't used to so much light. My eyes had always been a bit weak as well. But please, God, don't make me blind now that I've got out. People would even think I was crying. But there wasn't anybody around at the time, and the machines at the blocks of flats were a long way away. The man with the donkey had gone. I said a quiet prayer and amen.

But I had to get up and go on. Otherwise I'd be there on that stone and never be able to get up again. My Creator Father had preserved me, but not that much. There'd been some inside after they'd been arrested that had been sentenced and executed. Priests. A Catholic priest, a Reformed priest and a Romanian Greek Catholic. Their crime was treason and plotting against the authority of the state. I hadn't known any of those who were executed. They weren't from these parts. And a lot were the sort that went among the people and preached. And I'd heard about a lot of Protestants and nonconformists. The leader of the Jehovah's Witnesses too had been executed. No women had been executed, as far as I knew. God didn't have such great plans for women that he'd stand them up against walls in front of firing squads. But the Nonconformists had rather been imprisoned, and there'd been some that had died there of disease or weakness. Or lost their marbles. Some had gone completely insane. Lost their faith and gone mad. There was one deaconess, not even ordained yet. She shouted, had hallucinations. She was taken away, and the word was that the trolley had come for her. It could be heard in the corridor. The trolley, that is, that always made a characteristic sound, a rumbling, when a corpse was being removed on it. There were some, too, that committed a greater sin and did away with themselves, so heavily had their sin weighed on their souls. But the Lord preserved me, showed me mercy and now had brought me here. And now up I had to get, say a prayer of gratitude, and be on my way. It wouldn't do for me to give in. I asked God for the strength to get to my feet and to go from where I was in the fields into the road, as our house was on the edge of the fields, and to call on my relatives. If they were alive, and if I hadn't been given up.

I looked at the sparrows. They were taking a dust bath. Then when I went to move, they suddenly flew up into a bush. Then when I stood up the same thing happened, suddenly, on a word of command, into a tree. Then off again. How nicely they moved together, not one stayed behind. God leaves nobody to themselves. They moved in a fine garland, like us, when there'd been a number of us and we could pray the rosary together. Twenty religious! It was a long time ago.

Oh, to see my sisters again!

And the other one. My blood sister.

When I turned into Borháncs utca and saw the little houses and the big gardens behind them, such joy poured over me, it went right to my feet. For the first time since I'd been released. Now I was going where I wanted to go, I'd sit in the sun. There weren't many houses in the street. Even in the past it hadn't been built like a proper street, because then it had still been a field, and then poorer people had come there. Those better off had been over towards the sugar factory, mainly in Magyar utca, those not so well-to-do had been in the Pillangó area and the worst off here. The poorer had always been able to have a nice big garden and a house. It was rather quieter this way now. Perhaps people weren't yet back from the fields and the market. No sound of animals either. The silence seemed quite strange to me. It had been unusual not even to hear animals in the outer Hóstát.

Oh dear, I'd almost gone into the wrong house! The little Hóstát gates were so alike, all green and carved. I hadn't been this way for a long time. God was my guide. It was just as well, as I couldn't remember. I was inside the gate and I looked—the porch hadn't been like this. The entrance to this was from the end, and ours was in the middle. I left quickly, and fortunately nobody noticed me.

Our house was a couple of doors further. I stopped at the gate. Since the news had come last autumn that we were being released there'd been no further message. It could be that they'd thought we'd be home straight away. My father had disowned me, that much I knew because I'd been sent a document. But that didn't really mean that he'd disowned me, it was just customary, like a husband divorcing his wife on paper so as to be able to be able to live in the world. My father likewise had disowned me for the sake of work, I thought, so that he could get a job. So I wasn't upset.

I went into the yard, which was all overgrown with grass. So there are no animals now, I thought, for it to get like this. There were some chickens shut up in the chicken-run, and a little dog with bulging eyes barked at me. The house was locked and there was washing hanging on the porch. Good heavens! Baby clothes. So there was life there.

Where no oxen are, the crib is clean, says Holy Scripture. Everything was very clean. So there was certainly great poverty there. Not even a horse or cow these days.

There was a bench on the porch. I sat down because I was worn out, and went to sleep. They got a shock when they came home to find a stranger asleep on the porch, and a man called out: 'Anni, come quick, there's an old woman lying here.'

It was as if I'd returned from another world, I could hardly wake up, sleep had enclosed me like the grave. Then I sat up with an effort, because my one side was numb, and said to him, 'God forgive me, don't be angry, I lay down here because I thought this was the right house.' Because I meant that I'd made a mistake.

But then I saw my Annush's face. She let out such a cry that it frightened me. She screamed as if she was seeing a ghost. My Creator, I must have become such a sight for her to be so startled. A child in its pram began to wail at once. Annush paid it no attention but rushed, flew to me. I couldn't sit up straight, the way she threw herself onto me. Heavens, how she hugged me and kissed my face, held me tight—she was beside herself.

She cried all that evening. Cried when she looked at me or took my hand. I caressed her little girl, held her on my lap. She cried. The little girl also cried. The little boy was still a baby. Then I told her that I couldn't eat fat bacon, because she'd put some on the puliszka, it was nicely cooked, I said, but I couldn't because I'd had typhus and nearly died, but God's plan for me had been that I should survive. I wouldn't have any fat bacon because my innards would be so painful. So I told her. She began crying again. So we had a good cry all evening, and her husband put the children to bed because they'd go to the factory with him in the morning and go into the child care there so that he could work. Their mother was still in the garden and the market, and also went cleaning in shops. The older child was a girl, just like Annush, and a little boy, still quite tiny. He too cried a lot.

Such was Annush, I hardly knew she'd become such a lovely woman. She too was just a bit on the thin side. Her eyes were just the same as ever. She laughed, even when she was crying. They'd fallen on hard times, no longer had the field, all three parts had been lost, not only mine. There was only that small garden, thirty ares.

I told Annush that I would stay with them until I could find myself somewhere better. She replied that she wouldn't let me go anywhere else. She would never let me go. I said that I would work, she wouldn't have to keep me, only let me have my sleep out. I might not go, she wouldn't let me go anywhere.

I didn't ask about my father, but waited for her to tell me herself. When her husband Mihály had gone to bed, Annush told me that he had died five years previously. She hadn't wanted to let me know so as not to upset me. He'd suffered greatly before dying. He'd been buried beside Mummy. Well, poor Mummy, I said. That just slipped out, and I apologized. Annush laughed out loud, for the first time since my arrival. Oh, she's a beauty, my sister! Thanks be to you, dear God, for giving her such great loveliness.

She'd got a good husband. Made a good choice. He kissed my cheek as if he were my brother. He was hard-working, even saw to the children and put them to bed, teased them, played with them and sang to them. A good man. The children were so fond of him, sat on him like on a pony.

He was rather small, was Mihály. In fact, quite tiny, shorter than a woman. But anyone that's been given his great holy name couldn't short-change the world. Annush must have been slightly taller, and when she wore her high heels to go dancing, taller by a head. When he was going to bed, he said to Annush, 'Don't go to market tomorrow, darling. Stay with your sister.'

Annush said that she'd got to go to a shop the next day, to clean.

By then she was asking all the time for me to tell her about it all. I did say something, but she could hardly hear me, so weak was my voice. What should she do, what did I want, what would be good for me, what would I like now? I asked if she had a tomato. As if she hadn't . . . who's ever seen a garden without tomatoes? And out she ran. Mihály said, 'You see how lucky it is that you weren't let out in February or March, when most were released. Where would we have found you a tomato then? By February we'd even run out of tomato juice.'

I ate half a tomato. It was like . . . what did it taste like? Like the soil. I daren't eat any more, half was enough, and I wasn't sure my stomach would stand it, so let's see. And it was a nice big one, my dear sister had brought the biggest there was. She said hers were all the old sort. She wasn't an innovator, didn't do other sorts, because a lot of people did, they yielded more and ripened earlier, but she preferred the old kind, didn't know what they were called. Every sort had a scientific name. Well, I knew where my sister had obtained instruction, because she'd told me a long time ago. She'd certainly been very wicked. She'd mended her ways, done the right thing and got married and become a mother.

She ran me a bath. They'd got running water in the house, had had the gas brought in, and there was a toilet, though her husband didn't like having that indoors. There was a sort of little cubicle, with a little window, and you could put the light on. They'd bought a boiler and a tub. I'd never in my life taken a bath in warm water from a boiler. Annush came in when I was undressing, and I was so embarrassed because I'd got horrid grey underwear on, prison issue. She cried again. I told her 'Look here, Annush, if you're going to go on crying, I can't stay here. I can't bear seeing you cry all the time. Now, I'm not dead, you can see that. Don't keep looking at me, I'm not a picture, to be looked at.'

'I can't bear to look at you, Rózsi. I can't. What did they do to you? Just look at you!'

'Don't look at me. Be so good as to leave the room, even if you are my sister. I'm not letting anybody see me naked.'

She didn't leave the room, not at all! Previously I'd gone to sleep at table. The children were sitting there and kept laughing at me as nodded off and I went to sleep. What if I went to sleep in the bath in all that water? She wouldn't leave me alone in case I even drowned. A child couldn't take a bath by itself, had to be watched.

'Well then, turn your back,' I said. She sat on a stool with her back to me, and told me to keep talking so that she' know that I hadn't drowned. What was I to talk about? I'd got nothing to say. So I should tell her what happened.

'Were you been beaten up?'

'No, because they were sorry for me—*şchiop*. That was what they said—*şchiop*.'

'What does that mean?'

'It means lame.'

'Were other people beaten up?'

'Yes. Monks and nuns not all that much, the religious reactionaries. Women from the farms more so. Thieves, immoral people, all the time. There was a lesbian woman, she was beaten up. And they did other things to her. Treated her very badly. Well, perhaps she'd been granted the holy wounds. Because she got a thrashing every week.'

Oh, but the water hurt my skin. Either the water or the soap, I don't know which. It was painful, it burned. I daren't say anything to Annush. It was like being stung all over. I daren't say anything, she'd have been alarmed and started crying. My skin was all red cracks, especially my legs. The doctor hadn't given me anything for it in the prison. I'd have to get treatment when I got out, he said. It would be a lengthy treatment, and he didn't even begin because he hadn't got anything to use. A lead cream should be applied. It must be erysipelas. A long time ago he'd eaten too much pork and developed erysipelas. Well, I certainly didn't get it from pork on that occasion. A woman in prison called it St Anthony's Fire. She was a bit of a herbalist, and she'd been jailed for fortune telling and foretelling the end of the world. Because it burnt me something awful.

When Annush turned back and saw my legs, because I'd lifted them out of the water to stop the burning, she clasped her hands together.

'You've got scabies, Rózsi! Jesus! Oh, I hope the child doesn't get it.'

'It's not scabies, don't worry. It's erysipelas. It's worse. Harder to get rid of. St Anthony punished sinners with it. I need alum for it.'

'Are you sure, Rózsi? You need a doctor for that.'

'Have you got any alum? Your husband must have some, for when he cuts himself shaving, isn't that what he uses?'

'Don't put anything on it, go and show it to the doctor, Rózsi, You don't want alum for that.'

'Look here, Annush, if I go round with all my problems, you won't be able to sell enough in a year to pay for the treatment.'

I had to tell Annush to scour the tub out in case the child caught it. And to boil my headscarf. I was bringing nothing but trouble.

She brought me a clean blouse. An embroidered one, and she said I'd be comfortable in it. I said I wasn't going to put on her best blouse, no way, she could give me some old torn one. She would not. So we had an argument. Then she cried again, because she had to help me put it on as I couldn't raise my one arm very much, hadn't been able to for a long time. I had to lift it with the other one when I was dressing. She asked what had happened to it, but it was only rheumatism, I thought. Something of the sort. Because I hadn't had spa treatment for six years and I'd been very cold. But I didn't tell her that. I didn't want her feeling sorry for me, she was crying enough as it was.

She said that she was going to get me better and I'd be as good as new. I was a beautiful young girl, I'd see. I might even get married. I said that I already was married. Annush clasped her hands together. Surely I didn't mean to go on with that way of life, did I? she asked. But I'd never left it, never left my Lord.

She had thought that if God had messed me about like that, I'd have given Him up.

There was one thing on which Annush and I couldn't agree. At all events she meant to put me in the living room, to sleep in the bed. Certainly not! I'd just sleep in the kitchen, on the bench, that was definite. I wasn't going to sleep with her husband. I was somebody else's wife, I told her.

In the morning she could hardly rouse me. In fact it wasn't morning, more like midday and time for lunch. But I was scarcely able to rejoin the world. When I woke up I didn't know where I was, in which world. I looked at the little kitchen, there was so much light that it hurt my eyes. There was too much light in the world, I was almost blinded by it. She made me some vegetable soup and beat a raw egg into it. I daren't have more than one bowl of it because for a long time, I'd had such diarrhoea and my innards were very delicate. I had to be careful.

Annush had to go with me to the police station to take my release documents. I had to report in either that day or the next. If I didn't I'd be re-arrested. She too had to have a document stating that I had an address. *Carte funciară*, proving that she owned the house. Fortunately she found it quickly in the drawer, and off we went. When she saw that I had trouble walking she said that we should take a cart to the little market and then get on the bus.

I told Annush that I wouldn't stay long with them, but I'd find a place once I'd had my sleep out. I wasn't too badly treated at the police station. They took my documents, we sat about for an hour, then I went to be interviewed. Where was I going to work? I was asked. I said that I'd try to go back to the hospital. I wasn't allowed to work with people, was the answer. So I said there was a printer's, I'd worked there as a packer, but my health broke down, I began to cough badly, so I'd become a nun. I wasn't allowed to do ideological work, so I couldn't go to the printer's. So I'd go to the hospital and they'd find me a job, perhaps in the kitchen or the laundry. I was a trained nurse, I said, even qualified with the Protestants, and my certificate was recognized. That didn't count, I couldn't work with people any longer.

Well, I thought, there are a lot of teachers who've all been in prison, and priests. What about them? Can't they work with people? Were they going to preach to sheep or the forest trees? And all the university lecturers that there were.

I was back in solitary, I thought. At liberty, indeed, but in solitary confinement. Was this what clemency meant?

'Do you understand?' he asked. Yes, I said. 'You can't go begging, can't cause trouble in public, can't go calling on people, can't assemble with people. But most of all, you can't go calling house to house.'

'So where was I going to go?' asked the policeman. I'd have to think some more, I said. I couldn't say there and then where I'd go. I'd help my sister, I said. I must remember, he said as I left, that in the bublic, there was work for everybody.

On the way I was so weary that I could hardly walk. I told Annush that I'd like to go into the church. The Franciscans' church, where I'd always gone. She had to go home to see to things, the child, the garden, everything. I'll make my own way home, I said. She gave me five lei so that I could take a taxi. Or I could take a bus all the way to the little market. I sat on a damaged bench in the square in front of the church. There was a sign that said not to feed the pigeons, *interzis hrănirea porumbeilor*. How rotten the world had become. You weren't even allowed to feed God's birds. Inside was our dear St Francis with pigeons on his shoulders, but there you weren't allowed to feed them.

I didn't want to see this world, I preferred to shut my eyes and wait for Mass.

I dozed off and was only woken by the ringing of the bell.

The light was so strong when I tried to open my eyes that I was afraid I'd gone blind. There was too much light in the world. I could have done with black glasses, like those that we were always made to wear when we'd been arrested. Iron glasses, so that we couldn't see anything or know where we were. We were taken from one place to another in the prisoner transport, to the Securitate, to Várad, Temesvár, this cellar, that cellar. Nice cold black glasses, so that we couldn't see anything. They always put them on us when we were taken for questioning.

I'd told Annush that I hadn't been beaten, and I hadn't, even during interrogation. My father had beaten me plenty, so that I'd be afraid and confess to everything. So when I was asked whether I'd be beaten or would I confess, I knew straight away what to do. I lied about everything, confessed, signed my name without protest. I didn't tell them my secret name for them to mock. We were dead as far as the world was concerned. That is our vow. Because my real name I owe to the Lord. I put down my lay name, but that meant nothing to me.

I'd told Annush that I'd admitted and signed my name to having sympathized with the revolutionary people of Hungary, that I was opposed to the people's democracy and the power of the workers, and I'd uttered anti-Communist propaganda. I admitted that, along with my companions in the order, I'd praised the 1956 Revolution in Hungary and criticized the Soviet intervention and foreign suppression. And I'd expected that revolution to spread to Romania as well, because I'd been hoping for the collapse of the people's democracy. I'd prayed for it, I said, but that was later crossed out of the record. And I'd uttered propaganda in favour of Transylvania being reannexed to Hungary, or becoming an independent country—I couldn't remember which—and I accused those in power in Romania of not respecting the rights, guaranteed in the Constitution, of the Hungarians and other minorities. Annush clasped her hands together, saying, 'Jesus, Rózsi, had you done all that?'

So when my name had been signed—Rosalia, not Rózsa, Butyka—it was clear that we nuns were great politicians, and had almost succeeded in overthrowing the authority of the state. We had to write an awful lot, and use expressions such as we never understood. What was meant by 'authority of the state', I asked, because we recognized only one authority, that of the Father, the Son, and the Holy Spirit, but it wasn't permissible to record that in worldly proceedings.

And then we'd effected and incited even bigger reactionary clerical propaganda, I told Annush. We'd gone from house to house, as we had, in proclaiming the gospel, and in so doing had sold copies of the poem *Mary and the Three Lambs*. We didn't sell them, just received alms. We'd been begging, I said, as we were a mendicant order under our original charisma. No! We'd been uttering propaganda, was the reply. They'd come across the whole of the songs of Mary, and I'd copied them by my own hand, as I had nice writing. I'd made at least fifty copies. The Three Lambs were the three aspects of Jesus. Did I recognize my handwriting? Did I admit it? 'Mary and the Three Lambs'. The first was when He was born of the Holy Spirit, the Father, and Mary; in the second he was grown up and was the great teacher of the world and the Evangelists: and the third was the resurrected Jesus, who propitiated the sins of mankind and went to heaven.

When they asked why I went around in black, I confessed that I was in mourning for the Hungarian Revolution, and so it was put down in the records. But I didn't say that the appearance that we had in common, our uniform, with the little blue collar and cuffs and light blue headscarf, was because we were wives of Jesus and children of our Virgin Mother Mary. I was afraid that it would be ridiculed.

I was afraid, I really was. Not for myself, but for our Lord Jesus.

I told Annush all that straight out. I told her what I hadn't been allowed to say under interrogation.

Then I'd signed the omerta, I told her. So there. I'd infringed all God's commandments, one or two at the most I hadn't, because I'd merely wished my father dead, not killed him, except in my heart. But isn't that as great a sin? Killing in the heart? Or that I hadn't acted immorally. It's easy for anybody to remain free of sin that nobody leads astray. Christ called me. Called me to himself, enticed me, and I couldn't resist. As a true Christian, He's put every other sin in my way. I've even infringed the omerta, but that didn't count, it was only a worldly affair.

I didn't make any more copies, I told Annush, because my right hand and arm had developed a nervous twitch, and that arm was the one that I couldn't raise properly. Nor could I straighten my fingers out any longer or pick things up. In the prison I'd been lucky to be able to stay in the kitchen, and it hadn't been noticed. But I'd already had difficulty holding a knife.

Then after the bell had rung I went into our church. There weren't so very many in there. I didn't see any of my sisters. It was a ferial day, nothing special to bring people in. But no day was ordinary for us, because we had to give thanks to the Lord every day. Our church was dilapidated. There was a new priest, and I didn't know him or the sacristan, only the beadle. I didn't sit at the front. I preferred to be in the shadows, in front of Little Teréz, she always pointed to my place. But in there I couldn't catch that nice smell of Jesus. I closed my eyes and felt better like that. God had preserved me, dear God, thank you. The praying did me good, and I was almost afraid that it would never end. I ought to have confessed, but I'd come too late. Nor had I the strength, I was inwardly worn out once more. I'd have to wait, dear Jesus, to be able to recount all the sins that I'd accumulated. Because it had been six years since I'd confessed to a priest. I so yearned for the body of Christ to be placed in my mouth. I dearly loved the Blessed Sacrament. With all my heart.

It was shocking, the people hardly knew the liturgy. It looked as if they didn't understand the sacred acts being performed at the altar. They no longer knew when to stand, sit or kneel. As I went forward to take the Holy Body to me, I noticed how creased and soiled the altar cloth was. Wasn't there a verger, then, to keep things in order?

I looked to the right along the benches—what had become of the monks from the monastery which had been next door to the church? It was still there, and had been turned into a school. All the monks had been dispersed, had to leave. That had happened fourteen years previously. We had to bear on our shoulders the silent church. And go about the world without distinguishing marks, because we might not wear our habits.

Meanwhile, my longer leg was very painful. It had always hurt at the hip, but this time the sole of my foot too was burning as if it was covered in pitch. It was all hard skin and there were a couple of large corns on it as well, and

I'd cut them some time before. I used to have a razor blade, but I'd left it with a fellow prisoner when I was released. She hadn't been granted clemency, wasn't a political. Now my sole was so painful that I couldn't feel my bunions at all. If I could find a job, I'd get a cobbler to make me shoes so that my legs would be the same length.

I ought to have stayed after Mass and spoken to somebody, to ask if they could give me some work around the church. Did the church accept back people that had been torn from its bosom? In Szamosújvár a nun had told me that it was no longer the case that the church decided whom to employ or not. The ministry had to give permission for every job. The church ministry. The Ministry of Cults, as it was called. Certainly Rome was no longer in charge. So if the ministry had to give me permission, I wasn't likely to get anything. I wasn't allowed to work with people any longer. But somebody ought to be dusting the saints, changing the water in the flowers, sweeping round. And washing and starching the altar cloths. Just then I wasn't strong enough to speak to anybody and inquire. Perhaps they wouldn't even remember me. If I didn't look after the sick, the weak and the poor, what on earth would I be able to do? I'd come another time.

Annush said that I'd slept round the clock. It had been Thursday when I went to bed and Saturday when I woke up. She'd been making pastry in the kitchen and the cat had knocked a pan over, but even at such a noise I hadn't woken. I was on the bench in the kitchen, lying on a nice big bench with a horsehair mattress, in fact two! I'd slept from Thursday to Saturday. Dear Jesus, what a lazy servant you have!

There was no way I could be left alone. I so longed for solitude, but I simply couldn't. I was always clinging to somebody. Either I was running after Mihály to the shed, where he was soldering a piece of fencing to sell, or reading aloud to the children, or was constantly asking poor Annush what I could do for her. I even talked to Etelka next door, she was so full of woes, couldn't pray, and just kept complaining to people. I couldn't find silence in the evening so that prayer might speak within me. I talked to myself all the time. I ought to have observed a verbal fast. In the past our Mother, Sister Jusztina, had been with us. Where are you now, dear Mother? Are you still alive? Or have you been laid in a mass grave at the drainage? And then I couldn't get to sleep. Every sound disturbed me. There's always a bit of noise in a house. The children snuffle, and perhaps there's a mouse as well. And all the talk in my head! It will not stop! A fast. Fasting, prayer, and good works. Be content with those three, sister! I said to Annush that I must keep a fast of speech, that was my penance. She shrugged. How can I be left alone in the world like this, dear Christ, without my sisters?

I didn't know where to go first. The hospital or the church. Annush kept telling me to stay at home, have a thorough rest. I was sleeping as much as a newborn. I thought that I was always in their way. They were feeding me, giving me clothes, giving me everything, working round me, and I wasn't helping them at all. If I did a bit of work in the garden I had to sit down. I could hardly eat a thing, my digestion was out of order, I was forever in the toilet. I'd had diarrhoea like that for more than six months. It had come on during the previous winter. Sometimes Annush had to sleep with me so that I could get to sleep. She warmed me up with her body heat, because I was so cold all the time, and my feet were like ice. I was beginning to recover, I thought. My body was telling me, 'Well done, you survived it all, so now you can actually be ill.' Such is the wisdom of the human body. But I couldn't stay and be a burden to them forever. Annush kept saying that this was my home, my garden. Daddy hadn't really wanted to disown me, he was talked into it. Because if somebody was disowned their relations could stay in the collective and everything. Annush has forgiven our father completely, I could see that.

Mihály was a good man, loved Annush dearly, didn't spare himself, gave her his full support, backed her up, washed the children, bent over backwards, as Annush put it, to be in her good books. They'd left the church, hardly ever went, and preferred taking the children for walks on Sunday. They used to dress up smartly and stroll in the town. They liked to be in the centre, went to the Sétatér and the Fellegvár. But that Mihály was a poor boy, hadn't brought much property with him, there'd been hardly any land or garden to give him because it was next to his parents' house and couldn't be shared with his two brothers. So he'd gone to work in the shoe factory and was paid a wage. He'd moved into Annush's house there when they married, but brought nothing with him. The tub and the boiler came out of the wedding presents, and they'd later bought a big cupboard with a mirror. Mihály never drank a drop, worked, and organized the children better than I'd ever seen a man do. He even pushed the pram. But he was such a small man, God had given him such a fault. So that he shouldn't be overconfident.

I asked Annush how it came about that she'd married. Because before I was taken away, she'd told me that she had someone, hadn't she? An important man, and she was his lover, so there. And I prayed that she might not live in sin.

She said, 'Aunty kept telling me to marry Sándor, because he would have me. But he would have all the girls, once or twice, even three times. He was quick-tempered, that was what people said about him. That big-talking Sándor and his brother, they were real drones! Then her uncle said he'd rather show me another lad, who was a worker. Because that Sándor wasn't going to tie up tomatoes for me. He was an absolute drone, liked to knock about, let everybody hear what he had to say, in the pub too, though he didn't drink much. But him cutting bean sticks for you and setting them up—no chance. Only the other stick, and he winked. That Sándor preferred to go and work in the factory, and he'd gone. There he had his shift, from this time to that, and after that he was off out having fun. If you didn't work very hard in the factory it wasn't noticed. But in the garden you have to bend your back, and if a tomato stem has fallen down people do notice. Give that Sándor up. He's all right as a boyfriend, go about with him a bit, but he won't do for a husband. Then Uncle said, there's that little Mihály there. He's gone into the factory now, but the way he used to work for his parents, he was like a machine! He was a good farmer, even if he's gone into the factory. Which one I don't know, said Uncle, one of those at the station, that's the way he always goes. Mihály Kilin. The only thing about him that he didn't like was that he was so small. Never mind if he's small as long as he's got a good head, said Aunty. He'll be given everything, you'll see. Well, I'd got the house and the garden, didn't need anything. And he wasn't. And then we met at Aunty's one Saturday evening. Then a week went by and we went for a walk. Then we even went dancing as well one day. He was very nice! Tell the truth, he was as nice as Vili, but not as good looking. You know, Vili, he that . . . I waited and waited, and I thought "I'll find out what's wrong with this Mihály." Because every man's got some fault, some *cusur*, that's Aunty Mária's word—defect. As women have as well. Including me, you know. Well, it turned out that Mihály didn't have any defects, none at all. He didn't drink, didn't waste money, worked, was polite to his parents and to me, even to the dog and to Szőke their horse. He even talked to plants! Just like Vili. Vili would say to a flower, 'You're rather dry, my dear, I must give you a drop to drink, mustn't I?' And that's how Mihály did—'Oh dear, little plant, you're all weak and dry, how are you going to make a two-metre tomato bush?' As early as in March, Mihály would rush home after his shift in the factory to open up the plants that were under glass and let the sun caress them, so that they shouldn't sweat and begin to go mouldy. Because his mother would be in the market and couldn't do anything, because she had no pension, his father couldn't move as his legs were paralysed, and he only received a very small disability allowance. Then if the weather in March was bad and it snowed now and then, and the cold frame was open, he'd run home and close it. So when I'd seen that, after six months or so, I said to myself this Mihály is going to be mine. He hadn't proposed to me by then, and oh, he was scared stiff of me. He was a bit of a *papalaptye*, as Aunty Mária used to say, so slow he didn't come and hold me and drive me mad. He just waited for something to happen. I preferred the sort that drove me mad, to bring everything into the open myself, but he went on saying nothing. So in March I said to him, "I'm marrying you, OK?" It came as a surprise to him. What was he surprised at? What had he been thinking? Did I mean to take him on as a servant? I'd been thinking, never mind if he wasn't the sort of man that Vili was, and that I'd think of him all the time, never mind if he wasn't so dizzy with love that he couldn't breathe. And I told him in advance that I had a thing or two to tell him, so that he should know and not say later that I hadn't told him. "Shall I write it down?" I asked, would that be better? No, I should just tell him. So I told him both my two big facts. How I'd been with Vili. I didn't say his name, only that I'd had somebody, I'd been quite young at the time, and he'd loved me, but not exactly, so to speak, as a wife. And the other thing was that I had the habit of discussing things with my dead relatives. My mother hadn't appeared for a long time, but if she did and I spoke to her, I wouldn't be embarrassed, wouldn't keep it a secret. Mihály became a bit serious and asked for time to consider, I said, all right, but don't tell your mother, because then the whole street will find out. It knows as it is, said Mihály. I didn't think so, how could it? We didn't meet for a fortnight, and I was thinking that he'd never come back when he came out again to the market as he knew that I was out there. After that the wedding soon followed. But he's always been just a little serious, not a problem, because he's always had at the back of his mind not my second fact but Vilmos, and it worries him.'

I said to Annush that the Lord had listened, she'd corrected her error and was now living as she should. I mustn't think, she replied, that she didn't miss Vilmos a bit. That went through me like a red-hot knife. Dear Annush, may God have mercy on you. I shall always, always, pray for her sinful soul.

By then I was on good terms with Annush's little girl. When she caught flu I stayed with her, and she wasn't taken into childcare at the factory. Mihály went off to work, Annush to the market, and I realized that the two of us were left together. We lay on the bed, and I told her stories about Jesus and the children. She listened wide-eyed. Then we slept like logs. The bench was just a narrow thing like the one in prison. So little Zsuzsa and I had to cuddle up close together. I would say a nice cheering rosary for her. She liked my rosary, played with it. It was still the old one that I'd made in prison out of flour and salt, with a little wooden cross. I hadn't obtained a new one. And it hadn't even been consecrated. I started to say it for her, but by the first big bead she was fast asleep. She didn't even know the Lord's Prayer, and she was four. I just said it for her.

The sisters and I had arranged to meet on the first Monday of the month. However widely scattered we were, we had to get together on that day in the Fōtér at six in the evening. That we'd said even before we were arrested. God, grant that I might see my sisters! What day was it today, I wondered? I had to ask Mihály or Annush, because the child didn't know. Well, I too was a child, I knew nothing about the world.

I had to summon up my strength and go to the Franciscans' church, to talk to a priest there. I didn't know why I was nervous. It was the first time that I'd been nervous since being released. When I set off one day my legs were shaking something awful. Don't desert me, my faith, don't desert me, Holy Mother Church. Before I went into the church, I sat on the bench for a bit. I said a rosary, just on my fingernails, so that nobody should see the rosary in my hand. I went inside, and there wasn't a soul there. In the old days there even used to be a stall selling holy pictures and rosaries, but now there was nothing. I realized that I'd gone to the wrong place. There was a little door on the left, that was where I should look for the priests. It wasn't open. I pulled the bell-pull once and a second time. After a long pause, out came the elderly sacristan. I asked whether he remembered me. How should he remember me? We were the . . . I said no more. He didn't remember me. What did I want, he asked.

'I'd like a word with the Father. An interview,' I said. I no longer knew the right thing to say. I just spoke as we did in prison.

'Come another time, he's busy at present. What's it about?' he asked.

'In that case, at least let me speak to the secretary.'

I went into the secretary's office, she gave me a seat and took out a book to see when I could go and see him. Then a door at the back opened and in came the Father. He said that he had a funeral at two o'clock, could he have the deceased's biography because he hadn't known them. Tell the family to phone him. I stood up and greeted him. Glory be to Christ Jesus. Forever, amen, he responded and turned to go back.

'Father, excuse me, could I have a word?'

He turned. What did I want? He was a completely new priest, rather on the young side, and I'd never seen him before. I'd like to have a talk. Come into the office, he said. How was I to begin? I had no idea. I told him plainly what the situation was, I'd just been released. I'd been arrested in '58 with my sisters. We'd been in the Rose Garland according to the accusation, but we'd never called ourselves that, the state had made the name up. We were Franciscan nuns. Had he heard of us? He hadn't, he took no interest in politics. He closed his eyes, put his white hand over his mouth, and stood there silent. That meant that I must say nothing, and neither must he. He stood there for a long moment, perhaps praying.

So what was I to say? It wasn't for me to say that I'd suffered in Christ, he must know that.

'God forgives all sinners,' he replied

I nodded and said, 'I know, Father, I know God's infinite goodness.' He asked if I wished to confess.

'Yes, Father, but I haven't been able to eat the body of Christ for six years, or drink His blood.'

I couldn't confess six years' worth, he couldn't spare me so much time, he said, and he laughed. Oh, he was a Franciscan! The way he laughed! He didn't even need to wear his habit, even without it he was a Franciscan!

'I'll make a list for next time I come, I promise.'

Had he really not heard of us, I asked again. Mother Jusztina and the nuns. Leona, Melánia, Paula and me, Eleonóra. We used to live up Monostori utca in a grace and favour flat. It had no longer been called that officially, it was just accommodation for five people. He hadn't even been in Kolozsvár in those days, he said, hadn't heard of us. He repeated his gesture, placing his hand—what fine white hands he had!—over his mouth and closing his eyes. And I was so stupid, I kept talking, did I mean to tell him everything? Our leader had been taken off to the drainage in the Danube delta, had he heard of her? Sister Jusztina, did he know anything about her? Was she alive or dead? No, he hadn't heard about anybody. We were members of the order, I repeated, we'd all taken our final vows. Brides of Christ. He took a sheet of paper, wrote, and as he did so he spoke.

'You're now living as lay persons, is that right?' he asked.

'That's right.'

'I'm listening,' he replied.

So what could I ask? And want? I ought to have summoned all my courage to ask whether our good and gracious Lord had preserved Bishop Áron, because I knew nothing about him. I didn't know how to ask, how to approach the subject. If somebody would only mention him and I would find out. So what was I to ask?

He passed me the piece of paper. *Tuesday, 5 p.m. Sub Rosa, be there.* Oh, it was nice of him to use the informal address.

'What could he do for me?' he asked aloud.

'I've just been released,' I said like a fool. 'There were five of us, one was Sister Jusztina, who was sent to hard labour on the drainage. The four of us were in Szamosújvár.'

He did it for a third time. Placed his hand on his mouth and closed his eyes. His other hand he placed on my mouth, and he whispered very softly, 'Be quiet.'

He would hold confession for me any day, he said aloud. Then I made a supreme effort and asked 'I'd like to find a job in the church. Anything, even cleaning.'

Unfortunately, all their positions were filled. It was pointless asking for a new one, authority wouldn't allow it. There weren't many of them and they hardly needed help. I should submit a written request, but not state what I'd been doing previously and where I came from, and on no account mention prison. That was all that he could suggest. It would be scrutinized, I should come back in a month's time.

One more question, because this he would surely know: What had happened to our confessor, Father Fidel? He had been on the staff here. Had he come out yet? Yes, he wrote on the paper, he'd been transferred, he was in Szilágyi County but no longer had a parish. 'Which parish is he in? What's it called? What do you mean, an ordained priest can't celebrate Mass?' I asked, scandalized, because I'd only just caught on. What if he wasn't a priest, but perhaps a rag-and-bone man? Had the church still any say in who was a priest and who was not?

'Let's leave it at that. Don't ask to know any more. God is gracious and forgiving to all his children.'

'Did I want anything else?' he asked. Glory be, I said, I'd bring in the note, forever, amen. First, I thought, I'd say a nice rosary of Light to purify myself. I started, but then it was only my own words that came to my heart, and my thoughts couldn't calm me.

I prayed to my Creator not to take away my faith in Holy Mother Catholic Church and not to turn me from the sacred heart of our dear Lady Mary. We were so scattered and couldn't talk to one another in the Lord's house. I begged my dear God to enlighten me, and that I might have the strength to see the kindly Holy Mother Church and distant Rome, which, alas, was now very far from us. Perhaps silence was imposed on Rome too.

I was now feeling an abject spiritual emptiness. What should I believe in? Whom was I to believe? Would our church receive us back? Would we ever be able to break with it? Had it let go of our hands? Oh, what dark misgivings filled me now. It had never been like this in prison! My heart was completely dried out, as Father Fidel used to tell me. *Taedium cordis*, that was the one thing that he'd taught, all he'd ever said. I had to write a piece on *Taedium*! The Father tested us in that way, in writing too, not only *viva voce*. The exercise book had been there on the table and Mother had asked us all to write in it and read out each other's contributions.

All the same, I begged my Father not to let me have doubts in my church, but rather to strengthen me on my chosen way, which led me in the bosom of Holy Catholic Mother Church, as I knew no other. I prayed for dear Father Fidel, for Sister Jusztina, and my dear Sisters Paula, Melánia and Leona, and for all religious. Oh, if only someone would take my hand too now. I was so weak.

I was bodily so exhausted, and I had to go home. Fortunately, Annush and her family were out in the afternoon, because my heart was so weary when I got there. I'll go out into the garden and do some work, I thought, because Annush, my philosophical sister, was always saying that the soil would heal me. Not praying, not getting paid work at the hospital, but simply bending over the red onions and fresh lettuce. Because the Lord's most holy word told me that. The Lord spoke to men in the language of plants because it was with them that He fed them, so you just go and talk in the garden with the Lord's words. That Annush didn't go to church, neither did the children nor her husband, and she only received the Lord's supper on red-letter days.

I didn't go into the garden. I sat outside on the porch, but then I began to feel cold and so went into the living room. In there Annush had a cupboard with a mirror. Wherever I went I could see myself in it. If I took a couple of steps backward it was big enough for me to see myself from my head almost to the tips of my toes. I began to look at myself. I put on the light, drew the curtains, fastened them together with a pin, and bolted the door. Then I took a good look at myself, something that I'd never done in all my life.

The Lord had given my body to me and to the world and there I was judging it. But it was not for me to judge, nor to live according to the flesh.

Why did I do such a thing? Not in order to amuse myself. If the Father whom I'd talked to hadn't hurt me, I might not have done it. Only the dried-up soul does such things. It's indecent. One's body doesn't exist for one to keep looking at it. How often had Father Fidel said that man didn't live according to the flesh. Not according to the desires of the flesh. Where would we get to if we just lived according to the flesh! The apostle Paul only expressed his teachings in Romans 8 in terms of the flesh because that was what simple people would understand. That meant us. The Lord had to send His Only Begotten Son in flesh because before that we had been unable to comprehend His love. We can only understand in terms of the flesh, we're so stupid.

But we're told that we must live not according to the flesh but to the spirit. 'You are not in the body but in the spirit,' he said. Because the flesh is only weak. But what did Father Fidel say? How strong your bodies are! You will see, when Christ puts them to the test! Give thanks for that too, and the dear Father laughed so much that his black back teeth showed.

I looked at myself in that mirror. And I could see that the Lord had put me to the test in my body. I looked at what I was like in bodily terms. But it is God, not we, that must rejoice in us, and perhaps even in that ugly body that was mine, He could find something to delight Him. If He didn't speak to me while I was still young, in my body too, He didn't call me to follow Him so as later to mock me. I looked, and could see what the Lord could see in me. Because we must see Him in ourselves. And certainly this body of mine was pleasing in the eyes of God. Pleasing in the eyes of God. But in the eyes of men, loathsome.

But if you looked at yourself there for much longer, Rózsi, you'd have been quite scandalized. Do not scandalize God, it is said. Only the day before little Zsuzsa had asked, when she saw me getting dressed, why I was so floppy. She'd pulled at my skin and could see that I didn't really fit it, it was too big for me. I didn't look at myself then, but now I have. My whole skin was hanging off me, empty, in folds. Then I could see under my breasts when I lifted them, it was all raw, that was what made it itch so much. They too have become all empty, like damaged sacks. I ought have worn some sort of combinations so that my breasts didn't dangle like that, and underneath didn't get damaged. It used not to be like that. My hips were so lopsided when I lowered my shorter leg, the right, to the ground. That was getting worse and worse, I thought. My leg was shrinking because there's TB in it, wasn't that so? And as I lifted my arms the skin hung from them like a dishcloth. And those red legs, the erysipelas had almost reached my knees.

I looked on and thought that, at the most, what appeared in the mirror pleased gracious God. Because He'd have to be gracious, to love anything like that. Man either turned away in loathing from such a body or pitied it. Oh dear, oh dear, everything has worn it out, both time and neglect. What did our St Francis reply when his younger brother asked how it could be that God had chosen him of all people for the great glory of becoming so great a saint? Because he was the most worthless! Francis replied that God wishes to be great in His most worthless and most sinful children.

Dear Annush, if she could have seen me, how she would have howled. Or a man. Being seen like this by a man had never entered my head. No one saw our Virgin Mother of God naked in her human condition. But the world saw Christ our Lord naked on the cross, that it might see His pain.

I had to get dressed. I'd done a foolish thing. God forgive me.

If the sisters and I could live together again, and again be the Rose Garland, because for that, twenty religious were required, and especially if Mother Jusztina joined us too, our dear sister, for whom we prayed daily, we would again be strengthened. I would never again do such a thing as stare at myself in the mirror behind drawn curtains. I would not have to see such a thing. Nor should our faith utterly fade away. I began to weep copiously as I dressed. Annush was always giving me new, colourful clothes, youthful dresses, but in fact the truth was as Mihály had said when he saw me, that there was an old woman lying on the bench. That was what he said when I arrived. But he'd seen nothing but my hands and feet, as I'd covered my face with a piece of cloth. I wept bitterly, and even went out into the garden to weep.

Then I had a wash, and I thought I'd give the others a surprise. I hadn't done any cooking since I couldn't remember when. I didn't cook in the prison kitchen, only washed dishes. Before that too I didn't do much, as sister Leona had been our cook. I thought I could still make pastry. The Lord was with me once more. What sort of pastry could I cook? I ought to make a pitta. I took a jar of plums and made a sort of lattice. But I didn't know how to use the gas. I could see the tap, but I was nervous. I hadn't watched how it was lit. I had to go round to the neighbour and ask. I wasn't embarrassed. I found somebody in at the third house, as the rest were still at the factory, the collective, or the market, because they were all Hóstát people and knew nothing else. I said that I was staying with Annush Butyka, my sister, and wanted to cook something but didn't understand the gas. Had I come back, then? asked the old lady. As I recall there had been a Bányai family, and only she was left. Yes, I said, the merciful God had preserved me. Did she have gas, so that she could show me? She had, because it had been brought into all the houses in the street, she said, because it had had to be brought into some place called the Station. Had they built stations? A Calvary? I asked, and was pleased. Not at all, these people only build factories.

So she showed me the gas, no need to be afraid, just light it. Then turn it off when you've finished. To be certain that it was turned off, put a lighted match to it.

So there was my pastry, see, just ready to eat. There hadn't been much fat either. Annush had hardly anything in the pantry. Whatever did they eat? Főzelék from all sorts of vegetables gleaned from the garden, and puliszka. Mummy had still been alive when I cooked my first pastry. She said that it was very tasty, but I'd never get married for it. It had been slightly burnt. Anybody that marries Jesus doesn't need to be a good cook.

That evening Mihály had a good wash, changed into Hóstát costume and went to choir practice. The men used to sing on one Thursday a month, in a secret house. Singing in a choir wasn't permitted, but all the same they did. It was a traditional Hóstát activity. And they sang at dances and in church, but women didn't take part. Annush put the children to bed early, and as she was doing that I went and picked things for the next day's market for her while it was still light. She told me what was needed and how much, and I brought carrots up out of the cellar, because they'd already been lifted. Then we sat in the kitchen, and she asked if I'd like some wine. Are we celebrating Mass? I asked. I hadn't changed my ways so much that I'd actually drink wine.

I asked her to tell a folk tale. She put a little glass of red wine in front of her, and wine, they say, loosens the tongue. But she said that she didn't tell folk tales.

'You haven't signed it as well, have you?' I asked.

'Signed what?'

'The omerta, of course.'

She hadn't, but certainly she wasn't going to tell a nun anything about how it had been. And if the nun gave a full account, she would desert her faith. I said to her, look here, Annush, even bigger men than you have tried to make me desert my faith. The Securitate men, the prison warders and the informers in prison. There was one sergeant whose greatest glory it was if somebody abandoned their faith. He got a big reward if anybody signed, saying that they'd left their order. He tried to get me to do that during interrogation. He was a very clever man, cunning and intelligent. The devil had taught him how to go about it. He actually told me that all my sisters had denied Jesus, and where did I think Jesus was when I was locked up in there? Why wasn't He rushing to my rescue? I really couldn't give him an answer. Not because I couldn't think what to say. The way they went about it, the way they talked, I couldn't answer them. I sat there like a torn sack and said nothing. And then he was abusive, did I know that the Romanian People's Republic punished polygamy? That alarmed me, because I hadn't understood what he was talking about. We weren't all Arabs! Then I got it, and I didn't answer.

Afterwards I kept thinking what I might have replied. Because Jesus too had said that anybody that wanted to follow Him was setting out on a hard road.

'Why did you follow him, then, if it's so hard?' asked Annush.

'Whom should I follow, my dear? My own mind?'

But Jesus hadn't been listening when that sergeant was going on at me, He'd taken my hand and didn't let go of me. Sorry, my dear, you don't understand.

Anyway, I said to her, you tell me how it was with you. Because you drifted about a bit. Old news, all in the past, she replied. She'd been a lover, then became a wife. And now she'd got that good husband, that Mihály. She'd tired of being a lover. She'd got that very good husband. She loved him to bits. Just the way that he loved her.

'Love, now, that's another matter. You've really no idea about that, my dear Rózsi,' she said. Her eyes were sparkling now with the wine. But I didn't mind, she was so beautiful like that.

'I do, you know, Annush. We love our Lord Jesus passionately. That's why we become his wives. We couldn't give ourselves to Him if we didn't love Him.'

'I mean physical love, my dear. That you don't know.'

'Look, I'll tell you something. I found out even more about it today. I already had known, just hadn't realized. We nuns have no bodies, do you see? Not in the sense that they don't exist, because they do, you can see me sitting here, drat it, my hip hurts even when I'm sitting down, and I have to eat and I'm always having trouble with it. But to us that's nothing. Doesn't matter. That's not what we live for. We don't live according to the flesh.'

'When I'm asleep it doesn't matter for me either,' and Annush laughed.

She'd changed. She'd steadied up, she's a wife and mother. She and Vilmos hardly ever saw each other. She didn't talk about him any more.

So she wanted me to tell the tale, she wanted to know everything. Never mind, I replied. A nun doesn't talk about herself, get that straight. If I chatter I cease to be Sister Eleonóra, I'm not worthy of my name. I was in the church today, looking for work. I should leave the church, said Annush. Go into the factory, there are so many, workers were being brought in from the south all the time, lots of Romanians coming in. Big blocks of flats were being built for them. They'd surely offer me a job. I said that first I'd go to the hospital, and if I didn't get anything there I'd see what was to be done. I didn't tell Annush so as not to upset her, but perhaps life was harder out here than in prison. Inside I just had to take care not to lose my faith, because that would have been the end. What did I have to beware of out here? It was harder outside than people thought.

And was everything that I'd done and admitted written down? Annush went on. Had they given me my affidavit? They hadn't given me anything. All I'd been given was my certificate of discharge, my *eliberare*, which I'd given in at the police station to get my *identitate*. And after that there was no other evidence. In prison, under interrogation, I'd written such a lot of statements and things that I had a dossier so thick! and I showed her. And what's happened to that? she asked. What is that to you, Annush? Here I am, out of prison, I'm free. What is that dossier to you? Just so that we know, she replied. Because Vilmos had told her that it had been known for people to be given a *rehabilitare*. They'd spent years in prison, then been rehabilitated, their case had been reviewed, the verdict annulled, and their house restored to them. So he asked about the dossier and where it might be. I wasn't interested in it, it didn't contain a word of truth. At most it showed on what date I'd gone for interrogation and how many hours I'd sat there. Every interrogation was timed to the day, hour and minute. They were astonishingly interested in time. The truth was of no concern.

So would I tell her what an interrogation was like?

Long, I said. Very long. I'd be taken in at eight in the morning and released at two o'clock. Or it took even longer. Did they hit me? Only once, at the start, even before judgement was pronounced.

And then you wrote down what you'd said. They twisted it about until it contained what they wanted it to. The way they did it was amazing. Absolutely letter by letter. And you got so tired. It was all written down, and in the end you signed it. Every page. In fact, there might only be two. You'd been sitting there for eight or ten hours, and then produced two pages. Two pages, as much as the priest reads out in church, in the course of an hour-long Mass, in the epistle. That doesn't take long. And you'd been sitting there all day, almost falling off your chair. They talked and argued with me so much, in Romanian and Hungarian as well, so that I should understand, because there were a lot of Hungarians working there, even men from Szék. And then it came down to your two pages. It would be better if those documents were never made public. If they were, nobody would understand a thing. I just can't tell you the way it used to go on in there.

They asked: Had I betrayed the fatherland? You answered: Yes. Of course that wasn't true, but that was how it was put down.

And I wasn't allowed to answer like that, but it had to be in long, complete sentences, so that it could be seen that every sentence came from my mouth, for example:

'Yes, I betrayed the fatherland.'

'Were you in sympathy with the counterrevolution in Hungary?'

'I was in sympathy with the counterrevolution in Hungary and supported it.'

Is that how people usually speak? If anyone were to catch sight of those documents, they would immediately think that we really had wished to overturn the world, so great were our crimes! We wished to indeed, and we did wicked things, but only in the name of our Lord Jesus, and of our Mother Mary.

Two pages, that was all that was in writing. And the rest was the omerta.

I told Annush to wake me next morning when she was leaving for the market. Not to put the children in the crèche, I'd look after them. But that was out of order. If Mihály didn't take them in he'd have to tell the doctor that they were sick. And couldn't they stay at home with a relative? I asked. No, not once they were registered. And in any case, who'd be able to wake me first thing . . . I slept as if I never intended to wake up.

Oh dear merciful God, forgive me! God had made idleness the greatest of my sins. I was sleeping so much since coming out of prison that a day-old child had its eyes open more than me. It wasn't because I didn't want to see the light, just that I was so tired out. And I didn't dream of anything, my sleep was completely dreamless. Sometimes it was afternoon before I got up. I'd be soaked in perspiration, and have to wash the nightdress that Annush had given me.

Heavens, how I hurried down to the meeting on Monday. I no longer had pain in my hip. I'd been so looking forward to it all day. I didn't go straight to the Főtér, to hang about and be noticed, but all the same I was there by half past five. Merciful Creator God! Sister Melánia was already there behind the statue! And what a nice light blue headscarf she was wearing, like in the old days! I recognized it at once. Our habit had been a black ankle-length skirt, round collar, light-blue apron and headscarf. She'd brought a scarf for me too as a surprise. That gave me greater pleasure that a rosary. Not for the sake of vanity. God had spared us from great vanity. She put it on my head herself in place of the awful little white one. There was nothing wrong with it, I didn't mean to offend Annush by saying that she'd given me something tatty, but it just wasn't right. Not our style. We were so pleased to see one another, hugged each other, sat hand in hand on the bench. It had been six years since I'd hugged my sister, we hadn't been able to without somebody shouting at us, because she'd been in the other wing. When we were in the lorry, being taken to Várad, Melánia had stood up in her place and given me a hug. She'd been given such a slap in the face by the sergeant that was escorting us that she fell flat on her back. After that we weren't allowed near one another. Next time we saw one another was in the autumn of '63, when the big ideological training sessions were starting and political prisoners were beginning to be released. Until then we'd only been able to make occasional contact if somebody helped, but further hugs were out of the question. She'd been held in a very distant block. When the treatment of prisoners began to improve and meals were taken in one big hall my sister got word to me three times. Texts written on paper, the power of which sustained me, and all three were there in my heart. The scraps of paper were confiscated in a search, because I had been careless.

So God had great plans for us if He'd preserved us both. We waited for an hour. We could have gone to Mass, but we waited there on that dilapidated bench in case some of the others came.

We were sitting on the bench and tapping started. It was just like in prison! And as quietly.

Melánia said that she'd heard nothing about Mother. Our Mother, Sister Jusztina. She didn't speak, just tapped quietly on the bench. I was so impatient, I could hardly understand her. She had to do it twice. She knew nothing about her. Her mother lived somewhere near Temesvár, and she was a great age now but still alive. It was possible that she knew something. If Jusztina had been released she must have gone there. Mother too was turned sixty. Released from there? From the canalization? I asked. She didn't know. There was no way of finding out. She'd only heard about somebody that had been exiled. Where had she heard?

We ought to think of something cheerful when we were feeling so gloomy! That was what the original Franciscan charisma taught us. There were pigeons galore there. They were flying round Mátyás's head all the time, they should cheer us up. Oh, Mother, Mother, how nice you looked in your short skirt!

Good Lord! We'd had to stop wearing our habits, our lovely black skirts with the blue blouses and aprons. People had been rude about our dress in the old days, and said it was a monkish habit. Our outward, visible sign. When we took them off, Mother made them into skirts and blouses. Then when we saw her in a short skirt! That was how we were going to dress from then on, she said. But when we saw her for the first time in skirt and buttoned blouse, because she'd had to be the first to wear them, we laughed our heads off! We couldn't control ourselves. She was neither man nor woman. And she didn't tell us to shut up, wasn't cross with us, as she was at other times; she let us laugh as we stood in a circle in the kitchen, with her in the middle. Poor thing, she looked like a scarecrow in a Hóstát garden, and her hair was standing up on her head! Things like that are erected in gardens in the Hóstát to frighten away crows. And we had no official hairstyle, but some wore plaits under the veil while others had their hair cut short. We had to remove all symbol of Christ. So we got used to short skirts and to going around in ordinary clothes. And when we were dispersed, we were very alarmed. I wasn't all that much, but the older sisters were, who hadn't lived outside the convent since childhood, and other sisters from other houses. What was to become of them, how were they to lead the life that they'd promised to Christ? We had to find work outside, go among the laity, but we received no help from our convent or from the church or our superiors and had nowhere to hide. Had life no longer any pattern to which we could conform? Then Mother said that in dispersal we had to be like the very first Christians. Do you think that they had everything ready-made? That they had been received into the world for their amusement? They'd had to work things out for themselves individually. There were some people to whom they'd kept silence and others to whom they'd confessed their faith. Their examples must be followed.

Then Sister Melánia was silent and said nothing. She indicated with her eyes alone that we had to speak quietly. Tapping. There were a lot of people about in the Főtér, and so good was her sense of smell that she would sense if something was wrong. She put her arm round my shoulders and tapped behind my ear on the back of the bench. Nobody at all could hear it but me.

There had been a Reformed Church clergyman and his family who had returned from the drainage. So it was possible for Mother to be brought back as well. Lots of clergy had been taken from the area. Clergy that had organized. All Reformed.

What about the others? Leona? Paula?

Talking by tapping was such a slow business. You had to pay close attention, even more than to a rosary. I asked one-word questions. Leona? Paula? The answer was nothing, just the five longs. Five longs meant: nothing.

And shouldn't we visit the grace-and-favour houses? What had happened to them? Were they too broken up? Where did they meet? I couldn't inquire precisely about all that in this fashion. When we were inside, tapping on the pipes hadn't enabled anybody to preach. Only to ask: are you ill? Does it hurt? Your heart? That your heart was pure was not in doubt, or whether it had dried up.

Bishop Áron? Had the merciful God preserved him? All I said was: Bishop Áron. Sister Melánia replied: not prison, not freedom. I didn't understand. Later, she replied. What is later? I asked. She would tell me when we could speak in words. And she tapped three times. Palace arrest. Palace arrest. Palace arrest. So that was prison again. It was prison if he couldn't go among the people.

'And the Szentszék?' I inquired. What about the Holy See?

She didn't understand. 'Szék?' she asked.

'What *szék*?' I asked.

'Szék. The village?' she asked. 'Are you going to Szék?'

Our wires were completely crossed!

I tapped some more. I wasn't going anywhere. *Szentszék!*

I gestured for her, as she hadn't understood. I gestured a halo for 'Holy'. Holy Szék. I gestured for *szék*—the one we were sitting on.

'Bench?'

Oh dear, I couldn't stand it. Simply couldn't. Suddenly I went off like a bomb and laughed aloud. I hadn't done that for ages. Just when I was asking the most solemn of questions, had Bishop Áron been abandoned by the Holy See? I simply had to laugh and couldn't stop.

Melánia couldn't get it at all, but she laughed. My laughter was infectious, like a disease.

'Say it then!' she whispered. 'Speak the words.'

'No I won't,' I replied. 'Listen. Pay attention!'

Again I tapped out *Szentszék* as clearly as I could.

'Rome?'

'Yes.'

'You're going to Rome?'

She didn't understand. I tried again. Rome? What did I mean? The Holy Father? Leave? Rome is leaving the bishop under arrest?

So I grabbed that Melánia and whispered in her ear: Is the Holy Father letting Bishop Áron be in prison for life?

'We don't do politics,' she replied, and laughed so loudly that the pigeons near us took flight. She was scattering crumbs from her pocket, but that wasn't allowed, there was a sign up. *Interzis.* And in prison they'd said that if we even once engaged in political activity that would be our lot!

We were never allowed to do politics because we didn't live in the world. Our politics were in Christ. If ever Christ was persecuted in this world! What were we to do, His wives and followers? What we said wasn't heard in distant Rome, that we knew very well. We'd been banned for fifteen years, a whole fifteen years. Only the Lord heard us.

'There's a new pope,' said Sister Melánia very solemnly.

If he was new, he wouldn't do anything. Not for us, anyway.

Was she going to work? I asked. Who? She, of course!

'Teaching?' I asked. She wouldn't be allowed to practise, would she?

Formerly she'd been a secondary school teacher, but then had joined us. We'd never taken any notice of what life a person had led. She was a couple of years older than me, though she looked younger and more active, and was in better health. But she wasn't allowed back among children. They'd told us that we weren't allowed in places where there were people, especially children, because we were ideologically harmful. Melánia had lost her parents and had only an aunt and uncle out in the village of Kolozs, where she was now living. There were no children, she said, so she couldn't teach. Their children had left home. But she was going to have to leave Kolozs because her relatives there were afraid to have her staying, as she'd been released from prison. She produced a list of places that she'd been to, as we'd been out of prison for three weeks. She showed me that she'd crossed them all out where she'd been. To the cemetery, in fact two. The patisserie, the florist's, to Avikola, the furniture store, the shoe shop, the match factory. The pub? I asked. Not yet, she said. There wouldn't be people there, I said, they were 'non-people', just animals, when they came out. She'd been to Carbochim, the abrasive maker, for a job as a packer. They might be able to offer her something, they said, come back later in the week. If they gave her a job she'd have to find somewhere to live in Kolozsvár, perhaps with some old woman whom she could help by paying rent. And so we talked and tapped until it became quite dark. If she came into town to live, perhaps I would join her.

Wouldn't she join the collective? I asked.

I had to tap that three times as she didn't understand. Then I whispered it. Oh, she knew about that, she replied. She couldn't, that would be the end of everything. She'd lost her parents, she had nothing to take to the collective so as to become a member. And nobody could adopt her now, she was too old. Only God could.

It took me a while to understand being adopted by God! That she might have whispered, but she didn't, merely tapped. Half an hour went by before I could realize what she meant.

That Sister Melánia had been preserved by madness. God loves the mad, making the world less grim for them. Mother had once said that anybody that wanted to follow Jesus was quite mad, but when she heard Sister Leona call Melánia mad she told her off.

'Get a job in the church,' I said.

'What?'

'If we went as a pair it would be nicer,' I said.

'In a factory?'

'No, not in a factory.' I replied. 'I was in the church. I was told to write in and it would be considered. I had an interview in our church.'

I said that word by word. She didn't understand. I said it again. By that time there was nobody about in the square, so why were we tapping? There probably wasn't even a Securitate person going by. So we went on tapping. It had become a habit. So I preferred to whisper in her ear.

Melánia was very surprised. The churches had been told not to accept back people that had been in prison; she'd been speaking to an ex-deaconess who was now working for a Reformed clergyman and his family, having just come out of prison. That was what she'd told her. Mária was her name, or Márika. That was the situation with the Reformed, she said. An order, a *circulare*, had been sent to the bishops to the effect that if a clergyman went to prison his position might be filled, and then he'd be unable to return to it. So that must apply to all denominations. She'd heard of a family with seven children in which the clergyman had come back from the canalization and had no post. It was just as well that our priests didn't have children. That was why our denomination was so much better, blessed be the Holy Mother Catholic Church! If we were sent to prison our families didn't suffer. In the case of a Reformed clergyman, his imprisonment punished the family as well.

'We criminals have no place in the church,' she whispered. 'Because criminals is what we've been. And the Securitate obviously saw at a glance that our hearts were guilty.' And Sister Melánia really laughed. 'They saw them and could read our great big crimes straight off them. And what we liked!! Because when the fight for freedom was taking place in Hungary we were pleased, we certainly were! There were going to be convents again! And we'd be able to go about the streets in our original habits, and nobody would be able to ask us any longer what we were dressed like that for. Perhaps we'd even be able to get a papal blessing from Rome and have an independent convent.'

Rome, I thought, Rome was as far from us as the Milky Way.

We parted.

We'd brought each other texts. I'd also brought texts for Sisters Leona and Paula, but I had nobody to give them to. We exchanged texts as we'd always done. I would open the Bible, Annush's, which had also been Mummy's, and we would shut our eyes and each put a finger on a verse and write it down on a scrap of paper. Then we exchanged verses and remained silent. The text that Melánia had given me was like an arrow in my heart. 'He was not that Light, but was sent to bear witness of that Light.' She whispered to me that I had to consider why the Lord had sent us. It may be, I thought of myself, that God had not stricken me with vanity. I had been given it so that I should be aware that I was not that light. I was saddened too by it. I was not. That I knew. I was not that light. We least of all. Nevertheless, it hurt. That was the Lord's message for me.

Melánia and I hugged each other. In a month, on Monday, she tapped on the bench. Then I went home in the dark, because the town was completely unlit.

My pleasure in looking forward to seeing my sister, however, had been spoiled. And anger rose in my heart, that the Lord had sent word through her of all people that I was vain and wicked and couldn't pray with a pure heart. I went to bed and tossed and turned so much, I was hurting all over, my hips and my shoulders ached, and my legs too were bright red and swollen, and itched so much that I couldn't get to sleep. I knew that I was not that light, it was the Lord's message to me not to hold my empty head so high. Anyone who holds their head high like an empty ear of corn stands rigid. If the ear is a full one it's lowered and bows to the ground. Perhaps Scripture said that too, I didn't know, forgive me, God, I'd forgotten everything. We hadn't read the Scriptures in prison, we didn't have them, just tried to remember everything. There was a Greek Catholic priest's wife, because they too had been banned, and she knew the whole Bible and quoted it freely, but then she was taken off to somewhere else. She knew the whole book, but spoke in such strange language that I couldn't understand half of what she said, it was Romanian and yet not. So it wasn't only idleness, but vanity too was a great sin of mine.

We kept the arrangement as we'd said, the first Monday of the month there in the Főtér behind the statue of King Mátyás. He was still on horseback, not like my poor Annush, who hadn't got a single horse now. She was a girl of the soil, but had neither land nor horse.

All she had was that stupid donkey. What did she look like, going around with a donkey? I said to her 'Look here, Annush, wouldn't it be better if you didn't harness up that terrible animal but went in the shafts yourself and pulled the cart?'

'What terrible animal?'

'Well, that grey donkey.'

'Now Rózsi, are you calling God's creation terrible?'

'Compared with a horse it certainly is. It bites and brays all the time. It's got a lot more to say than a horse. It's not nice.'

'I'm glad to have it, all the same!' replied Annush. 'Donkeys are permitted, but these days horses are not. Everybody's got a donkey now.'

She wasn't ashamed of it, she said. All she'd got was a little cart, after all, and the donkey could pull that. But there was one terrible thing in particular that that donkey did. It was for ever dropping its dung all over the place, and children would stand round and laugh at it.

'Didn't you use to have a horse? I asked, because I could remember. Annush was fond of horses, and even when she was a child, it upset her badly to see a farmer beating a horse.

We were sitting out on the porch at the time, and the sun was warming us nicely. The children were playing in the dust, drawing things, then one of them would chase a chicken while the other tossed pebbles at a tin.

Annush didn't reply, and I could see that tears were in her eyes.

'What became of that horse?' I asked. I remembered how she'd worshipped it, and before I was arrested, she'd bought a red leather whip for it out of the little money that she had. It hadn't been a particularly good-looking horse, and I'd often seen her out with it. It was just a nice quiet one. And I'd seen Daddy as well once or twice, working as a carter in the town.

Annush couldn't bring herself to speak. She didn't say what had become of the horse.

Then when I asked again, she snivelled.

'So you're embarrassed by that poor donkey, are you, Rózsi?'

'Jesus rode that donkey in order to cause a scandal,' I replied. 'He picked the most stupid and ugliest animal.'

Annush was quiet for a moment, then she said, 'Jesus loved all animals.'

I didn't mean to upset her, and I could see that the horse was a painful memory. But that stupid donkey didn't understand a single word. I remembered that Mummy had been mad about horses, and obviously Annush took after her. She'd always been talking to the horse, even singing psalms to it, because in Mummy's opinion horses were intelligent animals and could understand psalms. But it was a waste of time anybody trying to teach that donkey its name, or to come here or stand there. It didn't understand a word that anybody said, hadn't even learnt its name. You could say to it 'Dimmo'—that was its name—and it wouldn't so much as move its ears. We knew why it was called Dimmo. If you said to it 'Come', it didn't move. If you had a carrot-top in your hand and called it, it just looked at you. One thing it did understand was a good poke in the ribs.

That Annush was a proud girl. Or rather, married woman. Pride was what the Lord had afflicted her with. She so loved nice clothes, having her dress starched, stiff, and every Sunday the sleeves of her dress too were pleated, as if she were going to a dance. She was a lovely young wife. She would go walking arm in arm with her husband, the children out in front. I would see them on a Sunday as I came out of church in Egyetem utca, eating pretzels on the Főtér. Because that was what the Főtér was for, so that the Hóstát people could look at one another on Sundays, until when there was nothing to see—so said Annush. She always had such great things to say about the Hóstát folk, such as I never heard from a woman. What was this young wife so proud of? The garden was lovely, for its size, and her goods at market were the best, because she used to sprinkle the greens with water from a pot to keep them fresh, But the amount that she was able to take for sale was becoming smaller and smaller. She no longer had any land, but neither had the others, and those that had joined the collective didn't cultivate their own. They lived just from that thirty-are garden and went to all sorts of places to work as best they could, into the factories and the collective. Annush divided her time cleverly between the shops that she cleaned, as she could always go selling between times. She had to live, by hook or by crook, as they said in the old days.

By then it was time for me to go and look for work, I'd had my sleep out. I'd been at liberty for a good month, and I'd slept more, it seemed, than I'd been awake. On one occasion Annush even bought some coffee to see if it would stop me sleeping so much. It did no good, but it was too much for my innards and ran straight out of me as I drank it.

So I went to the hospital. I'd put off going once or twice, for a whole week. That was how I was. Cowardly. Idle, Especially cowardly. Cowardice was the sin that the Lord had given me, to test me. It wouldn't be possible, in such a big hospital, for everybody to have been replaced and nobody to remember us. By then I was simply afraid that nobody would remember us. It seemed that we'd never existed! Because surely the Lord had given me such a sin, and a great one. Conceit.

What day was it? I didn't know. I was so idle, was sleeping so much, that like a child I didn't know what day it was. In fact I'd almost forgotten that it was 4th October, our patron St Francis' Day. Today I had to say a rosary of enlightenment. Only children might not know about time, adults certainly must. I didn't know what day it was, but I should have prayed according to the days. A rosary of delight was set for Saturday and Monday, and one of enlightenment for Thursday and so on. In prison we'd known even though we had no Bible, nor a directory. We'd prayed to both Romanian and Hungarian saints alike, making no distinction, and how often it had turned out that the two were one and the same. A saint had always performed miracles. We couldn't give one another texts, and we prayed in either language indiscriminately, though at first we didn't understand Romanian, not until we'd studied it. The Jehovah's Witnesses were with us as well. Once I received the Lord's Supper too, when one of our companions was taken; she was so afraid of death that she couldn't stop moaning. Certainly, that was because her faith had collapsed. She was the only one afraid. She thought that she was going to be taken for execution. How long her sentence was I can't remember—whether it was fifteen years or the same as us. She trembled like an aspen leaf when they came for her.

'*Fa-ti bagajul.* Pack your things,' was what they always said when it was time to be off.

She'd said that she then wanted to receive the Lord's Supper because she was Reformed, for us to take leave of her. She received it in puliszka and water, and we sang a psalm for her. It was a sorry occasion, but so, of course, is anything Reformed. I couldn't recall a Lord's Supper like it. It was too simple in my view, and there was no mystery about it. It was simple, but nobody knew how it had to be done. Even though I knew best I just didn't want to interfere. People were ashamed of their past, even there in prison, locked up as we were. The past was the past. What I was ashamed of was that I'd been born in a different denomination and had gone badly astray until I found my way to Holy Mother Church and was able to convert. So I wasn't upset about the Lord's Supper. It didn't matter that it was of *turtoj* and water—*turtoj* was what everybody called puliszka in prison—it was transformed into the body of the Lord before our eyes just the same, into bread and wine. Bread and Wine. If I thirst truly for the body of Christ, the miracle takes place. That's why I so love the Sacrament of the Altar. That girl had not acquired faith, did not ask for the Lord's Supper because she had. But she was afraid of death. Perhaps she believed that death was afraid of the Lord's Supper.

I kept wondering what day it was, and if it was St Francis' Day, then it was my sister's birthday. What could I give her apart from a nice prayer? I had nothing. I looked at the alarm clock, because her husband needed that when he went to the factory. It was one in the afternoon. I'd slept until then, and I'd intended to go to the hospital that morning. What kind of worker goes asking for a job in the afternoon? Who would take them seriously?

What had happened to the way I used to get up of my own accord for matins? Oh, how we used to jump out of bed when Mother called us at half past two in the morning! And we used to sit together and say the liturgy. Now I couldn't even get up for lauds. Vespers was the service for me, I managed to be up by that time. God could see everything, and must have been shocked at my idleness. I could have done with a good thorough confession. So that I could obtain a bit of relief, a good Father would hear my sins and give me a thorough ticking-off, and I'd be able to make a proper confession with my whole heart. Merciful God, lead me to my Father that I may purify my heart.

Then it occurred to me that it was rest time in the hospital from two to four o'clock, so I might go up then when nobody was working in the wards and there were no visitors to cause disturbance. Staff sat in doctors' rooms. They ate, sometimes even slept, and drank coffee. Perhaps I would call first on the director, Dr Erzsébet Constantinescu. A Hungarian. A Jewess, but very fair, as I'd heard, she'd been in prison as an illegal Communist. I'd go and see her first, she ought to remember me. Yes, of course. She knew Annush, she'd been to see her so often afterwards. Annush had tried to find out whether Dr Constantinescu knew the prison doctor so that he could help me. She too had been in prison, this Mrs Constantinescu, because she was known by her husband's name. She'd been a Communist and had been imprisoned during the war. Her husband too had got a divorce while she was in prison, as was the custom in Romania at the time.

I took the bus from the end of Patak utca to Mócok útja. The porter wouldn't let me in as it wasn't visiting time. I realized that he was expecting a bribe. Give a bribe to go into the hospital where I'd worked all those years? Nine years, almost nine years. He kept explaining to me that I should come back during visiting hours. I knew that, hadn't I worked there?

'*Nu mai lucri, nu intri,*' he said. If you don't work here, you can't come in. An oath almost slipped out, may the gracious Lord forgive me the thought. I took out two lei.

'*Ná. Deschide,*' I said. There. Open up!

He took them, not a word of thanks. If you give, do not expect thanks or gratitude, said the Lord. Even if you're giving something extra, not even then.

There nothing had changed, nothing had improved. Only the main door had been closed and one had to go in round the side. I could hardly find the entrance. There was no name on the door of the director's room. They told me in the nurses' room that Dr Constantinescu had retired, but she came in every Tuesday. Well, if she'd retired she wasn't going to help me. Whom could I go and see? Which of the old doctors was still there? I looked at the names, there were several. Dr Márton Szabó, the obstetrician, was still working there. I considered, should I go and see a male doctor or a female? Who would be more sympathetic? Should I go to a Romanian, because they were better connected? Rather to a Hungarian, I thought, because they would know our situation and might remember us. Also, I was wearing the blue headscarf that we'd worn in the old days. They'd been left in the hospital. Dear God, show me what to do, whom to turn to.

And what should I tell them, how should I open my heart? How must I speak to people? I could speak to God and He would hear what I said, but with people I was dumb and stupid. I sat down on a bench, but the iron was so cold. I'd sit for a while in silence, I thought, and say an enlightenment rosary. Just on my fingernails, that would do.

I'd tell the truth. Nothing else would come to mind, only the truth. My name, Sister Eleonóra, Róza Butyka Eleonóra OFM perpetually vowed, and that I am a bride of Christ, and I worked at the hospital between the dates given. Then I was imprisoned with my sisters. No. I would have to give my name, my lay name, and say that I'd worked in the hospital. The OFM, *Ordo*

Fratrum Minorum, didn't apply to us and we might never use that in future. It never really had applied, because it was the name of the order of the younger brethren and only meant men. Our Mother, however, had chosen it so that we should be closer to our Francis, and she'd said that when we were given a licence, we'd be able to change our name. Or we would stay as we were, because that was how Rome was going to license us. But Rome was so far away, far away and silent.

And when I had to introduce myself, I'd say that I'd taken a course of training as a nurse. Now I was applying for a job here, to look after the sick.

Dr Szabó recognized me when I knocked at the door with his name and those of three other doctors. He recognized me from my blue headscarf, but didn't know my name. He said that he had half a job there, Why still only half, I asked, because it had only been a half when we'd been there. The other half was in Dés, and he commuted by train every other day. He didn't know whether I'd get a job there or not. Had I any documentation? What sort? My nursing certificate.

I had not. It had been taken away when everything had been seized and confiscated as property. We were given nothing back because we were traitors and as such weren't given anything. And we were only granted *graciere*, not amnesty. Dr Szabó had to speak softly, so softly that I could hardly hear what he was saying. He said that I should bring my certificate and take it to Senior Doctor Muntyán. I didn't know him, had he been there as well in the old days? He didn't know, but he was a good man.

So I went the next day to what used to be called Horthy Miklós út—now it's an offence to call it that—and before that Wesselényi út, to the place opposite the Mariánum to get my document. That was where we went, the Reformed Church Deaconess Training School, where the nursing course was conducted by Reformed instructors. But nothing remained of it. I asked what had become of it, but nobody knew. There was a dispensary there, full of sick people, absolutely packed, but nobody to ask about anything. But it was a state dispensary, not Reformed. Should I go to the Reformed church to get my certificate? We Hóstát people went to the Kétágú church. So, I thought, I'd go to the church district, or as it's called, the clergy office. There was a sign up in Hungarian as well.

I wouldn't say blessing, peace, as they greet each other, and they'd even think I was a Reformed. I would say 'Good morning'.

A clergyman came out, a tall young man, rather stooping, with a suffering, grieving face. But he spoke to me politely and noted down what I said. I only gave when I'd been at the nurse training, which class I was in and even who was with me, and where we'd done our practical. We'd been placed in the Jewish Hospital on the Szamos bank. I asked where I had to go to get a certificate. The school was closed, he told me. He wrote down the address where I lived. He would send a copy if there was one, but I'd have to wait until he found it. He'd have to find out where the things had been taken.

The next day, I went to see senior doctor Muntyán. I could speak Romanian well, because I'd done it for six years at school. Dr Szabó told me that he'd been working in the hospital in my time, but he'd still been on the wards. I didn't remember him. He was a decent chap, said Szabó. No need to be afraid of him. He was a big, well-built man.

Dr Muntyán asked me in, though I had to wait a little while. He wasn't in a hurry, didn't talk down to me, but gave me a seat and listened to me. I could see at once that he had a heart. I told him that I'd worked there and then gone into the penitentiary. Not of my own accord, or rather I said in Romanian, 'Nu din buna voie.' Another four sisters and I had worked there.

He remembered us, he said. That was interesting, as I didn't remember him, but I didn't give that away for fear of offending him. But a woman, even a nun, was bound to remember a tall, elegant man like him. He was so . . . quick-witted, as they say. And a pleasant man too.

Maică, he called me. That's what a nun was called in Romanian, maică, little mother. A nun or a female religious. We were little mothers. I'd come back, I said, but some of us had been lost. Sa pierdut, I said. We'd been given graciere, but our crimes hadn't been expunged.

'*Rehabilitare*?' he asked.

'I don't know. I've never heard of such a thing happening,' I replied.

That would mean our crimes being wiped out and our civil rights restored. Even if I'd not had anything, as we were sworn to poverty. What we'd had taken off us went in one box. I'd inherited a little bit of meadow from Mummy, but that had had to go to the collective, like it or not.

I sat there and told him how it had been previously, that we hadn't all been put into one unit, one department, when we worked there, but had all been different. I'd been in the internal ward, others in surgery, *kirurgia*, the children's ward, *la copni*, and one of us even in the ENT department, but I couldn't remember her name, I'd forgotten it. I no longer had my certificate to prove my qualifications, but I would have. All I'd got was my identity document. If the old books could be produced at the hospital, we'd be in them as working there. He said that they'd had a great flood in '61, all the records had been soaked and there was nothing left. It was my calling to care for the sick, and we, followers of Christ, wanted to be constantly at the patient's side, to hold the hand of the dying. We didn't know how to cure people, but we were perfectly capable of cooling the fevered brow. The doctor didn't interrupt me at all. I went on telling him and didn't stop. There was so much to be said between us! I was completely exhausted.

Then I asked whether my other sisters had come back there. Not one had.

Then I stopped. We sat in silence, and he looked into space and stroked his forehead.

'*Maică*,' he began. Then he stopped. God forgive me for loving the way he said that. Little mother, because we'd only called Sister Jusztina 'Little mother'. Again: '*Maică, stai așa*—Just a minute, little mother,' he said, and left the room. He said that he was going up to the finance department, where he could have a word with somebody in accounts. He asked for my ID.

He left, and I had to wait. I looked through the window. Outside was a little garden, and a couple of patients, wearing pyjamas and slippers, were sitting on benches that had seen better days. One was eating from a glass bowl. I didn't want to do anything, and I just continued from where I'd left it the enlightenment rosary that I was saying before I could come in. If I was with people, I had to keep saying so many words, talk such an awful lot. There I sat, went on with the rosary, and didn't have to think of words in order to pray. I'd got all the words that I needed for a lifetime. And as I'd been speaking so much Romanian with Dr Muntyán I didn't notice that I was saying Our Father in Romanian, *tatăl nostru*, and I'd finished the three Hail Marys, was in the fifth bead and could then begin to say the mysteries. The first mystery came after ten Our Fathers. The language didn't matter to me. It made no difference which I used. That was nothing. It only mattered between people. The language in which I expressed myself, wanted something or tried to explain myself, was to me like clothes, something we have to wear. Because ever since we were put out of Paradise and ruined our prospects, we've certainly had to be dressed, in both clothes and language. We can't go about any longer as the Lord created us. That's how we have to be in this world. It doesn't matter to me what rags I'm wearing. I speak Romanian or Hungarian as need dictates. I even know a few words of Spanish as well. We learnt those in prison from Maja, whose husband went off to fight in Spain. And for us Catholics the liturgy, the set prayers and rosaries, is the same in every language. Wherever we go it's always the same.

But the enemies of Christ had taken away our proper dress, our lovely black monastic habit with the light blue collar and headscarf.

Dr Muntyán came back. Almost half an hour had gone by, as I'd finished my rosary and was looking out of the window again. I stood up when he came in, but he quickly told me to sit down, not to stand up. Never stand up for anybody, he said.

'*Maică dragă, nu poți să stai printre oameni,*' he said. I wasn't allowed to work with people. I said nothing, and my little finger stayed bent, as I'd finished and was about to begin another rosary. I could feel my hand at that bead, the last in the decade, and I was holding my little finger with the index finger and thumb of my left hand. The Lord is with you, the rosary went on inwardly—I didn't actually say it but it spoke, because the rosary told me that God's name was to be blessed for that too.

'*Pot să te trimet la subsol,*' the doctor went on quietly. He could send me to the basement. He could take me on there but nowhere else.

Again I was silent for a moment.

'*Maică, ştii . . .* '—You know . . .

'I know,' I replied.

That was the place from where the Lord lifted up His children to Himself. The mortuary.

'Even for that permission will have to be applied for,' he said.

'When can I start work?' I replied.

Then he asked, had I got somewhere to live? I had, but . . . I would move. Perhaps the sisters and I could get together again in a living garland. We were still scattered, weren't we?

'*O să rezişti tu. Eşti dirza.*' What did he say? *Dirza*. What did that mean? I asked. Strong, he replied. You're very strong. He knew how strong those nuns and monks were.

Oh, that was what they always said, that we were the strong ones. But in fact we were very weak, the weakest little flower stalks. Our Jesus had enticed us, and we'd been unable to resist Him. He'd called us and we'd just gone. We'd been such weak, worthless flowers in the Lord's great garden that worldly things hadn't even tempted us, isn't that true? That was what Father Fidel had always said. You're so weak and sinful that Jesus didn't even give you temptations, so be glad that you're such a little nothing.

Dr Muntyán asked whether I was up to this work. At first I didn't understand. He asked whether I was *apt*, that is 'fit for work', whether my health was in order. I wasn't coming for hydrotherapy. I admitted. God forgive me the vanity, I'd actually taken some of Annush's rouge. She had some that she always put on her cheeks when she went out dressed up on Sunday.

I hadn't done it out of vanity, but so as not to look so pallid. My fingernails were clean and, except for two which I kept concealed, had grown back where they were ragged. I'd also smeared my fingertips with a little butter, so that they'd be less dry. My hair didn't show from under my scarf, fortunately, because it had become very sparse and dry, it was inclined to break off, and by my left ear, Annush told me, quite a big patch had fallen out. But that couldn't be seen at present. I'd got a long black skirt from Annush, I couldn't wear new shoes yet and was still going about in my old gumshoes. Annush had given me some stockings, because my legs were still unsightly from the erysipelas. I didn't wear them because I was embarrassed but because I didn't want the sight to alarm people.

She said I was going to have to have them seen to when I started work.

She's given me some formulae, written me out five. I asked if I could buy them? I'd be able to from my first wages. She opened her table drawer, didn't take things out of the medicine cupboard, and gave me some vitamin pills, foreign things. I had to take one every day. And a little bottle of liquid, of which I had to take two spoonfuls daily. I saw that it was something for children, but never mind, I'd take it. She offered me some phials as well, containing vitamins.

This was God's plan for me. Working with the dead. At least somebody would be praying for them and they wouldn't depart naked, without a prayer, in sin. I would be able to start on 1 November, All Saints Day. I had to go a week later for an examination, to be given the *apt* certificate.

I kept an eye out for the document from that Reformed clergyman but it simply didn't come. I even went in and saw him twice and he was quite cross—he'd said that it would be sent. But they didn't know what had become of the records of that deaconess school after it had closed. Then he said that I should go to the church district and speak to an elder there, or rather not him, because laymen weren't allowed to work there. I should ask for somebody, as he knew that they intended to establish an archive, and that was the person to find.

How many more times was I going to have to state my business from Abraham on? If I went there too, I'd have to start over, who I was, who I had been, who I'd been before that, tell my whole life story. Omerta, omerta, it would have been very nice to keep silent. By then I was telling my entire business, without a thought, as I also had to say that at the age of fourteen, I'd converted to Roman Catholicism and joined the Rose Garland Society of Franciscan Sisters, though we hadn't been called that and officially didn't exist, we were just a nice community of sisters, and at the age of sixteen, I'd taken free of charge a course of nurse training at the deaconesses' place in Horthy út, otherwise known as Wesselényi út. Then I'd taken my final vows in secret. Then I'd worked in the hospital, then been given twelve years for treason, spent six years in prison in Szamosújvár, been given clemency, *graciere*, but my crimes were not expunged because it was only clemency. I'd said all that, told that tale through to the end, so often that it seemed that it wasn't my life but rather something that I'd read in a book. I couldn't even believe myself that I'd found so much to say.

My sisters . . . Stop there! an elder there told me, or rather not an elder, there were no such any longer, but a secretary or something. He also asked for my baptism certificate. I told him that it had been confiscated. So in which church had I been baptized? My record book and my certificate had both been confiscated, and the training establishment shut down. I was sent over to an office where the official record was produced and the certificate issued. On the spot! I only had to wait an hour and it was done. It was certified that I'd attended nurse training between certain dates and done my practical. It was all nicely written out for me. You see, God had performed another miracle for me. Our dear Lady Mary watched over me and was here with me. There was no sign of a record book or anything of the kind, so they just put that this appeared to be true.

The document was given to me in a folder so that it shouldn't get wet, because it had come on to rain. I tucked this under my waistcoat—Annush's knitted black one, which I was wearing although it was too big for me in the bust. I went straight from the Főtér into the Franciscans' church, knelt, and gave thanks to the Lord. That was the first time I'd gone back to our church to pray. It was cold and I was freezing, I could have done with a shawl on my back. At the time I was always freezing, which I thought was caused by illness. I felt that I had a slight temperature all the time. Annush had commented on my rosy face. Sometimes it was rosy, sometimes grey. But what should a girl look like that had given her life to the Rose Garland?

I went along to see Annush, as it was her day at market. What she did was to take her baskets out first thing in a wheelbarrow, sell for a while, then run round to three shops to clean them—there were seven that she did altogether—and between them she returned to her stall. Her husband went to the factory early and took the two children in to be looked after. The *crèche*, they called it, and in the old days there was no such thing. Annush went cleaning in the morning and in the afternoon, going back to the market between times. Her husband was always telling her that she ought to go into the factory with him, by the railway or out by the Hóhérok bridge, but she said that she wouldn't go anywhere but the big market, never mind the money. I waited and looked and looked among all the Hóstát people, but I couldn't see her. There was one covered basket that might have been hers, I didn't know, there was nothing on it to say whose it was, and all the Hóstát goods looked alike. Then I caught one old woman's eye and asked if she knew Annush, was she there? Was I a customer of hers? No, I said, a relative. She was around, she'd be along directly, I should wait.

I went to the toilet, because my stomach was still very shaky even though I was only eating soft foods. I was cooking light things for myself, and it was a bit better but not much. I was quite worried when I had to come into town. I'd have to tell Dr Muntyán, though he'd see in any case if he examined me that my belly was full of wind. I had to use the toilet urgently, and I went round to the back of the market where there were two little cubicles. Annush was there, talking to a gentleman by the wall. A rather older sort of gentleman. She spotted me and blushed deeply, and so did I. I'd known that Annush had a secret. This wasn't her old affair? I didn't recognize him. That girl was up to no good. But she told me that she loved her husband sincerely and respected him. And he was a good man, wonderfully good! In all my born days I'd never seen a man handle the children the way he did, I told her. But love didn't depend on marriage, she'd said. Marriage was something else. Love was a sort of permanent merger. Help me, gracious God, what was I to do, what should I say to my sister, how should I pray for her?

I told Annush later that I'd found a job at the hospital, where I'd been previously. They were taking me back. I didn't tell her in which department. And I received the document, the *adeverinca*, stating that I'd trained as a nurse. She showered me with kisses and hugs. Anybody that does that has a troubled conscience.

Then I went to call on Dr Muntyán again. As he had so many patients, I had to wait something like three hours, and I'd gone rather late so that he would have finished seeing them. He had patients in the wards and in out-patients. I didn't mind waiting, I had nothing at all to do but allow the Lord to fulfil His plan for me. In the old days I'd always had a little New Testament on me, an old pocket-size one. That too had been lost, of course. And when Annush gave me her bible, which had also been Mummy's, I was simply overjoyed. For the first day I couldn't read anything from it, I just held it tight in my hand. I slept with it by my pillow. It had been six years since I'd had a copy of the Word of the Lord. Next day I meant to read a bit and opened it in one or two places, but I could hardly make it out. Since then too I've kept trying, but I've so lost the habit of reading that I couldn't make out the letters. Not that I couldn't see them, I was simply unaccustomed to reading. I quoted everything from memory. And such was my memory, of course, that it let me down. I thought that Christ had put something one way when in fact He'd expressed it differently.

I had to obtain the document from Dr Muntyán to the effect that I was *apt*. He wasn't prepared to give it to me just like that, but he wanted to take a good look at me. He was not a slipshod doctor but thorough. I wasn't worried. I wasn't afraid of doctors or men. In prison I'd been examined naked every time. I had to regard myself and illness as if it were someone else's body that had to be cured. Both erysipelas and stomach trouble. There was nothing to be done about my teeth, and I didn't want false ones. Those that had fallen out, for goodness' sake, what was to be done about them, and those that were left weren't much good. He listened to my heart and lungs and shook his head gravely.

'*Maică, maică, ce faci*?' he repeated. What have you been doing, little mother? Oh, I did like him to call me *te*! He did it out of respect, as if I were his colleague. But something inside there wasn't to his liking.

He took a blood sample and sent it to the laboratory. He gave me some ointment for the erysipelas, and told me to watch my diet, keep off pork, fatty things and dairy produce. I told him that I'd been fasting all my life. All the same, I'd do as he said. *Postesc*, I told him. I was always fasting.

I was to go up to orthopaedics, and he gave me a referral. What was I to say? I told him straight: 'Dear doctor, I haven't come for a full medical, but, with respect, may I have that document.' *Cu stimă*, respectfully.

'Go up to orthopaedics, *maică*. When they've finished, they'll give you a report and you'll bring it back here.'

I was to come back in a week's time for the result of the blood test, and he took a sample of urine as well.

A week later, he shook his head and told me that there was nothing right.

'*Nimic de tot*. Nothing at all. You see, it's a miracle of creation, dear *maică*, that you're still on your two feet.'

'What have you discovered, doctor?' I asked.

'I haven't found anything. There was nothing wrong with your blood. No sign of anything. Just that there's all this inflammation.'

He said that I ought not to start work then, but all kinds of tests should be carried out. He even sent me to the ORL. Oto-rhino-laryngology Department. But some nurse couldn't say that correctly when it was opened so it was changed. The ear, nose and throat department. Had I any buzzing in the ears, I was asked. None at all.

He told me to take a lot of vitamins and fresh green stuff. I was doing, I said, my sister's a Hóstát girl. *Hostezenica.* I wasn't one any longer, but I didn't say so. Spinach would be good for me, and apples, I must avoid things like cauliflower and cabbage, have grated carrots etc. I should have an egg a day, and put a nail in an apple to go rusty. I was very short of iron, he said.

'*Domnu doktor,*' I said, 'What goes in at one end soon comes out at the other. My blood requires it, but my stomach can't absorb it. My innards won't stand it. My intestines, you know. *Intestinul mare, gros,* my large intestine can't take it, in my opinion.'

I mentioned typhus, that had left me with this digestion trouble. I could only eat semi-liquid things. Unfortunately, I didn't know the Romanian word, so I said soft, *subcire,* like soup. The body wasn't such a simple thing, one part depended on the rest. You couldn't treat just one part if the rest was sick as well. So I put in nice, tasty food at the top, and wallop! it ran out of the bottom. My digestion wasn't working.

Then he was going to examine me with a speculum. Please would I swallow this tube, said he. From top and bottom. Swallow it from above, from below it would be inserted into my anus. God will be my helper, *dumniezó ajuta,* I said. Swallow that great thick tube, I'd never tried it, but I knew that it was so painful for the patient that it still hurt three days later, some had bleeding throats, because they strained themselves, unable to swallow it easily, and afterwards could only drink water. And with the other he'd be looking for ulceration, it couldn't be seen any other way. Was my stool bloody? Had been at one time, I said.

'*Maică, maică,*' and he shook his head.

Was I sleeping well? Excellently, just couldn't wake up! All I did was sleep. My greatest sin was laziness. I didn't tell the doctor that because he was asking from a medical point of view. That was because of blood pressure, he said. Did I drink coffee? I should have three a day. I said that I'd drink it, but I didn't know how I could afford coffee, nor did I know whether I'd be able to obtain fresh coffee from the shop, because instant coffee wasn't much good, was it? But my stomach couldn't tolerate such stuff.

'*Maică*,' he said, 'it's really been the Holy Spirit that's preserved you, not your health. *Sfântul Duh.*'

The Lord must have big plans for me if He'd preserved me in such a feeble body. *Dumnezó are mari nagy planuri cu minye ca ma tinut in acest corp slab,* I told him. He'd preserved me in such a feeble body. *Să fie binecu-vântat numele Domnului.* Praised be the name of the Lord, I said to Dr Muntyán. When I see that a person respects the Lord, we can talk openly like that.

He looked at me with such big eyes, or perhaps his glasses made his eyes seem big.

'*Maică, maică, lasă . . .*'

What did he mean? That I shouldn't give thanks for that? Who has preserved me, if not the Lord? But I was so afraid of having to swallow that thick tube. And of having one poked up my backside.

Dear merciful God, have pity on me, dear mother, Virgin Mary, help me.

At that, Dr Muntyán left me in the consulting room to get dressed. He'd prodded my stomach with his big cold hands, felt all my innards, and it hurt so much that I could hardly straighten up. He went through into the office to write up the *foaie de internare,* the internal observations. I got dressed and sat there in silence. Perhaps I ought at last to go to confession today, so as then to receive the Sacrament of the Altar. I so desired the Body! Perhaps I really was as sick as Dr Muntyán was saying, and I would leave this world without having made a good confession.

I said to the doctor, '*Draga domnu doctor,* don't put me in hospital, I'll go mad if I'm made to stay in one place again,' and I hadn't had the slightest intention of crying, but my eyes flowed and so did my nose. A nun isn't made for lying in hospital.

'I won't, I won't, *stai aşa, maică.* But *esti bolnava.* You're a sick woman. You must eat well and get your strength up.'

'I don't like the taste of anything. Not of earthly food, you know, *domnu doctor. Nam gust la nimic. Nimic pamantesc.* I've no taste for earthly food, no taste at all.'

'Look here, *maică,*' he replied, and he handed me the folder with the *internare,* to take to the Gastroenterology Department. 'You're not in a convent, you're living in the world. You're not allowed to give up on yourself, you have to look after yourself. *Ai grija de tine.* Take care of yourself. I can't take you on to work in the state you're in. You'd just collapse. Even in the basement, down below, there are people, even if they're dead.'

Down there, there are only bodies, I thought, but I wasn't going to say anything. Bodies, from which the souls have departed and have appeared before the face of their Lord, for Him to pronounce judgement. It's the most high Holy Spirit's doing, I thought, that my soul doesn't leave me.

That doctor was certainly the sort of man who could see through me like a priest. He could see how weak my faith was. Perhaps if somebody doesn't want to be in this world their faith has collapsed. I was dried out in spirit, didn't want to live in the body any longer. God in His mercy had given me great sins to test me. And once more I've failed the test, spilling my oil on the road, before appearing before the Lord.

Dear Mother, our most high lady Mary, virgin of virgins, strengthen me in my faith, don't let me abandon myself in this world. The Lord preserved me in my hours of greatest tribulation, and now that I'm out in the world of liberty don't allow to fade my desire to serve my master for ever, my husband, my dear Lord, to whom I have given my life because He has called me. Give me strength to look after this body of mine so that I can serve the dying, because they indeed need prayer to be able to appear before the Lord. Strengthen me that I may spread your Holy Word in the world. Although our light blue caps were taken off us when I was still only a girl, and I left home to join my sisters and Sister Jusztina took me in as her beloved child, brought me up, and would have put on me the blessed dress, the wicked world attacked our faith. And so fifteen years ago, we were cast into the world, torn out of our order. And you have defended us in our weary imprisonment. Give us back our dear Sister Jusztina, who has been lost in the evil world that persecutes Christ. Let not the others too, all our religious brethren, lose their faith. And perhaps I too have so foolishly deserted my Christ, because anybody that allows their body to decay and doesn't keep it pure until their final hour is deserting their Christ, who had sent them into the world to proclaim the glory of His name. Make my body whole, that I may for many more years be able to preach your Holy Word.

Once again I was praying in my own words, haphazardly, making much of them. And my Holy Mother Church had taught me the holy word and mysteries of the Lord in the set prayers, and there was I rejecting them in favour of my own! But I didn't have my *Little Seraphic Guide*, in which are all our Franciscan prayers in Latin and Hungarian. It had been confiscated. The Lord's holy mysteries strengthened me, my own words weakened me, and only doubts remained in me. When the Redeemer Christ became obscure to my sight I could see only the Corpus, the dead body, as He hung and suffered on the cross, even then only doubt remained in me as to whether He would be resurrected. But dear Mother had said that Darkness had descended upon even the greatest saints, so that they did not see Jesus and the Father, did not glimpse them even in prayer. Little Teréz, our greatest saint, said in her *Life* that she could not see them, pray though she might. Darkness came upon her, the Father and Christ vanished from her sight, and she sought them in vain. She was in that condition for days and months, acting the apostle but not seeing the Lord. In my opinion, even Mother must have been mistaken or had misunderstood it, because she hadn't actually read it as little St Thérèse of Lisieux was French and her *Life* was written in French, and Mother had only heard it expounded by other religious. But the idea of Darkness descending on a saint? And her not seeing the Lord for months? I didn't believe it. So how could she become a saint? It was true of us, weak flower stems, wild flowers, that we should lose sight of the Lord.

But the great Saint couldn't have gone wrong! It wasn't possible. I hadn't believed Mother. She'd also said that little Teréz had been granted the Darkness. Granted the grace of the Darkness. God had so loved little Teréz that He'd tested her even with the Darkness. He'd sent doubts, because that was the greatest grace to a saint. How could such a thing be grace? To me, Darkness was the most fearsome torment. Father Fidel too had said, and how often, that doubts and Darkness had come upon the greatest saints. I hadn't believed him. I'd heard what he said, but I hadn't believed it.

So now I'd have to go to hospital, take care of myself and get better. Dr Muntyán would find out what was wrong with me, and wouldn't let me start until I was better. I didn't tell dear Annush how sick I was, she'd got quite enough problems. I told her I was looking for work at the church and so on. Who knows where a Franciscan goes? Everybody knows the old joke: the Jesuit does nothing but study, the Benedictine does nothing but pray, and the Franciscan does nothing but walk about. Members of the order have to be on the move, not sitting still.

My muscles were wasted, said the orthopaedic doctor to whom Dr Muntyán had sent me. I know, I said. They'd been wasting since I'd been twelve. I'd trodden in mud barefoot, brought cold water, because I'd had to tread mud for bricks. Daddy had said that others had done it and made their children do so, and no harm had come of it. But my leg hadn't been so short then. It stopped shrinking when I turned twenty. Hadn't shrunk any further. I knew, because at one time I had a shoe with a thick sole, but I couldn't get on with it. What had happened to that? It had been confiscated with all my personal possessions when I was arrested, because I wasn't wearing it at the time. I didn't explain about my prison history. The doctor had to take an X-ray. Then she wrote down what corset and shoes I should have made—I needed a corset as well because my back was bad. She said that I should sleep wearing the corset and come back in six months' time for her to see if it had done any good to my hip. Surgical shoes would be good, they would ease the pain in my hip. As it was, I was having trouble walking. She told me to go to an orthopaedic shoemaker.

I didn't know whether to bother. I didn't have the money for that sort of thing, nor anyone to ask for it. Nor did I really understand money any more, everything had changed so much. I was like the God's birds, what was given to me I lost. Annush fed me, I went about in her clothes, slept on her pillow. In fact I'd covered the pillow with my old headscarf, because the way my hair was falling out I didn't want to keep soiling it.

And there was a little wren there too. When I'd got up, it must have been nine o'clock, I went out onto the porch. Along came this little bit of a wren or something and took a dust bath, because it was all so quiet, everybody had gone out, even the dog was in its kennel. That bird was so small, smaller than my fist. The cat almost caught it.

'Shoo, just you stop that!' I said to it and tossed a pebble at it. That was Annush's as well.

Annush had a black cat because of the mice, and it was always having kittens, but she never killed a single one but reared them and then gave them to the neighbours or they were taken to the factory. That cat had almost eaten the wren. It was all over in a flash, but the bird had been quicker.

What was a wren like that in the world for? Such a tiny creature. What use was it to anybody? What was God's plan for it? I didn't know, couldn't see into the great mystery. Because I had to pray the mysteries.

So I went to see the shoemaker that the lady doctor had recommended. His shop was down in the old town, so I decided to go and look. Fancy sending me to the old town! Who did she think I was? A countess? I'd never even looked in the shop windows in the old town. Should I go back for her to name a different shoemaker? The sort of additional sole that I could get in the market and either tack or glue on wouldn't make the sort of shoe that I'd be able to walk in. A surgical shoe. The window was full of nice corsets and shiny orthopaedic shoes. What should I do? I went in. He would tell me how much I'd have to pay for a shoe with a raised sole. I'd only be paid a monthly wage if I was taken on at the hospital. More fortunate still, corset and shoe had been prescribed separately, because I was only going to inquire about the shoe. But it didn't turn out that I'd just show him the prescription and sketch and he'd quote a price. There had to be explanation, measurements taken, colour chosen, discussion. But, I said, I'd only like to inquire the price in the first place. The price of what? This isn't a simple matter, if you don't mind. I remembered that there'd been a shoemaker there previously, the shop had been there because I'd been that way to the Franciscans' church. Now it had become a collective. Then he talked for a long time, but first put it all down on paper and worked out the price by the centimetre. How many centimetres' elevation was needed? Eleven now, previously it had been ten.

'Just six hundred to you, madam.'

How much were wages those days? More to the point, how much would mine be there in the basement, because there'd been no mention of that at the hospital. And it was irrelevant that I'd worked there in the past, that wouldn't count now, would it, because traitors and the rest like me had no continuity. Weren't continuous, the term was. Our past was wiped out. Well really, how could it be possible to just wipe it out? What had we been, then? Lambs born that day?

I didn't know whether what he was quoting was a lot of money or not all that much.

'Why? How much to somebody else?' came straight away to my lips. He wasn't offended but gave me a reduction, because he could see that I wasn't a princess and that I was married. I had my ring, that hadn't been taken from me, the little silver ring that the Lord gave us when we made our final vows because we were His brides. But he'd make me a shoe that I could dance in. Did I like dancing?

'I did dance once in my dreams,' I replied.

I didn't give anything away to that shoemaker. People don't say that sort of thing out of malice, but because they speak flippantly, without thought. How boring all the talk is that people do. If they kept quiet, at least they would think. All that I said was that I was engaged. So that was why I needed the shoe, did he understand now?

He showed me what he'd be able to let me have for a little more. It wasn't the sort that's made of wood. He handed me a nice platform sole with two straps on it, like a sandal. Oh, the sandalled sisters! What had become of them? The poor teaching sisters of Temesvár. They always went around in sandals. I should try it on, it would give me confidence. It was so light as I held it, it wasn't solid wood but something like cork. 'That's right, it's cork,' said the shoemaker. I stood up on it, fastened it up, and wearing that even I could have danced. If I had to work for a year for a shoe like that I'd take it. He gave me the other half, just a sole, of course, with straps. It was as if they'd been poured onto me, they weren't too long either. I stood as straight as a tree in them! A poplar. He told me to take a few steps. So I did. I wouldn't have called it light, there's no word for how light it felt! It was like going barefoot. And there was no sound at all, I was walking but there was nothing to be heard, though there was no carpet, just a hard floor. I shut my eyes and walked in a little circle. I'd never in all my life known such silent shoes, it was as if I weren't there. Dear God! Perish the thought. I'd have gone and run off in them straight away, I could even have run in them, they were so light.

'*Bine, bine, lasă*—that's fine, that'll do. How much deposit shall I give you?'

I was so embarrassed. What was I to say? I'd come without any money. I said I was a nurse, a sister, and was just starting at the hospital.

'A nurse?' he asked. Could I give injections?

'I certainly can,' I laughed. He didn't need to know that I hadn't injected anybody for six years.

He had a bedridden wife, paralysed from the waist down, and the nurse who looked after her was about to leave to get married. He would put it to my account if I would attend his wife, they lived behind the market, next to the Jewish church, in the yard at the back. He could see that I was a decent woman, not the difficult sort who would come one day and not the next, because the awkward woman who was coming at present was never willing to come on Sunday. She was a nonconformist, a churchgoer, and said that it was sinful to work on Sunday. So had we a deal? Yes, I said, just tell me how it would work out.

He took a piece of paper and began to calculate. He only wanted me to wash and inject her every day. He calculated that I should go for the price of the shoes. I asked, what if I had to go to work at the hospital and couldn't come first thing every morning. As far as he was concerned, I could even go at five in the morning, he was up by that time because (he lowered his voice) he had a job on the side. He worked at the market as well, one had to live, you know. He multiplied and divided, and it worked out that I should work for him for two months and he would pay me four hundred lei.

Four hundred lei. If he'd said forty, it would have been a lot to me! How could I have come by money like that? I wouldn't even have asked for it from the church foundation. I would now, I decided, and was about to walk out. There should also be the Foundation for the Relief of the Poor. The Lord was with me. Our Lady was holding my hand. If only it wasn't so hard to negotiate with the church. Nobody remembered us anywhere.

Or should I ask Dr Muntyán? He had said in the past '*Daca au envoie de ceva, spune, tu maică?*'—If there's anything you need, let me know, all right, little mother?

So I should ask him. Asking for something is no shame. Dr Muntyán called me *maică*, mother, and used *tu*. People had to use that to us, and we liked it.

The shoemaker told me to go out into the street and walk about a bit, and I'd see. That four hundred wasn't a lot. 'Go on, take a walk,' he said, I would see. He didn't even watch me go, just went back into his workshop and left me. I stood there by myself in the shop, then made up my mind to go out. In fact it wasn't exactly a summer's day, it was November, of course, but I wasn't cold, I had thick stockings on. My dear Annush had given me winter stockings because she could see how bad my legs looked, red with cold, and the blood was hardly circulating in them. I had to keep warm.

I left the shoemaker's and went for a walk, and by that time it was pitch dark. I looked up at the clock, but all the hands had fallen off. The clock faces on all sides of the church were blank. I would know the time when a bell rang. But there wasn't a sound. I waited a little, then some more, but no bell was heard. Perhaps ringing bells was prohibited now, or perhaps only in the main square. Our church was there, it was open, only it all had to be silent, bell ringing was not permitted. Perhaps that was the situation. I'd already been quite surprised, when I came out, to see the churches all still open. Ours, the Orthodox, the Reformed as well, open at the usual times. From early Mass until evening. But the faithful might not be summoned by bells or other means. I wasn't allowed to go round proclaiming the Gospel in the land of Mary and the Three Lambs.

I was silent, and I was letting Him down. Father Fidel too had always said that. We couldn't remain silent! We had actually promised not to be. I felt a bit strengthened, that nice Dr Muntyán was making me better, I'd find my sisters and we'd once again be in the service of the Lamb. And how well I was going to be able to walk in those sandals! Or he'd make them into nice light shoes for me, I thought, and then I'd proclaim the kingdom of the Lamb.

Fortunately, I was no distance from the Franciscans' church. I sat down inside for a bit, on a seat at the back, in front of my little Teréz's altar. I said a rosary of gratitude for Dr Muntyán, and in Romanian. I didn't know them all in Romanian, but that one we'd often said in prison because there were two Romanian women who hadn't abandoned the Greek Catholic faith, and they honoured the Lord Jesus every day and taught everybody that wished. *Rozario* is the Romanian word. We'd been allowed that by Rome, so that we should understand each other in all languages and our faith, our Mass, should always be one and the same. Our churches aren't so different, the Greek Catholic and ours.

Then I got up, went and prostrated before St Francis, and said, '*Bucura-te ceea-ce esti plina de har, Maria, Domnul este cu tine, binecuvantata esti tu intre femei, si binecuvantat este rodul pantecelui tau Jezus. Sfanta Marie, Maica lui Dumnezeu, roaga-te pentru noi pacatosii, acum si in ora mortii noastre. Amin.*'

I had to be very careful. I may have confused that with the enlightenment rosary. I knew Romanian well enough for no one to say that I was anything else. But I didn't know the prayers so well, and I mixed the languages up in them.

I had prostrated on the cold stone, as I had done in the old days. But my body didn't feel the cold of the stone because the warmth of the prayer was with me. If I prostrated, prayer was different. I knew how tiny I was, and how powerful the Lord is over me. So I had to prostrate during the adoration.

We began to learn from Teofila, Maica Teofila, the Greek Catholic lady, because we were in agreement that a different one of us six brides of Christ in the big cell would always say the prayer; there were 48 of us altogether. Teofila was Mother, and she said how it was to be. She was a a brave lady, and had been arrested as Greek Catholic Mass had been celebrated in the public street, as had been forbidden. They had been unafraid, as they had known that the Lord would preserve them. Both their priest and themselves. Then more and more of us prayed, because the Word of the Lord came to all that heard it. Perhaps if we hadn't been in prison everybody would have spoken in their own language, because what was fine among us was that everyone said the same thing, but in different languages. In prison only the Lord took care of us, no one else. And see, He so preserved me that I was able to walk out. But in freedom we're so tossed about, we're far from the hearts of men and the sisters have been scattered. When at first we spoke in Romanian it was certainly odd to me, because that was not how God's word spoke to me. When we said the Lord's Prayer, *Pater noster*, in the rosary I found it very hard to say *Tatăl nostru care ești în ceruri* in Romanian. It took some getting used to. First, I had to learn the words thoroughly so that the prayer should flow as smoothly as the air that poured in and out of me without my thinking about it. And then, after all, I was saying something quite different in Romanian. We always say Our Father, and our hearts think of our Creator, our Lord, our God, the father of Christ our lord. When we say *Tatăl nostrum*, it's such a commonplace word, almost like Dad or Pa. The sort of word I didn't care to use. I had to get used to the way that they said it. It was vulgar. Or maybe not vulgar, merely plain, and it didn't go down well with me.

Because that's how I was. I believed that the prayer was in the language. But the Word of God couldn't be that, because I had to understand it while God understands all languages. We people, of course, can't conceive of that. Everybody believes that they can only say really sincere, heartfelt prayers in their own language. But it's possible to learn to do it in another language, you just have to want to very hard. Struggle. Even against Daddy.

The last time I saw the poor man was at the hearing. How ashen he looked. He was certainly in disgrace because of me. When the verdict was pronounced, we were permitted to say goodbye. I was able to give him a big hug, from my heart. He hugged me as well, and tears were streaming from him. When one is like that and the executioner puts the knife to their throat, they're no longer thinking of what's happened. I hadn't hugged anyone in a long time, nor had he, I think. And perhaps both of us were thinking that we wouldn't see one another again in this world. But as it was, of course, I was having to go first. But God had other ideas. And I couldn't ask for forgiveness. Nor could I pray *Tatăl nostru*, and I only said, *O, Iisuse, iartă-ne păcatele, fereşte-ne de focul iadului şi du în cer toate sufletele, mai ales pe care au mai mare nevoie de mila Ta.*

God had granted me to be tested.

Then I wrote down the name of head doctor, Kornél Muntyán, on a slip of paper, as there were some by the altar. I thought I must write it down as I wasn't used to writing in Romanian. The custom there was to write notes to St Francis, and there were paper and pencil set out. There was a little iron bag in the saint's hand, notes were placed in it and the sacristan took them out. I dropped mine in and from the sound as it fell it seemed that there were no more in there. Goodness, but I found it difficult to form the letters, my hand was completely unused to writing. My knuckles were really painful as I bent them. It must have been rheumatism, as it's called.

I turned and left the church, and there was nobody else there. What was the time? I'd better hurry to the shoemaker's. It was wonderful to walk in those sandals! God bless the man who invented them for the feet of the sick. And see, the rosary had helped me again. It had worked a miracle, because in them I could step out as proudly as a bishop in an Easter procession. I felt so strong as I left the church. Dear Lady Mary, our dear mother! I didn't care that I wasn't going to have shoes like these straight away, but I would have when I worked for them. Dr Muntyán will help you, Rózsi, you'll see! Oh dear, I called myself Rózsi, but I wasn't Rózsi any more, I'd given up my lay name. The one with the painful hip was Rózsi, and the one that said the rosary in church was Eleonóra. Róza Butyka Eleonóra OFM.

Eleonóra! Nobody has called me that for a long time. Merciful God! When I heard as I took my vows that my new name was to be Eleonóra I just couldn't believe that I was worthy of it. When Mother asked me what name I would choose, I said Eleonóra. She said that many longed for that name and it had to be earned. She didn't believe that that name would suit me, I still had a lot to learn and committed many indiscretions, wasn't sufficiently obedient. Because in our life there were three rules: poverty, chastity, and obedience. These we had to obey until death, and to remind ourselves of them every hour for the sake of Christ. But I found obedience not yet my greatest virtue, and so Mother said that I wouldn't deserve that name and would be given some other. So when, three years later, after investiture— which to us meant nothing at all, just the blue headscarf, as we already had to go about without distinguishing marks—I was able to make my eternal vows to Father Fidel in secret, nevertheless merciful God granted me the name of Eleonóra. 'God is my light' is what it means. When I took my vows, we were already scattered, and the sisters weren't living in the convent. When I heard my name, I was so happy that tears ran down my cheeks. The sisters had all known that that was to be my name, but Mother had kept it from me so that I could rejoice as I stood before the Father. That was my second birth, from which I gained my strength for eternity.

And now I had such strength that I decided to mend all Annush's damaged clothes and to accustom my hands to delicate work. I was to start work at the hospital and wasn't able to bend my fingers very well. I had to teach myself again. I would teach the children to write on pieces of paper and learn again myself. Already that day I was making a doll for little Zsuzsanna. My God, what a joy it was to hug that child, that little lamb. She so loved Jesus, it was wonderful! Annush just laughed, she didn't mind. I was looking after the child, putting her to bed, doing more and more with her. Little Mihály was not like that, he was still very unresponsive, and I was still training him not to soil himself. But we really mustn't deal with children, Ferenc Páll the Securitate man had said, and it hadn't been permitted even before then. So I had two children and one roof over our heads.

A long time ago Dr Constantinescu had allowed Sister Leona to work with children. But we who had been prohibited and had our veils taken off, we weren't permitted to work with children for fear of corrupting them. And how cleverly the little lady doctor had contrived that! At the time we weren't at all surprised, only later. She took Sister Leona, and when the Greek refugee children came—I can't remember whether it was 1949 or 1950, I hadn't yet taken my vows and still wore a white headscarf and had only been a novice for a year. The doctor allotted my sister to the Greek children. She allotted me too at the outset, as there were too many for a single nurse and two were kept busy with them. But it was decided that she could put only one of us in a ward and a floor in case we formed a group again. What nonsense! We'd been a group even before then. We'd still been wearing the veil, and the sisters, the eternally sworn, could still go about in the distinctive habit. We'd still done what we wanted, people everywhere were glad to see us and respected our cheerful black-and-blue clothes. So Sister Leona could have stayed on in the children's ward. But we'd been allotted to the Greek children because nobody could talk to them, no interpreter had come with them as there were so many refugees that there couldn't be interpreters everywhere. So if we couldn't talk to them, we couldn't have corrupted them. Then our dear Father Fidel taught us the Lord's Prayer in Greek and wrote it out for us to read more easily. So we were able to say the prayer with the children: *Pater hēmōn, ho en tois ouranois, hagiasthētō to onoma sou*. I'm afraid I can't remember any more, it's been fifteen years now. There was a Greek teacher in the prison, so I heard, but he was with the men, so of course we couldn't learn from him. Men were able to go to school much longer even in prison. In fact the agrarian criminals, who had opposed collectiviza-tion, they too had actually become university lecturers! And how many there were with four years school or five. Seven years were officially compulsory, but quite a lot had done fewer. We couldn't talk to those Greek children, but pray with them we certainly could! We played with them, dandled them, fed them, and prayed with them. We said Hungarian prayers for them and read the Bible in the evening. There isn't all that much which you have to say to a child. In the end they could even say the Hail Mary in Hungarian. It was easy with children, they understood everything, so we didn't have to explain such a lot. There were thirty Greek children in one big room, and one would give a disease to the next. We slept in the ward too, that was per-mitted. It was obvious that so many were orphans, separated from their homes, goodness knows where their parents were, or whether they were alive. There was one little girl, about four or five years old. When she was brought in she sat on her bed—there were two of them to a cot—and she howled and shouted 'Mummy, mummy.' That was the one word we did understand, because it's the same in all languages, isn't it? I picked her up, hugged her, dried her tears, and in a week she was no longer shouting. There was one that kept having tantrums, throwing everything about. They said I should tie her down. I didn't have the heart. I took everything off her and left her a rag doll and a spoon, she could throw those about. I knew what it was to be an orphan. My dear Lord God had granted me to be an orphan when He took Mummy to Himself when I was very young. The poor orphans were with us for six months and were then dispersed and went to orphanages, and some were adopted for money. Perhaps we would have been given some too, to take home and raise as our sisters. I'd have taken a little girl. After that Sister Leona stayed there, working in the children's ward. She stayed there, and nobody asked what she did or didn't do. I would have stayed as well, but I was needed more in gastroenterology. But among the children, even if we couldn't talk to them, nobody bothered us for taking the veil and made life difficult. Especially these days, when such a thing is a disgrace. First of all, even Scripture acknowledges that some are incapable of marriage because they're born that way. And there are some that people consider unsuitable for marriage, and there are those who, of their own accord, decide against marriage because they take another road. These are the three kinds that don't marry. Children understand the word of the Lord better, and in adults the world is a confusion. They don't know which truth to serve.

Praying in the church had certainly done me good, and had showed me that I could earn my shoes. But the Lord wouldn't let me down when I learnt to walk properly upright in the world. Now I would earn that money and help that shoemaker's wife.

By the time that I got to the shoemaker collective the light inside was out and the shop was locked. How long had I been in the church? I didn't watch the time when I was praying. If I'd said two rosaries it would have taken an hour, no, more, perhaps an hour and a half. When I said it the first time I didn't really succeed, because I tried to do it in Romanian and I kept getting stuck, said it with my head and my tongue, not from the heart. The second time I said it from the heart.

The shop was shut, and my boots, or rather Annush's, were still inside, but that didn't matter. But the expensive sandals were on my feet. I thought that the shoemaker would have gone straight to the police to report me. A lame nurse, because he knew that I was a nurse that worked in the hospital, so it wouldn't be hard for the police to catch me. I'd have to go home wearing the sandals and come back next day. Like a thief.

As I went home in that footwear, I thought I'd keep them and not give them back. I'd pay for them, but I couldn't give them back now. When I was so erect, hardly limping any more. I wouldn't give them back, I'd earn them.

The next day I overslept again, nobody woke me, but I wanted to go down to see the shoemaker. I no longer knew whether I'd ever be able to return properly to this world. Like a normal person who had their place in the world, get up, wash my face, say my morning prayers and do my work. Annush had taken the cart out by that time as it was Friday, she'd gone with the cart and the donkey, and her husband had taken the children off. She must have seen me not getting up, just sleeping like a log. She couldn't find any use for me. Once I was up I hurried, looked at the alarm clock. It was only half past ten, not too bad. Then I went outside to the loo as my bladder was giving me such trouble again, it was pouring out of me. I'd have to ask Dr Muntyán for a little phenol cream to apply down there, it was all so sore.

I sat out there for a long time, even though it was cold. There was a toilet in the house as well, but I preferred going outside. And now there was going to be drainage as well! There was so much development in those parts, blocks of flats were going up over towards the Kövességó and Eperjes. I said my morning prayers. If I wanted I could even say them out loud, there was only the cat to hear. It did me good to pray out loud! I felt that my whole heart was in it, I didn't have to whisper or be silent. Even with the sisters we'd always prayed silently, not like a church organ. Up there in our nice little cloister we'd had the end flat in the yard, but there was no knowing what could be heard outside. But now I could say my prayers nice and loudly.

I had to go to the hospital for Dr Muntyán to go on with his examinations of me. and give me a note for gastroenterology. First I'd go to the shoemaker's as I had to return those nice sandals. I looked at the clock again, but it was still only half past ten. Had it stopped, then? What time could it be? I couldn't tell, I had nothing to go by. It was so gloomy, November. Friday the sixth. I worked it out. But in prison I'd always known the time. I told myself every morning, and worked out what day it was with somebody else.

Anybody that was in prison and didn't know what day it was never going to get out.

I put on my thick stockings and the nice sandals.

The shoemaker's shop was shut. It was a sanitation day, and it had to be disinfected. Next day was Saturday. So I'd come back on Saturday. I wanted to go back next day, I told Annush to wake me up, because I'd got to go somewhere. I hid the sandal with the high sole so that she wouldn't see it. And in the house I wore tatty leather slippers. She asked where I'd got to go next day? To the hospital, I said, for an examination. She didn't think they'd be working on Saturday, she said, as it was a holiday, and the market couldn't open either. What holiday? Well, I thought to myself, in that case I shan't be able to take them back before Monday. Now what I was doing was pure theft. Should I break the shop window? I could, although there might be somebody working inside. But if I did, the police would catch me. I couldn't remember the holiday either. I tried to think what holidays we had about that time. All Saints had gone. It had been really nice out there by Mummy and Daddy's graves. What other holiday could there be, I wondered?

'It's 20th November—Revolution Day,' replied Annush. 'Mihály has to go in the procession. We'll stay at home, because anybody with little children doesn't have to go. I've got the *adeverinca*.'

So too bad, now I wasn't going to be able to take them back.

Mother, dear Mother Lady Mary, mother of Jesus. Enlighten me, what could I do about those stolen shoes? They aren't mine. I thought I'd see if I could get an idea from the Bible. Where should I turn to? Should I ask Annush? Or her husband? What could he say? I needed the word of the Lord, not of man. The Lord spoke, because I had asked for a sign from Him as I usually did. He quoted to me from the book of Ecclesiastes: Woe to him that is alone when he falleth; for he hath not another to help him up. I wasn't alone, not at all. I had my relatives and the Lord was with me. The Lord meant to tell me that I had now fallen. Had I gone astray, fallen, and was there none to help me? And was it pleasing to the Lord that I should look for a sign because of shoes? Look here, I said to myself, look here, you servant of God, you're always thinking of yourself and your foot? You want to get a better shoe? Because since Thursday I'd had nothing else on my mind. And there was Annush, dear Annush, saying nothing all the time and crying. Her two little ones had gone into the living room to play. Mihály had gone off to take part in the procession and then to be in the choir, because he hadn't given up singing in the Hóstát choir, and they were asked to sing in church on Sunday at a confirmation.

Annush was still crying, stirring the soup and wiping away the tears with the edge of her headscarf. I could hear her snivelling. So I went to her, put a hand on her shoulder, and said, 'Come on, Annush, let's say the Lord's Prayer together, that'll cheer you up. Come on, the child will come as well. Young Zsuzsa knows it already, I'll sit the little one on my lap and we'll teach him. Let's say a prayer together.'

She said nothing, just wept more and more. Everybody weeps that abandons God's living word. What could I have said to console her? What but the word of the Lord, 'Console the weary by speech'? Perhaps I ought to say a rosary for her? Then, after lunch when she'd put the children to bed, Annush went out into the garden and I went out after her in my slippers. She was pulling up the dried-up tomato vines and I helped. She let the chickens out into the garden, she'd only got seven at the time and a bit of a cockerel. She said she wasn't going to have the other garden any longer that she'd been renting from the old people in the next street, Büdöspatak utca, they weren't going to let her. She could look for another. Why wouldn't they let her? Because the garden had been surveyed, which meant that it was going to be broken up. I said, perhaps she'd be able to find another to rent. But look at the way she'd improved the soil by that time! She'd only just brought in three loads of manure when the greens had finished. You don't know, Rózsi, what a struggle it was for me to get a load of manure! Now I've got no horse or cow to provide any. I had to go round begging a boss to help me get some from the Brotherhood collective. She'd brought it out and dug it all over. All for nothing, 'cos now she was going to lose it. Is that why you were crying, Annush? The Lord will give you a better garden, you'll see. A finer garden than Gethsemane or any you care to mention.

She was laying into the tomato vines, and swearing something terrible. Really, Annush, I didn't know you knew such language!

'Now look, my dear,' I started to say, but she shouted at me to leave her alone, because God had afflicted her and nobody could help her. How would she be able to run her business from thirty ares of land? First all the field had been taken away, been collectivized because Daddy had joined, then that little bit as well which had been mine, because all my property had been taken off me, hadn't it, while I was in prison, and now she'd rented a garden from an old man and that was being broken up. And she hadn't got a fucking horse any more.

Good heavens! That's how Annush was talking, she was so desperate.

'You've got a useful donkey,' I tried to console her. 'Didn't our Lord Jesus ride a donkey? And why did he do that? To give offence, that was why. So that people should see that he didn't need a showy animal to ride.'

'These days all the Hóstát uses donkeys! So is everybody imitating Jesus? And your Jesus didn't mess up the local land workers.'

At that I immediately gave up on Annush, I wasn't going to listen to that.

'Dear sister, don't abuse Christ in my hearing, because . . .'

'Because what?' she asked angrily, and her eyes were blazing as if she meant to bite me. 'What do you know about what was happening here while you were in prison! And that my poor Puju was taken off me? And what they did to him! What do you know, Rózsi? All you do is pray, and the world can go its own way.'

'So what can be done with a horse?' I asked. It was made to work, I thought to myself, didn't just get its ears stroked the way Annush did it. And she took it bread, because Puju worshipped her so. Didn't she even sing to it like a child?

She didn't tell me what became of the horse because the sky would have fallen.

'Look, Annush, the sky isn't so fragile as to fall because of us.'

'Not because of us, but because of an innocent animal.'

'So what did that animal do?' I asked.

'It got eaten,' she answered.

'What? A horse?'

'Killed and eaten.'

Oh, I couldn't stop myself laughing. In all my born days I'd never heard of such a thing! Eating horse? Like primitive man. What had gone on here while I'd been inside? A war? When I asked 'They were eaten?' Annush straightened up, looked at me, and then we laughed fit to burst. Annush gathered up her skirt because she was laughing so much, nearly wetting herself. She bent forward, couldn't control herself, quickly pulled her briefs down and peed on the spot, fortunately missing her shoes.

When I asked again what had happened to the horse, Annush replied 'Sándor ate him!'

'What Sándor?' I asked, as I knew nobody of that name.

'Our Sándor, the minister, Sándor Mogyorosi.'

Once again she burst out and could hardly catch her breath.

'How did he do that?'

'With a knife and fork, he's a minister. Off fine china.'

Oh, I could stand no more. My sister and I hadn't laughed like that since I'd left home. Tell me what became of that horse.

Annush pulled herself together and brought a little bench, as there was still some warmth in the sun. We sat there and she brought herself a little glass of red wine.

As she told me the story, she was halving the remaining green, unripe tomatoes and putting them into a glass jar for salting. In the old days we threw such things away. Oh, my stomach churned at once at the mere thought of salted tomatoes like that, and my innards wanted to be on the move. I was never going to eat such a thing again, I thought, though in the old days I'd been so fond of them. Merciful God, let me not have to have my innards cut out. Heal my body, sweet Jesus, so that I don't have to think about it all the time, because when I'm in such pain I can't be with you, only with all my own troubles. Have mercy on me, Virgin Mother. Amen. Annush had no idea how painful my innards were.

She began to tell me what had happened to her dear Puju. She didn't know exactly, but he'd been put on the train. Because the poor creature had no mouth to talk with, and she had to speak for him.

'You know, my dear,' she said, once she'd calmed down and wasn't laughing, was just cutting up the tomatoes with a little knife, after first whetting it razor-sharp on the whetstone.

'Oh, I'm so glad you've told me that, my love. See, you dear, dear . . .' and tears came to my eyes. For what reason I didn't know, but it wasn't from laughing, but because I'd got such a beloved sister, blessed for ever be the name of the Lord, our Lord Jesus Christ, and of our Lady the Virgin Mary, who brought into the world our redeemer. Oh, you dear Annush, my sister.

'Listen, my dear,' said poor Annush again, and her nose was running so that she had to wipe it with her apron, 'if somebody hasn't got a mouth, we have to speak for them. We people have to speak even for a poor green tomato.'

'A tomato doesn't have a soul,' I replied. My sister was too much of a philosopher. 'Nor do horses. Only people.'

Annush looked at me so shocked that she dropped the tomato she was holding.

'Is that what you say, Rózsi? Do I have to hear you say that?'

She said that that dear little horse could do nothing but be dumb. Because in fact he'd been eaten just when I'd had to go to prison. Now we weren't laughing any longer. Daddy had taken to the drink that winter, at the end of the winter and in spring. In 1959. And as he was no longer a carter after that he couldn't keep a horse either. All the horses that didn't belong to carters had been taken away even before then. She couldn't go and be a carter, she was still a minor. If she'd worked as a carter, she could have kept the horse and had a licence and a workbook, but she hadn't been old enough, so she couldn't. She was just six months short of eighteen. She'd always gone to see Puju in the collective. She wasn't allowed to take dung away, but she could go and visit him if she gave a bribe. She went to see him while he was still alive in the *Infracirea*—Brotherhood—collective there in Szopor. She even took the poor horse out for a walk once a week. She always filled her pockets with cabbage leaves or some tasty morsel, even a couple of handfuls of oats. He wouldn't eat oats from a bucket while he was in there. And because horses weren't taken out much, didn't work, they just stood there in their stalls, in the muck and all. It was all tractors and more tractors, and horses didn't count against that. Then once she went when the frosts were beginning and she saw that the stall was empty, the floor had been washed down and scrubbed. She asked what had happened to her horse. What horse? In fact, what had become of the horses altogether? At first they wouldn't tell her. Then she slipped ten lei into the foreman's hand and he told her that they'd all been put on the train together.

Horses on a train?

Now we weren't laughing at all. Who'd ever heard of horses going by train?

They'd had to be taken away because the hay had run out. There'd been nothing to give the cows, so, of course, they'd given less and less milk. And so the minister—one Magyarósi, a Hungarian, that was his name, or Mogyorosi—went and said that the horses were eating all the cows. That's what he said, at the Party Conference, the horses were eating the cows. Nobody understood that, said the foreman. Then it turned out that they were actually eating the cows' hay. Well, of course, a townsman, a worker of some sort, didn't know what cows and horses ate.

Then they rounded up all the horses in the collectives and put them on trains. They weren't allowed to tell anybody. All the horses were taken from the whole country, even those from famous stables where there was some bloodline or something. There were saddle horses that had been brought from England during the monarchy, entered for all the races, their semen was worth a fortune! Even one that such a horse had bred by mating was worth ever such a lot! Such beautiful, tall horses, not cold-blooded, that had been racing and which kings had ridden. They were put on trains as well, and eaten. Some were slaughtered at the slaughterhouses here. Eight hundred thousand horses, the foreman said. Eight hundred thousand! Eight hundred thousand horses went to their deaths.

I asked Annush, how did that foreman know this tale? I don't suppose it was in the papers? Certainly not! How then? A foreman doesn't let a thing like that be known, such things are done in secret. Nor did Annush find out from the foreman, who was a big Communist and wouldn't divulge such a thing. His girlfriend told her, she knew about it from him. He was a big man, something in the Party, he knew everything. And all the other farmers knew as well, and they'd all gone there, Hóstát farmers, to groom their horses that were in the collective by then. And where did the collective hear from, I asked?

'Listen, Rózsi, I'll tell you how I found out. Only you won't believe me, because you only trust in Jesus Christ and not in people.'

'Only the Lord never lies.'

'And do even you tell lies, Rózsi? You who . . . '

'Perhaps, Annush, I stole a pair of shoes yesterday and didn't tell anybody, so I'm a liar. And a thief.'

'It's just as well you didn't steal the cross off the Főtér church! That I would believe!'

'And I believe everything you tell me, because you're my only dear sister,' I replied.

'In that case listen, Rózsi, my dear. How did I find out? From the horse's mouth. Nobody else told me what happened to that poor horse, just the horse himself. Do you understand? Puju told me, he was being taken and put on the train, taken to France and sold for dollars.'

'That old horse? For dollars? Who would give dollars for an old horse?' I asked. I could see she wasn't on this planet, she was talking such rubbish. How was I to believe her?

'The whole lot were sold from here for dollars, and the younger ones were taken to the slaughterhouse. They were eaten still in this country, sold to butchers as beef. The Communists all hate horses, all they care about is tractors. Since the Communists came in, all the horses have been finished, do you see? They had to be given in, you weren't allowed to keep one. And so, now they've killed them. Puju told me that when the foreman and the collective man were talking in his hearing about putting them on the train, they said that they'd have to smarten them up first. The foreman told the collective people to give the horses a good wash-down, because they'd have waybills tied on their legs. And Puju had come to say goodbye to me, his owner.'

'How did he come, Annush?'

'He got out at night, came and stood at the gate and said goodbye. He hadn't been far away, just over the Békás, in Szopor. where the Brotherhood collective is. He stood by the gate and gave a neigh, and I put my lékri on and ran out. I knew him straight away by his voice. It couldn't have been anybody else. He was there just five minutes, saying goodbye.'

I asked Annush whether there were any other horses in the street? Or only Puju?

Just he by himself, no other horses. He told me he'd come to say goodbye because he was going abroad on official business. All the horses were being cleared out of the country, he said. He'd be travelling with great, famous horses like those that came from Mongolia and from the big stud farms. From Radóc and even the mansion at Bonchida! He was honoured that he, a little nothing of a horse, was going to travel in the same wagon as such big animals! He'd overheard, when they were talking, the foreman being told what to do. Because he'd got three grooms under him. They thought he was a stupid animal and couldn't understand anything, but Puju heard and understood everything. And he came over to say goodbye to me.'

What could I say to poor Annush? I would pray for her. I'd never seen her so completely confused as to be on another planet.

'Do you believe that, now, Rózsi? That it happened like that? Do you believe?'

'I believe,' I said.

But I didn't believe a word of it. I was lying. But I was doing it for my sister's sake, so that her soul should be at ease.

The next day she ran over to see her old lover, said Annush, because he's an important man, to ask him to save her horse, and he replied that he couldn't save people, let alone horses.

'I went over to see him because he's got such a big garden up there, you know, he's got a place in Borháncs, the Station. He could take a horse there, Puju, and say that he needed him for carting because the area's so big that they can't take all the tree seedlings around by hand. I'd give him my cart as well, I told him. He didn't need it. He couldn't take the horse into the Station, it wouldn't do. So he didn't help me. Then when I went out to the collective, the stall was empty and clean like never before. It was being turned into a pig farm.'

I got up, went over to Annush and put an arm round her shoulders. 'Listen, Annush,' I said, 'you'll have another horse. You will, believe me. You'll get a clever little horse, not all that young, just nice and quiet, and it'll do the job.'

'I'll have a horse, but I shan't have a real garden. A bit of land to bring manure for and to plant a bit of lettuce.'

Then she began to cry again, and I could hear the child starting as well. There she was, standing at the gate, and she could see her mother crying so she joined in. The poor little thing had come out barefoot, even though the ground was cold.

Annush brought out the spade. She could dig with the strength of a man, and I watched as she turned over great big spadefuls. She said that she couldn't sit at present, it hurt too much. She was having her monthly trouble. Why didn't she go and lie down, I asked? It always used to be customary for girls and women to lie down for a day or two, even three in the case of gentry. She preferred to tire herself, have a workout, bend, strain, and then it didn't hurt. That was how she looked after herself.

'Look, Rózsi,' she said, 'if I lie in bed my belly hurts all the time, but if I bend and exert myself it doesn't.'

'I don't have that kind of trouble any more, haven't for ages.'

'You don't mean that your periods stopped when you became a nun, do you?'

I told her that I never even noticed when they stopped. Sometime in my first or second year in prison. I couldn't remember. It had stopped, praise be to God, that was one thing I didn't have to worry about. Some people were like that. I didn't matter, of course, you were given something to keep yourself clean with. Annush said that I was very young for that to happen.

'Aren't you a woman at all now?' she asked. What answer could I give, such I was. 'What if you changed your mind and wanted to have a child?'

'I haven't changed my mind, Annush. I've given my life as a woman to another, and He's accepted it.'

And then I asked her whether she would mind calling me Eleonóra, as I liked that. Nobody was doing that those days, because I'd been separated from my sisters, and I liked that name so much.

'Look, will you call me that if I ask nicely?'

She looked at me and replied, 'I'll have to get used to it. I'll call you what you want, just let me get used to your being somebody else's sister. You as Eleonóra. You weren't given that name as a little girl, of course.'

'It isn't given for an everyday name, only to sisters who are pledged to Christ.'

'Well, listen here, Eleonóra my dear. If we're put out of our house here . . . '

'How should we be put out of our house?'

'My former lover told me, and he's an important man. He said I should keep my eyes open and sell the house and garden while I've got the chance. I said, how should I sell? Where would I go? Buy a flat in a block, he said. Or somewhere that isn't going to be demolished. Because round here we're all going to be demolished and there'll be big tower blocks housing eighty people. A block will be as big as a little garden the size of mine, or rather ours. He'd been into town . . . '

'Annush, my dear, is he still your lover?' I was horrified.

'Leave it, will you? You've got yours, Christ, and I've got mine. I don't tell you to give him up when you love him, and nobody's going to tell me to either. Vilmos, that's his name, Vilmos, told me that he'd been into town to see what developments there were going to be and what land he was going to be given, because he's got the Station, the research place. And in town he was shown the systematized plan, as it's called. And I made a note of that, so that if I see it in the paper, I'll know what it means when they talk about town planning. All the streets have been given numbers. The first to be built up was in Szopor, and that's now finished, and all the streets have been given names like Borszék, and whatever, famous baths, Snagov. That's a sort of Romanian spa place. And then it's coming further up the Borháncs, along the Kövespad to Eperjes square. They'll come further up the hill and he could see which houses they mean to demolish. He saw a little cardboard model of the town with all the big blocks on it. And see, here where we live, in this very street and all around, the town is going be extended with blocks of flats.'

'Who needs all these blocks of flats, Annush? There aren't enough people in the town to need them.'

'They won't be building just blocks of flats, there'll be factories as well. People will be brought in to work in them, and they'll need somewhere to live, so the blocks will be for them. This good soil that we've made so that we take greater care of it than silver spoons—it will be taken away and covered with concrete. My lover's an important man, and in town he was shown everything about how it's all planned. Perhaps there'll be nothing left of us.'

There had been a time when there were as yet no Hóstát people, but I didn't want to upset Annush by telling her. The Hóstát gardeners hadn't known everything at first, they had only learnt and hadn't done it all by themselves. A Bulgarian gardener had come along, one János Jordánov, bought a little land, created an irrigated garden and produced a lot of vegetables for market. He made a huge wheel, what became known as a Bulgarian wheel because he was a Bulgarian, and this turned by itself and it took all the water from the Malomárok and other streams and diverted it into the garden. He'd bought a garden exactly where water could run down into it. That became known as Canaan, because it was a garden that produced for him at all times. Afterwards he bought bigger and bigger gardens, out of town towards the Kölesföld. There too there was a wheel, and he made a downflow for it and irrigated everything. So then the Hóstát people scratched their heads and began to see that they ought to make a Canaan there in Kolozsvár from Jordán's river. So they all made wheels.

Annush went on digging and I just sat there, because there was still a little sunshine and I turned my face to it. Would I tell her, said she, with her back to me, why we had actually been arrested? What had we done? She was thinking all the time but couldn't understand it at all. I should tell her, it had been no use my saying until then that she wouldn't understand what our crime had been. I said, shall I speak about it out here in the yard? People will hear. There was no fence between the gardens, there usually wasn't, There was nobody about that I could see. It was a big garden, thirty ares, and Annush was in the middle, digging in the manure, turning over the soil. I couldn't help her, and I just sat on the little bench because my guts were hurting again. I was weak now, perhaps I'd got a temperature, because my back was all wet.

But I mustn't repeat that all men are sinful, because she didn't believe it. Nor did she believe that I'd committed a crime.

So I said to her, just a minute, and I'll prove it. I went into the house and brought out the raised sole that I'd taken away and not paid for. I said, 'Look at this, Annush. I stole this sole from the shoemakers' collective. I didn't mean to, but I did all the same.'

She stopped and stared at me, but said nothing.

'Do you see this? Well, I've stolen it.'

'Where from?'

I had to tell her all about it. I wasn't going to take them back, as I'd be reported to the police if I did. The nice boots that she'd lent me were still in the shoemakers' collective. This sole cost four hundred lei. I would have to pay that much to have it made into a shoe. I wasted my time explaining. Annush was shocked, couldn't find words to say.

I only showed her the sole because she didn't believe that all men were sinners: just look at what I'd done. So there! Not that we were born sinners because such we were, but because of what we did. So you see, I had certainly done this. Because she believed that we were innocent.

To her, a crime meant something different, she said, and stuck the spade into the soil.

She asked whether I'd been to the police. We had to report every month—until when, had not been stated. Hadn't another month gone by, I asked. How was I to register worldly time? She said I ought to be quick, because a good six weeks had gone by, and I should take the *adeverinca* saying that I had a job. All Saints had passed. Any that dodged work were punished, weren't they, and I might be re-arrested. So I must go quickly and see kind Dr Muntyán to obtain that document, because I had certainly not been taken on. He could give me a medical certificate that I was still being treated and would be taken on when I was better. I would go straight to the police because I knew the way. Only I'd lost the name of the street as it been changed. I couldn't ask anybody for the right name. One person said one thing, another something else, so I'd never find it. The whole Pillangó quarter had been renamed in the second Hungarian period as well. Orbán Balázs út was now named after some actor. Why an actor was better than Orbán, who had been a Hungarian, was unclear.

So I went to the police station. There were a lot of people there, workers from the factories, all seeking residence permits. They were only being given temporary permits because they didn't live in the town, were only 'of no fixed abode', not permanently resident. Anyone that was moving to Kolozsvár was given a place in a block of flats and a *definitiv*. It was explained to them that if they had an address and a job, they qualified for a *definitiv*, but if not they were given a *flotant*, a temporary residence permit. First I was only allowed a *flotant* to live with Annush, later I would be given a *definitiv*. We that had been released from prison had to report not at the window but in a room. An unmarked room in which there were two policemen. How cold the walls were. I had to wait a long time; there was nowhere to sit and I had to remain standing like a horse. But wearing my stolen sandal, I was comfortable. No one had reported the theft, no one had been punished for it. I thanked the Lord very much for forgiving my sin in this way.

I was standing by the cold wall in the police station. How long was I going to have to wait, how long was I going to have to keep coming here, I wondered. I wasn't strong enough to stand for all that long.

Dear Lord, Redeemer Christ, dear good Virgin Mother, help me, let me not constantly be thinking of myself, of my body and my illness. If you cure my body, I won't have to worry about it so much because then it will be at peace and won't make itself felt. But when it's sick it does, it clamours. The spirit ought to clamour! We have to go about the world unmarked, nobody can see a sign on us of who we are, and so we must become symbols. Our dear Father Fidel gave us that command before we were scattered abroad.

Help me to look on your face, your kindly, radiant gaze, and to ignore my own misery. I have indeed had no misery but that your blessing and mercy have upheld me. And your infinite, enduring love. Amen.

Then I was able to say my prayers again. I was always saying them with my sisters in my mind. Oh, if only we could be together again, how I longed for that! It's time well spent, saying one's prayers. That's what dear God has given us nails, hair and fingers for, so that we can say our prayers as and when we like. If one says a good prayer with pure heart and full concentration, even a horrid place seems sanctified. Prayer is spread about in it and it becomes quite different. In secret we do what we want to. We go about the world unmarked and nothing betrays us. But a half hour or an hour of adoration and everything is sanctified.

Then I knocked on the unmarked door. I'd gained courage, because the prayer had given me strength. 'Come in,' came from inside, and there sat the sergeant whom I needed.

He didn't look at anything, nor did he ask any questions. He told me to come again in a month's time, noted the date on my document, but warned me not to be late as I had been this time. I'd been a fortnight overdue.

I hadn't known the date, it was no good them hitting me, I didn't know. I only got one slap in the face, I told Annush, in the first week when interrogation was beginning.

I told her about the first slap. What was a slap compared to the Lord's agonizing death? Nevertheless I was afraid, and why not? Christ had been afraid too! Did I admit I'd been there on 24 August 1956—or was it 24 September? Because I just stared and thought what year was it then, when must it have been, because it had been St Gellért, our martyr's day, hadn't it? Did I admit that I'd been there in Gyulafehérvár? I did, I said, and my heart warmed when he mentioned Alba Iulia. Gyulafehérvár! Bishop Áron had celebrated Mass and we'd all been there. But I couldn't remember when it could have been. I mustn't deny it, because the others had all said. If they'd all said, why need I say? We didn't tell lies. I couldn't remember what year or what day, only Bishop Áron's hand and his radiant face. Because he was then in Christ, everybody could see that looked at him. Anybody who looked at Bishop Áron knew at once why those that were not in Christ were afraid of him. Because afraid of him they were, that was why he was held in prison so long. How many prayers for him went up! Such songs of Mary resounded in Gyulafehérvár cathedral that even the Securitate men were taken aback! Did the word have such power? There were some that crossed themselves, some three times, not knowing that three times wasn't our custom. It was obvious at once that it was out of place there. Some did it sincerely, some incorrectly. There was no telling which was which. We couldn't see into the human soul.

Did I admit that we'd been in Gyulafehérvár Cathedral out of sympathy with the Hungarian counterrevolution? I was asked during interrogation. How could we have sympathized with a revolution? We were in Christ, not in the revolution in the world. Christ's revolution was what showed the way for us, that was for sure, it was Him that we followed. We'd only been glad and confident that Holy Mother Church too was at liberty and that we'd returned to Rome. That had been in 1956, I was told. So it must have been. Not a single interrogator believed that I couldn't remember what year it had been.

You'd gone to celebrate the anniversary, it's written down, they told me, the four hundred and sixtieth anniversary of your society. I answered that it was true, because that was what they wanted me to say. For us the cause for celebration was that Bishop Áron had been released from the hardship of prison and was able to address us in the cathedral. But I didn't venture to say that to the man who was asking and who disbelieved in the Lord. I knew that we'd been there for ages as a Society because our fine order had been founded in Kolozsvár for the service of God a very long time ago, and in secret, because even then it had had to be secret, Father Fidel had told us. But I couldn't remember what the problem in the world outside had been at that time. Something to do with the Reformed, perhaps. We weren't considering numbers, we were just celebrating, and I didn't know what anniversary it was.

'You know more about it,' I said to the interrogator, Valter somebody, a Hungarian. 'We don't keep notes.'

We didn't keep diaries or anything, that didn't suit the religious, we liked to pray living words.

'You'd been laying wreaths? With Hungarian flags and ribbon? On whose grave? Did you come out of church with flags? Foreign flags?'

Certainly nobody had gone processing or scattering. In the old days we'd scattered rose petals round the church. Going outside wasn't permitted now. We weren't allowed to do anything outside the church, we knew that. It was all forbidden. Flags in particular. Outside church everybody was unmarked

'What did the Bishop say?' we were asked.

Oh, I remembered that sermon! It will never leave me as long as I live. When I heard him preach—for the first and last time—my life was changed. I acknowledged my sin, confessed everything to the Father, such had been the effect on me of that sermon. He too had understood that previously we had been walking in sin, but now we're going to take up the inward battle against it. He absolved us. Because until then we'd been silent, that had been our great sin.

Bishop Áron had said that the churches were standing empty, there was nobody to bury the dead, and nobody brought children forward for baptism or sought the blessing of God on marriages. There were no priests. The faithful had all left or abandoned them. Or they'd put off the cassock, been scattered abroad. The houses of God in the countryside were deserted and silent.

He'd quoted from Luke. He'd said, the stones will speak if you don't.

He reproached priests that remained silent in the names of Jesus and Holy Mother Church and in his own. Us too, sinners. Bishop Áron was stern. He was very stern with us that had sworn to Christ and he demanded a lot from us. Although we went about the world without distinguishing marks it was our job to spread the Word. The Word was the Truth, said he. He that spoke the living Word brought the Truth. It was our job to tend the sick, put the word of Christ into the mouths of children, to pray for the dying and to struggle against spiritual withering. We should visit families that the Word of God does not reach. Or follow Christ and speak in the world with His holy words, or . . . I no longer remembered what we had to do, because the Bishop's words so resounded in me, and I was in such a passion, that I swore that as long as there was life-giving breath in my nostrils and sound came from my mouth, I would spread the word of Christ.

Christ is never silent, said Bishop Áron. The disciples might never be silent. Those that were silent were the ones that betrayed him. Remember Peter!

There and then he forgave every priest that went astray and had regard not for the church and Rome, but for the things of the world. He urged them strongly to return to the right way.

How his words rang out within us! Like the organ with the song of Mary. I had never before loved like that, nor been loved so much with true, ardent love. At the end we laid a wreath on a grave in the crypt. That of János Hunyadi.

I told the interrogator that I remembered Bishop Áron's sermon.

'Did he urge you to take action?' asked Valter.

'Yes,' I said.

'Against the Romanian People's Republic?'

'No, only against those that don't speak out.'

That was a silly thing to say and I ought not to have said it, because I was letting Bishop Áron down, and he already had so many enemies. If I remained silent I was letting Christ down. Merciful God, enlighten me as to what should I have answered. If I spoke it was a sin, if I kept silence it was a sin. Man is always sordid and sinful. He can wash himself and pray all day, yet when he appears before the face of the Lord he's very sinful.

Then they went on questioning me this way and that, so as to bring out incitement as they wished. Then came another slap to help me remember. I signed to the effect that the Bishop had encouraged action against the Communists. There was no mention of our Bishop Áron, but our business was not finished. All that was established in the *procès verbal* was that I had been present in Gyulafehérvár Cathedral on 24 September 1956 when Áron Márton had preached. I had come completely under his ideological influence. Did I sign that? Yes. And did I admit that after that I too began going round the houses with songs? Because when we'd heard what Bishop Áron said we too began going round the houses with songs. With the song about Mary and the Three Lambs, the Three Lambs being the three forms of Jesus. We mimed the song with our hands, here's proof.

I admitted to everything, but they were never satisfied with our crimes and wanted more and more. They found everything too little.

Father János too was not satisfied with my sins. He had become my spiritual father in the Franciscans' church since I returned, but I couldn't get on well with him as a priest. And I came properly prepared, I even wrote down what I was going to confess. I put everything nicely in order, and there was just the right amount. To him, however, it wasn't enough—would I please now say something serious!

When I went to see Dr Muntyán for the document, two days previously I'd eaten three whole eggs. I wasn't supposed to, but I had. I was fasting, keeping a conscientious fast, and I wasn't allowed to eat protein, least of all eggs. The doctor said that I shouldn't have done it, but even without that I knew that I was bloated. Eggs were acceptable as ingredients of pastry but not by themselves. When I got up one day it was almost midday, I'd been so fast asleep, and there was nobody at home, so I helped myself to three eggs and thoroughly enjoyed them, as I hadn't for a long time. Next day I confessed to Father János that I'd broken my fast with the three eggs, but he didn't show much interest. I should say something of importance, as was his usual response. I went to see Dr Muntyán; two whole months had gone by and he again wanted to examine me with a speculum, and then I'd just eaten the eggs. One thing was certain, down below I was going again non-stop. Perhaps I did it on purpose before going for the examination, so that it should affect me, filling my innards with air, and he would write me another note and I wouldn't be able to work because I was sick. Perhaps I was so weak that I didn't want to go to work, and I was making myself ill when I was about to be given the document saying that I was APT, *apt de lucru*—fit for work. When I told Father János, he gestured and was cross. That was nothing. Say something important.

'Father, this is something important. It's sinful, it's gluttony. I imposed a fast on myself, and then it seems there's no humility in me, my faith in Christ has fallen away, all I think of is my own advantage. Instead of dis-regarding myself so that Christ may grow in me. Even if I'm sick I shouldn't have done it.'

'It's nothing, daughter, don't concern yourself. Confess the important things that you've done.'

I just couldn't agree with Father János. I remember once confessing to Father Fidel that I'd slapped a child's hand when it tried to take another apple after lunch. It was while we were still dealing with the Greek children. The child hadn't waited for me to give it one, kept trying to take. I'd slapped his hand and even come out with 'For goodness' sake!' I'd used bad language. And I told him that I'd wept to Mother, because I'd told her first, not because of the language but because I'd hit the poor child. A poor orphaned child, hungry, and I'd hit him. Father had actually interceded for me. He took my hand and said that I'd given offence to God. Now I must beg for forgiveness.

Father János was always asking me to say something serious! Not just footling childish nonsense about three eggs.

Later sister Melánia said that when Father János asked us for something serious in confession he was questioning our faith. Asking about our hearts, whether they had dried up.

I once told Father Fidel, as he was also a monk, that I hadn't given alms, but I'd had in my pocket a slice of bread left over from lunch, and half an apple as well, and hadn't given them to a beggar. I hadn't, because I hadn't liked the way he persistently cawed at me, wouldn't leave me alone, kept following me. Father's reply was that he would pray for me, that I should not be so dry of heart. And he said that the drying up of the heart was the greatness sin. And that I was very much inclined to it. Father even spoke to Mother about my sin, and I was given a seven-day penance. The practice of prayer, fasting, forgiveness of sin and good deeds. I had to beg pardon every day from a person that I'd been angry with, been heartless to, or had bad thoughts about.

Father asked me afterwards from whom I'd begged pardon. He hadn't taken me into the confessional but into the Sub Rosa hall for serious questioning. I said one of the sisters and nurses who knew better about everything and was bossy towards me.

'Did you thank her for teaching you?' he asked.

In fact I hadn't thanked her, but I had begged their pardon for thinking badly of her.

'And who else?'

'Sister Melánia, because she's always singing loudly and won't leave me alone, and I'd been angry with her.'

'And who else?'

'The man next door, who tried to grope Leona, I told him he was a filthy swine.'

'Did you beg his pardon?'

'I told him I wasn't angry with him any longer.'

'What did he say?'

'That he'd never even wanted to grope me. I wasn't angry, because my heart was pure.' He laughed heartily and said, 'You see? The Lord has granted you that men no longer want to grope you! And who else?'

'Sister Melánia again. I knew that she'd had some ice cream. One of the doctors brought some to the hospital, she was given some, and I thought a bad thought. Perhaps I was only envious because I didn't get any.'

'And why didn't you ask for some if you wanted it so badly?'

'Because I'd have been ashamed to,' I said.

'Because you're stuck up,' said the Father sadly.

'I begged the pardon of one of our patients, an elderly woman, because when I was on nights, I'd had to change her sheet three times, and the third time I cleaned up after her, I told her she ought to be ashamed of herself.'

'And? Who was number six?'

'I asked forgiveness of the Virgin Mother because I'd been envious that her face was so beautiful and shining, her whole appearance like the radiant sun and that her whole form was so marvellous, with the resplendent Lamb sitting on her arm.'

'You compared yourself to the Virgin Mother?'

'No! Didn't you say that we should measure ourselves by Jesus?'

'That's right, daughter, always by Christ and the Virgin Mother, but not by their man-made images!' And the Father laughed aloud. 'And the seventh?'

'There wasn't a seventh,' I replied. 'Because when I recognized how I felt towards the Holy Virgin, I couldn't regard anybody else with admiration or affection. I'm unworthy to be a living person, unworthy of the habit, or of my vow, or of even once receiving the body and blood of Christ our Lord.'

That was what I said, and I began to cry. Then Father sent me out to the big market, because that was where the beggars were. He told me to look for the physically filthiest, foulest of mouth and drunken, the most repulsive that I could see, go up to them and put in their hand a slice of bread with my blessing.

Father gave me another week's penance. He said that he could see that my heart wasn't broken, and until it was, he was going to give me penances.

Then he sent me out again.

When I went to see him again, he asked me what my father's name was. Would he be Ferenc Butyka? Yes, I replied. He'd been to see him, but not actually him, but Father Superior, who had sent him on. Ferenc Butyka had been drunk and had threatened Father with being reported to the police for enticing away his daughter, Rózsa Butyka. He, Ferenc Butyka, knew that being a nun like that was forbidden and all the same the priest was enticing away unfortunate girls. Couldn't he see that his daughter was a cripple? Father had said that he would pray for him, and that his conscience was clear, he had never enticed anybody away. Ferenc then declared that he was not to pray for him of all people, because firstly, he was a Calvinist, and secondly, God was wicked. His daughter hated him, what was more, had deserted him, and she, his daughter Rózsa, had told him that if she had to live with him, she'd kill him. After which Ferenc Butyka had walked unsteadily out of the house of God.

Father Fidel told me to go and see my father and beg his forgiveness. Had I said such a thing as he had alleged? Yes, I said. Then I must go and beg forgiveness. I replied that if I found him sober I would, and he asked me to apologize to him even when drunk.

He asked me later at confession whether I had been to see Ferenc Butyka, and on both occasions, I could only say that I hadn't. When he asked a third time, I replied that I had no father. He became very sorrowful. He quoted Luke, saying that sin of the heart was the greatest sin, the rest didn't count. While my heart was like that, every day I was letting down Christ, who had died for me. And that mine was the heart that had dried up.

He said that he could do no more for me than pray, and that God was shocked at me.

Where now was Father Fidel, to see that my heart had been purified? Merciful God had helped me, led me out to my father's grave, and I'd been able to say the rosary of sorrow for him from a pure heart. Annush too had been there and was my witness.

Father János, however, wanted a serious sin from me. Surely I wasn't going to lie for his gratification? Where would serious sin begin in his opinion? Did he expect me to say every week that I had killed somebody? Would that be enough? Or that I had behaved licentiously? That I had broken my sacred marriage to Christ? I'd always only been able to think that I committed sin with my lower body. Or with my hand. Or that I had polluted myself only because I was a nun? Would that be sin enough? Father János didn't know to what heaven the sins of the heart rose, and that they drove people into all sorts of doubt. Or cruelty of a kind.

Father János only livened up when I confessed to him that I was beginning to have doubts concerning Holy Mother Church. I said that it hadn't rescued Bishop Áron from his wicked imprisonment through Christ's vicars on earth, the Holy See and the Holy Father. And that neither did Father Superior care about the clergy that were scattered and gather his lambs together. Our beloved Holy Mother Church, Rome, everybody, left us to ourselves. Nobody was fighting for us.

When I mentioned Father Superior he woke up sharply. How did I know what Father Superior was supposed to do? Then we talked like two politicians. What mattered to him was not that I had doubts about my leaders, but that I criticized them. He wanted to talk, but not about my sins. Sin didn't interest him.

Father János said that we were not an order now, I should get that idea out of my head. It was dangerous and stupid to have anything to do with it. I should walk in Christ and forget everything else. I should say my prayers. And what would become of my vow?

Well, there you have it! I confessed to almighty God that I certainly couldn't fully reveal my soul and all my sinful thoughts to Father János.

'I'd like to visit the brethren in Dés, we've got male brethren there.'

I asked Father János to help me. I'd better not try, I'd make trouble for him! But they were still together in Dés, I'd heard, because all the Franciscan monks had been relocated to there, and I'd have liked to confess to the

Minister General. Father János could see no reason for that, and would do all in his power to prevent my going to Dés. I would go to them for at least one Mass. I thought that the Minister General celebrated Mass. I must get it right, there were now different ministers! And he ordered me to stay where I was. Or he would stop taking care of me, would have nothing more to do with me, if I wouldn't do as I was told! What about your vow of obedience? he asked. But I hadn't vowed to desert my brethren. Where were they?

We hadn't had a single visitor from the convent since we'd been back at liberty with *graciere*. How could this be, I asked Father János. Had everybody forgotten us? Did we no longer exist? Did nobody need us now? I meant to tell him (because this most of all I ought to have said in confession, because until then I wasn't worthy to touch the sacred communion wafer, because I hadn't given an account of my true sins), that if we stayed as we were, I was certainly going to be disappointed in our Holy Mother Church, the whole of Rome and the Holy Father, because I could now see that he didn't need us there either. I'd been thinking, however, that the sanctified life that we had chosen, monasticism, meant that we were the blood vessels in the holy body of Mother Church, the inexhaustible source of faith, eternal movement, eternal prayer, unwearying evangelization. And that God, in His mercy, had been testing us when we went to prison, and had released us even stronger. But perhaps, after officialdom had taken away our habits, the church now thought of us as just a kind of excrescence that it could pare off if it was annoyed with us. Because Father János had said that we must not start evangelizing again. Begging had been forbidden for a long time, and we weren't allowed to go collecting. We had to receive money for our work, but it said in the Rule that we might not be given money except in the form of alms or oblations. But what was our monastic status worth if we were neither needed by Holy Mother Church nor allowed to go about the world? What sort of a gospel was it that might not be proclaimed? Or the word of Christ, that no one might speak it?

I couldn't say these things to Father János. What, then, was the value of confession? Perhaps my heart was in fact dried up, as Father Fidel had said long ago. Man is not sinful in general terms. How could I, Rózsa Butyka Eleonóra OFM, receive the Sacrament of the Altar after such a footling confession? But I did so desire it as I saw it on the sacred corporal.

So I confessed what I could, uncertainly. The Father gave me absolution, but I experienced no relief, couldn't find peace. Father János didn't say what I so much desired to hear. That the Church needed us at all costs, after being in prison, without habits, in the world, that Holy Mother Church knew about us, that we were its most passionate believers in Christ, its lay arms extended to believers and seekers. He didn't say that Holy Mother Church had been praying for us while we were in prison, or that it had celebrated Mass for its incarcerated children and for all that were innocent, which we had been.

All that Father János had said was 'Don't excite yourself, daughter. The Church is always there, for you too.'

In the prayer hour he then gave a talk of a societal nature. It was dull. I want to hear the living words of Christ, not talk of the sovereignty of the people. In those days it was all the rage. Politics. Father János had a lot to say about sectarians and reaction. I knew about sectarians, I'd seen plenty in prison—Jehovah's Witnesses, Pentecostalists, Adventists, Baptists, Nonconformists, Reformed Bethanists, all sorts. Lots of sectarians and lots of Romanians. But numerous monks and priests, who weren't sectarians. Who said who was a sectarian? Should I have asked Father János? Perhaps he considered that we too were sectarians and reactionaries. He said that sectarians fell into the sin of subjectivism, that they worshipped their inner god. A subjective god. One mustn't serve the inner god but the God of the Church. I couldn't make head or tail of what he said. What other god did we have except our inner God and guide?

The Father said that making converts was not allowed, had been forbidden. One had to be very careful, he said. It had already been prohibited, but he was reminding us. If there was an order that we must confess the faith, what was one to do that had chosen the consecrated life? So how would it be possible to walk in Christ if one might not confess it? I actually asked the Father that during the spiritual hour, because at five on Tuesdays we had a spiritual hour in the Sub Rosa hall. He replied that faith had to be confessed in church. That was what churches, Holy Mother Church, and confessor priests were for. Everything had to have its place in life. Then he produced from his cassock pocket a typed copy of one of Bishop Áron's sermons. Once more he placed his hand on his mouth and closed his eyes. What a great present, I almost shouted out.

'Then how are children going to come to the faith?' I asked him then. Because we weren't allowed to do anything, were we, except hold Scripture classes in the church? And so I left the spiritual hour completely at a loss instead of being at ease and pure at heart. A spiritual hour, and even in the Sub Rosa hall one might not speak out.

I went on postponing, I asked Dr Muntyán for the *adeverinca* that I was sick and not fit for work and went to the police. When a year was up that would be that, either I'd go and work in the basement where Dr Muntyán had accepted me, or I'd be registered as a chronic invalid. It wouldn't be possible to temporize any longer. Dear Christ, why were you sending me among the cold dead? What's become of obedience? God's name be praised for it. That's where I'll have to proclaim your name from now on. Would I be strong enough for that? 'Another shall carry thee whither thou wouldst not,' says John the Evangelist. But I knew that there among the dead was the greatest task. Those who had already gone on their way must not be left without a prayer. I would have to pray so for that basement that even a Communist would shit himself at the word of the Lord. God forgive me for thinking such a thing! I wasn't ready to go that way. I wasn't going to a genteel bourgeois place, to sit in some office or other where nothing is to do with people. I wasn't keen on paperwork. I needed people to love, even if they were dead. Dear Christ, how could I be equal to so great a duty? I prayed and implored to be granted strength for that mighty task to which you were sending me.

Dr Muntyán looked and looked at me, but my injuries wouldn't heal, because after all I had injuries all over my body. I wasn't worthy of the holy wounds, I hadn't been granted those that the great saints had, but mine were simply ugly human scars. I couldn't stop picking at the skin of my hands, though I prayed to be able to, wicked person that I was that couldn't control myself. 'It's not people in general,' as dear Father Fidel used to say, 'that are bad, it's just you, Sister Eleonóra, that you're talking about. You must say that you're the bad one, not some figment of the imagination. You must acknowledge sinfulness personally, not concern yourself over others.' So my hand didn't get any better, but there on my right thumb there was by then a sort of open wound where I'd been biting it. Dr Muntyán said that it was because of sugar. I was diabetic, and so had less capacity for healing. He would register me as a chronic invalid if I wanted, and he could put me in front of the board with half of what was wrong with me. I said I was going to get better, I promised. And if he registered me, he said, I wouldn't have to pay any taxes, not even the 'virgin tax', that women with no children were going to have to pay, which was being introduced.

I'd really been looking forward to Monday and meeting Melánia. I'd be able to relax with her, such was her cheerful nature. That crazy Melánia! I was sitting on the bench below the statue of King Mátyás, when all of a sudden she came up behind and covered my eyes with her hands. Her hands were so warm and smelt of soap. She whispered in my ear that she'd brought me a surprise. She kept her hands on my eyes so that I shouldn't see anything, and then somebody took hold of my hands. Gosh, who could those slender little hands belong to? Gracious God, Leona! You've found her! I was almost shouting! All three of us hugged one another, and so tightly that my arms were painful. Here was Sister Leona!

First we had to give thanks to the Lord for working the miracle. Now three of us five were there. Mátyás and his five men there were of bronze, and the Lord had created us too of such durable material that the five of us were still alive.

Then I said to Leona, 'You must tell us absolutely everything, we won't let you go until you have, never mind omerta.'

Melánia whispered, 'Keep your voice down, we're not alone.'

We weren't allowed to assemble anywhere, that had been in the omerta. Nowhere, but here at Mátyás's feet the Lord had worked a miracle for all to see. Perhaps the people that were watching us would even follow us into the church or even overhear confessions. Melánia said 'Let's say nothing for a bit and see if they go away.' I didn't know which she thought were watching us as there were certainly a number wearing similar coats. One was reading a paper, another smoking a cigarette, and there were another two standing there, all looking in our direction. Or perhaps women were the attraction? That too was possible.

We sat on the bench and linked our little fingers. Leona and Melánia sat one on each side of me, each of my hands touching one of them. That was how we'd used to sit in a ring, joining hands, each linking little fingers with the next. That was what the Rose Garland had been like, nobody had been alone. Sweet Christ, bring back our sisters so that the five of us can sit in a ring, linked together. Work a miracle on us.

While we were sitting like that I had no fear of anybody, and I even closed my eyes. How long we were like that I didn't know, but I was so relaxed. I could actually smile, I felt. I wasn't bothered about Father János any more, only my sisters were my confessors. By the time we opened our eyes again it was completely dark. Melánia looked round and tapped out on the bench 'The Securitate had been holding a quiet time.'

At first I didn't understand the end of the sentence. Then it dawned on me, and Leona and I laughed so loud that Mátyás immediately turned to look at us. I could only see two men, one to the left and one to the right, who were sitting and keeping silence with us.

Leona quickly tapped out her address. She had to do it letter by letter three times, because I hadn't understood. Roman was the name of the street, and I'd have to visit her—we'd all exchanged street names. She said I wasn't to go to her flat as her relatives were nervous. But at least I new where she was living. Was she working, I asked. She'd found work in a cloth-mill. Oh merciful God, help Sister Leona to return to human company. We swore that as of now, every Monday, we'd sit at the king's backside where everybody could see us.

Never before had I felt such love, such eagerness. Melánia was still worried about young children, because how old had I been, fourteen, when I'd joined our Mother and the sisters. Anybody that hadn't experienced love in the flesh wasn't able to recognize love for Jesus either. We were all lovers of God. Anybody that didn't have a passion for God and their redeemer Christ didn't completely surrender themselves to Him.

Father János forbade us all to be present at the bible class or prayer hour. All three of us. He kept telling us to be careful. But the sisters and I agreed to go one day to the rosary hour. It was forbidden, but we didn't care. We tapped out where and how to meet. It took a long time, tapping quietly on the bench, and then Melánia really burst out laughing, because she could see the Securitate man straining his ears as he read his paper because he couldn't hear what we were tapping out. Well, if he didn't know prison language, he wouldn't understand. All of them ought to spend a bit of time inside, there was a lot that they could learn. Leona said that we ought to dress as youngsters, wear trousers, then we wouldn't attract attention. I wasn't going to wear trousers, that was for sure.

At the prayer hour in the Sub Rosa hall, Father János was startled, but strangely amused, to see the three of us, all wearing our blue headscarves. 'Are you still all right? Do you mean to get together again . . . ?'

What were we to say? Anyway, he knew who we were. He said nothing, just made the sign of the cross over us, closed his eyes, and prayed inwardly.

Now we have a number and God will take care of us. It was with just those words that Mother Jusztina, on telling us the number, told us to look out for ourselves and God would look after us.

We held a spiritual practice and chose Sister Melánia as our leader until Mother came home, so now she was Mother Melánia. She told each of us in what way we should improve. She spoke to me too, and I didn't know which of my sins she would most likely choose as I had so many. But all she said was 'Sister Eleonóra, what's become of your Franciscan good humour? Think of Father's face, and always have him with you until he comes.'

Father Fidel was in fact always laughing and joking so much, he was a perfect clown. When he saw a nun looking sorrowful, he would ask, to cheer her up, 'Has your faith deserted you, dear sister? Why are you so gloomy?'

She would take offence: 'Not at all, oh dear no, dear Father, don't say such a thing, don't threaten me.'

'Then why so gloomy, my child? You haven't been much of an apostle today.'

She would reply, modestly, saying that she certainly had been an apostle, tending the sick, praying for beggars and all sinners, for Communists, for the leaders of our country and saying the rosary with a pure heart for all that were unfortunate.

'Nevertheless, it is your faith that has deserted you,' the Father would say, looking at her with a very gloomy expression. Then he would ask her to confess, be given a penance, and her soul would be lightened and her good humour restored.

Eventually Mother had told us what our number was. That which we had been given by the hand of the Holy Father, 8956. We memorized it as if it were our name, but it wasn't actually our final number, but merely indicated that our request had been received. The Holy See had taken in our application and would discuss admitting us; we must not operate outside the law like a sect and our convent would receive the Holy Father's permission to have our own spirituality as Franciscan nuns. We would be nursing sisters, and also have a convent too! Mother wished for nothing less than to establish a real convent with us. The application had been sent to Pope

John XXIII in secret, his signature was on our number, and we were now waiting for the approval of Pope Paul VI.

Even before that Mother had opened correspondence with Rome, but she hadn't told us for fear of alarming us, as such a thing could lead to imprisonment. Mother had not been caught with the licence, and yet God had tested both her and her faith. She had asked independently for a licence to function and for us to establish a convent in the little house in Fogadó utca. She'd bought that part of the house because the people there were kind and helped us financially. She had told us that the people who lived there previously meant to sell it, and we would be once again allowed to collect donations and to beg in order to buy that as well. And when we owned two parts, we'd also get the whole yard and be able to set up our own nursing home, for which we asked permission from Rome. Now, however, building and contents had been confiscated from her.

That which was movable could be removed, but that which was as firm as a rock could not, said Sister Melánia. Such was our faith. And I should understand that Father János, when he asked if we were still all right, meant only had we kept our faith.

But where was Mother?

When we were taken away in the lorry, Mother said that the Holy Father had sent our number so that we might establish the convent, and that she had taken it with her in her bosom, under her clothes, along with a monstrance. The number was 8956. We were to make a note of it, and never to divulge it to our tormentors. That was now our name: 8956.

That was the last thing that I told Annush, and there was nothing more for me to say, and then we so fell out over this that I would have done better to say nothing. I ought not to have told her so much, not because of the omerta, as that was a worldly restriction and we had no regard for it, but because she had to understand that it was not right for a religious to keep talking about herself and her person. A nun should only open her mouth to the glory of God. Anything that does not serve His glory must remain unsaid.

'So I suppose it was to the glory of God that you and so many other innocent people all got arrested?' asked Annush. 'And that you were interrogated? And made to admit to things that you hadn't done at all? Because you did indeed admit everything, and signed your names to it. So that was to the glory of God?'

Annush was angry, she was indeed! I didn't want to go into all my woes. Not the prison, nor what my illness was, nor where God was sending us to work in earthly life, I wouldn't, so there, I said, it was none of my business, nothing for a religious to be concerned with. Nor what was to happen about the house and the garden being sold. Oh, wasn't she just angry! She was so worked up that she didn't say another word, simply seethed.

The next day she began again: 'When are they going to apologize to you? And rehabilitate you? Because that's happened to some people. When will you be given compensation and rehabilitated? You ought to get back what was taken off you, land and everything.'

I told her that the Romanian People's Republic certainly wasn't going to forgive us. I told my sisters that as well, and Leona replied 'Neither shall we forgive it!' and she laughed and laughed. She really could laugh, that Leona. Not, so to speak, nicely, Franciscan-style, subtly, but quite wildly! Father Fidel actually ticked her off once, and told her that Franciscan good humour was a good thing, but losing control was not.

'The Romanian People's Republic isn't going to forgive us, so we shan't forgive it either! It can do with it, but too bad!' she said, and we laughed fit to burst.

Mother Melánia allowed us to have a good laugh at ourselves now and then, because by the grace of God Franciscan good humour was completely restored in us, just as Father Fidel's final instruction had been. He had told us that if Franciscan good humour succeeded in making us laugh, he would come back from Siberia, where he believed he was to be sent, and when he did we would be given the greatest penance of all, a verbal fast! And perhaps he would even bar us from the Sacrament of the Altar until our good humour was restored. How could one receive the sacrament sorrowfully? We'd better be careful, there'd be such a great penance, we'd never forget it. We'd very much like to go begging, Father, said Leona, and he laughed with her. Begging is such a fine thing to do, but religious aren't allowed to any more. Religious have to work like anybody else, earn money and go about unmarked.

When we'd laughed ourselves out and quietened down, Mother Melánia asked whether we remembered our most important prayer, the *Pater noster*, and in it the words 'as we forgive them'. Because, she said, there were no words more important in our lives on earth than that we should forgive as our Creator Father forgives us. That 'as' implies that we must first forgive others, all that trespass against us, and then we too shall be forgiven. We take the first step and He only comes after. And we must forgive for the sake of Bishop Áron, of ourselves, and of our many brethren. Then Leona and I said to Mother Melánia, because we weren't sufficiently accustomed to obedience to her, but we had sworn, that we didn't believe that it would be possible to forgive on behalf of Bishop Áron and all our brethren. Our Creator Father didn't require that we should forgive on behalf of the Bishop. Then forgive on your own account, said Mother. At the very next spiritual hour she would make a point of asking Father János, as our principal, to whom we owed obedience, whether we must be able to forgive or not. I, however, that was the weakest in obedience, said that I wouldn't accept Father János's reply because we didn't have Father Fidel, and Father János was quite different. But Mother Melánia ticked us off severely for judging the priesthood, as we weren't acquainted with them all and she certainly knew no one more steadfast than Father János, though he might not display his fidelity in some particular. And he'd had to test us first to see if we'd remained faithful. 'Father János is directly the disciple of Bishop Áron, you just haven't got to know him very well!' We asked Mother whether in that case Father János belonged among us? To which she replied, 'What did you think, perhaps he belongs among wolves?'

In answer to that, Annush told me that it was certainly great foolishness on our part. This forgiveness. Wasn't it I who had told her that in the church there were mortal sins, which couldn't, might not at all, be forgiven? Hadn't I said that? she asked. So what was I on about now? Would I please tell her what mortal sin was?

'What one does deliberately and with clear intent that is contrary to the Law.'

'And how do you know,' said she, 'that action against you has not been deliberate? How can you tell?' And wasn't action against us deliberate, to take everything off us and leave us with nothing at all?

She would never, but never, on her own account, forgive if action were taken to deprive her of her house and garden, because there was no law on earth that compelled her to forgive such gross, swinish behaviour. Such as made her homeless, reduced her to poverty, forced her into a block of flats, so that she should own not a bit of land, not a single animal or anything, have no means of sustenance, no work for her hands. Wouldn't she have to control the children strictly so that they didn't get out of line? And what would the world come to if everybody forgave, asked Annush, because obviously people would be uncouth, do as they pleased, and there'd be no shame left in them!

Well, I very nearly pointed out that this was not the situation. I had to turn my back, I was so inclined to laugh. Annush mustn't see me laughing, because she was really worked up and would be angrier still if she did.

I replied that we weren't going to agree on this, because she talked all the time of laws about land and the state, but we took a different view. We had no common ground.

Annush suddenly threw down a stone that she'd just picked up to press down the edges of the greenhouse with, so that the wind shouldn't blow on the seedlings that she was protecting. She hurled it down almost at my feet, and it hit the spade and even struck a spark. So she wouldn't forgive, I was to leave her alone, because I didn't care about anything, the land and the house didn't matter to me, I didn't consider other people, I was stubborn. Nobody was going to tell her what to do when such a great injustice was coming upon her and the Hóstát people and they were all being destroyed. A Catholic nun had better not tell her, or she'd pick up another stone and throw it at me!

I told her that if she meant to be like that, a child of wrath, and never ever forgive anybody again, not even that nasty-looking tomato that she had in her hand—it hadn't ripened and had fallen off because she'd kicked the plant in her fury—if she did stay like that, she'd see what kind of a life she got. She and all her children who could do nothing but be angry. I didn't mean to be like that myself. So then she shouted, now I'd really better shut up, she wasn't interested in what would happen to her and the child of wrath, I'd better shut up with my stupid talk and eternal cackling. It was easy for me, she said, because I'd have no children who'd inherit anything from me. I was like a silly child. I should speak for myself and she'd do the same.

And so it is, my dear Annush, I prefer to say nothing, I said, for fear you'll throw that stone at me and might even kill me. Not so as to cause pain but for the sake of kinship. Forget what I said, I told her. It was all foolishness, forget it. I hadn't been speaking in praise of myself in the least. Anyway, if anybody speaks in their own praise, they're forgotten. Whatever we say in praise of ourselves, fortunately, will all fade away.

Epilogue

Kali died young, and Vilmos took her child and brought him up. The boy didn't continue growing roses. Sister Eleonóra nursed Kali in her final months. Nobody studied her folk tales, but an ethnographer from the university recorded them on tape and preserved them. Even today many wear folk costumes in Szék, and a lot of the women from Szék go to Budapest as maids.

The biologist Vilmos Décsi was retired early. He continued his crossbreeding in his garden but lost interest in adaptation experiments based on Michurin theory. His hybrids are no longer cultivated and only the published experiments on them remain. The state has not yet restored the Station land to the more than ninety Hóstát families that owned it previously. No stock of the rose Vilmos Décsi has been identified anywhere, though it is possible that it flowers unnamed in a few Kolozsvár gardens.

The house in Borháncs utca where Annush and her family lived was demolished in the late 1960s and they moved into a block of flats. All but a few of the houses in the Hóstát were torn down, and several farmers committed suicide. There remain of the Hóstát only a few streets on the far side of the railway line, but to this day a number of elderly people grow produce for the Kolozsvár market, where one can still run into them. After 1990 many recovered their land. One of Annush's children has moved to Hungary.

Sister Eleonóra retained her faith until her death. She lived quietly, blending into society, evangelizing, and in 1968 returning to work as a hospital nurse. After her release from prison, Sister Jusztina returned to live with the sisters. They were watched, but the effort made to arouse mistrust among them failed to disrupt the community. Their lifelong vow was renewed in secret and symbolically dedicated to Bishop Áron, who was at the time under house arrest in his palace. The number 8596, that of the sisters' application to the Holy See, equalled that of registered and relocated nuns in Hungary in 1950. No precise figure is known for Transylvania. Sister Eleonóra and her companions now lie at rest in the cemetery, their graves marked by their religious names and the legend *Franciscan nun*. The state did not rehabilitate them after 1990 and has not officially deleted the crimes for which they were sentenced.

Translator's Notes

Part I: Kali's Tale

PAGE 4. **but for anybody from the 'Óstát**: A reference to Hóstát, the novel's setting, intricately interwoven with its themes and narratives. The eastern and northern outskirts of Cluj-Napoca, the unofficial capital of the Transylvania region in current Romania, was known as Hóstát until it was violently demolished in the 1970s and '80s under the dictatorship of Nicolae Ceaușescu. This area was home to a distinct community called the Hóstátians, whose livelihood was rooted in vegetable farming. Proud of their dual identity as city dwellers and farmers, they developed unique traditions and customs, forming a separate cultural group within the Hungarian minority in Cluj, Romania. By the twentieth century, Hóstát became an identity marker for long-established residents, distinguishing them from newer rural immigrants. The dramatic destruction of Hóstát culture, the nationalization of their lands since the 1950s, and the demolition of their gardens and houses led to the dispersal of these people. However, their semi-urban culture and traditional attire remain recognizable among older generations.

PAGE 8. **we was back in Hungary again**: Tensions regarding Transylvania are more than a millennium long. The region was part of the Kingdom of Hungary until the end of the First World War, which led to the collapse of the Austro-Hungarian Empire. The 1920 Treaty of Trianon transferred much of Hungary's territory, including Transylvania, to Romania, leaving around 1.5 million Hungarians within Romania's borders. Adolf Hitler's Second Vienna Award of 1940 gave Northern Transylvania back to Hungary. Towards the end of the Second World War, the Second Vienna Award was annulled by the Allied's

Armistice Agreement with Romania in September 1944. The 1947 Paris Peace Treaties reaffirmed the Romania–Hungary borders as originally established by the Treaty of Trianon, officially returning Northern Transylvania, including Kolozsvár, to Romania. These state borders remain valid today.

PAGE 9. **tasty, rich puliszka**: A Hungarian and Romanian dish of ground cornmeal porridge.

PAGE 12. **King Mátyás**: Matthias Corvinus (Hungarian: Hunyadi Mátyás, 1443–1490), king of Hungary and Croatia from 1458 to 1490. Subsequent kings were not Hungarians, mostly Habsburgs.

PAGE 15. *gatya*: Traditional peasant trousers, typically made of white linen, of medium-length with very wide legs.

PAGE 21. **What does *déo* mean?**: Refers to *d.o.*, the Romanian abbreviation for *domiciliul obligatoriu*, forced address or location, for people considered *burzhui* (bourgeois) and forced to leave their homes.

PAGE 28. **ev'ry bani was needed**: Romanian currency: 100 bani = 1 lei.

PAGE 32. **It seemed the world 'ad been turned upside down**: On 3 March 1949, the majority of Transylvanian aristocrats—most of whom were Hungarian—were arrested in their homes during the early morning hours and taken away for internal deportation, marking a significant event in the region's communist takeover under the Romanian Workers' Party. Essentially, this was a large-scale dispossession of the landed gentry by the new regime. For more on the subject, see Miklós Bánffy, *The Phoenix Land* (Patrick Thursfield trans.) (London: Arcadia, 2003); Jaap Scholten, *Comrade Baron* (Budapest: Corvina, 2010); and in Hungarian, Kovács Kiss Gyöngy (ed.), *Álló- és Mozgó képek, Vázlat az erdélyi főnemességről* (Kolozsvár: Korunk, 2003).

PAGE 36. **watery ludaskása**: Goose (more likely chicken) and rice.

PAGE 47. **Enyed**: A reputable wine area north-west of Budapest—a long way from Kolozsvár.

PAGE 47. **savanyúleves . . . kaszásleves**: Savanyúleves and kaszásleves are soups, both with a distinctly tart flavour, made with sour cabbage.

PAGE 49. **Korond**: In Romanian, Corund; a village in central Romania, renowned for its peasant ceramics.

PAGE 50. **Nagybánya**: In Romanian, Baia Mare, in north-western Romania.

PAGE 50. **can tell a loom from the loo**: A play on words in the Hungarian—'loom' is *szövőszék*, 'loo' is *árnyékszék*.

PAGE 53. **There was one shoutin' out as well**: The practice of *kurjantás*, 'trumpeting', the shouting of couplets while dancing *csárdás*. For example, *Ha elszakad az a húr / Megfizeti ez az úr*—'If that string breaks, this gentleman will pay for it'.

PAGE 50. **I went to church, to the Kétágú**: The Kétágú ('two-branched') Church in Kolozsvár, officially known as the Lower Town Reformed Church, Hóstát people's main church in the town. It is the largest and one of the most beautiful nineteenth-century classicist churches in Transylvania.

PAGE 65. **the Romanians kept Christmas too**: More than 85 per cent of Romanians are Eastern Orthodox Christians but keep Christmas on 24 December. Transylvania, though, has a significant Catholic following, up to 11 per cent of the populace.

PAGE 84. **you've kindly made me a nice bean soup**: A play of words in the Hungarian. Vilmos has said *tetszett főzni*, 'it has pleased you to cook'—heavily ironic use of the ultimate in politeness. He usually addresses Kali in the informal second person, while she uses the polite third person to him.

PAGE 90. **play a *ritkább***: A slow movement, the *lassú magyar*.

PAGE 93. **two or three 'old**: A hectare (100,000 square metres) equals 2.5 acres. A 'hold' is about half a hectare.

PAGE 108. **'E'd never before addressed me in that formal way**: Vilmos usually addresses Kali by the informal *te*, while she always addresses him as *kend*, a polite peasant address. This time he calls her *maga*, which indicates an abrupt change of relationship.

PAGE 120. **studied up in Enyed**: More correctly, Nagyenyed; in Romanian, Aiud. The high school and teacher-training college date from 1662 and are named after Prince Gábor Bethlen.

Part II: Vilmos's Tale

PAGE 143. **Miklós Horthy** (1868–1957), Hungarian admiral and statesman, served as Hungary's regent from 1920 to 1944. Though he disapproved of Adolf Hitler, Horthy supported Germany's anti-Soviet campaign and initially accepted Hungary's alliance with Germany during the Second World War. His subsequent attempts to withdraw Hungary from the conflict resulted in his forced abdication and capture by the Germans in 1944. Freed by Allied troops in May 1945, he was exiled to Portugal.

PAGE 144. **Nativity of the Virgin Mary**: Christian feast day celebrating the birth of Mary, occurs on 8 September.

PAGE 147. **Károly Kós** (1883–1977), Austro-Hungarian and Romanian architect, writer, illustrator, ethnologist and politician.

PAGE 147. **Lajos Jordáky** (1933–1974), Hungarian journalist, historian, sociologist and university lecturer, Social Democrat, who lived and worked in Romania; jailed several times for being his political views.

PAGE 149. **Carol II** (1893–1953), king of Romania from 8 June 1930 until his forced abdication on 6 September 1940.

PAGE 149. **father plant**: the rose that provides the pollen; the mother, the one that provides the carpel.

PAGE 157. **feast of the Virgin Mary**: On 8 October, the Hungarian Catholic Church celebrates a special feast day honouring the Blessed Virgin Mary as the Lady of the Hungarians and the patron saint of Hungary.

PAGE 158. *Falvak népe*: 'People of the Villages', the journal of Hungarian agriculturists (from 1991, farmers) in Romania. Founded in 1932, it appeared between July 1952 and December 1989 as *Falvak Dolgozó Népe*, 'Working People of the Villages'.

PAGE 162. **Szőreg and Tétény**: Szőreg is a village in south-east Hungary, close to the city of Szeged, which holds an annual rose festival and has a variety named after it. Tétény or Budatétény is an area south-west of Budapest.

PAGE 166. *lucskoskáposzta*: 'sloppy cabbage', a Transylvanian dish. See George Lang, *The Cuisine of Hungary* (New York: Bonanza Books), p. 288.

PAGE 176. *mic burghez*: Romanian term for bourgeois.

PAGE 183. **every rose only declared the praise of the boss**: The translator's nightmare, a pun. Kali has called Vilmos *úr*, 'boss, master, gentleman', to which he objects on political grounds. Then she speaks of *az úr dicsősége*, 'praise of the boss', which is indistinguishable from *az Úr dicsősége*, 'the glory of the Lord', which he likes even less.

PAGE 186. **I wasn't to call her *maga***: The formal mode of address, with the verb in the third person. So as not to feel his social inferior, Kali always calls Vilmos *kend* (translated as 'mister'), while he addresses her by the informal *te*. In using *maga*, Vilmos is being ultra-polite and conciliatory.

PAGE 189. **The Iron Guard**: In Romanian, Garda de Fier; Romanian militant revolutionary fascist movement and political party founded in 1927. It was strongly anti-democratic, anti-capitalist, anti-communist, and anti-Semitic. It differed from other European right-wing movements of the period by its spiritual basis, as the Iron Guard was deeply imbued with Romanian Orthodox Christian mysticism.

PAGE 190. Gheorghe **Gheorghiu-Dej** (1901–1965), Romanian politician, served as the first Communist leader of Romania from 1947 to 1965, holding the position of the country's first Communist prime minister from 1952 to 1955.

PAGE 192. *Scânteia*: More correctly *Scînteia*, 'The Spark', the name of a Communist Party central newspaper. The title is a homage to the Russian-language paper *Iskra*. It was known as *Scânteia* until the 1953 spelling reform, which replaced the letter *â* with the phonologically identical *î*.

PAGE 194. **MAT**: Magyar Autonóm Tartomány, a Hungarian autonomous region of the Romanian People's Republic, centred around Marosvásárhely, established in 1952 under Soviet pressure and modelled after the Soviet system.

PAGE 194. **Bolyai**: University named after mathematician János Bolyai (1802–1860), founded in 1945 in Kolozsvár as a Romanian state institution teaching in Hungarian. In 1959, it was merged with Victor Babeş University (founded in 1919) to form Babeş-Bolyai University. This event was considered the liquidation of the Hungarian university by nationalistic Communist Party politics.

PAGE 207. **RNK**: Román Népköztársaság, Romanian People's Republic.

PAGE 208. **EMGE**: Erdélyi Magyar Gazdák Egylete, Association of Hungarian Farmers in Transylvania.

PAGE 208. **vernalization**: A process of cooling seed before planting in order to accelerate growth.

PAGE 214. **Since then we 'aven't 'ad a good 'Ungarian king**: Mátyás I (1458–1490) was, as stated above, the last native Hungarian king; all his successors were foreigners. He was born in Kolozsvár, though not behind the post office; the house in question is preserved in his memory. Many folktales tell of his various exploits. If such is implied here, he was not born illegitimate, though his father, the celebrated Hunyadi János, may have been.

PAGE 219. **László Luka**: Vasile Luca (born László, 1898–1963), Austro-Hungarian-born Romanian and Soviet Communist politician, a leading member of the Romanian Communist Party from 1945 until his imprisonment in the 1950s.

PAGE 219. **kulak**: A Russian word meaning 'fist', but a colloquialism meaning 'wealthy peasant', referring to the petty-bourgeois at the end of the Russian Empire and the early decades of the Soviet Union.

PAGE 220. **MNSZ**: Magyar Népi Szövetség, Hungarian People's Union—a left-wing political party in Romania active from 1934 to 1953, claiming to represent the Hungarian community. Before 1944, it was known as the Union of Hungarian Workers of Romania.

PAGE 220. **Mezőség**: Cîmpia Transilvaniei, the Transylvanian Plain, an area between the rivers Someșul Mare and Someșul Mic to the north and west and the Mureș to the south and east.

PAGE 222. **Petru Groza** (1884–1958), Romanian politician, prime minister of Romania (1945–1952), president of the Presidium of the Great National Assembly (1952–1958).

PAGE 225. **If you think so, read the Bible**: A reference to Proverbs 14:4, 'Where there are no oxen, the manger is empty, / but from the strength of an ox come abundant harvests.' (New International Version).

PAGE 230. **fifty ares of outdoor beds**: An are is a unit of area in the metric system that is equal to 100 square metres.

PAGE 238. **Sándor Mogyorós**: Alexandru Moghioroş (1911–1969), Hungarian-born Romanian labour activist and Communist politician. He played an important role in the collectivization of Romanian agriculture and the eradication of 'kulakism'. At the end of the 1950s, he was deputy president of the Council of Ministers, but after Nicolae Ceauşescu came to power, he was pushed out of the Party leadership and died soon after.

PAGE 238. **József Méliusz** (1909–1995), Transylvanian writer, poet and translator.

PAGE 244. **How old was she? No more than fourteen**: Kálmán Mikszáth (1847–1910), the renowned Hungarian novelist, says that no Hungarian woman will admit to being less than fourteen or more than forty.

PAGE 247. **Edgár Balogh** (1906–1996), Hungarian journalist from Slovakia and then Romania. After the merger of Babeş and Bolyai Universities, he lectured on journalism at the Department of Hungarian Literary History. From 1957 to 1971, he was deputy editor-in-chief of the relaunched *Korunk*.

PAGE 247. **Jilava**: The maximum-security prison on the outskirts of Bucharest. Between 1948 and 1964, during the Communist regime, the prison served as a transit and triage centre for 'counterrevolutionaries', including members of banned political parties, spies, accused war criminals, and individuals involved in anti-Communist organizations.

PAGE 248. **Ana Pauker** (1893–1960), a Romanian Communist leader of Jewish origin who made history as the world's first female foreign minister, taking office in December 1947. She held the position until 1952.

PAGE 250. **János Fazekas** (1926–2004), Hungarian journalist, politician, and historian from Romania. He spent his final years in Budapest, researching for the Hungarian Academy of Sciences. Between 1945 and 1982, he worked to protect the rights of the Hungarian minority in Romania while holding various state and Party roles. After 1982, he lived in internal exile and struggled to find his place even after regime change due to his unwavering communist beliefs and support for national minorities, as a result of which he was rejected by both Hungarians and Romanians.

PAGE 251. **that little pumpkin seed**: A reference to Ceauşescu's short height; he measured 1.68 metres or 5 feet 6 inches.

PAGE 256. *tejtestvér*: A child not related by blood but having shared the milk of the same mother; a milk sibling.

PAGE 258. **Anna Novák**: Zimra Harsányi, aka Ana Novac (1929–2010), Transylvanian Hungarian playwright of Jewish origin. *Kovácsék* (1955) was her first play.

PAGE 259. **Arrow Cross**: The fascist party that had governed Hungary in the last months of the Second World War, named after its emblem featuring a barbed cross. The emblem symbolized the Magyar tribes who settled in Hungary in the late ninth century. Like the Nazi swastika, it was used to suggest the supposed racial purity of the Magyars.

PAGE 260. **Regina Elisabeta, named for the queen of Romania**: Elisabeth of Wied (1843–1916), the first queen of Romania. She held the title from her marriage to King Carol I in 1881 until his death in 1914.

PAGE 260. **Queen Erzsébet, for the queen of Hungary**: Born Duchess Elisabeth Amalie Eugenie (1837–1898) in Bavaria, Elisabeth, affectionately known as Sisi, was the empress of Austria and the queen of Hungary through her marriage to Emperor Franz Joseph I from 1854 until her assassination in 1898.

PAGE 266. **we weren't baptized and didn't have godparents**: In the baptism of infants, the name of the child is stated by the godparents, not the birth parents.

PAGE 267. **T. Attila Szabó** (1906–1987), Transylvanian Hungarian linguist, historian, literary historian and ethnologist.

PAGE 267. **László Szabédi** (1907–1959), Transylvanian Hungarian poet, journalist and translator who died by suicide after the liquidation of the Bolyai University.

PAGE 269. **23 August**: On this day in 1944, King Mihai I of Romania dismissed and arrested Ion Antonescu, the fascist wartime dictator. He ordered an immediate end to Romania's alliance with the Axis Powers, initiated armistice talks with the Allies, and began military cooperation with the Soviet Union.

PAGE 269. **Gergely Márk** (1923–2012), Hungarian horticulturalist; notable for creating a large rose garden in the Gardening Research Institute and another in the Szent István Park, both in Budapest.

PAGE 270. **Romanian national anthem**: 'Deșteaptă-te, române!' (Up, Romanians!) originated from a poem written during the Wallachian Revolution of 1848.

A Romanian favourite, played during various historical events, it was notably broadcast after the 23 August 1944 coup when Romania joined the Allies. Outlawed under Communism after 1947, it was adopted as the national anthem in 1990, following the 1989 Revolution.

PAGE 271. **can't be destroyed even though the world is in ruins**: A reference to Horace, *Odes* 3.3.7–8: *Si fractus illabatur orbis / Impavidum ferient ruinae*— If a shattered world were to fall on him, the ruins would leave him unperturbed.

PAGE 272. *The Silent Knight*: *A néma levente*, a comedy scripted by Jenő Heltai (1936); there is a stage version and more than one film.

PAGE 272. **Béla Horváth** (1927–1981), Romanian-Hungarian actor.

PAGE 274. **Carmen Sylva**: The nom de plume of Elisabeth of Wied (1843–1916), the first queen of Romania, referenced earlier.

PAGE 276. **Don't tell me we've got the nobility back**: A play on words in the Hungarian. A rose grower is *rózsanemesítő*, 'rose-ennobler', and Vilmos has used the word *nemesítés*, 'ennoblement', to mean 'variety'. In Hungarian *nemes* means 'noble', and under Communism the nobility had ceased to be.

PAGE 277. **Duiliu Zamfirescu** (1858–1922), Romanian novelist, poet, short-story writer, lawyer, nationalist politician, journalist, diplomat and memoirist. In 1909 he was elected a member of the Romanian Academy, and for a while in 1920 he was the foreign minister of Romania. *Viaţa la ţară* was first published in 1898.

PAGE 278. **Twentieth Party Congress**: The Twentieth Congress of the Communist Party of the Soviet Union, held 14–25 February 1956, is notable for Nikita Khrushchev's 'Secret Speech' denouncing Joseph Stalin's personality cult and dictatorship.

PAGE 278. Trofim Denisovich **Lysenko** (1898–1976), Soviet agronomist and biologist. A strong proponent of Lamarckism, he rejected Mendelian genetics in favour of his own idiosyncratic, pseudoscientific ideas later termed Lysenkoism.

PAGE 279. Constantin **Daicoviciu** (1898–1973), Romanian historian, novelist, archaeologist, Communist politician, rector of the Babeş-Bolyai University, and member of the Romanian Academy of Sciences.

PAGE 283. *The Six-Acre Rose Garden*: A short story by Mihály Babits (1883–1941), the respected editor of the famous literary journal *Nyugat*, and a celebrated as poet, essayist, translator and literary historian. Babits is, however, less interested in the roses themselves than in the psychology of the young people who visit the garden.

PAGE 285. *menü házak*: Cheap restaurants offering a very restricted *table d'hôte*.

PAGE 286. János **Hunyadi** (1407–1456), famous warrior and regent of Hungary, father of King Mátyás I. The Dacians were an ancient people that inhabited what is now Romania, and from whom modern Romanians like to trace their descent.

PAGE 286. **Áron Márton** (1896–1980), Hungarian Roman Catholic bishop of Transylvania from 1938 to 1980; opposed both the deportation of Jews during the Second World War and Romania's Communist regime. Arrested in 1949, he was sentenced to life imprisonment but released in 1955 after Stalin's death when the Romanian political climate changed slightly. Re-arrested in 1957 for his continued defiance, he spent a decade under house arrest before his release in 1967. A staunch advocate for religious freedom, Márton remained uncompromising until his death. For a concise account of his career in English, see Nyáry Krisztián, *Eminent Hungarians* (Budapest: Corvina, 2017), pp. 281–91.

PAGE 289. *bocskor* and *opinca*: *Bocskor* is a cross between a boot and a moccasin in Hungarian, while *opinca* is the Romanian word for it.

PAGE 289. *Szabad Nép*: 'Free People', a Hungarian daily that circulated between 1942 and 1956.

PAGE 294. **Mócvidék**: Ţara Moţilor, a hilly region of Transylvania.

PAGE 297. **Piski**: A town in western Transylvania; in Romanian, Simeria.

PAGE 297. **Miron Constantinescu** (1917–1974), leading member of the Romanian Communist Party as well as a Marxist sociologist, historian, academic and journalist.

PAGE 300. **I paid a better worker six hundred lei**: A very low wage.

PAGE 303. **Nicolae Labiş** (1935–56), Romanian poet whose rise was marked by growing tensions with the Communist regime, culminating in a tragic and mysterious death at the age of twenty-one. Remembered as a symbol of youthful rebellion and creative integrity, his works, including the posthumously published *The Fight Against Inertia*, continue to influence Romanian literature.

PAGE 303. **Petőfi Circle**: Established in 1955, this was a forum for young intellectuals in Hungary to discuss political and social reforms within a Communist framework. Initially aligned with Imre Nagy's reformist policies, the group's debates and activities contributed to the intellectual momentum behind the 1956 Hungarian Revolution, but it was banned before the uprising and its members faced severe reprisals afterwards.

PAGE 304. **István Nagy** (1904 –1977), Transylvanian Hungarian writer and member of the Romanian Academy.

PAGE 305. **people went out to visit the dead**: A reference to the Hungarian custom of visiting family graves on 1 November, All Saints Day, a national holiday in Hungary but not in Romania.

PAGE 306. **Tartós Gusztáv apples**: A late-ripening Hungarian variety, it has smallish fruit.

PAGE 309. **Dávid Gyula** (b. 1928), studied at Bolyai University from 1947 to 1951, assistant lecturer there between 1956 and 1957, and a political convict between 1957 and 1964.

PAGE 310. **Ernő Gáll** (1917–2000), editor, sociologist and philosophical writer; at the time, a professor of philosophy and pro-rector. Deported to Buchenwald in November 1944, he was released in April 1945.

PAGE 313. **'The club of those to be shot in the head'**: *Nekrassov* is a satirical drama written by Jean-Paul Sartre in 1955.

PAGE 316. **Mary's country**: The driver is evidently a Hungarian, since he refers to the Virgin Mary, the patron saint of Hungary.

PAGE 319. **the marriage of paprika and tomato**: An allusion to the biological research made by I. V. Michurin.

PAGE 328. **Zsigmond Móricz** (1879–1942), major Hungarian novelist and social realist. *Tündérkert* (Fairy Garden) is the first volume of Móricz's trilogy *Erdély* (1935).

PAGE 331. *keringő*: In the ballroom, *keringő* means 'waltz', but it is also used in folk dancing to mean a form in which couples revolve.

PAGE 334. **the pact with Hungary had been signed**: Presumably, a reference to the Warsaw Pact, established in May 1955, which was a collective defence treaty and military alliance led by the Soviet Union, uniting eight Eastern Bloc nations—including Hungary and Romania—as a counterbalance to NATO during the Cold War.

PAGE 335. **Murfatlar**: town in south-east Romania, on the Danube–Black Sea canal; famous wine region.

PAGE 336. *Szél fuvatlan nem indul*: The most significant item in István Asztalos's oeuvre is this short novel, published in 1949 and filmed in 1950. The title is a Hungarian proverb, the equivalent of 'There's no smoke without fire'.

PAGE 339. *The House of Bernarda Alba* (1936, first performed 1950) by the Spanish dramatist Federico García Lorca. Commentators have often associated it with *Blood Wedding* and *Yerma* as a 'rural trilogy'.

PAGE 339. **Lili Poór** (1886–1962), actress, life member of the Kolozsvár Theatre, wife of Jenő Janovics, the legendary director of the National Theatre in Kolozsvár.

PAGE 341. **first Romanian period**: The first period of Romanian rule in Transylvania dated from 1920 until the Second Vienna Award (1940), and the second period from September 1944 to the present.

PAGE 341. **Jenő Janovics** (1872–1945), a Hungarian silent-era film director, screenwriter and actor, legendary director of the National Theatre in Kolozsvár for three decades.

PAGE 342. **Cursing. Swearing**: A play on the Russian word *mat*, with five possible meanings. Vili picks the wrong one!

PAGE 343. **second Hungarian period**: Having been under Hungarian rule since 1002, Transylvania was ceded to Romania by the post–First World War Treaty of Trianon in 1920. The second Hungarian period was from 1940 to 1944.

PAGE 344. **misinterpreted as little short of kulak**: Because *nemesítő* (rose grower) contains the element *nemes* (noble), and literally means 'ennobler'.

☐ PAGE 344. **János Kádár** (1912–1989), Hungarian Communist leader, who became general secretary of the Hungarian Socialist Workers' Party during the Hungarian Revolution of 1956 and remained in the position for 32 years.

PAGE 345. *horă*: a traditional Romanian and Moldovan ring dance in which the dancers hold one another's hands and the circle spins, usually anti-clockwise, as each participant follows a sequence of three steps forward and one step back.

PAGE 345. **Kállai . . . Iliescu**: Gyula Kállai, prime minister of Hungary, 1965–1967; Leontin Sălăjan (1913 –1966), Romanian Communist military and political leader; Ion Iliescu (b. 1930), Romanian politician and president, 1990–1996 and 2000–2004.

PAGE 346. *Pendely*: long shirt-like woman's garment; *katrinca*: a kind of apron.

PAGE 347. **mujdei**: a spicy Romanian sauce. It is made from garlic cloves crushed and ground into a paste, salted and mixed energetically with vegetable oil.

PAGE 347. **Géza Simó** (1870–1946), Transylvanian journalist, teacher, educator and Communist politician.

PAGE 349. **to change trains was a miserable business**: For a long time, there was no direct rail connection between Kolozsvár and Marosvásárhely, a distance of 110 kilometres; changing trains could mean a delay of as much as three hours. See Andrea Tompa, *The Hangman's House*, Bernard Adams trans. (London: Seagull Books, 2021), p.53.

PAGE 350. **Regát**: the Romanian word for 'kingdom', is a term used by the Transylvanian Hungarians as a collective noun denoting the historical regions of Moldova, Oltenia and Dobruja, the 'Old Kingdom' of Romania.

PAGE 353. **Christ's coffin**: Proverbial saying—even Christ's coffin wasn't guarded without payment, that is, don't expect people to do something for nothing.

PAGE 362. *An Inspector Calls*: J. B. Priestley's highly successful modern morality play was first performed in the Soviet Union in 1945.

PAGE 363. **Virgil Fulicea** (1907–1979), sculptor, poet and university professor.

PAGE 367. *Alja* **or something**: Vilmos fails to understand the Hebrew *aliyah*—'ascent', emigration to Israel.

PAGE 371. *Utunk*: 'Our Way', a Kolozsvár-based Hungarian literary journal published from 1946 to 1989, after which it continued as *Helikon*.

PAGE 372. *Igaz Szó*: 'True Word', a literary journal published bimonthly in Marosvásárhely from June 1953. Published monthly from August 1965, it underwent several changes of name. After the 1989 change of regime in Romania, its successor was *Látó*.

PAGE 372. **Földes . . . *föld***: An untranslatable play on words—*föld* is 'land' while *Földes* (here a surname) is 'landed', 'landowning'.

PAGE 375. **Miklós Tompa** (1910–1996), theatre director, acting teacher, founder of the Székely Theatre (later the Hungarian Section of the National Theatre in Marosvásárhely), son of poet László Tompa and father of theatre director Gábor Tompa.

PAGE 375. György Kovács (1910–1977), Transylvanian actor, dramatist and performer.

PAGE 420. **ENSZ**: Egyesült Nemzetek Szerkezete, Hungarian for United Nations Organization.

PAGE 420. Aladár **Szoboszlay** (1925–1958), a Kolozsvár parish priest, wrote *Confederatio*, which sought the relaxing of ethnic tension and the end of the Communist dictatorship. The trial took place in 1957–58 with 57 accused, of whom ten were shot and the rest sentenced to twenty-two years' hard labour. The survivors were amnestied in 1964, and in 2010 all were exonerated.

PAGE 422. *The Doctrine of Salvation*: Late in life, mathematician János Bolyai's thoughts took a philosophical turn, and the book *Üdvtan* (Salvation, here translated as *The Doctrine of Salvation*) was a result. It was published only in 2003.

PAGE 424. **Working on earth! Perhaps he can also work on heaven?**: An awkward play on words here: *földi mű*, 'earthly work', contrasted with *égi mű*, 'heavenly work'. In his reply, Vilmos goes into the plural, *földi művek*, which can only mean 'tilling the soil'.

PAGE 425. **As they usually did in a synthesis**: The Hegelian dialectical form in which the opposition of thesis and antithesis is resolved by the introduction of a third concept.

PAGE 428. **Nicolae Mărgineanu** (1905–1980), Romanian psychologist with a distinguished career, imprisoned from 1948 to 1964.

PAGE 429. Miklós **Molnár** (Löwinger) (1922–1959), economist, university professor, head of the Economics Department of Babeş-Bolyai University.

PAGE 431. **Zoltán Csendes** (1924–1959), Hungarian statistician from Romania and university professor, deputy rector of the Hungarian Bolyai University. After the liquidation of the university, he died by suicide, like László Szabédi.

PAGE 438. **Házsongárd**: The famous Kolozsvár cemetery.

PAGE 438. **four copies for checking**: *Verifikálás*, that is, checking for loyalty to the Communist Party line.

Part III: Annush's Tale

PAGE 453. **building sanatoria there at the time**: An allusion to the Soviet-style system adopted in Central Europe. Here, 'sanatorium' means holiday accommodation for workers rather than a medical facility. Workers could apply for passes to stay there.

PAGE 454. ***aprozár***: A Romanian word for an industrial concern producing vegetables.

PAGE 457. **Brétfü**: An area north of the city of Kolozsvár, beyond the Nádas stream; formerly vineyards.

PAGE 474. **Murokország**: Literally, 'carrot country'. *Murok* is a species of white carrot, and the name Murokország is humorously given to an area on the River Nyárád, where a number of villages specialize in producing vegetables.

PAGE 486. **'We're all born children of wrath'**: Ephesians 2:3—'All of us also lived among them at one time, gratifying the cravings of our flesh and following its desires and thoughts. Like the rest, we were by nature deserving of wrath.' (New International Version)

PAGE 505. **Bács Forest**: Forest about 5 kilometres north-west of Kolozsvár.

PAGE 514. **'Judge me, oh God . . . innocence'**: Similar to Psalm 26:1— 'Vindicate me, Lord, / for I have led a blameless life; / I have trusted in the Lord / and have not faltered.' (New International Version)

PAGE 537. **shredded cabbage**: Sarvalt káposzta, similar to the German sauerkraut—raw cabbage, grated, and fermented for a few days in a salt solution together with herbs such as dill and parsley. In a restaurant, often listed as 'káposztasaláta', cabbage salad.

PAGE 548. **national daily, *Előre***: The name translates to 'Forward'; a Romanian newspaper that was the propaganda organ of the Communist Party. It was originally published as *Romániai Magyar Szó* (Hungarian Word of Romania) in Bucharest in 1947, but changed its name to *Előre* in 1953.

PAGE 554. **a bit of vakarék**: 'Scratchings', leftovers of dough lumped together and baked. From the verb *vakar*, 'to scrape, scratch'.

PAGE 560. **All men are sinful. That was what she'd said**: A play on words in the Hungarian. *Bűnös* can mean 'guilty, a criminal' or 'sinful, a sinner'.

PAGE 563. **Gherla Prison**: Located in Gherla (Hungarian: Szamosújvár), Cluj County, Romania, the prison dates back to 1785. It is notorious for the harsh treatment of political prisoners, particularly during the Communist era.

PAGE 563. **Sándor Rózsa** (1813–1878), a famed Hungarian outlaw. His life inspired numerous writers, including Zsigmond Móricz and Gyula Krúdy. Often compared to England's Dick Turpin, he also embodies elements of the Robin Hood legend.

Part IV: Eleonóra's Tale

PAGE 585. **Lóna, Magyarlóna**: A village 12 kilometres west of Kolozsvár.

PAGE 596. **that small garden, thirty ares**: Small by Hóstát standards—3,000 square metres, about three-quarters of an acre.

PAGE 598. **granted the holy wounds**: The five holy wounds of Jesus—his hands, feet, and the spear wound in his torso—symbolize his suffering on the cross. For centuries, Christians have meditated on these wounds to reflect on his Passion and seek mercy. Prayers like St Clare's *Litany of the Sacred Wounds* invoke their merits, such as: 'By this holy and adorable wound, I beseech you to pardon all of the sins that I have committed.'

PAGE 604. **Little Teréz**: Thérèse of Lisieux (1873–1897), a French Discalced Carmelite nun venerated as Thérèse of the Child Jesus and the Holy Face. Known in English as the 'Little Flower of Jesus', she is celebrated for her 'little way' of spiritual simplicity and trust in God.

PAGE 608. **some *cusur***: Mária uses a Romanian word *cusur*, 'defect'.

PAGE 615. **'You are not in the body but in the spirit'**: Romans 8:9—'You, how-ever, are not in the realm of the flesh but are in the realm of the Spirit, if indeed the Spirit of God lives in you. And if anyone does not have the Spirit of Christ, they do not belong to Christ.' (New International Version)

PAGE 617. **főzelék**: a traditional Hungarian vegetable dish with a thick consistency, often compared to pottage. However, it's not quite a soup nor quite a stew, but rather a distinct culinary creation in its own right.

PAGE 629. **'He was not that Light. . . . '** : John 1:8—'He himself was not the light; he came only as a witness to the light.' (New International Version)

PAGE 634. **I managed to be up by that time**: The liturgical hours; *lauds* was said at daybreak, *matins* either earlier or at the same time, and *vespers* at sunset.

PAGE 634. **because she was known by her husband's name**: In Hungarian usage, a married professional woman will generally use her maiden name.

PAGE 636. **Horthy Miklós út**: Later, Horia út. Miklós Horthy, Hungary's regent from 1920 to 1944, was a staunch anti-Communist. Unsurprisingly, a street bearing his name in Transylvania was renamed by Romania's Communist regime.

PAGE 645. **they'll give you a report . . .** : An untranslatable detail. In the Hungarian, the doctor stops using the informal *te* and changes to formal lan-guage, showing that this is an order.

PAGE 646. **put a nail in an apple to go rusty**: An old folk remedy for anaemia—an iron nail was driven into an apple and left there to rust, after which the apple was eaten.

PAGE 649. ***Little Seraphic Guide***: An instructive prayer book for members of the Transylvanian Franciscan Order.

PAGE 656. ***Bucura-te ceea-ce esti plina de har, Maria***: Traditional prayer 'Hail Mary, full of grace'; correct form in Romanian: *bucură-te! Ceea ce ești plină de har, Marie*.

PAGE 657. **such a commonplace word**: In Hungarian, the Lord's Prayer begins with *Miatyánk*, a unique form of *atya*, meaning 'father', used exclusively in religious contexts, such as addressing a priest. The common term for father is *apa*, as in *apánk*, meaning 'our father' or 'daddy'. Romanian, by contrast, does not differentiate between these uses.

PAGE 659. **whether it was 1949 or 1950**: During the Greek Civil War (1946–1949), fought between the Greek government and the Communist-led Democratic Army of Greece, many members and supporters of the defeated Communist forces fled Greece as political refugees. By 1949, over 100,000 had relocated to Yugoslavia and the Eastern Bloc, including more than 5,000 children evacuated to Romania, where many were reunited with parents in refugee camps.

PAGE 663. **Woe to him that is alone when he falleth**: Ecclesiastes 4:10— 'If either of them falls down, / one can help the other up. / But pity anyone who falls / and has no one to help them up.' (New International Version)

PAGE 670. **Radóc**: In Romanian, Rădăuți; town in the former Bukovina, near the Ukrainian border.

PAGE 676. **Orbán Balázs** (1829–1880), Hungarian writer, ethnographic collector, parliamentarian and correspondent member of the Hungarian Academy of Sciences.

PAGE 679. **the stones will speak if you don't**: Luke 19:40—'"I tell you," he replied, "if they keep quiet, the stones will cry out."' (New International Version)

PAGE 688. **sacred corporal**: The corporal is a square white linen cloth on which chalice, paten and ciborium are placed on the altar during the celebration of the Roman Catholic Eucharist.

PAGE 689. **'Another shall carry thee whither thou wouldst not'**: John 21:18— 'Very truly I tell you, when you were younger you dressed yourself and went where you wanted; but when you are old you will stretch out your hands, and someone else will dress you and lead you where you do not want to go.' (New International Version)